THE WAYS
OF WOMEN

THE WAYS
OF WOMEN

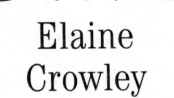

Elaine
Crowley

ORION

The right of Elaine Crowley to be identified as the author of this work
has been asserted by her in accordance with the
Copyright, Designs and Patents Act 1988.

First published in Great Britain in 1993 by
Orion
An imprint of Orion Books Ltd
Orion House, 5 Upper St Martin's Lane, London WC2H 9EA

A CIP catalogue record for this book is available
from the British Library

ISBN 1 85797 014 4

Typeset by Selwood Systems
Midsomer Norton
Printed and bound in Great Britain by
Butler & Tanner Ltd
Frome and London

For Yvette, my editor and friend

PART ONE

CHAPTER ONE

The street was decked with flags and bunting. In the brisk January breeze the little red, white and blue pennants danced between the gas-lamps to which they were strung. Women, elderly and young, wearing slippers and crossover pinnies, went in and out of the open-doored houses carrying chairs and small tables, arranging them in the middle of the road, laying cloths, standing back to admire their work and praying for the day to remain fine well into the evening when the party would begin.

A woman called Cissie said to her lifelong friend, Lizzie Mangan, 'It'll be the best party Dublin's ever seen.'

To which Lizzie replied: 'So it should. It's no more than Jack Harte deserves after four years in the trenches and getting a medal for saving Barney Daly's life.'

'I wasn't surprised,' said Cissie. 'Jack always had it in him, even as a child. Well able to defend himself, though never one to start a fight. Stand his ground without losing his temper – a good, kind, upstanding young man.'

'Isn't it a pity his mother and father didn't live to see his return, the Lord have mercy on them.'

'Thank God, he has your Julia for a wife,' said Cissie then, nodding her head in the direction of a house opposite, she continued, 'I noticed Rosie has steered clear of anything to do with the party.'

'Surely that came as no surprise. Rosie Quinlan's a stuck-up nothing. The street's not good enough for her. She can't forget she worked for the gentry.'

'I believe,' said Cissie, 'that she didn't even give to the collection. With Barney courting her daughter and him being one of them the party's being thrown for, you'd have thought she would.'

'Ah, we got plenty without her contribution,' said Lizzie.

Other women came with cups, plates, saucers and spoons, which they laid on the tables. Children too young for school hovered round and were warned not to dirty the cloths or touch the Delft; if they were good, later on they'd get custard and jelly.

Lizzie and Cissie carried on talking, Cissie commenting on the publican's generosity in lending the tumblers. 'He's very decent, giving a bottle of whiskey as well.'

'Decent me arse!' retorted Lizzie. 'He can well afford it out of the profits he makes from the eejits of men. In any case there's lashings of whiskey from the men's own collection.' Surveying the tables she said, 'That's all we can do for the time being. It's going to be a great night. Everyone will light the gas in their parlours and bedrooms. We'll bring out a few oil-lamps and candles if the wind doesn't spring up, and there'll be no shortage of music.'

'No,' agreed Cissie. 'There's the gramophone, a fiddle and a melodeon. I'm getting all excited. Like years ago, Lizzie, when we were girls and going to hooleys.'

'You were always romantic,' said Lizzie.

'And you,' replied Cissie, 'let on to have the hard heart but I know you well. You're as thrilled and excited as a child at the thought of Jack and Julia being reunited. Amn't I right?'

'Will you go way out of that,' said Lizzie, affectionately giving her friend a little push.

They had been born and reared in the street. Married and lived in their parents' homes until the old ones died. Cissie had never had a child. For years she prayed for one then accepted her loss as God's will. Lizzie had had many pregnancies – but they all culminated in stillbirths, miscarriages, or babies who lived for only a short time before succumbing to one of the many fevers and childhood illnesses that were prevalent in Dublin before World War One. Then, on the change of life when like Cissie she was accepting her childless state, Lizzie had Julia – who, like all change-of-life babies, was affectionately referred to as 'the shakings of the bag'. It wasn't unusual for women to start their childbearing at twenty and finish at forty-five or six.

Lizzie and Cissie were now widows. Cissie thought of Lizzie's daughter as if she were her own – there was nothing she wouldn't do for her. Night and day she had prayed that the girl's husband Jack would be spared and today, preparing the party for his homecoming, her heart was overjoyed for him and Julia. Leaving the tables and walking towards their houses they began to talk about the murder of two policemen the previous day. 'Between that and the Irish Parliament having its first meeting today I feel uneasy,' said Lizzie.

'I hope there won't be trouble like during the Rebellion. More civilians were killed in that than soldiers or volunteers.'

'Like many a one I had no time for them that started it, but I changed my mind after the executions. Fifteen in nine days, and poor James Connolly already at death's door propped on a chair to be shot. I never paid much attention to the stories before, about the British and their brutal ways of treating the Irish. The executions changed all that.'

'You weren't on your own,' said Cissie. 'Thank God anyway in the street we'd be well away from trouble, with it being secluded and no one here having ever bothered with the illegal organisations.'

'Thank God again,' Lizzie echoed.

They reached their front doors, agreeing to finish laying the tables later that evening.

The street was narrow and not very long. You entered it after crossing a piece of vacant ground through which feet and cartwheels had embedded a fairly wide track. Fifteen two-storeyed, redbricked houses lined either side, their front doors opening directly on to the pavement. At the back of each house a long garden ran down to an embankment beyond which was the railway line. Another large piece of vacant ground stretched from the end of the street for a quarter of a mile to more terraced streets.

It was said by people living there that fifty years ago or more, plans had existed to build houses on both vacant lots, but the builder had run out of money. The present-day inhabitants congratulated themselves on the builder's bad luck. The street, they said, was an ideal size, the vacant lots a god-send for rearing children — ready-made playgrounds. The young and not-so-young played football on them and pitch and toss, knocked hurley balls about and even had some makeshift games of cricket.

Wild flowers grew there; daisies and buttercups from which the little girls made chains to hang round their necks, and dandelions and docks. They tore off the golden dandelion heads and made whistles of their fat, milk-leaking stems. When the flowers seeded they called the beautiful fragile heads 'ginny joes', and with puffs of breath helped propagate the seeds as they sent them on their journey up into the sky; counting how many breaths it took to strip the head, and when they were very young believing the number of puffs told them the time of day.

It was, everyone agreed, a great place to live. They had good, comfortable houses, some with two and some with three bedrooms. There was a parlour, a big kitchen and a lean-to scullery and wash house. The men were tradesmen or semi-skilled. Ill health and bad weather knocked them off work but seldom for long, so that they were comfortable — all except for the Dalys, whose father hadn't a trade or skill and relied on

3

labouring work. A poor lookout it would be for his sons when they left school, the men and women commented. If your father hadn't a trade to land his son into, or a responsible job like Jack Harte's father, who was the foreman in the sawmills, labouring was all that faced you.

On warm evenings they gathered outside their front doors to gossip, the men leaving the women to go to the public house for a pint or two of porter. In bad weather they congregated in each others' houses. They talked a lot, sang a lot, and God, they said, was good and the Divil not as black as He was painted. From morning till night their hall doors stayed open and when, rarely, they were locked, a key on a piece of string could be reached through the letter box. Everyone in the street knew each other. Many had been born in it; many of their parents or relatives before them.

There was one, however, who remained virtually a stranger although she had been there for over twenty years. Her name was Rosie Quinlan. From the moment of her arrival as a young married woman with a new baby, she had made it clear that she didn't want to be neighbourly. Peering from behind their curtains, the women of the street had watched her move in, the unpacking of the cart with her furniture. They felt a mixture of curiosity and sympathy for a young woman with a baby faced with the ordeal of setting up home; she was maybe unfamiliar with the vagaries of the range, not knowing where the shops were, probably gasping for a cup of tea. So two of them went to bid her welcome and enquire if there was anything they could do to help. They invited her to come and have a cup of tea with them, or mind the baby while she sorted herself out. To their amazement, all offers were refused politely but firmly.

'It's very kind of you, but no thanks all the same. I have all my wants and can manage.'

They reported back, 'She never asked us inside the door !' An unheard-of thing in the street.

'Is she Dublin ?' someone asked.

'She is, but puts on the talk.'

'One of Them, eh.'

'Definitely one of Them.'

Rosie Quinlan kept them out of her house, but she couldn't actually pass them by : the paths were so narrow it would have meant stepping into the road to do so. She didn't have that much nerve and in any case, she welcomed the opportunity to boast – make it clear that she wasn't one of them. Where she came from in Dublin she never divulged, although she did admit that her husband, a plasterer, had been reared on the northside ; her manner suggested she was apologising for his origins.

4

She talked about having worked for the gentry, for a Lord and Lady Glenivy – of the position she had held there as Lady's maid. How she still had connections with that noble family, who apparently thought the world of her.

Every woman in the street in turn heard about the Glenivys. They listened, suppressing their desire to laugh or to mockingly express their surprise that she had ever deigned to settle in the street, let alone marry a plasterer from the northside. In time, if they saw her when they left their own house, they would invariably find an excuse to turn back. And all agreed she was a stuck-up beggar – a skivvy who'd lost the run of herself working for the gentry. No one ever called to her house again nor she to theirs.

The child, Sarah, grew up into a pretty little girl. She was never allowed into the street or on to the vacant lots to play, but after starting school she began to go around with Julia Mangan. From their first day in school, she and Julia had formed an attachment for each other.

Mr Quinlan kept himself to himself, just like his wife. He never went to the public house, though men who sometimes worked with him on the same job said he was decent enough – a quiet sort of a bloke, downtrodden, they believed. The women found no difficulty in believing that. Anyone with a wife like Rosie Quinlan couldn't avoid it.

So the newcomers were left to themselves. The other families might sometimes quarrel, usually over children, they never stayed bad friends for long. No one knew what loneliness was. A neighbour was always on hand to go with another to a doctor. For invalids they cooked egg custards, calf-foot jelly and dainty morsels to tempt flagging appetites. At times of birth and death they helped and consoled. Children were watched over by everyone in the street, shielded from danger, corrected for impudence and any form of destruction.

In idleness they had a gracious way of slipping a man a sixpence for a smoke, his wife a loaf, a pint of milk, sticks and coal for the fire, shoes and clothes out of which their own children had grown.

During the war they prayed for the men from the street who went to fight, for their safe return or a merciful death. Eight of the ten who had volunteered were killed: only Barney Daly and Jack Harte survived, and tonight, they were coming home. The street rejoiced. And the party for their welcome would be the best Dublin had ever seen.

In the Quinlans' kitchen, Sarah picked up the photograph of Barney from the mantelpiece. It had been taken not long before he went to France. Her mother watched her bring it to the table, sit and begin studying it. Rosie's hands itched to snatch the frame from her daughter's fingers, hurl it into the fire and watch the picture in its tortoiseshell frame go up in smoke. As many a time during the war, she had wished a similar end to Barney Daly, who had come into Sarah's life and ruined Rosie's plans for her daughter's future. Sarah was taller and stronger than her now. A tussle for the photograph was out of the question: Sarah wouldn't be beyond lashing out with a blow. So she had to be content with speaking her anger and disappointment.

'Whatever possessed you to take up with him I'll never know. Into service you should have gone – you'd have been well established by now. But not you – oh no, you threw it all up for him.'

'Give over, Ma,' said Sarah. 'You said yourself, any time I changed my mind I could still go to Glenivy. It's not too late.'

'Five years you've lost. You were meant to start at fifteen. By now you'd have been a parlourmaid, maybe even her Ladyship's maid. You threw it all away for that scut. God knows I tried to stop you, but you're the wilful child.'

God knows you did, Sarah remembered, putting down the picture of Barney in uniform and asking herself how she'd feel towards him after four years' separation. Would she still love him? Had she ever loved him? 'You tried all right,' she said to herself, as the memory of the night her mother found out she was seeing him came to her mind as vividly as if the scene was happening now.

It was a summer's evening just before her fifteenth birthday. She was going into service the following month, to work in Glenivy, the fairy-tale palace which from her mother's endless stories she knew so well. The place where her mother had worked until she married; the place where lords and ladies danced until dawn, strolled arm in arm through gardens filled with sweet-smelling flowers and the ladies wore gowns of silks and satins whose colours outshone the flowers.

Glenivy was a magical place where servant girls, not half as beautiful as she, married lords and lived happily ever after. She fantasised about all the wonderful things that would happen there and daily, with more stories, her mother encouraged her.

While other girls in the street found jobs in laundries, sewing and biscuit factories, Sarah counted the days until her departure for the Big House – until that summer evening when she stood with a crowd of boys and girls at the top of the street, tricking. Not that *she* was tricking. She stood on the edge of the crowd watching as they hurled mock insults at each other, pushing and shoving with pretended ferocity. Boys stole girls' scarves and ribbons and ran away with them, and the girls, sqealing as if they really objected, gave chase. They caught the boys and tussled each other . . . their arms pinned to their sides, brought close to the boys'

6

bodies, with their shining ringlets touching their cheeks, their faces and the boys' became flushed with the pleasure of experiencing thrilling sensations.

'All except me,' Sarah recalled. 'I was left like a lemon. It had happened before and I never minded – knowing I was too good for any of them. I didn't want to be pulled about by the rough common boys – *I* was going to work for the gentry, not spend my life in the street. I had nicer clothes, I didn't talk common. But that night, that lovely warm night when all the others were squealing and laughing and tricking with their flushed faces and shining eyes, I suddenly felt lonely. For the first time ever I wanted to belong, to be one of the street. And for the first time too I became frightened of going away to live in a strange place.

'I wanted to be like Julia – my only friend, though sometimes I hated her. In a way I knew I always had. Everything came easy to her. She never bothered to put rags in her hair and still it always looked nice. In school she was the best in the class without always having her nose stuck in a book. Everyone liked her. And Jack Harte loved her. I could have killed her for that. Jack Harte was the only boy I would have bothered with but no one stood a chance with him except Julia. She loved me. I was her best friend and most of the time I loved her too, except when I felt jealous.

'So there I was all on my own – they'd started chasing each other again – when Barney Daly appears, looking better than usual. He had got a start in the foundry and his mother had bought him his first suit. He was all done up in it. He started making jokes about the fellas and girls up on the vacant lot chasing each other.

' "Paddy Mac runs like a carthorse – one of the Guinness's big ones. And Jemser's after Allie – she'll give him a run for his money."

' "It's a wonder you're not in there with them," I said back.

'He went beetroot red, shuffled his feet and couldn't look me in the eye while mumbling, "I might if it was you I was chasing." And then in a flurry of words: "I've always had a smack for you."

'I was thrilled, forgetting that I'd never given him a second look, forgetting all my mother had pumped into me about being above the others in the street. Forgetting Glenivy. *Someone fancied me.* I said to him, "You're mad, so you are," and pushed him the way the other girls did. He stole my hair-ribbon and ran off with it. I let on to be furious and chased him, when he caught me struggling and twisting in his arms. It was gorgeous being held against him – more gorgeous than all the dreams of Glenivy. It was real and gorgeous . . .'

Her mother moved about the kitchen preparing the evening meal – a shepherd's pie from the remains of Sunday's cold mutton. Sarah aban-

7

doned her reminiscences of the evening she got off with Barney for the moment to aggravate her mother.

' "Another one of your concoctions", that's what my da'll say when that's put before him,' she commented as her mother layered mashed potatoes on the pie.

'A lot I care what he says, or does either,' replied her mother. 'Just because the women in this street know how to cook nothing but a lump of boiled bacon or corned beef served hot on Sunday and cold on Monday with fried cabbage and brown sauce doesn't mean I have to do the same.'

While Rosie went back to fluffing up the potatoes with a fork, Sarah returned to her thoughts, recalling her mother's fury when as it got dark she left Barney and went home. Like someone demented she was. Her eyes were narrowed, glinting; she almost frothed at the mouth. 'You whipster!' she'd screamed. 'I saw you. You and him! And he dog-mauling you.'

'We were only tricking.'

'Tricking – is that what you call it! I'll give you tricking. Take that!' Then she'd hit me hard across the face . . .

'My father was asleep by the fire,' Sarah remembered. 'My screams woke him. "Da, make her stop, she hit me for nothing. She's doing it again – make her stop it, Da!" The slaps stung but it was the shock that knocked me sideways. She had never in her life hit me before. My father got out of the chair and without a word went to bed.

'I hated her. I hated him. I was raging. In my temper I could have killed her. She came for me again. I raised my hand to hit her but she was bigger and stronger than me. She went hysterical, screaming at the top of her voice: "Raise your hand to the mother that brought you into the world," knocking away my arm and grabbing hold of my hair, twisting and pulling it until I was in agony and expected to see it come out in handfuls. And all the while she ranted and raved about the Dalys and Barney.

' "To get mixed up with one of them! But I'll put a stop to it. I'll kill you if you ever go near him again – I'll swing for you! You won't put a foot outside the door. I'll tie you to the bed and lock you in."

'She looked like a madwoman. Then there was a loud knock on the door – a neighbour, probably thinking someone was being murdered. The shock on her face when she realised she had been overheard. The show she'd made of us! Her that was so respectable, coming down to the level of a tinker. She let go of my hair. And while she was off-guard, I gave her a hard punch in the chest. She let on she was dying. Clutching her chest, gasping as if her heart was giving out, collapsing on a chair and crying quietly. Sobbing that she was sorry for hitting me. That it was only for my own good. "I wanted the best for you. I didn't want you finishing up married in the street. Everything was for you.' Her tear-filled eyes pleaded with me, but I saw something other than pleading in them. She was afraid. Afraid of me: of me screaming again, defying her about Glenivy, hitting her. I wan't sure which. Maybe all of those things. In any case she knew something had altered in our relationship. No longer would my mother hold sway over me. She stopped crying and spoke again. Her tone had changed – all the bullying gone. Now it was whining, persuasive.

' "You'll still go to Glenivy like a good girl, won't you ?"

' "Why wouldn't I ?"

'She looked relieved. I didn't bother to add, "I'll go if and when I feel like it, and in the meantime see Barney when I want to." And I did. Not that I was mad about him, but it passed the time. Besides, all the other girls had fellas. Without a fella you were no one . . .'

Sarah's mother finished with the pie and took a yellow turnip from the vegetable bag. While washing, peeling and cutting it into slices she brought up Barney's name. 'I wouldn't say he'll find it easy to get work.'

'We'll just have to wait and see,' said Sarah.

'And now the war's over I'd say your job dispatching uniforms from the warehouse will be a thing of the past.'

'I suppose so,' Sarah replied and waited for the question about when, if ever, she would go into service in Glenivy. However, for once she had read her mother's mind wrong. When Rosie spoke again it was on a different subject. Sarah didn't listen, recalling instead how she had slipped into seeing Barney regularly and how her mother had taken the news that she didn't want to go to Glenivy until she was sixteen.

She saw again the colour drain from Rosie's face on the day she had told her, heard her coaxing and wheedling which quickly changed to complaints. 'You'll regret what you're doing for the rest of your life. He'll never earn a living for you.'

'I'm only going out with him, not thinking of getting married,' Sarah scoffed. 'Next year I'll go into service.'

'D'ye promise me that ?'

'As true as God.'

Watching her chop the turnip now, Sarah thought what cowards her father and mother were. If she had a child who defied her so openly, *she* would have found some way of bending his or her will – certainly, she wouldn't have gone on keeping them for nothing! But her mother wouldn't send her into a factory or shop or service in Dublin. She would have starved rather than let the neighbours think she couldn't keep her daughter, though there was more to it than that, Sarah mused. 'She couldn't have made me go out to work but more important, she was frightened that if I did get a job I might like it and give up the idea of the Big House altogether.

'All she did was moan and complain and point out how without experience Lady Glenivy liked her staff to start young. To all of which I slung the deaf ear, for life before the war was great. Getting up when I liked, hours to do myself up, at the weekends going round in a foursome, sometimes the whole crowd from the street going with us. Usually, though, it was just me, Jack, Julia and Barney going up the Park, up the mountains, riding on top of the tram to the seaside. And if there was anything good at the Olympia, getting seats in the gods. It was a great time before Jack and Barney went to France. Some nights we'd play cards in Julia's parlour for ha'pennies. And then there was the bit of courting with Barney. He was very respectful. Never trying his hand on.

'Days and weeks flew by. Before I knew it I'd been going out with him for almost two years, only giving Glenivy a thought when my ma nagged, then telling myself I'd pack him in soon and go into service. For pleasant though my life was, I had no intention of settling for the street.

'Then Jack bought Julia an engagement ring and Barney bought one for me – a little bit of a thing with a half-circle of what was supposed to be diamonds. That's the way it is in the street – everyone copies the next one.'

Rosie Quinlan finished the preparations for her husband's meal and sat at the table. 'I see,' she said, 'that you're wearing his ring again.' Since Barney had gone to the war Sarah had seldom worn it.

'He'll be looking for it when he comes.'

'I often wonder where he got the money for it. Not honestly, I'd bet.'

Sarah had heard all this before – the accusations of Barney's dishonesty. In the beginning she'd defended him, saying he had probably saved it, won it on a horse or borrowed it from his brothers. She eventually found out that his mother had lent him the money, though she never bothered to let Rosie know this. She took pleasure in aggravating her, no longer caring how much she gave out about Barney or the Dalys, for when it suited her, Sarah would send Barney packing.

Now and then she felt a stirring of pity for Rosie, as on the night when she'd brought home the engagement ring. Her grief seemed genuine enough then. 'May God pity you for throwing yourself away on him,' she'd said, and her face had a woebegone look.

'Who said anything about throwing myself away?'

'You're engaged to him, aren't you, even if it is with a ring that looks as if it came from the Penny Bazaar or out of a Lucky Bag.'

'Engagements,' Sarah told her, 'like promises are made to be broken.'

'Aye, like all the promises you've broken about going to Glenivy. I doubt if they'd have you now.'

'That took the wind out of my sails,' Sarah admitted to herself, for one day I did intend to go there. One day I'd tell Barney to take his ring and feck off. He was like a cringing dog. I swear to God he'd have killed for me. It got in on my nerves and at the same time I liked the power I had over him. But I'd have to be desperate to marry him.

' "You're not serious about Glenivy not wanting me?" I asked her.

' "You're older than the usual inexperienced girls they take on."

' "But with your influence, couldn't it be done?"

' "Well, maybe," she admitted, "but I'll only try if you swear to God you'll go soon."

'I swore and that shut her up for a while. I half-meant the promise, only something always seemed to crop up when I was nearly ready to pack Barney in and go. Christmas was coming or St Patrick's Day and a dance. Then it was the summer. Before I knew it there was talk of war, some foreign Duke and his wife shot in a place I'd never heard of, the cause of all the talk. Me and Julia were eighteen. Jack asked her to marry him. Barney proposed to me. I said I'd think about it. I wasn't completely lying, either. Such an atmosphere there was – drums and flags, rousing music. Uniforms everywhere. Every other one getting married. I was caught up in the excitement, especially when I saw Barney in uniform: he looked really handsome. I really fancied him in it.

'I tried out the marriage question on my mother, and then realised that I hadn't completely cowed her as I had thought. She went mad. Not caring about who heard her, she screamed at the top of her voice: "You cock-crowed it over me once. Struck me – your mother that brought you into the world. That's branded on my memory till my dying day. And well I know you'd do it again. Do it again, then – I don't care. Batter my brains out with the poker. Kill me stone dead. For that's what you'll have to do if you want to marry and bring that excuse for a man to live on my floor."

'I knew she meant it. Marriage was serious; marriage was for keeps. Young couples with little money had to live with parents or relations, and my mother would go to the ends of the earth to prevent me marrying. Not that I'd been considering it seriously, though I suppose in the climate that was in it had she been willing I might have married him.

'He was broken-hearted when I refused. "Oh Sarah," he said, and he was crying. "I love you. The thought of you being my wife would give

11

me something to fight for, something to live for. Every day I'd be thinking about you. Telling myself I had to live for you."

'I let on to be as broken-hearted as he, promised I'd wait for him and wouldn't go into service while he was away. And was relieved when he left for France.

'I liked the job in the warehouse, dispatching uniforms. I enjoyed having money of my own. The girls were common but a good laugh. We joked about our fellas who were at the Front – how far they had tried to go, using the excuse that they might be killed before they ever knew what it was to have a woman. Not all of them joked – other wans were dead serious, always praying and doing novenas for their blokes to come home safe.

'I never gave that a thought, though I did write to Barney and sent him parcels. All he wrote about was how much he loved me. His letters were a scream – at least until the war ended, when he started on again about us getting married . . .'

Rosie Quinlan got up from the table. 'I'm going out for an hour,' she announced. 'Put the turnips on a slow boil and the pie in the oven before you go for your walk with Julia.'

They looked at each other. Both of them were dark-haired, though Rosie's was faintly streaked with silver. Their cheekbones were high and their eyes deeply set. They had good teeth: when they smiled you were very conscious of their white even teeth, for they appeared to have more to their mouths than other people. And if you had a morbid turn of mind they made you think of skulls . . .

Sarah remembered something she had meant to say to her mother earlier while they were talking about the pie. 'I was thinking, Ma. You and my da don't hit it off. I often wonder why you ever married him.'

'Because I was a fool. Because I thought I was in love. The same thing will happen to you if you aren't careful.'

'Me?' said Sarah, as if she had no idea what her mother was alluding to. 'I don't know what you're talking about.'

'That ring you're wearing to meet him. He'll be expecting to marry you. I don't know what you feel for him, but if you delude yourself it's love you're finished. And don't interrupt, just listen. I let myself be deluded and look where it got me – in this house in this street, tied to a man I can't abide, who won't change out of his working clothes, won't wash the plaster off his hands, and eats like a pig, shovelling the food into his mouth and cups of tea at the same time.

'A man,' she went on passionately, 'that if he'd had any go in him would have had his own plastering firm years ago, and provided me and you with a decent place to live. But no, there's not an ounce of ambi-

12

tion in him. Work, food and stretch out in front of the fire asleep and his mouth hanging open catching flies, that's all he's capable of. And that's your future if you marry Barney Daly. Worse, for at least your father has a trade, and he's earned enough for us to find somewhere to live. You'll be in a tenement room infested with rats and have a streel of children in no time. Why did you have to be such a stubborn child? Why, when he went to the war, didn't you go to Glenivy?'

'I promised him I wouldn't.'

'You've a great way of breaking promises. How come you kept your word where *he* was concerned?'

'I just did,' she said. Though that wasn't the real reason. She liked the way her life was – the company in work, having Julia all to herself with Jack away. She just liked everything the way it was. She didn't want to change it for a place in the country, for Glenivy, which wasn't so much in her mind these days. But now with Barney coming home and wanting to marry her, Sarah was having second thoughts, beginning to admit that Rosie's warnings might be right, after all. Barney wasn't much of a prospect.

Her mother continued talking: 'I don't know where I went wrong with you. God knows I did my best. Forever from the time you could understand I told you what life in Glenivy was like, the chances I lost through marrying the wrong man! There were plenty in Glenivy after me, many a man on the staff that's now coining it with places of their own – small hotels and boarding-houses. I didn't want you making my mistake. I wanted only the best for you.'

Sarah heard none of this; her mind had wandered into the past, where she listened to her mother telling of Glenivy, her own childish voice prompting Rosie whenever she paused in the telling. 'Tell me more, Mammy. Tell me what the ladies wore to the balls.'

'Gowns you've never seen the likes of – silks and satins, velvets and brocades. Silver and gold, creams and whites, pinks and cerises, apple green and lime green, azure blues and blues as deep as the night. And their hair would be curled up on the top of their head with jewels in it, and at their throats and bosoms. Like magic it was. Like something out of a fairy tale.'

'I wish I could see it, Mammy.'

'You will one day, my little dote. You will.'

'And were the ladies and gentlemen nice, Mammy?'

'Lovely. The nicest people on earth. That polite and well-mannered and handsome and beautiful, like fairy princes and princesses.'

'Could I marry one of them when I grow up?'

13

'And why not? Aren't you as beautiful as any one of the fine ladies . . .'

'Sarah, you're not listening to a word I'm saying!'

'Sorry, Ma, I was miles away, remembering the stories you used to tell me about Glenivy when I was a little girl.'

'Not so little. Wasn't I still telling them until you took up with that scut. It's him I want to talk about.'

'I thought you were going out,' said Sarah, hoping to escape more of her mother's nagging.

'I've decided not to; mind yourself tonight at that party.'

'How d'ye mean, *mind* myself?'

'That fella will have had little to do with women during the war, and deprived men are like wild beasts. Go getting yourself into trouble and it's the Union or down the country with the nuns in a home for fallen women you'll land.'

'For God's sake what d'ye take me for?'

'I'm warning you, that's all.'

'Will you not change your mind and come to the party?'

'I'll do no such thing. Street parties are common. You should have seen the one they had at Glenivy when Master Patrick came home from the war. Remember, I was asked to go down and help? And Lady Glenivy asked if you were ever going to work for her. I made an excuse about your war work – you know, the uniforms – the gentry are all for that sort of thing. Anyway, that was a party and a half. They roasted an ox. The tenants were all there. There was a fireworks display, barrels of beer and crates and crates of champagne for the gentry.'

'And Master Patrick, what's he like?'

'The handsomest man you've ever seen. Over six feet tall and with gorgeous red hair. If anyone asks about me this evening, say I have one of my headaches. That's no lie, either. In fact it's that bad I'm going to throw myself on the bed for half an hour.'

Left on her own, Sarah thought over the things her mother had said, admitting to herself that her father *was* a slob. He could have worked harder and got them out of the street. She didn't want to finish up here. She didn't want to marry Barney unless the war had worked a miracle on him – had given him more brains and go so that he might make something of himself. That would be a miracle, all right. Anyway, she'd wait and see what he was like. Four years might have changed him. 'God!' she said aloud, looking at the clock. 'Is that the time? I said I'd go for a walk with Julia.' She took the pie from the oven and went out.

A little later she and Julia came out of the Mangans' house carrying cups

14

and plates. After placing them on the tables they linked arms and walked down the street. 'For a breath of fresh air' they had said earlier, when deciding on the walk, 'and to calm our strung-up nerves'. Julia was ecstatic at the thought of Jack's return, though nervous at the same time about their reunion after the long separation. Following the talk with her mother, Sarah's mind was now in turmoil, but nevertheless, she said what she thought she believed: 'As long as I live I'll never forget it to your Jack for saving Barney's life.'

They were a pretty pair of young women with good figures and abundant hair. The front of Sarah's curled naturally, making a nimbus of tendrils round her forehead, while the wintry sun low in the sky highlighted the auburn tints in Julia's nut-brown curls. Affectionately she squeezed Sarah's arm and assured her that Barney would have done the same thing for Jack.

'I suppose so,' said Sarah, 'but all the same I'll never forget, nor Barney either. You're lucky being married. I'm all mixed up, one minute wanting to be and the next not.'

'But you love him?'

'I don't know, and that's the God's honest truth.'

'That's only nerves. They've been gone a long time – but wait'll you see him, then there'll be no more doubts.'

'I hope so,' said Sarah. 'Will you stay on in your mother's?'

'Oh, yes. Her and Jack get on like a house on fire and there's plenty of room.'

'I want a place of my own when I do marry.'

'Where, for instance?' asked Julia surprised at Sarah's pronouncement, for nearly everyone started off living on someone else's floor.

'I'm not sure exactly, but out of the street. A better neighbourhood – a good address.'

Julia said nothing, except to herself: 'I hope it keeps fine for you. It's grand ideas you have and I know where you got them. After your mother you're taking – Lord and Lady Glenivy's ex-parlourmaid, who doesn't think the street is good enough for her.' Sickening everyone with her constant talk of her time in the Big House in Kildare. The beautiful daughters who had married an earl and a duke. The handsome young master. The fishing and the shooting, the balls and house-parties, the Season in London and Lady this-one and Lord that-one.

Lizzie Mangan didn't like Julia being friends with Sarah, and often said that Rosie Quinlan was an unlucky woman, meaning not that ill-luck attended her but that by associating with her or Sarah, ill-luck could come into your life.

Now, walking with Sarah, the gist of these conversations returned to

Julia's mind, and Lizzie's comment: 'There's something about that young wan. Her face, her smile – they give me the shivers. I wish you'd find someone else to pal round with.'

'But I like her, Ma. We've been pals all our lives. We started school together, she was my partner for my Holy Communion.' Julia didn't add that now at sixteen they were close confidantes, sharing their secrets and hopes, which centred on marrying Jack and Barney.

She knew Sarah's faults even back then. Like her mother, she boasted about their connections with the gentry. Repeating how beautiful they were, how handsome; the magnificence of their home. It was enough to make you sick if you paid too much attention. Julia didn't, for she knew well how the gentry looked. Weren't you falling over them in Grafton Street, seeing the women going in and out of the Shelbourne, and their men into the Kildare Street Club.

They were stylish, elegant, some handsome and beautiful. You'd look and admire their clothes, but only as you would the clothes in Brown Thomas'. They were things to stare at and fleetingly long for, like pictures in a book, not real, not connected with your world. And so you passed on and put the images from your mind.

But Sarah and her mother lived through them, talked as if they were on intimate terms with the Glenivys, when in fact their only connection was the presents sent at Christmas, which her own mother dismissed as charity, looking after the peasants and proselytising.

Now, nearing the end of the street, Julia recalled how once she had challenged her mother when she decried the sending of the presents. 'Tell me this, Ma. You're a city woman and you were never in service, so how come you know so much about the gentry?'

'Aren't they in the city, too. Aren't they everywhere – all over the world and behaving the same way. Natives they call us, meaning savages, quaint characters, not to be trusted or taken seriously. Wasn't my mother and hers acquainted with the Big Houses, and like them, haven't I the long memory. At their knees I heard the stories of the Famine and the evictions. And tales of the same gentry who evicted and then stayed dancing till dawn at their balls and carousing at the levees in the Castle. Very civil people they are. They'd enquire about your health and with as much concern about your dog. But for all that I'm not a flag-waver or a drum-beater. The time will come when they have to go – but to hasten it I wouldn't wish one drop of anyone's blood shed. I rarely give them a thought. What brought up this coversation, anyway?'

'You,' Julia remembered having replied to her mother. 'It was you on about the Quinlans.'

'So it was,' Lizzie nodded. 'Them and their likes are the ones that make my blood boil – the arse-lickers, the worshippers of the gentry; the Irish that have suffered as much down the years as anyone else. The gentry live in a world of their own – they know no better, but as for the Quinlans, the toadies with their admiration and aspirations, I could set fire to the lot of them! And on top of everything else, the Quinlans are unlucky, mother and daughter. Remember what I'm telling you: never confide in Sarah anything you care about. They are grabbers who'd do anything to further themselves. Hang you, for a leg-up in the world.'

All these memories passed one after another through Julia's mind in the time it took her and Sarah to walk up and back down the street. As they reached her front door and she asked Sarah in for a cup of tea, a shiver ran over her so that her flesh stood out in goose pimples. 'Someone is walking over my grave,' she said.

Sarah laughed, a nervous laugh. 'Don't you be talking about graves. You're cold, that's all. Sit over by the fire and I'll make a hot cup of tea. You wouldn't want to catch a chill.' She smiled, showing her pearly teeth – a smile that never reached her eyes.

An image of a skull flashed across Julia's mind – a grinning skull, a death's-head. All teeth. 'Her mother has the same smile,' she shuddered and moved closer to the heat. 'I'm getting as bad as *my* mother. Seeing things that don't exist. Thinking about unlucky women and all because Sarah said she wanted to better herself.'

While Sarah made the tea, Julia wrestled with her strange thoughts. Dismissing her mother's superstitions and premonitions was easy, – *if* you ignored how often they had proved right. Hadn't she dreamt that Jack would join the army? 'I saw your Jack in uniform last night in my dream, as plain as I'm seeing you,' she had said one morning just after the war started. 'He's going to join the army, never mind what he may have said to you.'

'I was just sitting down to my breakfast when she said it,' Julia remembered. 'I nearly died. My heart dropped like a stone and left a hollow sick feeling where it should have been. And my mother kept talking. "I saw him going away, and I saw him coming back."

'I screamed and banged the table. "Shut up! Shut up! I don't want to hear." I kept screaming and banging the table with my fist. The cups danced and the cat got the fright of its life and ran from its place by the fire. I was still screaming. Hysterical I was. "Jack's not going to the war. He promised. He's not going. He's not. *He's not!*"

'And she said: "I only told you my dream. Stop that screaming this minute or I'll slap your face. And don't, married woman though you are, ever raise your voice to me again."

17

'She was right about that, Jack *did* go to the war. My tears and pleadings and threats did not move him and in the end, though I was broken-hearted, he made me understand. He couldn't hang back when everyone else was going – Barney, all his pals, the fellas in work, half the Boxing Club. Everyone was going. Someone had to stop what was going on over there. The Germans couldn't be allowed to get away with it. No country could go marching into another one, into little countries like Belgium, committing the atrocities the Germans were.'

And Lizzie was right about other things, too. She dreamed other dreams – ones about the deaths of young men they knew. But she never again mentioned Jack's name in the mornings when she related her dreams.

'You haven't touched your tea. Are you sure you're not sick?' Sarah's voice recalled Julia to the present. Sarah, with a smile on her lovely face. Sarah, looking like her old self again.

'I don't know what came over me. Excitement, maybe. The thought of seeing Jack again after all the years. Wasn't God good to us! I can't believe he and Barney are coming home. Can you believe it, Sarah? Our men are safe. Isn't it wonderful? Weren't we lucky? Imagine it – everything will be like it was before, the four of us together again. If you move from here don't go too far away. Don't let anything split us up, sure you won't.'

Sarah sat beside her, a look of discontent appearing in her eyes. 'It's all very well for you – you're married. You still have your work. Tonight you'll be in bed with Jack. I'll be lucky if we can find somewhere for a bit of a court.'

'You'll get more work. You knew the job in the warehouse dispatching uniforms would come to an end once the war was over, but you'll get another one and so will Barney. And then you'll have such a wedding! And with God's help, long and happy lives before us. Come on now, Sarah, don't look so down in the mouth. Whatever it was that happened to me a few minutes ago is happening to you now. Nerves – that's what it is. Four years is a long time to wait for someone but you'll see, everything will be all right. I suppose in a way we're a bit frightened about seeing them again. Wondering if they'll have changed, if they'll think we have changed. It's only nerves.' Julia took hold of Sarah's hand and squeezed it encouragingly.

'Don't mind me,' said Sarah, letting go of Julia's hand and standing up. 'Listen, we'd better start getting ready. I'll go now and see you later.'

Soon after she left, Julia's mother came in. 'The tables are looking grand. If the rain only keeps off we'll have a great night,' she said.

'Whether it does or not, we still have a grand night. I'd better go and dress myself.'

'What are you wearing?'

'What I was married in. I wore it to say goodbye and I'll wear it again to greet him.' She cried then. 'Oh, Ma, isn't it marvellous? In no time he'll be here.'

'And if you don't get a move on, left standing on the quay,' Lizzie said, turning away so that Julia shouldn't see the tears of joy shining in her eyes. As she left the room her mother called after her, 'I hope the dress still fits you!'

'It does,' she called back with certainty. She could afford to be certain, for once a week during the long four years she had tried on her wedding dress, the blue crêpe wool georgette with its softly gathered skirt and sweetheart neckline, and had taken from its box her bridal hat, also blue with a pale-grey grosgrain ribbon which on the day of her wedding Jack had said was the colour of her eyes. Now she dressed in the outfit once again and while she waited for Sarah's call her mind went back in time . . .

. . . Back to the night before her wedding. Everything was ready: her dress laid out and the hat, covered in tissue paper, on a chest of drawers. The dress was carefully arranged on the spare single bed next to her underwear, which the girls in work had made and given her as a wedding present. It was of white cambric, faggoted and threaded through with ribbons of the palest blue, while her nightdress was made of satin and had a matching bed-jacket. They were delicate, beautiful garments such as she had often made in the workroom for other women's trousseaux. Admiring them, joining in the other girls' jokes about 'first nights'. The older, married ones looking smug, never imparting the secrets that were theirs; secrets that the younger and not so young (for there were many old maids) longed to know, and imagined as best they could from overheard snatches of conversation. References to picking a date when you wouldn't be unwell because men wouldn't like a refusal on their 'first night'.

Julia had picked up the nightdress and held it in front of her, imagining the following night. Having to get undressed in front of a man, even though the man was Jack, scared and excited her at the same time. Supposing Jack turned out to be one of those men she had heard about who became like an animal – pouncing on you, hurting you, with thought only for themselves. But no, she told herself, Jack wouldn't be like that. Jack wouldn't turn into a mad thing. Maybe it would hurt, but no bride she had ever seen looked the worse for wear the morning after her first night. They looked pretty, happy, coy – some as if nothing out

19

of the ordinary had happened though everyone knew it had. It all depended on the girl's disposition.

No, she repeated, it wasn't the thought of intimacy that frightened her. She loved Jack so much, adored him. The smell of him, the taste of his mouth, the hardness below his waist when sometimes their courting almost got out of hand. That was what marriage was about. Being close, being one. What frightened her was the seriousness of the commitment. Marriage was a sacrament, one that bound you together for the rest of your life, for thirty, forty, maybe even fifty years. Sometimes when she was in school and after a nun had spoken about becoming a Bride of Christ, she had felt that maybe she had a vocation. She imagined a life of prayer, a life in the convent in an order like the Presentation Nuns, who never went outside except in a closed cab, who prayed before taking classes and after classes, who devoted their every moment to God. The lessons they taught, everything they did, was offered up to God. And she remembered the beauty of early-morning Mass in the Oratory chapel, the flowers and the incense, the black robes of the nuns which in school were pinned at the hem to make their movements easy, undone, trailing behind them as they glided to their prie-dieux. She was overcome with a sense of vocation: this was how she wanted to spend her life. Her conviction had become so real that one day she spoke of it to the Mother Superior, who listened and when she had finished speaking, told her that she was to pray every day for God to direct her. Not every woman was meant to be a nun: God didn't want that. God wanted nuns and mothers, women who married and women who didn't. God wanted for women what they wanted for themselves.

'So pray, child. Every day say a special prayer for God to direct you. You're a good, lovely child, but a child is still what you are. Pray and we'll talk about it again. A lot of girls at your age believe they have a vocation, and we are delighted when it turns out to be a true calling. D'ye see, Julia, a vocation is for life. If you are given the gift of one you would come into a convent for the rest of your life. Think about that and what it means.'

For almost a year she was convinced that she had received the call, and then doubts set in. Supposing God directed her, made known to her that a nun was what He had ordained her to be. And then supposing once she was in the convent she didn't like the life, but because she had made her vows, there she would have to stay for the rest of her life ... She was terrified. All her life would be lived as a lie. She'd be praying while her mind was outside the walls. She'd be in a cell praying when she wanted to be outside in the world.

She'd have her hair cut off and wear long black robes. She hated black.

At about the time that doubts and fears began to fill her mind, Jack Harte, who until then had simply been a friend, took on a new importance. When he caught and imprisoned her in their games of Relievo, pleasureful sensations coursed through her body, through her developing breasts, in her private parts. And though Jack had never handled her roughly in their games, now his touch was tender. Not even to Sarah, her confidante, did she mention what was happening. Not for a long time, until one evening when she was nearly fourteen, Jack had whispered after catching her in a chasing game, 'I'm going to marry you when we're grown up.' Then without waiting to hear if she had anything to say, he ran back and joined the crowd of boys. And Julia knew without a doubt that what he said was true: he *would* marry her. And that was what she wanted.

All thoughts of a vocation were banished from her mind and remained banished until the night before her wedding. While holding up the nightdress of her trousseau, fear of the enormous commitment she was about to undertake overwhelmed her. The sacrament of marriage: something for the rest of her life; something that would last until she or Jack died. And Julia recalled now how, standing before the mirror, she had prayed: 'Please God, let me be a good wife. Let me never do anything to displease Jack. Don't ever let me have doubts, or want to change my mind like I did about the vocation.' And when her prayers brought no consolation she went down to her mother who was with Cissie seeing to last-minute plans for the wedding breakfast, and cried telling of her fears.

'Child of grace,' said Cissie who was like a second mother, getting up and putting her arms round her. 'Your fears are natural. You're taking a big step. Every girl and boy who marries take the same one.'

'Nerves,' said her more prosaic mother. 'Nerves, that's all it is. But just the same, love, it shows the seriousness of how you're approaching the sacrament. There's many a young girl with no more thought in her head than the dress and the hooley. It's a long road and a hard one, marriage, but you've nothing to fear. Yours will be a good marriage. You've picked the right man – you were made for each other.'

'Indeed you were,' rejoined Cissie. 'I remember the night before I got married – D'ye remember it Lizzie?'

'Will I ever forget! You wanted to call it all off and run away,' said Lizzie.

'You weren't that brave yourself,' retorted Cissie, 'for all that you were letting on.'

'You're right, I wasn't,' admitted Lizzie. The two older women began reminiscing about the night before their wedding, laughing at the nervous girls they had been, their fears of the changes being a married woman would bring, recalling their hard and happy times as wives, and in the long run calming her and making her laugh.

And how right they had been, Julia thought. The next morning, when she entered the church and saw Jack waiting for her before the altar, she was the happiest, most contented girl in the world. And her first night had been magical : Jack, finding an excuse to leave the room while she undressed — no wild beast waiting to pounce on her — lying together, tenderly and with awe exploring each other's bodies that neither one had ever seen naked before. Making love oblivious of the music and singing that came up from the downstairs where the wedding was still being celebrated.

God, she thought, had been so good to them. Jack had lived through the war. She adjusted her hat to a more becoming angle. She began to think about the night ahead while she waited for Sarah to call her.

CHAPTER TWO

Mrs Quinlan fastened the hooks and eyes down the back of Sarah's plum-coloured dress – a hand-me-down from Lady Glenivy – and warned her daughter: 'Don't you forget what I said about tonight, and remember your Confirmation Pedge – don't let drink pass your lips. And if there's any talk of marriage, sling the deaf ear.'

Sarah sighed exasperatedly. 'Honest to God, Ma, you're making me think I shouldn't even go to meet Barney! It was supposed to be a happy affair, something to look forward to, and all you're doing is trying to put the fear of God into me.' She turned before the full-length glass. 'How do I look?'

'A picture,' Rosie told her. 'Any man's fancy, and you had to pick Barney Daly. I hope you know he's not going to walk into a job. Get yourself into trouble and have to marry him – what sort of a future is that? Where will you live? What'll you live on? Romance won't pay the rent. And to think how you were reared. The hopes I had for you. You were the best-dressed girl in the street. Half the night I sat up, cutting down and altering clothes from Glenivy for you.'

'I was that well-dressed I frightened the fellas in the street off. No one except Barney ever asked me out.'

'You were a child. It wasn't to get a fella from this place that I kept you nice. The chances you'd have had if you'd gone into service. But no, you knew best and threw them away for that excuse of a man. And even when he went to France and you were free and could have taken a situation, into a warehouse handling rough khaki you had to go.'

'I promised him I wouldn't go to work where I had to live in. He's awful jealous. He was worried about me. He said that young girls living away from home could be taken advantage of,' Sarah explained as she put the finishing touches to her hair.

'And I suppose that buying you a ring without the decency to as much as ask me or your father wasn't taking advantage of you.'

'People in the street don't ask if they can get engaged.'

'Exactly – and isn't that just what I mean about them being common! Now the gentry ... do you think one of *their* daughters would do such a thing? Oh no. There's a proper way of doing things. I tried to bring you up like that. I taught you nice manners, corrected you when you spoke common. Listen, love,' now her voice took on a coaxing tone, 'you're only engaged. It's not too late. You could break it off.'

'You might let him get here first before you talk about breaking it off. Let me meet him, see if I feel the same about him.'

'With God and His Holy Mother's help that you won't. But in case you still do, there's to be no wedding until he gets work, so make sure there doesn't have to be. And another thing: if you do marry him, remember that you're a woman now, and any woman worth her salt can manage a man. Start as you mean to go on: consider your wants first. You can have him like a lapdog so long as he doesn't know you're the one pulling the lead.'

'You didn't succeed that well with my da.'

'That I can't deny, but can you imagine what he'd have been like if I didn't have the strong hand over him? When did you ever know him to come in here with the signs of a drink on him? When did he ever open his wages before I handled them? I failed over the business and I never got out of the street. Isn't that all the more reason why I want the best for you! Every mother does.'

'I know in one way you are right. I'd love to get out of here. Anyway, who knows what will happen? First I have to meet him and I'd better get a move on. Me and Julia are getting the tram into O'Connell Street. We'll walk from there to the North Wall.'

'How about coming back?'

'We'll get a cab. Arrive in style.'

Julia saw Jack long before he spotted her, picked him out from the soldiers coming down the gangway loaded with equipment. For a moment her heart seemed to stand still at the sight of him, then it raced, filling her with exultation and she called his name. 'Jack, Jack! Oh, Jack,' and tears of joy spilled from her eyes.

Sarah, also scanning the descending men, couldn't see Barney. And didn't until he called her name. Other wives, mothers and sweethearts called their men's names. It seemed as if each voice found wings and flew to the ears of its beloved, for beneath peaked caps soldiers' eyes smiled at the sound of their names being called by those they had loved and waited so long to see again. From the throng on the quayside they recognised them, calling in return and waving excitedly.

Sarah heard her name called and searched in vain for Barney. When at last she saw him, as he was about to step ashore, she was overwhelmed with disappointment. He wasn't like the picture she sometimes had of him in her mind, nor the real photograph of him, taken in Mary's Street before he went to France, which she kept on the mantelpiece. He wasn't

24

as tall as she remembered, low-sized really. He was fatter and scruffy-looking. She wanted to turn, fight her way through the embracing lovers, rejoicing mothers and relations, and run far away from Barney who was struggling to push his way forward.

Julia and Jack stood before each other, looked into each other's eyes and the lost years were as nothing. As if they had never been. This was the first time he had said, 'I love you.' The night he asked to marry her; the day of their wedding when the priest declared them man and wife; their wedding night when, for the first time, seeing her undressed he had kissed the hollow between her breasts – all their wonderful, magical, beautiful moments come together here on the quayside as he took her in his arms, holding her as close as the bulky equipment would allow. For a moment neither spoke, content to hold each other and gaze into eyes which shone with the relief and delight of being reunited; of being real, alive. Together after the years of fear and longing and wondering would such a moment as this be granted to them.

Then they kissed and spoke their thoughts, kissed again then held each other at arms' length, exclaiming how well the other looked, how they hadn't changed. Though Julia noticed that round Jack's lovely eyes were webs of fine lines that hadn't been there before he went to France.

Sarah didn't run away. Rooted to the spot she waited while Barney came nearer, heard his voice saying, 'Sarah, Sarah. Ah darling, God how I missed you.' Everyone, she knew, was watching them, saying to themselves, 'What can she see in him?' 'Oh love,' he said and held her and kissed her and kissed her again.

'You're squeezing the life out of me and them things, that equipment is digging into my breasts.'

'Bloody awful yokes. I'll take them off the minute we're in the cab.' He kissed her again, a long passionate kiss. For four years she hadn't been kissed and now despite herself she responded, though part of her mind was occupied with the sight she felt Barney to be. Opening her eyes she swivelled them and spotted Julia and Jack oblivious to everyone about them, embracing. 'Look,' she said, pushing Barney from her. 'There's Jack and Julia.' She called to them, noticing as she did so how smart and handsome Jack was.

They moved toward each other. 'Julia.' Barney's arms enfolded her. 'Ah Julia, it's great to see you. You haven't changed a bit. You look marvellous.'

With great warmth Julia kissed his face. He was exactly as she remembered him: short and stocky, cocky-looking, his brilliant blue eyes twinkling as they always had, not a trace of a line near them. She loved him. She remembered having minded him when he was a little boy younger than herself. A cheeky, cocky little boy – all front, easily quashed, easily led. The first to run to the canal bank but always the last in for a swim. The little boy who time and time again Jack had to rescue from a situation into which Barney's bravado had led him. 'Poor Barney,' she thought affectionately. 'I'm glad Jack was there when it was more serious than a couple of young fellas giving you a goingover.'

Genuinely glad to see Sarah again after such a long separation, Jack kissed her cheek and held her for a moment. He remarked on how well she looked, letting go of her without seeming eager to do so, which he was – for although he had known her all his life he had never taken a liking to her. If he had been asked to explain why, he couldn't have. There was just something about her that he didn't warm to. But she was Julia's friend and he was Barney's so he was careful never to let his dislike of her show.

'I suppose we'd better make a move,' Barney suggested. 'Will we share a cab?'

'No,' said Jack. 'Not tonight. Me and the wife are travelling alone.'

Barney and Julia laughed and Sarah quipped, 'Mind your wife now,' as they went for separate cabs.

'Will I pull down the blinds?' Jack said when they were alone and the cab driving down the quay.

Julia laughed. 'Do you want us to be arrested? In any case, there's no blind.'

'Wouldn't it be grand if there was, though.'

Julia blushed and laid her head against his chest. 'We'll be home soon. Do you remember the last night?'

'God, I was so sorry about that. All the times in France I thought about it and cursed myself. The night I was leaving you and for that to happen.'

She put her fingers on his lips and said, 'It didn't matter. Don't talk about it.'

He lit a cigarette and looked out of the window, talking now and then, telling her how marvellous it was to be driving through Dublin with her beside him. To be coming up the side of Trinity, looking across at the Bank, everything the same.

While he talked she remembered their last night together – the farewell party and how he drank too much. As they went upstairs to bed he had been very amorous and then in the time it took her to get undressed, he had collapsed across the bed fast asleep. She had had to undress him down to his vest and drawers, vexed and at the same time feeling love and pity as she imagined you might for a small child. For with his hair tossed and flushed face, like a small boy he looked, and her heart broke when she thought of what lay in front of him. So moved was she by his look of helplessness that she reached to kiss his parted lips.

His breath reeked of porter, quickly dispelling her pity, turning it to disgust. Angry and disappointed, she moved away from him, lay tossing and turning, poking him several times to silence his snoring. Then the realisation came to her that the next day he started for France and she left him undisturbed.

She fell asleep and woke drowsy and warm with his arm around her, his hand on her belly stroking her flesh. She turned to him, her mouth searching for and finding his, unaware now of his still drink-laden breath, yearning for him, moving into him as close as she could get. Wanting to be one with him. Their legs found ways of accommodating their need for closeness. And then there was a loud knocking on the bedroom door and her mother's voice shouting. 'Quick, get up! Quick, the alarm didn't go off. The cab's at the door and you'll be late reporting to barracks.'

It was all panic. Her mother in the room with hot water for Jack's shave. He frantically dressing. And the tears – so many tears, even though she had promised to send him off bravely. Tears and more tears all through the long lonely four years. But now he was home. Beside her in a cab driving up Dame Street. At home forever. They'd make a good happy life, please God. They'd have a family, and love each other always.

They held hands for the rest of the ride, now and then kissing, smiling and laughing with the joy of being together again. The street was out to greet them. Jack was taken from her, embraced, kissed, clapped on the back, blessings showered on him. Exhortations to hurry and ditch all that webbing, rifle, tin hat, the rest of his gear and let the party begin. Which it did, and went on into the small hours of the morning, with dancing and singing, accordions, melodeons and fiddles playing. Eulogies began and never finished in praise of Jack's heroism.

A neighbour brought out her gramophone, a child carrying its large green horn and little tin box of needles. Records made popular during the war were played. *Roses in Picardy* brought tears as the ones who should have been here too were remembered in their French graves where the poppies grew.

Sarah sat on Barney's lap. Without his cap and having unbuttoned his tunic, he didn't look so fat nor scruffy. The joyful atmosphere surrounding her, the fuss made of Barney lifted him in her estimation; the feel of his body, all convinced her that she did love him. He kissed her face and nuzzled her neck, telling her how lovely she was, that he was mad about her. He jigged her on his knees, exciting her. And he coaxed her to drink from his glass of whiskey. 'Have a taste, go on, only a sup,' he urged, holding the glass to her lips.

She pushed it away. 'You know I don't drink. The smell of it makes me heave.'

He persisted. 'The taste'll take the smell away. It'll do you good — keep out the cold.'

She laughed. 'Cold is the last thing I am.'

He tilted the glass, dribbling drops between her lips. She swallowed the spirit, then coughed. 'It's burned my gullet, it's horrible.'

'That'll pass in a minute. Drink another drop.' She did, and liked the feel of the whiskey spreading its warm glow inside her belly. 'I love you,' Barney said in her ear and with his free hand caressed her breast.

'I love you too,' she whispered and kissed him passionately, their tongues exploring each other's mouths. Again he offered her the whiskey. She was about to drink when into her head came her mother's voice: 'You mind yourself with that fella tonight.' She pushed away the tumbler. 'I don't like it. I don't want any more.' She reached for her glass of minerals and after drinking some made an excuse to get off Barney's lap. All her doubts and discontents returned.

In the early part of the night only the women danced, the young girls, their mothers, grandmothers and Mag the smiling good-natured simpleton. Mag was the mascot of the street, spoiled and petted, with the freedom of every house — even occasionally the Quinlans'. Mag refused partners and danced solo, laughing and shouting with glee.

The men were called, coaxed, encouraged to take the floor and as the porter and whiskey worked their magic, courage and their estimation of their footwork grew in leaps and bounds. Soon all were coupled and waltzed, one-stepped and two-stepped.

They danced and sang and ate and drank. As the night wore on the laughter grew louder, the voices slurred and ballroom dancing gave way to sets and reels and jigs. Couples buzzed until their heads reeled. Jack, remembering the night before he went to France, drank sparingly, tipping glass after glass of whiskey under the table. During a pause in the music someone called for a toast to the man who had saved Barney's life.

They were drunk and tired and it was the umpteenth toast. Those sitting found it difficult to rise; the dancers, once the dancing stopped, felt drained. Barney, befuddled by drink and Sarah's desertion — for after leaving his lap she had avoided him ever since — stood propped against a wall watching as she bade Julia and Jack goodnight and walked to her house without once looking in his direction.

It was a great party, everyone agreed, and silently wished that someone in the name of God would call it a night. Then the rain came, first as a shower, then in torrents which lashed and hopped off the ground. Everyone except Mag and Barney ran into their homes and closed the doors.

The tables, chairs, Delft and glasses were left. The flags and bunting hung in strings. The street was deserted except for Barney and Mag. In the torrential rain he made his way to Sarah's house, where no lights showed, and stood outside looking at the closed door, his hand raised as if to knock. Mag, oblivious of the clothes soaked and clinging to her like another skin, wandered slowly up the street, singing softly *Two Little Girls in Blue*. Barney lowered his hand and dejectedly made his way home. Jack and Julia with their arms round each other went up the stairs to bed.

CHAPTER THREE

'It was a pity Julia couldn't have time off,' Jack said to his mother-in-law, who was frying breakfast for him.

'What a hope,' she replied, turning the bacon.

'Still, please God I won't be long about getting work and then she can give it up altogether.'

'Don't build your hopes too high – there's not much work about.'

'I'll go down later on to the sawmills. They'll look on me favourably, at least.'

'Look might be all they'll do. Don't expect to be taken on as a foreman again – you weren't gone ten minutes to France when someone else was in your job.'

'You couldn't expect them to let the place run down because I went to be a soldier.'

'I suppose not. All the same, it's hard to see men who thought they were doing the right thing walking the street idle.' She brought the plate of rashers and eggs to the table and sat down with Jack. 'Yesterday's paper is there behind you on the press. Have a read of it for I'm going out for my messages in a minute.'

He reached for the paper but left it unopened and talked about last night's party. How much he had enjoyed it.

'It was a grand night,' Lizzie Mangan agreed. 'Barney got the worse for wear, didn't he? Will her and him get married?'

'That's all he thinks of – all that kept him going in France. I think they will.'

'I wouldn't bank on it, not if her mother has any say. Unless he falls in for a job right away and gets married quickly I wouldn't bank on that match coming off.' Lizzie poured him more tea, asked if there was anything else he wanted. 'I'll do the table when I come back. If I hurry I'll get ten Mass before I go for my messages. Why don't you ramble into town – it's not a bad day.'

He said he might. When she was gone he settled himself nearer the fire and opened yesterday's paper. He read about the two policemen who had been shot in Soloheadbeg while escorting dynamite to a quarry, and about the first meeting of the Irish Parliament. He was reminded of how little he knew of Irish affairs, had ever known. Jack had been brought up by parents with no interest in politics, not Irish, English or any other kind. Sometimes his mother sang a song about Sarah Curran, the sweetheart of Robert Emmet executed for his part in the Rebellion of 1803. It was the broken-hearted lovers which interested his mother, that and Robert's speech from the dock, which she knew by heart and had taught him. Judge Curran, she said, was 'a hard-hearted oul bastard who wouldn't defend poor Robert and publicly denounced his daughter.' Often when in Thomas Street she had shown him St Catherine's Church, outside which Robert had been hanged, drawn and quartered. Of his part in the United Irishmen or his attempted rebellion she expressed no opinion.

What little he knew of Ireland's history and her struggle for independence had come from songs, street ballads and poems learned from an occasional patriotic teacher. His lack of knowledge had never bothered him before he went to France, for he was always either working, courting Julia, playing football or boxing; every minute of his life was occupied. In France, for the first time he was alerted to his ignorance of Irish history.

There was a soldier he liked – a Londoner called Alf, an intelligent fellow but like himself, uneducated. Shortly after the Easter Rebellion in Dublin, he and Alf and some others from their platoon had been withdrawn to a rest station for a few days. There were newspapers there. Alf was reading an account of the Rebellion, the five days of fighting, surrender, the arrests and executions of the fifteen leaders including two brothers, a man already dying with consumption and another so badly wounded he had to be propped in a chair for his execution.

'A bad move that,' he said, putting down the paper. 'Makes martyrs of 'em. If the Irish didn't rally to the cause before, they will now, I don't know much about Ireland and its troubles – what brought all this lot about?'

Robert Emmet, Wolfe Tone, Father Murphy and Vinegar Hill, Brian Boru and *The Harp That Once Through Tara's Hall* all came to mind in a jumble, but not for the life of him could Jack have given Alf a proper reply. Eventually he said, 'D'ye know, Alf, I'd make a better fist at explaining what caused the Indian Mutiny. We did that in school but our own history was glossed over.'

'Your education sounds like mine – full of stuff about the victories and heroes. But there's another side to history, like this bleedin' war. That didn't start only because some Duke and his missus was bumped off, nor to defend poor little Belgium neither. Men like you and me and thousands more were fooled up to the two eyes. Maybe knowing won't make much difference in the long run. Maybe if we knew the real cause of this war we'd still have gone like lambs to the slaughter. But we should know our history. And if there isn't a bullet or shell or canister of gas with my name on it, when I get back to Blighty I'll start to find out what the school didn't teach me. And the likes of you living in a country that doesn't even rule itself have even more of an obligation to.'

Jack remembered how impressed he had been by Alf's pronouncement and how he had promised himself that if God spared him he would find out about Irish history. He owed it to himself and to the memory of Alf, who was killed a week after they went back to the Front.

He made himself another pot of tea and sat down again to read about the Soloheadbeg raid and the meeting of the New Irish Parliament.

Sarah sat to the table for the breakfast. 'Will I do you a fry?' her mother asked.

'Only toast,' she replied.

Mrs Quinlan cut slices from a loaf, moved her chair in front of the fire and began toasting the bread. After bringing it to the table she talked about the previous night. 'I waited to hear you come in, not that I could have closed my eyes in any case with the noise that was going on. Did you enjoy yourself?'

Sarah shrugged. 'It was all right.'

'And your man, what about him?'

'He was all right.' She wouldn't give her mother the satisfaction of knowing Barney had tried forcing drink on her.

'A party they had the nerve to call it. More like a drunken brawl if the noise was anything to go by. The screams and roars – what were they doing to cause such a commotion?'

'Irish dancing.'

'I might have known. Even that they couldn't get right. Done properly it's like Scottish country dancing. Many's the time I've seen it done at a ball in Glenivy, but never in my life did I hear the roaring and shouting that went on last night. But then as I've told you before, the gentry do everything in style. Are you sure you wouldn't like a rasher?'

'No thanks,' said Sarah. 'You really loved working there, didn't you?'

'Adored every minute of it. So would you if you'd taken my advice. And the mistress, she's the greatest lady I've ever met. And God knows I met plenty in my time. Of course I was her maid, but apart from that I was her favourite. We're the same age to within a month of each other. She used to say to me, "Rosie, you're a treasure, an absolute treasure. I don't know what I'd do without you." Mind you, it caused a lot of jealousy, I can tell you.'

'Who was jealous?' As usual her mother could always catch and hold her interest when she talked about Glenivy.

'The other servants. You see, her Ladyship treated me as one of the family. We were like sisters. She'd confide in me. "I know I can trust you to keep a secret," she'd say.'

'What was the secret?' asked Sarah.

'Oh, some man she had fallen in love with. I'd be brushing and arranging her hair and she'd tell me all about him.'

'What happened? Did she run off with him?'

Her mother laughed. 'Indeed she didn't. Wasn't she always falling in love with someone and falling out as quickly.'

'What about her husband? Did she love him?'

'She never said she didn't, and aren't they still together all these years. You'd get on great with her. Being my daughter you'd be special to her. She was broken-hearted when I left to get married. I thought she'd cry, but the gentry have great control. "How will I manage without you?" she said. "Who will I find to do my hair the way you do?"' Mrs Quinlan smiled and looked far away, lost in thought for a while before concluding, 'They were the happiest days of my life, working for her Ladyship.'

'But didn't you mind living in, Ma, being away from your own home?' Sarah asked as she buttered another piece of toast.

'All the times you've asked me that – you've a terrible memory! Wasn't I at home where I was? Amn't I always telling you we were like sisters. Didn't I have the run of the place? Didn't she confide in me and ask my advice on everything? She never bought a frock, a gown or hat in Dublin or London that she didn't show to me the minute she arrived home.' Rosie sighed. 'Ah, Sarah, it breaks my heart all that you're missing out on. I can tell you till Tib's Eve all about Glenivy but to know what it's really like you'd have to see for yourself. If only you'd not be hasty – you know what I'm getting at. If that fella starts on about marriage don't do anything rash. You'll live to regret it, mark my words.'

Rosie went on dreamily, 'Living there was like being part of the happiest family in the world, but not one of your come day, go day, God send some day families like them around here. Everything at Glenivy ran like clockwork. Everything was peaceful and orderly, the height of comfort. In the summer the sun could be splitting the trees but inside the house you'd be as cool as a cucumber. In the winter the rain could be lashing, or the snow up to your knees, or a bitter east wind blowing and inside you'd feel neither damp nor draught.'

'Was everyone that comfortable – the rest of the servants, for instance?'

'You don't think the gentry would neglect their staff! Everyone was well looked after. Of course, I was special being her Ladyship's maid. As

I said, like one of the family. And that's how it would be for you. Mind you, in the beginning you'd have to start at the bottom, seeing as you're not experienced. That's how the gentry do things: a proper training. But being my daughter and with your appearance, in no time you'd have a grand position.'

Bewitched like always when she listened to her mother's stories, Sarah thought of a future married to Barney, never escaping from the street, and compared that with the magical Glenivy. Her mother got up from the table. 'Be a good girl and wash the Delft while I run out for my messages.' She was hardly gone when Sarah heard the letter box flap. Barney, she thought, as she went into the hall and saw an envelope on the floor. He must have watched for her mother's departure. Her name was written on the envelope.
She read:

Dear Sarah,

I'm terrible sorry about last night. It wasn't out of disrespect. You know how I feel about you. I was wondering if you'd come into town with me this evening. I'll be at the top of the street from seven on. Please don't let me down.

Love, xxxxxxxx
Barney

'I might as well,' Sarah said to herself. 'What else is there to do except listen to my mother?' Back in the kitchen she threw the note in the fire. As she cleared the table she thought more kindly of Barney and, remembering last night's kissing, felt pleasurably excited. A pleasure which was dispelled when she met him later on. He was wearing civvies – a suit he'd had before the war. 'Jesus, the cut of him,' she thought. 'That thing should have been given to the ragman years ago. I'll be ashamed to be seen walking with him.'

'You look gorgeous,' he told her. 'Will we wait for a tram?'

'Get on a tram with him looking like a twanger! Surely to God he must know what he looks like. It's an insult, so it is. After four years wouldn't you think he'd try to make an impression.' These feelings went through Sarah's mind, but she held her tongue except to say, 'No, we'll walk.'

'I didn't know about wearing the suit. I suppose I should still be in uniform until I'm discharged.'

'Don't ask me,' said Sarah with an edge to her voice which Barney didn't notice.

'What'll we do?'

'Whatever you like,' she replied. It was one of the things that irritated her about him. 'What'll we do? Where will we go?' Hardly ever in all the time she'd known him did he make a decision.

'We could go for a drink.'

'A drink! That shows what you think of me. Only oul wans and bad women go to public houses.'

'How about an ice-cream parlour?'

'All right, but not round here.' She would die if anyone saw him looking like a mendicant.

Once they were served with their ice creams he said, 'Out there I used to dream of this. Of being home, being with you. Every single night and day I'd be thinking ...'

She cut him short. 'I know – you were always telling me in your letters. When d'ye think you'll get work?'

'Give us a chance – I only came back yesterday.'

'Well, don't let the grass grow under your feet.'

He was used to her short manner. He believed it wasn't her true self. Like a lot of people she was often in bad humour but he didn't mind. He loved her. 'I'm going out with Jack in the morning to look for a start. With the help of God we'll be lucky. Did I ever tell you about this bloke I served with? He was a howl. Afraid of no one – officers, NCOs, no one.'

'You told me about him. We ought to go. That ice cream was like water with ice in it. In any case, I'm tired after last night. I'm going to bed early.' She allowed him only a perfunctory kiss before saying goodnight.

For several nights she kept him at bay, unreceptive to his attempts to make conversation, quizzing him about where he'd been to look for work, never even pretending to be the least entertained when he attempted to amuse her. But towards the end of the week she stayed with him later and allowed more kissing. Kissing and being held by him was the only pleasure he gave her. And more and more her mind toyed with the idea of Glenivy, but for all that she didn't want to burn her boats in case Glenivy wasn't to her liking. Bad and all as Barney was, a man – even a clumsy, fumbling eejit like him – was better than no man at all. Nowadays after the thousands killed in the war, men were no longer ten a penny.

A few days after arriving home, Jack went to the sawmills to see if there was anything doing. He decided to go to the library afterwards — it seemed the obvious place to start learning the history of Ireland. First he'd go through the back numbers of the newspapers to bring himself up to date with fairly recent events, and if the Librarian seemed a decent skin he'd ask his advice on further reading.

'Isn't it queer,' he thought as he went into the sawmills, 'how nothing is as big as you remembered. This place seemed so enormous whenever I recalled it in France. At least the lovely smell hasn't changed, but I don't see a single familiar face. They're all young men. I must have looked like them before I went to France. A lot of kids, too. I was only a kid the day my father, Lord have mercy on him, brought me on my first day, fourteen and just left school. I was so nervous and uncomfortable in the new long trousers, the first pair I'd ever had.' Jack overheard again the conversation between his mother and father the week before he started work. His father was telling her, 'Wouldn't the knickerbockers do him for the time being? A lot of the young fellas wear them.'

'Well, he's not. Look at the size of him, he's a man already.'

They weren't old. He had expected if he was spared to see them again, never thinking they'd die from what was called the Spanish Flu, within a few days of each other. Dying so suddenly that they were dead and buried even before news reached him in France. Them and thousands all over the world.

'Jack, is it yourself! God, I'm delighted to see you home safe and well.' It was a man from his father's time, a man looking hale and hearty, coming with his hand out to greet him. 'I was very sorry about your mother and father, God rest them.' He shook Jack's hand. Asked when he'd come home, how Julia was and congratulated him on his decoration. Then he said, 'I suppose you've come about a job.' Jack said he had. 'There's nothing doing, a terrible slackness, though with the help of God things may pick up, only don't build your hopes too high. Go into the office and see Kennedy. He might fix you up with something. I'll see you again.'

He'd never seen Kennedy before, so had to explain who he was, where he'd been, his father's position in the firm, his own involvement. 'I was a foreman before I went to France. I'm not expecting to step back into that job. I'll take anything.'

Kennedy was pleasant. He invited Jack to sit, gave him a cigarette and explained as the man in the yard had done that there were no jobs — and no prospects of work increasing.

'I'd do anything,' Jack said.

'I've no doubt of that, nor that you'd do it well, but there's nothing.

If and when things pick up I'll let you know. Have you thought about Guinness's? They employ a lot of ex-servicemen.'

Jack thanked him and left. Before going to the library he had intended to walk into town, ramble through the streets and saunter along the quays, have a look at The Green, familiarising himself with Dublin again. Now, disheartened after the sawmills, he didn't feel like the walk into town and decided instead to set out for the library.

The Librarian was a tall scrawny man with receding gingery hair and a very prominent Adam's apple. Jack waited behind two women who were having their books stamped, noticing that the man had a pleasing manner. 'What can I do for you, sir?' he asked in a well-spoken country voice which Jack thought could be West Cork. He had soldiered with several men from that area and thought it was the loveliest accent in Ireland.

He explained how he'd been in France for four years, how his reading had always been sketchy and how he now desired to remedy that fault. 'You've come to the right place, so,' said the Librarian, and introduced himself as Seamus Harrington. 'Have you any idea where you'd like to start with the books, any favourite authors?'

'What I really want to do is learn about Irish history, a bit more than I got in school or from hearsay. I know that'll take time.' Then he told him how he had read about the Soloheadbeg incident and the opening of the Irish Parliament on the very day he had come back from France. Also, although this only struck him as he was talking, that no one – not his wife, his mother-in-law nor the group he had been with the previous night – had mentioned either incident.

'That's fairly typical – most people are not political. Maybe if twenty policemen had been shot it might have taken their notice.'

'Mind you,' said Jack. 'There *was* a party to welcome me home.'

The Librarian laughed. 'Well, then, weren't they better employed fêting you than concerning themselves with the newspapers! But for a quick idea of what's been going on, it's the papers you want – the back numbers. Where would you like to start?'

'Before the war – 1913.'

'As good a time as any. Come on, I'll show you.'

Seamus Harrington took him to the Reading Room, sat him at a table and chair and went to fetch the papers. While he waited Jack looked round the room at the other men, who were mostly elderly and shabby. Some, he noticed, were reading avidly while others were just turning pages without appearing to be reading; he guessed that many had come in just for the shelter and warmth. One man, sitting at the next table, had the appearance of a tramp. Little of his face was visible, as it was obscured by a tangle of beard and moustaches. His boots were broken, the soles gaping, and his trouser legs were bound with rags. With a magnifying glass he went down the page line by line. Jack wondered who he was – who he had been before he took to the roads, and what had sent him on to them.

'Here we are,' said the Librarian, returning with a large leatherbound book. 'A year's supply. I'll be in there,' he nodded to the library, 'if you need help.'

A whole year's papers. No wonder it weighed a ton, Jack mused as he arranged the volume and himself to begin his reading. At first he read about only what he had come for, but as he turned over the pages looking for this information, other items caught his interest – accounts of robberies, accidents, place-names he knew, even the death notices distracted him from what he had come to seek. The room became intolerably stuffy; he felt sleepy and made little progress. He looked at the clock, it was half-past five. He'd been here for hours! At this rate it would take him a week to go through one year's papers, *if* he was lucky.

Before he knew it, the library was about to close. The other readers left their papers and went. He was alone when the Librarian came to ask how he had got on.

'Not very well,' he admitted.

Seamus smiled. "Tis the way unless you're an experienced researcher. Other things catch the eye, isn't that so?'

'That's what happened to me.'

'Listen, then. I know a fair amount about the last few years. If it's them you're particularly interested in I could give it to you in a nutshell, a grounding from which you could then go on and do your reading. After a while you'd get the knack of ignoring what you didn't want and find searching the papers no bother.' He looked at his watch and asked, 'Do you take a drink?'

'Not a lot but I enjoy a pint.'

'And are you in a terrible hurry to get home?'

'I amn't. Tonight the wife is working late.'

'That's very convenient. Would you meet me in the Long Hall after I've locked up here? We could have a jar and start your education. D'ye you know where it is?'

'George's Street.'

'The very place,' grinned Seamus. 'I'll be with you in about twenty minutes.'

'Grand,' replied Jack and shook hands, thinking as he did so how he warmed to the Librarian. It was kind of him to go to so much trouble for a stranger.

He told him so when they were seated waiting for their pints of porter.

''Tis nothing,' said Seamus. 'I like to help and in a way I suppose to show off what I know.' After a long swallow of their drink, Seamus first talked about run-of-the-mill things and asked Jack a few questions: how long had he been at the war? Had he a job? Any family? In return for the answers he spoke about himself. He was a bachelor from West Cork – Bandon. 'Where the pigs are Protestants,' he joked.

'I never heard that before,' said Jack.

''Tis a well-known saying in Bandon, going back a long time. Richard Boyle, you see, or to give him his title, the Earl of Cork, founded the town after robbing the ancient stock of their land. Then he planted their properties with English Protestant settlers – so you see how the saying came about.'

Jack laughed. 'Aye, indeed,' he said.

'And I'll tell you another thing about Bandon. It is said that on one of the gates of the town wall there was this inscription: *Turk, Jew, or Atheist may enter here ; but not a papist.* And someone, a local wit no doubt, added: *Who wrote it, wrote it well ; for the same is written on the Gates of Hell.* The land and the people are full of myths and legends, Jack, but it's truth and hard facts you're after, am I right?'

'I enjoy the stories, that was a great one you just told, but it is facts I want.' He noticed that Seamus' glass was nearly empty. 'Will you have another?' he asked.

'I will, thank you, and then we'll get down to business. I think,' Seamus said, wiping the froth of his second pint from his lips, 'I'll start a bit before 1913. Did you learn anything about the Union in school?'

'I don't remember.'

'Did you know, for instance, that the Bank of Ireland on College Green was once the Irish Houses of Parliament?'

'I heard it called the Old Houses of Parliament by my grannie but I never paid any attention, thinking she was in her dotage.'

'She was right. That's where they were until 1801 when we were made part of the United Kingdom. After that, Irish MPs sat in Westminster. The Union was supposed to bring prosperity to Ireland. It did to parts of the North, but divil the bit of prosperity came our way. Not having a say in our own affairs rankled in the hearts and minds of fair-thinking Catholics and Protestants. Then in 1870 it was a Protestant, a grand young man called Isaac Butt – who was a Queen's Counsel at the age of twenty-nine – the last bridge on the Liffey is named after him . . . where was I? Oh yes, well anyway he started an organisation to press for Home Rule. That's all they wanted – no talk of a separate Ireland, still keeping the ties with Great Britain, but having the right and privilege of managing our own affairs. The movement grew from strength to strength until the British government was forced to notice it. Will you have another drink?'

Jack refused and curbed his impatience for more about Home Rule until Seamus came back with a whiskey and began again to talk. 'The Home Rulers were men who wanted to win an independent Parliament by constitutional means. And they made grand progress once the secret voting came in. The Ballot Act worked in their favour, and in 1874 Butt's new party won more than half of all the Irish seats! By '77 Parnell was on the scene and he took over from Butt. Other branches of the Home Rulers were formed – one I know for a fact was in Manchester. Even so, it wasn't until 1886 that Gladstone introduced a Home Rule Bill into the House of Commons. It was defeated. And again and again – getting through the Commons only to be turned down in the Lords. In 1913 it was defeated *again* in the Lords. Nobody could accuse us of not being patient, but in Ulster the Home Rule question was causing great unease. The Ulster Unionists formed their own Volunteer Army. As I said, we'd been patient. That's not to say that everyone had been in favour of Home Rule. There were some that would settle for nothing but a fully independent Ireland. And an independent Ireland was what the Northern Unionists feared as a result of Home Rule. That was why they formed their Volunteer Force. Naturally those who wanted a free Ireland did the same. So there we were in 1913 with three armies – the Irish Volunteers, the British Army and the Ulster lot. Are you getting tired?' Seamus asked as Jack stifled a yawn.

'No, I'm not. Go on, I'm taking it all in,' urged Jack. But Seamus decided to call it a night.

'It took longer than I thought,' he said, 'and as for putting it in a nutshell, well . . .' he smiled and spread his hands in mock despair, '. . . it wouldn't bloody well fit. I'll tell you what, go home now and before you next come into the library I'll have some books ready that will bring you fairly up to date. How's that?'

'Great,' said Jack. 'I'll look forward to it,' and he bid him goodnight.

The night was cold and frosty and as he walked home the air cleared his head and he regretted having yawned in the public house. He hoped Seamus had taken it for what it was – a drowsiness brought on by the porter and stale air in the bar, not a sign that he was bored. Far from it. He would have enjoyed listening all night to what Seamus had to say. He had liked the way he presented his information – as facts, seldom if at all letting whatever he felt personally show through.

He'd let a few days go by before visiting the library again. Give Mr Harrington time to sort some books for him and he time to go on looking for work.

CHAPTER FOUR

It was April. The weather was warmer, and everywhere in the parks and gardens, in the birdsong, there was the promise of new life. And it was with hope in his heart that every morning Jack set off to tramp the streets looking for work which he didn't find. The constant refusals dejected and humiliated him. He felt a failure. A married man not able to support his wife.

Every morning on her way to the firm where she embroidered top quality underwear and table linen, Julia went into Whitefriars Street chapel to hear Mass and prayed that today Jack might succeed in getting a start. Every night when she came home and saw his dejected face she wanted to cry for him but didn't, knowing it would only make him feel worse. Moreover, she was so grateful to have him home safe and whole. Him being spared was more important than a job. They could manage to live with her earnings, two pounds a week, more than many a man earned. Jack had savings and so had she, the marriage allowance paid to her during the war.

And if God blessed them with a child she could work until the last minute. Only after the birth if Jack was still idle would they feel the pinch, for her mother was too old to mind an infant and she would have to finish work. But it wasn't in her nature to let gloomy thoughts of the future spoil their present happiness.

Every day and all day Sarah fumed that Barney hadn't found a job, blaming his failure on lackadaisicalness – a belief her mother encouraged. Her mind was in turmoil trying to decide whether she should give him up and go into service at Glenivy. The spring weather made her restless, desperate for a change in her life. Her body was constantly plagued by sensations even when Barney wasn't attempting to seduce her. She ached with desire though she wasn't sure if it was him or just any man she wanted.

Barney wanted her and marriage with or without a job. He never concerned himself with looking too far ahead. Something could always turn up. He adored her, worshipped her. Would do anything she asked of him – rob or kill for her. She was the only girl he had ever loved. The only one he had ever kissed. He remembered it and how he had felt ten foot tall because Sarah Quinlan, the prettiest girl in the street, had kissed him. How he had held her and placed his lips on hers, trembling with the delight and wonder of it.

After his fruitless daily search, Jack would come home to a meal made by Mrs Quinlan, who would enquire about his morning, rail against the injustice of men who had gone to fight now walking the streets idle, and promise him that something would turn up. Knowing how he loved to read, she would then leave him to it.

Jack had brought himself up-to-date with events since 1913, arriving at the 1916 Easter Rebellion, of which he had read in France: the summary executions of all the leaders except de Valera, who claimed his American citizenship. He learned of the imprisonment of thousands of men implicated or suspected of being implicated in the Rebellion. How at the beginning of the Rebellion, the majority of the Irish people had scorned it as in France he had himself, feeling it was a betrayal of those Irishmen fighting in the war. Of the surge of sympathy and hatred of the British government after the executions.

Jack read how the survivors of the Rebellion, buoyed up by this feeling, had stood at by-elections on the Sinn Fein ticket even though some were still in gaol, and were elected. Those of them not imprisoned had refused to take their seats at Westminster. The anti-British mood was intensified in 1918 when conscription for Ireland was threatened. It led to an overwhelming victory for Sinn Fein at the General Election in that year, followed by the first meeting of Dail Eireann on the day that Jack had come home from France. Ireland's Independent Parliament hoped to be achieved by peaceful means. What worried Jack was the Soloheadbeag shooting of the policemen in the dynamite raid, suggesting as it did that not all were hopeful or in favour of the peaceful means of settlement.

On the nights when Julia worked late he visited the library and afterwards, went on to the Long Hall with Seamus, of whom he grew fonder. He was also flattered that the Librarian, an educated man, found him interesting enough to spend some time with him. Jack learned more about his new friend. One evening he asked Seamus where he had gone to college.

'I was in a seminary.'

'You were going to be a priest?' Jack asked, surprised. The thought of Seamus as a priest had never occurred to him.

'I thought I had a vocation, but there were conflicting loyalties.'

It was on the tip of Jack's tongue to ask if Ireland and her independence, and how this was to be achieved, was the loyalty that conflicted, but he didn't. You couldn't pry into the personal motives of another man. For his part, Seamus was always interested in how Jack's search for work was going, and promised he would keep his eyes open for anything that might arise.

One night Julia, though very tired and wanting nothing more than her bed, looked at Jack engrossed in a book. He seldom talked about what he read; she seldom enquired. Often she resented his preoccupation with the books. Now, looking at his lovely face bent slightly towards one, a thought came into her mind: maybe he would welcome a few questions. After all, for someone who had hardly ever opened a book before the war, it was a great achievement to have taken to it as he had. She should be encouraging him. So, pretending an interest she didn't feel, she asked what he was reading.

Looking up at her, smiling that gorgeous smile which always melted her heart, he said, 'One of the usual – dates, names, facts, figures,' in a deprecating manner.

All the same she knew he was pleased by her enquiry and pursued it. 'Tell me about it.'

'It's that dry you'd fall asleep.'

'Try me.'

Julia's mother, always quick on the uptake, guessed what she was about and because she loved Jack as if he were her own son, went along with Julia's pretence and also coaxed him to tell them what he was reading. Again he tried to put them off but both women knew by the expression on his face that he was delighted to be asked. Finally Mrs Mangan said, 'For the love of God will you tell us! If it's as dull as you say we'll fall asleep but give us the chance to find out for ourselves.'

'All right then, it's about all the attempts there were to get Home Rule.'

'I remember once when we thought it was a sure thing,' said Mrs Mangan musingly. 'There was dancing in the streets and bonfires.'

'Why didn't we get it?' Julia asked.

'Mainly because of the Northern Protestants' opposition to it,' her husband told her.

'They're a bitter lot, the Northern Protestants,' Mrs Mangan nodded. 'An aunt of mine, God rest her soul, went up to live in Dungannon, to work in the Moygashel Mills and they set fire to her house.'

'In any case we don't need Home Rule now that we've got our own Parliament. Wasn't de Valera elected the President a couple of weeks ago?' asked Julia.

Jack said he was and Mrs Mangan added, 'And he made Michael Collins his Minister of Finance. You hear a lot about him nowadays.

43

Someone was telling me in the pork butcher's yesterday that he's supposed to be behind the Soloheadbeg raid.'

'D'ye think our own Parliament will work?' Julia enquired.

'If England doesn't ban it, it has a good chance,' he told her. 'And they're going about it in a peaceable way.'

'Not according to the woman in the pork butcher's. She says she has it on good authority that Michael Collins is spoiling for a fight.'

'Ma,' said Julia, 'I never knew you bothered your head about such things.'

'For all the good it'll do, or difference it'll make, I do if I think the things I hear may lead to bloodshed.'

'Do you think it will, Jack?' Julia asked, looking alarmed.

And not wanting to worry either of them, he lied and said he didn't think so.

One day, after another fruitless search for work, Barney and Jack went into a public house on their way home and while they sat waiting for their porter to settle and Jack watched the peat-brown liquid slowly turn black and a creamy collar rise to top it Barney asked, 'Would you do it again?'

'Do what?' asked Jack.

'Join up. Go to France. Do you regret it, I mean?'

'Often. I have nightmares about it. I wake screaming, thinking I'm back. No, given a second chance I wouldn't have chosen to witness what we did. But,' he shrugged, 'it's done. No use complaining now.'

'I suppose not. All the same, we were shaggin' eejits. And look at us now – wearing the clothes we wore five years ago, not a penny to jingle on a tombstone and no sign of work. And we had good jobs. You were a foreman in the sawmills and I was doing all right in the foundry.' Barney drank deeply from his pint, wiped the froth from his lips and asked Jack if he had any cigarettes.

They lit up and continued to talk. Looking around the bar, which was filled with men as shabby as themselves, Barney said, 'The drink's the last thing to go to the wall.'

'Aye,' replied Jack. 'In the long run it's the women who make the biggest sacrifices. I never drink a pint nowadays that I don't feel guilty at the thought of Julia blinding the two eyes in her head. I never thought it'd finish up like this. I was going to keep her.'

'At least you're married – what about me and Sarah? I love her. I'm demented with the way things are, you know.'

Jack nodded his understanding of Barney's predicament but neither man enlarged on the subject.

Barney drank again from his glass, almost emptying the pint tumbler, lit another cigarette and became less despondent. 'Surely to God things will pick up soon. I mean, with having our own government, even if England doesn't recognise it. Something's bound to come of it – that fella de Valera being President, you know what I mean.'

'Maybe,' said Jack.

'We were shaggin' eejits. We should have stayed at home and gone out in 1916. That would have been something to see. We should have been fighting for our own country, fighting for its independence. Wouldn't you have done it if we weren't in France?'

'I don't suppose I would.'

'You wouldn't? You mean you'd have stood aside without lifting a hand!'

'I do, if I'm to tell the truth. Sure I never gave the state of the country a thought before I went to the war, no more than yourself. No more than the other thousands who laughed and jeered at the men when they did take over the General Post Office, and jeered them on their way to gaol. It was only after they were executed that anyone began to take notice – the majority of people, anyway.'

'I wouldn't say you were right about me never being interested. Wasn't I reading about our heroes morning, noon and night?'

'That's true, you were,' confirmed Jack, not wanting a contention but saying to himself, 'Yes, you did have a book. A book of heroes – pictures, mostly, with small paragraphs under them, of men like Brian Boru, Sarsfield, Father Murphy, Clive of India, Robert E. Lee, Nelson and Greek heroes that we couldn't pronounce the names of. I remember it well. Its pages were dog-eared. You probably had it in your knapsack in France, though I don't remember seeing it.'

He felt a great affection for Barney, a love that was tinged with pity, for part of Barney was still a child. Anyone with a stronger character could influence him. He could be swayed as wind swayed a field of barley, not his own man. Inflamed to anger one minute, the next his pity aroused and always his opinions changing as quick as lightning.

Had Barney been in Ireland at the time of the Rebellion and met a supporter able to spin him a convincing yarn, out he'd have gone, though half an hour later he might have regretted his decision.

Barney finished his drink and offered Jack another. He refused. 'I won't either,' Barney decided, 'but listen, before we go tell me this – what d'ye think of the situation now? Which way d'ye think things will go?'

'Honest to God I don't know. I puzzle my brains wondering. We have an elected government proclaiming to be the true government of Ireland, with ministers doing their best to run the courts and sort out our finances. I'd say a great many of the people are supporting them – *but will England allow it?* Will the impatient ones be prepared to let passive resistance have a chance? The way I see it is that the more Royal Irish Constabulary that are shot, the more British soldiers will pour in. The more killings there are, the more there will be. I think, though I hope to God that I'm wrong, that the raid at Soloheadbeg was the beginning. The next step will be England outlawing our government and then the real trouble will start.'

'I suppose you've hit the nail on the head,' said Barney, looking wise as if he had followed every word of Jack's, weighed it up and agreed with his conclusion.

Jack knew he hadn't, but contented himself with saying: 'I'm all for an Independent Ireland, we've waited a long time – but not at any price.'

Coming out of the gloom of the bar, the bright sunlight blinded them for a moment and its heat beat fiercely down on them in their unsuitable clothes. Jack pushed his cap back on his head and Barney, observing what he was doing, said, 'Jaysus, you're going grey.'

'It's worry,' laughed Jack. 'My father and mother lived to a good age with hardly a grey hair between them.'

'May God spare you to live so long.'

'You too,' rejoined Jack.

They walked up George's Street, Jack thinking of Julia working not far away in a poky, badly-lit workroom. His lovely Julia that he wanted to look after. Well, he would one day. If necessary he'd take her to America. He'd take her anywhere that he could earn a living for her.

His gentle-natured Julia who never complained about his lack of a job. Julia with her joyous laugh, her gaiety, her enjoyment of the simplest things. He thought of her when himself, Barney and Sarah went up the mountains on a Sunday, the same mountains he could see as if they were at the top of the street. There were few places in Dublin from where you couldn't see the mountains. Julia always loved the ride on the tram, the hike afterwards to Glenasmole or Glencree. Like a little girl – each time greeting the mountains as if she was seeing them for the first time. He hoped America wouldn't be necessary. Julia would miss the mountains.

Trams swayed by, also an occasional car, its occupants swathed in veils, heads covered with motoring caps, eyes protected by goggles. Coal-carts passed, bakers' vans, carts with rattling milk-churns, rag-carts afloat with balloons to exchange for rags or jamjars, and in between them people wove their way to the other side of the street. Shabby men propped up corners, coughed and spat. The pavements were speckled with gobs of phlegm, some of a repulsive colour.

At the corner of Kevin's Street Jack bid Barney goodbye, saying, 'I'll pass an hour in the library till it's time to meet Julia.'

'I'll see you later on, oh no I won't,' Barney corrected himself. 'I forgot, I'm seeing Sarah. See you tomorrow.'

'Right,' said Jack, and they went their separate ways.

'I'm warning you for the last time – get yourself into trouble for that fella and you'll get no help from me. So don't come crying and think you can live with him on my floor.'

Used to such haranguing, Sarah didn't bother answering her mother but went on filing her nails. She knew that Rosie was doing it for her own good. And she was right: Barney would make a useless husband. Only she couldn't give her mother the satisfaction of agreeing with her. Sometimes she thought she'd marry Barney to spite her. It wasn't that she didn't like her, she did. And she knew how much her mother loved and wanted what was best for her. It was true, she *was* looking for trouble the way things were going with Barney. She wanted to finish with him – wanted to go into service.

As if able to read her mind, Mrs Quinlan changed her tactics. Sitting down by Sarah and lowering her voice, she said, 'Ah dote, why are we always rowing? We never used to. I know I'm hard on you over Barney, and maybe like me with your father you do love him at the moment. Sure didn't I think that way myself. But you must admit, he is dragging his feet about finding work, so why don't you give him a fright?'

'How d'ye mean, a fright?'

'Raise a row tonight. Get yourself in a right wax and break off the engagement. Listen, don't interrupt. It doesn't have to be permanent. Give Glenivy a try. He'll be mad with jealousy and quick about finding work. What have you got to lose? A lover's tiff – they happen all the time. You'll write and make it up while you're away. The rest is up to you. Glenivy isn't a prison. You can leave any time you like – a week, a month, as you please. Do that, love. It will sort everything out one way or another.'

Sarah felt an overwhelming sense of relief, as if a heavy weight had been lifted from her shoulders. A solution such as her mother's had never crossed her mind, but it was the right one, she could see that. A lover's tiff – work herself into a frenzy and break it off. As her mother said, rows between courting couples happened all the time, whereas if she tried finishing it in a reasonable way, it wouldn't leave her the opportunity for blaming it later on on her fiery temper, telling him how sorry she was, how he knew what her temper was like. Making it up if she had to.

She didn't really want to marry him while he was idle, but neither did she want to lose him. There was many a wan who'd snap him up with the shortage of men, and Barney would be better than finishing up an old maid. And now she had the answer. Definitely tonight she would break it off. He'd sulk for a few days : long enough for Glenivy to be fixed up. All done on the spur of the moment, *moryah*. He'd soon stir himself once she left, and get work.

Then, when it suited her, she'd write and patch things up – if nothing marvellous happened before that. Going off into a fantasy world she imagined meeting someone fantastic who'd sweep her off her feet. Someone as different as chalk and cheese from Barney, a man she couldn't resist. Dreamily she began doing her hair, still conjuring up visions of a tall, handsome man who'd fall madly in love with her, who could kiss and do all the things Barney got into a hell of a fix attempting. This one would know all the right things to say and do. Then coming back to reality, she told herself, 'And well, if I meet no one like him, there's always Barney.'

'You won't go back on my advice, will you, love ?' her mother asked as she was about to leave.

'Definitely not.'

'Good girl. You won't regret it.'

Under the railway bridge where there were no street lamps was a recess in one wall, where Barney and Sarah did their courting. And there Barney pleaded, 'Please, Sarah, I won't hurt you. Oh, please. You don't know what it's like.'

'No I don't want to, not until we're married,' said Sarah, angrily pushing him away and rearranging her clothes.

'OK. All right, I won't touch you, promise. Just let me put my arm around you.'

She allowed him to and said she was sorry for pushing him away like that. 'You know I love you, and I have my feelings, too. It isn't easy for me either, but I can't. I could have a baby and finish up in the Union or with the nuns in a convent for fallen women. And it's a sin. You know that as well as me. It's a sin unless you're married.'

'Then we'll get married. Tomorrow we'll see the priest and put the Banns in. I'm mad about you. You don't know what you do to me. I could – oh God – I don't know. I just can't stand much more of this. We'll see the priest. We'll get married.'

'Are you mad or what !' She moved away from him. 'Married – how can we get married and you not doing a tap. What would we live on ?

Where would we live? Never mind being crazy about me – I think you are crazy full-stop.' Her voice was mocking.

'We'd manage – I have a few pounds. We could live with my Ma, and I'm bound to get work soon.'

'There's eight of you in that house.'

'We'll live in yours then,' said Barney, and put an arm round her again.

'We'll do no such thing! I want a place of my own. In any case, my mother wouldn't have us. She believes young couples should stand on their own feet.'

'Then you'll have to live in our house,' said Barney.

A train rumbled over the bridge, drowning the sound of his voice and impatiently when it had passed Sarah asked, 'What did you say?' He repeated his words and she sighed exasperatedly and asked, 'Are you deaf, or what? I just told you I wouldn't.'

'What'll we do, then? I can't stand much more of this. Night after night worked up to ninety. No man could stand it. What am I going to do?'

'What plenty of decent men do, men who have respect for their girls – pray for self-control. Think about all the poor priests and nuns. Otherwise we'll have to stop seeing each other on our own.'

'You're not serious!'

'Oh yes, I am. You frighten the life out of me when you get too passionate. Maybe it was the war but you didn't used to be like that, and I'm not putting up with it. So unless you change your ways until we can get married, I'll only go out with you in a foursome.'

Barney couldn't believe what he was hearing. Never be alone with her again – go out always in a foursome? He couldn't stand that!

'Ah, Sarah,' he wheedled. 'Don't be hasty. I'll do anything you ask. I'll go and talk to the priest. I won't lay a hand on you, as true as God, but don't say we can never be alone again. I couldn't bear that.'

'No.' She was adamant. 'I've changed my mind about the priest. You're not to be trusted. You'd let on you'd been to him and then start mauling me all over again. Until you get a job and there's the prospect of marriage I won't go out with you again.'

'Well fuck you, then,' said Barney, surprising himself with his reaction. 'And as for going out in a foursome, fuck that as well.'

'You blackguard!' Sarah's indignation was well-acted. 'You cur. Here, take this!' She worked the engagement ring off her finger. 'Go on, take it, or I'll fire it down the shore. You bowsie, five years of my life you've wasted, but I'm well rid of you. Are you going to take this ring or not?'

Speechless and stupefied he stood as though paralysed, confused thoughts swirling through his brain. How had all this happened? What had he done to offend her so? What had he done to make her break it off? He loved her. As long as he could remember, even as a child, he had loved Sarah Quinlan.

'Did you hear me? Are you going to take your ring or not?' Still he said nothing and she dropped the ring with its minuscule diamond by his feet and flounced away. He bent and with his hand swept the pavement until his fingers found the engagement ring. He picked it up and in the dark lonely street put it to his lips and tears ran down his face.

'Well?' asked Rosie Quinlan when Sarah came in. 'How did it go?'

'I broke it off. I gave him back his ring.'

'Good girl. He'll come to his senses soon enough. He'll stir himself and find work and I'll write first thing in the morning to Lady Glenivy. She'll find something for you. A year with her and you'll have a few pounds. You'll learn nice ways and see how the quality live. Write to him now and then, not too often, but enough to keep his interest, and you'll see the change that will come about. He'll get work and then let the talk of marriage come up. Wouldn't you have been the fool to throw in your lot with him as things stand. We've made the right decision, you'll see. And who's to say that in service you mightn't even meet someone more suitable.'

'I hope you don't think I'm looking for a footman. I love Barney in my own way. I don't want anyone else. He's the only man for me. But you were right about forcing him to get a bit of shape on him.'

'I was, you won't regret it. And I'll tell you something else – there's no such thing as one man for one woman. Tomorrow or the next day you could meet another, and all thought of Barney fly from your mind. Many a time I've seen it happen. Many a time. Didn't I see the proof of it with my own two eyes and I not more than a year in service.'

'What was that?' Sarah asked, undoing her hair and letting it fall round her shoulders like a shawl.

'I must have told you about the young Lord Beales, a relation of the Glenivys?'

'No, Ma. I never heard you mention his name. Go on – tell me.'

'I'll make a pot of tea first,' said her mother, and pulled the kettle over the fire. She laid a tray with a dainty cloth and two odd china cups and saucers, cut thin bread, buttered it and placed the tray on a small table before Sarah. While she poured the tea she said, 'Wait till you see how they do things in Glenivy. Wait till you see how the afternoon tea is served. They're the people who know how to live.'

'What about this Lord Beales? Tell me the story,' prompted Sarah.

'He used to come to the House for parties and the shooting and things. He was that handsome. Sometimes his fiancée came with him, too. She was a beauty, from England. She didn't have a title but had pucks of money. All the arrangements were made for this big wedding in London, and then didn't he fall madly in love with a maidservant from a castle in County Cork. You see the way it is with the gentry – they all know each other so it wasn't only to us he'd come. They said she was a beauty too, the maidservant, though there were them in the kitchen that said she was a tinker. How and ever didn't the pair of them run away and get married! I believe his mother was fit to be tied and his father threatened to disinherit him, but in the long run it all blew over and he was received back into the family. Though I never laid eyes on him or her in our place, but I've heard tell they are happy and have a family. So there you are, isn't that the proof of what I said?'

In the room which had once been her mother and father's, Julia lay in Jack's arms and listened to him tell her that he was sure any day now he would get work.

'Please God you will,' she said, and stroked his face. 'To have you working would be grand but I'm so grateful to have you alive I wouldn't care if you never worked again.'

He kissed her and told her how much he loved her and that it wasn't only talk about the prospect of a job. 'You know the fella in the library who keeps the books for me? Well, he told me today that there may be something coming up and if it does he'll put in a good word for me.'

'Honest to God?'

'Honest to God,' said Jack.

'And me giving out yards about that fella to myself.'

'Why?' asked Jack, surprised.

'Because he's set you mad about the same books. You're reading when I go out in the morning and every spare minute in the evenings your nose is stuck in one. I declare to God you must know more about the history of Ireland than any professor going. But if the same fella's the cause of getting you a job I'll forgive him.'

Within a few weeks Jack got the job. On the head of it he bought for Julia and her mother a box of sweets from Lemon's in O'Connell Street. Mrs Mangan said there was cause for celebration and sent him to the public house with money for stout, a Baby Power for herself and minerals for Julia. And because of the day that was in it she cooked him three rashers, black and white pudding, sausages, two eggs and fried bread.

'It's a bit of everything,' he explained when asked what he would be doing. 'Portering, handyman, messenger, cleaner, a bit of clerical work –

whatever comes up. The club is only starting. If it keeps going and expands, I might in time land a good job.'

'It sounds great. What sort of a club is it?' asked Julia.

'It's to foster and encourage Irish culture. You know how much I've learned through reading – before that I knew nothing about Ireland. About Irish music, poetry, all that sort of thing. Well, there's thousands more like me, eager to know. For after all, our lesson books didn't tell us much about anything, and what little they did was about England. Think of the songs we sing. Apart from *Moore's Melodies* every other one is about England. They'll have Irish dancing and Irish classes. I think I'm going to like it. And once we get on our feet you'll be able to give up work.'

'I wouldn't for the time being,' said Julia. 'It's not hard and I love the embroidery. You never said where the job is.'

'The northside – Parnell Square. In one of the big houses, but not all of it, only four rooms including the front and back drawing rooms. When things get going we can have functions there. One of these nights I'll have you both over when there's a dance.'

'A ceilidh, I suppose,' said Mrs Mangan. 'I wouldn't go to a ceilidh – all that leppin and roarin' and the arms being swung out of you.'

'There you are,' laughed Jack. 'That's what I mean! Like the majority of Dubliners you look down on your own culture. That sort of dancing you dismiss as being for the country people – the *culchies* – and yet it's your heritage. I'm telling you, after a bit of a practice there'll be no one to hold a candle to you when it comes to dancing a reel or a jig.'

God had been very good to them, Julia thought as she knelt to say her prayers, and she thanked Him. The stout had sent Jack to sleep before she rose from her knees. She turned out the gas and got into bed where she lay listening to his soft breathing, thinking how lucky she was to have him for a husband. How much she loved him. How every evening she watched the clock for his return. How kind and considerate he was with her mother.

She wished he was awake, but told herself he was tired when he came in and the drink had knocked him out altogether. All the same she wanted him awake. She moved closer to him and put an arm round him. The nearness of him made her want him more; she raised herself and kissed him. He made a little noise of protest at the disturbing of his sleep. Then she kissed him again and he opened his eyes and smiled into hers and took her in his arms.

CHAPTER FIVE

Lady Glenivy agreed to employ Sarah as a general maid. 'You'll be expected to help wherever you are needed,' her mother explained, 'but you're quick to learn and have a good appearance. The parlourmaid is getting on and so is her Ladyship's maid, so in no time you could fall in for either of those positions.'

'I only want to stay long enough for Barney to stir himself about a job. He passed me yesterday in the street, though I could tell he was dying to talk. Wait'll he hears I'm going away. He'll be leppin'. Mad with jealousy. I'll let him stew for a week or two before I write.'

Her mother, busy packing for Sarah, said nothing but her mind was making plans. If after a few months Sarah was still keen on Barney then she'd ask her Ladyship to help him find work. She had great influence like all the gentry. There was hardly a committee in the city that she didn't sit on, and on every one to do with ex-servicemen. She'd get him a job in no time, and take it he would, if Sarah went the right way about persuading him – letting him know she had no intention of coming back to Dublin otherwise.

The night before she went away, Sarah lay in bed thinking about Barney. She heard a train going by and remembered the nights spent courting under the railway bridge. She liked being held close by him in the dark. The kissing was gorgeous. Thinking about it made her go hot and cold. The state he got her in, though she tried not to let on. It hadn't been like that before he went to France. Of course, she was only sixteen then. At twenty you were bound to be more passionate. And in any case, he'd never touched her then the way he did now, on her breasts – squeezing them and doing things to her nipples, and if she'd let him he'd have had his hand up the leg of her knickers in a flash. Little would he ever know how near she came to letting him. But thank God she hadn't and wouldn't until they were married.

Since the breaking-off of his engagement, Barney often came to Julia's and Jack's of an evening. After having told them the news and showing them the ring he never referred to it again, which surprised Julia, who knew him for a talkative man. 'He's broken-hearted,' Jack explained. 'He idolised the ground Sarah walked on. He took it for granted they would marry. It was only the thought of her that kept him going in the trenches. And now it's over. He's broken-hearted and stupefied – no wonder he can't talk about it.'

'It hasn't had the same effect on *her*. If she's told me once how she threw the ring back at him she's told me a thousand times. I don't understand her. I thought I did, but there's been a change in her lately.'

And then Sarah landed her with telling Barney of her departure to Kildare. Julia protested that she couldn't do it, she wouldn't have the heart. And Sarah countered, 'Isn't it better for him to hear it from friends than a black stranger give him the bang of it?'

'As if there's such a thing as a stranger in the street. Though I must say yourself and your mother have kept the secret well – I've not heard until you told me word of you going. I don't like what you're asking me to do but I suppose you're right and it's better to come from us,' Julia agreed.

And so she had to break the news to Barney. He was sitting by the table where Jack was leafing through the evening paper, with that lost look about him that was nowadays his perpetual expression. Julia kept finding unimportant tasks to do, sweeping the hearth that didn't need sweeping, watering the geraniums in their clay pots on the windowsill, aware that water was the last thing they needed, fiddling and foostering in an effort to delay what it was she had to do. She cleared her throat several times before taking the plunge. 'Barney,' she said, 'I've something to tell you.'

Instantly, his lost look vanished and his face lit up. She could have cried for him, knowing that he hoped for news of Sarah, good news: a message asking to meet him, a sign that she wanted to make it up.

'It's not good news. It's about Sarah.' It was terrible to see the hope leave his face and an anxious fearful look take its place. Julia silently cursed Sarah for causing such pain and herself for ever having agreed to be the one giving the bad news. The quicker she got it over the better, and in a flurry of words she told him: 'She's going away in the morning, down to Kildare to work for Lady Glenivy. She asked me to tell you. I'm very sorry, Barney. I'm . . .' She could think of nothing else to say and sat down by the window busying herself with pulling off dead leaves from the geraniums.

'I'm going up there, up to her house this minute. I'll tear the door down. I don't care about her oul wan nor her da either. I'll show them what's what and bring her to her senses. I won't let her go. I tell you I won't. I won't let her go into service – live in. I'm not having it and that's that.'

He stood up and squared his shoulders. And Julia's heart went out to him and she was reminded of all the times she had seen him put on the brave front, get ready for a confrontation which before many minutes had passed he would talk himself out of. He was, she supposed, a coward or maybe only a gentle fool. Seldom giving offence, always looking for the easy way out. Often too quick to forgive and forget. And the most easily led man she had ever met. Even as the thoughts were going through her mind he was beginning his climbdown. 'They'd probably be in bed, asleep maybe. It might be better to leave it till the morning.'

'Definitely,' said Jack.

Julia looked at the clock. It was only half-nine – even the Quinlans didn't go to bed this early. Barney continued: 'I'd get no sense out of her. What time is she leaving tomorrow, Julia?'

'Early, on the eight o'clock train.'

'I'll catch her before she goes. I'll have it out with her then. I'll make her change her mind.'

'The very thing,' said Jack. 'I'll tell you what I was thinking, Barney.'

'What was that, Jack?'

'About two foaming pints of porter. How about it?'

'Gameball,' said Barney, and rubbed his hands together.

Later, when Jack came home from the public house, Julia asked how Barney was when he left him.

'Legless. He went on to the hard stuff. The way he spent tonight there won't be much of his savings left.'

'Drowning his sorrows. Poor Barney, is there any chance of him going to Sarah's first thing in the morning?'

'You know him as well if not better than I do. Only once in his life did he ever do what he threatened to do, and that nearly cost him his life.'

'In France you mean – when you saved him?'

'Aye,' said Jack.

'Tell me about it.'

'It was nothing, really.'

'It must have been something, didn't you win a medal because of it!'

'He was doing a performance like tonight, only the lads there didn't know him as we do. "Go on, then," they urged him. "Go out there and blow that fucking German machine gunner to hell. Go on Pad, don't let the side down." And they clapped and hooted. Our officer and sergeant had bought it the day before. There was only a lance-jack – a useless bugger who couldn't have stopped him even if he'd tried. "Go on then, Pad. Show us what the Irish can do," the lads kept on. And before I could try stopping him, he had a grenade and was up and out of the trench. I watched him running and thought – that's the last I'll see of you! I cursed him for all the stupid bastards God ever created and said a prayer for him at the same time. We could see him throw the grenade and then the machine gun opened fire. He fell. He was dead, I thought. It was as if I'd died myself. Barney was part of me, always around me. All my life he had always been around me.

'Then, when it got dark, I heard something. It was him, calling my name. I thought at first I was imagining it. No one else heard anything. Then I heard it again. And without thinking I went over the trench and crawled to where he lay, not knowing what state he'd be in. Maybe his legs were blown off, maybe his entrails were hanging out. You often found them like that. But all he had was a twisted ankle – a bad one. He could have dragged himself nearer our lines, only he confessed that he was afraid to budge. Anyway, I got him back. And that's all it was. We were lucky.'

'You saved his life,' said Julia.

'Maybe. I don't know. Maybe the Germans would have raked the place again with the machine gun, maybe not.'

'You don't have to belittle your action. Barney doesn't. I think he'd die for you.'

Jack laughed sardonically. 'I'm not so sure,' he said. 'There's very few that will die for another.'

'Oh, you,' said Julia. 'You let on to be so cynical and you're not like that at all. You're the fairest, decentest man I've ever known. I love you.' She sat on his lap and kissed him.

'Because I'm decent and just – is that the only reason? Supposing I changed . . . what about the love then?'

'I love you. Whatever you were I'd love you. Till God closes my eyes I'll always love you. And I want to die before you, for I couldn't bear to walk the earth without you.'

After bidding Sarah goodbye at the station, her mother walked back along the quays, her thoughts following the train on its way into the country and Glenivy. She imagined Sarah's arrival, her first impressions of the House, and hoped against hope that her reception would be all she had led her to believe it would. Admitting finally to herself how often she had let her tongue run away with her, exaggerating how wonderful life was in Glenivy. Ignoring her own painful memories in the beginning of her stay there – the homesickness, the bullying by the upper servants. The housekeeper with her jangling keys who seemed to appear wherever you went like a gaoler. It hadn't been all sunshine. Rosie Quinlan remembered the long hours, the back-breaking work, the cold of the attic rooms – the discomfort of them. Maybe she should have warned Sarah . . .

Then she consoled herself that Lady Glenivy was bound to favour her, bound to remember how it had been between the two of them when they were both young girls, the mistress newly married, coming to live in the House only weeks before her own arrival. The instant liking she had taken to Rosie; how much she made of her, and in no time had her as her personal maid. They were the great times – the laughing and giggling, the secrets they told each other, Lady Glenivy even confiding about her brief though numerous love affairs. She was so beautiful the men flocked round her like bees on blossoms. Some of them were so handsome that you couldn't blame her, for God knows his Lordship wasn't the handsomest of men.

Rosie crossed the road and turned into Capel Street, trying to ignore another memory fighting its way to the surface of her mind. One she hadn't shared with Sarah, hadn't shared with a living soul and never would. It was another secret, but one this time which she would regret having been told until her dying day . . . Clear in her mind she heard Lady Glenivy sobbing hysterically on that day more than twenty years ago, and her own voice asking: 'What's wrong, my Lady? What ails you? Tell me.'

And then her Ladyship told her how she was head over heels in love with someone else. Rosie had hidden her smile of relief, thinking as she did so, 'Not again!' But this time it turned out to be more serious. For one thing, he was a married man and usually her mistress only bothered with bachelors. And what was really terrible was that she thought she might be pregnant.

Rosie recalled not knowing what to do for the best. She had dabbed cologne on Lady Glenivy's forehead and told her not to be crying as it would spoil her lovely eyes, but nothing seemed to console her. Then she an idea, and told her mistress what it was. She stopped crying after that. 'You're a clever girl, Rosie,' she said. 'That's the solution. I haven't uttered a word about this to anyone, only you and him, so who's to say it isn't Glenivy's? We were careful – none of that business of going to his room. There's always someone prying.' She was smiling now, looking her beautiful self. 'Out in the middle of the night we went to a summer-house.'

'She never mentioned the business again, except once more when she told me that her lover and his wife had gone out to Kenya,' Rosie mused. 'I saw Patrick not long after he was born. He was a fine fat child with red hair. As far as I knew, there were no redheads in the Glenivy family. At least, none of the portraits up the stairs, on the landings and in a lot of the rooms showed men or women with red hair. Of course, it could have come from his mother's side. As they say, it's a wise child that knows its own father.'

Rosie went into a teashop in Dame Street and ordered a cup of tea and a buttered scone. She was starving and wished she had asked for two scones. While she ate and drank she continued musing over the time after Patrick's birth. How a change had seemed to come over her Ladyship. She was more distant, the laughing and giggling that had been between them finished. Rosie had put it down to her growing up and feeling her position. Or perhaps it was that she regretted giving her maid her secret. People often did that. In the heat of the moment they confided in you, then afterwards hated you for knowing their shame or guilt, or whatever it was they'd done or not done. Still and all, things were never the same again. Oh, Lady Glenivy was still very kind to her, but they weren't like sisters any more. Perhaps it was time for Rosie to be put in her proper place : to know that she was only a servant.

'I hope I haven't built Sarah's hopes too high,' Rosie muttered to herself. 'I didn't prepare her right. I always get carried away when I talk about Glenivy, forgetting that what I'm really remembering is the golden days when me and her Ladyship were a pair of young girls together – a happy-go-lucky pair like sisters who loved each other. It did change. Not that I felt one bit less admiration for her or the gentry, and still do. They're the finest people in the land, and I'm worrying myself for nothing. Sarah will do all right there – get a good training and that scut of a Barney Daly will go out of her mind. I was hungry, that is all it was. I'll order another cup of tea and a scone. Sure with her gone I've nothing to hurry home for.'

At the station Sarah was met by a pony and trap. The driver was an elderly man who had known her mother when she worked at the Big House. 'You're the spitten image of her,' he said as he helped her into the trap. 'She was a fine, handsome girl. There wasn't a man about the estate that didn't have a smack for her,' he continued talking as they drove off. 'Indeed, if she'd given me half a chance I might have been your father. What d'ye think of that now ?'

'Not much,' Sarah said to herself. 'You're an awful-looking oul ticket,' but she smiled sweetly and admired the passing countryside, remarking on the bright green fields and the rolling grasslands. ''Tis the best grass in the world,' the driver said. 'Limestone, that's what it grows on. It's what makes for the great horses – the finest that money can buy. Did you know that ?' Sarah admitted that she did not. 'And his Lordship is famous for his horses – and I'd say the young master won't be long making his own reputation with the creatures.'

'I thought he was a soldier,' said Sarah, remembering her mother relating his homecoming party after the war.

'He *was* a soldier. He went all through the war and got a medal, but he's handed in his papers this while back. We've this little hill then now,' said the driver, giving the pony a cut of the whip to encourage it with the climb, 'and once over the brow you'll see the House.'

It was everything she had heard of it. It was all the pictures she had conjured of it in her mind's eyes. And more, much more than anything she could have thought or imagined. For one thing, it was so big. A big white house with curved wings extending its size on either side. She shivered with delight at the thought of living in such a place. Memories of stories told by her mother came flooding back – descriptions of the ladies walking on the lawns and playing croquet. Strolling in the moonlight after supper. Of afternoon tea served under the trees. Of the hunt assembling there before a Meet. Of the balls and the sound of music drifting out into the night through the opened French windows. She clasped her hands together, squeezing them tightly. It was the most beautiful place in the world, and she was going to be part of it. She was going to live in that house! Tonight she would sleep there. She was so happy that she could have thrown her arms round the neck of the old man as he handed her down from the trap.

And was only a bit disappointed when, as she went to walk up the flight of steps to a pillared porch, he said: 'Not that way. We go round the back. You'll have to see the housekeeper but first you'll have a cup of tea and something to eat. God love you, you must be famished.'

The kitchen was, she was sure, half the length of the street at home and full of people. 'You must be Rosie's daughter. You're the image of her,' another old person greeted her – a woman with her hands covered in flour. 'Sit over to the table. Make this child a cup of tea and cut up some of the cake and soda bread. She's come all the way from Dublin.'

'Yes, ma'am,' a young girl replied, and the cook wiping her floury hands on her apron sat to the table and asked questions about Sarah's mother. After satisfying herself about Rosie's wellbeing, she spoke about Sarah's future. 'Your mother probably told you that to start off with you'll have to do a bit of everything. But then I'll put in a word for you. Get you into my kitchen and train you up. You'd make a great assistant-cook, I've no doubt.' Sarah thanked her while thinking, 'She can stick her assistant-cook up her jumper. I didn't leave Dublin for that! As my mother said, the parlourmaid's getting on and her Ladyship's personal maid as well. Except for the young wan that made my tea, they all look ancient.'

Before she had finished her refreshments she was summoned to the housekeeper's room. 'Go now,' said the cook. 'Mrs Bellows doesn't like to be kept waiting.'

The housekeeper's room was like a little parlour and an office, Sarah supposed, for there were ledgers and papers and a small desk, reminding her of the office in the warehouse. If the housekeeper had known or heard of her mother she had made no mention of it. Brusquely she told Sarah to sit down, asked for her name and age and her home address, all of which she entered in a ledger. Afterwards she outlined her duties. 'You must be clean and tidy at all times. Speak only when you're spoken to. Don't hang around the kitchen. There is always something to do . . .'

'Yes, ma'am,' Sarah said when the housekeeper finally paused after a lengthy harangue.

She glared at the girl and continued. 'Tomorrow morning you'll be up at six o'clock, your bed made, you washed and dressed and in the kitchen not a minute later than quarter after six. You will make a cup of tea before starting your duties. You'll find a list of them pinned up in the kitchen. You'll be paid sixteen pounds a year, have your keep and a free uniform. You get an afternoon off once a month, and a day every three months. Do you understand all that ?'

It was a question so Sarah supposed it was all right to reply. She said, 'Yes, ma'am, I understand.' What she really wanted to say was : 'Stick your job up your arse ! It sounds more like being in Mountjoy Gaol than working for the gentry.' But she consoled herself. Lady Glenivy was bound to ask to see her. After all, she was her mother's daughter – not just anybody.

'Very well then, wait outside. Don't forget your bag, and I'll have someone show you where you are to sleep. Tomorrow you'll get your uniform.'

After what seemed an age, the girl the cook had ordered to make the tea came along the corridor. 'I'm Mary Flynn,' she said. 'You'll be taking over from me – the dogsbody. Come on and I'll show you where you'll sleep.' She led her through a passage and then up a narrow flight of stairs covered with oil-cloth. After the first landing the stairs became narrower and the boards were bare. Wearily Sarah dragged herself and her bag up another two flights. All the while Mary was chattering, but such was her accent that Sarah hardly understood what she was saying. In any case she wasn't concentrating very hard for her mind was full of misery. None of it was as she had imagined living with the gentry would be, except for her quick glimpse of the house before she was whisked round to the servants' entrance. And she hadn't taken to anyone she met in the kitchen – not even the cook. Her only crumb of consolation was that when she met Lady Glenivy it would all change, for her Ladyship was fond of her mother. Didn't she send presents every year? And her mother had the highest praise for her.

They reached a long landing with shelves on one side, on which stood rows and rows of white chamber pots, candlesticks and bundles of candles.

'What's all this for?' Sarah asked.

'The pos are for what you'd think – the white ones for the servants and guests that aren't important. There's others with that many flowers and birds painted on them it seems a shame to piss in them. Then there's the master's, with his coat of arms, but they're kept in their bedrooms. It'll be your job in the morning to empty and rinse the pots – though maybe not the Family's to start off with. Here's your room. Some of us share but this is a single room.' The girl opened a door and Sarah saw a bare-boarded floor, a rickety chair, a small press and an iron bedstead with a wafer-thin mattress.

'This is a desperate room. I wouldn't sleep here!'

''Tis great comfort you must be accustomed to, so,' said Mary. 'We're grateful to have a bed to ourselves and a change of sheets once a week. But I suppose in Dublin you all live in palaces.'

'I want to see her Ladyship. I want to see her now – this minute!'

'You're tired and maybe a bit homesick. Unpack your things. The sheets are there – make up your bed and throw yourself on it for an hour.'

'I won't. I wouldn't sleep a night here. I want to see her Ladyship – she's a friend of my mother's.'

'And there was me thinking you were a servant girl like myself.'

Sarah wanted to lash out and strike the fat, grinning flat-faced girl who was making a jeer of her. She hated her, hated everyone she had met so far. She longed for Barney, for Julia. And no matter what happened, she would not sleep in this terrible room, on that bed.

'Listen,' said the girl. 'I know what it's like when you leave home for the first time. I'll help you make the bed.' She moved as if to touch Sarah, who if she hadn't been so wrapped up in herself would have seen that the maid was being sympathetic. A girl not much older than herself, a girl who was maybe as lonely as herself.

'You leave me alone,' she snapped. 'I don't want your help. I told you, my mother is a friend of Lady Glenivy and when I see her everything will soon be put right.'

The servant shook her head in bemusement. ''Tis a pity your mother

61

didn't prepare you better. See Lady Glenivy, indeed! Sure you could be here for a month of Sundays and never lay eyes on her or one of them. And take my advice, in case you should happen to cross her path: bid her the time of day and no more. She's kind enough – they all are. We get plenty to eat and our wages. If you were taken bad they'd see you had medical attention, and if you were dying, a priest. Apart from that you might as well not exist. It's how they are – the gentry.'

'Get out,' Sarah hissed. 'You're a liar. I know the truth. I've heard my mother tell it a thousand times. Go on, get out! For bad and all as it is this is my room, so go on, get out.'

Not until the door shut would she let herself cry. And cried herself to sleep every night for more than a week.

Exhausted after a twelve-hour day during which she emptied chamber pots, cleaned and laid fires, peeled vegetables and was the runabout for the cook, the housekeeper, and any servant more senior than her, she climbed the flights of stairs and threw herself on to the bed. Mice scurried about the room, and owls screeched, terrifying her for she didn't know what they were and thought of ghosts. On wild nights the wind moaned through the trees and she remembered all the stories she had been told of the banshee. And she longed for Barney, for the comfort of his arms around her, the warmth of his body against hers. For the noise of the street. Julia to talk to. And she cursed her mother for talking her into giving up Barney and for sending her into service. And the fat, flat-faced country girl for having the last laugh on her. Seeing in her eyes every time they met the challenge: 'Well, wasn't I right? How much have you seen of Them?' The galling thing was that so far, Mary Flynn was right: although it was more than a week since Sarah's arrival, she still hadn't laid eyes on one of the family.

And then one day she did. She was in the morning room where she had been sent to lay and light a fire. She was cold and miserable as she approached the room carrying her box of dusters, polish, newspapers and matches. Her eyes ached from crying and lack of sleep and her hands were sore and chapped. Manoeuvring her box in front of her, she opened the door. 'Oh!' she exclaimed, for so early in the day she had expected the room to be empty. But sitting in a green leather armchair was a young man reading a magazine. 'Oh,' she repeated. 'I'm sorry. Excuse me, sir, I didn't think anyone was in here,' and she began backing from the room.

The young man lowered the magazine and looked her up and down. She could tell by the length of his legs stretched out that he must be very tall. A giant of a man compared to the men she knew in Dublin. He was good-looking, she supposed, it you liked dark red, more a mahogany colour, tightly-curled hair.

'You must be new. I haven't seen you before,' he said, continuing to regard her and smile with a faint hint of amusement about his lips.

'No, sir. I mean yes, sir, I am. I only came last week.' She decided she liked his hair and that he was very good-looking. She relaxed and flashed him a brilliant smile, all curved lips and flashing white teeth.

'Stay,' he said. 'Light the fire. You won't be disturbing me. What do they call you?'

'Sarah, Sarah Quinlan. If you're sure then about the fire, I'll be quick.'

'Take as long as it takes,' he said, and went back to his reading.

She knelt and removed the fender, covered the area of carpet directly in front of the fireplace with newspapers and began her task, thinking as she did so that the young man must be Master Patrick, the one whose homecoming party from the war her mother had described. As she raked out the ashes, now and then Patrick looked over the top of his magazine, watching her bottom move as she reached and stretched into the large fireplace. A pretty little thing, he decided, with a fine figure. And such a tiny waist – one he felt sure he could span with both hands.

And Sarah, very aware of his maleness and sensing that his eyes were on her, exaggerated her wiggly movements, knowing that her bottom was nicely rounded and showed her hips to advantage. She lifted the ash and began laying the fire and while positioning sticks on the twisted paper heard him get up, the magazine fall to the floor and him without uttering a word leave the room. She waited a minute then ran to the window to see if he had gone into the garden. He had and was walking across the terrace. What a fine man he was, she thought. He paused and afraid he might turn and see her watching him, she hurried back to the fire.

For the first time since coming to the House she felt less bereft. He had smiled at her, the first man to do so since she left Dublin. For you couldn't count the gardeners, coachmen, the master's valet or the grooms and stable boys she saw about the place. They were either ancient, or big, thick-looking redfaced countrymen.

She sang snatches of popular tunes as she replaced the fender, rubbed and dusted it. Maybe she would see him again, and he'd smile at her. She put a match to a twist of paper and watched it ignite the sticks which sparked and spat. Golden showers flew up the dark chimney. The coals caught; crimson and yellow tongues of flame licked them, danced above them. She felt alive again like the fire – warm, glowing.

He was there in the morning room the next day. Expecting this, she had ironed her black skirt the night before, paying particular attention

63

to the sashes, knowing that nothing set off a figure seen from the back like a big bow well-tied. She had scrubbed her hands and sneaked a lump of lard from the kitchen to rub into them. They still had coal-dust ingrained in them but felt softer.

After greeting her he returned to his magazine, then a few minutes later she sensed him behind her. She turned and looked up at him, and there and then she knew this was the man. The one she had fantasised about the afternoon before she broke it off with Barney. He was gorgeous. The look of him made her feel weak.

'I'll never get this done if you keep standing over me,' she said, smiling at him.

'Who'll notice it?' he asked, grinning.

'Mrs Bellows for one. She checks up.'

'Bellows went to Dublin last night, so what's your panic?' He touched her hair. Then bending, put his hands under her arms and lifted her to her feet. 'You're beautiful. Too beautiful to be cleaning out a fire.' They were now facing each other, her heart galloping. He spanned her waist with his hands. 'You're the loveliest little thing to ever have come into the house.' He pulled her to him and kissed her. He held her closer and she could feel his thing growing hard against her the way Barney's used to when he got worked up. And she knew he was going to try something on. And she wanted him to. One day she'd known him and she wanted him to.

Still kissing her, he manoeuvred her to the armchair and took her on his lap. Now and then she became aware of where she was and how at any minute someone could come into the room. She grew frightened but the fear only excited her. Slowly he unbuttoned her blouse and pushed it, her camisole straps and her vest from over her shoulders. She remembered that her vest was thickened and yellowed from all its washing and for a minute felt ashamed for him to see it. Then her breasts were exposed and she didn't care about her underwear, for Patrick was licking one nipple and then the other. Then the licking changed to a gentle biting. Her body took on a life of its own, her hips and belly arching, thrusting themselves upward. She clenched her teeth so as not to cry out when he bit harder. Her knickers felt wet, sticky-wet. His hands lifted her skirt, slid up over her black woollen stockings, past the garter and on to her flesh. 'Like silk,' he said, slowly sliding as far as the leg of her drawers, then sliding them away, up and down until she wanted to scream for him to go on. When he did and parted the lips of her vulva and his finger moved backwards and forwards, sliding easily, she moaned softly with the pleasure of it. And then something else happened. The sensation was different; his finger slid as before but now there was something in the way that it hesitated and massaged, its rhythm quickening her insides, convulsing as if a hand was squeezing, tightening everything inside her. She thought she was dying and didn't care. Tighter and tighter the squeezing became and then something burst. Then followed the most wonderful feeling she had ever experienced in her life. Something burst and a delicious throbbing contracting, pulsing thing went on inside her. She clung to him and he kept his mouth clamped on hers. If he hadn't she would have had to cry out. He took her hand and placed it over his penis, his own above it showing her how to move her hand up and down, up and down, his mouth still glued to hers. Faster and faster he moved her hand until with grunts and groans and enormous sighs he came into her hand. She looked down and saw it spill on to part of her black skirt, but she didn't care.

'Oh God,' he said, when his breathing was even. 'You're ravishing. I could eat you. I want to carry you up to bed and do it properly. We will, won't we, darling?' He cleaned her hand with an exquisite linen handkerchief and dabbed at her skirt. 'I'm sorry, have you another one?' he asked, and kissed her mouth tenderly.

The question brought her down to earth for so happy, so contented and so lazily warm did she feel that nothing in the world concerned her and certainly not her skirt. Now he had broken the spell. 'No,' she said. 'Next week I'll get a clean one. What'll I do?'

'It'll dry in a minute then you can rub it off.'

'Are you sure?'

He grinned. 'Quite sure. It might leave a little stain, but who'd notice?'

She was back in the world of a dogsbody. 'Anyone, Mary Flynn, the cook, one of the men. I'll have to wash it off – but where? I can't go downstairs in case someone sees me and that's the only way I can get upstairs to my room.'

'You silly little thing. After what happened between us, you're worrying about something like that. Regretting it, are you?'

'Oh no,' she said. 'Oh no. It's only the oul skirt.'

'Next time I'll take it off,' he grinned at her. 'There will be a next time?'

'Maybe,' she said, beginning to tease him. 'Maybe there will and maybe there won't.'

'You little vixen.' He held her tightly, pretending to be angry, shaking her but not hard. 'There'll be a next time?'

'All right, all right. Yes, there will be.'

'Right, then, I'll fix your skirt. Come with me to the flower room and I'll wash away my seed.'

'Will anyone be there?'

'Not at this time. You come after me.'

She waited for a few minutes before doing so. She shivered in the flagged-floor room while Patrick filled an earthenware pot and with a rag and cold water sponged her skirt, kneeling before her. She touched his hair. He looked up at her and smiled. Rising, he told her to inspect the skirt.

'Look, it's fine now, only a damp patch – that could have happened anywhere.' He kissed her. 'In the morning room, in the morning?'

'Oh,' she said, 'the fire! I forgot all about the fire. I'll have to fly.'

'Off you go, then.' He smacked her bottom and she went.

He wasn't in the morning room the next day nor for several more days. And she sank again into despondency. At night in bed she thought about him and what they had done. Reliving it, she recaptured some of its thrill. When reliving it wasn't enough, she masturbated, copying what Patrick had done to her. And as she stroked herself, what she had thought of as the little lump raised itself beneath her fingers and massaging it as he had, she eventually came. But it wasn't as sweet, or as exciting as with Patrick. Afterwards she thought about the little lump, wondering what it was. And then remembered a girl in the warehouse, one who was considered fast, telling her about 'the little man in the boat', and how he was the one to get you going. 'Where is he?' she had asked. And giving her a knowing grin, the girl had said, 'Where d'ye think?' She was curious to look at herself, something she had never done before. But you couldn't by the light of a candle – imagine if it set fire to your brush. Thinking about that she fell asleep laughing.

In the morning she again stroked herself; it was very pleasant. She should have tried it before, then she remembered it was a sin – though lately she didn't pay too much attention to sins. Beneath her finger the little lump became erect, and holding a hand mirror between her legs and parting the lips of her vulva, she saw it and laughed out loud, for it did look like a little man in a boat – a little man in a little boat wearing a sou'wester.

While she dressed she thought about Patrick and when he would come to her and how he would want to go all the way. Fear of pregnancy had stopped her with Barney, but maybe it was also more than that. Barney had never touched her down there. Barney wasn't like Patrick and once he got her going, even though before and afterwards she might be terrified of falling, at that moment when he would have her on fire, pregnancy would be the last thought in her mind. If you wanted to go all the way, there was little you could do except hope you didn't get pregnant. And she wanted to go all the way with Patrick.

The following week he was in the morning room for three successive mornings. He hushed her fears about Mrs Bellows with kisses, undid her skirt and each time came nearer to going all the way. She wanted him so much she would have lain down on the floor for it. He restrained her. 'You are a passionate little thing. But we'll wait. Not too long, I promise. I'll come to your room.'

'Oh, please,' she pleaded, and asked why not when he refused.

'What about Mama's carpet? I can't very well lug that to the flower room.'

So she agreed to wait.

CHAPTER SIX

After Sarah went away Barney lost interest in everything except drink. He went for days without shaving. His boots, in which you could once see your face, were left unpolished and he no longer looked for work. 'It's his way of grieving,' Julia explained to Jack, who worried about the deterioration of his friend's appearance and attitude to living. 'Give him a bit of time and he'll pull himself together.'

'Kill himself more likely at the rate he's drinking. And who in the name of God's going to give him a start looking the way he does. If he's in the pub I'll try talking to him. Maybe he'll listen.'

'There's no harm in trying – though I wouldn't bank on you succeeding,' said Julia.

On the way to the public house Jack bought an evening paper. 'He's been and gone but I think he'll be back,' the barman said to Jack's enquiry as he pulled his pint. 'Her going is the ruination of him. Any chance of them patching things up, d'ye think?'

'Not as far as I can see.'

'Women,' said the barman, giving him his pint of porter. 'More bloody trouble than they're worth.'

Jack settled himself to drinking and reading the paper, now and then looking up when the bar door opened. With a sinking heart he learned of more raids on Royal Irish Constabulary barracks, four policemen shot dead, arms and ammunition taken, and of more policemen resigning. Trouble, he thought, was definitely brewing; more members of what was now called the Irish Republican Army on the run.

'You're deep in thought.'

'Ah, Barney, sit down. I'll get you a drink.'

'No,' said Barney. 'I'll get them.'

Watching him go to the bar Jack said to himself, 'He's well away already, and look at the cut of him. You'd think he'd slept in his clothes.' He probably did. He'd have to haul his friend over the coals. He was destroying himself.

After Barney brought the drinks they sat for a few minutes without saying anything. Then Jack spoke. 'Why don't you drop her a line? Julia has the address.'

Barney laughed sardonically before asking, 'Are you mad? She broke it off for nothing. You don't think a letter's going to change anything.'

'You never know, it might.'

'What'll I write – "Dear Sarah, I hope you're well. I'm grand. Still not doing a tap. Apart from that everything's gameball. Any chance of you taking the ring back?" '

'Stop feeling sorry for yourself – get work.'

'You bastard – you above all to say that. What d'ye think I was doing, tramping the streets with you!'

'You've stopped looking. Start again. Take anything – casual, anything. Anything at all.'

'It was anything at all we looked for,' said Barney, 'before you were landed into a job.'

'We could have got a day here and there. That ould fella in Charlemount Street, the coalman, he'd have given us an odd day. But we thought we could do better than that.'

'You did,' said Barney.

'That was just a stroke of luck. If it hadn't come up, by now I'd have taken anything. I hate to see what you're doing to yourself. I don't want to interfere, but when did you take a good look at yourself? When did you last have a shave? Look at your clothes – you're like a mendicant.'

'There's not another man I'd take that from.'

'I know, Barney. And it's only because I care about you that I took the liberty. Here, have a smoke.' He took out his Woodbines and shook two on to the table.

After lighting one, Barney said, 'I've nothing to live for. No one to get work for. I can't get her out of my mind. I dream about her every night. I worshipped the ground she walked on.'

'Don't I know that well! But you're destroying whatever chance you might have. Supposing she packs in Glenivy – comes home unexpectedly, and finds you looking the way you are. Then you can say goodbye to her for good.'

'There's as much chance of her packing in the job as of me finding a leprechaun with a crock of gold. I've solved my problem. I'm joining up again. I'm going back in the army so you can stop giving your advice. Stop worrying about me. I'll pull myself together without any help from anyone. I'm going to be a soldier. Maybe they'll post me to India – I've always wanted to see India.'

'Joining up – you're not serious! You can't join the army again, Barney. Have you forgotten what it was like? You hated every minute of it.'

'Ah, but that was different – there was a war on then.'

'You shaggin'eejit, what d'ye think is going on here! They're using real bullets. And as for being posted to India, with your luck you'll be stationed here and finish up mowing down your own countrymen.'

'I don't care. I'm joining up and that's an end to it.'

Jack tried another tactic – reminding Barney how, after they had come from France, he wished he had stayed out of the war, that he had taken part in the Easter Rising instead. 'You haven't forgotten saying that, surely to God.' At the time, Jack had known it was just more of Barney's talk. It meant nothing. And he wouldn't have brought the subject up again except that he felt this time, because of his crazy grief about Sarah, his friend might just do what he threatened and join the army. He might very well be posted to India, putting an end to whatever hope there was of a reconciliation between him and Sarah. He wanted that for Barney; he wanted him settled. He had neither love nor liking for Sarah Quinlan, but Barney loved her more than anything in the world – and if he could help him to have her, he would.

Barney didn't deny that he had expressed a wish to have been out in 1916. 'At the time I meant every word of what I said, but like you I've changed my mind.'

'What d'ye mean – like me you've changed your mind?' Jack asked, puzzled.

'You taking the job in that Republican Club. Everyone knows that's just a front for the gougers that's doing the killings.'

'Jesus!' Jack said. 'Why do I bother with you? The Club has nothing to do with violence – nothing whatsoever.'

Barney looked sceptical. 'Are you telling me you haven't gone stone mad over everything Irish, and me sick of seeing the books you get from that fella in the library?'

'It wouldn't do you any harm to read a bit more, then you might appreciate what the Club is about. You'd learn about our heritage, Irish culture, and that it's got nothing to do with bombing and shooting. Honest to God, Barney, I wouldn't lie to you. And as for my reading, I've learned more about Irish history from that than I ever did in school.' Jack gave Barney another cigarette, took one for himself and when they were lit went on, 'I didn't know a fecking thing about my own country, and neither do you. How could we, taught as we were to see Ireland through England's eyes. I'd like to learn Irish.'

Barney gibed, 'The next thing, you'll be going to ceilidhs.'

'And why not?' asked Jack.

Barney waved a hand dismissively. 'Go way out of that. Go home to Julia. Don't be bothering about me, I can mind myself.'

'Well?' asked Julia when Jack came home. 'Did you get anywhere with him?'

'I could have saved my breath. He's going to join the army.'

'That's all talk. You should know him by now. Will I fry you a rasher and egg?'

And while she cooked they continued talking, Jack asking, 'What does his mother think about him giving over looking for work?'

Julia turned the bacon and basted an egg. 'You know Mrs Daly – an easygoing poor soul.'

'Any mention about Sarah giving back the ring?'

'Not much, but I got the impression she wasn't sorry. She's getting on and not in the best of health but she's nobody's fool and knows Sarah mightn't be the best wife nor easiest of daughters-in-law.'

'She wouldn't either.'

'No,' agreed Julia. 'Not unless by some miracle Barney came in for a fortune to fulfil her ambitions. She wants out of the street – somewhere with a good address. It's only lately I've realised there's more of her mother in her than I thought.'

'Isn't it you that's the innocent, uncritical eejit. Anyone with half an eye could see that. It was sticking out a mile. I could never understand you being her boon companion.'

'Having ambitions and taking after her mother couldn't wipe out all the years. I don't remember a time when I didn't know and like her. But to come back to Barney and his mother. This is ready, sit over to the table. She believes the war has changed him. She thinks he's suffering from shell shock, God help her. He's her favourite – she'll always make excuses for him.'

Then, in between eating his supper, Jack talked about his luck in getting the job, how pleasant it was and how the members were a great crowd. 'Of course I owe it all to Seamus Harrington.'

'Who?'

'The fella from the library.'

'I keep forgetting his name. God bless him – would you never ask him up to the house? I'd like to meet him,' Julia said, pouring out tea for herself and Jack.

'I've hinted at it. He's never taken it up, though the hint was plain enough.'

'Why d'ye think that is?'

'He's very busy. There's the library, the odd night he has a drink with me and I think he may have many more friends and acquaintances – part of a life he won't include me in. Maybe he can't – I don't know. I'd say in the future we'll have a real friendship but not yet.'

'I don't understand that.'

'No, well, that's how it is. God knows what else he may be mixed up in. I wouldn't pry, for his sake but more for my own.'

'How d'ye mean?' asked Julia, looking puzzled.

'Love, there's all sorts of things going on in the country. Plans and plots, organisations . . . how does anyone know what's going on? And a man valuing his family's safety and his own wants to know nothing about any of them. That is, a man not committed to the aims and ideals of certain people.'

'Are you saying Seamus belongs to something?'

'It's possible.'

'Then he could be dangerous,' said Julia.

'Not if he's only stamping out books for me or us having a drink now and then. I know nothing about him. He keeps it that way and being the decent man he is I'd say that's as much for my protection as for his own.'

'Well, whatever he is or isn't, God bless him for getting you the job. God answered my prayers,' Julia said, and then to herself; 'And may He if it's pleasing to His will, grant me the gift of a child. A child would be the crowning glory.'

Before the week was out Barney apologised to Jack. 'I don't remember what I said the other night but if I gave offence I'm sorry.' Jack put an arm round his shoulders and told him to forget it. All of their lives Barney had at one time or another given offence when he was drunk and apologised afterwards. Jack took no notice of the offences so the apologies weren't necessary.

For days after she had left, Sarah Quinlan had been the main topic of conversation in the street. Few had a good word to say for her: all the sympathy was with Barney, though the majority felt he had had a lucky escape. One evening when Julia, her mother and Cissie were sitting outside, the two older women on the windowsill and Julia on a chair, Cissie said sagely, 'It would have been all her mother's doing.'

'That wan's gone past her mother's tutelage. She's full of herself and suffering from delusions of grandeur. I'd put nothing past her.'

'Ah, Mother, that's not fair,' Julia protested. 'She'd like to marry Barney but he's gone to the dogs.'

'Only since she gave back the ring,' said Lizzie. 'Before that he was looking for work the same as Jack.'

'I wouldn't say he was putting his back into it. You know what Barney's like, he'd think nothing of getting married though he was idle. Sarah wouldn't hear tell of that, and long engagements are a terrible strain on a couple,' Cissie said, to be fair.

'I'll grant you,' said Julia's mother, 'it's better to be in a job if you're getting married, though many a one starts and is a success with idleness. Wouldn't the families help – couldn't they live on their parents' floors the way we all did in the beginning. But not Sarah. She's looking for a Belted Earl and a house in Rathgar. Cut down off her mother who's a dissatisfied oul bitch. She didn't find the man she was looking for and had to settle for poor Quinlan and the street. An unlucky woman. It's written all over her face. I'd light a bonfire if they left.'

It was a warm evening. The sun was still visible above the railway arch, and there wasn't a breath of wind, yet at the sound of her mother's words Julia felt a shiver run up her spine, just as she had on the afternoon she and Sarah went walking while the party was being prepared and Sarah's smile had reminded her of a grinning skull.

She knew her flight of fancy was nonsense – all her mother's fault. Lizzie was always harping on that Mrs Quinlan was an unlucky woman, and hinting that Sarah as well could bring bad luck to others. Her mother and her superstitions and premonitions! Before it could take breath in her mind, Julia stifled the thought of how often her mother had been proved right. Instead she concentrated on the children playing. The younger ones with joined hands were moving in a circle chanting, 'Ring a ring of roses, a pocket full of posies', and the older girls with their long ringlets and ribbon bows, two with raised arms and with hands touching, formed an arch under which a line of girls passed. All sang, 'Here's the robbers passing by, passing by, my fair lady. What will the robbers do to you, do to you, do to you, my fair lady?'

The childish voices rang out in the street and more quietly the voices of her mother and a neighbour continued talking. And Julia thought how it only seemed like yesterday that she had played the same games, excitedly worried that when she passed beneath the arch the robbers would be chip, chopping off heads. Then it would be her turn to take the place of one of the arch-holders. Not another worry did she have then. Never a shiver to chill her spine or the nameless fear that caused it.

There were young boys also playing in the street, keeping their distance from the girls. Their games appeared disorganised – mock battles with a lot of shouting, and blows being rained on each other with homemade wooden swords, and sticks used as rifles. A lot of flinging themselves to the ground, clutching their chests and lying as if dead. Their exuberance and the high sweet piping voices of the girls lifted Julia's spirits and she thought of babies, of a particular baby, hers and Jack's. And though she knew it was flying in the face of God to wish for anything but a healthy child, she hoped that if she was blessed with the gift of one that it would be a son. She allowed herself to dwell on a time when her prayers would be answered and she imagined a baby, a boy who would look like Jack, who would grow healthy and strong and play in the street, the same games as the boys were playing now, the same games that Jack had played in the same street.

Then a commotion broke out where the girls were chanting, 'Here's the robbers passing by.' And Julia saw that while she hadn't been looking, Mag had come along and like a large playful pup was disrupting the game, trying to nudge one of the arch-bearers to one side, wanting to take her place. She was shouted at and told to go away, not to be spoiling their game. And Mag with her ambling walk like a drunken man, not affronted or offended, went walking over to the circle of little girls playing Ring of Roses, and broke up the chain, taking a hand on either side and towering above the five and six-year-olds, prancing clumsily around while her raucous voice roared out the rhyme. Poor unfortunate Mag, Julia thought. She would never have a man to love her. She would never know what it was to be a woman. If she lived to be seventy, she would still amble up and down the street with a permanent smile on her moon-like face.

After a while the games broke up and the children wandered further up the street. Mag came to where Julia, her mother and Cissie were sitting and, reaching out, she stroked Julia's hair, a habit of hers. 'Me oul segosia.' Julia hugged her and asked, 'What have you been doing all day?'

Mag simpered and rocked on her heels. 'I saw someone doing dirty things.'

'That'll do,' Julia's mother remonstrated. 'You're not to be telling lies.'

'I did,' said Mag. 'I did so. Last night under the bridge I saw a man doing his pooley.' She clapped her hands and laughed delightedly before walking away.

'She's dangerous.'

'Ma, the poor child's simple.'

'But there's nothing wrong with her sight. She sees things and she can talk. She has the run of everyone's house. Less attention is paid to her than a stray dog wandering in and out. She sees and hears plenty and repeats what she sees and hears. One of these days she'll see something and name someone.'

'But Mother,' Julia protested, 'no one takes any notice of what she says.'

'Someone might some day. And another thing – she's out half the night.'

'Half the night!'

'That's what I said.'

'But what's her mother and father doing to let her?' asked Cissie.

'They're a pair of drunkards and they sleep the sleep of the dead.'

'But how do you see her during the night, Ma?'

'I've had a chill on my bladder this while back. I'm up and down during the night. I often look out the window, and like the cats Mag is prowling.'

'You should get a bottle from the doctor. I had that complaint and the medicine cured it,' nodded Cissie.

Fear again returned to Julia. Was her mother sick? Was there something seriously wrong with her, God forbidding all harm? Never before had she heard her complain. Never had she been sick in all of her life. 'Please God, don't let anything be wrong with her. Not now when our worries are over,' Julia prayed, 'when Jack is home safe and now has work. Don't let my mother be sick, not seriously sick.' Then her mother laughed loud and long at some remark Cissie had made, and looking at her face, Julia saw it as it always had been – the picture of health. Nothing ailed her. She was becoming morbid, letting her imagination run away with her. Worrying about nothing.

Sunday was a glorious day and Jack suggested going up the mountains. 'Take advantage of the day, we may not get many more fine ones,' said Julia's mother. 'It won't take me a minute to put together a few sandwiches. Take a kettle and you'll be able to make a cup of tea.' In no time they were ready. The sun was warm on their backs as they walked for the tram which would take them part of the way. From there on they would hike the remainder of the journey to their favourite spot in the mountains.

Jack carried the food and the kettle in an army knapsack. They held hands and exclaimed as they always did when they reached the mountains, on the sweet freshness of the air, the singing of birds and the fields golden with buttercups. They laughed at the mournful-eyed cows who appeared to watch their passing, motionless except for their swishing tails.

'I could live here forever and ever – in a little cottage, a whitewashed one. I'd make a garden. You could plant vegetables and cut the turf. Just me and you – imagine it.'

'I am,' said Jack. 'I'm seeing it in the winter. Not able to cross the door, me laid off because I can't get into the city and you going melancholy for lack of some women to talk to.'

'You,' she said, in mock annoyance. 'You're not a bit romantic. Anyway, there's no harm in dreaming.'

He put an arm round her, pulling her close to his side and kissing her. 'In a cottage up the mountains, in your mother's house, in a tinker's caravan,' he said, lifting his face from hers. 'I'll live with you anywhere, love you anywhere, and for always. Now is *that* romantic enough for you?'

'Oh, Jack, I love you too. And I don't care where we live, where we finish up, so long as we are together.'

They kissed again and again. The sun beat down on them. A lark rose soaring into the sky, singing. Still with their arms about each other and stopping now and then to kiss again, they left the path and moved into a sheltered place. The haversack was slung down and their shoes kicked off and on the soft springy grass for the first time in their lives they made love in the open and in daylight.

CHAPTER SEVEN

It was three weeks since Patrick had gone to England. Three weeks since their last time together in the morning room. In the kitchen they said it was the Season in London. God knows when he might be back. The glow which had surrounded her since Patrick had been paying her attention was fading, all her disappointment and dissatisfactions with Glenivy returning.

Even the menservants weren't teasing her like they had when Patrick was here. It had amused her, the way they flocked round her once the business in the morning room had started – almost as if they knew and thought either that she was easy or special because Master Patrick was attending on her. Almost as if she was a bitch in heat – as if they could smell the sex. She liked the attention. She liked making the other women jealous. Now everything was getting like it was before and always there was Mary Flynn pretending she wanted to be friendly.

Every so often she thought of Barney, more so the longer Patrick stayed away. She should write to him. Patrick could have sent her a picture postcard. Maybe he had gone off her. She should write to Barney, for if Patrick had given her up she wouldn't stay in Glenivy, for all that she was coming to love the house and admire its beautiful things, the way it was run and to see that her mother was right – the gentry did know what was what.

Once, when her Ladyship's maid was sick and she away, she had sneaked into the bedroom and gasped at the luxury of it: the silken hangings round the great bed, the soft, deep-piled rugs. She had fingered the cut-glass scent bottles, tempted to squeeze the bulb and shower herself with perfume but knew the smell would be noticed in the kitchen and someone would ask where she had come by it. Instead she turned her attention to the mother-of-pearl-backed hairbrushes, the trinket-boxes, the porcelain ring-tree shaped like a hand decorated with minia-ture flowers and birds.

She moved round the room, one ear cocked for anyone approaching and though she had been told not to linger, couldn't resist opening a floor-to-ceiling press where her Ladyship's gowns hung. Fingering the satins, silks, brocades and velvets, she marvelled at the colours – pink and lavender, violet and purple, rose and cerise, silver and gold lamé, kingfisher-blue, pale blue, deep blues . . . She was dazzled by the clothes, by their touch, and intoxicated by the scent exuding from the press. She longed desperately to own and wear such things, imagining the feel of them next to her skin. How she would love to shower herself with scent, to sleep in such a bed, to step barefooted on to the rugs. Looking and touching, smelling and wanting, she remembered her mother's story about the lord who married a servant, a beauty. Well, she was a beauty. To confirm her opinion she moved to a chair before the looking glass. Over its back lay a peachy lace peignoir. She draped this around her and smiling at her reflection in the glass, told herself again that she was a beauty. So a lord married a servant girl, she mused. It could happen again, to anyone who was beautiful. *It could happen to her.*

Lost in a fantasy world, she didn't hear the door open nor the derisive laugh of Mary Flynn. ''Tis grand you look – the colour becomes you better than it does her with the raddled cheeks. Paint and powder is no substitute for youth. All the same, the cheeks of your arse may be raddled if you're not in the kitchen in one minute. There's potatoes for peeling and the cook's a fierce woman when raised.'

Ignoring the girl who always seemed to get the better of her, Sarah swept out of the room with her head held high, telling herself that one day, maybe quite soon, Mary would get her comeuppance. For if her dreams came true she would soon send the likes of Mary Flynn packing. Her earlier despondency was gone, banished by her reflection in Lady Glenivy's looking glass. She was very beautiful. Her fears were foolish. Patrick wasn't losing interest in her – that wasn't why he had gone to London. It was as they said in the kitchen, the Season – he had gone to that. She did feel he should have said goodbye, but then again, men weren't always considerate. What mattered was the times they had had in the morning room and the times they'd have when he came to her room. She had no doubts that come he would. And then all her dreams would be fulfilled.

The next day while the staff were having their dinner, the old coach-man said, 'He's coming home tomorrow. I've had my orders to pick him up.'

Sarah's heart somersaulted. He was coming back, coming back to her! He missed her. 'Cutting short the Season?' queried the cook, carving generous slices from a Limerick ham that the Master and Lady Glenivy would have for lunch the following day (served sliced they'd never know it had been savoured already). 'It's peculiar that, him coming back,' she continued.

'I overheard her Ladyship telling the master he hadn't been well in London – something he ate, she said. And his Lordship said it could have been shellfish, that Master Patrick didn't take kindly to it.'

Sarah smiled a little smile and thought how Patrick's return was nothing to do with shellfish. He couldn't bear being parted from her, that's why he'd cut his visit short. She went off into a dreamworld, imagining being in Patrick's arms, and was only brought back to reality by one of the grooms saying, 'They must have been grand thoughts you were having, Sarah. You blushed like a rose.' He drew the other men's attention to her and they teased her. She soon would have slapped the one down who first spoke, had they been alone, but with so many present they'd get the better of her when it came to backchat so she smiled demurely and said nothing.

An older stableman brought up the talk of de Valera. 'Between him and Collins we'll soon have our rights,' he said. And was pounced on by the cook.

'Get your rights, indeed! From a lot of bog-trotters like them? What would they know about rights or how to run a government, even supposing England went mad and let the one they've set up stand. The cheek of them starting up their own courts. I wouldn't like to be tried in one o' them. Michael Collins and de Valera, is it? All of a sudden you're full of admiration for them. But tell me this, when did one of them ever put a bit in your mouth? It's the gentry you have to thank for that and for the roofs over your heads. God bless and protect them always.'

She talked for so long and with so much passion that her face went puce and her bust was heaving like a bolster stuffed with live chickens. Sarah thought she would have a seizure – not that she'd be sorry if she did. Always on about training her up to be an assistant-cook. She was another one who would have to watch out when Sarah became mistress of Glenivy.

'Have another bit of ham, child,' said the cook, who after a glass of stout had recovered from her harangue. While eating the delicous meat Sarah suddenly realised that even if her dreams of marrying Patrick came true she wouldn't be able to dismiss the cook and Mary Flynn immediately, for while Lord Glenivy was alive she wouldn't be the mistress. But he was getting on. One day he'd die and then she'd come into her own.

The coachman now had his say, telling the other young men to be careful where they aired their views. 'Terrible times are coming, I feel it in my bones. God knows there's been enough killing in this country already but there'll be more.' The young men when the coachman wasn't looking in their direction winked and grinned at each other and pointed to their heads, making screwing motions then nodded towards the old man. A screw loose. An oul fella, his mind going astray.

She caught a glimpse of him early on the morning after his arrival and clapped her hands with delight. 'He's back, he's back. Oh, he's so handsome. Look at him on that horse. Oh, I love him. Will he come tonight,' she wondered. 'Please God let him. I'll tidy my room. The minute I've finished work I'll tidy it up. And I'll put on my best nightie – the one my mother said I was to keep in case I got sick enough to have the doctor. I'll wear that. And not plait my hair – I'll leave it loose.'

Walking on air she went to the kitchen for her early-morning cup of tea. Mary Flynn was there. 'You're looking great,' she said. 'Have you had good news?'

'How,' snapped Sarah, 'or from where at this hour of the morning would I get good news?'

'I was only trying to make talk,' said Mary. 'You and me are near enough in age, 'tis a pity we can't hit it off – everyone else is old. I wish to God I could go home to my own people but they couldn't feed another mouth. There's tea wet – will I pour you a cup?'

'No thanks,' said Sarah.

'Guests came with Master Patrick, a young man and woman,' Mary said.

'How d'ye know that?' Sarah was indignant that Mary should know anything about the family that she didn't.

'One of the upstairs maids told me. Well, I'd better be going I suppose.' Sarah ignored her leaving.

She had to endure another week without him. Despondency began to plague her again. He was busy, she knew that, entertaining the guests from England – with fishing, boating, picnics, visits to other Big Houses in the county. All the same, she reasoned, he could have spared her a minute, got a note to her. Maybe she was an eejit codding herself that he loved her. Dreaming all the stupid dreams about him – about them. She definitely wouldn't stay if he gave her the cold shoulder. She couldn't bear to be in the same house and be ignored. She missed him so much. The feel of him, not just a glimpse of him riding away into the distance. And she missed so much his attention, all the things he'd done to her in the morning room. All the kissing and stroking – and the end of it. That above all she missed. It wasn't so easy doing it on your own – and it was an empty sort of thing without him, not making you feel good.

Again she thought about writing to Barney, telling herself that a bird in the hand was worth two in the bush. God knows, she thought, he wasn't much but better than nothing, and nothing was what she'd have if Patrick abandoned her, unless she settled for one of the red-faced thick-necked grooms. Barney was no oil painting but compared to them he was passable. And moreover, she could manage him.

Before she got round to writing the letter, however, she heard news that gave her fresh hope of seeing Patrick soon. While pegging out white linen sheets with Mary Flynn in a place behind the kitchen garden Mary said, 'I hear the guests are leaving on Sunday evening.'

For once Sarah didn't cut her short and asked, 'Who told you that?'

'One of the upstairs maids, the one with the queer name – Abigail, that's it. She was complaining about new beds to be made up. So they'll be off the day after tomorrow. Isn't it well for them going here, there and everywhere, never having to soil their hands, everyone at their beck and call. Thanks be to God we all have to die.'

'Why,' said Sarah, 'are you thanking Him for that? I don't want to die. The thought of it frightens the life out of me.'

'Well, we all have to – them as well. The thought consoles me when I envy them too much. No matter what they eat and drink, no matter about their fine clothes and ways and fine feather beds, into the grave the same as us they'll go.'

Sarah thought she must be mad. Anyone talking about death on a day with the sun scorching and the birds singing and the smell of flowers had to be mad. She clammed up and concentrated on Sunday. Sunday evening they'd be gone. Patrick was bound to make a move then. She silently prayed that he would. She willed him to.

On Sunday she was detailed to serve afternoon tea on the lawn beneath the giant Cedar of Lebanon. She was thrilled. It would be her first opportunity for ages to see Patrick close up, and she could have a squint at the guests.

The girl, she had to admit, was attractive, dressed in the height of fashion, painted, and powdered but with not a pick on her. And as flat-chested as a young fella. Like a skeleton she'd be in her skin.

She was raging to see Patrick laughing and joking with her, letting on he didn't notice her, though she supposed with his mother and father there he couldn't very well. She'd soon remind him. Moving closer than was necessary to pick up his cup, she let the weight of her breast lean on his arm. Their eyes met; quickly his smile came and went. It was enough for her. He was still interested. He'd come to her – and before long.

On Sunday night, or maybe it was early Monday morning – her candle was out and she couldn't see the clock – he came. She let on to be asleep while he lit the candle after a lot of fumbling with matches that didn't catch first time. On her back in the bed with her hair arranged around her and her best nightie with its top buttons undone she lay as he brought the candle near and looked down on her. Then he put the candle-holder on the washstand and bent and kissed her. She opened her eyes and pretended surprise. 'Oh Patrick,' she said. 'I was just dreaming about you.'

'You little liar, you weren't asleep. You little witch, letting on you were.' Then he took her in his arms and kissed her again before laying his head on her breasts and saying with such fervour, 'I've missed you so much. Every minute I thought about you.'

'You had a queer way of showing it.' She moved him from her, sat up arranging the pillow behind her and pouted.

'Don't be like that, not tonight. Don't fight with me. Tonight is special.'

'I don't see what's so special about it.' She looked up at him from under lowered lids.

'This is going to be our honeymoon. Look – I've brought you presents all the way from London.'

She gave up the play-acting. 'Presents! Let me see, please let me see.'

'First you have to say you're sorry for being such a crosspatch.'

'I'm sorry. I'm sorry – now let me see!'

'This and this. Chocolates and scent. Handmade delicious chocolates and scent.' Like a child she reefed off the wrappings, ate a chocolate, gave him one, ate another, then turned her attention to the scent. It was in a black bottle, a big bottle with its spray and tasselled bulb. 'Smell it,' Patrick said. 'Here, let me do it.'

'It's like flowers,' she whispered. 'Flowers that grow in the spring. Blues and mauves. I fecked two from a dealer's basket in Grafton Street once. Hyacinths – that's what it smells like. So gorgeous. I've never forgotten the smell. If you kept smelling them you'd think they'd make you go to sleep, not like ordinary sleep but as if you were drugged. Thank you, oh thank you. And thank you for coming back to me. I love you. I missed you all the time.'

He put the chocolates on the washstand, lay beside her and kissed her lips, her neck and her breasts. Then he got up and took off his dressing gown and pyjamas. 'Let's pretend it's our honeymoon night.' He took off her nightdress. 'Now,' he said, 'I'm going to anoint you.' She was too excited to be frightened by the word, which at other times put the fear of God into her with its connotation of dying. 'Lie back.'

She did. And beginning with her ears he squirted perfume on them, on her forehead, under her chin, on and between her breasts, on her belly and into her navel, on her thighs, behind her knees and on the soles of her feet and the palms of her hands and the fold of her elbows. The smell was overpoweringly sweet, intoxicatingly so.

'And now,' he said, and starting with her ears he licked them and moving slowly down her body every other place he had anointed, finishing at the soles of her feet and beginning then to journey upwards. Parting her thighs before laying his head between them, he said, 'Here has its own perfume.' Her hands wound in his hair. He was doing with his tongue what he had done in the morning room with his finger. That, she had thought, couldn't be bettered : she had been wrong. He came up to her mouth, his body on hers and entered her. They were going all the way. No thought or fear of pregnancy touched her. No thoughts at all, only wonderful, wonderful sensation.

They were upstairs, Sarah and Mary, each carrying an armful of towels to be placed in the various bathrooms when a figure came into the long passage. Out of the corner of her mouth Mary said, 'That's her, the Lady herself. Thank God I'm going in the next room. Remember what I told you – don't speak unless she talks to you.'

Patrick's mother! Sarah was filled with a joyful anticipation. At last she would meet her employer face to face – not the few fleeting glimpses in the distance. 'How tall she is and so slender,' Sarah thought. 'Maybe I should talk first. What'll I say ? Are my hands clean ? I hope my hair's not a show. Thank God for my cap, it'll hide the worst.' Thought after thought raced through Sarah's mind : 'She's a picture. Her costume's gorgeous. Dove grey really suits her and that shell-pink blouse is lovely.'

They were almost within touching distance. Lady Glenivy stopped and so did Sarah, who smiled. 'Ah,' said her mistress. 'You must be Rosie's girl. Settling in all right ?'

'Yes, ma'am. Yes, your Ladyship,' Sarah replied, flustered.

'Good, good,' said her Ladyship, and walked on leaving behind a flabbergasted Sarah and a smell of scent.

It was the same scent that Patrick had brought and used on her. She leaned against the wall until the shaking that had taken hold of her eased. She couldn't believe what had happened – couldn't understand why it had happened. She could only begin to reason that maybe her Ladyship had found out about her and Patrick. That had to be it. She was upset, annoyed about it, the way the parents of Lord Beales who married the servant girl from Cork were in the beginning. But in the end it had all worked out, according to her mother. And so it would for her and Patrick. The shaking had stopped. She felt grand again and went on her way with the towels.

Lady Glenivy as she went on hers thought about Sarah and her mother. The girl was the image of her former maidservant, pretty and forward-looking. The mother had had a way of insinuating herself – overfamiliarity. It probably ran in the family. She must have a word with Bellows – tell her that if they kept the girl on, she was to stay downstairs, become assistant-cook or something.

Her maid had become very over-familiar – although that really had been her own fault. She was so young – a bit over-awed with the responsibility of Glenivy. A bit frightened of Bellows, of the cook. They'd been here for ages, acted as if they owned the place, while Rosie was younger, just like herself. It was only natural that she should turn to her. She could do such wonders with her hair, and she was amusing, too. The young Lady Glenivy used to forget she was only her maid.

'It must have come as a shock to Rosie when I suddenly put the barriers up,' Lady Glenivy reflected. 'I wonder, does she remember what I told her when I was expecting Patrick? Did she ever tell anyone? Probably not – not the servants, anyway. She thought herself a cut above them with her delusions of grandeur. Poor old Rosie. How we used to laugh. We were so young. It was all such a long time ago. She probably thinks I keep in touch and bring her back from time to time because of the secret. Silly cow. She was a good worker, very honest and goes back a long time.

'What an innocent I was then. So worried about my affair with Sam. He was a bastard but such a gorgeous one. I really loved him. I wonder, was he Patrick's father? He has exactly the same dark red hair. It could have come from some long-ago ancestor, though. Poor old Sam – such a terrible end, though sooner or later it was bound to happen. A knife in his back and her throat cut. Ghastly business. Supposed to have been a native, but no one believed that. Everyone knew it was her husband. I mustn't forget to mention Sarah to Bellows.'

Two things marred Sarah's nights of bliss. Before Patrick left her on the first night of their pretended honeymoon, he said, 'You'd better wash that scent off.'

'You did a very good job with your tongue,' she replied, smiling languorously up at him.

'Seriously, you must have a scrubdown.'

'But why would it matter if I don't?'

'Oh, you rather reek of the stuff. Who'd want a pong like that on the teacups?'

She had to admit he was right, so, afraid she might sleep too late for an all-over wash, she rose and with cold water and the strong carbolic soap supplied to the servants, washed and scrubbed her body. The smell of scent and sex was replaced by one of disinfectant.

The second spoiler of her pleasure was the fear of pregnancy. Before and after they made love the spectre of it rose in her mind. During the day she was kept too busy to give it much thought but when she heard his footsteps on the stairs her heart beat with excitement and at the same time her mind told her, 'Don't let him go all the way tonight. Ten days you've been doing it now. Maybe it's already too late. Maybe it was on the first night you should have stopped him. Still, you mightn't yet have fallen, please God. So don't let yourself get carried away.' But once she was in his arms and when his lips and hands began exploring her body, all thoughts of anything but the immediate pleasure fled her mind. Nothing in the world mattered except what was taking place between them.

It was only after he had left her, after the shock of cold water and the vile-smelling soap brought her to her senses that the fear came again to haunt her. She would be disgraced. Her mother wouldn't stand by her. She'd be the talk of the street. Her mother would put her in a home for unmarried mothers down the country run by nuns. They'd have her on her knees praying or scrubbing. And after the child was born, what then? How could you keep it? Where would you live and on what? Definitely she would in future have to refuse him, and make him understand why. But even as she thought this she knew it was hopeless. She could never refuse him. Once he touched her she became frantic with desire and gave herself to him as joyfully and as passionately as he took her.

Sometimes she found consolation in thinking about married women who waited months, even years before they fell pregnant. Julia, for instance. And others who miscarried, or were barren. Though her consolation was always shortlived, remembering that the majority of married women were expecting within the first month. At other times she felt sure that if she was having a baby Patrick would marry her. Gentlemen were honourable and did the right thing. They did marry servants and ladies married stableboys and footmen. Not every day in the week, but sometimes they did. All the same, if her period came she would find out where she stood before they made love again. She would tell him of her fears. Try him out – see if there was any talk of marriage.

As well as all that she could suggest that he wore something. What it was, she wasn't sure. The fast wan in work who had told her about 'the little man in the boat', had said toffs used things when they went with prostitutes. 'Not,' Sarah remembered exactly her words, 'that they give a shite about putting a pro up the pole. It's to protect themselves from the bad disease but it works the other way too.'

She would have a serious talk with Patrick while she had her next period, please God, for that would be the time when she could refuse him. Not all his pleading or passion would make her budge then. Everyone knew you got cancer doing it while you were bleeding and God forbidding all harm you'd be out of your mind to risk that. For about another ten days she'd have to risk getting pregnant. Please God she wouldn't. She'd say a prayer every night after Patrick went, and just in case anything did go wrong, tomorrow she would definitely write to Barney.

Barney couldn't believe his eyes when the letter came for him. In it Sarah described the worst of her life at the House – the drudgery, the unfriendly staff. But she lied that she had met all the family and they were true ladies and gentlemen. She missed him very much, she said, the street, Dublin and Julia, and couldn't wait until her first day off when they would meet again. She signed it *love, Sarah* and crossed in a line of kisses.

He read it several times before bringing it to Julia's and Jack's, and as there was nothing personal in it, passed it to each of them in turn, asking for their opinion.

'Poor Sarah,' said Julia after reading it, 'You can tell she's regretting her choice and longing to see you.'

'I thought the same myself,' said Barney, his face wreathed in smiles.

'I hope to God,' said Jack when he was done with the letter, 'it's changed your mind about joining up.'

'That was never certain,' Barney admitted, 'but after the letter I wouldn't give it another thought.'

'Good man, and go easy on the drink and smarten yourself up. You mightn't get warning that she's coming up.'

'As soon as I've scribbled a few lines in reply I'm off for a haircut. You wouldn't have such a thing as a sheet of notepaper?'

'I have,' said Julia, 'and you're welcome.' She found two pieces of writing paper and an envelope. 'What about ink?'

'I saw a bottle somewhere about the house. Listen, I'll go now and write this.'

'What did you make of it, Jack?' Julia asked after Barney had left.

'I wouldn't say it was the letter of a woman pining for her man,' he shrugged, 'but then maybe Sarah's not the sort who could write such a letter.'

'Do you want to know what I think, without having laid eyes on her letter?' asked Julia's mother.

'Nothing good, I suppose,' said Julia.

'I think that one's hedging her bets – playing the field down there and if she doesn't back a winner – well, there's always Barney the eejit.'

There was a time when Julia would have taken her mother to task for her suspicions of Sarah, but lately her mother didn't seem herself. It was nothing you could put your finger on, but she was permanently out of sorts. No amount of persuasion would make her see a doctor, the lot of whom she dismissed as quacks. She could do without the annoyance of being contradicted, Julia decided, and changed the conversation.

At home he read and reread Sarah's letter, and the oftener he did so, the more he read into it. She'd pack that kip in if he had work. She was missing him. Regretting having broken it off. Missing him as much as he missed her. She'd marry him in a minute if he had a job. Work – any sort of work – that was the solution. It wasn't a bit of good answering her letter until he'd found something: a start, even if it was casual. Once his foot was in the door they'd keep him. Then he'd write and he'd take a bet on it she'd be no time about coming back.

It took him the best part of a week to find something, and that night he wrote his letter.

Dear Sarah,

I hope this finds you as it leaves me in the pink. I was delighted to get your letter and I'm sorry for not answering it sooner, but I was out looking for work, and thanks be to God found it. It's not the sort you'd have liked for me but it's a start, with a coalman. He seems a decent skin. He only has me a few days, at the weekend and on Mondays. I know it doesn't sound like much, but he says things will pick up in the winter. That he might, if anyone had a few pounds to invest, buy another yoke. I knew what he was getting at: if he had another yoke I'd have the driving of it permanently. What d'ye think of that?

I'm dying to see you. I do think about you all the time. Soon, please God, you'll come back and we won't be parted any more. Julia and her mother's grand. There's nothing else strange. Hoping to see you soon.

Love, xxxxxxxxxxx
Barney

He left the posting of the letter to his mother, who put it behind the clock and forgot for a couple of days that it was there.

Jack enjoyed his job, though he wished the wages were enough for Julia to be able to give up work. However, he had been promised that the membership was growing by leaps and bounds and that soon he could look forward to a rise. The work wasn't arduous. He was on hand to note who came in and out, to sweep the small premises and pin up announcements of forthcoming events. This left him with plenty of time for reading, catching up on all the lost years before his interest had been aroused, and the wasted ones in the trenches. Seamus continued to advise him and put under the counter books in which Jack would be interested.

The place where Jack worked was on the northside of the city – three to four miles from where he lived on the southside. He walked, whatever the weather, down the Rathmines Road with its Victorian houses, town hall and the church with a cupola that was a copy of St Peter's in Rome, pausing sometimes to lean on the canal bridge where turf boats were moored or moving according to the level of the locks.

On the other side of the bridge there was Portobello Barracks with its contingent of British soldiers and almost facing it, Portobello House – a fine building. He admired it and remembered that once it had been a hotel where people stayed or arrived before beginning or ending a journey across the country on the specially designed canal boats.

Leaning on the parapet one day he mused on the names of the streets leading from the bridge to the city – Richmond, Charlotte, Charlemount, Camden, and George's Street. Every one of them named for a King, Queen, or member of the English aristocracy. And he reflected how it was the same all over the city – Irish streets named for Englishmen and women. Until recently he had taken it all for granted, never given it a second thought. But now, with his newfound awareness of the injustices Ireland had suffered down the centuries, he saw everything in a different light.

If the country got its independence, would the street names be changed, he wondered. And if so, what would they be renamed? After saints, men who had fought and died in uprisings, mythical heroes even? He must raise the subject with Barney, see what he could come up with. Of course, it depended *how* Ireland got her independence, for what did it matter what a street was called if even one man should die so that the name might be changed . . .

A chill wind blew off the water, making him shiver, depressing him so that he left the bridge and walked on briskly. Dark thoughts went with him, a foreboding that many men might die in the months to come. Rumour had it that Collins was in favour of an armed conflict: bloodshed, he believed, was a cleansing and sanctifying thing, the nation who regarded it as the final horror had lost its manhood. He believed that there were things more horrible than bloodshed, and that slavery was one of them.

Would he, Jack asked himself, talk so glibly about bloodshed being sanctifying had he served in France? Could anyone who had watched blood gush like fountains from severed arteries or seep in a flow that couldn't be staunched call it 'sanctifying'?

Walking on he thanked God for the little out-of-the-way street where he and Julia lived. It was well apart from the city – unlikely to become a part of gun-battles, should it come to that. And with Britain banning Sinn Fein it might very well. It was the excuse for which the hardliners were waiting.

'If I had the means,' he thought as he came into the city, 'I'd emigrate, not to America as I once believed, but to Australia. There, me and Julia would start a new life. I'd forget about street names and independence, live only for my wife and family when God blesses us with one. That's all I want from life – to live happily with Julia. Earn enough money for our needs. Nothing grand – maybe a bit of a garden, books, nothing much. Only to grow old with Julia, to see my children live in a country where they couldn't get dragged into anything. Where they would know peace.'

Once in work and busy, however, Jack's black mood passed and in great humour he finished that evening in time to visit the library.

Inside, there were a few elderly men reading the newspapers, and a woman and a little girl talking in whispers as they scanned the shelves. Seamus was behind the counter sorting tickets. He nodded and smiled at Jack, and pointed beneath the counter. Jack grinned back his acknowledgement of a book put by for him.

''Tis a grand evening, Jack. I think you'll like this. It's by a fellow called O'Sullivan – *The New Ireland*. Move nearer the counter, I want to ask you a favour.' Mystified, Jack went as close as he could to the wooden barrier between him and the Librarian. 'It's this way,' Seamus whispered. 'I was praying you'd come in this evening. It's very important. I've a friend in trouble – he needs a shelter for the night.'

Immediately Jack understood the implication of what he was being asked to do. The 'friend' must be a Sinn Feiner on the run, wanted by the British; rightly or wrongly suspected of one of the recent murders of policemen or informers. Fear paralysed Jack for a few moments. To shelter a man on the run could mean his own death, maybe even Julia's.

'I know it's a lot to ask but he's desperate, and you've told me often enough how your place is off the beaten track, about the railway line and that. He'd not come till it was dark, slip along the line. You could leave a door open. He'd be gone before daylight.'

'Oh my God,' thought Jack. 'I never wanted this. I love Ireland – I'd love to see my country independent, only I'm a coward. I don't want any part of the struggle. I don't want to bring the threat of violence into my own home. What am I going to do?'

And then he pictured the man, no doubt a young man, a boy even. A boy in dread and in fear for his life. Hounded. Nowhere to lay his head for a night's rest. If he refused, tonight might be the night when weary and worn out from the running and hiding, he was caught. He remembered the trenches, what lack of sleep could do to you. You became clumsy, lost your concentration, made wrong moves. If he refused shelter and the man was caught and shot, how could he live with his conscience?

So he agreed. 'I'll do it this once only. There's a light on half the night – the mother-in-law doesn't sleep well. I'll let on to her and the wife it's someone from the army, a country fella catching a train out early in the morning. Then if they hear a disturbance they won't get a fright.'

'Good man yourself. The less anyone knows the better. You could have met your soldier pal in town – bumped into him.'

Julia and her mother accepted the story without question for it was the most natural thing in the world to give shelter to someone without a roof over their head. They went to bed at their usual time. Jack said he'd stay down a bit longer in case his ex-buddy was late. When he did go up he lay awake for a long time but heard nothing. Neither did Julia's mother, despite her nocturnal wanderings.

'If your friend came he left no sign,' she said the next morning. 'Not a cigarette butt, not a crease on the sofa cushion and the tray I left out in case he wanted a cup of tea was untouched.'

'An old soldier,' laughed Jack. 'They trained him well.'

The next time he saw the Librarian, Seamus winked and nodded what Jack knew to be his thanks.

CHAPTER EIGHT

Barney's letter eventually arrived. Sarah skimmed over it, for her mind was on something else. She was pregnant. Not for an instant did she think her missed period was anything to do with the weather, a chill on her stomach or something she had eaten. At fourteen she had had her first period and one every twenty-eight days since. Every night for the last three weeks Patrick had come to her room. She was pregnant.

She wasn't unduly alarmed, although she would have preferred it hadn't happened so soon, that there had been time to talk of marriage. But he would marry her. He was a gentleman and would do the right thing. He loved her. Not that he had said it in so many words. All the same, she could tell he did. She loved him. Everything about him. The things he did to her, his height, his handsomeness. And who he was. He brought her presents, paid her compliments. Made her feel wonderful. Oh yes, she loved him, and could live happily with him for the rest of her life. There was a lot she'd have to learn about running a Big House, God forbidding all harm, when his parents died. But there would be her mother to advise her and the cook and even Mrs Bellows would have to toe the line once she was the mistress.

During the day she went about her duties trying to decide when was the best time to break the news to Patrick — before or after they made love, finally deciding that afterwards would be better, when he lay contented, lazily stroking her before drifting to sleep for a few hours as he always did.

She whispered what she had to tell him. In an instant his drowsiness was gone. He shot up in the bed. 'Good God, are you sure? How can you be, so soon?'

It wasn't what she had expected. 'I am, definitely,' she said. He sat on the side of the bed, lit a cigarette and inhaled deeply. She waited for him to say something else and when he didn't she prompted, 'Well, have you nothing to say?'

'I'm stunned. The suddenness of it. You'd better have a word with Mama.'

'You mean her Ladyship?' Her voice was puzzled.

'Yes, my mother.'

'What's it got to do with your mother?'

'Well, you know, she handles any serious problems with the servants.'

'It's not a problem with a servant. It's me,' Her voice rose. 'It's *me* having your child!'

'Don't make such a fuss. Don't shout, you'll be heard.' He got off the bed and moved to where his clothes draped the back of a chair. She looked at the great length of his body, his beautiful pale-skinned body. The candle cast shadows on it. She knew every inch of it. She adored and worshipped it. He put on his pyjamas and dressing gown.

'We only have to get married.' Now her voice was quiet, humble, pleading.

'That's out of the question.'

'But why?' she asked. 'We're both single, we love each other.'

'No, we don't. It was just a lark. I never said anything about love. In any case, I'm about to become engaged.'

'You never said! You never mentioned an engagement!'

'Hardly.'

'I suppose it's to the skinny bitch, the one who was here last month.'

'Caroline? Yes, as a matter of fact it is. Oh come on now, don't cry. I'm very fond of you. You're a sweet little thing. Everything will be all right, you'll see. You'll be taken care of. Mama will see to that. I'll have a word with her, then she'll see you and fix things up.'

He was gone before she could plead, castigate, rant or rave. She lay watching the candleflame waver, burn lower and eventually go out. He had rejected her: put her in her place. A servant with whom he had had a 'bit of a lark' – that's all it was to him. For her it was the end of a beautiful dream. What would become of her now? She would be dismissed or worse still, kept on as daily her belly grew bigger and the servants sniggered. Kept on until almost her time and then be packed off home to Dublin. Maybe that's what the gentry did with pregnant maids – she had no idea. It wasn't something the sour-faced housekeeper had talked about. And her mother – how would Rose react? She'd put her into a home with the nuns for fallen women. Oh God, she was in terrible trouble. And Patrick was going to marry the skinny one and do to her all he had done with Sarah. She had loved him so much and for him it was just a lark. What a fool she had been. Tears of rage, self-pity and fear fell down her face until eventually she fell asleep, forgetting to wash away the scent with which for the last time he had liberally anointed her.

It was just after midnight when Patrick left her. He went to his mother's room, knowing she read until the early hours: that she and his father no longer shared connecting rooms. She was pleased to see him and said so. Laying aside her book and patting the bed, she said, 'Sit here and tell me to what I owe this visit.'

'A spot of bother, Mama.'

'Oh,' said his mother, and thought as she always did when confronted by her son how handsome he was, how much she loved him. 'What sort of bother, darling?'

'I'm sorry. It's a thing with one of the maids.'

'Which one?'

'That pretty little one, Sarah.'

'Oh Patrick – not Sarah!'

'I thought her rather fetching.'

'It's nothing to do with her looks. I knew her mother – she was my maid. She'll have felt her daughter would be looked after here. You are an idiot. I suppose she's pregnant.'

'So she says.'

'Is it your child?'

'I suppose so. Yes, I think so. I think she was a virgin. I'm not sure. Ma, can I leave it with you? I wouldn't know how to handle it. I'm sorry for her but what can I do?'

'Absolutely nothing. Leave it with me and I'll see to it.'

He kissed her. 'You're a brick, Ma.'

'I won't tell you what you are. Goodnight, darling.'

Her darling Patrick, how she loved him! Never being sure who his father was had made him seem totally hers. No one else had a claim on him. It was as if she alone had created him. She would do anything for him. If he impregnated every girl in the county of Kildare she'd see to all of them.

This time last year, she remembered, he was in France, one of the Poor Bloody Infantry being shot in their thousands. Her days were spent in fear of the dreaded telegram, and all the while because of who she was she must keep a brave face, bottling up her fear and grief. Visiting the mothers of soldiers on the estate, women who could beat their breasts, cry, call down curses on the Germans, plead aloud to God. But she, Lady Glenivy, had to give calm, comfort and strength. As if she was less human. As if he was less precious. As if she hadn't carried him beneath her heart and pushed him into the world like every other woman.

God had spared him, sent him home to her. She was grateful. She'd see to Sarah. She felt sorry for the girl. She'd do what she could for her. Wasn't there some mention of another man in the letter Rosie had written when she asked for Sarah to be found a place? She'd look it up in the morning before writing to Rosie. Had it been the other maid,

Mary Flynn, she would just have sent her packing. Sarah as Rosie's daughter deserved a more gentle severance.

Next morning she found Rosie's letter and skimmed through it. '*It's years ago she should have come to you, my Lady. Only she took up with a young man who didn't want her to go into service. She has been seeing him until recently, but now has come to her senses.*' There was a young man. Things could probably be worked out for the best, thought Lady Glenivy, putting away Rosie's letter and preparing to write to her. After the child was born, if the date coincided with the time Patrick had been with the girl, she'd send her some money, and that would be the end of that. The end, too, of her relationship with Rosie. No more being brought back for casual help, no more presents or passed-on clothes. Nothing to give Rosie the impression that there was any connection between the two families.

She wrote the letter and yawned. It was years since she had been awake so early – at half-past five. By lunchtime she'd be out on her feet. She summoned a servant at six o'clock, and gave instructions for the letter to be posted, to catch the post before midday, thus ensuring its delivery the next day in Dublin. Rosie should arrive in the afternoon. She also told the servant to see to it that Sarah came to the morning room as soon as breakfast was finished.

Sarah was dreaming that Patrick was going to marry her. Telling her he loved her. There was no engagement to the skinny bitch. He was about to take her in his arms, then his voice changed into a rough scolding one. He was shaking her hard, not lovingly at all. She opened her eyes and saw the face of the elderly parlourmaid and heard her say, 'Why didn't you come down this morning? Get up this minute and make yourself presentable. Her Ladyship's waiting to see you. Ten minutes, not a minute later, be in the kitchen.'

'I was sick in the night,' said Sarah, wiping the sleep from her eyes. 'I was up several times, that's why I slept it out,' she excused herself, looking at the clock.

'Ten minutes. And wash away that smell, whatever it is. Breathing that in, no wonder you were sick.'

She scrubbed herself all over in cold water and the carbolic soap, dressed and carefully arranged her hair, for after all it was her Ladyship she was going to see, and in less than ten minutes she was in the kitchen. Everyone knew there was trouble brewing for her, but no one was sure exactly what though they hazarded many a guess. The cook, taking pity on her, said; 'Drink this, child. It'll give you strength,' She handed her a mug of milky porridge, but before she had swallowed more than a few mouthfuls of it the parlourmaid was back and ordering her to leave it and come with her.

From the kitchen she followed the older woman, noticing when she bent to pick up a dropped handkerchief and her long skirt lifted, how swollen her ankles were, spilling over the flat black lace-up shoes, and how slowly she walked, how bent were her shoulders. For a moment she forgot why she was going to see Lady Glenivy, thinking of her original plans fostered by her mother and her own impressions that the upper servants were all ancient and soon she would step into one of their pairs of shoes and cockcrow over anyone who had made her life a misery. But all too soon they had left the cold draughty passages, were in the family's part of the house and approaching another morning room, one in which she also lit the fire. She wondered who had done it this morning. She liked this room : it was prettier than the one in which she had met Patrick. The walls were covered in a pink and blue ribbon-patterned paper. There were soft, cretonne-covered chairs and lots of cushions, and miniatures of babies and young children, brightly coloured magazines and always flowers from the gardens and greenhouses.

This was the room where Lady Glenivy wrote her letters. Several times Sarah had sat at the escritoire fingering the writing implements, touching the creamy headed writing paper, and the sheets of card on which her Ladyship wrote the day's menu for the cook. Often she tried the drawers but they were always locked.

The parlourmaid knocked on the door and Sarah, remembering why she had been summoned here, felt apprehensive. A voice called, 'Come in.' The maid opened the door and announced Sarah's arrival. 'Send her in,' the voice commanded and she was ushered into the morning room.

Lady Glenivy was sitting at her desk. After dismissing the parlourmaid she beckoned Sarah to a chair in front of it – a chair Sarah noted that wasn't usually there.

'Sit down,' Lady Glenivy said, and smiled. And Sarah saw how, despite her over-painted face, she was very beautiful. 'This,' she thought, 'is the woman my mother worships, and she's Patrick's mother. She looks kind. She'll make everything all right. She's a lady – they always do the right thing. She'll soon put a stop to the engagement. After all, I am carrying her grandchild.'

Lady Glenivy said, 'I've written to your mother. She's a sensible woman who'll know what to do, don't you agree ?'

Sarah said nothing and her mistress continued, 'I believe you were courting a young man before you came here. Have you kept in touch ?'

'A few times, ma'am,' replied Sarah, with one hand clasped in the other. Lady Glenivy wasn't smiling any more, she noticed.

'Good. Now here's what we'll do. You aren't well – a stomach upset, so you'll stay in your room today and tomorrow. Your mother should arrive by late afternoon to take you home. You'll get your wages to the end of the year and after the event, fifty pounds. If you marry this other young man I'll see to it that he finds employment. So you see, things aren't so bad after all.'

'But, ma'am,' Sarah protested as Lady Glenivy rose, went to the fireplace and tugged the bell-pull.

'Ma'am,' Sarah tried again.

'That will be all,' her mistress said, sitting back at her desk, reading a letter. The parlourmaid arrived. Without raising her head Lady Glenivy said, 'Sarah Quinlan is sick. She's excused duties. See that her meals are sent up.'

Sarah was back in her attic room before fully realising what had taken place. Patrick's name hadn't been mentioned once, neither had her pregnancy. There had been no recriminations, no lecture – nothing.

'The hard-faced oul bitch, the oul cow. It was as if I wasn't there. The bloody oul bitch. It meant nothing to her. No flustering, nothing. Not even asking how far gone I am. Dismissed – just like that. Flicked out like a piece of fluff before a broom.' She spoke her thoughts aloud, her face contorted with fury.

Mary, the maid, was right. They fed you, they'd get a doctor or a priest while at the same time making you feel as if you didn't exist. If anyone had told her she'd stand there like a dummy when she had so much to say – had the *right* to say, she'd have called them a liar. She wasn't afraid of anyone. She could fight her corner. With the mother of any other man whose child she was carrying she'd have given the length and breadth of her tongue. But in front of that woman she had been like someone mesmerised – a rabbit in front of a weasel. How had she managed to do that to her? Another woman would have been hurling accusations, insults, questioning if the child was her son's. Lady Glenivy had said nothing, or almost nothing. Smiled once – the smile of a Judas. Made little of her without saying one insulting word. How had she managed that?

It was a knack, Sarah supposed. A knack for managing people. They'd been at it for hundreds of years. They didn't get their hair in a knot: at least, not with servants. What a bloody hard-faced oul bitch. But all the same you had to hand it to her. She had the knack and knew how to use it. If only she had it, too. What couldn't you do with your life if you had that ability! No wonder they got where they were.

She moved about the room packing her clothes, still thinking about Lady Glenivy, calling her names but at the same time grudgingly admiring her. Then her mind switched to thoughts of Barney and she thanked God she hadn't burnt all her boats. She had sent him the letter and had an answer. He'd have to do. There was no use crying over spilt milk or remembering her fantasies of marrying Patrick. Barney would have to do. But she'd change his ways. She'd move heaven and earth to get on: she'd manage Barney.

Wasn't I lucky, she said to herself, not to have waited for months before I told Patrick about being pregnant. God must have directed me. If I'd waited until I was three months gone, I couldn't have fobbed off the child as Barney's. He's not *that* much of an eejit!

In less than four weeks she would be married. And Barney would never know the child wasn't his. No one except herself and her mother would know the truth – not in Dublin, anyway. But she'd never forget it – never forget she was carrying one of the gentry. And another thing: she'd do everything in her power to give the child every advantage.

They caught the last train from Kildare back to Dublin. There was another passenger. He left at the next station and immediately Rosie started on Sarah. 'Well, you made a right hash of it. What possessed you to let him?'

'There was two of us in it – it wasn't *all* my fault.'

'It's always the woman's fault. You might have caught him, you're beautiful enough – but not *that* way – not with one of them. You're supposed to show the dog the bone – not throw it at him. What's going to become of you now?'

'Listen, you had my head so full of Glenivy, lords and ladies, lords marrying servant girls ... when the other kids in the street were learning their prayers I was learning about Glenivy. I believed every word.'

'More fool you,' sniffed her mother. 'I mean, thinking they married their servants. Lord Beales was the only one I knew to do such a thing. I won't be able to lift my head in the street,' she wailed. 'We'll be on the market cross. I can just hear them.'

'I don't care what they say. I don't care about anyone. I don't even think badly about Patrick, though I'm jealous that he's marrying someone else. I'm going to have his child – the grandchild of Lord and Lady Glenivy.'

Her mother was so angry and disappointed, so ashamed at the brazenness of Sarah sitting opposite her smiling as if she had just announced her engagement that she was tempted to wipe the smirk off her face. To say, 'You're carrying a bastard and maybe the son of one.' Still and all Rosie thought, when all was said and done, Sarah was still her daughter, and she had been badly let down. 'I won't hurt her more,' she vowed silently. 'And I won't break the promise I've kept all these years to Lady Glenivy.'

Instead she said aloud: 'The child of the gentry or not they'll never acknowledge it, so who's going to keep it?'

'Me and Barney,' replied Sarah. 'We'll get married.'

'How can you be so sure he will?'

'He will – he's mad about me.'

'If he does, never tell him the truth.'

'D'ye think I'm mad?'

'No, but sometimes the woman feels a need to confess and the man to forgive. That doesn't last. Sooner or later he'll turn sour, upbraid the woman and have a down on the child.'

Outside their doors, in their kitchens, in the shops, on the way home from Mass, the women of the street talked about Sarah and her hasty return from Glenivy.

'D'ye think she fecked something?' one asked another.

'She might have, though I never heard that the Quinlans were light-fingered.'

'Knowing as little as we do about them, it's hard to tell what they are,' the first woman said. They went into the pork butcher's where a neighbour buying a backbone and pig's tail asked: 'Did you hear the latest? Sarah Quinlan's back. Very sudden, wasn't it? Stomach trouble, so I was told.'

Then almost in unison the three women said, 'In that case we'll have to keep an eye on her stomach.' They roared with laughter.

Sarah watched for Julia coming home from work. 'You're back!' Julia cried. 'I'm delighted to see you. I missed you. Are you back for good?' She was so pleased to see her friend again that she almost blurted out her secret. Nearly said, 'I think I'm having a baby.' In the nick of time she held her tongue. For one thing it was too soon to put her hopes into words, and for another she wanted Jack to be the first to know.

She listened to Sarah's explanation as to why she was home. 'I got this terrible vomiting and diarrhoea. My stomach was desperate. I hated it there anyway. 'Twas freezing cold and you had to work like a dog. I couldn't stick it a day longer. If you'd seen the face on the housekeeper! I hated her – miserable, bossy oul bitch. Lady Glenivy, she said, wouldn't be at all pleased. Servants didn't come and go as they wished. And then trying to make me change my mind, she said, "Her Ladyship took a liking to you. You'd have done well." I didn't need her to tell me that.

Lady Glenivy favoured me because of my mother. All the same I stuck out for leaving and here I am.'

Believing every word, Julia congratulated her on having done the right thing. 'I'd have hated it as well. Barney's overjoyed. You know about the work? He was ten foot high when the coalman said he could start. He's mad about you. I think he'd have gone out of his mind had you stayed down there. Don't delay too long about getting married, will you? Married life is lovely.'

'I don't think so, though we'll have to live with my ma for the time being. You'll be my bridesmaid and Jack, Barney's best man.'

When Sarah left, Lizzie came in from Cissie's house, where she had been sitting at the window. She had seen Sarah go into her house with Julia and had waited until she saw her leave to come home.

'I couldn't face seeing that wan even though it meant you waiting for your dinner,' she said as she began to make the meal. Julia told her all that Sarah had had to say and Lizzie gave one of her contemptuous sniffs. 'There's more to it than she told you. That's the cute little girl. She wouldn't let her left hand know what her right was doing.'

'All the same I'm glad she's back. I missed her.'

'More fool you,' said her mother. 'I hoped she was gone for good. There's something about her . . . an unlucky woman, that's what she is. And remember my words – never give her the keeping of a secret, for if she could use it to her advantage, no matter what the consequences of her telling it, tell it she would.'

To change the subject, Julia asked her mother there was any buttermilk. 'I'll make a brown square for Jack's tea.'

'Oceans,' replied her mother, 'but we're short of flour. I'll go and get some. Is there anything else we want?'

Julia said there wasn't, and her mother went to the shop from whence she returned with another topic of information: a detective from the Castle had been shot outside his house in Drumconda. 'He wasn't killed straight out, but he's dying. 'Tis a fella called Smith, Dog Smith so I'm told was his nickname. They say it's all Collins' doing. He's outwitting the British left, right and centre. Did you see the picture of him in the paper? He's a fine, handsome man. God knows I'm not in favour of bloodshed, but the British government are trying to provoke things. As Mrs Dempsey and me were saying, the bloody cheek of them to ban Sinn Fein after the people of Ireland elected it. I believe Michael Collins has a scheme to sell bonds to raise money to keep them going. How and ever, all it'll lead to is more bloodshed. Half the Royal Irish Constabulary barracks in the country are deserted. Ran out of them they did, in dread and fear of their lives. It'll have a bad end, mark my words. Britain will

99

come up with something, and knowing their record it won't be for the benefit of the Irish.'

A coalman, that's what she had finished up with. Ingrained in his skin the dirt from the coal, never out of his ears or from under his nails. But in her circumstances, Sarah knew she had to put up with it for the time being.

Her mother consoled her. 'When Lady Glenivy wrote to tell me about the business,' she nodded towards Sarah's flat belly, 'she said that if you married and your husband had trouble getting a job, to write and let her know. So after the wedding I will.'

Sarah lost no time in letting Barney have his way under the railway bridge, putting up just the right amount of resistance to make him believe he was seducing her. The following week she cried and told him she had missed and was afraid she might be pregnant. He cuddled her like a baby, showered her face with kisses and with his coal-black hanky wiped away her tears. 'Don't cry. I love you. It'll be all right, we'll get married. Tomorrow night we'll go to the priest and put in the Banns.'

'Don't say a word about me being "in the way". I won't tell it in Confession, either. I'd die of shame talking about things like that to a priest. And I won't be married in the Vestry – that's where Protestants and pregnant women have to get married.'

'You'll have to tell it in Confession, love. If you received Holy Communion without confessing you'd be committing a mortal sin.'

She pretended hysteria, sobbing and shaking, tears running down her face, saying over and over again : 'I couldn't confess that. I'd rather not get married. I'd face anything, but not telling a priest that me and you done things. I'll run away. I'll kill myself, honest to God I will.'

'Don't talk like that, Sarah,' Barney pleaded. 'Don't say them things. I'll tell you what, don't confess it before we get married and the following week tell it as a past sin. God forgive me for what I'm suggesting is probably a worse sin. How would I know? Only a priest could answer that.'

'You're so good, Barney. What would I do without you? Only, make sure you don't blurt out anything when we go to see the priest,' said Sarah, calm now and relaxed knowing that a wedding before the altar would give anyone in the street remarking on her hasty marriage something to puzzle them.

The neighbours never stopped talking after Barney and Sarah's Banns were called. Cissie said to Lizzie Mangan, 'That's very sudden, wouldn't you say?' as they walked home from Mass where the Banns had been called for the first time.

'Very,' agreed Mrs Mangan.

'Still and all though, I believe she's not getting married in the Vestry, so it's not "Haste to the Wedding".'

'So it would appear.'

'Because surely to God a Catholic little girl wouldn't perjure herself in Confession.' Never one to spread the first whiff of scandal, Mrs Mangan kept her thoughts about some little Catholic girls to herself, not even commenting on Sarah's hurried wedding to Julia, whose loyalty to Sarah was unshakeable. Time and time again she had tried to open her eyes to what she saw as Sarah's scheming nature, her contempt for everyone in the street. The begrudgement in her eyes when she saw Jack and Julia beginning to get on their feet. How they couldn't see through her she could never understand. And then for that again she could. They were open and trusting, deceiving no one. Consciously never harming anyone and believing everyone else was like them. She hoped and prayed they could continue to go through life like that, that her own suspicions – more than suspicions, a real fear that somewhere, somehow Sarah had the power to hurt them – would be proved wrong.

The week before the wedding, Michael Collins launched his bond-selling, hoping to raise a quarter of a million pounds. The British government proscribed the scheme : anyone found selling the bonds was arrested, and so were people who spoke out in favour of the scheme.

CHAPTER NINE

The wedding was a quiet affair, not because of Sarah's pregnancy, for no one except Barney and her mother knew of the expected baby. She hadn't confessed her sin and was married before the altar in a white dress with a large silk hat, a hand-me-down from Glenivy. The wedding was quiet because Mrs Quinlan wouldn't open the door to the street. Weddings in the street were normally joyous, lavish affairs – even if the lavishness was provided by borrowed money, and food and drink bought on score. Weddings were celebrated with a great breakfast after the return from the chapel. People packed into the house, sitting on borrowed chairs and stools, and using cups, plates and cutlery brought over by the neighbours. Drink was served from early morning until late into the next day, and the party resumed again in the evening.

Bride and groom were traditionally showered with presents bought on credit – bedding, towels, clocks, china and many religious statues and pictures. These were often duplicated, so that images of Our Lady and the Sacred Heart had to be hung and stood in more than one room.

Few invitations to a wedding meant few wedding presents. Sarah had four – a blue and gold lustre jug from Julia and Jack, a quilt from Julia's mother, a large chalk statue of St Patrick (a combined gift from Barney's family) and a pair of linen sheets given by her mother, who had received them from Glenivy on her own wedding day. They were yellowed along their creases from more than twenty years of lying in their folds.

The table was correctly set, the glasses sparkled, the china gleamed, but the food was sparse and the drink, a bottle of the cheapest port wine sufficient only for the toast. Later in the day Barney suggested a visit to the public house to replenish the wine and get some minerals for the women. His mother-in-law's expression left him in no doubt of what she thought of such a suggestion. He contented himself with tea and more tea and tea again. Julia's mother complained of feeling unwell. Jack jumped at the excuse of escorting her home, and Julia said she'd have to go as well and see her mother to bed. The Dalys fell over themselves in their eagerness to leave a house in which they instinctively felt unwelcome and choked with thirst. And Barney consoled himself with the thought that in a while he could plead tiredness and take his bride to bed.

'The hungry cow,' said Julia's mother when they got home. 'I wish I had the price of my quilt back. Not a bottle of stout nor a glass of whiskey – did you ever know such a wedding in your life? And did you notice something else?'

'I didn't,' said Julia.

'There was no present from the gentry – I wonder why?'

'She was there no time – I suppose that was the reason.'

'Wasn't she supposed to leave through sickness, and wasn't her mother a great favourite of the family's?'

'According to her,' Julia said.

'They never forgot her at Christmas, though. I'm telling you, there's more to her leaving than meets the eye.'

'Maybe you're right, Mother, I don't know. I don't care either. I'm that tired, all I want to do is sleep.'

'You're always tired nowadays,' said her mother, giving her a knowing look.

'She's like a witch,' Julia thought with affection. 'She knows, I bet you anything she knows. Please God let her be right, let me be pregnant.' She yawned.

'Go to bed,' said her mother. 'I'll make a bit of supper for Jack.'

'Not yet,' said Jack. 'I'm going to have a few pints.'

'I don't blame you. Go on then, I'll boil a sup of milk for Julia. Go to bed now, I'll bring the milk up in a minute. Shhh, what's that?'

'I don't hear anything,' said Julia.

Her mother opened the back door. 'I knew I heard something. That young wan, Mag, she must have been outside the window. She's gone haring down the back. Look, there she is – climbing up the embankment. One of these nights she'll be put in bits under a train. The poor unfortunate. All the same, she's a danger to herself and everyone else.'

Jack went to the public house, Julia fell asleep in the chair and her mother sat by the fire gazing into it and rubbing a hand across her stomach as though she were trying to shift a pain.

A month later Sarah, simpering, smiling and blushing, told Julia she was expecting, adding that of course she couldn't be sure as she had only missed the once – but never having missed before and with being married, well . . . it stood to reason, didn't it? So delighted for her was Julia, so carried away with the idea of them both expecting babies that she told her news even though her mother and Jack still didn't know.

They hugged each other and then talked about dates though neither knew how to calculate an expected date of birth and agreed they would have to ask their mothers.

'Though,' confided Julia, 'I think I know when it happened.' She blushed scarlet and talked in a whisper though no one else was in the house to overhear her. 'It was on a Sunday and we went to Glenasmole and . . .'

'Go way! You didn't, I don't believe you. In the daytime – in the open air?'

'It was beautiful,' said Julia, 'So beautiful. I'll never forget it as long as I live.'

'When was that? When did you go up the mountains?'

'Not long after you went away. Julia, the last Sunday in the month.'

Sarah watched the ecstatic expression on Julia's face and thought, 'God she's gorgeous. She was always nice-looking but now she's beautiful. She's nicer-looking than me and she didn't used to be.'

'I must be about two months gone.'

'Yes, oh you're sure to be,' said Sarah, 'and I'm probably a month. I must have fallen the first night. We've a long way to go yet. Just think, this time next year we'll have them.'

'Please God. I think my mother knows, though I haven't said a word. Of course neither would she, not until I'm over the three-months mark.'

'Why three months?'

'Because it's so easy to miscarry until after that.'

'That's news to me,' said Sarah, and thought how her baby and Julia's might be born at the same time, or at least very close to each other. But of course hers would be premature. She'd have to be careful when the time came not to talk about dates to anyone other than her mother. Julia's baby would be born in April, and hers expected in May. She'd have to get that into her head and then be overwhelmed with surprise when it arrived in April.

'Don't mention it to anyone, not even your mother,' requested Julia, 'and especially not Barney. He'd be bound to say something to Jack and I want to be the one to tell him.'

'Her face looks like an angel's, one of them you see in holy pictures, her skin like pearls.' Sarah didn't remember ever feeling jealous of Julia before, always so sure that she was the prettier, smarter one, the one who had connections with people Julia would never know. Which she still had in a way, she told herself; even the fact that Julia looked prettier didn't matter. It happened to some women when they were carrying. It was Julia's contentment of which she was jealous. Her love of Jack, wanting him to be the first to know about the baby. When compared with the reception Sarah got when she broke the news to Patrick . . . but Sarah wasn't one to live in the past. What was done was done. She'd get her looks back, and then she'd set about achieving her ambition to move

104

out of the street, to make something of herself and her son. How, she didn't yet know. But do it she would.

Lady Glenivy kept her word and found Barney a job as a porter in a club on St Stephen's Green.

'So,' said Jack when Barney told him, 'we're doing the same sort of thing!'

'Yeah, you could say that. Only this is a gentleman's club. It's a mansion! You can sleep and eat there. They've everything – bedrooms and billiard rooms, a library and bathrooms. You should see them – all mahogany, even the jacks – well, the seats – and the baths are that big you could fit two men in with no bother. I'm telling you, they've everything. And as for magazines – there's *Blackwood's* and *Punch, Country Life, The Field*, the *Tatler*, the *Illustrated London News* and God only knows what, and all brand new. This now you won't believe – the newspapers have to be ironed. Honest to God,' he swore when Jack looked sceptical, 'if there's as much as a wrinkle in them I have to give them a belt of the iron.'

'It's a change from coal-heaving. But d'ye like it?'

'Landed, so is Sarah. The wages are better and I get good tips. I'm not keen on the uniform – a shaggin' monkey-jacket done up with brass buttons.' He patted his belly. 'And I'll have to watch out for this. The grub's that good and we get pucks of it.'

'A belly's the last thing you want in a monkey-jacket. How d'ye get on with the members?'

'Grand,' said Barney. 'Being an ex-soldier I'm used to that sort of person. It's like being with the officers. I know how to take them – to be respectful but never familiar even when they seem friendly.'

'I don't like to see you still working,' Lizzie told Julia as she neared the end of her sixth month.

'But Ma, I'm grand. Since the morning sickness finished I've never felt better. It's not for long, anyway. Another month and I'll give it up.'

Her mother said no more about it but tackled Jack instead. 'I know she looks grand and please God that's the way she'll stay, but I'd feel happier if she was home. The last few months are the ones that make inroads on the mother's health. You talk to her – she looks that drained some evenings when she comes home, my heart goes out to her.'

Alarmed, Jack asked, 'There's nothing wrong with her, is there?'

'Please God there isn't, nor won't be. All the same I think she's worked long enough. I know there's women with a houseful of children on their feet until the last minute, but they're at home, not having to please an employer, able to leave what they're doing. It's the money she'll be concerned about, but I've a few pound put by. She won't go short.'

Jack talked to Julia and reluctantly she agreed, afterwards admitting how relieved she was at not having to go to work. How pleasant it was to spend time gossiping with Sarah, holding hanks of fine soft white wool for each other to wind into balls from which they knitted matinée coats, bonnets, bootees and shawls. To cut yards of flannel into gowns, bibs, pilches and binders. She taught Sarah how to sew French seams and do simple embroidery stitches with which to decorate her baby's gowns.

While sewing and knitting they talked about their neighbours and their husbands' jobs, Sarah inevitably boasting of all the important people Barney met at the Club, name-dropping generals, viscounts, lords and admirals. Sometimes, but not often, they talked of the terrible happenings throughout their country – the people killed by both sides – and congratulated themselves on living in their small, safe street.

If Lizzie was out they talked of their expected babies. Mrs Mangan thought it unlucky to talk about babies not yet born. They wondered was it true what some women said about childbirth – were you quartered and stitched up like an old boot? Was the pain so unbearable that no man would endure it more than once? Then, after frightening themselves imagining the ordeal, they consoled themselves by saying that there was nothing to be done about it. The babies were there and out they had to come.

Once during a gossiping session Sarah asked, 'How did your mother have only one child?'

'She had seven more,' Julia said, and went on to explain. 'Four misses, two were dead born, one lived for eleven weeks and then there was me. I was the last.'

'I never knew that.'

'You'd have been too young. Sometimes my ma still cries about the baby who died at eleven weeks, after all this time. Did your mother lose any children?'

'Not according to her. So either she didn't let my Da or took the black pills.'

Julia knew about the little black pills which according to her mother were a sin to use, even though they seldom worked in their function to get rid of a child. She sympathised with the pill-takers and them that resorted to crochet hooks, knitting needles and carbolic douches. Women more often than not were driven to such measures because of drunken, violent husbands, so desperate that they risked their own lives in order to lose the child they were carrying. Julia shared her mother's views and thanked God for her good, kind and considerate husband.

Once a week she went to pray before Our Lady Of Dublin in Whitefriar's Street chapel. There, kneeling before the Virgin's statue, which was black in appearance because it was made of bog oak, and had been looted by Cromwell's troops, lost for centuries and not found until late in the 1800s, she prayed for a safe delivery.

Julia's belly grew so all the neighbours joked that you could see her before she turned the corner. In contrast, Sarah's bulge was barely noticeable, and her natural smallness was further aided by a tight corset which she wore at her mother's insistence.

They counted the weeks to Julia's expected date in April and Sarah's fictitious one in May, and said they were glad to have the summer before them for rearing the babies and drying their clothes.

The statue of St Patrick stood on a chest of drawers under the window. Light from the gas-lamp outside shone down on the saint through the gap where the scanty curtains didn't meet. In reality the statue's hair, visible beneath his conical-shaped hat was brown but, looking at him in the gaslight, Sarah saw it as red, dark red, the colour of mahogany like his namesake and she remembered the nights in her attic bedroom, her fingers wound in the red curls, the smell of the perfume and her response to Patrick's lovemaking. Such things happened to her. The screams she wanted to scream as his hand came down over her mouth. Screams and curses – the sort of curses only men said. Men standing at corners. Curses you weren't supposed to know existed, never mind want to shout out.

Instead of all that magic there was Barney beside her, like a big lump of lard. No fear of him making her scream or curse, except with annoyance. The weight of him, for one thing – twice as heavy as before they married. It was all the food he ate in the Club. Roasts every day and the puddings, ones she'd never heard of. There was Spotted Dick, Cabinet puddings and this Fool and that Fool – and him the biggest fool of all. Bringing home that magazine with the picture of Patrick's wedding to the skinny one, admiring them, asking her what was Patrick like. Had she ever seen his wife?

And she had told him: 'Only once did I ever see him and never her.' Well, what else could she say without fear of giving the game away? She recalled the look of admiration and adoration on Barney's face as he studied the picture. He had become a great admirer of the gentry since he started in the Club. Little did he know how soon he'd be rearing one of them.

The baby heaved itself round inside her. God, how she wished it was all over. She was fed up with the discomfort. There didn't seem to be enough room inside her for it as it heaved over and kicked and poked and prodded her. One thing was sure and certain – she'd never have another. Once the child was born she'd never let Barney near her again. She'd be delicate, her insides delicate. The doctors would have told her to have no more children. He'd believe it – Barney was such an eejit he'd believe anything. She'd tell him another child could be the cause of killing her. She'd do anything for him except let him stick it in her. Bouncing up and down and it all over in a minute. He had his glue if he thought that was going to carry on.

If he had his way she'd have her belly up to her chin every ten months, and how could you better yourself with a streel of children at your heels? Barney turned in the bed, moved closer to her and his arm reached towards her. She gave it back to him and continued with her thoughts. They'd made a start anyway. His tips went straight into the Post Office. Their savings were growing but not quick enough for her liking. What they needed was a windfall, someone to die and leave them money – only neither of them had a relation worth tuppence. There was the fifty pounds Lady Glenivy had promised after 'the event', and if that arrived it would boost the nest egg. The baby was still, had been she realised for a few minutes. She wondered if they slept inside you. Then, what it would be like to give birth. Then, if it would have red hair. She hoped so. She had loved Patrick's hair. She supposed she had loved him too. Barney was a poor substitute. She was fond of him, though. She'd look after him, be a good wife in every way except that one thing. She'd cook, wash and clean for him, so long as in return he'd do her bidding. Now and then she'd recall her nights with Patrick, but thoughts of him or what might have been wouldn't ever occupy her mind for long. What was past was behind you. It was the future you had to think of.

Julia also found it difficult to sleep during the last month of her pregnancy. She was hugely pregnant. Lately her legs, feet, hands and face had swollen and her head ached often.

'It happens to some women,' her mother had told her, not adding that to many women who swelled their babies were born dead: that often the women fitted, often they died.

She made Julia stay late in bed and lie down again in the afternoon and did the only other thing possible. She prayed morning, noon and night for a safe confinement and a live, healthy child, aware of how often such prayers weren't answered. Every time a woman gave birth she held her life in her hands, sometimes for it to be snatched from her.

Julia was also aware that many women died during childbirth, but she was young and the thought of her own death was impossible to imagine. Even so she prayed fervently for a safe delivery, and though dreading the prospect of going into hospital, had yielded to Jack's wish that she should, for there she would be in safe hands.

CHAPTER TEN

Sarah started her pains a week before Julia's baby was expected. Immediately Mrs Quinlan put her plan into action. She ran with a distracted air about her to Julia's mother, saying, 'Oh, Mrs Mangan, would you ever have a look at Sarah. She's not well!'

Alarmed by the woman's anxious appearance, voice and the unexpectedness of a visit from her, fearfully Julia asked what ailed Sarah.

'God forbidding all harm I think she might be starting, and she not due for a month or more.'

'If you're in doubt as to what's the matter with her, get the nurse,' Julia's mother advised brusquely. Then relenting, because a woman in trouble was a woman in trouble even if you couldn't abide her, she added, 'I'll come and have a look at her. It might be no more than cramps.'

Sarah was clutching her back, pacing the floor and moaning now and then. After timing several pains Mrs Mangan proclaimed what Sarah and her mother had been aware of for hours: 'She's in labour. Send for Nurse Gannon.'

'But she won't be expecting the call. It was next month Sarah booked her. She mightn't be in.'

'She doesn't travel far. Try the public house – if she's on a case she leaves word there.'

'I'd go but I don't like leaving Sarah on her own. Would you ever ask someone to do the errand?'

'I'll go myself, and if you like come back and give a hand with the confinement.'

Mrs Quinlan's thanks were effusive as she beckoned Julia's mother into the hall. 'I'd be only delighted of another pair of hands, and such capable ones. God bless you – you're kindness itself. But herself,' she nodded to the kitchen, 'she's become very pernickety all of a sudden. Not minutes before her pains started she said to me, "Ma, I want you to promise that only you and Nurse Gannon will be with me when I have the baby. I don't want anyone else gawking at me." She's a very modest little girl.'

'It's up to you, ma'am, but if you want anything you know where I live. Now I'll find the nurse.' Lizzie made allowances for the refusal:

Sarah was entitled to have only her mother and the nurse present at the birth. All the same they were quare people. Never in a million years could she warm to them. Nothing would please her more than to hear they were leaving the street. Whenever she was in their company she felt a strange unease, though it was seldom or ever she saw much of the oul wan, but Sarah since Julia had finished work was in and out of the Mangan house every minute of the day.

Mrs Quinlan and Sarah congratulated themselves on having managed everything according to plan. Julia's mother would spread word of Sarah's labour and how her mother was beside herself with worry because the child was coming before its time. Nurse Gannon was half-blind and seldom sober: unless the child was hanging alive in fat and weighing a ton she'd be none the wiser that it wasn't premature. And neither would anyone else, for no one – not even Julia – would lay eyes on the baby for many a week to come.

With little or no trouble Sarah delivered, as she had known she would, a son. He didn't have much hair and what he had wasn't red. He went greedily to her breast, reminding her of his father. That in turn reminded her of the promised fifty pounds and when the nurse had left she told her mother to let Lady Glenivy know that the 'event' had taken place.

Barney gazed on the baby in wonderment. 'Hold him, he won't break,' Sarah said, a hint of ridicule in her voice.

Tentatively he lifted the child from her arms and awkwardly held him, all the time looking down at his face adoringly. 'My son,' he said, 'my little son,' and kissed his cheek. 'Look at him, he's gorgeous. Look at the fat cheeks of him.' He walked the room with him, talking to him. Telling him all he'd do for him. His face glowing with pride and love.

Before the end of the week a registered letter arrived, addressed to Mrs Quinlan. Inside the envelope was a fifty-pound note and a brief letter hoping all were well. It was signed by Lady Glenivy.

'Open a separate account for that,' Sarah's mother advised, handing over the money. 'Otherwise you'll have him asking questions.'

'I'll do that,' replied Sarah, 'in my maiden name. As soon as I'm up I'll go to a Post Office in town where I'm not known.'

Without any complications Julia had an eight-pound girl, and within a few days after the birth the headaches went and her swollen face and limbs returned to normal. She fell in love with her daughter as soon as she looked at her, marvelled at her perfection and prayed for God to bless and spare her. Lizzie and Jack visited every evening, Lizzie bringing in freshly cut tempting sandwiches, small bowls of milk jellies and fruit.

Jack brought her sweets and pawned his father's gold half-hunter to buy her a silver locket and chain.

Discharged after fourteen days with the baby dressed in the finery she had prepared, Julia felt as proud as a peacock, only sorry as she rode home in the cab with her mother that Jack couldn't have had time off work to be with them. Cissie and the other neighbours came to see Julia and the new baby, to bring presents or put silver into the baby's palm. And while there, they commented on how Sarah was still confined to the house and no one had laid eyes on the baby.

'He must be very dawny,' Cissie said. 'May God spare him.'

Another neighbour tut-tutted, 'In all my years in the street I never knew the like : a new baby and no one to lay eyes on him. I've seen premature babies not the size of a rabbit wrapped in cotton wool and so small they had to lie in a shoebox, but you were still brought in to see them.'

'Maybe it's newfangled ways picked up from the gentry,' Lizzie said.

'Aye,' said the neighbour, 'you could be right.'

Jack was less demonstrative with his daughter than Barney was with his son. In the beginning he seldom held her, only occasionally stroking her cheek, marvelling at its softness, her beauty, considering her too fragile for him to handle. He was terrified of touching her head, where a pulse beat visibly in the fontanelle, wondering if such an opening was normal.

He continued to worry and wonder until one Sunday morning he watched his mother-in-law washing and drying the baby's head vigorously then put a hand on either side of the unclosed skull and pushing it gently towards the centre, afterwards making the Sign of the Cross over the opening. The Blessing gave him the opportunity to ask a question. 'Why ?'

'For God to make it close in the right time.'

'It's normal, then ?'

Mrs Mangan hooshed the baby up in the air and answered Jack by talking to her. 'Listen to your daft father. Tell him of course it's normal. Tell him you're perfect, a little beauty. *My* little beauty – the image of your mother. Tell him that.' She lowered the child on to her lap and addressed Jack. 'You weren't worried about it, were you ?'

'I was,' he admitted.

'Then why didn't you mention it ?'

'I didn't want to be upsetting Julia.'

'Men,' his mother-in-law scoffed good-naturedly, but when he left the room she thought about him, his kindness and consideration. Afraid that something ailed the child but not wanting to frighten or worry

Julia. Not many men were that sensitive. Her own husband had been a good man but not like Jack. Watching him with Julia she sometimes felt a pang of regret for the things she had missed. How, in passing, Jack would touch Julia's hair, slip an arm round her shoulders or waist as she stood by the window or table. Little things. Little signs of affection for which all women craved. Then the pawning of his father's watch to buy the locket. She knew how much he treasured the watch. Jack was a lovely man, and as Lizzie dressed the baby she again talked to her. 'A lovely man, that's what you have for a father. You're a lucky girl. May God bless and spare him to you.'

Seamus Harrington sent a present for the baby – a silver and ivory teething ring. 'It's beautiful. He's very generous. Did you ask him to come to the christening?' Julia asked, still handling the present.
'I did.'
'And?'
'He made an excuse. Said he isn't sure what he'll be doing on the day.'
'He's quare all the same,' said Julia.
'He's not. I told you before, he's a very private person. The decentest and most generous man you'd wish to meet, but that's as far it goes. He has his reasons, I'm sure. Maybe it's as well not to know what they are, as I said before. And another thing – he may feel awkward with being what they call a spoiled priest. I don't know – I'm only guessing.'
'So I'm not likely to meet him?'
'I wouldn't think it likely. Certainly not for the time being.'
'The man's entitled to his reasons. Thank him all the same for the beautiful present. And you can tell him I remember him always in my prayers.'

'Wasn't it a pity the way things worked out over the christenings,' Julia said one day when she and Sarah were having their usual gossip.
'With me going early it couldn't be helped – I had to have a friend of my mother's to stand for him. I never saw her before in my life. I'll probably never lay eyes on her again. And then I was sick for so long after the birth I couldn't stand for Eleanor,' said Sarah, looking down at the little girl on her lap. 'She's a dote. What made you call her Eleanor?'
'Jack wanted her christened Ellen after his mother. I wasn't keen on that so I thought Eleanor was near enough and nicer.'
'Much nicer. Very uncommon, very aristocratic. Don't go calling her Nellie or shortening it to Lena. That's what'll happen to him,' Sarah said, nodding towards her son on Julia's lap. 'The minute he goes to

school he'll get Paddy or Pat – but at home he'll always be Patrick. This one is gorgeous – the image of you. Look at the fat on her, bracelets of it on her wrists. And look at my fella – like a skinned rabbit.'

'He is not, God bless him. D'ye hear what your mammy's saying about you?' Julia asked, bending to kiss Patrick's cheek.

'I suppose considering that he was premature he's not too bad. Who d'ye think he's getting like?'

Julia, who could never spot a resemblance in an infant to anyone else nevertheless gave the answer she was sure all mothers of sons wanted. 'Barney, he's the spit of Barney,' she said, and seeing the smile spread over Sarah's face knew it was the right one.

Barney's mother and father died within a week of each other, his father of pneumonia, his mother, the neighbours said, of a broken heart – though the death certificate stated the cause as kidney failure. Mrs Daly had kept up the insurance policy, so there was enough Society money for a good funeral: oak coffins with brass handles, a hearse pulled by four black-plumed horses, their bodies draped with black-velvet-tasselled palls. There was a mourning coach for the immediate family, three carriages for relations of a lesser degree and close friends, while neighbours hired hackney cabs.

For the wake Julia's mother lent what was known in the street as the 'Dead Bundle', a set of linen sheets and pillowcases, a small white cloth to cover a bamboo table which would hold a crucifix and a dish for Holy Water, in which a feather rested so that people paying their respects could sprinkle the body with the Blessed Water. Included with the Dead Bundle was a pair of brass candlesticks and wax candles. Julia's grandmother had started the custom when she was in comfortable circumstances and when many in the street were not. Her mother carried on the tradition and it was taken for granted that in her turn, so would Julia. After the wake the deceased's family had the linen professionally laundered if they could afford it and replaced the candles.

As for the street party, the neighbours made cakes and sandwiches, lent chairs and crockery; Barney's family supplied the drink. There were tears and laughter, reminiscences, jokes, story telling and many a song. Because the street was isolated, only friends and neighbours came to the house, unlike less secluded streets, where passing men, seeing a crêpe on a hall door, often claimed acquaintance with the dead man or woman, knowing they would be sure of a drink.

They called down blessings on the corpse, sprinkled it with Holy Water and spoke of all the good times they had spent together. They were seldom challenged.

A few days after Mrs Daly's funeral, the single and married family members and their wives and husbands gathered to dispose of their parents' possessions.

The single brothers and sisters decided to go and live in England, saying: 'You could take over the place, Barney. The landlord wouldn't raise an objection.'

The joy of leaving his mother-in-law's home showed on Barney's face. Sarah kicked him so he said, 'I'll have to think about it.'

One of his sisters added, 'Sarah, we've all agreed that apart from a few keepsakes, everything else will be yours.'

'Mine?' she said, and looked contemptuously round the shabby, though comfortable, room.

'Thanks all the same, it's very kind of you, but I couldn't fit another thing in my mother's.' And she thought, the nerve of them offering me their leavings! The whatnot with its cracked and mended ornaments — I'd back the fire with that. The deal dresser with its common thick cups and saucers. The religious pictures and chalk statues. What did they think she was? She longed to give them a piece of her mind, but Barney's sister was in her opinion a common rossy who'd go for anyone she thought was making little of her family. So she thanked them again and repeated about her mother's house being already over-furnished.

Afterwards in the public house, without openly criticising Sarah, Barney made excuses as to why he wouldn't be able to take on the house and resigned himself to life with Mrs Quinlan until such time as he found the means of moving out of the street. Where he would find these means he didn't know, but every day Sarah reminded him that he must. The thought of it was imprinted on his brain. Sometimes he dreamed about robbing someone, coming home to her with hundreds of pound notes. Throwing them up in the air, handfuls at a time, watching her face as they showered down round her. For seconds after waking the dream lingered and then reality took its place. He wouldn't know how to set about robbing anyone. He didn't *know* anyone he could rob.

'When are you ever likely to earn more money?' Her voice was quiet but Barney who had just come in from work and sat for his meal knew it was the calm before the storm. A knot formed in the pit of his stomach. He hated rows. Sarah's tongue was like a knife: it cut into his heart, into his soul, leaving him after the row feeling as lifeless as if her weapon had been real and drained his life's blood. Yet never once did he turn on her; never once feel that he wasn't entirely to blame for not having a better job. Now as ever he tried to placate her.

'I thought I'd give it a bit more time before asking for a rise.'

'What you mean is that you haven't the spunk to ask for one!' Her voice was rising.

'I've been there no time. They mightn't think I was entitled ...'

'You're not a man. A man wouldn't see his wife and child stuck in a dog box of a back bedroom, but that's the way you were reared. Three or four of you to a bed – like pigs in a sty. Well, I'm telling you I won't live like that. I want a place of my own. I want a house away from the street. Just because your mother didn't care how she lived doesn't mean ...'

He had loved his easygoing mother. This was the first time since she died that Sarah had brought her into one of their rows. He missed her. He was grieving still for her. It gave him the courage to turn on her. 'Leave my mother out of it! Let her rest in peace. She never harmed you.'

'Oh, didn't she. Well, let me tell you she did me the greatest harm of all in having you. You've destroyed my life. Ruined it.'

Mrs Quinlan put her head round the kitchen door, saw the dejected figure of Barney and Sarah standing with her hands on her hips, and thought – good girl. Keep at him if you want to make anything of him, and then withdrew. Sarah now tried another tactic. She began to cry. 'You don't know what it's like having to live with my mother or how I worry about Patrick. About when he's old enough to play in the street. You know what they're like here – as common as dirt. He'll be cursing and talking like all the others. You don't want that for your son, surely to God?'

Moved as he always was by her tears he got up from the table and went to put his arms round her. She pushed him away. 'Don't try soft-soaping me either.'

'I was only going to say that you were reared in the street and you speak lovely. And honest to God, at the first opportunity I'll ask for a rise. We can manage for a little while longer. Julia and Jack do and they've no more room than us.'

'Don't mention her name to me.' The tears were gone and she was shouting. 'She's like a contented cow. She has no ambition. She'll live and die in the street. What else does she know? I'm different, I was reared different. And I'm warning you, if you don't do something to improve our life I'll leave you. I mean that. I'll walk out of here and take Patrick with me.'

'Don't even think such a thing. Don't, Sarah. I'll do anything for you, anything. Only have a bit of patience.'

Her father came into the kitchen and put the kettle on. Many times he had heard Sarah fighting with Barney. He longed for the courage to take him aside and say, 'Give her a dig in the jaw. It's what I should have done to her mother years ago,' but like Barney he didn't have the courage. Instead he asked, 'D'ye want tea, either of you?'

Without answering her father, Sarah stormed out of the kitchen and Barney made an excuse to go to the lavatory where he stayed for a long time. When he came in Sarah and her mother were in the parlour. He passed the door quietly and went to bed, telling himself that for tonight it was over. She wouldn't row upstairs for fear of waking Patrick.

When he called his daughter anything, Jack called her Eleanor, but he secretly thought of her as Ellie. It was the name by which his mother had been known, and it also had a softer sound. When she woke for her middle-of-the-night feed he brought her from the washing basket which Julia had padded with wadding and lined with pink stuff and, while she took the breast, he made tea and toast for himself and Julia. Ellie didn't always settle after her feed. On those nights he took her and, after lowering the gas-jet, walked the floor singing softly whatever song came into his mind, singing and gently patting her back. Her head lay on his shoulder, her whisper of breath on his neck. When she slept he laid her down and before getting into bed again, after putting out the light, he always parted the curtains and looked into the garden. And thanked God for seeing only what was supposed to be there.

One day during the first week of June 1920, a warm beautiful day when Ellie was five weeks old, Julia sat in the garden feeding her. Feeling relaxed and happy, she gazed at the face of her daughter while random pleasant thoughts went through her mind, like how blue the sky was. The garden was a show – millions of pee-the-beds, though she liked their bright yellow colour. Eleanor was thriving and she herself had never felt better in her life. The baby would be shortened soon. Sarah seemed very happy with Barney. She would make a blue dress for Eleanor, smock it. When she was six weeks old, she and Jack could . . . From the kitchen her mother called, '*Julia, Julia, child!*' The voice wasn't right – something was wrong. All thought of when she and Jack could resume their lovemaking fled from her mind as she shouted: 'Ma, are you all right? I'm coming. I'm coming.'

Her mother lay on the couch still in her outdoor things, her marketing bag on the floor; a head of lettuce, its roots crusted in earth, a bunch of scallions and several potatoes had spilled out. 'Oh Ma, what ails you?' Julia asked, trying to hide the panic she felt, for her mother's face was the colour of a tallow candle and sweat beaded her forehead.

'I took a weakness as I was coming out of the vegetable shop. It came over me all of a sudden. I didn't get half of what I wanted.'

'It was the heat. It's roasting out,' Julia said, as much to reassure herself as her mother. 'I'll put Eleanor down and make you a cup of tea.'

'Let me have her.' Her mother held out her arms.

'You'll do no such thing.' She arranged cushions in the armchair and laid the baby down, then made tea and before giving her mother a cup, laced it with whiskey. Drawing a chair up to the couch she sat and began to scold.

'You do far too much. I'd have got the messages. You're always on the go, not letting me lift a finger before nor since Eleanor was born.' As she talked, Julia looked at her mother's face, asking herself when had she gone so thin and taken on such a bad colour. How hadn't she noticed the changes in her? Was it with seeing her every day, being so used to her face that she never really saw it? Or because she had been so concerned with her own small discomforts during pregnancy?

'That's after putting new life into me – I feel better already.' The baby whimpered. 'That she may grow up to be as good to you as you are to me.' Lizzie handed Julia the cup and closed her eyes.

'Would you like another?'

'No thanks, love.'

'Is there anything else I can do for you?'

Her mother opened her eyes and smiled. 'One thing if you will.'

'Oh Ma,' Julia said, and laid her head on her mother's breast. 'Anything at all, anything in the world.'

Her mother stroked her hair, and Julia choked back her tears. If anything happened to her mother she'd die. The feel of her hands, the fingers massaging her scalp, reminding her of warm olive oil being rubbed in as it was once a month during her growing. 'To nourish your scalp,' her mother used to say. Once a week the same fingers searching, parting strand after strand of hair, searching out nits. Those hands soothing her headaches, rubbing away pain, tying ribbon bows in her hair, shoelaces. Gently spreading ointments and liniments. Hands that had washed her face, one wrapped in the corner of a towel to make a face cloth. Drawing boils, lancing whitlows, knitting gloves and socks and jumpers. Smoothing back a lock of her father's hair before his coffin was closed.

Raising her face she took her mother's hands in her own and covered them with kisses and tears she could no longer check. They fell like rain as in between sobs she implored, 'Oh Ma, I love you. Don't be sick. I love you. How would I manage without you?'

'All that ailed me was a weakness. It was the heat and I'd been to Communion so I'd nothing in my stomach since last night. You're worse than a child. Stop that crying or you'll send your milk astray.'

Julia recognised the hint of irritation in her mother's speech and was glad of it. Mrs Mangan could be short at times if you fussed her too much. She took it for a good sign.

'I'll make you toast, fry an egg, make a bit of porridge.'

'A bit of toast. Look at me now, amn't I grand?' Her mother sat up. 'Not a feather out of me.'

'You have to promise me one thing,' said Julia as she made toast. 'You'll have to go to the doctor. Please.'

'I'll see how I feel through the week. Before all this started I was asking you to do something special for me, remember.'

'Anything, anything at all,' said Julia, plastering the toast with butter.

'You'll have to ask Jack as well. It's about the baby. I know you don't want her name shortened, but Eleanor is a bit of a mouthful and not right somehow on a baby. Could I call her Ellie?'

'Ellie? I never thought of that, even though everyone who knew her well called Jack's mother that. He'll be delighted. We'll all call her Ellie. Here now, eat the toast and then have a little rest.'

'But what about the dinner?'

'Now Mother,' Julia wagged a finger, 'I can make a dinner. Don't forget I'm a married woman with a child.'

Thankfully her mother lay down and let a blanket be tucked round her. She slept for hours, all through Ellie screaming, through Sarah and Patrick coming into the kitchen. Julia cried again as in whispers she related the morning's happening. They moved with their babies into the garden. 'I'm afraid she's got cancer, God forbidding all harm.'

'You're very morbid, Julia. How could anyone with the go in her your mother has have cancer? Why, the day I went into labour she ran all the way for the nurse. She never stops, polishing this, washing that, carrying pucks from the shops, cans of paraffin oil, stones of potatoes. Your mother's as strong as a horse. She had a weakness, that's all.'

'But look at the colour of her, and she's as skinny as a rake.'

'I wouldn't mind her colour – did you ever see yourself after you've fainted? And as for being thin, she always was. She doesn't eat enough for a sparrow. You've nothing to worry about. It was the heat – that and not having broken her fast since last night.'

Julia allowed her fears to be allayed and thought what a kind comforting person Sarah was, how lucky she was to have such a friend. She hoped she'd never move from the street, envisaging the babies growing up together. Starting school at the same time, being best friends as she, Barney, Jack and Sarah were. She looked ahead to all the good times they'd share as families: Christmas, Hallow's Eve, St Patrick's Day, the First Holy Communions and in the summer, going up the mountains, to Glenasmole, and the pine forest. Or to the seaside – out to Howth on the top of a tram. They'd have lovely happy lives, please God.

Sarah talked about Barney's job, how settled in he was, and Julia was reminded of something she had been meaning to ask her. 'You never said how he took to the Glenivys finding him the work.'

'Didn't I ? He was delighted. My mother had mentioned the possibility of Lady Glenivy using her influence so it came as no surprise. He loves it. All the members are gentry – Lord Glenivy's one of them. Barney says he practically lives there nowadays.'

'Another thing I've always meant to ask you,' said Julia, pretending more interest in the gentry than she felt. 'Have the Glenivys children ?'

'Three,' replied Sarah, 'all married. One son and two daughters. All living in London.' She hoped Julia wouldn't ask their names. Though she wasn't a suspicious person you never knew if she might think it a coincidence that the Glenivys' son and hers were both called Patrick.

Julia however changed the conversation by saying, 'My Jack's going to have his reading curtailed.'

'I don't blame you. Books make the place very untidy.'

'It's not for that reason. I like books but I'd like a garden better. I want a plot of grass for Ellie to play on, and potherbs near the door so that in bad weather I won't wet my feet. I'll have oceans of wallflowers, they're my favourites. And roses, a lavender bush, stocks and pinks, mignonette and London Pride. I'll buy a trellis for the end of the garden and plant honeysuckle. In front of it there'll be vegetables.'

'Talking about gardens, you should have seen the ones in Glenivy.' But to Julia's relief before Sarah could start her description, Patrick woke and started to scream. 'He's dirtied himself, I'll have to go,' said Sarah. 'I'll see you tomorrow.'

Lord Glenivy was forty-eight, a handsome man who in no way resembled his son, Patrick. Before inheriting his title he had had a distinguished military career. Now he bred fine racehorses, was a local magistrate and greatly involved in founding and maintaining an intelligence network to help defeat the present troubles. Lately this had necessitated frequent visits to London and Dublin. In his Club he kept an eye open for likely members of staff who might be recruited for his network of spies. He wanted local men, men who knew the city – who were at home in its public houses. Vain, weak men, easily flattered, preferably with some sort of military background. Gradually he was building up a dossier on the porters, waiters and odd-jobmen who worked in the Club.

★

'How are you feeling now?' Julia asked when eventually her mother woke up.

'Grand and I'm a bit peckish.'

Her mother's request for food convinced Julia even more than her improved appearance that nothing serious ailed her. 'I kept your dinner warm, a centre loin chop and the cabbage is lovely.' Watching her eat, Julia felt happy and carefree with the weight lifted from her mind. And as for her mother's thinness, she'd see to that if it meant stall-feeding her.

Jack was told of the decision to call the baby Ellie. 'I hope you won't mind, son. It was me that suggested it,' said Mrs Mangan, in between stripping the chop-bone with her teeth.

'Let me tell the two of you something. To myself I've been calling her Ellie since the day she was born.'

Julia gave him his dinner and afterwards while the three of them were eating bread and butter and drinking tea he said, 'The town is full of rumours today. Not a good lookout if they're true.'

'What are they saying?' Julia asked.

'There's a force being brought over from England – the excuse is it's to help with the shortage of RIC men.'

'Soldiers?'

'No, Ma. Well, they were during the war. Rumour has it they're a tough bunch, recruited at ten bob a day. I don't like the sound of it.'

'Neither do I,' said Mrs Mangan, 'though I'm not surprised. I said as much, didn't I, Julia? Remember that day before – it's a long time ago now, but I did say something like this would happen.'

Julia, who could never keep track of her mother's warnings and prophecies, lied and said yes, she remembered it well, then asked Jack: 'If these fellas aren't soldiers what're they called?'

He shook his head. 'No word of that yet, but it'll be all out in no time.'

In the following weeks it was 'all out' and the Black and Tans had arrived. 'Gaolbirds, murderers,' the Irish dubbed them from the minute of their arrival. 'The scum of English prisons let out to come here and slaughter us.'

Jack righted the rumour about them being gaolbirds. 'Unemployed soldiers,' he explained to Julia and his mother-in-law. 'Probably excellent soldiers when under a tight rein. Here they won't have that and I hate to think what the consequences will be.'

'Did you hear they're getting ten shillings a day?' Mrs Mangan asked.

'That seems right enough.'

'That's three pounds a week if you don't count Sunday. Mother of God Almighty they'll go mad on that, be drunk morning, noon and night. Why are they called the Black and Tans?'

'Some say it's because of their kit – khaki uniforms and the dark green belts and hats of the RIC, then there's another rumour that it's after a pack of fox hounds. I don't think anyone knows for sure.'

'Animals, savages probably. God keep us far from them,' Mrs Mangan said.

The Black and Tans were followed shortly by ex-army officers given the rank of Sergeant in the RIC and paid ten pounds a week. In town Jack saw the two bodies of men, often drunk, swaggering, throwing their weight about. Driving through the city in their Crossley tenders, the backs of which were covered in wire mesh so that anything lobbed at the vehicles rolled off. These men were stationed in Dublin and through- out the country. They were shot and ambushed, and they retaliated with ferocity. And as news of their methods – on-the-spot executions without trial, civilian homes raided, looted and burned down (in many cases homes that were not connected with the Republicans) – they came to be feared and hated.

Julia invited Sarah, Barney and the Quinlans to Ellie's shortening party. The Quinlans made an excuse not to come. Ellie wore her new pale- blue hand-smocked dress and was greatly admired by all. Sarah said that because of Patrick being premature she'd leave him a while longer in gowns, and Julia promised to make his outfit when the time was right.

The men talked about the continuing killings and bombings, and speculated on how, if ever, it would all end. Barney related amusing anecdotes about the night porter, admiring ones about the gentry and asked how Jack was getting along in his place.

'Much the same as usual,' Jack replied. 'It'll never make me a fortune but I'm content. I like the crowd. I like the atmosphere and, you can laugh if you want to, but I'm learning Irish.' Barney did laugh. And Jack went on to explain that if and when Independence came, he could foresee the day when Irish would be taught in schools. 'And then wouldn't I be a right eejit, not understanding a word of what Ellie was saying.' She was so small and so beautiful, he thought, looking at her on Julia's lap. It was hard to imagine her old enough ever to talk to him. But she would be one day, please God. He'd watch her mind developing, talking, asking questions. He'd read to her and teach her how to read. Tell her stories – fairy stories and Irish legends. Teach her songs and poems.

'You're miles away and me trying to organise a trip up the mountains for the four of us.' Barney corrected himself: 'The six of us.' Jack apologised for not listening.

'Glenasmole, I thought,' said Barney.

'Delay it until next year,' Sarah said. 'With him on the bottle I'd have to lug too much stuff.'

Julia looked at Patrick with his boat-shaped feeding bottle and thought it was a pity that Sarah hadn't persisted with breast-feeding. The minute she ran into trouble, like Patrick wanting sucks oftener than suited her, the bottle was mentioned. 'I'm too tired. He has the back dragged out of me,' she'd complained. And so Julia gave her a rest, feeding her friend's baby from her breasts, but telling Sarah it couldn't be done too often. If Patrick didn't suck from Sarah regularly, she'd lose her milk. And then Sarah had put him on the bottle altogether, taken massive doses of Epsom Salts and plastered her breasts, sending away her milk.

'Next year then,' they all agreed.

Mag came in and nursed Patrick and Ellie in turn, closely supervised by Julia's mother, for sometimes she got rough and overexcited with the babies. When they were safely back with their mothers Mag helped herself too liberally to the cake and Mrs Mangan sent her home.

CHAPTER ELEVEN

It was 1921, and oh how the years were flying by, Julia thought as she walked home from the doctor, who had confirmed that she was three months pregnant.

'You're expecting again,' her mother had said before she was even a month gone.

'You're like a witch, Ma. How can you tell? I'm not even sure myself.'

Julia remembered herself saying this, Lizzie replying, 'There's something about a woman's face that gives her away. You learn as you get older to recognise it. Don't go pulling and hauling Ellie nor lifting anything else heavy for the time being. Will you go into hospital on this one?'

'I'll see nearer the time,' she had said.

She stopped at the baker's and bought a piece of snowcake for Ellie and an apple puff each for herself and her mother. When she got home, the kettle was singing on the hob and Ellie was on Lizzie's lap playing with the teething ring Seamus had given her. 'Well, was I right?' asked Lizzie.

'You were, as usual. I'll tell Jack tonight.' She took off her coat, gave Ellie part of the cake and wet tea for herself and her mother. Lizzie put Ellie down and she walked round the furniture.

'She's getting steadier every day on her feet,' Lizzie said. 'God bless her she's a lovely child, not a cranky streak in her. You were a demon at her age. It's after her father she takes.'

Ellie gradually made her way to where Julia sat and she picked her up and kissed her, and gave her more cake. Thinking as she did so how happy and how lucky she was. How much she loved Jack and Ellie. How she loved her mother. And for a minute a dark thought crossed her mind: Lizzie was getting old. She was nearly seventy, having been well into her forties when she had had her. 'On the Change', as she often said – the shakings of the bag. And Julia wished that like her, her mother had given birth in her twenties. That she was only fifty. Then she told herself that for all she knew, her mother could live to be ninety. She looked grand. She never complained. Julia had to stop being morbid and put her trust in God.

★

'The pair of you can wash the Delft,' said Lizzie after she had put Ellie to bed. 'I'll go up to Cissie's for an hour.'

'That's unusual for your ma to go out before doing the table,' Jack said.

'You're not objecting to doing the Delft, are you?' asked Julia, pretending seriously to question him.

'Amn't I always offering? Only you know how fussy she is and – what are you smiling at?'

Julia came and sat on his lap. 'She's gone out because she knows there's something I'm bursting to tell you.'

'Oh,' he said, 'and what's that?'

'Guess.'

'Like your friend you want to move out of the street.'

'I do not!' She was genuinely indignant.

'You're sorry you married me. You want to be a nun.'

'Definitely. How did you know?'

'You've got a holy look about you these days.' He kissed her neck.

'I'm going to have another baby, please God.'

'Oh love,' he said. 'Oh, that's grand. Another little baby. Poor Ellie will have her nose put out of joint.'

'Not much chance of that where you're concerned. The other one will be lucky to catch your attention at all.'

'Is everything all right?'

'Great. August, the doctor said. Imagine that – we'll have two children, please God.'

'Maybe it'll be a little . . .'

Julia shut his mouth with a kiss, afterwards telling him, 'You must never say or even think that. Only pray for a healthy child. Now get up and help me with the Delft.'

'You know your mother was joking about that. She'd have a fit if she thought I'd really touched them. It's not a man's work, she'd say. I'm going out to do the garden.'

'Go on, then. You'd have smashed more than you washed anyway.' She kissed him again before getting off his lap.

Jack had worked hard in the garden. By Good Friday he'd have a few drills of potatoes sown, and the slips of honeysuckle planted by the wire near the embankment were showing signs of catching. As the evenings lengthened he worked until it got dark, happy and contented, creating the garden Julia wanted. Envisaging the square of grass where Ellie and the new baby could play. One evening thinking of the swing he would build for them, he suddenly felt a great sadness that Ellie, still not yet two when the other one arrived, would no longer be the baby. Out of

125

her cot and pram – the eldest. His Ellie that it seemed only such a short time ago was born. She was beautiful and never mind what his mother-in-law said about turning her head, he would keep on telling her so as she grew up. She had spirit, too – you could detect that already. Sometimes she was a little divil. Julia's mother said it was because she only had to whimper and he'd pick her up. He didn't believe that. He didn't think you should leave a baby to cry, even if they weren't hungry, wet or dirty. Couldn't they be lonely up in a room on their own, wanting their mammy and daddy, frightened, and how else could they let you know only by crying? God knows they'd grow up soon enough. You only had to look around you to notice that once a child was walking and talking it was little nursing they demanded.

The feckin' weeds, he muttered to himself, you only had to turn your back on a patch that minutes before had appeared free of them and look round to find them sprouting. He began raking them out when he saw Barney come out of the scullery and call to him, 'You're always making a rod for my back.'

Laying down the rake he went to meet him. 'I haven't seen you this two days – and how am I making a rod for your fine broad back? We'll go in and have a cup of tea.'

Barney went before him into the house, talking as he went. 'You seem to have taken the Pledge, that's why.'

'I can seldom afford a drink nowadays,' Jack said as he pulled the kettle over the fire.

'Where's Julia and her ma?' Barney asked.

'In the parlour doing something with a frock.'

'I was joking about you and not drinking – I seldom go myself now. It's Sarah that's my trouble. Nowadays she's ready to fight with her nails. I don't know what ails her.'

'She might be fed up living with her mother. I wouldn't say she'd be easy to get on with. Maybe she wants her own place,' Jack said as he wet the tea.

'She could have had one. After my mother died and the others got married our house was idle for weeks. But you're right, she does want a place of her own but not here, not in the street. Somewhere with a good address. On what I earn, what chance is there of that?'

'Little, I'd say.'

'You know I love the ground she walks on. I'd do anything for her, anything, but she's so hard to please. She bites the head off me for nothing. You should have heard her at teatime when I forgot and called the child Paddy. If I'd called him a bastard she couldn't have given out

126

more. Of course I know she's not well. Delicate, since the birth. Ah well, I suppose things will change.'

Sarah delicate? Jack would never have said that. She looked as strong as a horse.

'I was thinking,' said Barney, 'when the weather gets fine maybe we could go somewhere – up the mountains, take a picnic like we used to. The children are old enough now. It might cheer her up. What d'ye say?'

'That'd be great. I'll tell Julia, get her and Sarah to arrange something. Easter Monday if it's a good day.'

'D'ye remember all the times we had up there when we were courting? D'ye remember one day ...' Barney reminisced for a while longer and then said he'd better be going or else Sarah would have a face on her.

In bed that night Jack told Julia what Barney had said about Sarah being delicate. She laughed. 'Sarah's never been sick in her life. I never even remember her having a cold. She doesn't like housework and she doesn't want any more children. Her mother does all the work. Poor Barney. You know what she's using her delicacy for.'

'But that's a sin – she'd have to confess it,' said Jack.

In the darkness Julia smiled at his innocence. 'Sarah,' she said, 'is a law unto herself even in Confession, not that I think she often goes.'

'She's on at him to move out of the street, to a good address. Did you know that?'

'Since the night you were coming home from France. I wouldn't mind that, she's always had notions of grandeur. Nothing will come of it – how could it, and he earning no more than you? Every time I'm expecting I get sleeping sickness. I dozed after dinner for an hour and now I can't keep my eyes open.' They kissed goodnight and in seconds she was asleep.

The urge to pee awoke her. She got out of bed and used the chamber pot. Then she heard a noise from outside, a sound as if something had hit or fallen on metal. She thought of the meat safe in the yard with its metal frame. Something had struck it. Moving to the window, she looked through a chink where the curtains didn't meet and saw a figure hurrying over Jack's plot. She couldn't tell if it was a man or woman. It was biggish and stocky. And then she saw what at first she thought was a large stick being carried by the person, hanging down by their side: *it was a rifle*. For a second she froze with terror then went to the bed, pulling at Jack and crying: 'Jack, Jack! There's a man in the garden – a man with a rifle! Quick, quick,' she urged as she went back to the window. At her side Jack looked through the chink in the curtains. She put an arm round him. 'D'ye see him? He's got a rifle.'

Her voice was panicky. She moved in front of him to see out as Jack said, 'There's no one there, love.' She didn't detect the catch in his voice, any more than she had noticed his trembling.

'But there was! I saw him – walking down the garden. *And* he had a rifle. I saw him – I'm telling you he was there!'

'Come back to bed. It must have been a nightmare,' he said placatingly.

'A nightmare?' Her voice rose, which it seldom did.

'Shh,' Jack said soothingly. 'You'll waken the child.'

'I don't care. D'ye think I'm mad, or what? A nightmare! How could it have been a nightmare – I was up, awake, using the chamber.'

'All right, all right. But get into bed. There's no one there now.' He covered her. 'I'll go down and make a cup of tea and when I come up tell me all about it.' She knew he was humouring her. She was angry. She wanted to shout, to scream at him, at anyone to relieve the fright she still felt. But remembering Ellie and her mother sleeping in the next room she remained quiet.

While he waited for the kettle to boil he smoked two cigarettes, lighting the second from the butt of the first to calm his nerves. Julia wasn't an alarmist. Julia didn't see things that weren't there. Who was it in the garden? 'Oh God,' he prayed, 'don't let them be using the house again. Not now when the city is like a powder keg just waiting for a spark. Don't let them be endangering my family. Bringing trouble into my home.' He had thought it was all finished. Long done with. Over when the Librarian had gone away, no one knew where. Gone without a word, without a goodbye.

'Put something round you,' Julia told him when he came upstairs. 'You look terrible. I hope you didn't catch a chill.'

To please her he draped a baby's shawl round his shoulders. 'Drink this and then tell me exactly what you saw,' he said quietly.

In between sips of tea Julia related what she had seen. He questioned her. 'Are you sure it was a rifle?' She admitted that at first she thought it might have been a stick, a hurley even. He grasped at straws. A man on the run would hardly carry a hurleying stick. 'Was he tall?' She wasn't sure. What difference did it make whether he was tall, short, fat or thin? She had *seen* him. 'I was just wondering if it could have been Mag. I've seen her myself wandering at night. Down through our garden, into other gardens, around about and then up on to the embankment.'

'I'd have known Mag.'

'Not if it's still dark, you mightn't. It must have been her – sure who else could it have been round here?' Jack needed to convince her, for he needed to convince himself. He didn't, but she pretended to be satisfied with the explanation and lay down again and he held her hand until she slept.

His own fears kept his mind in ferment, and sleep from him. Over and over again he told himself it had to be Mag. It was last year, before Ellie was born, that anyone had used the house. He hadn't wanted to get involved. It just happened – out of pity and gratitude, and owing to his own weakness and inability to refuse the Librarian. His sympathies were not with the men on the run, not when they shot and bombed and killed. Never that – not if Ireland had to wait a million years for her independence, never that.

'Sweet Jesus,' he asked, 'why did I let myself be drawn in? If only I had the time over again.' He had tried to dissociate himself from the obligation. Plucking up his courage, he had gone during his dinner-hour some months before to see the Librarian, to tell him to put the word about that his home was no longer a safe house. The stranger behind the desk had shrugged when he asked for Seamus. 'He's vanished, you might say. Here one evening, and not been seen since.'

'Could I get in touch with him – write or anything? He must be in another branch.'

'If he is,' said the man, 'it's one I've no knowledge of. I'd leave it there if I were you.' And so he had drawn his own conclusions. The Librarian had been tumbled. The Castle had a powerful network, but Michael Collins had a better one and had reached the Librarian first. He could be anywhere by now – spirited to America, Australia or England, or even still in Dublin or Ireland, like Collins himself, moving from place to place under the nose of the authorities. He would never know.

Jack had liked him. He was a good friend, who might have mis-understood his interest in Irish history. In different times they could have enjoyed each other's company. 'Oh God', he prayed silently as the early-morning light came into his safe warm bedroom with Julia snoring softly and Ellie now and then moving in her cradle, 'don't let word have been put out again that my home is a safe house. Not now when this war is at its height. When night after night the Tans are raiding homes, not caring if the people living there are innocent.' Picking people up who were out after curfew, including one poor unfortunate prostitute known as Honour Bright (her word of faith), who had been found shot dead and dumped in the mountains.

Things were really hotting up. There was a price on Collins' head. The authorities were under pressure to finish this Anglo-Irish War as they called it. Even the English papers were appalled at the brutality of the Tans, not that they were any more brutal than the other side. But the Tans, even if in name only, were supposed to be representing the Crown.

He got up, washed and shaved. His thoughts became more rational for as long as he wielded his cut-throat razor. Its movements demanded concentration and the sweet-smelling soap and warm water had a soothing effect. Unfortunately, this reprieve lasted no time. Again he was thrown into despair at the thought of not knowing where to turn, or whom he could trust to put word about that his home wasn't to be used? With whom could he talk over his fear? For all he knew, the new Librarian could be in the pay of the Castle and use the information against him. Or he could be with the other crowd and brand him as an informer.

What a time to live in. Not to know who anyone is, to have no one to turn to, no one to trust. He could only put his trust in God – pray to God to guard his family. He went out to the lavatory. It was going to be a lovely day. Already the sun was warm and not a cloud in the sky. Despite his fear and depression, Jack's heart lifted. He looked in the garden for a clue as to who it might have been during the night – a hurley stick would put his mind at rest – but he found nothing. It had rained towards dawn but had there been footprints of Mag or someone else, he didn't find them. Then he remembered something that gave him some consolation. Whereas once the back and front doors were left unlocked all night as in the daytime, since the arrival of the Tans Julia bolted and locked them before she went to bed. So if it was someone other than Mag last night, they'd have found no welcome and would put the word about to leave the place alone. For the first time since the night before, Jack breathed more easily. Saliva flowed again in his mouth; he even whistled as he boiled another kettle for the women's early-morning tea.

It wasn't until he was walking to work that he remembered the outside lavatory. It had a little bolt on the inside, but outside, it was open to the world. A desperate man could spend a night there.

Patrick had been cross during the night; he was cutting back teeth. Barney had walked the floor with him singing every song that came into his mind while from the bed Sarah complained that the crying was giving her a headache. Her black hair was spread on the pillow and her creamy rounded arms were outside the sheet. The child quietened. Barney slowed the pace of his singing and patting. He felt the baby's body relax against him. He was asleep but for a little while longer he walked and soothingly patted the child's back.

When he laid him in his cot, Patrick whimpered. Barney rocked the cot gently until the whimper of protest subsided and he went back to his own bed. At his approach, Sarah turned on to her side, her nightdress riding up as she did, so that when he turned back the sheet her fine rosy arse was exposed. He wanted to jump on her and have his way but didn't, knowing exactly where that would get him. For not once since the birth of the baby had she let him make love to her. He was going out of his mind for the want of her. It wasn't her fault that she refused him, he knew that. Another baby could be the cause of killing her. Every so often she went to the doctor to see if her insides had improved. They hadn't. She cried when she told him this, telling him how sorry she was for not being a good wife. And she did what she could to relieve him. But it wasn't the same as the real thing.

The next morning as he walked along the side of the Green to work his mind was full of his grievance. Thinking about it gave him an erection. A bedraggled prostitute passed him. Out all night, he thought. Last week after he had knocked off, one had approached him. 'Are you doing business, sir?' she asked. He was sorely tempted. Up like a ramrod his yoke had stood. The feckin' thing – just the thought or mention of sex and up it shot. He had mumbled a refusal to the prostitute and walked on with her, 'Fuck you, then!' ringing in his ears.

It was money that had stopped him. His tips never fluctuated by the amount a wigger would have cost – which was five or maybe ten bob, according to the fellas in work. How would he have explained the shortage to Sarah? You couldn't lie to her. Her eyes were like magnets drawing the truth out of you. And if he looked away to avoid them, the game was up.

The fellas in work had the highest praise for the brassers. They were the cure, they said, for a man with his wife up the pole or delicate. They'd do things that the missus would think were a mortal sin. He'd love to commit a mortal sin with a prostitute, Barney said to himself as he stepped over the heavy looped chains edging the pavement, hastily adding, 'God forgive me' to his unspoken thoughts.

'There y'are,' said the night porter as he entered the Club. 'Thanks be to Jaysus you're a great timekeeper. I'm out on my feet. There's a message for you.' He handed Barney a folded sheet torn from the desk memo pad. 'From his nibs, Glenivy. He wants to see you in the private room at eleven sharp.'

Barney immediately imagined the worst. 'I've slipped up somewhere. Forgot something – didn't pass on an important message. I'll be sacked. Sarah'll kill me.' He read the note confirming what the night porter had said, and while putting on his monkey-jacket, worried aloud. 'That's strange – the private room and all.' He held in his belly to button the jacket.

'Usen't your wife to work for him? Maybe he wants to ask after her. He's bound to know you have a chiseller – he'll be wanting to congratulate you, slip you a few bob. The gentry are very correct about things like that.'

'Not nearly twelve months after the child is born they're not. In any case, something like that he'd have done at the desk, not in the private room.'

'That's right enough – now you have me puzzled. I know,' he said, after giving the impression he was thinking. 'D'ye ever go in the Gallery?'

Barney looked genuinely puzzled as he said, 'Never, why?'

'There's pictures and statues in there, of cherubs or angels they call them – little boys, and do you know what? Now that I come to think of it, you're the spitten image of them! With that butter wouldn't melt in your mouth sort of face, and with that pot belly, you're one of them to a tee. Some ould fellas like that look. You'd want to watch yourself with Glenivy – in the private room and all. I've heard a few things about him.' Playfully the porter made as if to jab Barney in the belly, drawing back his fist at the last minute. 'For the love of Jaysus will you take that worried look off your face. The oul bollocks can't eat you. I'm off. All the best. See you tonight.'

Barney began his work, sorting the mail, putting letters and small packages into their pigeonholes, checking that the ashtrays were emptied and properly cleaned, and that the newspapers and magazines had been delivered and in the correct numbers, putting aside any with wrinkles for ironing. He went about his tasks, every now and then looking at the tall clock in the hall, willing its hands to move faster, on to one o'clock so that his meeting with Lord Glenivy was behind him, then panicking at the prospect of the encounter, he wished for a momentous happening like a gun battle in the Green, a fire or a bomb in the Shelbourne Hotel, something big like the burning down of the Customs House – *anything* that would lead to the meeting being cancelled.

At five to eleven he stood quaking outside the private room, trying to pull in his belly and tugging at the monkey-jacket. On the first stroke of eleven he knocked on the door, but several minutes passed before he was called to come in. The extra wait increased his apprehension.

He opened the door and stood just inside its threshold. Lord Glenivy wore a lovat tweed. His face had the silky sheen about it which Barney had noticed on many of the gentry. The maroon leather, brass-studded armchair came high above the back of his head. He was reading a newspaper and continued to do so while Barney, despite his nervousness, noticed on the occasional table a coffee pot, cream jug, suger basin and one cup. The smell of coffee and cigar smoke was in the room. He waited while Lord Glenivy turned several more pages before raising his head and saying, 'Ah, Daly, there you are. Shut the door like a good chap, then come and sit down.'

'Yes, sir.' Barney controlled his desire to salute.

'Here,' said Lord Glenivy, indicating a chair at the other side of the occasional table. 'Now then, how are you getting along in the job?'

'Great, sir. Grand.'

'Not the sort of thing you were used to is it? A bit dull after the army, wouldn't you say?'

'You could say that, sir. It's not a bit like the army.'

'Ah, yes. Nothing like the army if you like soldiering. Which reminds me,' here Lord Glenivy told a deliberate lie. 'I met your CO last week, in London. Your name came up.' He had, it was true, met Barney's CO and they had talked about many things including the situation in Ireland, but of Barney and the other ranks who had served with him no mention was made. 'He told me you were a damn good soldier.'

'Major Barrington, sir. You know the Major?' Admiration was audible in Barney's voice. The Major was one of his heroes.

'We were at school together.' Lord Glenivy took his time preparing and lighting a large cigar. When it was going to his satisfaction he spoke again. 'Served in India together.'

It was very warm in the room. Barney, though now less apprehensive since the mention of the Major, was physically uncomfortable. His jacket kept riding up, the crotch of his trousers was too tight, he was gasping for a smoke, but was afraid to light up and didn't have the nerve to ask permission. And he was ill at ease sitting in the presence of an officer or gentry. Lord Glenivy was both. Only in the trenches had he ever sat while they were about.

In between puffs of fragrant smoke Lord Glenivy continued with his fabricated line. 'Major Barrington spoke highly of you, Daly. Thought you were quite heroic.' Barney's face flushed with pleasure. 'Very impressed indeed. Said if the war hadn't finished when it did, you would have been made up and possibly decorated.'

'It was the time I went out with the grenade,' Barney thought, and rewrote the scenario. The grenade hadn't fizzled out on the wrong side of the parapet. The gun and its crew were blown sky high. He heard the cheers of the lads go up. Then he'd lain doggo until it got dark and crawled back to his own lines.

'No need for me to explain to a chap like you who spent years at the Front that there's a war going on here, too. More sinister than in France,

133

though. There at least you knew your enemy. Not so here, eh, wouldn't you agree, Daly?'

'I suppose so. It is hard to tell who's who.'

'Damnably so. That's why I sent for you – someone I can trust. Someone with your proven record. There are few men of your calibre about, and if this ghastly business is to be stopped, we need your help. Look at that dreadful thing with the Customs House. Appalling. Innocent men and women being murdered. Property destroyed. The streets not safe for our wives to walk in.' Lord Glenivy laid down his cigar and enviously Barney eyed it. 'What I have to say now is in the strictest confidence. As a soldier you'll understand the importance of that.'

'Indeed, sir. Security and all that.'

'Exactly. The thing is, we need all the information we can get. Only with the right intelligence network can we hope to stop this ghastly violence.'

Barney was sweating profusely and finding it difficult to understand what Lord Glenivy wanted of him. Was he suggesting that he should rejoin the army? Sarah would never stand for that. Or worse still, did he want him in the Black and Tans? He'd be strung up in the street if he joined them. Gathering every ounce of his moral courage he forced himself to query what had been said. 'I'm not exactly sure, sir, where I come into any of this. Were you wanting me to join up again? I'm married and the wife . . .'

'Good God no, man. Nothing like that. It's intelligence work. Here in the city – in the Club. Just a matter of keeping your eyes and ears open when you go on errands to other clubs or hotels, or when you're in the public houses and on the trams, where you live . . . You get on well with people, don't you? I can tell you do. So talk, but most important – *listen*. As a soldier you'll be observant and have a good memory: ideal for the job. What we want to hear is anything that seems, if only slightly, out of the ordinary. You'll be paid, of course – a weekly sum, somewhere in the region of thirty shillings. Think about it. You might be the one who cracks this thing, who catches the big fish, on whose head there is a substantial reward. Let me know by Thursday, same time as today.'

Barney had risen when Lord Glenivy did. He was dizzy from the heat and his restricting clothes, but most of all with the sense of pride surging through him.

'Very well then, Daly. See you on Thursday.'

Knowing he was dismissed he almost saluted, almost about-turned, but not quite and left the room.

★

'How did it go?' the night porter asked when he came to relieve him.

'You were right. He asked about Sarah and Patrick and into the bargain slipped me a few bob.'

'A few bob?'

'Five quid,' lied Barney, and began changing into his outdoor things.

At about the same time as Barney stood outside the door of the private room, Sarah with Patrick arrived at Julia's to gossip and talk about the proposed outing to Glenasmole at Easter. She put the baby on the floor beside Ellie and Julia gave him a blue sugar bag that still had a few grains in it to rattle.

'I saw your mother on her way out.'

'She's gone for ribs for Jack's tea,' Julia said, putting cups and saucers on the table.

'You're looking very tired – did she keep you awake?'

'No, she's as good as gold.'

'Not like him, he's a crying jinnet.'

'I have to get up a few times to pee, you know what it's like.'

'Will I ever forget it,' said Sarah. The babies, fed up with their rattles, started crawling towards the fireplace.

'Put the chairs down, will you Sarah, while I wet the tea.'

Sarah laid two kitchen chairs on their sides and wedged them so they wouldn't tip and penned a child between the rungs of each chair saying as she did so, 'You should have seen the things they had in the nursery in Glenivy. Chairs, small high ones you could feed a baby in, another thing on wooden wheels like a sort of basket with holes for the legs. I suppose a child not able to walk could, in a yoke like that. Not that there were any babies while I was there.'

'Go way, imagine having such things – they'd be a great help in rearing children,' said Julia, sitting down and pouring the tea.

'Barney was telling me about going up the mountains. I'd love that.'

'We'll go then if the weather's fine.'

They talked for a while about the outing to Glenasmole, planning what they would take to eat, what time would be best to set off, recalling other times when as a foursome they had gone up the mountains. The babies became tired of their imprisonment and started crying, were freed and taken on their mothers' laps, given sips of milky tea and buttered crusts. Then Julia asked a question: 'Do women ever go mad when they're pregnant?'

'Not that I've heard of, though some do after the birth. Why?' Julia told her about seeing someone in the garden during the night, how Jack hadn't believed her; he'd humoured her, said she'd had a nightmare.

'That was because you broke his sleep. My fella's the same – like a divil if he doesn't get his sleep,' Sarah said. Her mind wasn't really on what Julia was telling her. She was looking through the kitchen window now and then as Julia continued with her story, thinking of how, when she had her own place, she'd show people what a garden should be like.

'I think he had a rifle,' Julia was saying. 'Anyway, he was carrying something. I suppose it could have been a stick or a hurley. Jack tried to convince me it was Mag, so I let on I believed him.'

'It could have been. Well, who else would you get around here in the middle of the night?'

'Anyone, I suppose, in the times that are in it. I was afraid of my life.'

'Put it out of your mind – it was Mag for sure. Would you never ask her?'

'Poor Mag, a lot of sense I'd get out of her.'

'You're right.' Sarah sighed. 'I could stay here for hours but I'd better be going. My ma's gone into town. She's very cranky these days, you know, about Patrick pulling the house about. We had a row before she went. She wants it tidy by the time she gets back.'

Julia saw her to the door carrying Ellie, picking up her hand, waving it and saying, 'Patrick's going home. Wave "day, day".'

CHAPTER TWELVE

Fifty pounds in her own account and a few pounds in the joint one ...
that wouldn't take them far. At this rate she'd be stuck in the street for
years. Patrick would grow up as common as all the others in it, Barney
was a useless husband – only the one thing on his mind. Well, he could
whistle for that. If only there was some way of making money. She'd do
anything for it.

She looked at the clock: her husband would be home soon, looking
for food. Her mother and father were in bed, more's the pity: it'd give
him an excuse to get up to his tricks. Not that he'd get anywhere. She
clipped the rinds on a couple of rashers and put the frying pan on a low
heat. Marriage was a cod – well, it was if you had no money. Scrimping
and saving, trying to better yourself for the sake of the child. And if
things had gone different the life she'd be leading now. Patrick with his
nursery and a nurse to mind him. Lovely clothes, never having to soil
her hands. It wasn't fair, life wasn't. Why should that skinny bitch have
had Patrick and not her? It all came back to money. To get anywhere
you had to have money. There must have been a time when the Glenivys
had nothing – in the beginning when no one had, hundreds and hundreds
of years ago. There wasn't always castles and mansions. Someone belonging to them would have started off in a small way and worked their way
up.

Well, she'd see to it that her son had his chance. Tooth and nail she'd
fight for it. By rights he was owed that chance. She heard Barney
whistling as he came into the hall, then he called her name. 'Sarah, are
you there, Sarah?'

'No,' she called back. 'Like every other night I'm out.' He got in on
her nerves. 'Wait'll you hear the news,' he said, entering. 'Make a cup
of tea.'

'Mind your orders now – I was just going to fry your supper. Can't
you wait for the tea?'

'I'm that excited I couldn't eat. Wait'll I tell you. We're made!'

'Made? What are you on about now?' she asked impatiently. He was
used to her impatience, her abruptness. He didn't mind – it was her way.
Fiery, she was. He loved her in all her humours. She made the tea and
joined him at the table. 'Well, go on. Tell me what's so marvellous.'

'Lord Glenivy sent for me this morning.' For a second she held her breath – surely to God he hadn't said anything about the baby – about Patrick. Then told herself she was a fool. The Glenivys had never acknowledged that the child was anything to do with them. 'I wish you could have been there. The things he said about me. I was ten foot high.' She was bored already imagining him being complimented on how he ironed the papers. And eejit that he was, he'd swally every word. But as Barney unfolded the story and mentioned the extra money and maybe a reward, she sat up straight and listened to every word. And when there was no more to tell he asked, 'Well, what d'ye think?'

'Think of what?'

'Should I do it, what he wants?'

'I thought you were full of the idea.'

'I was. All the way home I could think of nothing else, but now I'm not so sure. What do you think of it?' he asked again.

She took her time about answering the question. Poured him another cup of tea and offered him a piece of cake before saying, 'Sure you know as well as me I've a head like a sieve. I rely on you to make the decisions. You look very tired – we should go to bed early. Sleep on it and maybe in the morning it'll be clear in your head.'

She was so understanding. He'd been the lucky man to get her for a wife. He ate the seed cake, which he didn't like – she must have forgotten. He began to talk again. 'I suddenly saw what Lord Glenivy suggested in a new light. I'd be a traitor, wouldn't I? I'd be betraying my own people.'

'I suppose some people might look at it like that – red-hot Republicans. No one with an ounce of sense would. You never belonged to any of the organisations. You never gave them a thought. To betray someone you'd have to belong, be part of them. At least, that's the way I see it.'

'There is that to it,' Barney agreed.

'You took an oath to no one except the King. In one way what you were asked to do could be considered no more than doing your duty. You have to admit most of the Republican army are no better than murderers.' She let that sink in before continuing, 'Look at what they did with the Customs House. Do you know that in years to come if we wanted a copy of Patrick's birth certificate we mightn't be able to get one. And in any case, you probably won't find out a thing. Don't let it worry you. Finish that tea and we'll have an early night.' Going up the stairs she told herself to go very easy. Let Barney believe he was making his own decision. One false move and he might go to Jack for advice. Then she'd be done for. High-minded Jack would finish her chance of extra money.

138

'You forgot to ask about the doctor,' she said, sitting on the side of the bed, her skirt up, rolling down her stockings in a leisurely way.

'I'm sorry, love, it went right out of my mind with the other thing happening.' Her thighs were fat and the colour of cream. She was that beautiful he could eat her. He sat beside her and stroked her leg. 'What did he say?'

'I was never so embarrassed in my life. He was too, I could tell. He kept fiddling with things on his desk and not meeting my eyes. I don't suppose many women talk about such things to their doctors, but as I said to him, it's not fair on my husband. I know my insides are delicate but I do be that upset refusing him night after night. So he suggested something.'

'What?'

'Come here and I'll whisper it to you.' She held his head close to her lips and told him her mother's advice on how to let a man have his way without getting pregnant. Advice given ages ago and ignored, but tonight she'd let him and make sure he made no mistakes.

Afterwards he talked. 'I've made my decision. It's my duty: it's to the authorities I owe my loyalty. Them gougers are nothing but a crowd of murderers.' Sarah lay very still and silent. Barney continued: 'I'll keep my eyes and ears open and report to his Lordship on Thursday.'

She kissed him. 'You're a good man and a brave one. I'm only sorry the war didn't last long enough for you to get a medal. Talking of which reminds me – will you mention anything to Jack?'

'I hadn't thought about that. What d'ye think?'

'If it was me I wouldn't. But it's different for you – he *is* your best friend, though he has too much admiration nowadays for everything Irish. I wouldn't even tell my mother.'

'Not tell your mother!'

'No, no one. But that's my way of thinking. This is your business.'

'I'll have to think about it.' Shortly before he went to sleep he told her he had decided not to mention a word to Jack.

On the following two Thursdays he reported to Lord Glenivy. At the first meeting he repeated gossip heard in public houses, hotel kitchens and in the Club itself. 'Docherty, sir, he works in the Shelbourne. I heard him talking about going down to Cork during next week. A wedding, so he said. As far as I know he hasn't friends nor relations in Cork.' There were similar incidents to relate about other men. He gave names and their place of work. And when he'd finished Lord Glenivy said, 'Keep up the good work, Daly,' and handed him a brown envelope with the thirty shillings in it.

Life had never been better. Sarah was very considerate and he could pass a prostitute without giving her a glance. Now and then a little niggle agitated his brain. Had any one of the staff, he wondered, copped on that twice now he had been up to the private room? After considering the question he was able to dismiss the niggle. For his first visit he had a good excuse and no one knew about the second. That had been arranged between himself and his Lordship – the same as the next one. He was in the clear. Even if someone did get nosy he always had the excuse of Sarah having worked for the Glenivys, her mother as well. Lady Glenivy was interested in their health, in the child, in arranging an errand she wanted done in town. Tons of excuses he had for going to the private room.

By Wednesday of the following week his spirits were low. Docherty was as large as life hailing cabs outside the Shelbourne and regaling anyone willing to listen with how legless he got at the wedding in Cork. The same as the others whose names he had given to his Lordship – not a bother on them. And had they been interrogated, all of Dublin would now be the wiser. He couldn't understand it: maybe they were being watched, but he didn't think that was how it was done. Not with things as they were. You couldn't afford to let the grass grow under your feet, not with bombs going off and people being killed left right and centre. What it meant was that his information was duff.

Going to the next meeting he felt a failure and had a sense of foreboding. After making his report he apologised, 'I'm not sure, sir, if what I'm bringing you is of any use. I'm doing my best, but . . .'

Brusquely Lord Glenivy cut short his attempt at further excuses. 'I'll be the judge of that. Carry on with the report, Daly.'

He left the room believing he was finished. Tomorrow there'd be a note cancelling any further meetings. It stood to reason. He could tell from his Lordship's manner. No mention of, 'Carry on the good work, Daly,' just the envelope pushed across the desk. The last one he'd ever handle. Sarah would go demented, her nerves get bad again, her insides affected. All finished and just when things were going so well between them. If only something big would come his way . . . something definite, something important to report, but in his heart he knew nothing like that was likely. He was finished. Gone down in his Lordship's estimation. In Major Barrington's, too. They were bound to talk about him when they met again in London. But worse than anything was breaking the news to Sarah.

By the time he got home he had convinced himself he was no longer spying for Lord Glenivy. Frightened and abject he stood before her holding out the envelope with the thirty shillings. 'That's it,' he said.

'That's what?'

'The last you'll handle. I'm finished. I've failed, I'm no use.' Tears pricked his eyes.

'You've lost your job? You've been sacked!' Her hands went to her hips, her eyes narrowed and glinted like granite chips. 'You lost your job?'

'Not exactly. Not the portering – the other part.'

'Lord Glenivy finished you?'

'As good as. Nothing was said but I got the feeling. I'm bringing him nothing worthwhile. He's not going to keep throwing good money after bad.'

'You stupid fat bastard. I could kill you.' She kept her thoughts to herself, fearing that if she gave them free rein she'd go mad. Go for him with the carving knife. Scald him with the boiling kettle. Oh Jesus, to be married to such a man. She had to get out of the room before she did something desperate.

'My head is opening,' she lied. 'I have to go to bed. Make your own tea and mind the child, my mother and father are gone out.'

The fool, he hadn't lost the job, not yet, but he would the way he was going about it. She tossed and turned on the bed, hating and despising him. Thirty shillings wouldn't have taken them out of the street in a hurry, but she had hoped that the war with the Tans and Republicans would have gone on long enough for the money to accumulate. Now the fool stood to throw away their one chance.

She despised him, him and his great big belly, his fumbling and farting. He was robbing Patrick of his chance of a better life. She wouldn't care if he dropped down dead this minute. She'd be a respectable widow, free to look for another husband. She wouldn't care if he was an oul fella so long as he had money.

From the street came the sound of Mag's raucous voice. It grated on Sarah's nerves: she had enough to contend with, without her roaring like a jackass. She would soon put a stop to it. Sarah started to get off the bed and then she remembered something which had slipped her mind, something which, if she handled it right, could turn her fortunes round. It was worth a try. Back on the bed she lay scheming and thinking, planning her every move. When she heard Barney coming upstairs she closed her eyes and pretended to be sleeping.

'That young wan Mag must have the fourleaved clover all of a sudden.'

'Why d'ye say that, Ma?' Julia asked.

Her mother was lightly kneading brown soda bread, forming it into a round cake, scoring a cross on it. She talked as she worked. 'Haven't you noticed she's practically living in Sarah's? Every time I pass the door or

141

look out she's either going in or leaving. That's not like the Quinlans.'

'Mrs Quinlan and him are down the country for a few days. I suppose Mag's company is better than no one.'

'What company? The poor child is simple.'

'She loves the baby. Sarah wouldn't leave her alone with him, but she's handy to give him a nurse. She sings him songs and says rhymes to him.'

'I wouldn't have thought she knew any.'

'You'd be surprised. She can learn things off by heart and then never forgets them.'

'You learn something every day,' said her mother philosophically, testing the oven by throwing in a handful of flour. Satisfied with the time it took to brown she placed the soda bread on the rack, brushed the flour off her hands and sat by the table where Julia was cutting vegetables.

'You're looking great, Ma, but you never went to the doctor as you promised.'

'I did no such thing as promise. I said I'd see how I went on – and I've gone on fine. Amn't I eating and sleeping – what more d'ye want?'

'You're still too thin.'

'I was always thin. I haven't a pain or ache,' Lizzie said, but never mentioned, nor wouldn't, that frequently she bled. She had months ago faced the possibility that something serious ailed her, and had told herself that something had to come for your end. She was almost seventy. She had had her three score years and ten. She was going near no hospital to have them pulling her about, cutting her open, experimenting. Bringing unnecessary worry to Julia. She would hold out for a while yet. God would be kind to her and in the end she would go quickly. Every night she prayed for a merciful death if it was pleasing to His will.

'I can't drag you to the doctor, that's for sure and certain, and you are looking well – but will you try to eat a bit more?'

Mrs Mangan gave her promise and thanks for the good daughter and son-in-law she had, knowing she could die with an easy mind. Jack was a good provider. Julia and Ellie would be safe with him. She had her policies paid up, the grave receipt. They wouldn't be out of pocket. Her small pension would die with her, but she had the savings. So long as Jack had work they would be comfortable.

'If you don't say it again I'll put Patrick upstairs in his cot and I won't let you come in to play with him.'

Mag looked up from where she sat on the floor playing 'This little piggy went to market', with Patrick's toes. 'Can't,' she said, scowling at Sarah.

'Right, out you go then. Up, come on, out you go.'

She walked towards Mag, who grinned and said : 'I was in my garden and I saw the man in Julia's garden and he had a gun – a big, huge gun.'

'Good girl. Say it again and I'll give you a bar of chocolate and you can play with Patrick.' Mag said it again, had her chocolate bar and when she'd eaten it Sarah made her say it again.

For four days she'd had her in the house coaching her in the story she was to tell Barney when he asked her. The sight and sound of Mag disgusted her. She had a horror of all physical abnormalities. She loathed seeing Mag's pudgy hands with their bitten fingernails touching Patrick, but for her plan to work the lunatic had to be endured. Sarah had to be careful how hard she pushed her. Mag was stubborn, and once in one of her moods, not all the chocolate, pennies, even Patrick could coax her out of it. So in between reciting her lines there had to be long rests.

One more day, she'd have to endure her for one more day before she told Barney, and then hope that when he questioned Mag her mind wouldn't go blank. Sarah gave her a glass of milk, let her lift and hold the baby and listened to her nonsense for more than an hour before putting her through her paces again.

Her mother would be home the day after tomorrow. Mag had to be word-perfect by then, for her mother mustn't know anything of what was going on. As she had told Barney when he first went to work for Glenivy, she wouldn't take anyone into her confidence. Her mind worked this way and that thinking of the best way to approach him with what she believed could be the makings of them.

The night after Mag's final rehearsal, she pleaded a headache and went up to bed early. When Barney came into the room later, she opened her eyes. 'You woke me,' she said, mildly accusing.

'I'm sorry, love.'

'It's all right.'

'How is your head ?'

'Not too bad. I have so much on my mind, that's what caused it. I wanted to talk to you but with my mother being there I couldn't.'

'What is it? Tell me.' Barney's voice was full of concern and his face anxious-looking. 'You're not sick or anything, like you know ...'

She laughed. 'No I'm not, so don't look so worried. In myself I've never felt better. I feel nearly as well as before I had Patrick. If this keeps up, maybe a little sister or brother would be nice for him. No, what ails me is something I have on my mind. Something Julia told me a while ago, but it slipped my mind at the time. Then all of a sudden this morning

I remembered it, and it might be important. Come to bed and I'll tell you. See what you think about it.'

In bed she moved close to him and repeated to him how Julia had told her about the man in the garden. He only half-listened, his mind on other, pleasanter things.

'You're not listening!' She took his hand away from between her legs. 'It's serious, Barney, now listen. Move over there until I've finished what I have to say.' She related the story again.

'So,' he said when she had finished. 'Jack was right. It must have been Mag.'

'Ah,' she said, 'but it wasn't, for I asked her.'

'She's half-daft – you couldn't believe a word out of her mouth.'

'Not about this, she's not. But more than that, wasn't it a funny thing that Jack did nothing about it, about the man I mean? You'd have gone out to see if there was anyone there. You might have reported it to the police.'

'I'm not sure about the police but I'd certainly have gone out. Jack though isn't like that. He's a cautious sort.'

'A bit too cautious if you ask me. Maybe he had something to hide.'

Barney sat up in the bed and pulled the string that ignited the mantle. Leaning over Sarah he asked, 'What in the name of God are you getting at?'

'I'm not sure. That's what's been giving me the headache. Not knowing if I should mention it to you with Jack being your best friend.'

'I still don't see what a man in their garden has to do with Jack. It could have been anyone.'

'Then tell me this: why did he go to such lengths to make Julia think she hadn't seen a man? D'ye know what she asked me – did I think she was going mad? He must have something to hide if he went that far to convince her she hadn't seen anything.'

Barney got out of bed and sat on the side. He lit a Woodbine before saying anything else. 'Are you trying to tell me he's implicated in something?'

'I don't want to believe it, not about Jack. Then things keep coming back to me. You told me yourself he was sorry he ever went to the war. How he'd known nothing about Ireland before he got the job and started reading. And look at the way he goes about learning Irish. He's changed since he went to work in that place.'

'That's right enough, but he hasn't got anything to do with the Republicans.'

'He wouldn't have to join them to hide someone.'

'Not Jack, never Jack.'

'You just think about what I've told you. And Mag *saw* the man.'

'For Jaysus' sake will you give over about Mag – she's not right in the head. I wish you hadn't said anything. You've got my head going now.'

'Ah darling, I'm sorry. Come back to bed and I'll kiss it better. I'm really sorry but I had to tell you. If it's true it's your duty to know.'

'What d'ye mean, my duty?'

'Well, the work you do for Lord Glenivy.'

'Fuck Lord Glenivy – it's Jack you're talking about. Jack my best friend, the man who saved my life, don't forget.'

'And might be the cause of you, me and Patrick losing ours.'

'How d'ye say that?'

'Supposing I'm right and it's a big bug he's hiding, you could have the Tans up here, a battle, the houses burned from under us.'

'What are you saying? That I should inform on him?'

'Oh love, I wouldn't tell you what you should do. You'll make up your mind to do what's right. I know you.' She stroked his face, her fingers slowly moving to his ear which she caressed.

'Even if I wanted to I couldn't – not inform on Jack. They'd shoot him.'

'No, they wouldn't. He'd be lifted and go to gaol, that's all. I've done all I can – you think about it and see Mag. She's not such a fool as you think. Ask her.' Her hand moved down his chest, stroking, and down and down. 'Will you do that for me, only that, please?' She paused for his answer before guiding him in.

He looked ill when he came home on Wednesday night.

'What ails you?' Sarah asked.

'What d'ye think! It keeps going round and round in my brain until I think my head will burst. One minute I tell myself there's nothing in it – Julia was dreaming or it was Mag in the garden. Then the next minute I remember some of the quare things he says about Ireland – about a free and independent Ireland. And if it is true, whoever it was could have stayed the night in the lav.'

'I thought of that myself. And another thing, this street being so out of the way the authorities would never have given it a second glance.' She put his tea before him – a piece of fried pork steak smothered in onions.

He pushed it away. 'I couldn't stomach anything.' She coaxed him to taste it, but he refused.

'Will you, at least hear what Mag has to say. I know she's a bit soft in the head, but just hear her out. After that we'll say no more about it. I'll go for her now while my ma and da are doing their novena. All right?'

145

He nodded resignedly and she went running to fetch Mag, hoping she'd be in good humour, hoping she'd remember what she was supposed to say. She had in the pocket of her pinnie a bar of chocolate which she fed to her on the way back. Suddenly she realised she had forgotten the most important part of the plan – Patrick. Without him Mag wouldn't talk. She'd think she was being punished if he wasn't there, and sulk.

'Listen,' she said, just before they got to the door. 'You stand here just for a minute, here's sixpence. Stand here and I'll bring you in in two shakes.' Mag, engrossed in examining the sixpence, mumbled what sounded like, 'yeah'. Quietly Sarah went into the hall, thankfully saw that the kitchen door was shut, crept up the stairs and lifted Patrick roughly from his cot. He started to cry. 'Barney,' she shouted as she came back down the stairs. 'Did you not hear the child?' By the time he opened the kitchen door she had Mag in the hall with her arms outstretched for the baby, who willingly went to her.

'Barney wants you to tell him what you saw.' Mag looked at Sarah blankly. 'You know, in the garden – in Julia's garden,' and Sarah willed her not to go dumb, not to forget. 'Ask her Barney, go on.'

Barney began hesitantly, 'Sarah was saying, Sarah was telling me ...'

'Not like that, for God's sake, you'll get her all confused. Ask her out straight. Say, "what did you see in Julia's garden?"'

He asked. Sarah held her breath. Mag said, 'Ehhh,' looked away from Barney and into the baby's face and then repeated her lines, word perfect. Sarah sighed with relief. Barney muttered, 'Sure she could be making that up – it means nothing,' but without much certainty.

He wasn't convinced. She hadn't expected it to be that easy, but knowing him so well she had detected a note of uncertainty in his voice. There was still plenty of hope. She wanted Mag out of the house now, before her mother came from the chapel. Mag was so unpredictable: instead of as she was doing now, saying 'Goosey, goosey gander,' she could start reciting what she had learned by heart in the last few days.

'I think he's getting tired, Mag. Will we take him back to bed. I'll let you carry him. God love him, he's falling asleep.' Mag tickled Patrick too vigorously and he cried. Sarah wanted to slap her across her grinning face. Instead she said, 'I told you – he's jaded. We'll take him up.'

'It's not fair. You said I could play with him. I hate you.'

'Give her the coconut creams, Barney, quick before she starts a performance.' He brought the biscuits and Sarah took them from him. 'I'll hold him while you eat them. Here, give me the baby.' She held out the biscuits and Mag handed over Patrick, took the coconut creams and crammed both in her mouth, talking while she ate them.

'She'll choke,' said Barney.

That she might, thought Sarah. Nevertheless she watched Mag masticating until the last crumb was swallowed safely. 'I'm going home now and I'm going to tell my mammy.'

'What are you going to tell your mammy?' Barney asked, and Sarah crossed her fingers.

'I'm going to tell her,' she stopped and looked to Sarah as if seeking a prompt, then began to talk again, 'I was in my garden and I saw the man in Julia's garden and he had a gun, a big, huge gun and he went into the lav to do his pooley. I'm going home now and I'm never coming back.'

'Let her go,' said Sarah when Barney tried to detain her. She knew he wanted to ask her more questions and was afraid.

'That's done it,' he said when Mag left. 'She's not right in the head, we know that and I wasn't convinced in the beginning but the thing about the lav – she couldn't have made that up. Didn't I say that's where whoever it was would have hidden – in the lav? She saw him all right.'

'So it was worthwhile asking her.' That's all Sarah would say on the subject for the time being. She couldn't believe her luck that Mag should have come out with something she had never mentioned. She *must* have seen something that night: there *had* been a man with a gun in Julia's garden and he *had* spent the night in the lavatory. It was true! All the same, she'd say nothing more to Barney until they were in bed.

'You were right,' he said, once the bedroom door was shut. 'You were right all along. The thing about the lavatory put the finish to my doubts. Of course it doesn't mean it was Jack. Some fella might have just hopped over the wire, chanced finding a shelter.'

'I suppose that could have happened.' He was almost there. She mustn't rush him. With a little bit of help he'd talk himself around.

She undressed provocatively. 'Sure, how do we know who anyone round here is? Someone other than Jack could have arranged it, and your man got the wrong house. I wonder who he was – I wish I'd seen him. I could have trapped him in the lav.' She didn't remind him that the lavatory bolts were on the inside.

'I could have barricaded the door and you could have gone for the police. Imagine that – I could have captured him. He might even have been the big fella.' In his drawers and vest Barney sat on the side of the bed smoking one cigarette after another. 'There's a lot on his head. Surely to God Jack couldn't be implicated. I know lately he's got quare ideas – but all the same he was a British soldier.'

She couldn't resist saying, 'So were a lot of them that's up to their necks in the Republicans.'

'That's right enough. Put the light out and we'll keep nix at the

147

window. If I was to see anything, best friend or not I'd have to report it.'

In the dark, Sarah said, 'I don't suppose someone like the big fella would use the same place every night. From what I hear about Michael Collins, he moves on each time. You don't have to see anyone, Barney – you've enough evidence as it is.'

'All the same I'd feel easier in my mind if I saw someone.'

'Are you sure we can't be seen from the garden or embankment?'

'Definitely. They learned us about looking out from dark places in the army.'

Nothing moved, not a cat, not Mag, not a man. Sarah was cold, tired and impatient for an end to his dithering. 'I'm shivering,' she said. 'I'll have to go back to bed.'

'I'll stay for a few more minutes. It's not an easy thing, to blow the gaff on a mate. Maybe someone will show up.'

'I know it isn't easy for you. Stay as long as you like but put something round your shoulders. The weather's treacherous.'

He didn't stay long after her and when he was in bed she said, 'I wish I'd never mentioned it in the first place. It has you in a terrible state, torn between your best friend and your duty. If Collins *is* hiding round here and is caught, d'ye know what that'll mean?' She didn't wait for his answer. 'Well, I'll tell you – an end to this terrible business. No more killing, no more broken-hearted mothers and wives, no more fatherless children. You'd be making your bed in Heaven.'

'What would they do to Jack, though? The Tans are not like the British soldiers – some of them are bastards.'

'Arrest him, question him.'

'They've shot fellas before now.'

'Only them that put up a fight. Jack's no fool. He's not going to do that. He'd be lifted and home again in a few days.'

'Supposing he suspects me?'

'In the name of God why would he?'

'Supposing it went all right and we did get the reward, you wouldn't want to do anything hasty like moving too soon.'

'D'ye think I'm an eejit or what? . . . He's almost there,' she thought. 'I'll try the next move and if that doesn't work, nothing will.'

She kissed him, and told him not to think any more about it. In any case, there might be nothing in it. And to feck his Lordship and the thirty shillings. 'We managed before and will again. I love you,' she whispered in his ear. 'Feck Michael Collins and the reward. It's only me and you that matters. I mentioned it before about a baby – I'd love another one. It's not good for Patrick being an only child.'

'You mean,' Barney said, hardly able to breathe for the passion she was rousing in him, 'You mean – I don't have to pull out?'

'No, love, you do not.'

After he had come and lay on top of her getting his breath back, she thought, first thing in the morning I'll go to the chemist for the little black pills and if I fall and they don't work, that oul wan in Dorset Street's supposed to be very reliable.

'Sarah.'

'What, darling?' She ran her hands gently up and down his back. 'What is it, love?'

'I'll do it. I'll report to his Lordship tomorrow.'

'You've made the right decision. You're only doing your duty, I'm very proud of you.' Another go will fix him for sure. 'Wasn't it lovely, making love the way God intended us to?' Her hands were busy reviving him. Open-eyed, smiling and lying passively she thought about her new home.

CHAPTER THIRTEEN

They were having their evening meal : finnan haddock poached with an onion in milk. Jack flaked fish from the bone and fed morsels to Ellie, who made grabs for the spoon, wanting to feed herself. Julia talked about the planned trip to the mountains at Easter, saying that Barney could get someone to change with him and asking, 'What about you, love ?'

'I think it'll be OK. Let's hope the weather is fine.'

Mrs Mangan brought an applecake to the table, thinking as she did, 'Why can't they go up the mountains on their own ? The years haven't changed my opinion of Sarah. Ill-luck shines from her eyes.'

Jack said the town was alive with rumours of a Truce. 'I hope there's more to it than rumours,' he added.

'It wouldn't be before time,' announced his mother-in-law.

'Imagine, no more killings, shootings and bombings,' Julia said.

They lingered round the table, talking, laughing, playing with the baby.

'Anyone for more tea ?' Mrs Mangan asked, then cocking her head to listen, said, 'That's a peculiar noise. What is it ?'

Jack recognised it at once and his blood ran cold. 'A lorry,' he said casually. No point in alarming the women. The Black and Tans' Crossley Tender might be only passing through the street, having taken a wrong turn.

The noise grew louder. Mrs Mangan ran into the parlour and looked through the lace hangings. All the lace curtains in the street twitched. Signs of the Cross were made and prayers prayed for this symbol of evil to pass by and be gone from the little peaceful street.

Sarah and Barney watched, too. His face was ashen, his bowels loosening. 'It's them, they've come for him. Oh, Mother of the Divine Jesus, why did I do it ? They'll kill him. They're bastards. No mercy – they've no mercy.'

She grabbed and shook him. 'Keep your voice down. You did it – there's no going back. If they do anything, it'll only be to lift him, so shut up. Say or do nothing that'll bring suspicion on us. Don't forget – not even my mother knows, so keep mum. Act natural whatever happens, if you don't want to be branded as an informer.'

'Me – an informer ! You're not serious.'

'That's how you'll be seen if you give the game away. I hope Lord Glenivy has taken it into consideration.'

'If there's any trouble I'm to go immediately to the Club.' He had difficulty steadying his hand to light a cigarette.

'Me and the child as well?'

'He only mentioned me.'

'You're not scarpering and leaving *me* to face the music! It's passed by Jack's,' she said, craning her neck to see up the street.

Sighs of relief and prayers of thanksgiving were heard in every house, none more fervent than Jack's silent ones as the lorry left the street and headed on to the vacant lot. And then it turned on the waste ground.

'It's coming down again. I don't like it. There's trouble for someone, God protect us all. Let's go back in the kitchen,' Julia's mother said.

The watchers saw the Tender, the six armed men in the back, the wire netting forming a canopy above them, slow down and stop outside Jack's house. He waited for the knock or the door to be kicked in, warning the women, 'If they come here say nothing. They don't listen to reason. They'll have drink on them – you'll only inflame them.' And he thought of his position – the most terrifying, helpless, humiliating one a man could find himself in: here were the people he loved more than anything in the world, who looked to him for protection, and he would have to stand by whatever happened.

'I don't know why they've stopped here. It has to be a mistake. But say nothing, not even if they should take me. Many an innocent man they take. Maybe they'll lock me up for the night. They'll soon find out they've got the wrong man and I'll be let out. So say nothing. Don't aggravate them and it may blow over.'

He cursed himself while he waited. Cursed himself for ever having sheltered anyone, for exposing his family to such an ordeal as he was positive they would have to endure in the next few minutes. He remembered also the night Julia had said she saw someone in the garden. There must have been someone there – and another person had seen him besides Julia and they had informed on Jack. But who? Who in this street would do such a thing? How would you know, he mused despairingly. How would you know anything any more? Informers existed even within families. He had no one but himself to blame. God, how he wished to have the moment back, when he let his heart rule his head and agreed to what the Librarian asked.

He saw Julia's terror-stricken face, Ellie's laughing one and his mother-in-law's resolute expression. 'I'm so sorry,' he said mutely. 'For the world I wouldn't have harmed a hair of one of your heads, but I did. Whatever the outcome of tonight, I've changed your lives for always.'

151

The front door was burst open. The six armed men clattered down the passage and crowded into the kitchen, their guns levelled. 'Jack Harte?' the one in charge asked.

'That's me.'

'And these?' His head nodded to Julia and her mother. Jack told him who they were. 'Anyone else in the house?'

'No, no one.'

The Tan was as tall as him, about the same age. In the trenches, Jack thought, they might have been mates. Shared fags, covered each other. Got drunk together when they went for brief respites out of the lines. Tonight or tomorrow he might kill him. The world was a queer place.

Without taking his gaze from Jack the Tan gave an order. 'Search the place, everywhere – the yard, the shithouse.' Three men went noisily upstairs, another began ransacking the kitchen, the fourth and fifth men kept their guns trained on Julia and her mother. Ellie, frightened by the crashing of Delft to the floor, began to cry. Julia rocked and soothed her, their tears mingling. Flour, oatmeal, peas, lentils and custard powder were swept from the shelves and trampled underfoot.

From upstairs, resounding noises crashed above the kitchen ceiling. Flakes of plaster fell like snow, settling in the butter-dish, on the apple-cake, in the jug of milk, on Jack, Ellie, Julia's and Mrs Mangan's hair.

'Where's your gun?'

'I haven't a gun. I've never had a gun except in France.'

'Fucking traitor. You've been hiding someone. Who? Where is he?'

'No,' Jack said. 'No one.' He could control his voice but not the expression in his eyes.

'I want answers.' He remained silent. 'Ever heard of dumb insolence, mate – no, and you an ex-soldier?' the Tan said, advancing towards him. 'Punishable, dumb insolence is.'

'No!' Julia screamed, as he punched Jack in the mouth, splitting his lip. Mrs Mangan moved for a towel on the rail above the fire. 'Leave it, not another step,' barked the Tan.

'Nothing up there, nor out the back, nor in the parlour,' the men reported, returning. Blood poured from Jack's mouth. Julia swayed. Fearing that she and the child would fall, Jack spoke through his smashed mouth. 'Let my wife sit down.'

'Sit down, missus. Run a brush up the chimney,' he ordered his men. Only clumps of soot fell down. 'Right – take him out.'

'Please, oh please don't. He's done nothing. He's not a Republican.' Julia attempted to stand up and was pushed down.

'I'll be all right. Don't worry, I'll be all right. I love you.' He didn't resist. Six men, six guns, an old woman, Julia and the baby. What could he do? Tears mingled with his blood.

The guns covered Julia and her mother until the men were out of the kitchen. Fearfully they followed and saw Jack hoisted and heaved into the lorry, fall and the Tender pull away.

All the doors opened. All the neighbours came running out, Barney and Sarah amongst them. 'Why?' the voices asked. 'Why Jack, and him an ex-soldier with a medal and all? They got the wrong man.' Barney's voice was the loudest.

Sarah took Julia into the house. Brushed the flakes of plaster from her hair. Wrung out a face cloth and held it to her head. The women set about the kitchen, calling down curses on the heads of the men who had caused such wanton destruction. Upstairs the men restood upended wardrobes, did what they could with slashed mattresses and restored a semblance of order.

Sarah got Ellie ready for bed while talking consolingly to Julia, who sat as if petrified – cold, devoid of any feelings, unaware of people coming and going, hearing voices but not what they said. Sups of hot tea and teaspoons of brandy were forced between her lips. Her mother sat by her, holding her icy hand and saying, 'Pray, child,' over and over again.

The men went home and the women stayed, taking it in turns to make tea, bring in bread and butter from their own houses, keeping the fire going and talking to each other when they went into the scullery to fill the kettle.

'I think poor Julia's mind is unhinged.'

'It's hard going with her sitting as if she was turned into a stone, you know what I mean. At a wake even you have a bit of a laugh, but this – I've never seen anything like it.'

'It was all a terrible mistake – Jack Harte to be lifted.'

'A mistake it was, no doubt about that. But someone gave the Tans his name.'

'Go way! How could that be, and how d'ye know?'

'Lizzie told me. She said the minute they came in the door they said his name.'

'You know what that means? They didn't come to the wrong house. They knew who they were looking for. Some rotten bastard made it up and reported it.'

'Isn't that what I'm telling you.'

'If I knew who it was I'd swing for him.'

'Wouldn't we all.'

Julia stayed awake all night in her chair. Towards morning, her mother dozed off and then came to with a start. 'I heard something!' A look of terror was on her face.

Julia shuddered and spoke for the first time. 'You didn't dream anything bad, Ma? You didn't see anything happen to Jack – sure you didn't?'

And Lizzie replied: 'No, love. I didn't dream – honest to God. I only heard a noise as I woke.'

One of the women, as old as Mrs Mangan and well acquainted with her dreams and presentiments, laughed gently and said, 'What you heard was me. I knocked down the enamel basin – knocked the arse out of it, no doubt. It made a terrible clatter. You all heard it?'

'I didn't,' said Julia.

'Sure, you were miles away, child,' the woman assured her. 'You might have dropped off for a minute and the noise woke you like it did your mother.'

Julia appeared to accept the explanation. The sun came up. In the daylight she came alive again and began to hope. They'd locked him up for the night. Now that it was morning they'd find out their mistake. He'd be home. He'd be home soon.

She'd wash her face and comb her hair. She must look a sight – she'd tidy herself for Jack. She was thirsty and hungry. She drank a cup of tea and ate a slice of bread. 'I wouldn't say they'd keep him too long now, Ma, would you?'

'I would not, love. They'll find out Jack is an innocent man. Stretch out on the couch for half an hour – you have to mind the child you're carrying.'

She let herself be led to the couch and covered up. Hardly had her head touched the cushion when she slept.

CHAPTER FOURTEEN

A farmer doing his morning milking found the body, face down among the grass and wild spring flowers. It was riddled with bullets. By the time he got to the village and reported the killing, and the police came for it and then contacted the Dublin police, it was midday before the knock came to Julia's door. She was still sleeping.

'Good day, ma'am. Are you Mrs Harte?'

'I'm her mother.'

'I'm terrible sorry. I've bad news, I'm afraid.'

'He's dead. They shot him. I heard it, about six this morning.'

'They did, ma'am. About the time I wouldn't know. A farmer found him up in Glenasmole. It's his next of kin I have to notify.'

'It would come easier from me.'

'It would that, but it's what I have to do.'

'Wait then for a minute. She's asleep. I'll wake her.'

She lay on her side, one palm supporting her cheek – like a little child, her mother thought. She bent and kissed her face and whispered, 'Julia,' her voice broken with grief and pity. 'Wake up love.' Julia opened her eyes, turned on her back and smiled. 'Julia, child,' Lizzie began. 'Julia, listen,' and she saw the smile die and the fear come into her eyes.

'He's dead, isn't he? Jack's dead.'

'Oh, my poor little child. My little girl.' She took her in her arms, rocking her as she had when she was a baby. 'They shot him. They killed our lovely Jack. Lord Jesus have mercy on his soul. There's a policeman – he brought word. He has to see you.'

Around the room the women who had stayed sat with downcast eyes, their hands clasped in each other, crying silently.

Julia sat up and told her mother to bring in the policeman. 'I'm terrible sorry, ma'am, to bring you the bad news. It's desperate times we live in. Your husband was found dead this morning in Glenasmole. He had been shot. And you'll have to identify him.' She nodded her head but said nothing. 'I'll leave you so, and may God comfort you. Good day to you now.'

'What time?' Mrs Mangan asked as she showed him to the door. 'And where?'

'As soon as you can. The city morgue, that's where he is, the Lord have mercy on him.'

'Glenasmole,' Julia kept repeating. 'He died in Glenasmole. Fancy that, they killed him in Glenasmole. Jack to be dead in Glenasmole.'

Her mother and the women willed her to cry, to scream, to curse the Black and Tans, but after a while she repeated no more her incredulous statements about Glenasmole and went into a trance-like state again. Not answering questions, not responding to the women's words of sympathy, not responding even to Ellie when she woke and was brought down from bed. Seeing only in her mind the sunlit fields, the larks soaring and Jack with an arm round her walking through the soft, bright-green grass.

She broke down when Sarah came. They clung to each other, crying and babbling about the mountains and the picnic they were to have had at Easter. And Julia cried and asked, 'Why, why? Why Jack? Why did they take and kill my Jack?' Then she took Ellie from her grandmother and held her close, crying into the child's hair.

Sarah talked. 'Wait'll poor Barney hears, the effect it'll have on him. He loved Jack. His best friend.'

Julia was coaxed to drink a glass of milk when she refused food. Her mother waited until almost two o'clock before gently reminding her about the identification. 'It's better to go soon. It's for Jack's sake, love. You wouldn't want him spending a night there.'

'We'll bring him home.'

'Of course we'll bring him home. Drink the milk, wash your face and run a comb through your hair. I'll get a cab and we'll go.'

'Mrs Mangan, you've been through an awful lot. I'll go with Julia,' Sarah volunteered. 'You mind Ellie. Look at her poor little face, she's never seen her mother crying. I wouldn't be surprised if she senses something.'

Mrs Mangan looked at Sarah who, had she been more sensitive, would have seen the hostility directed towards her from the older woman's eyes.

In a lifeless voice Julia said, 'She's right, Ma. Ellie will make strange if we both go, and you look so tired. Sarah will come with me.'

She didn't talk in the cab. She looked out through the window seeing nothing. Because the day was warm she wore a light coat, but she wasn't aware of the morgue's icy atmosphere, nor the reek of formaldehyde. She didn't see the other bodies on their marble slabs nor smell the smell of death.

The attendant, a talkative little Dublin man smoking the butt end of a cigarette, led her to Jack. His head was bandaged, his body covered up to the neck by a stiff white sheet. His poor mouth, she thought, looking at his swollen, bruised lips. His mouth that was so beautiful. She gazed at him in disbelief. She expected him to open his eyes, smile and make everything all right. From somewhere in the room she heard the little man's voice talking to Sarah. 'Riddled him, they did. Like a colander he was. A right lot of bastards. Every day in the week I get bodies in here like that.'

She bent and kissed his broken mouth and touched his face. He was so cold. Never in her life had she felt such cold. Sarah came and took her arm, unable to speak for the sobs that racked her body. So that eventually it was Julia who said, 'We'll go now.'

'It was him?' the attendant asked.

'Oh, yes,' replied Julia. 'It was him.'

'I won't keep you a minute – there's a few forms you'll have to sign. Then if you hurry you'll get an undertaker to fix things up.'

The undertaker was sympathetic but it was late in the day to arrange anything. 'Please,' Julia pleaded. 'I couldn't leave him there tonight. That'd be the second one out of the house. I couldn't do that, not to Jack. Help me, please.'

She was taken pity on. The undertaker talked to the coffin-maker, who said, there was a coffin in stock. It was on the big side, but that was better than being too small. They could disguise the fault by padding out the head and foot. Yes, they would do it, though it might be late before they brought him home.

The parlour was made ready for his reception: the mirror was covered, the centre of the floor cleared of furniture. A font of Holy Water, the Blessed candles and crucifix were all laid out and hung.

'I can't look on him.'

'You have to. What would people think, and you his best friend not going to pay your respects!'

'It's because I *was* his best friend, because I turned him in – that's why I can't look at him.'

'But, love, it wasn't your fault he was shot. You never thought that would happen! I didn't, either. Remember, we thought he'd be lifted, questioned, kept in gaol and, if he had been hiding anyone, maybe do a stretch. Never killed. We never thought that.'

'Sarah, stop talking. That's all you ever do. "Get out of the street. Get on. Make money." On and on and on your voice goes, and now you're full of excuses for what I did. I'm not as clever as Jack, nor as quick-thinking as you, but I'm not a complete eejit. I knew what would happen to Jack: and I went ahead and did it, God forgive me. I loved him. He was my brother, my mate, my hero. I wanted always to be like him. And I had him murdered. How can I look on his face ?'

'I don't know, but you will. You'll come with me. You'll look at him. Get drunk, stocious. Cry, don't cry – do what you like, but you're coming. There's no excuse you could make. If you were dying you'd have to crawl there. You'll come and stand by the coffin, for if you don't, conclusions will be drawn and before the week is out the other crowd will be here for you.'

At that moment he wished it was himself coming home in a coffin. Then he wished it was Sarah lying dead. Without her nagging, raging, whining and prompting, or her favours, he would never have done what he did. Then she put her arms round him, kissed his cheek, told him again it wasn't his fault, that it had gone wrong, and he was sorry for his thoughts. He worshipped her; he always would. But there was still Jack's face to look on ... He would get drunk before he even set foot at the wake.

He went to the public house and drank more whiskey than he had ever consumed before. Those watching him said, 'Poor ould Barney, don't you feel sorry for him. Going through the war together, Jack saving his life, and now for him to see the work of them murdering bastards.'

He was coming back, and as on the night when he came home from France, the street was preparing for him. The same women brought plates of sandwiches and cake, the men armfuls of stout and bottles of whiskey. Jack was coming home. Home to be waked.

He came at nine o'clock. The coffin was opened and the lid with its brass cross and nameplate stood against the wall. The crying was heartbreaking. Men and women, old and young, children, boys and girls, they all came to see Jack. To cry and rail in disbelief at someone they had seen yesterday walking up the street from work, in a coffin, in a shroud. *Murdered*. There was none of the usual easy consolation that he was a good age, or that he was out of his suffering and that it was a relief to his family. None of that. They wiped their eyes. They prayed, and thought their thoughts of the men who had done such a thing. Then they talked to Julia. Gave their sympathy, and to her mother. And to Barney, who was inconsolable, his eyes swollen and red from crying, his voice incoherent as again and again he related how Jack had saved his life.

It wasn't a wake where people sang and danced. They ate and drank and talked quietly about Jack. About the terrible mistake – about how powerless they were. Not that anything could bring him back. But an admission, an apology – if not now, later, would be a consolation for the widow. They knew from experience how the smallest of gestures helped comfort the bereaved. Poor Julia could whistle till the cows came home if she expected sympathy from the government or them owning up to their mistake. The Tans were a law unto themselves. You couldn't even have the satisfaction of complaining – who could you complain to?

His body was taken to the chapel the next night, the same chapel where he had been christened, confirmed and married and where, tonight he would lie alone.

She dreamed about him but never that he was dead. Wakening she found the empty space in the bed and remembered. And then she didn't want to face the day. Didn't want to face life with the certainty that never again on earth would she see his face, hear his voice, touch him. But Ellie was there, standing up in her cot, clamouring for attention. And so day by dreary day she rose and washed and dressed and saw to the child, listened to what Sarah had to say, promised her mother that she would go out the next day. And the next day promised the same thing.

When kindly women came to the house and said, 'Time is the great healer,' she nodded and smiled, for she knew they meant well. Some of them were widows, war widows, but they could console themselves that their men had volunteered knowing the possibility of being killed. The husbands of others had died from cancer. Consumption, pneumonia, blood poisoning, accidents – all the things people died from every day in the week. It was the Will of God, but not her Jack. How could his death have been the Will of God? Not the God she believed in. If it wasn't for Ellie and her mother, she would walk to the canal when it was dark, slip into the water, wade out to where it was deeper and let it drown her.

Mag called at the house most mornings. Mrs Mangan ran her from the door, saying, 'Julia's sick. Julia's in bed. Come back tomorrow.'

Sometimes she stuck her tongue out and said she hated Mrs Mangan. Sometimes she just went away. But one morning she refused to go. 'I won't,' she said. 'I won't.'

'You're a bold girl. If you don't go home I'll tell Julia and she won't like you any more.' More fool me, Lizzie thought, giving my senses to the poor unfortunate creature. And while she mused on her foolishness in arguing with the girl, Mag began to recite.

'I saw the man in Julia's garden and he had a gun, a big huge gun.'

'*What* did you say? What did you see in Julia's garden?' Mag repeated her line. Mrs Mangan gently pushed her down from the step, went outside with her and closed the door for Julia not to hear anything. 'I'm going to tell your mother. You're a wicked bold girl saying such a thing.' Mag rocked on her heels and grinned. 'Sarah told me,' she said. 'Sarah told me. Sarah told me.'

'All right, all right, you're a good girl. I've got something nice for you. Look,' she took from her apron pocket a shilling. 'You go now and buy sweets. There's a good girl and tomorrow you can play with Ellie.' She couldn't get rid of her quick enough. If she didn't get to the Quinlans and confront Sarah, her heart would burst. She pressed her fist into her chest and prayed, 'Jesus direct me.' Mag grabbed the shilling and went ambling up the street.

At the Quinlans' house she didn't, as was usual in the street, walk in without knocking. Sarah came to the door. 'There's nothing up with Julia, is there? Is she all right?' she enquired.

'She'll never be all right again,' Lizzie said bitterly. Then she repeated what Mag had said.

Sarah ventured, 'You don't look well, Mrs Mangan.' And because she felt far from well, Lizzie sat. 'You know what's she's on about – the night it happened,' Sarah spoke. 'She'd have seen the Tans in the garden with their guns.'

'I'm not a fool. Everyone would have seen them. She was on about something else – something she said you told her.'

'Ah now listen, Mrs Mangan. Everyone knows Mag isn't all there. She makes things up on the spur of the moment, you know that as well as me. God, I'm surprised at you giving your senses to her.'

It was a reasonable explanation and yet it didn't satisfy her. Something she had heard recently, something about Mag, niggled in her mind, but what she couldn't remember. 'I suppose you're right,' Julia's mother said, though she didn't think so for a minute. If only she could remember what it was about Mag. Always she had had a premonition that she could be the cause of trouble: she remembered saying so to Julia, and Julia poo-hooing it. It wasn't only Julia who was in danger of losing her mind – she was heading that way herself. Coming down here making an accusation she couldn't back up. For the more she thought about it, the more senseless it all was; even supposing Sarah *had* told Mag about someone in Julia's garden, someone other than the Tans, what could poor Mag have done with such information? All the same, she'd give Sarah something to mull over.

'I'm sorry for saying anything. I shouldn't have come. But mind you, I hope she doesn't go round the street repeating what she said to me. People are quare. They might take it up the wrong way.'

Sarah laughed. 'Well, more fool them if they listen to another fool.'

Sarah, however, wasn't as unconcerned as she appeared. For the rest of the day she pondered the possible consequences of what Mrs Mangan had told her, and by the time Barney came home she had decided how she would deal with Mag.

'Father Dunphy's having his supper,' the housekeeper said.

'I'll wait,' said Sarah, determined not to be fobbed off with excuses.

'You're only supposed to come to the Presbytery if it's for a sick call.'

'It isn't, but I still want to see him.'

'Couldn't you come back in the morning?'

'No,' said Sarah. 'It's urgent.'

'I suppose you'd better come in.' Sarah followed her into the hall and was shown into the parlour, where she sat looking round the cold dreary room. She observed the large crucifix hanging over the fireplace, the fan of red crepe paper hiding the empty grate, the Holy Pictures and religious books, and she breathed in the smell of damp overlaid with furniture polish.

The priest who had married her and Barney and christened Patrick came after a while. 'Good evening,' he said. 'You're . . . ?'

'Mrs Daly from Springfield Terrace.'

'Ah yes, of course. What can I do for you, Mrs Daly? I believe it's urgent.'

'I think so, Father. I've been very worried all night. I suppose I should have come before when I realised Mag wasn't a child any more.'

'Mag who?'

'Mag, the girl in our street, Mag Venables. She's an imbecile, God bless the mark. Her mother and father are a bit careless. To tell you the truth, Father, they drink and Mag has the run of the streets night and day. That was bad enough when she was a child but she's sixteen now. Anyway as I say I've been worried about her for a while. You know, that someone might . . . take advantage of her. I kept meaning to come and see you, but with my husband working late and the baby, I kept putting it off.' She paused for breath and the priest prompted her to go on.

'Last night Patrick, that's the baby, was cranky – he's cutting back teeth. I was walking the floor with him and I happened to look out the window, and there was Mag on the embankment. She was not on her own. There was a man or a boy with her, and I didn't like the look of things. I ran out and the fella cleared off. Mag's clothes were disarranged. I don't think anything had happened – I must have been in the nick of time, but there'll be other nights and other fellas. Father, that's why I came to see you: poor Mag, I'd hate to see anything bad happen to her, and I'd be wasting my time talking to her mother or father.'

'You did the right thing. The poor unfortunate child, she must be protected. Did you by any chance recognise the man?'

'No, I didn't. He ran like a hare.'

'May God bless you for doing your Christian duty, and rest assured, I'll see to the matter first thing in the morning.'

'I'm sorry if I disturbed you from your supper.'

'Not at all, not at all. A child's welfare, her spiritual welfare, is at stake. The parish needs more people like you. I won't keep you any longer from your duties.' Sarah rose and the priest saw her to the door. 'Good night and God bless you.'

'Goodnight, Father.' And she hurried home to tell Barney that Mag would soon be out of the way.

Before the end of the following week, Mag was down the country in a home run by nuns for girls in need of care and protection. People in the street were sorry to see her go and gave her sweets and chocolates, rosary beads and ribbons, and wished her well, though doubtful of how she would be treated. The nuns had a fierce reputation for dealing with children in their care.

Julia was sorry for poor Mag's loss of freedom but her mother, who hadn't been fond of the girl, said it was all for the best. She was at an age when she could be taken advantage of. All the same, it seemed that the move had come about very suddenly – and was it only a coincidence that it should have happened so soon after her conversation with Sarah?

Mrs Mangan's illness was troubling her more each day. She couldn't give into it, not with Julia still locked in her grief, dragging herself round as if she had no wish to live. Never mentioning Jack's name, never shedding a tear. It wasn't natural. Her own pain and discomfort had to be ignored, every ounce of her will brought into being to muster her fading strength. Julia needed her. Julia had a small child, was carrying another. They all needed her. She prayed for God to spare her until Julia recovered, and then for a quick and merciful death after that. And lately she asked Him not to let her lose her senses, for her mind was working in a strange way since her visit to the Quinlans'. There was something that had been said, before Jack was shot – something about Sarah and Mag ... Try as she did, Lizzie couldn't remember what, she that had always prided herself on her memory. Secretly, she was afraid that whatever ailed her insides had spread to her brain, blocking the memory that was almost within her grasp. It might be nothing – but it might be something important. What, she wasn't sure, only that it had to do with Jack, Mag and Sarah. It might be something so terrible that Julia's stupor would give way to anger. And anger would at least make her come alive again.

CHAPTER FIFTEEN

On 11 July 1921 a Truce was signed between the IRA and the British Army. And two days later a letter came, addressed to Julia. There was no signature, the postmark was indecipherable and nothing in the letter showed where it had come from. It read:

Dear Mrs Harte,

I was unable to write at the time of Jack's murder to express my sympathy, but I couldn't have been sorrier had he been my own flesh and blood. Jack was never a member of the organisation. Once, a long time ago, he gave shelter to a man in desperate need. That incident had nothing to do with his murder.

A conspiracy of lies was spun to implicate him in something he hadn't done. It was spun by those close to you, a couple you consider your friends. They gave their false information for money. They will get their just desert. In our own time the punishment meted out to informers will be theirs.

In disgust Julia threw down the letter. 'God, haven't I enough suffering without the likes of that, cranks and mad people writing to the afflicted.'

Her mother took the letter and read it twice before saying, 'This is genuine.'

'Now don't *you* start! How can it be genuine?'

'For one thing, the writer of this knew Jack, and he also knows that someone *did* stay here before Ellie was born. The close friends are Sarah and Barney.' Only the anguish on Julia's face stopped her from adding, 'I warned you, didn't I?' Julia paced the floor like a demented person. 'Listen,' her mother asked. 'Was there ever a time when you confided in her?'

'Millions of times.'

'I don't mean about your husbands, your pregnancies – all women do that. Something out of the ordinary.'

'How would I remember? Would I want to? As it is I think I'm going mad.'

Watching her, Mrs Mangan despaired for her lovely, generous-natured daughter who was being destroyed by a sorrow she couldn't mourn, for the bitterness that occupied her mind. Her heart was corroded with it. It was that more even than her terrible loss which drove her into herself.

'Mad,' repeated Julia, pausing in her pacing. 'Mad – that's it! I remember now, I *did* tell Sarah something out of the ordinary! I never mentioned it to you, because I didn't want to worry you. It wasn't that long ago – I mean, not long before they came for Jack. I thought I saw someone in the middle of the night out the back. At first I thought they had a stick or hurley, then it looked like a rifle. By the time I woke Jack, whoever it was was gone. He persuaded me it was Mag, tried to let on that I might have dreamed it, or had a nightmare. But I was so certain. The next morning I couldn't be sure and wondered if I was going mad. Anyway, I mentioned it to Sarah, half-joking, asking her if pregnant women went mad.'

'That's it, then. But your story was told in a different way to someone else.'

'Who? Who could they tell it to?'

'That you may never know, only the outcome, which you know too well.'

'I don't believe it,' Julia said in a trembling voice. 'Not Sarah and Barney. She came with me to identify Jack. Who could do that if they were guilty?'

'She could and did.' Lizzie's voice was implacable.

'I won't believe it. They wouldn't. They're my friends. Jack and Barney soldiered together. They couldn't have done such a thing. It's hard to imagine anyone doing it, never mind them. And how would they have stayed living in the street – wouldn't they have been afraid for their lives?'

'Why? What was to throw suspicion on them, who to say the first word?' She remembered Mag, and heard again, *'I saw a man in Julia's garden and he had a gun, a big huge one. Sarah told me.'* And the memory she had tried so hard to recapture now gave itself up: the week before Jack was murdered, remarking to Julia how much time Mag was spending in Sarah's. And Julia's explanation that Mag played with the baby. Mag could say rhymes she had learned off by heart ... rhymes or lines. And when Sarah knew she had twigged something, Mag was whisked into a Home before you could say Jack Robinson.

'Julia, stop walking the floor like a lion above in the zoo. Sit down and listen to what I have to say.' Mrs Mangan told her about Mag, what she had said, and about her visit to Sarah.

'You hate her, you always have! You're just jumping to conclusions, going on that lunatic's letter.' Julia buried her head in her hands and sobbed.

164

'I abominate her. She should be in Hell roasting – and him, for in a way he was worse.'

'Mother, Mother, will you shut up!' Julia banged the table with her fists. 'Do you realise what you're saying – that Sarah and Barney were responsible for Jack being dragged out of here and shot. But how? Tell me *how*? Who could they have told? Who would have believed Mag, poor Mag, no matter what lines Sarah taught her by heart. Just tell me that.'

'She's certainly alive now, angry, only her anger's directed at me, not them,' Lizzie thought. 'I can live with that and the truth will dawn on her before long. Have you forgotten where Barney works?' she demanded. 'For the gentry. The gentry is the army, the authorities. Who more than them would have jumped at the information? And as for Mag, the unfortunate dupe, she'd have been used to convince Barney, for I don't suppose he went willingly to being an informer. She'd have worked her wiles on him, an evil woman who'd stop at nothing. And Barney was never blessed with brains – he's one of the few who'd have heeded Mag's words. Now d'ye believe me?'

'I don't know what to believe. I don't want it to be true, not of them, the people I loved and trusted. Can't you see that? Can't you understand that?' When her mother said nothing she picked up the letter and read it again. Then she asked, 'What does this mean; "*Once, a long time ago, he gave shelter to a man in desperate need*"?'

'What it says. Don't you remember him once saying a mate catching an early train might come late at night?'

'But you said no one did.'

'No – what I said was that he'd left no trace.'

'If this letter isn't the work of a madman, then Jack brought a man here, a fugitive, to our home. He deceived me. He put himself in the way of being killed. Why? Why, Ma?'

'He'd have had his reasons.'

'What reasons?' Julia's voice rose. 'What reasons could he have had for sheltering a murderer, risking our lives, sacrificing his own? Dear sweet Jesus, why did they write that letter? To comfort me? To drive me completely mad?'

'To warn you. To expose them two. To make it clear that the man or men who stayed in our house or sheltered in our yard weren't the cause of what happened to Jack. Don't forget that whoever wrote that letter will have found out the real truth, for you may be sure that however many informers there are at the Club where Barney works, the others will have just as many.'

'I don't want to hear another word about it. Not one, d'ye hear? Not now, nor never.'

'I've said all I wanted to say. It's a lovely day, why don't you take Ellie out for a walk?'

'No.' Julia shook her head. 'I can't face anyone. I'll play with her in the yard.'

Since Jack died she slept badly; the slightest noise woke her. Now she was woken by a smell of burning. She had left the clothes horse too near the fire – it had fallen over! She ran downstairs. The smell was stronger here, though the horse was upright: it was coming from outside. Throwing a coat round her shoulders, she opened the front door. People were running, shouting. She went out. Sarah's house was blazing. A woman was screaming, 'They're in there! They'll be burnt to a cinder!'

Men shouldered the door, but it didn't budge. Another smashed the parlour window. Flames rushed out. 'Where's the Fire Brigade? Did anyone send for it?' several voices were asking.

Julia stood as if paralysed. Was this what 'a just desert' meant, roasting people alive? Roasting Patrick? 'No, no, no!' she screamed, and fainted.

She came to with her mother and a neighbour in attendance. 'The firemen are in, maybe there's still hope,' the neighbour said doubtfully. All Julia could think of was Patrick, a little child like Ellie. 'Drink that,' the neighbour said, holding a glass to her lips. 'It's bromide, it'll make you sleep.'

'For Ellie's sake and the baby,' her mother pleaded.

The smell of smoke and burning was still in her nose when she woke and the taste of them in her mouth. She retched, and when she put her feet to the floor, retched again. 'Stay where you are, I'll bring the bucket,' her mother said. She held her head while she vomited.'

'There's a terrible smell of paraffin oil,' Julia gasped.

Her mother wiped her face with a wet cloth and gave her a glass of water. 'I knocked over the can of oil when I was lighting the stove. I'll change my pinnie. Do you want to hear the news?'

'I suppose they are all dead.' She began to cry.

'Don't waste your tears. The oul wan and oul fella are dead – up in the bedroom, according to some in a locked room, though the fireman told me that's not for sure, as the door was burned to cinders and the lock and key melted into a ball. But the others are gone.'

'Gone? What are you talking about?'

'Gone, scarpered. After informing, they must have been on the qui vive every minute, had their getaway planned. Anyway, they got out – but wherever they were going, Mammy and Daddy weren't invited.'

So it was true. All of what her mother had said, the letter as well. Such a surge of hatred and anger went through her that had Barney or Sarah stood before her now, she knew she could have killed them with her bare hands. She got off the couch.

'What are you doing?' asked her mother.

Without answering she went upstairs and when she came down was dressed. 'Mind Ellie, I'm going out.'

'You're in no condition to go anywhere. You'll collapse in the street.' As before she ignored her mother and went.

She ran up the street and to avoid passing the burnt-out house, went across a vacant lot and by a roundabout way to a hackney stand where she knew some of the jarveys. They said, 'That was a terrible thing in your street. Is it true the oul wan and oul fella were roasted alive, locked in their room?'

'No one's sure about that, but they are dead.'

'Jaysus, ma'am,' one who didn't know her said. 'That's an unlucky street if you ask me. I'd get out of it if I was you. Were you wanting a cab?'

She couldn't think: her mind went blank. The horses' hooves step-danced on the cobbles. She saw their nosebags and heard them munch, smelled the fresh manure, heard the jarveys laughing and she couldn't remember why she was here. She couldn't remember leaving the house.

'Are you all right?' Someone had hold of her arm. She turned and looked into the face of a jarvey she knew. He was an old man, his blue kindly eyes rheumy.

'Ah, Jemmy, it's you.' She knew him well. Her head cleared and she remembered her reason for running from the house: she had to find Sarah and Barney. Find them and kill them. She had a good idea where they'd have run to. 'I'm all right, Jemmy, a bit shocked after the fire. You heard about it?'

'All sorts of rumours.'

'The old people died in it. I have to do an important message. Drop me at the corner of the Green.'

'Right y'are, love.' He put her into the cab where she leant back against the musty leather seat and closed her eyes. They had came home in a cab with the same smell the night Jack returned from France. *Oh, Jack, Jack, where are you? I'll never see you again. Sarah and Barney murdered you. And they cried with me, put their arms round me. Comforted me and all the time they had murdered you. But I won't let them get away with it. I won't. No. I won't.*

She walked along the Green, passed the Shelbourne, crossed at the corner and went up the other side to Barney's Club, which she entered.

Her dishevelled appearance led the porter to believe that she had come about a cleaner's job.

'No,' she said when he asked. 'I'm looking for Barney Daly and his wife.'

The man, another of Lord Glenivy's recruits, said: 'He's not in today. As a matter of fact, he's finished here. Didn't turn up this morning. He'll be sacked for that sort of thing – unless he's very bad. Dying he'll have to be.'

'You're a liar. If you don't know where they are, someone in this place does, and I want to see them. I have to find them, d'ye hear me?' She reached across the desk and caught hold of him. By now her voice was a scream.

'Now listen here, missus. For one thing I know nothing about them, and for another women aren't allowed in here. So take yourself off before I call a policeman.'

'Call one. Go on – call a policeman.' The feeling was in her head again. The muzziness. The man's face was receding. From far away she heard a voice ask: 'Something wrong, Farrell?'

'No, sir. This woman came in by mistake. I'll show her out.'

'I won't go. I won't leave until I know where they are. I won't.' The porter was handling her, pushing her towards the door. She resisted and screamed and for the second time that day fainted.

This time when she came round it wasn't her mother or a neighbour she saw. The face bending over her was a stranger's and unfriendly. She struggled to sit up. 'Lie down,' the stranger's voice commanded. 'Lie down and keep still.' The figure went away, and another voice said: 'She's an oul cow. Never had a man nor a child. No feelings. But you'll be all right love, now that you've come round from the anaesthetic.'

She looked to see where the voice came from and saw a woman in a bed next to her and other beds with other women smiling and waving at her.

'Where am I?' she asked.

'In Holles Street. D'ye not remember what happened?'

'No, nothing.'

'You collapsed on the Green and were brought in.'

She heard or imagined she heard, the crying of a newborn baby. And in her confused state believed she had had the baby. That was why she was in the Maternity Hospital.

'How far gone were you?' the friendly voice asked.

'Nearly five months.'

'God love you – a miss can be as bad as a birth. Was it your first?'

She knew then what had happened and couldn't answer. They'd killed

168

Jack and now they'd killed his son, for it would have been a boy – of that she was certain. Then she remembered Ellie and her mother. Did Lizzie know where she was? How could she? She'd had nothing on her to identify her, only the money for the cab in her pocket. Her mother would be out of her mind with worry.

'Missus,' she asked, 'how long have I been in?'

'Since yesterday. After dinner they brought you in.'

'Did anyone come to see me?'

'Only the doctor.'

'I have to go home – I have to. I've a little girl and my mother's not well.' She got out of bed. In a locker beside it she found her clothes bundled up.

'Jaysus, ma'am, what are ye doing?'

'I have to go home. My mother'll be demented.'

'Someone will have let her or your husband know.'

'He's dead. And the baby's dead. I'd nothing on me to say who I am.' She began to dress. The wadding between her legs was saturated with blood.

'Wait'll I tell you – if you're determined to go, do it this way. Put your clothes over your arm and drape my morning gown over them. You can dress in the lav. Put your shoes under the towel. Then watch for the coast to be clear and make a run for it. If they see you they'll stop you. But I don't blame you, I'd do the same myself. Have you any money?'

'Not a penny.'

'Take this, then.' The woman gave her two shillings. 'Don't waste time thanking me or Leather Arse'll be doing her rounds. Go and God bless you.'

In the lavatory she rolled her blouse into a pad and wedged it into her knickers. After dressing, splashing cold water on her face and drinking some, she felt revived, though her legs were shaking and when she bent her head stars spun and danced before her eyes.

She hung the morning gown on the back of the door, opened it a chink and peeped out: no sign of anyone. She walked slowly because she couldn't walk quickly, but it might be less likely to arouse suspicion than if she appeared in too much of a hurry. Holding tightly to the banisters she made it down the stairs. Her heart lurched as she saw a porter cross the hall. He looked casually at her and went to his little room, and when she passed by the glass panel she saw him inside, engrossed in a newspaper.

She was out. At the top of the street she'd get a cab. Halfway along the street she felt giddy and had to cling on to the railings of a house.

'Are you all right, daughter?' A stout woman in a black shawl came to her assistance.

'A bit weak. I was seeing the doctor.'

'Feckin' lot of quacks. Keep away from them, that's my advice. Pulling and hauling your insides about and them students gawking at you. Have you far to go?'

'The cab-rank on the Green.'

'Catch hold of my arm, I'll take you.' Strength flowed into her from the warm stout arm. 'Lean on me,' said the woman. 'I only live off Mount Street. You can come home and I'll make you a strong cup of tea.'

'You're very kind,' said Julia, forcing herself not to cry, for if she did she would never be able to stop. 'But I'd better go home. They kept me waiting and my mother's minding my little girl. She's a handful.'

'I'll cross you over and see you into the cab. Are you all right for the fare?'

'God bless you, ma'am, I have it, but thanks all the same.'

'Mind yourself,' advised the woman and waited until the cab drove off.

'Oh, Ma!' Julia threw herself into her mother's arms and let fall the tears that for so long she had withheld.

'Where were you? I was out of my mind with worry. When you didn't come home last night . . .'

'Where's Ellie?'

'Asleep upstairs.'

'I lost the baby. I lost Jack's son. Jack and the baby, they're dead. I've lost them. What am I going to do?'

Lizzie led her to a chair and let her have her cry out. In between sobs she got the story of the Club and the hospital. She comforted her. 'My poor child, you've had a hard road and a hard one in front of you. Hush now, there's a good girl.'

But Julia wouldn't take consoling and cried over and over again. 'What am I going to do? Tell me, Ma, what am I going to do?'

And her mother decided the time had come to tell her what she had to do. 'Jack is dead and you lost the baby. Now listen to me: you've had terrible things happen to you – things no woman should be asked to bear but we are, all the time. Babies die and men are murdered. You can't lie down and die with them. You have another child – someone has to rear her. There's no one except you. Do you understand what I'm saying?'

She wasn't even listening, Mrs Mangan could see. Not listening, never

170

mind understanding. And she knew the time had come when she had to be cruel to be kind. 'Julia, I'm dying.'

'You're not, you're only saying that. But you're right – I have to pull myself together. I think I can now. It's an awful thing to say, but in a strange way I feel better knowing about Barney and Sarah. The anger and hate in me for them is giving me strength. I thought it went when Jack was killed. I have to live to know they get what they deserve.'

'No, love, not that. That's not what I meant. Leave them to God. Try to put them from your mind. Don't let bitterness corrode your heart, it'll like rust eat it away. It'll destroy you and worse still, destroy Ellie. And I am dying.'

'Don't say that. That's not funny. Don't make a joke like that.'

'Love, it's true. I've been sick for a long time. Things happen to me that I haven't told you. I know all about them. I nursed my mother – she went the same way.'

'But the doctor – you'll go to the doctor!'

'I won't, not unless the pain got bad and please God it won't.'

'Are you sure? It might be nothing. They could cure you.'

'Not of what ails me.'

'And all this time you've been killing yourself looking after us. Since Jack died I've done nothing.'

'What's killing me has nothing to do with anything except what's killing me. I'm gone seventy. Everyone dies and something has to come for your end. Now that you know, you can take over your home again. I'll sit in the corner and enjoy the comfort.'

'I can't bear it, I can't! First Jack, then my baby and now you. What'll I do without you?'

'The same as I did without my mother. I'm depending on you now. Life goes in circles – me and my mother, you and me, and in the fullness of time, you and Ellie. And now I'll make you something to eat.'

Julia cried for hours. Crying into the jug of milk, on to the plate of bread and butter until at last her mother said: 'For God's sake use your hanky and dry your eyes. I don't like sodden bread.'

For the first time since Jack's death, Julia laughed out loud as she said, 'Well, whatever ails you it's far from your tongue.'

And her mother, catching hold of her hand, kissed it. 'You're a good girl, a fine woman. You'll be all right, so long as you don't let bitterness take a hold. Promise me you won't.'

And Julia promised.

CHAPTER SIXTEEN

Daily her mother grew weaker. She came down in the mornings, ignoring Julia's pleas to stay in bed or at least wait until later in the day. Sitting by the fire she prepared vegetables, amused Ellie and received her friends, who came regularly. They gossiped and laughed as they always had. Only sometimes she would fall asleep in the middle of a sentence. Julia feared she wouldn't last until Christmas, but was thankful that she didn't appear to be in pain and asked that God would call her before she was.

Sometimes, though not often, when alone in the evenings Julia sought consolation for her own loss by recalling all the senseless deaths there had been since the year of 1921 began: the British officers shot in bed, some with their wives lying beside them – the reprisal the same day, when the Black and Tans opened fire on a crowd of spectators in Croke Park, killing twelve of them.

The death after seventy-three days' hunger strike in Wormwood Scrubs, of Terence MacSweeney, Lord Mayor of Cork. Their deaths and the deaths of all the unknown. They had left wives and children, too, she'd tell herself. She was not unique. And for a little while she seemed to find a consolation, until remembering that all of those who died had died at the hands of strangers. They hadn't been betrayed by those they had trusted, and this not from patriotism, but for money or preferment. Money, money, money – it had to be that. Money to further Sarah's ambitions to get out of the street – as she had forecast on the day Jack and Barney returned from France.

But Barney – what part had he played in it? How could he have given false information about his friend? And yet he must have done so. What went through his mind when he looked at Jack dead? Did he walk – wherever he was – with an easy mind? She hated and loathed both of them. She wished for all the ill-luck in the world to attend them. While they lived, she would go on hating them.

World opinion was outraged by events in Ireland, by the savagery of the Black and Tans. To a large extent, so were the British public and some Members of Parliament. General Crozier, head of the Auxiliaries, had resigned and in May admitted that the Black and Tans had, without provocation, fired into the crowd at Croke Park. On 11 July 1921 a Truce was signed.

From her seat by the fire Mrs Mangan thanked God that the killing was over, not adding what was in her mind and Julia's – that it had come too late for Jack. Ellie played in the garden and sometimes in the street where an older child would mind her, telling her when sometimes she said, 'Dad, Dad,' that her Daddy had gone to Heaven.

Julia went out early in the mornings to do her messages, going the long way round to avoid the shell of the Quinlans' burnt-out house. Sometimes she wondered if her mother had set fire to it, remembering how on the day after the fire she had remarked on the strong smell of paraffin oil about her. She no longer cared if her mother had, only wished that Sarah and Barney had burned with it. Then, thinking of Patrick, was glad they hadn't.

In the early morning of the day when their house burned down Barney, who had been sleeping badly since Jack's death, woke and smelled smoke. He went out on to the landing and saw clouds of it billowing up the stairs. He had lived in dread and fear of such a reprisal; so had Sarah, and kept a small bag packed for such an eventuality. Barney called her while pulling on his clothes, then went and banged on his in-laws' bedroom door. 'Get up,' he shouted. 'The house is on fire !' They didn't answer. From the bedroom Sarah was screaming for him to come back and see to Patrick. He tried the handle. The door was locked or bolted. The smoke was choking him. He put his shoulder to the door and heaved. It didn't budge. He stood helpless, not knowing what to do. The smoke was growing thicker, while Sarah's voice and Patrick's cries were echoing in his head. He ran at the door once again. It held fast and no sound came from within. Maybe the smoke had already killed them, otherwise why didn't they answer ? He ran back to his own room, soaked the face cloth in the washbasin on the marble washstand and clamped it over Patrick's mouth and nose and carried him down the stairs with Sarah following.

They walked to the Club on the Green, going through narrow streets and back lanes so as not to draw attention to themselves. Now and then when they had to cross a main street, an occasional cab drove past, a few drunken men staggered by. No one seemed to notice them, and if they had would have assumed they were moonlighting – leaving a house where they owed a lot of rent, their bits and pieces gone on ahead on a hand-cart.

At the Club Barney asked the night porter for Lord Glenivy.

'In the middle of the night ? Are you mad ?'

'He said to come at any time. I'm in terrible trouble.'

'I'm not even sure if he's here tonight.'

'Will you look in the book?'

'All right. But keep your voice down – it's the middle of the night. And another thing. You can stay, but your missus and the child can't, not in the hall. We've members coming in at all hours.'

'For Jaysus's sake will you get a move on!' Barney hissed and cursed his luck that now of all times this eejit was on duty. A country fella no time in the job.

'I'll put her and the child in the storeroom. It's not bad, only cases of whiskey and that.'

'I know what's in the storeroom.' Barney's voice was impatient. 'Will you find out about his Lordship.'

'All right, I'll look,' said the porter, whose name was Paddy McGrath, 'Yes, he's here.' He shut the register and told Sarah to follow him to the storeroom. He said he'd go to his Lordship's room afterwards.

'Lord Glenivy isn't available,' he announced to Barney a few minutes later.

'But he's booked in!'

'So he is, and I went to his room where him and another gent were there drinking. He said he wasn't available, but the other fella'll be down. You're to wait in the dining room.'

The smell of thousands of rashers and eggs, curries, roasts ... the smells of all the meals served over the years, hit Barney's uneasy stomach and made him retch. Guilt, fear and the disappointment of Lord Glenivy's refusal to see him made him want to run from the dining room, run from the Club, run and keep on running. Run far away from everyone, so far that the sight of Jack dead would be blotted from his mind; the fear of them coming for him leave him; the fear of Sarah's fury be removed from him. He wanted to run and run and fall down dead. Then he thought of Hell and didn't want to die.

The man came into the room. It was someone he didn't know, had never seen before, an abrupt man who told him he was to stay out of sight in the storeroom with his wife. Tonight he would go out on the Holyhead boat and before that he would be given tickets and his instructions.

'They set fire to the house, sir, We were lucky to escape with our lives.' Barney was trembling visibly and his voice was unsteady.

'Get a hold of yourself, man!' It was a command, and Barney obeyed as he would any command delivered in such a voice. 'Now listen to what I have to say.'

'Yes, sir,' Barney listened. And Patrick McGrath behind the serving-hatch listened as well. Later in the day he would pass on his information. And in the course of time Barney would be taken care of.

Again Julia's mother extracted a promise from her. 'Bitterness is like rust. It's corrosive, it'll eat your heart out. Promise me you won't let it take a hold on you.'

Looking at the beloved face she promised, while her heart said, 'I can't. I can't do what you're asking me. They destroyed so much that I loved – Jack and our little son, and hastened your death.'

As if reading her thoughts, Lizzie whispered, her voice so faint Julia had to lean close : 'Don't forget Ellie, you have her. She's precious, part of us all. Don't inflict your suffering on her.'

'I won't, Ma, I won't. I promise.' And she tried. Going more often to the chapel, lighting votive lamps and candles, making novenas and imploring God to help her, but still her hatred and bitterness remained. Nothing would rid her of it except retribution. Her loved ones had to be avenged, and she had to have the proof of it.

She stopped confessing the sin of her hatred. Stopped going near the chapel except to Mass. Confided in no one what she was going through, not even to Cissie who spent part of every day and most of the evenings with Lizzie, knowing her time was near. When neighbours asked, 'How are you, Julia ?' she told them, 'Not too bad.' They replied, as ever, 'Time is the great healer.' She nodded her agreement, thinking as she did so that while Barney and Sarah walked the earth she would never get over it.

The priest brought her mother Communion and one day anointed her. Watching him apply the Holy Oils and her mother calmly accepting this Rite of the Dying, Julia wanted to rage against God for allowing such things to have happened in her life. She wanted to scream at the priest, ask him where was God the night the Black and Tans came. Where was God when Barney did his informing.

Into the parlour, where her mother's bed had been brought to make nursing easier, came the sound of children's voices playing outside. Amongst them she heard Ellie crying. Her mother did too and raised a hand. 'Father,' she gasped, 'wait for a minute, maybe the child's hurt.' The priest stopped what he was doing. 'Go and see what ails her,' Lizzie told Julia, who rose from her knees and went. Her mother, her marvellous, wonderful mother was getting ready to die but still even at such a time caring for her family. For a while this consoled Julia. God was good. God made her mother what she was. She was sorry for having railed against Him.

Nothing ailed Ellie, she saw with relief, and again thanked God. She was tired, that was all.

Her mother lingered on into November. Cissie and the other neighbours were praying for God to take their friend soon, before she had unbearable pain. 'It'll be a happy release,' they told Julia. 'You wouldn't want to see her suffering.' She didn't want her mother to be in pain, yet she couldn't pray for her to die. Without her, how would she survive? Turning back to God, she prayed for a miracle. And when one day her mother seemed a little better, asked to be propped up and drank some soup, she believed her prayers were being answered. She ignored the old women who said, 'That's the change before the end.'

Then one afternoon when she and Cissie were sitting quietly by the bed, Cissie moving her rosary through her fingers, Julia suddenly clutched her arm. 'She's not breathing! Oh Cissie, she's stopped breathing. She's dead, my mother's dead.'

Cissie went to the bed, looked down at her old friend, bent and kissed her forehead then closed her eyes. 'My companion,' she said. 'My childhood friend.'

'Oh Ma. You're gone. Oh Ma, what'll I do now,' Julia wept as she touched her mother's face, kissed it and lifting her hands kissed each in turn. 'All they did for me,' she sobbed. 'I love you.' Cissie left her to cry and grieve and kiss her mother, to stroke and kiss her hair, noticing as she did so how its smell was the same as her own hair and the same as Ellie's.

The day of the funeral was cold and damp; the mourning coach in which she, Cissie and two other close neighbours drove to the cemetery smelt musty. Ellie, oblivious of what was happening, practised her vocabulary. 'Dada, Nana, Mama. Dada gone' – now and then she said a short sentence. Julia hugged her and buried her face in her hair, inhaling its smell. Trying to shut from her mind the open grave which in a little while would confront her: Jack's grave and her father's. The hearse and carriages stopped outside the graveyard gates. The coffin was laid on the trolley, the mourners lined up behind it and the procession began. Along the narrow paths bordered by leafless trees dripping moisture it followed the coffin. Julia held Ellie close to keep her warm and for the comfort the child's body gave her. She pondered how, even though she had known for a long time that her mother was seriously ill, she had never really believed that Lizzie would die. Her mother would go on for ever. Her mother had always been there. Never had she been able to envisage a time when she wouldn't. Even now as she stood by the grave she expected to hear the familiar voice telling her it was a terrible day to have the child out in. 'You'll give her her end.'

The heavy clay struck the coffin lid; the priest swung the censer to and fro and intoned the prayers. One of the mourners took Julia's arm, offered to carry Ellie. 'It's all right, she's not heavy,' Julia said as they left the graveside. She didn't want to talk. She wanted no intrusion on her thoughts of her mother and yet as they proceeded back along the narrow paths her mind registered other things: sparrows perched on gravestones, swooping to peck in the damp earth; the tree with the long cruel thorns supposed to be the one from which Jesus' crown of thorns had been made. Remembering her father telling her the story of how the cemetery had once been a gentleman's demesne in the eighteenth century, when the nobility did the Grand Tour, and how a slip of the tree had been brought back from the Holy Land.

She was annoyed with herself for allowing such thoughts to distract her from her grief. But so it was to be during the afternoon, with people coming in and out to see her, enquiring whether she'd like someone to sleep in the house until she got used to the idea of her mother being gone, saying she must let them know if she wanted anything. If they could help her in any way, they would. They talked about other things: the ongoing Troubles. How Mag's mother and father were a disgrace with their drinking. The talk coming back now and then to her mother – the grand woman she was, the great neighbour. Cissie and the older women recalled incidents from Lizzie's and their childhoods, sometimes making Julia cry, sometimes making her laugh. They talked about everything and everyone except Barney, Sarah and how Jack met his death. But in a week, a month, a year – at some time that, too, would also be talked about. And while they talked, Julia decided that she would leave the street. The memories it and the house held would be unbearable. And as soon as Ellie was old enough to understand, she would learn how her father had died. She didn't want that. The story would go down the generations. Ellie must never learn that such people as Barney and Sarah existed, at least not until she was a woman. Julia would find a place where she wasn't known, and let no one in the street know of her move. She would sorely miss them all, but for Ellie's sake it had to be done. Ellie's lovely nature, already evident, mustn't be warped.

A week after her mother was buried, Julia began making forays into the city, walking through unknown neighbourhoods, sizing them up. In streets that she found acceptable, she enquired about the price of rooms to let. One day in a shop where she was asking, a stout pleasant-looking woman whom she judged to be about her own age told her that just before or after Christmas there would be two rooms idle in the house where she lived. She introduced herself as Maggie Simmonds and promised to have a word with the landlord. She pointed across the road to a tall house saying, 'That's where I live. Call in before Christmas.'

CHAPTER SEVENTEEN

For months talks had been taking place in London between an Irish Delegation headed by Michael Collins and the British cabinet, on the signing of a Treaty between the two countries. The talks were given much publicity and pictures of Michael Collins appeared in the papers. It was reported that he was a great success with many London hostesses and rumoured that one famous society beauty was his mistress.

After leaving Copperfield Street for the tannery where he swept yards, hosed them down and helped shift the untreated skins to where they were processed, Barney passed the Fox and Hounds at the junction of his road, Quilp Street and Great Guildford Street. Between there and the railway arches he stopped at a shop to buy his Woodbines and a morning paper. He never passed under the arches without thinking of his courting days with Sarah. Remembering how happy they were then. How delighted he was when he knew she would marry him; his happiness when his son was born. For a little while he forgot the reality of his life as it was now. How daily Sarah complained about his lack of ambition, her thwarted plans for moving from the street. How her voice could rise to a scream as she ranted and raved. In his memory all seemed to have been harmonious until their move to England. What had caused the move he studiously blocked out of his mind though sometimes, passing the Public Library – lit up he supposed for the cleaning women – his efforts to keep Jack from his thoughts failed him. Jack came back to him, talking to him about books, advising him to read. He came back to him as he had seen him in his coffin, his mouth bruised and swollen. He came back to him as he did in his frequent nightmares and stood over him, alive yet with the countenance of a corpse, asking, '*Why, Barney ? Why ?*'

On his early-morning walk to work, these thoughts overtook the other terror that also seized him, the fear of those who would come to get him. In the day that still wasn't light he shrank into himself, attempting to be less conspicuous, walking close to the wall for its imagined protection. The sound of footsteps behind him made him tremble and in his bowels he felt a loosening, making him tighten his sphincter muscles and pray silently that he would reach work and a lavatory before soiling himself.

Barney made the return journey in the same dread, and in fear of Sarah's reception, for every night she had a new axe to grind. And yet he still loved her, longed for a kiss, a touch, a kind word. But except as the recipient of her tongue-lashing, he might as well not have existed. Patrick was the only good thing in his life : Patrick, who was always still up when he came home.

The little boy would be wandering round the small room amusing himself, playing with a cardboard box, a sugar bag, a little lamb on a platform with wheels all made of wood which Barney had bought one morning in the newsagent's with one and sixpence which he had found in an old pair of trousers. Patrick's face lit up when he came through the door. He cried in delight, 'Dad, Dad, Dad,' and held out his arms to be picked up, then covered his face with wet sticky kisses.

Sometimes Sarah greeted him with silence, slapping his meal on the table and not uttering another word for the rest of the night. In bed she lay as far from him as the bed allowed, having made it clear that if there was anywhere else to sleep she would. On other nights she began complaining and listing his faults, her hatred of the cottage, the area, as soon as he came in. He didn't know which reception he dreaded most.

One night at the beginning of December he arrived home to find her in a fighting mood. As he bent to pick up Patrick she screamed, 'Don't touch him till you've washed your hands and changed your clothes. You could give him any disease after handling them skins all day.' On the kitchen table was an opened newspaper, the same one he had bought that morning. She knew what was happening; she'd have seen the photograph of Collins coming out of Downing Street, and read that the signing of the Treaty was in sight. He realised this as he changed his trousers. She'd be on about it for the night.

He came back to the kitchen and picked up the child. 'Have you seen it ? Have you ?'

She pushed the paper in his face. 'It was all for nothing. We didn't get a reward. They never caught the big fella, far from it. He's as large as life and being fêted by the Society ladies in London — the real London, not in shaggin' Borough. Not in a dog box of a place in Copperfield Street. It's all your fault. You never could do anything right. Nothing, ever! I hate you! I loathe you.' Her voice rose to a scream. Terrified, Patrick screamed as well.

Barney hushed and patted him, at the same time trying to placate her. 'It's not my fault that they had a Truce and are going to sign a Treaty. I did what you asked me — a terrible thing. A thing I'll regret all my life.'

'Shut up. Shut up. All you do is complain. You don't like where you work. You miss Dublin. But what about me ? How do you think I feel ?

I'm cooped up in here with him from morning till night. Out for my messages, that's as far as I go. To Borough High Street where I can't understand a word said to me. I ask for rashers and they look at me as if I'm talking Double Dutch. I say a quarter of potatoes and they laugh. 'They've never heard of lap of mutton, tumblers are glasses and basins are bowls, and they answer me in their Cockney voices. I'm like a fool saying, "I beg your pardon." Savages, that's what they are with their basins of snakes wriggling and writhing and they eat them.'

'Love, they're eels,' he told her as he had on numerous occasions. 'I'm sorry for the way things turned out but for the sake of the child let's not fight. Don't keep screaming, he's shaking like a leaf. And it'll soon be Christmas. Let's try and make the best of it. Is there any tea wet?'

'Christmas? Don't talk to me about Christmas, nor don't think I'll lift a finger in this kip to make one.' She put a loaf, a paper of butter and a knife on the table. 'The kettle's boiling – make your own tea.' She sat down by the range fiddling with the damper, raked the fire and complained about the cold, the damp, the cottage and the black beetles.

He made the tea while still holding Patrick, then poured and offered her a cup which she refused. 'Let me drink this,' he said cheerily, 'and I'll bring in more coal. I'll soon get a blaze going. If I stuff the window frames with paper it'll stop the draught and I'll get Borax for the beetles. If you sprinkle it round the skirting boards they eat it and it kills them, so a fella in work told me.'

'I thought they didn't talk to you in work.'

'Well, they don't – not like at home. And I don't encourage them – well, you never know where you'd be talking.'

'You should have changed your name, our name. I told you that on the train coming over.'

'I would have done but the letter from the Club had my name on it. Another thing we could do is buy a hanging for the hall door – that'd cut down on the draughts.' She said nothing. He talked to Patrick who was sharing his bread and butter. He seldom ate anything other than bread and butter, seldom had since the night the Black and Tans came for Jack. The flesh had melted from him. His face was haggard and his belly flat. 'Look at the size of you, you'll be a giant. Whoever you're taking after it's not me.' He bounced him on his knee.

'Put him down – you'll get him over-excited.'

He stopped bouncing the child but didn't put him down. 'Did you hear what I said?' Once again her voice rose. It was rarely he went against her. To do it now was madness, when given time she might have calmed down. He never knew why occasionally he defied her. Was it an attempt to assert himself, or the hope that such a small rebellion might make her regard him as more manly? He didn't know. So confused were his thoughts and feelings that now he never knew why he did anything. Sometimes he wished the assassins would come for him. Death was his only release. Then he would remember: remember that he had never confessed the sin of having had Jack murdered. That his fear of the confessional, even in the days when his sins were no more grievous than missed prayers and stealing coppers from his mother's purse, needed the summoning of all his courage. Even though after the ordeal of confining himself in the narrow dark box, and waiting with a thundering heart for the grille to slide back and through its wire gauze screen see the hazy image of the priest's face and hear the Latin intonation, once he had confessed and been absolved he left the confessional like a lark ready to soar. Knowing that his soul was spotless, filled with sanctifying grace and that if he dropped down dead he would go to Heaven.

Now, when he needed sanctifying grace more than ever in his life, he couldn't confess. Although he had been taught that it was to God, through the priest, that he made his Confession and in one level of his mind believed this, in another it was a man he heard and saw. And to no man could he tell what he had done to Jack.

'Did you hear me?' Sarah shouted.

'I'll put him down in a minute.'

'I hate you. I wished I'd never married you. Look where I've finished up, and all because of you. There's not a face here that I know. I never wanted to leave Dublin – I loved Dublin! It was all your fault, and then you made a bags of it. But I tell you what – I won't stick it. I'm going back, I'm going home. Me and Patrick are going back to Dublin.'

The threat struck terror in his heart. She mustn't leave him. He wouldn't let her. He couldn't bear to lose her and Patrick. He had to stop her. To frighten her. 'They'll shoot you.' He didn't think they would, but it might stop her.

'Me?' she shrieked. 'What hand did I have in it? You passed on the information. It's you they're after. Didn't his Lordship make that clear when we were leaving?'

'I never saw him again after I blew the gaff on Jack, God forgive me.'

'You must have done, while I was in that oul storeroom. The porter said he was booked in.'

'He wouldn't come down. Another gent did. He gave me the few quid and the letters. There was something else as well which I didn't tell you.'

'What? What was it, and why didn't you tell me?'

'You were upset about the fire. About your ma and da.'

'That wasn't my fault. You banged on their door. It was my father's fault – he always bolted the bedroom door. There wasn't time to break it down. They weren't that old or decrepit – they could have got out. Sure, how do we know for certain they didn't? Only the stop press we heard the young fella shouting when we got to the boat. Go on, anyway. What did the other fella tell you?'

'That from the minute we left Ireland we're on our own.'

'You mean . . .' She looked frightened and lowered her voice.

'I mean we are on our own – no looking to the gentry for help or protection. They'll be wanting to pull with Collins and de Valera from now on. We've only got each other. I love you: let's stop fighting. Maybe once the Treaty is signed the IRA will forget about the likes of me.' He didn't for a minute believe this – he knew they had long memories – but he wanted to give her hope. He wanted for whatever time he had left to live in harmony with her. 'We could make a life in England. I'll get a better job – we could move out of Borough. There must be nicer places to live in London. Even if not for our own sake, let's try for him.' He looked down at Patrick who had fallen asleep on his lap.

She bowed her head and said nothing. He didn't press her for an answer, believing she was considering his plea. She wasn't. Silently she was fuming with rage, quickly followed by fear. She had expected that one day they would hear from Lord Glenivy. That he would arrange for them to go to Australia or New Zealand. Their way would be paid, with maybe a pension. Now they were deserted. For the second time in her life the gentry had let her down. They were abandoned. Maybe it was true what Barney said – the IRA might shoot her if she went back to Dublin, though she'd never heard of such a thing. In any case, how would they know she had had anything to do with it? She hadn't, not really. All she had done was to tell Barney what Julia had told her. He did the business of passing on the information. It was all Julia's fault. If she hadn't said anything about seeing someone in the garden none of it would have happened. She wouldn't be stuck here in this hole. God knows she hadn't benefited from any of it.

The more she thought about her plight the more she realised that she must leave Barney. He was a millstone round her neck. The only hope of any improvement in her life was when she thought a reward might have been paid for the information Barney gave. That was the one and only chance with him. He was useless, he'd never amount to anything. Tied to him, how could she rear Patrick as she wanted to?

She didn't really believe the IRA would come for her, but while trying to kill Barney she could be accidentally shot. All the more reason for getting away from him, and the sooner the better. Their joint savings had been dug into since coming to London. Everything was dearer than over there. There she'd had her mother's bedding and Delft, and the housekeeping money was pooled. Now there was little or nothing left of Barney's accumulated tips and the couple of thirty-shilling payments he'd received from Lord Glenivy. But her own fifty pounds was safe and sound, in a Post Office account in her own name. That would give her a start. Never mind what Barney had said, she would write to Lord Glenivy – explain their position, or rather *her* position, for she would leave him and soon. She'd have to think where she could go. Not to Ireland, she wouldn't risk that. Maybe in years to come, but certainly not now. Lord Glenivy was bound to help her – he was a gentleman. It wasn't true that twice the gentry had let her down. What had happened between her and Patrick was altogether different. He was almost engaged when she told him about the baby. She never thought for a minute that he could be in love with the skinny wan ; the marriage would have been arranged. He was just weakwilled, not able to stand up to his parents and fight for her.

She was miles away thinking of when she would go and where, so that twice Barney had to say, 'He's fast asleep. I'll disturb him if I take off his clothes.'

'Take him up as he is. If he wakens during the night I'll undress him then.'

'I'll go to bed while I'm above,' Barney said.

'Go to hell for all I care,' she said silently, and went back to planning her leaving.

Julia went back to see Maggie Simmonds before Christmas, and the woman told her that the rooms would definitely be idle in January of the coming year. She had spoken to the landlord, apparently, letting on she knew Julia well and he had raised no objection to her moving in. 'I've mentioned you to Mrs Fahy, she's the woman who's leaving. She's a nice woman and she told me that when you called, to bring you up. You'll get an idea of the rooms, the size and that. Sit down by the fire and I'll go up and tell her you're here. Leave the door open and you'll hear me give you a shout over the banister if she's in.'

The shout came. The stairs were bare but well-scrubbed. Julia had been in many tenements but had never seen one as wellkept or pleasant-smelling. It wouldn't be the same as having your own house, she thought, but it would be cheaper, and Ellie would be safe from finding out what had happened to her father. Maggie she liked. The house had a good atmosphere. She felt she was doing the right thing.

Mrs Fahy had the front and back drawing rooms. She showed Julia how the folding door worked, and the little closet in the back room. 'If your family's mixed it gives great privacy for washing or at a time when you might be taken short. It's a pity the water's not laid on. Sometimes you get jaded going up and down the stairs. Still,' she said looking at Julia, 'you're a fine young woman, the stairs won't take a feather out of you. I'll leave you the table on the landing. It's handy for the water buckets, the bath you can see fits grand over it on a good strong nail and under the table a small sack of coal and sticks will fit.'

Julia thanked her and complimented her on how nice the rooms were, how well-kept. She said she loved the long sash-windows. 'Do the shutters work?' she asked.

'They do, and are a godsend in the winter. I do think the wind blows straight down from the mountains.'

How had she forgotten the mountains? She'd been so careful when choosing the street, to find out were the shops convenient and was there a variety of them so she would seldom if ever have to travel far from it; where the chapel was. And, even though it wouldn't matter for a while yet, where the school for Ellie was situated. And after all that she hadn't noticed the mountains, had forgotten that from almost everywhere in Dublin you could see them: a permanent reminder of all the good times, of the day on which she was sure Ellie had been conceived. Of the night or early morning when Jack had died on them. Being unable to see the mountains was one of the reasons she had wanted to leave Springfield Terrace. It frightened her to think how out of touch she was with reality that she could have walked up and down this street and not noticed the mountains.

'You're deep in thought,' said Maggie. 'Are you not sure about taking them?' She heard Maggie's voice but clearer than hers was Jack's. He was telling her to take the rooms. She was making the right move, for herself and Ellie. 'The mountains,' he said, 'haven't changed. The mountains are as beautiful as ever they were. It wasn't them that killed me. You'll be able to look at them again. Take the rooms.'

'I often do that, go far away. No, I'm sure enough. I'll take them. I think I'll be happy in them, and in the house. It has a good atmosphere. I like the smell in the rooms, Mrs Fahy. Were you happy in them?'

'I was. I came into them as a bride: I had my three children in them. We had more laughs in them than tears, but Tom died last year and the children are married. I'm getting crippled with rheumatism – old age, it comes to us all in one way or another. I'm moving in with my daughter where I'll be on the flat.'

Julia thanked her and said goodbye. Mrs Fahy said: 'God bless you, child, and I wish you and your family as much happiness as I've had.'

Maggie lived in the front and back parlours. She asked Julia in for a cup of tea. Her front parlour was crowded with good furniture: nice mahogany and walnut pieces which had once belonged to her mother. The mantelpiece was crowded with photographs in brass, wooden and shell frames. She took down one of the pictures. 'This,' she said, holding it out to Julia, 'was me and Jimmy.' Julia took the photograph. She recognised the photographer's backdrop – the balustrade with its climbing plants. She and Jack had stood in front of it when their picture was taken before he went to France. Jimmy looked as self-conscious as Jack had then, awed by the camera and uncomfortable in the stiff new uniform.

'That was taken a week before he went to the war. We'd been married a month. He was killed in the Dardanelles. A slip of a girl I was then and look at the size of me now.' Julia saw tears in her eyes. Then Maggie laughed. 'After the telegram I got great consolation from a bottle of stout. It works wonders.' She put the picture back on the mantelpiece and made the tea, pulled a small table between their two chairs, brought out a jam tart and a plate of lemon puffs and told Julia to tuck in. Then she asked the question Julia was dreading, for to answer it and the ones that were bound to follow would start her on a course of deception.

'Will your husband like the rooms, d'ye think?'

'He's dead.'

'The Lord have mercy on him – you never said. I'm very sorry. Was it the war?'

It would have been easy to say it was, only there was Ellie, at eighteen months too young to have been the child of a father killed in the war.

'No, not the war. He was shot in town, caught in cross-fire in Westmoreland Street.'

'The bastards, whoever it was that killed him. At least my fella volunteered for his death – not that at the time it would have been uppermost in his mind. All the same he'd have known there was a risk. It's not the same thing as walking across town and being killed. Have another biscuit. Lemon puffs are my favourites. Would you be entitled to compensation for that?'

'I don't know. I never thought of it.'

'Well, you want to, especially if this Treaty is signed. You might get something. I have a pension – you wouldn't buy many bottles of stout on that, but it's better than nothing. Where are you moving from?'

Julia gave the name of a street miles from where she lived, keeping her fingers crossed that Maggie didn't know it or anyone living in it.

She didn't appear to, but afraid that a memory might stir and remind her of someone or something about a street which Julia herself didn't know, she made an excuse about Ellie and the woman who was minding her. She would have to hurry back.

'I forgot to ask Mrs Fahy when she's moving out exactly,' she said as she rose to leave.

'New Year's Day,' said Maggie, walking to the front door with her. 'The first of January, 1922. God almighty, don't the years fly! Come down the following day – the landlord will be here and you'll get the keys. Goodbye now, I'll see you after Christmas, please God.'

'Goodbye and thanks very much. I think I'll like being your neighbour,' Julia said as she left.

Walking home she thought about Christmas, how she had made no preparations for it. How every other year of her life by this time in December her mother would have had the Christmas pudding made long ago, the turkey – a white hen turkey – and a Roscrea ham ordered. Last year she had bought Jack a new pipe. He wanted to stop smoking cigarettes and pipe tobacco, he had told her, worked out cheaper in the long run. She had gone into town to Kapp & Peterson's for the pipe. The man in the shop recommended a short-stemmed one and had then talked her into buying a tobacco pouch and a penknife for cutting the plug of tobacco. And after all that, Jack couldn't get the hang of the pipe! She still had it and the pouch and often took it out, fondling its soft black leather, thinking how Jack's hands had held it, and opening it, smelled the fragrant flakes he had never finished smoking.

She called into a shop and bought the makings of a small pudding and a bottle of port. The neighbours would come in on Christmas morning bringing gifts for Ellie. Her mother would turn in her grave if she didn't have the traditional slice of pudding and glass of port to offer them. They'd wish her a Happy Christmas and she them and never tell them that in a week she would be gone from the street. They'd think badly of her. They'd be hurt and puzzled that she had left without even a goodbye, but it couldn't be helped. She wanted a clean break: a new start for Ellie.

Later in the evening while making the pudding she wondered how she would manage the move without anyone seeing. Where would she get a carter who was unknown in the neighbourhood? A local one wouldn't be long about divulging her whereabouts. She wavered in her resolution to leave. Everything was too difficult; there were too many lies to tell. Already with Maggie she had begun them. If she moved into the new house she would have to continue. A liar needed a good memory, so the saying went. Forever she'd have to be on her guard. It would be a terrible way to live. And she asked herself as she gave the pudding its final stir, why was she really doing it? Wouldn't it be better for Ellie to grow up amongst people who had known her mother, her father and her grandmother – people who would talk to her about them, keep them alive in her memory.

When the pudding was on the range boiling she sat by the fire ready to top up the water when it boiled too low.

Ellie woke crying. Julia brought her down, changed her, gave her some milk then sat with her on her lap singing and repeating nursery rhymes like *See-saw Margery Daw, Ride A Cock Horse* and one her mother used to sing to her and Ellie: 'There was a little man and he had a little gun. And up the chimney he would run. With a belly full of fat and an oul tall hat and a pancake tied to his bum, bum, bum.' She bounced the child on her knees, squeezed her belly full of fat and then began to cry and cry as if she would never stop. She held Ellie close to her, asking, 'What'll I do, Ellie? What'll I do?' The toddler struggled out of her tight hold and chanted, 'Mam, Mam, Dad, Dad, Nan, Nan' and jigged up and down on her lap.

Julia had put out the gas when Ellie was changed and had been sitting with only the glow from the fire while she sang and recited for Ellie to fall asleep again. Shadows were in the room, cast by the fire, when a flame flared. Sitting by the table where the utensils, empty currant and raisin bags and tins of spice and other remains of her pudding-making lay she saw Jack. He was smoking a cigarette. He was as he was before, wearing an old pullover, a grey one her mother had knitted. 'Jack,' she said, 'is it really you?'

He smiled his lovely smile. 'Who else would it be?' She wasn't frightened. It was so natural to see him sitting there. To hear his voice. 'Don't cry,' he said. 'It makes me sad when you cry.'

'But I don't know what to do. I'm afraid. Afraid of doing the wrong thing for Ellie.'

'Go,' he said. 'Leave. I don't want Ellie to know what happened to me. It's nothing to do with the neighbours.'

'Oh my love. Oh, Jack.' She had stopped crying without realising it. Ellie had fallen asleep. She hadn't noticed that, either. 'Oh, Jack.' She rose to her feet. 'Let me touch you.' She began to walk towards him, holding Ellie close. 'Don't leave me again. Don't ever leave me again.'

She was almost by the table. 'I love you, Julia. I'll be minding you and Ellie.' There was a sound in the hall, then Cissie, her mother's friend called out, 'It's only me, Julia.' She looked away from him for a second and when she looked again he was gone.

187

Cissie opened the kitchen door. 'What are you doing sitting in the dark?'

'She woke up and I was putting her to sleep. The light's on, on the landing. I'll take her up. Sit down.'

When she came back to the room Cissie had relit the gas-mantle and was sitting down with the *Evening Mail* in her hand. 'I know you take the *Herald* so I bought you this. There's an advertisement to make boys' shirt-blouses at home. You were telling me you were looking for that sort of thing.' She gave Julia the paper opened at the page of Situations Vacant.

'Half a crown a dozen. That's not bad, especially if they're already cut out. I'd do eight dozen in a week at least,' Julia said, after reading the notice.

'And if you were stuck at any time, like if Ellie was troublesome, you could bring her into me.'

She was only half-listening, her eyes turning from Cissie to look at the chair where Jack had sat. She thought she smelt cigarette smoke.

'What ails you? What are you looking for?'

'I don't know. I'm tired – I made the pudding. I don't know what ails me, I'm all on edge.'

'I don't think you heard what I said. I'll keep an eye on Ellie if she gets cranky, you know – so that you could get out your eight dozen. It's a Box Number – I wonder where the place is? It'd be no good if you had to traipse miles to collect the stuff.'

'Maybe they'll deliver. I'll write in any case.'

'I don't think you're all that well. Are you eating?' Cissie asked concernedly.

'Like a horse. I'm grand, Cissie, honest to God.' And then she told her. She couldn't deceive Cissie, not Cissie who'd sat with her mother night after night when she was dying. Who'd made her chicken soup, egg custards and calf's-foot jelly. Cissie in her seventies who had just offered to mind Ellie so she could do her eight dozen. She couldn't leave the street without saying goodbye to Cissie.

'I'm going away. Leaving the street. After Christmas. Early in the New Year.'

'I don't blame you. I would, too, if I was in your shoes.'

'But I wasn't going to tell anyone – not even you. I don't want anyone to know where I'm going except you.'

'Listen to me, Julia. No one, no more than yourself, ever suspected that pair until after the fire. Though your poor mother, God be good to her, always had her suspicions. After the fire everyone knew. Ellie will hear it as soon as she can understand. Learn that her mother and father's best friends had her father killed for something he didn't do. God's curse on the pair of them. It could destroy her, leave her that she'd trust no one. Go, child. Go far away from here. This country's full of people brought up on the stories of the past. It's no good for anyone. Go and don't tell me where you're going.'

'I'd like you to know.'

'I don't want to. I'm an old woman – secrets I can do without. But if you're ever in any trouble, if you're short, or sick and need me, you know where I live. If you can't drop a line someone will do it for you. And don't be thinking that when you read my death in the paper you have to come to my funeral. I know you'll think of me and say a prayer for my soul. Wet a sup of tea and tell me how'll you get away from here without anyone knowing.'

'Oh, Cissie, no wonder my mother loved you.' Julia went to her and kissed her cheek.

'I loved her and you. Now make the tea.'

While they drank tea Cissie suggested a plan for keeping the neighbours in the dark about Julia's move. 'Are you taking everything from here?' she asked.

'The rooms are a fair size but everything wouldn't fit. I thought I'd take one of the double beds, two armchairs, the dresser and table and a press for the clothes. The tools Jack bought for the garden I would have no use for. I'll have to take the sewing machine. I don't want the furniture from the parlour, nor my mother's bedroom suite. I want her china cabinet and all the pictures and ornaments, and Jack's books. Oh, Cissie, isn't it as well we don't know what's in front of us! Who'd have thought this time last year I'd have been breaking up my mother's home. D'ye think she'll mind?'

'Your mother mind! "Sticks," she'd say, "bits of furniture don't make a home or happiness". Your mother wasn't sentimental. She'd be encouraging you to get out and start a new life. Now listen – I'll put it about that you're selling a few things. Everyone knows you're in bad straits, so when the cart goes off it'll be no surprise. But what about the things you leave?'

'You give them away. Give them to anyone who needs them.'

'There's many a one would be glad of them. Will I try for a few bob for them?'

'I don't want anything.'

'All right then, if you're sure. About the move. Go down to Camden Street, or better still the Coombe. There's lots of fellas with yokes who'd shift you. Fellas that have nothing to do with anyone round here. I'll give you a hand with Ellie while you're packing up. I'll pray for you and

Jack and your mother will intercede for you. You're doing the right thing, Julia. I'll go now, and remember what I told you – never let me know where you've gone. My mind's not all that it was and things slip out that I never meant to. But until God calls me I'll be at your beck and call if you need me.'

After Cissie left Julia thought about Jack, about him sitting in the kitchen earlier. She hadn't imagined it. He *was* there. He had talked to her, advised her as he had earlier in Mrs Fahy's rooms. He had come to her; God had sent him. For the first time since he died she didn't think of Barney or Sarah, but fell into a dreamless sleep.

CHAPTER EIGHTEEN

On 6 December 1921 the Anglo-Irish Treaty was signed in Downing Street. Collins had settled for the best of a bad bargain. 'In signing it,' he is reported to have said, 'I have signed my own death warrant.' For he knew well that hard-line Republicans would be furious that their country was not to be known as The Republic of Ireland but as the Irish Free State. That what the British had granted was Dominion status, not total independence, requiring all members of Dail Eireann to swear an oath of allegiance to the King. Six of the northern countries, Fermanagh, Antrim, Tyrone, Londonderry, Armagh and Down were given a month in which to decide whether or not they wanted to become part of the newly-formed Irish Free State. No one, especially hard-line Republicans, believed that at the end of the month the Northern States would opt in. The Republicans split, more than half of them regarding the signing of the Treaty as a betrayal.

However, the majority of the people joined hands and thanked God for an end to two and a half years of death and destruction. Julia, more concerned with plans for Christmas and her move, paid little attention to the news. The peace of mind that had come upon her after the vision of Jack had gradually faded ; once more, when she wasn't torn between which article to take to the new rooms and wondering if she would hear from the Box Number to which she had written, her thoughts again centred on Barney and Sarah. As she went about her tasks, she reflected bitterly : 'Only for them I'd be making our Christmas. My mother might still be alive. Ellie wouldn't be fatherless. I wouldn't be watching the clock for a letter telling me I can sew eight dozen shirt-blouses to earn a pound.' She wondered where the couple were and hoped life wasn't good for them, that they lived in dread and fear, had no friends. And from time to time she broke down and cried for what was happening to her, for the change in her nature. She had lost her joy in the ordinary, everyday things, but that was normal. Had Jack died of a disease or been killed accidentally, she would still be grieving for him – would, until she herself died, grieve for him. It was a natural thing experienced by all who lost someone they loved. It wouldn't be intertwined with her loathing and bitterness which, like a poisonous plant, was crowding out her necessary time of mourning.

★

There was nothing to distinguish them from the other men travelling steerage on the night boat to Holyhead from Kingstown. Their clothes were shabby, their collarless shirts fastened with brass studs. Both were dark, one with almost-black curly hair and blue eyes. He was a lot taller than his companion and his shoulders were big and square. They each carried in their jacket pockets brown-horn rosary beads and wore inside their vests sets of scapulars. One had an old leather travelling bag, the other a carpet one. In each bag was a parcel of boiled bacon sandwiches, a quarter bottle of whiskey, a Lucknow sauce bottle of cold sweet tea corked with a wad of paper, several packets of Woodbine cigarettes and wrapped inside a shirt and vest, a revolver. They looked like two Irishmen going to England for labouring work.

Steerage passengers travelled far down in the boat on wooden benches arranged one behind the other. The benches were packed with people of all ages, men, women and children. Once outside the harbour the boat pitched and tossed. People began to retch and heave. The two men were good sailors. They played cards, using their laps to place them on. They smoked and drank moderately of their whiskey. They looked after the two small children of a woman sitting next to them when she went to be sick.

Before the boat docked in Holyhead, most of the passengers had been seasick, many feeling too weak to make the lavatories. The stench was appalling. The two small children slept, one on the mother's lap, the other beside her. The young men went up on deck and sheltered behind a funnel from the driving rain. They could see into the first-class lounge, deserted except for a young man and woman sitting on a chintz-covered sofa, talking, laughing and drinking.

'I'd have thought there'd have been more of them,' the shorter of the two men said, nodding towards the lounge.

'It's easy to tell your sailing's been done in small boats and never over to England,' the other said.

'How so ?'

'There'll be fifty, sixty, maybe more of them tucked up in their cabins with a steward in attendance should they as much as fart.'

'Is that a fact ?'

'That's a fact. You'll see them when we dock, cock – powdered and shaved. Getting off the boat before anyone else.'

'And all the poor hoors down below.'

By the time they arrived at Euston the sandwiches, cold tea and whiskey had been eaten and drunk. The woman whose children they had minded called to them as they passed on the platform, 'Goodbye now and good luck and God bless you for your kindness.' They said,

'No bother, ma'am,' and waved to the little boy and girl. At a station buffet they had tea and toast before heading for Paddington, where one of them had a sister living. 'She'll cook us a breakfast. Then we'll doss down for a few hours. 'Tis a pity it isn't last week. We could have had a dekko at Downing Street and maybe seen Mick coming or going.'

'D'ye think there's any truth in what they say about him and Lady Lavery?'

'I'd say there is. Sure, isn't she a fine young woman married to an oul fella. And wouldn't Mick be any girl's fancy.'

They ate bacon, sausage, fried bread and eggs and drank cup after cup of tea. They slept until four in the afternoon, then talked to the sister for another hour before making their way to Borough where they went into the Fox and Hounds, drank pints of beer and nursed a whiskey apiece for half an hour. The public house was crowded. No one paid them any attention. The one whose first time it was in England asked the taller wide-shouldered man, 'Are you sure you'll know him?'

'As sure as if he was my own brother. He came in and out of the hotel where I was working, both of us looking for information for the other side. He was nice enough in an inoffensive way.'

After leaving the public house they hid in a deeply-recessed doorway and waited for Barney. It was dark and lashing rain. He came soon on the opposite side of the street at the time their informant had said he would. They had also been told he was a thin man now. They let him pass, stepped out into the street, and quickly looked up and down. No one was in sight. 'Daly, Barney, Daly,' the bigger one called across the narrow road.

His heart froze. Then a forlorn hope surged in it. It was an Irish voice – someone he knew, maybe. He turned and the younger man fired. Barney fell and the man ran to him and kneeling by him, whispered into his ear a short Act of Contrition. Coming back he said to his companion, 'You never know, it might be a long time since he went to Confession.'

'Aye,' said the other one. 'Let's head back for Euston now. There's a whore's melt been sitting pretty in Watford this while now – another of Glenivy's men. He'll be in heaven before the night's out.'

Barney was found by a porter on his way to Southwark Market; he wasn't dead. He was taken to Guy's Hospital. There was nothing to identify him, but the smell from his clothes suggested the tannery and later in the day the police went there with his description. By the time they had his name and address, Barney was dead.

They had come for him. They had got him. Of this Sarah had no doubt, knowing that nothing else would have kept him from home all night. It wasn't yet light when she woke. In less than half an hour she could be away. Hopefully no one would come before that to tell her what had happened to him, or to make enquiries. Her plan for fleeing was already made : the fifty pounds drawn from the Post Office. A bag was packed, at the bottom of it in a big envelope, her marriage certificate, Patrick's Baptismal Lines and newspaper cuttings of the Glenivys at different functions, and the magazine picture Barney had brought from the Club of Patrick and Caroline's wedding.

She woke and dressed Patrick. He was nearly trained to be clean but because of the travelling she put him into a napkin. She fed him, ate a cut of bread herself and drank some tea, wrapped him in a rug and banging the door behind her, walked to London Bridge Station from where she took a cab to Euston Station. There she bought a single ticket to Glasgow. She knew nothing about the city except that it was far away. Before boarding the train she bought minerals, biscuits and chocolate – a lot of biscuits and chocolate to pacify Patrick on the journey.

It was late at night when she arrived, dirty and dishevelled, Patrick soiled and smelling. Both of them had clogged-up noses and sore throats and eyes from the smoke and smuts that despite closed windows had found their way into the carriage as the engine belched its discharges throughout the long journey.

'Sir,' she said in her most appealing voice as she approached an elderly porter, tears in her eyes. 'I'm after coming all the way from London. I missed the train last night, and I'm in terrible trouble. The child was sick so I couldn't catch it and now I've missed the people who were to meet me – my employers. I daren't go near their place at this hour of the night. In any case, they probably won't want me now after letting them down. But I'll try them in the morning. It's tonight I'm worried about. D'ye know of anywhere cheap where I could lay my head for the night?'

The man took pity on her. He knew of a lodging-house, but it was a walk from the station. 'Too far for you and the bairn,' he said as he gave her the address. 'Now take this for a cab,' and he pressed a shilling into her hand.

'May God bless you,' Sarah said piously. 'I'll remember you in my prayers.'

The man was a Catholic, and her manner of thanking him warmed his heart, reminding him of his Irish grandmother. He carried her bag and found her a cab, and on the way told her that if she failed with the employers to try Father O'Hare in St Joseph's. He was a great man who never turned anyone away. She'd be sure of a few shillings and he might fix her up with work if the other thing failed.

The lodging-house was dirty with only one lavatory where the sink was. She had to wait ages before it was free. Patrick's bottom was raw. She washed him and herself. He toddled round the filthy room touching the vile lavatory. She washed his hands again, slapped him, sat him on the floor and warned him not to move while she rolled his soiled, stinking napkin in one of the sheets of a pile of newspapers beside the lavatory pan. She decided that when she left the room in the morning she'd leave the paper parcel behind her. They ate the last bar of chocolate and despite the sound of loud drunken voices, doors banging and people coming up and going down the stairs, they both fell asleep quickly.

From a remnant of blue velvet, bought for next to nothing, Julia was making Ellie a dress for Christmas. It was the blue of her daughter's eyes, and of Jack's. She was sewing it by hand, for hand-sewing she found more relaxing. Julia worked on after Ellie went to bed, sitting by the fire plying her needle and thinking her thoughts. Remembering the party when Ellie was shortened – when Sarah didn't shorten Patrick because she felt it was too soon to take him out of long gowns because he had been premature. How Mag (poor Mag, she often wondered how she was getting on) had dug into the cake. However kind the nuns were to her, her freedom would be curtailed. The last time Julia had enquired about the girl she had received a short answer from her mother, who was drunk as usual. 'You're very concerned about her all of a sudden, you and everyone else in the street! But you run her out of it – a child that harmed no one. Run her out of it, you did.' She never enquired again and avoided Mrs Venables.

When she had sewed all she was going to, she would put out the light and sit hoping when she looked towards the table that Jack might appear. Often she felt his presence about her, as she did her mother's. She talked to them, asked their advice and help. Her mother was disapproving, warning her as she had when alive about her bitterness. Urging her to forgive. She quarrelled with her. 'You,' she'd say, 'you that hated them before they harmed us, you to tell me to forgive!' And her mother would say, 'You'll never be whole again if you don't.' Her mother was the way she was when she lived. Her tongue sharp. Critical. Treating her as if she was a child instead of a grown woman, a widow tormented by how she was widowed. And she'd wondered why Heaven couldn't let her mother see into her heart, and know that she could never forgive either of them. Never.

Jack was more understanding. He'd encouraged her to leave Spring-field Terrace, reassured her that she was doing the right thing. Jack told her he loved her. They never mentioned Barney's or Sarah's names, but she knew he must feel the same as she did. What, she used to wonder, would have happened if Cissie hadn't come the night she did. Could she have touched Jack? Would he have felt warm and real? Ah, to be held by him once more, to lie with him ... to have him stroke her hair, kiss her face and whisper his love. To know that never again would she see him on this earth was the hardest thing to bear, so hard that sometimes she feared for her sanity. And her mother talked about forgiveness! Cissie didn't know her as well as she thought. She never told Lizzie about the move during these encounters. She didn't share Cissie's belief that Lizzie would be in favour of it.

She got an answer from the shirt–blouse people: they would deliver and collect, and eight dozen was the average they expected, for which they paid a pound. If you exceeded the amount by not less than another three dozen, they paid a bonus. All materials would be supplied. A high standard was expected, and on no account must the work be soiled. Pressing was not required. She wrote back accepting and giving them her new address. She could start at the beginning of the second week in January, she said, knowing she would need that time to get settled into the new rooms.

One evening while Ellie was still up she read the paper, skipping the news of the dissensions caused by the signing of the Treaty, and skimming the Deaths Column and the advertisements for clothes for Christmas. Then she turned to the small news items – three and four-line paragraphs, usually of some terrible tragedy befalling unimportant people. It was here that she read of Barney's killing. '*Bernard Daly, a Dublin man, was shot and fatally wounded in south-east London on the 9th of December. So far, police enquiries have been unsatisfactory.*'

He was dead. They had got him. She was glad – she hoped he hadn't been shot in the back, that he had been aware of what was about to happen. She was elated – until it came to her that Sarah probably still lived. And while she did, her hatred and desire for revenge would continue. Not until she who must have been the instigator of Jack's betrayal got her just desert, would Julia find peace.

Sarah combed her hair back and secured it in a tight bun. She dressed herself in the sober costume she had brought with her, and on her head placed a dowdy hat. She then set out with Patrick to find St Joseph's church. The city frightened her. Compared to Dublin, and even Borough, it was bedlam. The streets were so busy with traffic – the crowds, the noise! She stopped to ask the way from a woman who smiled and appeared to be friendly, but Sarah couldn't understand a word she said. She thanked her and moved on. Her second enquiry was more successful and she found the church, which was similar to many Dublin churches. In case someone – a priest or a housekeeper – might be observing her from the nearby Presbytery, she did what a good Catholic, especially one in the dire straits that she would present to the priest, would do, and entered the church where she proceeded to bless herself with Holy Water, genuflect, enter and kneel ostensibly to pray. She stayed for five minutes getting her story straight, then with her thoughts collected went to the Presbytery door and on the housekeeper's enquiry, replied that she wanted to see Father O'Hare.

The woman, stout, elderly and pleasant-looking, said : 'Father's on a sick call. Is it urgent ?'

Sarah let her tears fall and in between sobs said, 'It's only that I've been travelling all night. I'm destitute. What time will he be in ? I could come back.'

'Oh, you poor wee hen, you'll do no such thing. You'll no walk the streets on a freezing morning with the bairn. Come in and I'll make you something to eat.' She sat by a blazing fire in the kitchen eating porridge and melting toast, and between mouthfuls told her tale of woe. The housekeeper fed Patrick on her lap and murmured sympathetically. 'Consumption,' she said. 'It's a terrible scourge. It takes the flower of the flock. How did you come to settle on Glasgow ?'

'Barney, Lord have mercy on him, worked here one year.' She named a construction firm she had passed on her way to the chapel. ' "Go to Glasgow," he told me when he was dying. "Ireland's finished. The gentry are ruined." D'ye see, I used to work for the gentry before I got married. "Glasgow," he said, "is the place where you'll find kindness. Go and see Father O'Hare. If anyone can help you, he will." ' She hoped to God Father O'Hare wasn't newly-arrived in the parish.

'The poor young man,' her companion commiserated. 'He was right, too, about Glasgow and Father O'Hare. Eat up that toast, now. Are you sure you won't have a boiled egg ?'

'No, thanks very much. I'm bursting. It's work I'm hoping to find – a live-in situation where they wouldn't object to a child. I could get good references.' She sniffed and searched for a handkerchief, blew her nose and continued : 'With the way things are at home, the gentry will be leaving in their thousands.' She wrung the handkerchief between her hands and offered to take Patrick.

'Ah, leave him where he is,' said the housekeeper. 'He's a bonnie wee laddie. What's his name ?'

'Patrick, after Barney's father : Patrick Michael Kane.' Kane would be an easy name to remember, she had decided.

'Father won't be long and I've a feeling you might be lucky. God never closes one door but He opens another. Of course, it's not for me to say but I know for a fact there's a family, not in this parish now but out in Clarkston, that are looking for a housekeeper. Lovely people, great friends of Father's – the MacDonaghs. Poor Mrs MacDonagh had a bad stroke. Thanks be to God she's made a grand recovery, her speech is back and a bit of use in her legs, but she'll never keep house again. Only last week I heard him tell Father they'd have to find a housekeeper.'

'That's Barney interceding for me,' said Sarah piously.

'Don't build your hopes, not until Father comes in. But one way or another he'll see to it that you're not left destitute.'

Sarah had never met a priest like Father O'Hare in Ireland. She was genuinely impressed by his kindness and friendliness, by the attention he paid Patrick. And when he said he thought the job could be hers she felt like hugging him and kissing his red handsome face beneath its shock of silvery hair. 'Hold on there and I'll give Tom a ring,' he said.

'That's Mr MacDonagh,' fussed the housekeeper. 'He's a big contractor in Glasgow. All through his own hard work mind. He built it up from nothing.'

'Well, Mrs Kane, you're in luck. You couldn't have found a kinder, more Christian family to work for, and the child, God bless him, will be as welcome as the flowers in May. Tell me now,' asked the priest, sitting down to the table where the housekeeper was already pouring tea for him. 'How d'ye think things will work out in Ireland with the Treaty?'

'God forgive me, Father,' Sarah said, having decided that kind though the priest might be, he was a shrewd man, 'I've had no interest in it nor what's gone on for the last years. My mind was occupied with Barney's suffering. There wasn't another thought in my head.'

'Well, of course, that would have been natural. You stay now and after dinner I'll get a cab to take you out to the MacDonaghs.'

She thanked him sincerely.

'Make yourself comfortable,' the housekeeper told her. 'Have a look at the paper.'

Sarah did, and read a small paragraph reporting her husband's death. She read it again. Barney was dead : she was rid of him. An encumbrance she was free of.

CHAPTER NINETEEN

The move went without a hitch. The carter came to Julia's at eleven o'clock in the morning. Cissie was there to let him in, Julia having gone to meet the new landlord and take over the rooms.

'You're not taking the curtains?' Cissie had queried the night before.

Julia explained about the long windows which her own curtains wouldn't quarterways cover. 'And in any case, if I'd taken them down the neighbours would have wondered why.'

'You're right, they would. No one has an inkling of what's happening. In a day or two I'll let the truth be known.'

'I'll miss you all.'

'Please God your new neighbours will be kind to you. You're sure you don't want anything for what you're leaving behind?'

'I'm sure. They're not much but may do a turn for someone. You'll know who needs them most.'

'After I've disposed of them I'll give back your keys. Come to me in the morning for your breakfast, but go to bed now – you look jaded.'

On her way to Cissie's the next morning, she met a neighbour going to early Mass. 'You're up and about at the crack of dawn,' the woman said. 'There's nothing wrong?'

'Ah no,' said Julia, hating herself for her deception. 'I'm going about a bit of work. Cissie's going to mind Patrick.'

'I'll say a prayer you get it,' the woman said leaving her, and Julia fought back her tears. It was a new beginning: a new life for Ellie. No more crying. Soon enough she'd be of an age to notice. Her mother's sorrow and bitterness had to be hidden from now on. Even so, when she left Cissie's Julia did cry.

Maggie was at the hall door watching for her arrival. She brought her into her place, gave Ellie something to eat and something to play with, and sat Julia by the fire. 'Mr Crystal'll be here in a minute. He's a nice oul fella, not bad about repairs. He's a moneylender as well. Mad to die in Palestine.'

'Why in Palestine?' asked Julia.

'He's a Jewman, that's why. Did you get the work? Remember you told me about it the last time you dropped in.'

'I did, thank God. It'll be a help.'

'You're very unfortunate. Lord have mercy on your husband, if he had to die it was a pity it wasn't in France, for you'd have had a pension. It's a bloody disgrace the way widows are treated, thrown on Relief. Maybe this government of ours might remedy that. You take the Jazzer Doyle, he got rheumatic fever at the war. It left him with a bad heart and he's on a pension.'

'The Jazzer – is that his name?'

'It's what I call him. I'm terrible about giving people nicknames – not to their face, though. You'll meet them all. Hop the Twig, he lost a leg in Flanders and is on crutches. Then there's Gunner-Eye – one looking to the wall and the other at his nose – and Drim and Drew. There's no harm in it. I like them all, they're a great crowd of neighbours.'

'I suppose I'll be in the house no time before you've one for me.'

'Maybe,' said Maggie, 'but sure you'll never know. Don't look so serious – I'm only coddin' you. There's nothing funny or peculiar about *you*, but the others – take the Jazzer for instance. He's mad about dancing – out every night in the week, bad heart and all. You'll see him in the yard sometimes, giving the brush a twirl, whistling or singing the latest tune. What else would you call him except the Jazzer?'

'I suppose so. You'll have to tell me their real names, though. What about Drim and Drew, are they two people?'

'They are. Two sisters, Ethel and Maude – Protestants, can't you tell by the names. Decent, respectable women, and good neighbours, though they keep theirselves to theirselves. You can tell they've come down in the world and want to get back up. They're a bit withered and grey if you know what I mean. "An oul drimandrew", that's what my mother used to call anyone with aspirations and a withered-looking appearance. It's Irish, I think. But they're very nice really. That's your man just come into the hall.'

The landlord knocked and Maggie called him in and introduced Julia. He was an old man with very blue eyes. Julia was surprised; she thought all Jews had dark eyes. He shook hands with her and said the rent would be four shillings a week. 'Mr Crystal, she's a widow with a child. Mrs Fahy was only paying three and six. What ails you, for God's sake? She can't afford four shillings. Have a heart, now.'

'Maggie, Maggie, you're a terrible woman. How am I supposed to live! "The lavatory's broken, Mr Crystal. The roof is leaking, Mr Crystal. The banister's cracked, Mr Crystal." Repairs, repairs. Everything goes up – so the rent goes up.'

'You bloody oul robber. It's Palestine you're thinking about. Well,

Mrs Harte's sixpence a week extra's not going to get you there any the sooner. Sit down and have a cup of tea.'

'No tea, no cakes, no bread and butter. Look at this.' He patted his large belly. 'I'll tell you what I'll do. Three and six for the first six months and then four shillings. All right?'

'That's grand with me,' said Julia.

'It's better than nothing,' Maggie said. 'The rent-book now and the keys.' When the transaction was finished Mr Crystal left. 'He'll forget about the extra, he always does. Take up the brush and a duster and give the rooms a sweep before your stuff comes. Leave the child with me. If she gets too cranky I'll bring her up.'

The rooms were spotless, and to Julia's delight, Mrs Fahy had left the curtains – a godsend, as stuff for such big windows would have made a hole in her savings. There was a sack of coal coming on the cart, and sticks. She'd have a fire going in no time. A pity, she thought, that there was no range – no oven. But she'd manage without home-made cakes. Soda bread she could cook in the pot with a few sods of turf on the lid, and on the rare occasions she could afford a roast, that would do as well in a pot.

Looking round the front room she saw that Mrs Fahy had left the gas mantles. She attempted to light one but no gas flowed. The meter was behind the door. She fed it two pennies. By the sound of the coins landing she could tell it had been emptied. She tried the light again and it worked. Turning it out she said to herself, 'I like it here. I think I'll be happy. I like Maggie. She'll be curious but that's natural in some people.' She looked out through the window watching for the cart. She was impatient to have her things about her.

The MacDonaghs' house was detached, double-fronted, redbricked and set in a fair-sized garden behind a laurel hedge. A young, untidy-looking girl answered Sarah's knock.

'Come in,' she said. 'Mrs MacDonagh's waiting for you in the parlour.' Following her into the hall Sarah wondered who she was – surely not a daughter in that straggly skirt and hair that hadn't seen a brush in a long time. 'I stayed on,' said the girl as if to answer Sarah's wonderings. 'I do the cleaning. I finish at one, but I stayed behind to let you in. I'm Annie. This is the parlour.' She opened the door and put her head round, saying, 'She's here. Mrs Kane's here.'

'Send her in, hen, then you can go.'

'I'll see you tomorrow,' Annie said as she left.

Mrs MacDonagh was a little woman with a lot of sandy-greyish hair. 'Come in. Come up close to me, for even with my specs my eyes aren't good. Sit down now and take off your coat, and let the child run about. God bless him, he's a bonnie wee boy. Mrs Sharp'll be in at three – she sees to the food – the dinner. Tom makes the breakfast and Annie makes me a snack at midday. I've a woman that does the washing and ironing so you won't be killed.'

'It's very kind of you to take me on without seeing me or a reference or anything.'

'Father O'Hare's word is good enough for me. A great Christian, that man, and a great judge of character. Here am I blathering on and no doubt you want to ask *me* things. I'm that lost since the stroke. I was a great one for going out – shopping, the whist, into town to eat cream cakes with my friends. And talking. Now there's only Annie – the poor child, I have her moidered. Mrs Sharpe, she just does what she has to do. No lingering, no talking. I miss that sorely. I'll want you to do that – keep me company. And maybe do something with my hair: I used to pin it up, but my arms are weak if I hold them over my head for long. Tell me about yourself. Father O'Hare said you worked for the gentry, so this'll be a bit of a comedown. But we'll treat you well, and – what's the child's name?'

'Patrick, after his grandfather.'

'Fancy that – one of my sons is Patrick, Paddy we call him. I've two sons and two daughters. Grown up and gone away. Paddy's an engineer in Vancouver and Donald's a doctor out in Brisbane. They'll be home this summer, the first time in four years. Pray God you'll still be here and will meet them.'

Patrick toddled round the room. Sarah kept an eye on him, for the room was crowded with small tables filled with silver-framed photographs and ornaments.

'How old is he?' asked the old lady.

'He'll be two in April, please God.'

'And spare him. I lost a little boy at two – Edward, a lovely child. My mother used to say he had the face of an angel, and when he died of measles that God wanted him back in Heaven. He'd be forty next month.'

Sarah's head was splitting and she felt that if Mrs MacDonagh didn't stop talking it would burst open. Fortunately Patrick started to cry. She grabbed at the excuse. 'He has a sleep about now, that's what ails him.'

'The poor lamb and maybe he's thirsty as well. If you can find your own way about – to the kitchen and up the stairs. The second floor, the first room on the right, that's where you'll sleep. Tonight Tom'll bring a cot down from the attic – will he manage in the bed for now?'

202

'So long as it's not too high.'

'It's high enough. Put him in my room – there's a sofa there : the first landing and the first door on the right.'

'Are you sure ?' asked Sarah, musing, 'I know she isn't gentry, but I wouldn't expect an employer to be this kind. There has to be a catch.' There wasn't. The MacDonaghs were kind people who paid her thirty shillings a week, treated her as one of the family and Patrick as if he was their grandson. In return she kept house for them, did Mrs McDonagh's hair and when she wasn't shopping or taking Patrick out, kept her company, for hours during the day and many nights during the week. Mr MacDonagh, who resembled the priest in complexion and hair-colouring but who had features more like an ex-boxer, was greatly involved with the local Catholic church, spending several evenings on committee work for the Building Fund, the Sodality and the Society of St Vincent de Paul.

Sarah listened to Mrs MacDonagh and when she tired was expected to talk to her. She heard about their progression from the Gorbals where she and her husband had been reared and he worked as a bricklayer, to Clarkeston and his own building firm. How their daughters were missionary nuns in Africa. How, though longing for grandchildren, they had accepted God's Will when the girls professed their vocations. Now their hopes were pinned on Donald and Paddy marrying and having children.

Sarah made appropriate noises now and then while her mind compared the over-heated, over-furnished room with the elegance of Glenivy, wondering at the same time which of the questions would Mrs Mac-Donagh ask when she had finished talking about her family. 'How long did your poor husband have consumption ? Have you no relatives in Ireland ? Did he die hard ? Did you have a bad confinement on Patrick ?' Again and again she asked the same questions. Maybe the stroke had affected her memory. Maybe she was just that sort of gabby woman : gabby and religious, for when she wasn't asking questions or repeating stories of her children, she talked about novenas, relics that worked miracles, saints in whom she had great faith, pilgrimages to Lourdes. By the end of her first week in the house Sarah had decided that as soon as possible she would leave Mrs MacDonagh and Glasgow behind, but first she had to write to Lord Glenivy, asking for his help.

Halfway through her second week in the house, Mrs MacDonagh announced one morning that she had a great surprise for her. Sarah pretended eager curiosity. 'A surprise ? I love surprises. Tell me, I'm dying to know.'

'We're going to Lourdes, me and you and Patrick. It's all arranged –

203

Father O'Hare has fixed everything. We'll be off in the New Year. What d'ye think of that?'

Lourdes? She had heard all about Lourdes. Praying and processions. Praying and praying. Singing *Ave Maria* till you were hoarse. Being belted with wet cloths in a freezing pool. Sick and dying people everywhere. This was the impression of Bernadette's Shrine she had formed judging by the rapturous descriptions heard from returned pilgrims. Cynically she dismissed as rubbish tales of miracles: the peace that came to you there, the consolation for your own suffering in the face of so many worse off. And not if she had to sleep in the streets was she going to Lourdes. While these thoughts went through her head she thanked Mrs MacDonagh. 'You're very kind. I believe it's a marvellous place. The people I knew who were cured there! Please God you could get better in Lourdes.'

Delighted with herself, Mrs MacDonagh told her of the travel arrangements while Sarah composed in her head a letter to Lord Glenivy in which she told him that Barney had died in London, that she lived in dread and fear of her life in an unpleasant situation in Scotland. She begged him to help her, to get her and her son to some faraway place. She asked him to use the name Kane when he replied, explaining that this was the name she now went under. She wished to be remembered to her Ladyship and hoped she and his Lordship were in good health.

While Mrs MacDonagh was taking a nap she wrote the letter. Fearing that since the signing of the Treaty the Club might have changed hands, even be run by members of the IRA., she sent the letter to Glenivy House. His Lordship would reply, of that she had no doubt, and then her troubles would be over.

Julia met her neighbours. The Jazzer, whose name was Sean, was tall and slight, with black straight hair combed back and kept in place with brilliantine. His face was long and had a pallor about it which Julia thought might be caused by his heart condition, until she noticed that his mother, Mrs Doyle, had the same pale skin. He shook Julia's hand and hoped she would be happy in the house and offered to knock in a nail or picture-hook, should she ever want such jobs doing, then left her with his mother, who extolled his virtues as a son, as a handyman and his progress as a clerk in a firm making patent medicines.

'He's doing night classes and has the prospect of being a book-keeper. He got rheumatic fever in the trenches,' she said, and went on to tell her what Julia already knew from Maggie. 'Thanks be to God it doesn't affect him. His job is light work. Every six months he has to go before the Pension Board – not that they're concerned about his health unless the improvement is so great they can cut him off or reduce his pension. I'd love to see him settled down with a good woman. That would put a stop to his dancing. He's a divil for it. Every night of the week he'd be at it if I didn't discourage him.' While she talked, Mrs Doyle was scrutinising Julia as she did any single woman or young widow she met, sizing them up as a possible wife for the Jazzer.

Hop the Twig and his wife Mrs Sheridan had ten children – the five older ones married and living elsewhere. 'Maggie tells me your husband, Lord have mercy on him, was shot in one of them battles – an innocent bystander. Thanks be to God there's an end to that with the Treaty signed. Was he at the war?' Mrs Sheridan enquired.

'No,' Julia lied. 'He volunteered but didn't pass the medical.'

'It just shows you – your death is mapped out for you. If he'd passed he might have come home safe.'

'Mary's a great believer in fate,' her husband said affectionately. 'Tomorrow morning if I fell into the mixer and came out in bits with the bread dough she'd console herself that my number was on the blades. She's a great optimist, as well. Did you hear her now thanking God that the Troubles are over! I think they're just beginning. The country's split down the middle: Free Staters against Republicans. I'm telling you, you haven't seen the end of things yet.'

'Shut up for God's sake, Charley Sheridan – you're always meeting trouble halfway. What I wanted to say, Mrs Harte is that don't ever be stuck if you want someone to keep an eye on the child – she's a little dote. My daughters are well used to children. She'd be in safe hands.'

Julia thanked her and said she'd be delighted if now and then one of the girls could take Ellie out when they came home from school. 'For a walk in the park. I had a little garden – she was used to the fresh air.'

'Where was that – the street you lived in?' Mrs Sheridan asked inquisitively.

Two questions and two lies in less than five minutes. It was the way Dublin people were – *all* Irish people, she supposed. For a minute she had forgotten the street where she was supposed to have lived. She hated the deception. She hated Sarah and Barney for being the cause of it. She hoped he was in Hell, burning.

Drim and Drew asked no questions. They hoped she'd be happy in the house; she knew where they lived if ever she wanted anything. They admired Ellie. Julia could see what Maggie meant about them – dressed in shabby tweed skirts and jackets, with old-fashioned felt hats. Grey, everything about them a greyish colour. Long-faced, thin. Beautifully spoken. They had seen better days. She liked them – their manners were better than the other women's in the house. She didn't think she'd have to tell them many lies.

Gunner-Eye O'Brien, whose name was Dinny, and his wife Molly had no children. Maggie said it was because he couldn't see where to put his mickey. That she was good-natured, would give you her last ha'penny, but then would tell everyone she had given it to you. As well as that she had a wicked tongue and would take your reputation as quick as look at you.

'What does he do for a living?' Julia asked Maggie after meeting the O'Briens.

'He's in Jacobs in the dispatch bay. God only knows where the biscuits finish up with him dispatching them. He brings home bags of biscuits for the kids in the house – you won't go short of Mariettas.'

Julia thought that she must always address the men as Mr O'Brien, Doyle and Sheridan to guard against their nicknames slipping out. And Drim and Drew she would call the Misses Bruton.

She soon had the rooms to her liking, and once underway with the new job, was averaging eight dozen shirt-blouses a week. Ellie was good at amusing herself. She had a rag doll, a wooden pull-along horse and a ball. When these lost her interest, Julia half-filled a small tin with shirt-buttons and taped it shut. The child rattled it, banged it and tried to undo the tapes. Julia talked, sang and recited nursery rhymes as she treadled the machine. Sometimes Ellie slept for an hour and then she sewed furiously. After school the Sheridan girls if it was a fine day took her in the go-cart to the park.

In between times Julia went for her messages, cooked, washed and ironed. Maggie sometimes came at night after her visit to the public house and if she hadn't drunk too many bottles of stout, sewed pearl buttons on to the shirt-blouses while Julia embroidered the buttonholes. During these sessions Maggie related the happenings of the evening: who was giving whom the glad eye – how it wouldn't be long before he had her up against a wall in the lane getting his oats. If either of them were married she hadn't a good word for them, but single people, widowers or widows she felt were free to do what they liked. It was their body and their arse that would burn in Hell. Nothing to do with anyone else.

One evening as they both sat sewing, Maggie said, 'The Jazzer has notions of you.'

'Of me!' Julia said with incredulity, looking up and stabbing her finger with the needle. Quickly she put it in her mouth to avoid staining the shirt-blouse.

'Why shouldn't he? Aren't you a finelooking young woman? I'll tell you another thing: his mother would be delighted – she's taken a great shine to you. Have you never thought of marrying again?'

Julia took her finger out of her mouth and bound it with a bit of the shirt material. 'No,' she said. 'I never have,' glad that for once she could answer a question of Maggie's truthfully. A question, moreover, she bitterly resented. Marry someone else – lie with someone else after Jack! Where was there a man who could compare with him? She wanted Maggie to go, to leave her alone. What right had she to ask such a thing, to mention the word 'marriage' and Jack not a twelvemonth dead! Then she remembered her lies, the impression she had given her that Jack was a good while dead. Maggie wasn't to blame: it was a natural enough question for one widow to ask another.

'I wish you hadn't said that about the Jazzer. Every time I see him in future I'll feel awkward. He's nice, I like him. I wouldn't want to think that by being friendly, passing the time of day with him and smiling I was encouraging him.'

'It won't do him a bit of harm. There's never been anyone in the house like you before.'

'But he goes to all the dances – he must meet girls there!'

'It's my belief the only dancing he does is in the yard with the brush. He'd be too shy to ask a girl.'

'The poor man,' Julia said.

'Never mind the poor men, what about the poor widdawomen deprived of their conjugal rights. D'ye miss them, Julia, d'ye?'

She was flabbergasted. She blushed. She lied. 'No,' she said. 'I never think about them.'

'I'd have thought you were the sort of woman who would. Now take me, I'd rather have them than my dinner any day or night of the week. And I do now and then. If you listen to Molly O'Brien, she'll tell you I have a man in my room every night of the week. A bloody lie. Most of them in the pub I wouldn't piss on. But now and then, there's a fella, he goes to sea and when he's home we make hay while the sun shines. I'm going boss-eyed doing these buttons. I'll go home and let you go to bed. Goodnight and God bless you.'

After she had left, Julia put away her sewing and sat thinking about Jack and what Maggie called her conjugal rights. The tears ran down her face. 'Oh my love,' she spoke to the empty room. 'To call what we had by such an ugly name.' She recalled his face. His beautiful mouth, the taste of it. His hands caressing her. 'Oh my love, my love – and all the years we should have had. All the years and days and long lovely nights.'

★

207

'Well, I'm off again tomorrow.'

Mary Flynn, who'd worked at Glenivy with Sarah, looked up at her husband's words as they sat having breakfast together.

'Where to this time?'

'Only up to the uncle's. He's not well.'

'How do you know?'

'I had a letter yesterday.'

'And you never said a word.'

'You must have been out when it came.'

'Maybe I'll come with you. I wouldn't mind seeing Kildare again.'

'Would that be wise and him so cranky – worse if he's not well.'

'Maybe not,' Mary said. 'How long will you be gone?'

'Depends how he is.'

'How's Collins coping these days?'

'Don't mention that bastard to me.'

'You worshipped him one time. When you came back from London the last time you were full of him and the Treaty.'

'So were a great many more, till they realised the full implications of what he'd signed. Lackeys of England, that's all we are now.'

'Will trouble come of it, d'ye think?'

'That I wouldn't know. Cows is my business.'

'Aye,' she said, and began clearing the table. What, she wondered as she washed the dishes, was really taking him to Kildare? It wasn't his uncle. That oul fella had never been sick a day in his life. When his time came they'd have to shoot him. And for sure no letter had come. Yesterday she hadn't crossed the door. She had found the revolver after his last visit to England. She had a good idea what his trips entailed, and she believed he knew she had an idea. But nothing was said. Nothing ever would be by her. What he did was his business. He was a good man. She loved him. She was carrying his child. She thanked God always for the day she met him. And fearing that trouble was coming and with his animosity towards Collins he would throw in his hand with the Republicans, she prayed for his life to be spared. All through the day, the following one and the next she kept wondering what was taking him to Kildare.

'He won't write back straight away,' Sarah told herself as she sat listening to Mrs MacDonagh make plans for the pilgrimage to Lourdes. But Lord Glenivy would definitely answer and help her. By April she'd be far away from Glasgow, Sunday Mass, Holy Days of Obligation and everything else she hated about Mrs MacDonagh.

Her employer, meanwhile, was secretly thinking about Donald's visit in April, wondering what he would think of Sarah. He'd be bound to find her attractive. Now that she didn't wear her hair pulled back in a tight bun you could say she was beautiful – beautiful and good. A devoted mother, and kindness itself. What she'd do without her she didn't know. She ran the house like clockwork, was a great listener, and when she got going about Glenivy – well, you felt as if you were there. She'd make a grand wife for Donald. Tom would buy them a house nearby. Donald was bound to be happier at home. She'd have him and Sarah and Patrick whom she loved as if he were her own flesh and blood. God worked in mysterious ways – sending her the stroke and then Sarah as if to compensate her. Sending her a daughter to take the vacant places. Tom thought of her as a daughter, too. Not that he ever said, but you could tell by the pleasure on his face when he talked to her – the way his eyes lit up when she came into the room.

Tom came in just then as she was thinking about him. He went and kissed his wife's cheek and silently asked God to stop him making comparisons between her and Sarah. She was a good wife. He loved her. He would do anything in the world for her. But Sarah's hair, the way it went in little curls round her forehead, the walk of her, how her hips swayed and the small waist on her, her breasts pushing out the front of her blouse – they affected him in a way that wasn't fitting in an old man. It was sinful. She was a terrible temptation. Looking at her he remembered being young. He had confessed the sin and the priest told him to pray. Night and morning he did and still he was tormented.

'Time for my bed, I suppose,' Mrs MacDonagh said.

'I'll make your cocoa,' said Sarah. 'Will you have it here or above?'

'In bed, I think.'

'Upsadaisy then,' Mr MacDonagh said as he gently helped his wife out of her chair, then he and Sarah with arms supporting Mrs Mac-Donagh, took her up the stairs. He left the room while Sarah got her undressed and into bed. 'Take out my hairpins.'

'As if I'd forget,' thought Sarah savagely. 'Every night you say the same thing and I know what's coming next.'

On cue Mrs MacDonagh said, 'Tom always liked my hair loose in bed.' She shook her head and her wispy gingery-grey hair fell about her shoulders.

Mr MacDonagh went into the garden and smoked a cigar while Sarah made the cocoa. She took it up then went to her own room. Patrick had thrown off his covers. She rearranged them. In the glow from the nightlight she thought he resembled his father. She smoothed his forehead and talked to him: 'The letter from your grandfather will come soon. We'll go away then. I'll make something of you. You won't grow up the child of a servant.' She went to bed and thought about Glenivy, about the attic bedroom and Patrick. Wondering if his father would mention her letter to him. He was the most gorgeous man she had ever seen. She hoped Patrick would grow up to look like him. People would see the breeding in him. Maybe one day she would tell him who he really was. It would depend on how her life went. Who she married. And marry she would. Take her time about finding the right man – never, not if she starved, another Barney, but a man with money. She needed money for Patrick's sake.

Mrs Bellows had rooms on the ground floor so it was she who was woken by the heavy thuds on the front door. Uncorseted, wearing a dark dressing gown buttoned up to her chin and with a hairnet well down on her forehead, she looked pathetically ludicrous. 'Who is it? What do you want at three o'clock in the morning? Who are you?' she asked in her imperious voice.

'The Sergeant from the barracks, ma'am. We've an important message for his Lordship.'

'Can't it wait until morning?'

'Our instructions were that he must get it this minute.'

It wasn't within her powers to decide what was and what was not urgent business for his Lordship. In the last two years there had been many strange comings and goings at all hours. She opened the door and was confronted by six armed men, one of whom pushed her aside and came into the hall. 'Wake the house,' he said. 'Get everyone up and out. But first bring Lord and Lady Glenivy down.'

She went upstairs as quickly as she could, first to Lady Glenivy's room. She told her what had happened. 'I've to waken his Lordship and then get everyone out.'

'I'll waken him. You see to the others.'

'Very well, ma'am.'

Lady Glenivy got up and looked out through the window. She saw four men with what were drums of petrol, she presumed, rolling them towards the house. She had been expecting something like this: it had already happened in other Big Houses. But why, she wondered, hadn't they been alerted from the lodge? They had a phone to the House. Unless ... but would they have killed their own? From a drawer in the small bedside table she took and drank from her silver whiskey flask to stop the trembling in her legs and the racing of her heart, then she put on a warm coat, scooped the jewellery she had worn that night into a handbag along with two small photographs of Patrick, and then went to waken her husband.

210

She shook him gently. 'Get up, darling, we have visitors.'

He woke, startled and very old-looking. He hadn't been well lately. The local quack said it was his heart. Next week he was going to see a good chap in Fitzwilliam. 'What is it? What's up?'

'We have visitors.'

'At this time?' he said indignantly, and then in a different voice, 'Oh, I see – them.'

'I'm afraid so. We are to get everyone out – you know what that means.'

He got up, sat on the side of the bed and buried his face in his hands. She knew he was crying. Crying for what would happen to his beloved House. She said nothing, knowing that he would pull himself together. Even shave if she let him, which of course she wouldn't. Not with a crowd of madmen outside. He sighed, then reaching under a pillow, found a handkerchief and blew his nose loudly several times.

'Drink some of this,' she said, offering him the flask. 'It's freezing outside so put on a heavy coat, socks and your shoes.'

He went to the bathroom and came back looking more himself. Watching him straighten his back when he had dressed, she thought. 'We have to show the flag, keep a stiff upper lip, that's what they expect of us.'

'Come then,' she said, and linked her arm in his. The servants gathered in the hall made way for them.

'What is it you want?' Lord Glenivy asked. No one could have guessed that minutes before he had sat on his bed and wept.

'All the guns and ammunition you have in the place. No one will be harmed if they do what we tell them.'

'You're these breakaway fellows, eh?'

'That's no business of yours, sir. We're sorry for causing you an inconvenience, but it has to be done. Now the guns if you please.'

His accent wasn't local. West of Ireland, he would say. Yet there was something familiar about the fellow. You couldn't tell by his face with it blackened, the hat pulled down and the coat collar turned up. It was his size, his stance. He had seen him before . . .

'If you please, sir, the guns and ammunition.' The voice was soft, insistent. Silently Lord Glenivy raged, longed for a Lewis gun, longed to scatter these men to kingdom come. His wife holding his arm, squeezed it. He saw the reality of the situation and ordered two of the menservants to bring the guns and ammunition.

'That's the lot then, is it?'

'The lot,' Lord Glenivy said. In his pocket he had a pistol, of no use to him here, but they'd have to shoot him before he'd surrender that.

The other men moved the arms away and the big one said, 'Now I want you all to go a long way off – the further the better. We're going to set fire to the House.'

A servant screamed. Mrs Bellows commanded her to be quiet. Lord and Lady Glenivy led the procession away from the House. They huddled together. Most of the women were crying. One young girl remembered the horses and asked with hysteria, 'What'll happen to them? They'll be burned alive.'

Another servant hushed her. 'They'll be all right. The fellas are Irish – they'd roast us, maybe, but not the horses.' And as she spoke the sound of the horses being freed, the clapping of hands and the chasing of them to safety could be heard.

It seemed that they waited a long time in the cold February night, too far away to see what was happening up at the House. Then a flame shot up with a terrific *whoosh*! and in no time the house was ablaze.

Lady Glenivy consoled herself with the thought of leaving Ireland. She hadn't ever liked it. Patrick was in London, so were her daughters. She would go there. Beside her, her husband was saying in a voice devoid of feeling, speaking as though he were in a trance: 'All the years it has stood. Hundreds of years. All the beauty, all gone. It wasn't my house – it wouldn't have been Patrick's. We only mind them. We love them and mind them to pass down the generations, as we plant trees we will never live to see grow to maturity. We make something beautiful. Something to last and in minutes they destroy it.'

When the flames had reached the top storeys the tall man came and said, 'We're leaving now, sir. Someone will let the barracks know, though I'm sure they'll have seen the blaze by now. I'd say you'll be picked up soon. Goodnight, sir.'

Lady Glenivy put her arms round her husband. 'I'm so sorry, darling, so very sorry.' She held him close, not caring who saw or heard. He was trembling. She hadn't loved him or the House – she would shed no tears for that. But for him at this moment she would have done anything to console and comfort. He was a good man; they had been married a long time. He loved Ireland – thought of himself as Irish. She was so sorry for him.

They were picked up by car, by cart and by pony and trap. Other Big Houses in the vicinity had come to their aid; their servants would be put up and tomorrow sent to their own homes.

Lord Glenivy and his wife sat in the library of a close friend. The fire had been rekindled, and hot soup, sandwiches and whiskey and brandy were to hand. They related the happenings of the last few hours.

'We'll be next,' their host said. 'The fellows who've split with Collins are desperate for arms. There's a civil war coming.'

'They could have had the arms,' Lord Glenivy said, 'but why didn't they leave the House? Why such wanton destruction?' He launched into a diatribe about the Republicans. Suddenly he stopped, a look of amazement on his face, and died.

Sarah looked through the letters that had dropped on to the mat, searching for one with a Dublin postmark. There wasn't one. 'Tomorrow,' she told herself. 'It'll come tomorrow definitely. It has to come. It *will* come.' She picked up the newspaper and took it and the letters through to the kitchen where she laid a tray, made tea and toast for Mrs MacDonagh's breakfast in bed, then took the tray, letters and newspapers up to her.

She was dressing Patrick when she heard the scream. 'She's scalded herself or fallen out of bed,' she thought impatiently as she hurried to the main bedroom, carrying Patrick with her.

Mrs MacDonagh had the paper spread over the tray. She was crying and saying, 'I can't believe it – your lovely House. They burned it down. They set fire to it. Your beautiful House – it's gone, hen, and the poor man, Lord have mercy on him.'

Sarah believed she had lost her mind; had had a vision of the past – seen the house in Springfield Terrace on fire; was talking about Barney or her father being dead. Closing the bedroom door and putting Patrick down, she hurried to the distraught woman. 'Mrs MacDonagh,' she urged. 'Stop it. Calm down or you'll make yourself bad again, bring on another stroke.'

'But look!' Mrs MacDonagh said, holding out the paper. 'Look at the beautiful House. Look at Glenivy House burned to the ground and the poor Lord dead. Look!'

'Oh God! Oh my God!' Sarah exclaimed in horror as she took the paper and saw the pictures: Glenivy as it was on the day she first arrived, the magnificent House in all its beauty, and beside it another photograph of a burnt-out shell. 'What happened to Lord Glenivy? Did he die in the fire?' she asked.

'Read it. It's all there. He didn't – afterwards he had a heart attack. Read it.'

'I couldn't,' said Sarah. 'I'm too upset. It's like losing my own home, my own father.'

'Of course it is, my poor wee love. Of course it is. I feel as if I knew the place myself from all the stories you've told me about it. You've gone very pale. You've had an awful shock. Call Annie, tell her I want her.'

When Annie came she was told by her mistress what had happened. That Sarah was in a state of collapse. Annie was to leave the housework, take Patrick out and let Sarah go to bed.

Delighted to be able to go out, Annie assured Sarah that she would mind him well, have him back for his dinner and make a bit of lunch for the two women. 'Off you go and lie down,' fussed her employer. 'Annie'll get me up and help to dress me.'

Not wanting to appear too eager to escape, Sarah said, 'I'll mind Patrick while she does.'

'You'll do no such thing. He's my little lamb – what trouble will he be wandering round the bedroom? Off you go and sleep. Make yourself a hot toddy – you're the colour of a ghost.'

She didn't need sleep nor a hot toddy, she needed time alone to think. Her letter now would never be answered. They had found out about his spy ring, that's why they had set fire to the House. One by one they were tracking down their enemies. She could be next on their list, though she hadn't been involved directly. But how was she to know what Barney had told Lord Glenivy? She could imagine him saying. 'Well, it's this way, sir. I saw nothing myself but the wife has it on good authority that a man was in the Hartes' garden.' His Lordship probably made notes. Someone, one of them, would have read his notes. Spies and informers were everywhere. They would have the notes and amongst them would be her name. Thank God she had changed it. They'd be looking for a Mrs Daly. It would delay them – but not for long. She had to put an ocean between herself and them. But how?

She had some money left from Lady Glenivy's fifty pounds and had hardly broken into her wages. The MacDonaghs had bought Patrick's last outfit. What did steamship tickets cost? Where were the offices? What excuse could she make to Mrs MacDonagh for wanting to go into Glasgow? Supposing she didn't have enough money? She lay on the bed, a blanket over her in case Annie came to see how she was when she brought Patrick back from his walk. She didn't want to be disturbed. There was too much to work out. She hit upon a reason for needing to go to Glasgow: she wanted to send a wreath to Lord Glenivy's Club from the best florist's she could find. They would know all about the funeral arrangements. That excuse would cover her for all the other enquiries she had to make, and if she didn't have enough money she knew where she could find it.

'Of course you must send the wreath,' Mrs MacDonagh told her when later in the day she came downstairs. 'Annie will mind Patrick. You don't want to have the wee boy traipsing round Glasgow with you. I feel from all the stories you told me about the family I should send

214

flowers myself. Of course I wouldn't, but I'll give you five pounds so that you can send the best. Go to the French flower shop – they do the most beautiful wreaths you could imagine. As for now, you must take it easy for the rest of the evening. Annie has stayed on, she'll sleep the night and see to me and Patrick. We'll have a nice chat. When something terrible happens, like someone dying or the House being set on fire, it does you good to talk about it. Tell me now – what sort of a man was Lord Glenivy ?'

PART TWO

CHAPTER TWENTY

For a couple of days after Sarah had left Glenivy, Patrick had missed his nightly visit to the attic bedroom, and then all thought of her went from his mind as his marriage to Caroline became imminent.

He hadn't at first been madly keen on the idea. His bride-to-be was a bit on the lean side, and he liked his women plump. However, he raised no objection to the marriage being arranged. Now nearly two years into it, he adored her. She was a kind, gentle person, not very demonstrative in public – a bit of a cold fish, one not knowing her might think. He knew otherwise.

His mother's and his sisters' eyes went immediately to her stomach each time they met, but they drew the line at asking the question uppermost in their minds. One day and fairly soon, he expected his father to broach the subject of an heir. Patrick wasn't religious, but even so every night he did manage a prayer asking God to send him and Caroline a child. There had to be an heir for Glenivy : you couldn't just leave a place like that to fend for itself. His father had a black sheep of a brother who had been packed off to the colonies, and who had never married, by all accounts, though it was years since anyone had heard from him. He could have had a swarm of children, by now, but it was unthinkable that one of them should inherit Glenivy. What if he'd married a native !

The title and estate could only go to a male member of the family which, thank God, ruled out Caro and her girls. For that he was pleased. He didn't like his sister Caro. Isabella was sweet, he'd always been fond of her, but she'd produced daughters as well.

After harbouring such thoughts he would pull himself together, and give himself a pep-talk. 'Look here – you and Caroline have years yet in which to have a child. Papa hasn't got one foot in the grave. Don't think about it. But at the same time keep in touch with the Man Above.'

Since their marriage, Patrick and Caroline had lived in a fashionable

London Square. His sisters were not far away. Isabella was kind and sweet as she had always been, and Caro spiteful and shrewish, the way he remembered her from childhood.

Patrick visited Glenivy several times a year. One day in the far future, he hoped, it would be his and then in turn his son's. He had never spoken to Caroline about his longing for an heir. Their marriage was happy and normal, and talking could solve nothing. And in any case, as he told himself, it was still early days. However, when the shocking news of his father's death reached him, Patrick was brought face to face with the reality of his own mortality and the importance of an heir.

He grieved for his father of whom he had been very fond, never as close to him as he was to his mother, but they had got along very well. He consoled himself that his father hadn't been a young man and that for some time before his death, hadn't been in the best of health, but Patrick was in no doubt that the wanton destruction wreaked before his eyes had hastened his end. Glenivy ... which should have gone on for ever. All his childhood memories were of Glenivy – the lovely old House, the parks and gardens, woods and lakes. A paradise for a child to grow up in. His childhood there had been truly heavenly. And when he went away to school he cried himself to sleep for many nights thinking about it, missing the servants who spoiled and petted him and the villagers in whose homes he was always welcome.

His mother, who had apparently been wonderfully brave on the night of the fire, had cracked up since. He could personally have killed each individual who had turned her from what she was into an haggard-looking old woman. His beautiful mother, who still daubed her face with rouge and powder, not allowing a maid to see to her, now resembled a clown. His sisters assured him that she would get better. 'It's not the loss of the House,' they told him. 'It was the suddenness of Papa's death. The shock.'

'And guilt,' his younger sister, Caro had added once, when they were discussing his mother.

'Guilt – why guilt?' Patrick asked, startled.

'Well, you would hardly describe her as having been madly in love with him. They hadn't slept together for years.'

'You stupid bitch, what a thing to say! They were married for thirty-five years – they stayed together all that time.' He didn't like Caro: that day he realised he never had.

One morning while he and his wife were having breakfast a letter came: it was in a white, cheap envelope, very soiled and creased. 'Look – this was addressed to Papa, sent to Glenivy, forwarded from there to his Club and then on to me,' said Patrick, intrigued.

'Strange,' said Caroline not looking up from her copy of *Vogue*.

'It came from Scotland originally,' Patrick remarked, still scrutinising the envelope.

'Strange,' repeated his wife, who was neither fully reading nor listening. Her mind was preoccupied. Their second wedding anniversary was coming up and this morning she had started the curse. For almost two years it had come, as regularly as when she was a virgin. She adored Patrick and wanted desperately to give him an heir. She dreaded that one day he would tire of her barrenness.

Her friends with hordes of children said she didn't know how lucky she was. 'Look at your waistline,' they said. 'Look at your bosom. Childbirth is ghastly. You get fat afterwards and your breasts sag like a bitch's dugs.' She wasn't consoled. She saw their smug, proud faces when their offspring were brought in for showing off. Nor was she consoled by her batty, sentimental mother, who read romantic novels and when she knew her curse had come said, said, 'That's your womb shedding tears.'

She happened to glance up from her magazine as Patrick was slipping the grubby envelope into his inside breast pocket. Curious at last, she asked, 'Was it important, darling?'

'Yes and no,' he said. 'From one of Papa's old servants who retired to Scotland. I'll have Banks drop him a line.'

On his way to Isabella's house to see his mother, who was staying there, he pulled his car into the side and re-read Sarah's letter. Memories flooded back. She was a pretty little thing with a lovely figure. Good in bed. Had to leave because she was having a baby – said it was his. It could have been. Hard to tell . . . His mother had dealt with the situation.

But why had she written to his father? Surely he hadn't – but then one never knew. And she was very attractive. No, that was a crazy thought – he dismissed it. Who was this Barney fellow? Dead, according to her. And why was she frightened of staying in Scotland? It was a most peculiar business altogether.

He stayed in the car for longer than he had intended. Sometimes a smile was on his face as he recalled the nights in the attic: creeping up the stairs, the lark with the scent. He'd read about that in a dirty book. The excitement of the clandestine meetings – though in reality he supposed every one of the servants knew what was going on. What a wonderful carefree time it had been. His father alive and his mother well. The House, the lovely House. The beautiful things that were Ireland. All now changed. Dreadful thing to burn down the House.

They were Philistines, destroying in hours what had taken centuries to build. Didn't they understand it wasn't his father's house, nor his? It was in their keeping only. To be cherished, passed on. Passed on now to whom, though. No son. No child.

Unless, of course, Sarah had spoken the truth, that she *was* having a child and the child was his. He became quite excited and started up the car again.

His mother was alone. He was glad about that. 'Darling,' she said, looking up from her game of Patience. 'How lovely to see you.'

He kissed her cheek raddled with rouge. He touched her hair. 'How are you?'

'Better, much better. And you my love, what brings you so early in the day? At least, it's early for me. Before, you know, I never got up sooner than ten or eleven. It's a nuisance waking at the crack of dawn.'

'That's depression. The doctors say it will pass.'

'Perhaps,' she said. 'But it wasn't to tell me that, that you came.'

'Actually it's about a letter. Do you remember Sarah? She was a maid at Glenivy.'

'Oh, yes, I remember Sarah, Rosie Quinlan's daughter. A flighty girl. Pretty, with a bold face. She said she was having your child. Why do you want to know about Sarah all of a sudden?'

'What happened to her?'

'I sent for her mother who took her home.'

'And then?'

'She married someone she had been courting before she came to us.'

'Did she have a baby?'

'According to her mother, and it was born at such a time that it could have been yours. But who's to say? Who really knows the ways of women? It could have been born prematurely. Her mother was a grasping woman. I had promised to send fifty pounds after the event, and I was duly notified when the child arrived. For all I know it could have been a month old or more by then.'

'You mean it could have been a cock and bull story.'

His mother smiled at him. 'Dear Patrick, I love your innocence. Of course it could have been a cock and bull story. I don't doubt but that she had a child, but whose? Now for heaven's sake tell me what has brought all this interest in Sarah about?'

He showed her the letter. 'Ah,' she said after reading it, and her eyes filled with tears. 'Your poor silly Papa. He loved intrigues. He had this Intelligence thing going – mostly unreliable men, club porters, waiters, those sort of people. I wasn't allowed to know too much about it, for women aren't considered capable of understanding such matters.

219

Apparently we have to be protected from the nasty things of life. Barney, let me see ... yes, that was the name of the man your Sarah married. Papa found him work in the Club, and no doubt also recruited him for his Intelligence network. Oh, my God!'

Lady Glenivy's hand holding an ace of spades began to shake, and her face paled beneath the cosmetics. Alarmed, Patrick asked what ailed her. She waved to a side table. 'My smelling salts,' she gasped. After inhaling several time she told him, 'I remembered something. It gave me such a shock my heart began to flutter. Horrible sensation.'

'Wouldn't you like to lie down?'

'No, no, I'm fine now. It was something I read in the *Irish Times*, last year I think. About a Tan raid. Usually I skip them, but the address caught my eye. I remembered noticing that it was the street where Rosie and Sarah Quinlan lived.'

'So?' asked Patrick, his voice puzzled.

'Well, not long afterwards another paragraph caught my eye, mentioning the same street, only this time it was Rosie's address. Her house had been mysteriously burned down with Rosie and her husband trapped inside it. Sarah, her husband and their baby boy escaped. Oh, there was another thing – the child's name was Patrick. Now do you see, darling, that letter from her to your father is beginning to make sense.'

'Make sense how?' asked Patrick, still puzzled.

'Barney must have been one of your father's spies, and have informed on the man the Tans shot. Sarah says he's dead. She knows your father would read between the lines, understand that the IRA had got him. That's why she's frightened and wants help to get out of the country.'

'Do you think she is in real danger? Should I send money for a passage to Australia for her?'

Lady Glenivy looked at her son and grieved for him, knowing what was going through his mind. This child Patrick who might be his could be living an endangered life. That would haunt him. She personally doubted whether the IRA would bother with killing Sarah. Still, one could never be sure. 'Perhaps you should write to her first. But of course you must do what you feel is right. And now I will lie down.' He helped her from her chair, kissed the side of her face then rang for her maid.

He wrote:

Dear Sarah,

I must apologise for how long you have had to wait for a reply to your letter. Unfortunately my father died before receiving it. I am distressed to hear that you feel insecure where you are, and would like to help. Do write back and give me more details as to where exactly and when you would like to go and I will see to things.

Yours, Patrick

Early the following week his letter was returned, enclosed in a larger envelope in which was another letter, which read :

Dear Mr Patrick,

You gave no other name so I had to address your letter in that name and begin this one in the same way.

My wife and I decided to open your letter for two reasons. Firstly because there wasn't a return address on it and secondly, we hoped perhaps that it might lead to some news of Sarah. You see, she has disappeared. My wife, who is ill and was very attached to her and her lovely little son, is distraught not knowing what has become of them. As far as we knew Sarah was happy in our home where she was housekeeper.

She suffered a shock not long before she vanished. Her former employer had his house destroyed by arson. My wife told me that on the day Sarah discovered this she was greatly distressed.

It's a sad and worrying business. We had grown so fond of her and the child, thought of them as our own. If you do happen to find out any information about her we'd be grateful to know, not necessarily for us to approach her, just to put our mind at rest that she and Patrick are not in trouble or want.

Yours sincerely, Thomas MacDonagh

The writer didn't add that at the time of Sarah's disappearance a sum of money and a valuable gold chain had also disappeared.

Patrick showed the letter to his mother. 'Such kind people,' she said after reading it. 'Kind and foolish, for I'm sure Sarah wherever she is has fallen on her feet.'

'All the same I think I'll go and see them.'

'Whatever for ?' Lady Glenivy asked, though she had a good idea why.

'I want to find out more about the child,' Patrick replied, confirming what had been passing through his mother's mind.

'What could they possibly tell you ? He's scarcely more than an infant.'

He blustered, not wanting to confess that he was becoming obsessed by the thought that the child was his son. 'I'd just like to know what he looked like, how Sarah treated him – you know, that sort of thing. They might even know something they're not aware of, like some clue as to

221

where she could have gone. After all, she did seem pretty desperate in her letter to Papa. All things considered we do have an obligation to her.'

'I wouldn't say that, darling,' his mother said. 'I'm sure she and her husband were looked after in whatever way it's usual to look after such people. They're Irish – they knew the chance they took becoming involved with the thing Papa had going. They would have known the price informers have to pay. That's what it was all about – a price. Money and greed would have motivated them. Sarah, and I'm sure the man she married, wouldn't have given loyalty to us or the others a second thought. Take my advice and leave things as they are, for should you succeed in tracking Sarah down she'll interpret your interest as something other than *noblesse oblige.*'

However, he didn't take her advice and went to Glasgow the following day, telling Caroline that his father's old servant, the one from whom he'd had the letter, was dying and had asked to see him. 'He was rather special. He was in Africa with Papa during one of the Zulu wars, and he saved his life,' he said, inventing the story as he went along. 'Darling, don't mention this trip to Mama or the girls.' Knowing this was an odd request he blamed it on Caro. 'Mama and Bella would understand and approve, but Caro would accuse me of sentimentality. You know what she's like. If it comes up, say I'm away on business.'

Caroline put his mind at rest. 'Actually,' she said, 'I was thinking of going down to Surrey to see my mother for a few days. I'll bring the visit forward, and stay until you get back.'

The more Patrick thought about the child, the more convinced he became that the boy was his son. And when he arrived at the Mac-Donaghs', something happened to reinforce this conviction. During the course of a conversation Mrs MacDonagh, who had been studying his face intently, asked was he related to Sarah. He said, 'No, I was a great friend of her husband's. Unfortunately I was out of Ireland during the time he was sick, but I had always promised him to keep an eye on Sarah and the child. You see, I was Patrick's godfather. It's the sort of promise one makes. They called him after me.'

'I should have remembered, for many is the time Sarah told me she didn't have a living relation. It's just that wee Patrick is the image of you, though I suppose it's hard to tell a likeness in one so young.'

Her husband smiled indulgently at her, and explained to Patrick, whom he had judged rightly to be embarrassed by his wife's question, 'I never met a woman like her for trying to spot resemblances between people. Even animals, never mind people. We had a dog once she swore was the image of me.'

'He was too,' said Mrs MacDonagh good-naturedly. 'I hope you find them, young man, and I hope Sarah, God help her, is well and happy.' Her eyes filled with tears as she made Patrick promise to let her know how Sarah was faring if he managed to track her down.

He was very moved by the woman's obvious devotion to Sarah and the child. Her commenting on his resemblance to little Patrick left him in no doubt that Sarah's son was also his. He thanked them for receiving him. Mr MacDonagh said he was sorry they couldn't have been of more help, and as they shook hands, thought that for all the times his wife had been wrong about resemblances between people this time she had hit the nail on the head. This young man, obviously a gentleman, who had introduced himself as Mr Donleavy, was the child's father. He wondered what the story was behind it all, accepting as he watched Patrick leave the house that he was unlikely ever to know the truth. Hoping with real charity nevertheless that at some time, word would come that Sarah and her child were safe and well.

Patrick returned to Glasgow, where he booked into an hotel in a state of euphoria. His mind was filled with thoughts of his son – *his heir*. A son who looked like him. While bathing, dressing for dinner and during the meal he planned Patrick's future. Straight away his name had to be put down for school. He imagined him there. At first he'd be homesick as he himself had been, but that would soon pass. There would be nothing namby-pamby about *his* son. He would take him to Glenivy – show him the ruined house. Tell him how he would have it rebuilt, how one day it would be his. He'd learn to ride and fish, to do all the things he had as a boy. After school he'd join the regiment.

And then as he drank his coffee and brandy, a sobering thought brought him down to earth. How would Caroline accept Patrick? What about his mother and sisters? No sooner had the questions come to mind than he heard Caro's mocking voice. She had always sneered at his schemes and ideas. Her favourite name for him was 'Idiot'. She poked fun at his attempts to dam a stream, to skim pebbles across a lake. When they were children she had had the ability to make him feel small and stupid – true idiot. To a certain extent she still had this effect on him, and now she would have truth on her side. He could hear her say, 'Bring this child into the family? This is 1922, or have you forgotten that fact? The twentieth century, not the reign of Charles the Second, who brought his bastards to Court. And that's what he is, this newfound son – a bastard. He can't inherit.'

She was right. His joy, his plans for Patrick's future were just castles in the air. He ordered another brandy and sat despondently and a little drunk as the castles came tumbling round his head. Then he remembered something which lifted his mood again to one of hopeful expectancy – his father's black sheep brother, the remittance man somewhere in the colonies. Money would have been sent to him regularly to keep him out of England. He could find him – his solicitor would have the details of his whereabouts. Of course he might be dead, but there would be descendants. Patrick could be passed off as one of them, an orphan adopted by him. Glenivy flesh and blood – all legal and above board. In whatever hole-and-corner place of the Empire his uncle had settled, bribes in the right quarter would provide a birth certificate making Patrick a legitimate descendant of the Glenivys.

Caroline wouldn't be hurt by such an act. This would be an act of charity, a family obligation. There would be no mention of Patrick becoming his heir, well, not until such time as Caroline was past child-bearing. And if she should produce a son, nothing was lost by taking Patrick into his home. He sat back in his chair with another brandy and lit a cigar, congratulating himself on how everything would work out. Then once again he received an unpleasant jolt. Sarah – where was Sarah? Since leaving the MacDonaghs he had been daydreaming, making plans for the future of a child who by now could be anywhere in Great Britain, even on his way to some far-flung place. It was several days, a week at least, since she had disappeared. Where was she and where would he begin to look for her? He rose unsteadily to his feet. He must begin, but where, at nine-thirty? The railway station would still be open ... It was a long shot, and unlikely that anyone would remember Sarah. Nevertheless he would try it.

A train, its engine belching smoke and steam, was being loaded with mailbags. Porters went to and fro carrying the sacks, heaving them on board, while others pushed trolleys laden with crates and parcels. Patrick waited. When the train was loaded, the doors shut and the porters leaving it, he approached them and gave a description of Sarah. Had any of them seen her, he asked. He was a toff, that was plain to see, and toffs gave good tips. The men searched their minds. 'Hard to tell, sir, that many pass through,' one said. Then another said yes, he thought he did remember a young woman of that description.

'With a small child?' asked Patrick.

'No, there was no bairn. She was a bonnie woman on her own.' He gave a pound to one of them, thanking them for trying to help. They tipped their caps gratefully. He looked into the waiting room, not that he expected to find Sarah there, hardly after the lapse of time. It contained a few passengers waiting for trains. A fire burnt in the grate; an elderly porter swept the hearth then came out onto the platform. He was no more likely to have information than the others he had questioned,

Patrick thought, but what did he have to lose? So he stopped the little man and described Sarah, stressing that she would have had a child with her.

And to his amazement the porter replied, 'Aye, I saw her and the little boy, a lovely child. He wouldn't keep his sailor's hat on. That was the second time. The first time he was wrapped in a rug.'

'You saw them twice?'

'Oh, aye, twice I saw them.' And the porter described the night Sarah had arrived late, crying that she'd missed her employers, looking for lodgings. How he'd helped her to find a place to sleep. 'She seemed a nice wee lassie,' he said. 'That's why I was so disappointed when I saw her again.'

'When was that? When was the second time?' Patrick asked, hardly able to conceal his excitement.

'Well now, let me see. Four or five days ago.'

'You're sure?'

'Definite. A week ago I was laid up with lumbago, couldn't put a foot to the floor. Four days ago it was – a Tuesday, that's it. I remember because I came back to work on the Monday. My back was still giving me gyp, so my mates told me to take it easy that day. But the next day I was on the platform carrying luggage when I saw her and the child. I recognised her straight away even though she looked different. All done up. She was wearing lovely clothes and the child in a reefer coat and sailor's hat. Not like that first night when she cried and was shabby.

'This time she had a brand new portmanteau, not the little bag like before. So I went up to her, all friendly-like, to ask how she was, and would I carry the bag for her? She looked right through me. "You're all right, hen?"' I asked. "Did you get the job, or did you see Father O'Hare?"

' "I don't know what you're talking about," she said, as if she'd never laid eyes on me before. I'm a proud man, I know when I'm being cut. I wasn't going to remind her of the last time. "I made a mistake," I said, but as I turned to go, the child dropped a little fur dog he was holding. I picked it up. It had fallen by the portmanteau and I had a dekko at the label. My eyes nearly fell out. *The Adelphi Hotel, Liverpool*, it said, and her name *Mrs Kane* with a "K" was written on it. The Adelphi's very posh as you probably know, sir. Anyway I gave the child back his dog and left, but I hung around and watched till she got on the train, into a first-class carriage. I needn't tell you I was surprised. And I'm a curious sort of a man. It was going between me and my rest to find out how she'd come up in the world so fast.'

She might still be in Liverpool, in the Adelphi! Patrick couldn't believe his luck. He wasn't interested in how she had come up in the world, only in dashing off to find her. But after all the help the porter had given him, he felt obliged to listen to the rest of his explanation.

'So what I did was to go to the digs I'd found for her the first time, on the chance that she might have stayed there again. She had. That would have been a week ago.' The day she disappeared from the MacDonaghs', Patrick thought as the porter continued. 'I know the woman who runs the lodging-house. This Mrs Kane she told me, had booked in for a couple of nights. The next morning she went out early with the bairn, dressed the way she was on the first night she came to stay. But late that evening she came back all done up and the child too, in a cab. Another cab came for her in the morning, that'd been a day or two before I saw her setting off for Liverpool. Oh, and the other thing the landlady told me was that she left every stitch of her clothes and the bairn's and the old carrying bag behind. So what d'ye make of that?'

'I don't know,' replied Patrick, not interested in where or how Sarah had come by the new clothes. Only one thing was uppermost in his mind: to get to Liverpool as quickly as possible. He took two guineas from his coin case, gave them to the porter, thanked him and asked the time of the next train to Liverpool.

'You've missed it, sir. While we were talking out she went. There's one at seven in the morning.'

'Right. Thank you again,' Patrick said, and returned to his hotel, where he hardly slept for thinking that tomorrow he might see his son. He didn't expect too much trouble in getting Sarah to agree to his proposal of adoption. A sizeable sum of money should see to that. The MacDonaghs had said how much she seemed to love the child, even so she was bound to see the advantages for Patrick in being reared as his son.

On the way up in the train he resorted to his usual method of prayer – 'having a word with the Man Above' as he termed it. A chat, asking for His help. Once or twice it crossed his mind to wonder where Sarah might have obtained the money to stay in the Adelphi. Then, when he was actually in the hotel's grand foyer, he wondered if the label had been a sham, put on to impress other passengers. Yet the porter had stated that she went first-class and was wearing lovely clothes. 'Please God let her be here,' Patrick prayed. 'Don't let her have already left or worse still, that the label was a sham and she is staying in a boarding-house somewhere around me in the sprawl of Liverpool.'

After leaving the house Sarah went into Glasgow found the shipping offices and made enquiries. For America she would need a passport which would take time to get. But she could enter Canada. Only there wasn't a sailing until the following week. She had sufficient money to pay for a single passage and fifteen pounds to tide her over when she arrived. But if she had to hang around waiting for the passage she'd be ruined. Even though the lodging-house was cheap her money wouldn't stretch to staying there for another seven nights.

She walked away from the shipping office dejected. Patrick trailed behind pulling on her hand, beginning to whimper, asking to be picked up. She cajoled, coaxed and finally threatened to slap him. He walked a little longer. Her mind was in turmoil. What was she to do? Where could she go? Who'd take her in for nothing until the ship sailed for Canada?

The MacDonaghs would. They'd be delighted. Welcome her and Patrick with open arms. She would say nothing about her plans. Let it seem as if she had just come back from an outing. It would give her breathing space. The chain wouldn't yet have been missed. There might even be an opportunity to steal something else to pawn or sell.

Patrick sat down on the pavement. His tear streaked face and determined expression making it plain to her that he wouldn't or couldn't walk another step. She picked him up, kissed him, wiped his eyes and nose and told him she was sorry. The weight of him, she thought, he'll cripple me. I'll have to find somewhere to sit down. Sit and sort out what I'm going to do. She came to a little a park and went in. Patrick sat beside her amusing himself tracing the iron scroll work on the back of the bench.

The thought of returning to the MacDonaghs' even for a week filled her with revulsion. She couldn't bear that claustrophobic house for another minute. Mrs MacDonagh's cloying affection: her constant chattering. Her plans for Lourdes. A week in that atmosphere would send her out of her mind.

There was Father O'Hare. If she told him the truth. Part of the truth. That her husband hadn't died of consumption but was shot for being a traitor. How she feared that they might be after her. Plead with him to help her get away. He'd forgive her the lies she had told in the beginning. He might even give her a few pounds to swell what she had. Telling her they would help her to get settled in Canada. For a few minutes she thought her problem was solved. Then she realised that whatever Father O'Hare would do would include her returning to the MacDonaghs'. Returning to the good, kind, Catholic home he had found for her. There was no way round that. He knew they didn't ill treat her. Knew they welcome Patrick as if he were their own flesh and blood. She could of course hint that Mr MacDonagh made her feel uncomfortable sometimes. Suggest that a time might come when he would make improper advances. But even as she pondered taking this line she knew it was useless. Father O'Hare wasn't a fool. He'd know about men and their temptations. He'd also know there were men who never succumbed to them and be positive in his mind that Mr MacDonagh was one of them. For her to make such an accusation would avail her nothing.

Patrick got down from the bench and chased sparrows. Sarah decided that she'd rather go on the town, rather die than go back to the MacDonaghs'. Silently she cursed Barney, her mother and the Glenivys ... They were all to blame for the terrible predicament she was in. Patrick lost interest in the sparrows and stepped uncertainly over the looped white chain fence onto the smooth green lawn oblivious of the black letter plaque forbidding him to walk on the grass. ... A man came down the narrow path bordered on one side by laurel bushes and paused by the bench. Though aware of him Sarah continued to stare into space ...

'A nice day, ma'am,' he said. He was, she thought well spoken, though she couldn't tell if he was English or Irish.

'Mind if I sit down?' the man asked.

'No,' she replied and regarded him. He was old, forty or more, she guessed. Very well dressed. She knew quality clothes when she saw them. Tallish, thin. Gold cuff links. Prosperous-looking.

Patrick clambered up the small grassy rise beyond the plaque. 'Come back,' she called 'Ah, ah, no Patrick, come back to Mammy, there's a good boy.' Patrick ignored her.

'Would you like me to fetch him?' the man asked.

'That's very kind of you,' said Sarah and watched him go. He was smart, well made. Patrick ran, a wobbly gait as the stranger approached him, but didn't protest when caught and lifted into the man's arms.

'Thanks very much,' Sarah said, taking him back on her lap, kissing him. 'Be a good boy and then Mammy will buy you a lovely cake in a minute.'

'He's a fine child, how old is he?' the man asked.

Sarah told him and wondered what the man did for a living. What was he doing in a park when other men would be working. He wasn't forward, she decided. A shy man she would say. You could tell by how he devoted most of his attention to the child. Asking him if he liked the birds. Naming sparrows and pigeons. Taking hold of Patrick's small fat hand and playing, 'Walk Around The Garden.' He probably had a wallet stuffed with notes. A few of them would take her out of the hobble she was in. He'd probably be a soft touch if only she could find an opening to spin him a yarn. If she could prolong their time on the bench one would present itself. She began to plan what she would tell him. Then Patrick became bored with the palm-tickling and struggled to get off her lap.

'I expect he's remembering the cake you promised,' the man said.

'Yes,' she said. 'He'll be hungry by now.' He has a nice face, not handsome, just nice, pleasant looking. His teeth are very white and even. He doesn't work hard for a living. Not with them hands and nails. Even The glasses don't take from him. She was taking everything in about him. Patrick arched back on her lap, her restraint making him begin to cry loudly.

'I'd better go,' she said rising, 'before he throws himself into a fit . . .'

The man stood too. 'I was going to ask if you'd have a cup of coffee with me,' he said. She might get her opportunity yet, she thought, but didn't rush to accept the invitation. Saying nothing while she straightened Patrick's cap and wiped his face unneccessarily with a handkerchief.

'If you've no objection that is. Maybe you've a meal to make for your husband.'

'Will you walk for Mammy ?' she said to the child as she played for time. Her mind working out how to answer the question of a husband. Patrick sat on the path letting her know he had no intention of walking and she sat back on the bench sighing and saying, 'He has me worn out.' The man sat beside her. Patrick stood up and came to Sarah and laid his head in her lap.

'You're Irish, aren't you. A long way from home. Are you living here now ?'

'In a kind of way,' she said. 'I'm hoping to leave only . . . She looked away from him and felt a lump rise in her throat. A lump she could conjure up at will, as she could the tears that now filled her eyes.

'Only what ?' prompted the man. 'Are you in trouble ?'

She turned back to him and smiled bravely. 'Ah,' she said, 'it's nothing really. A little hitch, that's all.'

'I think a cup of coffee would be a good idea – that is, as I said earlier if you don't have to rush home. You know, to your husband maybe.'

'I've no husband. He died.' She let her tears fall. Patrick raised his head and began tugging at her skirt.

'I'm sorry. I shouldn't have said anything. I'm sorry.'

'That's all right. You weren't to know.' She smiled sadly, and again stood up. 'I'll have to go. It was nice meeting you.' She bent to pick Patrick up.

'Let me carry him. And let me buy him the cream cake. You did promise him.'

'You're very kind.'

Patrick wouldn't allow himself to be carried by the stranger. Sarah agreed to go to a café, where she ate toasted teacakes and told the story of her husband's death as she had told it to Father O'Hare. Then she related how she had worked for the MacDonaghs until a few days previously, when the husband who had been making free, came one night to her bedroom. 'I woke and there he was undressed standing over me. I nearly died. I thought at first I was having a nightmare, only I always kept a nightlight burning, as Patrick doesn't like the dark. It was real all right. He put his hand over my mouth, but I kicked and struggled and he left. So I had to go. First thing in the morning.'

'I wish I'd been there. I'd have killed him. You poor girl, to try and take advantage of a defenceless woman. You must have been terrified. Where are you staying now? How are you managing for money?' He apologised for the directness of his questions. 'It's just that you're so young, so helpless and with a child. Couldn't you go back home to Ireland?'

'I've no one there. All my relations died from the Spanish 'Flu. But I'll be all right. I've got some money, only . . .'

'Only what?'

'No, nothing. Everything's fine, really. I'll manage.'

'You can tell me. I'm old enough to be your father. I'd like to help you.'

'Indeed you're not,' said Sarah, thinking that he seemed to be a decent man, who might help and expect nothing in return. All the same he was a man and a bit of flattery never did any harm where men were concerned . . . And in any case, she wanted more now than just a few pounds pushed across the table. It was a gamble. Too many refusals and he might take her at her word. She knew nothing about him – not his name, if he was married, where he was from . . . She already aroused his pity. She thought she knew how to arouse it further. If she succeeded, then the chances were it was more than a few pounds across the café table she would get.

'You're not old at all, and I've never met anyone so kind. Look at all this,' she said, pointing to the spread of luscious cream cakes, tea-cakes, and milk for Patrick. 'You're terribly generous, and I'm not going to burden you with my troubles. But there is one thing I would be grateful for.'

'Just tell me,' said the man, who now not only saw her as a poor defenceless widow but also as a very attractive woman. 'Just you tell me what I can do for you.'

'You could get me a cab. It's a long way to where I'm staying. Patrick's

230

tired and he'll want to be carried. I'd be very grateful if you'd do that for me.'

'Of course,' he said. 'You finish eating and I'll find a cab.'

If things worked out as she hoped they would, he'd offer to ride in the cab with her. She had noted how the expression in his eyes had altered. First they were friendly, then they became curious as her story unfolded, curious and sympathetic. And now they were regarding her as a woman.

He came back, paid the bill and carried Patrick to the waiting cab. She gave the driver the address. 'I'll ride with you,' the man said when she was seated and he handing in the child.

'This is where you're staying?' he said, horrified, when they arrived.

'Yes,' replied Sarah.

'But no woman should stay in a locality like this. No woman should have to stay in such a house.'

Sarah shrugged. 'It's cheap.'

'It's disgusting. If the outside looks like this I can imagine what it must be like inside.'

'It's not great,' Sarah admitted. 'I don't mind for myself so much but I worry about the child's health. There's rats and you should see the damp. There's mould growing up the walls.'

'I wouldn't let a dog stay in there.' She detected the masterful tone in his voice. Her plan was working. She would finish up with a fistful of money, enough for her lodgings until the boat for Canada sailed and if he was as generous as he seemed, a good bit over.

'I'd like you to move out. If you won't do it for your own sake, remember what you just said about the child.'

'Where would I move to?'

'I'll find you a place. A decent place.'

This wasn't what she'd had in mind. The lodging-house would have done until the sailing. Now he wanted to organise her into some boarding-house — see her into it. For all she knew, come to some arrangement about picking up the bill. Maybe she had overplayed being independent. Maybe no cash would change hands.

'I can't do that. I have to stay here, for tonight anyway. I'm expecting a message about a job. From a priest's housekeeper. She's sending it here this evening.' The lies tripped off her tongue. 'And it wouldn't be fair on the lodging-house woman. She's expecting me to stay for another night at least.'

'Well, I suppose I am rushing you a bit. After all, I'm a stranger. You're right to be cautious, I admire you for that, but don't go in there now. Look, here's what we'll do. I'll take you to lunch at my hotel. You can

231

see what it's like. We can talk.' She watched his nice, pleasant, earnest face. With the right handling she reckoned he'd be like a piece of putty.

'But you'd bring me back here tonight?' She didn't wish to appear too eager, even now that the situation had altered. She was sure it had. He wasn't planning on booking her into a boarding-house and paying the bill in advance. She could feel it in her bones that something else would come of her chance meeting with a stranger in the park.

'I couldn't go in there!' Sarah exclaimed when the cab stopped outside his hotel.

'Why not?'

'Look at the state of me. Look at my clothes and the child's.'

'I only looked at your face,' the man said.

'It's more than my face they'll be looking at if I step over that threshold.'

'Unfortunately,' he said, 'I have to admit you're right. That's the way of the world. And I wouldn't for a minute want you embarrassed. But we can fix that.' He leant out of the cab window and gave the driver instructions to take them to the fashionable shopping area.

The shop outside which the cab stopped reminded Sarah of Brown Thomas's in Dublin, a shop she had never even been inside. With the man she had met in the park escorting her, a hand beneath her elbow while with the other arm he carried Patrick, they went in together. Her feet sank in the carpets, reminding her of Glenivy. 'You never told me your name,' he said as they went up in the lift to the Ladies' Department.

'Sarah,' she said. 'Sarah Kane.'

Having arrived at the floor she watched the assistants sizing her up and her companion. She remembered the hauteur of Lady Glenivy and other women she had closely observed in the House, and now assumed this manner, though inside she was shaking with embarrassment. The man addressed the assistant in a relaxed but authoritative manner – another sign of money, Sarah thought. 'Mrs Kane wants outfitting. Will you attend on her?'

'Certainly, sir.'

'I shall take Patrick to the children's department – that's if you trust my taste,' he said, and Sarah smiled her agreement and gratitude.

'Outfitting completely?' the assistant asked.

Sarah believed she detected a note of condescension in the girl's manner. 'Completely,' she said.

'Underwear as well?' enquired the girl.

'Outfitting completely would include underwear.'

'Yes, of course, madam,' the girl replied, wondering if by any chance she had an eccentric aristocrat on her hands. 'The underwear section is on the next floor down, madam.'

'Then have a selection brought here,' Sarah commanded, and thought, 'I missed my chance on the stage,' as the girl went to do her bidding. Pure silk stockings in shades of champagne, moonlight, gun metal, misty morn and oyster were brought and taken from their boxes and offered for her scrutiny. Shoes were sent up – a dozen pairs in assorted colours and styles, patent leather gleaming blackly, brown kid one-strap shoes and a two-buttoned slipperlike pair of shoes. There were T-bar leather shoes as soft as doeskin, ones that fastened with ribbon bows, all laid before her. White cardboard boxes and tissue paper soon littered the beige carpet. The lingerie was lovely – armfuls of crêpe-de-chine knickers in pastel shades, silk chemises, a new line in brassières called Bandeaus – the latest from America, Sarah was told. Corsets she waved away. She chose a bathrobe, sand-coloured doeskin leather gloves, a selection of underwear and a nightgown, sponge bag, handbag a darker shade of sand than her gloves and T-bar shoes to match it. And then a suit with a calf-length skirt. The skirt was narrow but not as restricting as the hobble skirts which had been the fashion earlier. The suit was made of mushroom-coloured fine velour, its waist lowslung and belted. The bottom of the jacket, cuffs and lapels were embroidered in a slightly darker shade of mushroom. The blouse she bought was shell-pink crêpe-de-chine. She dressed in the clothes and told the assistant to get rid of what she had worn coming into the shop. Had it been possible she would have made a bonfire of them and screamed with delight as they went up in flames and smoke to celebrate what she felt was the beginning of a new life.

'The hat, madam?' asked the assistant.

'Oh yes, the hat,' said Sarah, turning from the cheval glass. 'I hadn't forgotten the hat. But for that I'll go to the millinery department.' And there she bought a hat, its brim turned up on one side of her face. The hat was a darker shade of shell-pink, and where the brim turned up nestled a rose darker still, a silk rose.

Finally, she stood before the mirror to see the complete ensemble: faint with pleasure, hunger, excitement and disbelief, while about her clustered assistants complimenting her on her taste.

The man returned with Patrick who was also beautifully turned out, followed by an assistant laden with packages. 'That looks more like the Sarah I know,' said the man, gazing at the transformation in her appearance. He looked at his watch. 'We're a bit late for lunch now. In fact it's almost time for afternoon tea.' While he settled the bill Sarah sat on a gilt chair and Patrick looked at her adoringly.

She was sorry for having told her benefactor that she had to go back to the lodging-house, was tempted to explain it was a lie – that there was no priest's housekeeper coming with word of a job. Then she decided it was too soon yet for any form of honesty. Perhaps there would come a time to tell him the truth, or some of it. But not now. Not until she knew exactly where she stood with him.

He left her to speak with the doorman. Returning, he said, 'I've ordered a cab.' Sarah sat like a queen on her gilt chair, as at ease as if these surroundings and wearing such clothes was something to which she was quite accustomed. 'You forgot one thing,' the man said. 'You didn't get a bag.'

'I did. Look – see,' and she held up the new handbag.

'That will hardly hold a handkerchief and your powder puff. I meant a biggish one, a portmanteau.'

'Do I need one?'

'You do. You'll shop again tomorrow, and in any case, you always take some sort of luggage when you book into an hotel. Tell the commissionaire to hold the cab, and I'll get a bag.'

She could be dreaming, imagining all this was happening to her, as so often she had daydreamed of becoming the mistress of Glenivy. And later of Barney making their fortune from the information he gave Lord Glenivy. She must be dreaming. This morning she had been destitute. She closed her eyes, telling herself that when she opened them again the luxurious shop would have vanished. Like Cinderella she would be sitting in her rags on the park bench while Patrick chased sparrows.

'Do you you like this one?' She opened her eyes. The man stood before her displaying for her approval a leather portmanteau of soft cocoa-brown leather. A beauty, she thought. As good as any piece of luggage she had ever seen in the House, except for being brand new. At Glenivy the bags showed signs of wear – well-used, as were the tweed jackets, walking shoes and sticks, waterproofs and luggage. But in time her bag would lose its raw newness.

'It's gorgeous,' she said.

'You're sure? There was a great assortment – fabric ones, carpet ones. I can change it.'

'No, it's grand. I love leather.'

He called an assistant. 'Please pack Mrs Kane's packages in the valise.'

'Certainly, sir.'

Sarah's extra underwear, her toiletries and Patrick's parcels were packed in the bag. The cab arrived and they left.

'I don't know how to thank you,' she said as it moved off.

'All the things. All the beautiful clothes. Lord have mercy on my mother she'd have a fit if she knew.'

'Why?' asked the man, who sat beside her with Patrick on his lap.

'At home in Ireland it wasn't considered right for a woman to take personal things from a man, not even one you were going seriously with. A watch was all right, but then only near the time you were going to get engaged. But not clothes, never clothes or underthings.'

'Circumstances alter cases. You needed them – you felt that need. And your mother's not to know.' He smiled. 'You look beautiful, "pay for dressing" as the saying goes. So don't worry.'

She lifted a hand of his and kissed it. 'Thank you, thank you a hundred, a million times. I'll never forget your kindness.' She saw him blush. He wasn't a freemaking man. She wouldn't be surprised to find out he was a bachelor. Her mind began to spin fantasies . . . maybe this time she had found a Prince Charming.

The hotel was opulent. She waited while he collected his key from the desk and talked to the man behind it, and then signed something. She looked round at the people, thrilled to be there. To be on a par with the smartest of the women and more beautiful than the majority.

His suite was spacious and luxurious. Whoever he was, he had money and to spare. Whether he really was her Prince, or just a man who had taken a shine to her, she didn't care. If only for a little while she had landed on her feet, and she intended making the most of her good fortune. Gone now were the fantasies as she considered her plans: how to use her wiles, charm him, seduce him if he was backwards about coming forward. As well he might be if he wasn't a womaniser, and somehow she didn't think he was.

He rang for afternoon tea. It wasn't a novelty to her – many a one she had served at Glenivy. Many a one eaten in the kitchen illicitly. The novelty was in being waited on, addressed as 'madam'. She gloried in that.

Patrick yawned and rubbed his eyes. 'He's tired,' the man said.

'He gets sleepy about this time,' Sarah replied, and wished she knew the man's name. He had asked hers but never gave his. Maybe he was being cagey. Maybe her guess about him being single was wrong. She had kept her ears open when the porter spoke to him in the lift, and when the waiter brought the tea, but they only addressed him as sir. There was nothing to stop her asking him, however. She could say: 'After all you've done for me, I don't even know your name.' It would be a natural thing to do, but she decided against it. If he had something to hide he wouldn't welcome prying. Let him remain nameless for the time being.

'Why don't you take him for a nap? You look tired, too. Have a bath and a little doze. Your suite is booked. I'll call you in plenty of time for dinner.'

'I didn't know you had booked me a room.'

'I did while I was at the desk. Your keys are on the writing table. I'll ring for your things to be taken along. Are you ready to go now?'

Sarah yawned. 'Yes,' she said, 'I'm ready.' And she thought – 'this will be it. Patrick asleep, the porter been and gone. The two of us alone in my room ... and why not? I like him. He deserves it. It's a long time ago since I had a man, and God knows he couldn't be any worse than Barney.'

Her suite was several doors down from his. He had said 'suite' but it hadn't sunk in, and she gasped with pleasure when she saw it. It was as big as his, and as lavishly furnished. 'I'd no idea,' she said, going from room to room. 'A separate room for Patrick with a bed and a cot. I'm speechless.'

'I wasn't sure which he slept in so I ordered both.' She sat on the bed and wept with joy.

'Will I lay him down?' She nodded. 'In the bed or the cot?'

'The cot,' she said. He came back into the bedroom. 'It's so beautiful,' she enthused. 'Look at the flowers and the hothouse fruit. Sit down.' She patted the bed. He deserved kissing. He deserved a lot more. She smiled a beguiling smile, her eyes dewy with tears.

'I won't,' he said. 'I have to go out. I'm going away the day after tomorrow.'

'Oh,' she said.

'I'll be back in time for dinner. We'll shop again tomorrow. Have a bath and a sleep.' He touched her face. 'I like you. You're a decent woman,' he murmured, then he left.

'A decent woman.' No one had ever told her that before. She didn't know whether to be pleased or piqued. A decent woman – what was that? Someone like Julia – a butter-wouldn't-melt-in-your-mouth kind of a woman? Or like Mrs MacDonagh – she could imagine her ex-employer being called a decent woman. Someone who didn't get into debt, kept their houses tidy and didn't drink. Weren't *tempting* ... No, it wasn't the greatest compliment. He was a quare fish, Mr Whatyoumaycallhim. Spending a fortune on her, putting her in these rooms and yet not laying a finger on her. You couldn't count touching her cheek – anyone could do that, another woman, a priest even. Maybe he was one of those fellas who only did things to men. She'd heard tell they could be very kind. They might be given to taking people out of hobbles. She wouldn't know, never having seen one, much less met one. She didn't

236

care if he was. She had the clothes, and he'd talked about more shopping, hinted that she'd be staying after tonight in the hotel. So she'd have free lodgings. Tomorrow she'd suggest a watch: she could sell that, the clothes and anything she could pinch from the suite. Whatever the outcome, she'd finish better off than she started.

And than an awful thought struck her. Supposing he was a madman! A murderer. Another Jack the Ripper who, instead of killing women in dark alleys, did it in hotels. Only a very peculiar man would do all he had done for a stranger and want nothing in return.

The lovely airy room began to feel suffocating. She was sweating and her heart thumping. She wasn't staying here to have her entrails draped on the bed. She'd go, leave just as soon as she could. The bag wasn't unpacked – it wouldn't take a minute to leave, to get Patrick up. First she'd have to cool her burning face, though. And have a pee. She was bursting for one.

The bathroom was as luxurious as the rest of the suite. She had seen several of them in Glenivy – and scoured them with bathbrick until her hands were raw and her bones ached in the damp, cold draughty rooms. They had painted lavatory pans decorated with flowers or game birds and autumn leaves, lovely colours, mahogany fittings around mirrors and lavatory seats just as this one had, but there the resemblance ended. For here, warm fragrant air surrounded her instead of mouldy dampness.

She had never in her life had a bath unless you counted the tin one brought in from its nail on the yard wall, placed before the fire and filled from kettles. When she grew up the weekly bathing stopped and like her mother, once a week she stripped to the waist and washed to there. Then put on her vest, hitched it up and washed from her waist down.

She would have one now: use the sandalwood soap (there was a new cake in the dish), and pour in the coloured salts from the tall glass jar. She started the water running, went and undressed in the bedroom, checked on Patrick and returned for her bath. She lowered herself into the warm scented water. It was a glorious sensation. She played with the water, not afraid of splashing as she had been under her mother's cranky eye. Splashing with her hands, kicking, lifting handfuls and letting it trickle over her breasts. She thought, 'Ah, to live like this every day of your life!' She wanted such a life, had always wanted such a life. 'Imagine,' she told herself, 'if he isn't married, isn't a peculiar man who doesn't like women,' for by this time she had dismissed her fears of a mad murderer, 'imagine him falling in love with me. *Marrying me . . .*' She forgot that once she had imagined such an ending to her affair with Patrick. 'Imagine I could live in comfort all my life. Me and the child. I could give him everything.'

If only she knew his plans – how long he intended staying with her. If only she knew *anything* about him, except that he had money. She heard Patrick whimper and reluctantly left the scented warm water. Wrapped in a large fluffy towel she went to his room. He smiled and said, 'Up,' raising his arms. She lifted him out, kissed him, gave him a drink of water and while she dressed he explored the suite. Then she heard him crying and went to him. He looked disconsolate. She knew that expression : he had had an accident. 'It's all right,' she consoled him. 'It was an accident. Mammy's fault, giving you the water and not asking if you wanted to do a wee-wee. You're a good boy, you nearly always tell me.'

While changing his clothes, she thought more realistically about herself and the rich man. It was too soon for anything to come of it. She'd only known him for part of a day. If he fancied her, the night back at the lodging-house might whet his appetite. They were spending tomorrow together after all. A day dressed in her new clothes. She'd use her charm all day. Early in the shopping expedition she'd ask him for perfume, then move about in a cloud of its fragrance. They'd come back to the hotel for dinner. No doubt he'd see her to her room. She'd inveigle him in. Once she had him there the rest was up to her. For a little while she revelled in the outcome as she imagined it. And then as she had before consoled herself that if he didn't take the bait, hinted or bluntly told her that soon he would have to say goodbye, she would still be better off than when he had found her sitting on the park bench.

He bought her the perfume and the watch, a silver watch, its mount and face made of marcasite. More outfits ; more clothes for Patrick. Real tortoiseshell combs for her hair. Toys for Patrick. A set of luggage. She sprayed on the perfume. He set the watch and fastened it on her wrist. He was all fingers and thumbs. She believed it was because of the contact with her flesh and took it as a hopeful sign. He had the purchases sent back to the hotel. They lunched, then took Patrick to a park where they talked. He asked questions about Ireland, about the Easter Rebellion, the Black and Tans, about Michael Collins and de Valera . . . He asked how the ordinary people had felt about the happenings, and how she herself had felt. Sarah was shrewd and intuitive – she sensed the answers he wanted from her. She made a great showing of her sympathies with the men of 1916, her hatred of the Black and Tans and her admiration of Collins. She related how her father and fictitious brothers had been out in 1916, and described her husband's terrible grief that his health had prevented him from taking part in the struggle. She knew by his changing facial expressions that she was making the right responses. After mentioning Barney she allowed herself to cry. With his immaculate handkerchief he dabbed her eyes and she notched up another physical contact.

At the hotel she bathed Patrick, ordered him an early supper and arranged that while she dined he would be looked after. After her bath she powdered and perfumed her body, dressed in a gown that was slightly provocative without being too daring and went to meet her magical benefactor.

From Glenivy she knew enough Menu French but pretended not to, leaving him to choose the meal. She drank wine, her first real taste – she didn't count the dregs that came back in the glasses to Glenivy kitchen for washing up. She felt gloriously excited and expectant. She flirted. He was unresponsive but this, she felt, was inexperience not indifference.

He took her back to her suite and was prepared to say goodnight at the door, but she persuaded him otherwise. 'Do come in. Just for a minute. Just to see Patrick,' she urged, taking his arm.

'He'll be asleep. I wouldn't want to distrub him.'

'You fool,' she thought. 'You kind innocent fool, where have you been all these years? What sort of a life have you led?' She brought him into the room.

'He's beautiful, like a sleeping angel,' the man whispered, bending over Patrick's cot.

She manoeuvred him back to her bedroom, and ignoring the sitting-room area, led him to sit on the bed. 'I have to show you something,' she said, bringing the flask of perfume from the dressing table. 'Once,' she said, 'I saw a bottle just like this and I sprayed some on my wrists. It belonged to someone else so it was stealing, really. I've never forgotten how it smelled. I used to tell myself that one day I'd own such a bottle, knowing that I never would. And now I do, because of you. I'll treasure it all my life. Never use it, only smell it so that it lasts and I shall remember you.'

He took her hand. 'Tell me where it was that you saw and used the scent?'

'Somewhere I once worked. A horrible place. A place I never want to see again.' Then she told him about Glenivy – the slavery and drudgery. The indifference of her employers. The advances attempted and repelled of the eldest son. She moved a little closer to him. Their thighs were touching.

'A lovely girl like you shouldn't have had such a terrible life. A girl like you should be sheltered and protected.'

'Life isn't like that, not if you're poor. There's few men you can trust. I did find one but God took him. It was His Will. Sometimes His Will

is hard to accept. I fancy it's got very warm in here, d'ye?'

'I'm fine. Just right. You could have some lemonade or soda water, it's all here.'

'You'll laugh at this, but the only thing I find cooling is a hot cup of tea.' Ordering tea, maybe staying to drink it with her would keep him in the room.

'I'll order some. Anything to eat?'

She laughed. 'Oh no, I'm bursting with food. I feel a bit overcome. While you order the tea I'll splash cold water on my face. I think it's the wine that's done it.'

She stayed in the bathroom until room service had been and gone. Earlier in the evening she had left a nightgown, lacy peignoir and satin slippers there. She changed into them, let her hair down and came back into the bedroom. 'I was suffocating. After eating so much my clothes felt too tight.'

He looked at her and then hesitantly said, 'My God, you're beautiful.'

'Thanks to you,' she said, sitting beside him.

'It's more than clothes. You'd be just as . . .'

'They help,' she said, and laid her head on his shoulder and raised a hand with which she touched his cheek. When she felt little response she withdrew it, but he caught and held it then brought it to his lips and kissed it. She let her other hand rest on his thigh but didn't move it, afraid to frighten him off. She leant her weight against him and noted the change in his breathing. Judging the time right for her next move, she embraced him. One arm around his neck, her fingers stroking the back of his neck, the other round his waist. She kissed his lips. He returned the kiss clumsily. She'd have to lead him. She did slowly and gently until he was sufficiently roused to lay her on the bed.

She was almost naked but he remained fully dressed even to his shoes. She undid the buttons of his fly and smiled as he eventually entered her that he was still wearing his glasses. But it wasn't a smile of derision. She liked this innocent, sweet, clean-smelling man. She had liked their lovemaking which had in it a tenderness she had never experienced before. And for a fleeting moment was sorry that she must spoil it in some way for him by going into her act of a shamed young woman.

She cried bitterly, castigating herself for giving in to temptation. 'Never in my life have I ever done such a thing. What came over me? What will you think of me! I'm not a bad woman, I'm not. I'm so ashamed of myself.'

'It was all my fault, you've nothing to reproach yourself with. I'm the one at fault, if fault you can call something so wonderful. Don't feel any shame, Sarah. It was the most beautiful thing that ever happened to me.

I have only made love to a woman twice in my life. It was years ago when I was a student, and drunk. I don't remember who the girl was. And afterwards I never met anyone I wanted to marry. I believe that it should only take place between married people.'

So he wasn't married. Well, that was one obstacle out of the way, Sarah was thinking as once again she confessed her shame and fervent belief that making love outside of marriage was a sin.

'Don't keep blaming yourself,' he pleaded. 'Please don't. Give me time to think. Don't ever get the idea into your head that I've misjudged you, that I hold you responsible for what happened. It was me, my doing. If, and I don't think there is, any blame to be cast, I'm the guilty party.' He disengaged himself and went to the bathroom, from where he came back looking less disarrayed. He sat beside her and took her hands in his. 'I have to go to London. I mentioned to you that I was going away. I planned to stay two nights – I'll try to alter that to one. You stay here. I'll be back. I'll leave you some money – promise you won't do anything foolish like bolting.' He kissed her. 'Trust me and everything will work out fine.' He kissed her again and left.

She lay thinking, 'He never said he loved me. He talked about marriage, but not marrying me. How will everything work out fine? I suppose he'll pay me off when he comes back. What can I do? Nothing. I trust him. I know he'll come back. He's a good man. A decent man.' She smiled, remembering that was how he had described her: a decent woman.

Little did he know.

'Yes, we do have a Mrs Kane staying in the hotel,' the receptionist replied to Patrick's enquiry.

'With a small boy?'

A smile lit up the woman's face. 'Oh yes, with a beautiful little boy. She's in Room 107.'

'Ring her please, and tell her that Lord Glenivy is on his way up.'

'Certainly, sir.'

Going up in the lift his heart pounded with as much excitement as it had on the nights when he climbed the attic stairs, only this time the excitement was induced by the thought of seeing his son, and not Sarah.

'Come in,' she called to his knock. It was a suite, and Sarah sat in a chair by the window. He was amazed by her appearance, only ever having seen her naked or in her maid's black uniform. She was dressed like his mother, Caroline or his sisters. She was very beautiful. He felt a faint stirring of old desire. Her voice, abrupt and icy, quickly killed it. 'What d'ye want?'

He was nonplussed and had to search for an answer. 'I just wondered how you were getting along.'

'Fine, as you can see.'

'And the child?'

'He's sleeping.'

'May I see him, please?'

'If he wakes before you leave.'

He couldn't stand this formality any longer. 'Sarah,' he said, 'it's me, Patrick. Don't you remember? I've come all this way to see you. You've changed so much. May I at least sit down?'

'Do,' she said. 'I could order tea but I wouldn't want to delay you. So tell me how you found me and what has really brought you here.'

While she spoke she was thinking how handsome he was, how like Patrick. Charming, as were all the gentry. And she was remembering his reaction when she had told him she was pregnant.

He was telling her how the letter to his father had eventually come to him; about the MacDonaghs writing to him. He described his visit to Glasgow and the station porter. 'A great stroke of luck, wouldn't you say.' He felt far less sure that things would go smoothly than he had previously. This wasn't the laughing, giggling Sarah whose belly he had sprinkled with scent, who had pleaded with him to make love to her in the morning room. He noticed something else that he hadn't before – how hard an expression she had in her eyes. They glinted like chips of a shiny metal. He felt decidedly uncomfortable and sat clasping and unclasping his hands.

'You still haven't said what made you come here.' Her tone was that of an inquisitor. He felt like a small boy in disgrace. And she, watching his discomfort, wanted to say, 'I've learned how to do this from your mother. The morning after you arranged for me to see her. "Mama," you said, "sees to problems with the servants".'

'It was about Patrick, actually. I was thinking how with your husband being dead you might find it difficult looking after him.'

'So?'

'Well, I thought I could help out.'

'How?'

'For one thing I'd acknowledge him as mine.'

'I always thought the skinny wan might be barren.'

He was offended by her tone and reference to Caroline. He wanted to say, 'How dare you speak like that to me, or about my wife! Remember who you are.' But he told himself that she was Patrick's mother, and held his tongue.

'We haven't been married all that long; it's only two years. Not having a child wasn't the reason for my suggestion.'

242

'Which is just as well, for you are not having him – not if you gave me all the jewels of India.'

'But he is my son.'

'Have you proof?' For the first time since his arrival she smiled. A dreadful smile like the grin of a skull, Patrick thought.

'The MacDonaghs say he looks like me.'

Sarah thought, 'Oh, if only you had been prepared to acknowledge him the night I told you, to marry me and rear him as he should have been reared, how different everyone's life would have been. Glenivy would probably still be standing. I know your father had the Intelligence network, so it might still have gone up in flames – no one will ever know – but Jack Harte's death would have tipped the balance.' It was seldom she thought of Jack, but when she did, she exonerated herself from any part in his death.

'I would rear him as my own – think of his advantages. And of course I'd make it worth your while.'

'Pay me off? Forbid me ever to see him again? He's the only thing in my life worthwhile. The only person I have ever loved or ever will. Not if you were the King of England would I let you have him. I'll rear him and rear him well. He'll be a gentleman, I'll see to that. I'll never tell him you were his father, which you are. He'll never know you existed. I'd like you to go now.'

'Won't you at least let me see him?'

'No,' said Sarah, getting great satisfaction from seeing him grovel.

'Please,' he begged. From an adjoining room came the sound of Patrick crying. 'Oh, please, don't deny me that,' Patrick pleaded. 'Just one glimpse.' Sarah smiled her smile again and thought – why not? Let him see her beautiful son. Let him carry away an image of what he had forsaken.

She brought him out, his face flushed with sleep, his eyes brilliant with tears, his smile tremulous. Patrick felt his heart in his mouth choking him with emotion. He walked towards them, his arms held out. 'Let me hold him just for a moment.'

'No,' said Sarah, 'he doesn't like strangers. And now if you don't mind I have to see to him.'

'I could force you to let me have him,' Patrick threatened, desperate to prolong his time with his son, to break Sarah down. To force her by bribes and argument to agree to what he wanted.

'You know perfectly well you couldn't. And if you don't leave I'll call the police.' Her expression left him in no doubt that she would.

As a parting shot, a weak one he knew, he said, 'You haven't heard the last of this.' She didn't bother to reply.

★

After the door had closed, Sarah talked to Patrick. 'That was your father. He wanted to take you away from me – just walk in here and take you. That's what the gentry are like, reared to think of everything as their right. I used to think he loved me : I hoped he would marry me. D'ye see, I was reared on fairy tales and I believed them. But it isn't like that in the real world.' Patrick laughed and reached for her hair. 'No,' she said. 'No, don't spoil Mammy's hair,' capturing his fat dimpled hand in one of hers.

'You're one of them – gentry. All that he has should be yours, but he made you a bastard. And his mother treated me like the dirt beneath her feet. Today I got my own back, though a week ago it might have been a different story. Don't look like that, don't cry,' she said. 'I'm not cross with you. Oh love, I'm sorry I was holding your hand too tight. That's the state he got me in. I'm so angry inside myself at the nerve of him sailing in, Lord of the Manor demanding what was his.' She let go his hand and kissed his wrist where her fingers had marked it. 'A week ago I was so desperate I'd have begged him for help, for money. But I still wouldn't have let him have you. We're all right now. We don't need his money. He won't give up that easy, mind. He'll try for you again if he can find us. That he never will. We've someone else to look after us now. You'll never be Lord Glenivy, but you'll be reared in comfort. You'll have an education. You'll have his breeding that'll mark you out from others. And the love that has nothing to do with inheritance. You're lucky. We're both lucky. We found someone to love and care for us.' She held him close, kissed him and then rang for room service, saying to Patrick, 'We'll have our afternoon tea just like the gentry – little sandwiches, and scones with jam and cream. You shall have milk and I'll have a pot of China tea. And then I'll take you out for a walk. Wouldn't you like that?' Patrick looked at her with an adoring smile and clapped his hands and she repeated the rhyme, smiling as she did so : 'Clap hands till Daddy comes home.'

On the way back to London, Patrick fumed at Sarah's arrogance. How dare she refuse to let him have his son, to let him hold him ! The child was his – a blind man could see that. He was such a beautiful child, a son of whom any father would be proud. She was a fool if she thought he would give in so easily. She had money – or someone she had found had money. Remembering the alacrity with which she had let him have her, he suspected the worst. She was a kept woman. Some unsavoury character had installed her in the Adelphi, and bought the clothes – someone she had picked up before leaving Glasgow. She wasn't a fit mother for his son. This fellow, whoever he was, would soon tire of her, then she'd be glad to be rid of the child. First thing tomorrow he'd get someone on her trail. He'd have her watched; her every move reported to him. Her circumstances would change and then he'd pounce, have her declared an unfit mother. He would go to any lengths to have his child.

As the train neared London his thoughts turned to Caroline and the story he must concoct about his father's old servant. He had died, he had seen to his funeral. He must write to the MacDonaghs telling them he had found Sarah and she and Patrick were well, but with no hint of where she was. They were kind good people but probably interfering. In the event of him seeking custody of Patrick on the grounds of Sarah being an unfit person he didn't want them giving her character references, vouching for the good Catholic she was – the unsuitability of the child being reared as a Protestant.

Caroline accepted his story of the death and funeral. He wrote and sent the letter to the MacDonaghs, making it plain in the politest way possible that there was no need for further correspondence between them. Then he rang the Adelphi. 'Mrs Kane has booked out,' the receptionist informed him, and to his next question replied, 'No, she left no forwarding address.' He engaged a firm of private detectives to trace her. 'It might take a long time,' they told him. 'It will cost a lot of money.' He instructed them to go ahead.

Gradually, events in his everyday life let Sarah and Patrick recede further in his mind, although he never completely forgot his son. Time and a calmer attitude showed him the impossibility of ever claiming the child without Sarah's cooperation. But surely she wouldn't refuse the setting up of a trust fund for young Patrick's education. He owed the child that. They would eventually be found. The firm he had employed were the best in the business.

Reports came from them regularly. Every major city in Britain had been searched; every city and town in Ireland. All shipping lists were scrutinised, priests and domestic agencies interviewed, but all to no avail. Patrick paid the bills and instructed them to keep trying, but as time passed, so did the urgency of locating Patrick. Months and months went by when he forgot about the boy's existence.

CHAPTER TWENTY-ONE

In 1927 Ellie was six years old and being prepared for her First Communion. Now that she was in school, Julia had no trouble in sewing the eight dozen shirt-blouses; she often did more. When extra money was needed, as it would be to dress Ellie for Communion, she borrowed a small amount from Mr Crystal.

Seldom in the years she had lived in the house was it necessary for her to go into town. All her wants could be bought locally, for in the street and nearby were several small shops, like the pork shop, which delighted Ellie, for in the window standing on their hind legs were two almost life-size wax pigs carrying trays holding a variety of pork pies. There was a butcher who catered for all the wants of families, those with plenty of money coming in and those like Julia, who was living on Relief and what she earned sewing. He sold legs of lamb and mutton, sirloins and topside, steaks, centre loin chops, beef pieces, lap of mutton, the breast cut into strips which could be fried or boiled, offal of beef and lamb, cheap mince and beef sausages.

Two old women kept the vegetable shop. Farmers from the mountains tipped from their high-sided orange-painted carts mounds of cabbage on to the pavement outside it – cabbage so fresh that caterpillars still wove through the leaves and fresh earth clung to the roots. Cabbage, yellow turnips, carrots, onions and curly kale were the vegetables most in demand for their cheapness. Cauliflowers and fresh peas could be bought from markets and in more prosperous neighbourhoods. More potatoes were bought than any other vegetable. They were seldom served except boiled in their skins, occasionally peeled and mashed; left-over mash was turned into potato cakes.

Cooking apples were bought regularly for applecakes. Soft fruits, plums and damsons were bought in season and served stewed with custard. Lemons made an appearance in local homes on Shrove Tuesday for flavouring pancakes, and were sometimes made into hot drinks for coughs and colds. Oranges, bananas, nuts and pomegranates known as wine apples; were rarities, bought for invalids, or by children who had earned pennies running messages and chose to spend the money on rare fruits instead of sweets for a change.

A small draper's stocked all items of clothing except men's suits, women's coats, costumes and grown-up shoes. Layettes for babies were available, as well as knickers, vests, wrapover pinnies, knitting wool, art-silk blouses, babies' organdie sunhats, elastic, needles, pins, thread, hankies and at Christmas, fancy goods. In the fine weather they stocked children's white and black canvas shoes.

From a cool, flag-floored dairy you could purchase milk, kept in earthernware pans covered by snowy muslin. At the back of the dairy lived the cows in a commodious field.

If you kept canaries or horses in the yard for pulling carts not riding, another sweet-smelling shop sold hay and birdseed. Secondhand books and comics were bought or swapped in the store next door. There was a bicycle shop, a fish and chip shop and the favourite shop of all the children in the street – Ma Doyle's toyshop, which as a sideline sold paraffin oil and coal blocks. Ma Doyle was a cranky old woman, disliked by grown-ups and feared by children who nevertheless, with quaking hearts and pennies clutched in their hands, braved her glowering appearance and growling voice to buy the treasures with which the shop was stocked in abundance. She sold balloons on short bamboo sticks, the necks of the balloons decorated with shocking-pink feathers; packets of Japanese paper flowers which miraculously blossomed when placed in a saucer of water; multicoloured balls encased in net and hanging from elastic thread; black and white baby dolls; teats; feeding bottles; exotic birds of papier-mâché; sheets of transfers which, with a bit of spit and pressed to your arm, left a tattoo of strange animals, flags, ships and Kings and Queens.

There were marbles, pencils, tin whistles, rubber rats and mice, fizz bags and lucky bags, wooden tops and lashes, windmills on sticks. Nothing cost more than threepence and most things only a penny. Everything tasted or smelled of paraffin oil.

In the street there were shops catering for everyone's needs and wants: three public houses, a pawnbroker's and several provision shops. However with Ellie's First Communion not far off, a trip into town was inevitable. Julia dreaded the prospect. There was always the possibility that in town she might meet someone from Springfield Terrace. She missed all her old neighbours, longed to talk to someone from her past, to hear what had been happening in the Terrace. She knew that Cissie was dead – she had read the announcement in the paper. It was a trial for her not to go to the funeral. She consoled herself, remembering how Cissie had excused her of the obligation, and prayed for her soul to have Eternal Rest. Mag, as her mother had forecast, was killed by a train. Poor Mag who, having reached twenty-one, would have been sent home from the convent. Mag wandering at night was presumed, according to the paper, to have fallen down the embankment and under the train. Or had she? Julia wondered whether, confused after her long confinement, Mag had deliberately thrown herself under it. Another crime to be laid at Sarah's door.

However her day started – and sometimes she woke with a sense of peace about her – into it always came a reminder of Sarah and Barney, and so a part of her waking hours was always spent in bitterness and a longing for revenge, though to the outside world she appeared calm and placid. A woman who always had time to listen when her neighbours had a worry. To smile and laugh when they were happy. To be pleasant when she met the Jazzer.

After reading the report of the arson attack on Glenivy and the descriptions of the men, who weren't local according to the police, and noting that one in particular had been a big, burly man, Mary Flynn knew the reason for her husband's visit to his supposedly sick uncle. She remembered the day they had met outside the public house – his questions then and afterwards about Glenivy. How many staff did they have? Was there another entrance besides the main one? Questions about the shooting parties, leading to others about guns kept in the house. She had considered the questions to be idle curiosity about the gentry had answered them and walked him round the outside of the estate pointing out two other gates, grass and nettles nearly smothering them. They had rested by one of them, sitting on the verge. He had kissed her and all the time he was using her – getting information from her. It was probably why he had come on to her in the first place, because she worked at the Big House and could give him information to use in the future.

She was hurt and felt cheated. It hadn't been a great falling in love as she had believed, at all. This feeling persisted for a while after reading the account of the fire, but it passed. For though in the beginning he may have wanted her only for what she knew, in the long run that wasn't so. They loved each other deeply. She had two sons, a daughter and another expected. The uncle had died and they had inherited the land and bought more when part of the Glenivy estate was sold off. Her husband was now a farmer and an elected member of the Fianna Fail Party under de Valera, with hopes of becoming a cabinet minister if and when they won an election.

Once in every few months she went to Dublin, shopping. Often as she walked through Grafton Street or Mary Street she wondered if one time she might meet Sarah. Maybe now that she was who she was, Sarah would be friendly. They could talk about their days as the dogsbodies and gloat a little that those days were a thing of the past. Fewer and fewer

Big Houses were occupied: the gentry had gone back where they belonged, to England. Then she would recall Sarah's veneration of them and know that whatever else they talked about, it wouldn't be to crow over the gentry's comeuppance.

One day in Bewley's in Grafton Street, an old woman sat at her table. She was shabbily dressed, but her clothes had once been good. 'It's very warm today,' Mary said, attempting to get into conversation as Irish people did with one another in cafés, on trains and trams, anywhere. The woman said it was, without looking up from the toasted teacake she was buttering; she obviously didn't want to talk. Mary took the hint and was about to leave when she realised she had seen this woman somewhere before. It was Mrs Bellows – the Glenivy housekeeper. She said her name and the woman looked up.

'You know me?' Her voice wasn't friendly.

'Yes,' Mary said, and reminded her of where they had met.

For a few minutes the old woman didn't say anything. Then she said in a low voice, 'From Glenivy . . . you're the first person I've met from there since that terrible night.' Mary saw that there were tears in her eyes. She felt a pricking in her own for the part she and her husband had played in bringing that about.

'Of course,' Mrs Bellows said, having quickly regained her composure, 'I was seen to. The gentry are meticulous about such things.'

'Of course,' Mary agreed.

'Oh yes, they gave me a grand reference and a pension, but there were so many of us without positions, so many Big Houses burnt down. The gentry were leaving Ireland in droves – and then my age was against me.'

She wasn't working. She was living on whatever pension the Glenivys had given her. Not so badly off, Mary supposed, compared to thousands of women of her age all over Ireland, but after the life she had been used to, a terrible comedown. She longed to slip her a few bob, but knew instinctively it would be resented and refused. 'The heat,' she said, 'has given me a terrible thirst. I think I'll have another pot of tea. Would you like some?'

'Thank you, no,' replied Mrs Bellows. 'I have an appointment.' She put a threepenny bit beneath her saucer, gathered together her gloves and handbag. 'I don't suppose,' she said as she stood up, 'you ever heard anything about anyone?'

'My husband's people came from the village. Someone there who kept in touch with the cook told me she died and the coachman too.'

'It was the Family I was thinking about,' said Mrs Bellows. 'Well, it was pleasant meeting you.'

'Do you come often into Bewley's?'

'Every day – their coffee is so good, and a nice class of people use it.'

'I may see you again, so. I come up to Dublin once a month,' said Mary, and felt sorry for the poor old woman with all her silly pretensions.

'Perhaps,' said Mrs Bellows. 'Goodbye.'

Mary followed her out and up Grafton Street, up and into St Stephen's Green where Mrs Bellows sat on a seat facing the fountain and fell asleep. So much, Mary thought, for her appointment. A lonely poor soul killing time. The cook and the coachman dead, and the others, where were they? And Sarah – was she here in Dublin, she wondered as she retraced her steps down Grafton Street.

Patrick could have answered her last question. His enquiries had gone on for several years and cost him thousands of pounds. Assuming she hadn't gone to the Middle, Near or Far East, China, Russia or Europe, which Patrick didn't consider likely, Sarah had vanished from the face of the earth. He regretted not being able to help her and the child. Even after he realised that to help financially was all he could ever do, he still wondered how they were faring. Then, six years into their marriage, Caroline finally conceived, by which time Patrick had decided against having Glenivy rebuilt and had bought a country seat outside Salisbury.

It was there one morning that Caroline announced her pregnancy. He cried when she told him. Holding her close he cried, accused himself of being such a fool, became inarticulate. 'Oh my love, my dearest, I don't know what to say.'

'That you're thrilled, delighted, ecstatic, over the moon, you darling, sweet idiot.'

'Oh, I am. I am. It's wonderful. Marvellous. Oh my God, I can't believe it. Are you sure?'

'Absolutely. It's been three months.'

'And I never noticed.'

She kissed him. 'Don't worry, you soon will.'

A little later in her pregnancy she said one day, 'I know it's fashionable to have babies in nursing homes these days, but I'd like the baby to be born here. I wish it could have been at Glenivy, where you and all your ancestors were born.'

'Ah yes,' he said. 'I believe they did us proud in Glenivy when a baby was born. I suppose we supplied all the booze and sweetmeats, nevertheless the villagers threw themselves into the celebrations. Such contradictions in life. Then they burned us out.'

'Surely not the villagers,' said Caroline.

'If it wasn't an actual tenant who struck the match, then someone close to him would have had a hand in it. There's never been any proof,

250

of course. Anyway, it's all in the past. We'll start a new tradition. Adaptability, that's our strength.'

'I'm glad you brought that up, about the villagers. I've never been madly keen on the Irish, now less than ever. And I know it's a family name, but, keeping fingers crossed, if we have a boy don't let's call him Patrick.'

Remembering the little boy he'd last seen in Liverpool Patrick was relieved by Caroline's suggestion. Two boys called Patrick, one a constant reminder that his brother might be faring badly, wouldn't be pleasant. 'What name were you thinking of?' he asked.

'Oliver,' said Caroline.

'Oliver. Oliver Glenivy. It doesn't exactly roll off the tongue easily. What put that name into your head?'

'Roland and Oliver. I loved the legend, I love the name. Officially he could be Patrick, though for God's sake why should a Glenivy be called after Ireland's patron saint?'

'I suppose it started in the days when we were Catholics then, like so much else, it became a tradition. But my sweet darling girl, if Oliver is what you want, then Oliver he shall be.'

In the early part of her labour Patrick sat with Caroline, who said, 'I don't know what they make such a fuss about. There's nothing to it − I've had worse tummy ache after a blackberry pudding.'

Knowing nothing about childbirth Patrick believed her. Later, when the contractions wiped the smile off her face and later still made her swear, the attending nurse advised him to leave. 'It's better for madam, sir. If you're not about she'll rest between contractions.'

'God,' Caroline groaned. 'The pain is bad enough without feeling like bloody Anne Boleyn.'

'Anne Boleyn?' Patrick looked bemused.

'You mustn't mind madam, sir. Women say strange things at such times − often nasty things about their husbands. It would be better if you went.'

'Anne Bloody Boleyn, who had her head chopped off for not giving the King an heir. Oh God, get out, go on. I don't want to see you. It's all your fault. Oh my God.'

'Pay no attention, sir,' the nurse said, ushering Patrick out. 'She's doing fine. Sir Robert will be along shortly. He'll deliver her, give her a little whiff.'

He drank several whiskies. He walked in the grounds. Came back and drank more whiskey. He was drunk, asleep in the library when Robert, a friend and consultant obstetrician, woke him. 'Congratulations, old man. You've got a fine son.'

He sobered up immediately. 'A son. A boy. *I've got a son!*' then he remembered his wife. 'Caroline, how's Caroline? Is she all right?'

'Fine, absolutely fine, both of them. Come along, they're waiting for you.'

Oliver Patrick David James Glenivy lay in his mother's arms – a plump, red-faced infant with what Patrick thought was a faint covering of gingerish hair on a head that seemed to have an immensely high forehead.

'Isn't he gorgeous?' said Caroline.

'Thank you, darling. Yes, he's beautiful. I love you. Thank you so much.'

'So I get to keep my head,' she laughed, and Patrick did too.

Then he asked, 'There's nothing wrong with his head, is there? His forehead seems very high.'

'Brains,' said his mother sagely. 'He's fine – I asked Robert. It's from being pushed into the world. He'll look normal in a day or so. Poor love, was I horrible to you?'

'A bit,' admitted Patrick. 'I knew you didn't mean it, I forgive you. Let me hold him. Oliver,' he said, looking down on the child in his arms. 'Oliver. Yes, I quite like it.'

When the child was a year old, Patrick requested the detective agency to close the file on the missing woman and her son. He had given them the name of Kane, which she had used in the letter sent to his father, her maiden name of Quinlan, and Daly, her married name which he had obtained from his father's Club. He had done all he could.

Julia bought white crêpe de Chine for Ellie's dress, buckskin shoes, a complete set of new underwear, veiling and white silk crochet yarn for a mob cap to keep the veil in place. Maggie promised a silver Communion medal, the Jazzer's mother an imitation-pearl-covered prayer book and Drim and Drew asked would she be offended if they gave Ellie a present of her socks? Hand-knitted, they explained, in white silk and cotton, done in an openwork pattern.

Sitting alone in the evenings working on Ellie's dress Julia counted her blessings. She had made a good life for her child. Ellie was a lovely-natured little girl who so far didn't seem to have suffered being deprived of her father. Often she remembered the night Jack had appeared in the kitchen in Springfield Terrace, and longed with all her heart that he would come again. There was so much to tell him: how well Ellie was doing in school, that she was making her First Communion, how never a day passed without her missing him. She would put aside her sewing, lower the gas and wait. But he never came.

The neighbours admired her for the hardworking woman she was, for how well she looked after Ellie. She was always ready to lend a hand in sickness, run up a frock for a child, or pass on something that Ellie had grown out of. Mrs Sheridan who, as quick as a son or daughter left to get married, produced another baby to take his or her place, was especially grateful for Julia's kind help. But all the same they said to each other, 'I never met anyone so deep,' and someone else would add, 'as a drawn well,' and another that it was most peculiar she didn't have a photograph of her dead husband.

One day when such a conversation was taking place, Mrs Doyle the Jazzer's mother, who still had high hopes for him and Julia, said, 'You're not suggesting that she never had one?'

Mrs O'Brien of the bad mouth who had made the remark about the photograph, replied, 'I'll leave you to draw your own conclusions.'

'What you're saying is that Ellie is a bastard?'

'Maggie Simmonds, I never said no such thing.'

'What else would she be if her mother never was married?'

Mrs O'Brien, who was secretly afraid of Maggie, having many a time suffered at the length of her tongue, became flustered, raised her voice in denial of the accusation. Mrs Doyle and Mrs Sheridan, fearing that Julia might come into the yard and overhear, urged the two women to let the contention drop. They did and went up to their rooms, Mrs Doyle saddened that no longer could she consider Julia suitable as a wife for her son.

In blissful ignorance of her neighbours' suspicions, Julia continued to act her part. She lived her life as a performance – an actress playing a woman who was widowed, but now reconciled to her loss. Going about her business; talking and laughing with the other women; grieving when there was sorrow – all the things women did for one another. Lying when anything that touched on her previous life came up. But all the while her real self stood aside, a self that dwelt on Sarah and Barney. Wishing him in Hell and that she should get her just desert. Sometimes even including Patrick in her wish, but immediately afterwards regretting that wish. The child had had nothing to do with it. He too was fatherless. Sarah wasn't affectionate so he wouldn't be sheltered by love.

It worried Maggie that the seeds had been sown to mark Julia as a woman who had a child but no husband. One day she had hoped that her friend and the Jazzer might make a go of it. He wasn't bad-looking. He'd passed his exams and was earning good money, and he was crazy about Julia. In her presence he blushed and mumbled like a fifteen-year-old boy. They could have a good life, but now with the suggestion that Ellie was a bastard and her mother a fallen woman, Mrs Doyle would make sure that her son never got within spitting distance of Julia. She had to do something about it.

Sure enough, Mrs Doyle had already warned her son: 'You're to do no more turns for her. If her pictures fall off the walls, let them lie where they fall. And don't linger in the yard when she's there. She's a disgrace – though maybe she couldn't help it. She may have been let down. All the same, it's up to the woman every time. I don't want to have to tell you again. You can still buy a bar of chocolate for the child and I'll get the prayer book for her Communion. After all, it's not her fault, the poor unfortunate child.'

'Mother,' the Jazzer said, 'you should be ashamed of yourself. You're supposed to be a Catholic, to forgive the sinner. Not that for a minute I believe what you've told me. Though even if it was true, if Julia was to look at me as if I existed I'd ask her to marry me. But have no fear – I mean no more to her than one of the children in the house. Julia smiles at me and talks to me, but it's like as if she was talking to herself. She's not aware I'm there. Something isn't right with her, I'll grant you that, but it's not what you said.'

His mother watched him like a hawk, and if she saw him lingering in the yard when Julia was there, found an excuse to call him in. Julia didn't even notice the change in Mrs Doyle. Maggie did, however, and knew she would have to do something about it, not only for Julia's sake but for the child. The rumour would spread beyond the house, and one day Ellie would suffer the taunts that she herself had as a child. A bastard didn't have an easy life growing up, as she knew only too well. She'd have to let Julia know what was going on, but not before Ellie's Communion.

The women of the house came to see Ellie before she left for the chapel. 'Like an angel she is,' Maggie said, fixing the silver medal on its satin ribbon to hang evenly round her neck. 'A beautiful little bride,' Drim and Drew said, and admired the ankle-length dress falling from a short yoke to a deep frill picot-edged at her ankles. Mrs Doyle said as she gave the prayer book, 'It's been blessed already.' The other women each put a shilling into her bag for hansel.

Ellie believed what Sister Agnes had told her that Napoleon had said when asked what had been the happiest day of his life: 'The day I received my First Communion.' It would be hers, too. It had started already with all the presents, the gorgeous dress and veil. Even before she put that on, when she was being dressed in her set of new underwear – all soft and white and smelling new. Never before had she had so many new clothes at once. She loved the white silk knickers with a frilled pocket on one leg, and tucked inside it the daintiest handkerchief, trimmed with lace. She would never, ever blow her nose in it. She felt like laughing out loud, singing, dancing but you couldn't, not on such a holy day. Her thoughts must be about the Sacrament she was going to receive – the Body and Blood of Christ. She tried hard to feel holy and think only about the Sacrament, but other things came into her mind. In the afternoon her mother was taking her to tea in Woolworths. Only once before the day they went for the dress material had she been in town. After tea they were going to a studio to have her photograph taken. Ellie said a quick Hail Mary and tried to think about the Blessed Sacrament.

Watching Ellie walk up the aisle with her partner, Sarah came into Julia's mind. She tried to blot out the unwelcome vision, thinking instead how proud Jack would have been today. Then the reason why he wasn't here loomed large, and she saw herself and Sarah as innocent as these little children walking hand in hand to the altar. Fearing she would scream out her hate and bitterness, she pretended a weakness to the woman sitting next to her, who stood to let her pass. She left the seat and went outside. In the porch a sidesman gave her a chair and brought her a glass of water. 'It's the heat,' he said. She agreed it was and sipped the water until she was calm enough to go back inside, in time to see Ellie return from the altar.

On the day Julia collected the three studio pictures, Maggie came up in the evening to see her and she gave her one of them. For weeks the other woman had mulled over how to let Julia know what was being said about her and Ellie, and how she should do something to stop it. The photograph gave her an idea. 'I often meant to ask you,' she said, 'if you've one of Jack?'

'No,' lied Julia.

'Not even a sticky back – they were all the rage. My fella had dozens of them.'

'Nothing,' said Julia.

'That's a pity.'

'I have a clear picture of him in my mind.'

'That's not the same thing, though. Now supposing you had one like mine, taken on the day you married. That could solve a thing or two.'

'Maggie, I've known you for five years. Why all of a sudden are you interested in a picture of Jack?'

'It could put a stop to something.'

'I don't understand you, you're talking in riddles. Whether I have or haven't a photograph of Jack is nothing to do with you or anyone else.'

'Don't get angry with me, I'm only trying to help. You have to believe that. Listen to me now and don't jump before I'm finished. You know well like women everywhere we talk about each other – not out of badness, curiosity mostly, gossiping. No harm meant. Harm seldom done. We like to know things about each other, and when we don't sometimes we make them up. That's when harm can be done.'

Suspecting that Maggie was wanting to ferret information about her past, Julia tried to control her anger. Anger would confuse her. Interfere with her memory. And a liar needed a good memory. 'I know all about the gossiping,' she said. 'The only ones who don't are Drim and Drew.'

'You may be sure they do to each other about us.'

'They seem like good Christians to me – I doubt that they do. I don't know why you've brought up this subject or what it has to do with a photograph of Jack.'

'Supposing you had one like mine taken the day you were married. It'd stop them making up things.'

'Making up what things? Who's making up things?'

Deciding that she'd beaten about the bush long enough, Maggie came out with it: 'They're saying that maybe you were never married. And what does that make Ellie?'

'Oh my God.' The colour drained from Julia's face. 'They're saying that. Oh God. I thought of everything else, but that someone would think that never entered my mind.'

'It's natural enough. A woman on her own with a child – a woman who's guarded. You wear a wedding ring – but you can buy them anywhere.'

'D'ye think that? That I'm not married and that Ellie's a bastard?'

'I'm one myself. I know it's hard on a child, that is, but no, I never thought that about you. I know you've something to hide. I've imagined a husband in prison – one that deserted you, but I've always believed you were married to Jack.'

Julia cried. 'Oh, I was. I was married and loved him dearly. He's not in prison nor has he run off on me. He's dead. Shot. Who said it about me? Who said it about Ellie?'

'That's not important. What is important is to stop the rumour before it gets into the street, and into the school where from time to time they'll torment her.'

'What am I going to do?' Julia asked in despair. 'How can I prove I was married except by telling things that can't be told for a long time, not until Ellie's grown up. I left where I lived because of it – left neighbours that had known me from a child. Left the street where I was born and Jack, too. I had to do it for her sake. To know too young what happened to her father could destroy her.'

So it was something shameful, after all – something Ellie had to be shielded from. He could have been an informer. It didn't matter what he was. What *did*, was putting things straight about Julia being married. 'Couldn't you let a little of your past be known,' Maggie suggested. 'Mention one day in conversation where you were married, or talk about Jack when he was alive. You never do. It's as if he never existed. You told me in the beginning he was dead, and that was the end of that. Ellie sometimes says her Daddy's in Heaven. I know she was only an infant when you brought her here so she wouldn't remember him, but I don't think you talk much about him to her either.'

'Why d'ye say that? Have you been trying to sift information out of her?' Julia was angry again.

'I wouldn't do that to a child, but I'd expect that now and then she might mention something you'd told her.'

'She's not seven yet.'

Maggie got up and prepared to leave. 'I didn't come to scald your heart. It was Ellie I was thinking of. You too because I'm fond of you. But in the long run it's none of my business.'

'Don't go, Maggie. Don't leave me. I'm sorry. You're right – I'll tell Ellie more about him. You've been a good friend to me, and I'm sorry I can't confide in you. I will one day. You'll understand all then. Please don't go. I have a photograph – I'll get it.'

She went into the bedroom and returned with the picture taken on her wedding day, wiping the glass with the corner of her pinnie. 'Look,' she said, and handed it to Maggie who after the first glance began to cry.

'Ah Julia, God love you, he was a handsome man. But why in the name of God haven't you had it on the mantelpiece?'

'I don't know. Well, yes I do. I didn't want strangers gawking at it. I thought it would be easier to hide everything from my past. All sorts of other reasons. It even went through my mind that someone in the house might have known him – not well, but have made his acquaintance at some time. And everything had and has to be kept secret until Ellie is grown up.'

It must have been something terrible that he did, Maggie thought, and remembered that Julia had even denied he had been in the army. She wouldn't remind her of that. But Julia herself remembered the lie.

'I got carried away with covering up my past. There was no need to deny that Jack went all through the war, but I did. He wasn't killed in it though, that was the truth.'

'Ellie's the image of him: no one seeing that picture can deny you were married, or that Jack's her father. I'm delighted for her sake. I'm sorry if I was hard on you earlier on this evening. And another thing, until the time is right for you to tell me I'll never ask another question about who you were or where you came from.'

In bed that night she talked to Jack. 'I was doing it all to protect Ellie and forgot the most important thing, that people would think she was a bastard and take against her. Nobody should do that but they do. I didn't hide your picture not to be reminded of you. I see your face all the time. It was for the reason I told Maggie, but I was wrong to deprive Ellie of it. She has no memory of your face, but she will now. Can you see her? Do you know how beautiful she is? The image of you, Maggie said, and she was right. There's a little bit of me in her, but she's definitely a Harte. Why have you never come to see me again? Will they not let you? Maybe in Heaven they only give you the one chance of coming back. I love you. Goodnight, Jack.'

She didn't draw Ellie's attention to her father's picture until she came home from school. 'That's your daddy,' she said. 'I'd mislaid the photograph when we moved but I found it today in an old trunk.'
    'And who's the lady?' asked Ellie.
    'Me,' said Julia.
    'That was in the olden days when you were a girl.'
    'You're right, love, the olden days it was.'
    'And Daddy was a soldier. He looks nice.'
    'Will you not give him a kiss?'
    Ellie kissed the picture. 'One for him,' she said, then put her lips to the glass again, 'and one for you.' She handed back the picture, her interest in it gone. Julia was hurt and disappointed, having expected more of a reaction from Ellie. Then smiling, she asked herself, 'What did you expect, she's only a child. More interested in her tea and going out to play than old photographs. There's all the time in the world for her to know her father's face and ask questions about him. I'll have to tell her lies at first but the time will come when she must know the truth. Maybe when she's married or engaged. When she meets a good man, please God.'

She was back in Mrs Doyle's favour without ever being aware that she had been in and out. She dazzled the Jazzer with the smile she smiled at everyone. He convinced himself it was for him alone and cherished hopes that one day he might find the courage to tell her how much he loved her. In the meantime he was very attentive, using Ellie as an excuse to come to Julia's with pencils, rubbers and sheets of paper brought home from the office that she could draw on.

Maggie constantly teased Julia about the attention the Jazzer was paying her. At first Julia dismissed Maggie's teasing, assuring her he was just a kind thoughtful man who brought little gifts for Ellie.

'Julia, you were a married woman. Jack would have courted you. Don't you recognise when a man has a fancy for you?'

'I don't suppose I do. Jack was the only one I ever courted. Ever wanted. To me every other man I knew I thought of as a friend. Since he died I'm hardly aware of the difference between a man and a woman.'

'What sort of a statement is that? Not aware of the difference between a man and a woman!'

'Maggie, sometimes you drive me mad posing such questions,' said Julia, thinking back to the night Maggie had talked about conjugal rights. 'Of course I can tell Mr O'Brien from Mrs O'Brien – what I'm trying to say is that there was only the one man in my life. There'll never be another. I know what happens to widows. God knows I've seen enough of them since the war and the Troubles. Once they get over the shock, they change. They're free again, single again. You'll see them begin to do up. Giggle and flirt in men's company like young girls. Whether they are aware of it or not, they are looking for another man. I was never like that. With me and Jack there was none of that – no playing hard to get. We were sweethearts from our childhood, and when he died I didn't feel single. I didn't feel like a young girl again. D'ye understand what I'm saying? I didn't and don't want a husband. I had the one. I loved him, I always will. When I die I'll lie with him again.'

'You're special. I never met another woman like you.' There were tears in Maggie's eyes. 'I envy you having had a man and a love like that. Few ever have.' She blew her nose hard and resumed her usual expression. 'But for all that you ought to put the Jazzer out of his misery. He's pining for you.'

'Stop it, Maggie! I never in my life gave him any encouragement.'

'That's what you think. You may live in the past but you give out other signals. Have you ever taken a good look at yourself?'

'Seldom if ever. I look in the glass when I comb my hair or if I've altered a frock – why?'

'Don't you know you're the most attractive woman in the house? Though that's not saying much with the crowd that's in it. You're the most attractive woman in the street.'

'Ah, give over, Mag.'

'It's the truth. You have the "come hither" look about you, all the more enticing because you look as if butter wouldn't melt in your mouth – which I know it wouldn't. I see women in the public house with their diddies hanging out and only short of showing their arses that get men to take them up the back lane after closing time – men that wouldn't recognise them the next day. But if you walked into that public house, dressed as you are now in an old frock, and no do up, the same men would be wishing they were single. You could marry anyone you like. I don't know what they call it, even if there's a name for it, but whatever it is you've got it.'

'I think you've been drinking.'

'God forgive you at this hour of the day, Julia.'

'I don't know whether to be pleased or offended,' said Julia. 'The only thing though that concerns me is the Jazzer. I'm very fond of him. I wouldn't for the world want to hurt him. What'll I do?'

'Not much, I suppose, unless he declares his hand. After all, you can't stop him giving the child the paper and pencils. So we'll just have to wait and see.'

When Julia first put the wedding photograph on the mantelpiece, the neighbours noticed and commented, admiring her and Jack, and saying what a fine handsome man he was and how like Ellie. Gradually it came to be ignored by all except herself and Ellie who, as she grew older, took more of an interest in it and asked questions about her father. Questions about how he had died. Julia lied about his death, telling her as she had everyone else who had asked since the picture was displayed, that he had been caught in the crossfire of a battle between the English soldiers and Republican Forces.

'Was that in the Civil War?' Ellie asked one day. Julia told her no, the Civil War had been later, in 1922 and that it had been between the Irish themselves.

'Why?' Ellie enquired.

'I'd find it hard to give you a true explanation,' said Julia. 'It was something to do with a falling out over the Treaty. What had been one group fighting for Irish Independence split up after the Treaty was signed, for one side was not satisfied with the terms of it while the other side were, and formed a Government. Then they fought each other. Brother fighting brother. Terrible things were done in it. Terrible, terrible things are always done in wars.'

'Who was Michael Collins?'

Julia looked at her ten-year-old daughter in surprise. She never talked about anything to do with either the Civil War or the War of Independence, nor the Easter Rebellion. 'How do you know about him?' she asked.

'From school and some of the games we play in the street.'

'What sort of games?'

'All sorts. You know, like "Proddy, Proddy on the wall, half a loaf would feed you all. When the divil rings his bell, Proody, Proody goes to Hell." Like that, only instead of Proddies we have Free Staters and Republicans. Some of the kids are for the Free State and some for the Republicans. What was Michael Collins?'

'A Free Stater. He was killed, shot in West Cork.'

'Why?' asked Ellie.

'I don't know,' said Julia. 'I don't want you playing those games. You'll learn all about the wars when you're older. In school you'll read about them. Play skipping or piggy beds, marbles or something.'

Ellie heaved a sigh of exasperation and wished her father was alive. She knew for sure he would answer her questions. Her mother was always fobbing her off. She was very strict. Her father wouldn't have been like that, always wanting to know where she was going. Her father looked like a film star. A girl in school had a book about film stars. She was glad she looked like him, not like her mother. She was terrible old. When they quarrelled she hated her. She never used to, not before she was ten. But ten was nearly grown up.

'I never want you going near the canal,' Julia would warn Ellie during the summer holidays when with girls from school she went for walks. 'Children are drownded every other day in the week in the canal. And if you go in the park, don't go too high on the swings.' Ellie promised to obey and once out of the door headed straight for the canal, going down by the edge to watch the boys swimming. Often on hot days she and her friends said it wasn't fair – only boys were let swim in the canal. And for a little while they wished they were boys.

In the park she stood on the seat of the swing, bent her knees and jerked forward, straightening her body as she swung back and repeating the motions until the swing flew high, higher than the scrubby fir trees growing close by. High enough for her to look over the railings and into the distance where she could see the next stop on her outing: the Hospice for the Dying where she and her companions went frequently to look at the dead people. Some had pennies on their eyes. Some had lice crawling on their faces. Some were old and some very young – not babies or children, but young. After inspecting each corpse they knelt in the mortuary chapel and prayed for the souls of the dead people. Outside they dared each other to run backwards three times round the Devil's tree which grew near the deadhouse. You were supposed to see the Devil if you completed the runs. Always halfway through the third round everyone gave up.

She went to the seaside with other families from the house, out to Sandymount and Booterstown. Julia paid for her tram or train fare, gave her sandwiches, a bottle of minerals and a penny to spend. She didn't mind that Julia didn't go with her. She knew the shirt-blouses had to be ready for the weekend and in any case, the other women weren't as strict as her mother.

Wracked with guilt that seldom was she able to take Ellie anywhere, Julia treadled her machine, sometimes singing, sometimes not even thinking. Sometimes overcome with a wave of longing for Jack, followed always by hatred for Sarah and Barney for all the sorrow they had inflicted on her, all the deprivation they had caused Ellie. She often wondered where Sarah was. Was she still alive? She hoped she was, hoped she would live for a long time in poverty, remembering what Sarah was like and knowing how hard she would find that to bear. Real poverty, Julia gloated. Existing from day to day, not knowing where to turn for the next meal. Living in some terrible alley or court with what Sarah would consider rough, common, dirty people. Then Julia would treadle faster, snip threads quickly, attempting to beat her target so that at the weekend she'd have an extra half-crown which she'd spend on a tea in town for herself and Ellie.

Great excitement gripped everyone in the house and street when it was announced that Ireland had been chosen as the host country for the Eucharistic Congress, to be held in the spring of 1932. The announcement was made one Sunday after Mass in every parish throughout Ireland and a letter was read out from the Bishop explaining that the Eucharistic Congress was an international gathering which met to pay honour to the Holy Eucharist and to foster devotion to it. By increasing love for Christ in the Blessed Sacrament, the Congress thereby effectively fought against the unhealthy attachment to worldly concerns and possessions demonstrated in the modern world. After the Bishop's letter the priest announced that in the following weeks more information about the Eucharistic Congress would be forthcoming.

From pulpits throughout the land priests urged their parishioners to demonstrate to those people from all over the world who were coming to attend the Congress their devotion to the Blessed Sacrament by decorating their homes and streets with religious objects. The tenants in Julia's house planned how they would show their love and devotion. Flags in the papal colours were made and large banners with religious emblems, to be hung from their windows. Each window facing the street would have windowboxes containing yellow and blue flowers. The Jazzer volunteered to make the boxes for Julia, and she accepted his offer with gratitude. He was in and out of her front room oftener than ever before, measuring the sill, then trying the bark-covered boxes for size, and always refusing payment for either his time or work. Only after much arguing on Julia's part did he agree that she would buy the flowers and loam.

Flags fluttered in the street and the banners were secured in windows. The night before the Congress was to begin, when Ellie, almost sick with excitement at the thought of going to O'Connell Street the next day to see the procession and afterwards to the Mass in the Phoenix Park, had gone to bed, there was a tap on Julia's door. It was too early for Maggie, Julia thought, and anyway she just tapped and walked in. 'Oh,' she said. 'It's you, come in.' The Jazzer had never come so late in the evening before.

'I just wanted to check on the boxes,' he said. 'Make sure they hadn't shifted or anything, you know.'

'They're great. See for yourself,' she said, going towards the window, talking as she went. 'I watered the pansies. They'll last for the time being if there's no wind tonight. I'd say they were forced under glass, wouldn't you?' She bent to lift up the sash window.

'Don't – you'll strain yourself! Let me do it,' the Jazzer said, standing close behind her. Then his hands were on her elbows halfraising her to her feet. He was so close that when she turned her body was touching his. 'Oh Julia,' he said, his voice husky. 'I had to come. I've been wanting to tell you this long time.' She could smell drink on his breath. 'I love you, Julia.'

'Ah,' she said, and moved slightly away. 'Don't say that.'

'It's the truth. I think I did from the very first day I saw you.' And she thought, 'You poor man, you nice, good, kind man. How am I going to handle this without hurting you? But why did you have to pick me, me that will have to refuse your love.' 'I don't,' she said aloud, searching for words. 'I only ever . . . what I mean is that it's very nice of you to tell me that.' She moved further away from him. 'And I'm very fond of you. You're a lovely decent man. No one could have been kinder to me and Ellie. Will I make you a cup of tea?' She didn't wait for an answer. 'Only the thing is, I never got over Jack. The truth is, I never will. So it wouldn't matter who told me they loved me, I'll never be able to love anyone else.' 'Please God go home,' she silently prayed, 'or you'll have me crying in a minute.'

She backed towards the fireplace. 'I'll pull the kettle over,' she said for something to say, so that she could look away from his sorrowfilled eyes.

'I knew that,' the Jazzer said. 'I wouldn't expect you to love me, but I could look after you and Ellie. I hate to think of you on that machine

263

night and day. I earn good money. We could get a little house with a garden.'

'I couldn't,' she said. 'I'll never marry again. It's nothing about you. I know you'd be a good man, a good husband. And I'm sorry. I'm very sorry.'

'You won't think bad of me for coming or saying what I did?'

'I will not. I'll always remember that you paid me the honour.'

'I'll go now then,' he said. 'Goodnight.'

'Goodnight,' she said, going to the door with him and just before opening it she reached and kissed the side of his face. Without looking at her he went away.

After he'd gone she sat by the fire and cried. Cried for the courage it would have taken for him to come and declare his love. Cried for his embarrassment, for him going back to his mother's room and for the empty lonely life he led. She hoped that having found the courage to come and say what he had, to accept her refusal as he had done with such dignity, that he might now find the courage to go from the house and his suffocating mother. Make a new life for himself, find a woman who could love him. And before she went to bed she regretted not having told him that to no one would she ever tell what had brought him to the room tonight.

CHAPTER TWENTY-TWO

Ellie had many friends in school, but Chrissie was her special one. She was a clever girl who the nuns said would go far if she had more application. 'Intelligence is not enough,' Mother Angela frequently told her. 'You must work as well. There's days on end when you don't bring in your homework. I know sometimes it isn't your fault,' the nun said when she was scolding Chrissie in the privacy of her office, 'but for your own sake child, try. Pray for perseverance.'

After one of these pep-talks Chrissie would tell Ellie, 'She knows my father's a drunkard, just as likely when he gets in a temper to upend the table with my copy books and ink and everything on it. It's easier not to bother.'

Ellie loved her and felt sorry for her because of her father and her mother who was delicate. 'Would you not come home to my house to do your exercises?' she often suggested.

And as often Chrissie refused.

'My ma if she's had a bad day might be waiting for me to get her messages.'

Ellie didn't like going to Chrissie's home : there was an unpleasant smell there, though everywhere was always tidy. And the china was prettier than Julia's thick Delft. There was a piano on which Chrissie's mother sometimes played Tom Moore's melodies and selections from Gilbert and Sullivan.

Once when she mentioned the smell Julia told her she must never talk about it to anyone in school. Ellie said, 'But Ma, I wouldn't. Chrissie's my friend.'

'I know you wouldn't, I was only reminding you how cruel it is to talk about people's homes.'

'But why does it smell? Our house doesn't – well, not like that.'

'The poor woman's not well enough for housework, and her washing is only lathered out. You can see that by the cut of Chrissie. If he wasn't such a quare man I'd offer to help, but he has a dog's manner and likes no one across his door. D'ye know he ordered the nuns out when they came to offer help? It's the drink – it does terrible things to people it gets a hold on.'

'He plays in an orchestra in the Queens or the Capitol, I'm not sure.'

'And earns good money and constant at that. They could be very comfortable.'

'What ails her, Mammy?'

'I don't know. Sure, I seldom see the woman. Now and then I might meet her going to Mass or out for a message. I always ask how she is and she says great, though far from great she looks. She reminds me of another woman I knew who had the same look about her and wouldn't go to see about her health.'

'Who was that?' asked Ellie.

'A woman I knew years ago,' Julia said, and thought, 'There's time enough for you to know how and what your grannie died of.'

'I like her but not him. He has a quare look about him and makes me feel uncomfortable even when he's sober. The only good thing about him is the free passes he says he'll give me and Chrissie when we're older. We'll be able to get into the theatre for nothing then.'

'That won't be for a few years yet. After you go to work then you'll be able to go out in the evenings.'

'I know that,' said Ellie and Julia, detecting the impatience creeping into her voice, as it did so often since she turned twelve, changed the subject.

Ellie was a good, obedient child, loved by everyone in the house and in school. She smiled more often than she frowned, she laughed and when they did row, never sulked for long. But she was headstrong and eager to try her wings. Julia knew that many more battles lay in front of them as her daughter grew up. Please God they would never be more serious than an objection to be in at a certain time, or to let her know where she was going and who with.

Before her thirteenth birthday Chrissie and Ellie sat in the school playground on wooden chairs brought out from the classroom, waiting for the dancing display to start. The dancers were pupils who paid extra for the lessons. The dancing mistress came once a week to teach them and once a week the fortunate children went to her home on Adelaide Road for another lesson. They paid one and six a week for the two classes.

The display began with a performance of Swedish drill. The girls wore pale green short skirts, white blouses and green hairbands. The piano had been brought into the playground and the dancing teacher played *The March of the Gladiators*. The girls advanced in two lines almost to where the spectators were, then one line turned left the other right; down the playground they went and came back four abreast, repeating the manoeuvres until three lines with eight girls in each were formed. The front line took two paces forward, the rear line two paces back and the rhythmic exercises began to a Strauss waltz tune. After the drill there was Irish dancing. The dancers wore black pumps, threequarter length white stockings and tunics made from a cream material embroidered with Celtic emblems. Chrissie and Ellie's eyes never left the performers. A gypsy group with gold-spangled waistcoats, emerald and scarlet head-scarves, long golden hooped earrings and real, beribboned tambourines danced next. The following act, which Ellie whispered to Chrissie was her favourite, was a gavotte danced by eight girls, four of them dressed as men in satin breeches, wearing wigs, satin jackets and buckled shoes.

They clapped until their hands were sore. 'I'd love to have been in that,' Ellie said, walking past the slaughterhouse on the way home.

'So would I,' breathed Chrissie.

'And I'd love to have a tambourine. Did you ever try one?'

'Never.'

'I did – they're gorgeous. The sound they make! My ma said she might have been able to manage the one and six but never the costumes.'

'It was the same with me. Will we look under the door?'

'They'll all be killed by now.'

'They mightn't.'

'All right then,' agreed Ellie, and she and Chrissie lay down on the big cobblestones in front of the slaughterhouse gates looking through the gap where they didn't close. 'Nothing,' said Ellie, 'only the piles of sheepskins soaked in blood.' They stood up, wiped their hands down their dresses and walked on talking again about the dancing, Ellie now saying that she wasn't sure if the gavotte was her favourite. 'I think I'd rather be in the gypsies after all.'

'On Sunday my daddy's taking me to the zoo.'

'Next week my daddy's taking me out to Blackrock and is going to teach me how to swim.'

'My daddy said he'll buy me a fairy bike if he wins the Sweep.'

Ellie listened enviously to the girls in school talking about their daddies and wished she had one. She knew he was in Heaven and Heaven was beautiful, and no matter how much you missed anyone you shouldn't wish them back from Heaven. All the same she did. And would imagine coming home from school one day and finding her daddy sitting by the fire. Then she could boast in school about where he was taking her on Sunday.

'She's a good scholar,' Reverend Mother told Julia when the time for her to leave school was approaching. 'It's a pity you have to take her out. She could go on to our secondary school and of course there'd be no question of fees.' Julia thanked the nun and explained that much as she'd love Ellie to have the education and though they'd waive the fees, she still couldn't afford the uniform and books.'

'We could help there as well.'

'God bless you Mother for your kindness. But I need her wages. I sew at home. It's not as constant any more. Times are bad everywhere.'

'Have you found an opening for her?'

'I was an embroideress in Walpole's before Ellie was born. They give preference to children of ex-employees.'

'That'll be better than a factory. You've made a good job of rearing her. You'll get your reward in Heaven.'

Walking back from the school Julia thought how proud Jack would have been of Ellie. Had he lived, she could have gone to the secondary school. He would have loved that, loved to hear her speaking Irish. She remembered him saying the teaching of it would come to every school, justifying his learning of it so that when Ellie brought home the Irish they could converse in it. Barney had mocked him. There he was again in her thoughts, him and Sarah. They were the cause of all her misfortune: the move from Springfield Terrace where Ellie even without a blood relation would be surrounded by people as close as her own family – people who had known and loved Jack, who had known his parents and her own. Without Barney and Sarah, Ellie, if only for a little while, would never have been suspected of being a bastard, enduring that hateful slur. Julia need not have exiled herself from all those she had lived amongst for as long as she could remember.

Not that she was discontented in the house or with her neighbours. It was only that they didn't go back far enough. You needed that – people who remembered you when you were young. People to talk to about your mother and father, your husband. Sometimes she dreamed about Springfield Terrace, that she was still living there, and woke happy that she was. Then as the dream faded, a feeling of great sadness overcame her, so that to rid herself of it she was tempted to go back, to see the street and her old friends again. But once up and dressed she knew she could never do that – drop in and drop out again. Not until Ellie was a woman and able to to hear and bear the truth of what had happened to her father.

The firm she had once worked for had no vacancies, but they would keep Ellie in mind, they promised. Coming up to her fourteenth birthday Julia watched the papers for Situations Vacant. Ellie was bright, the nuns had told her so. She had lovely handwriting, was quick at figures. She might be lucky and get into an office. There were advertisements for school-leavers in offices, but everyone asked for qualifications or stated that only Church of Ireland need apply.

She left school in the summer of 1935. The same week, her periods started. From girls with older sisters she knew vaguely about them so that she wasn't frightened when she saw the blood. She told Julia who had been expecting them and preparing herself as to how she would explain them, calmly and with no embarrassment. In her own day a neighbour, Cissie in fact, had done the telling; matter of factly. Saying it was Our Lady's Gift, making her a woman. She had shown the pieces of sheet, explained how they were to be used; the importance of bathing every day; the dangers of washing her hair or immersing herself in water and above all, how in men's company what had happened to her must never be mentioned. It was women's business.

Unable to meet Ellie's eyes, she passed on the information about cleanliness, the steeping of the rags; Our Lady's Gift. How she was a woman now. And then something Cissie hadn't said to her. Turning her back on Ellie, pretending to be busy at the fire she mumbled, 'You're a woman now and have to be careful. Never let a man take liberties with you. And if one ever kisses you, never, on no account, let him put his tongue in your mouth.'

Ellie laughed. 'Ma,' she said, 'I don't know any fellas. And if I did, wouldn't he be the quare eejit putting his tongue in my mouth.'

'Just remember what I told you, that's all,' Julia said, not turning round until her fierce blush had subsided.

Ellie's periods were never as such mentioned again. They were referred to, when it was necessary, as cramps or headaches. Always aware of the time of the month, Julia would give her daughter hot jars, an aspirin and if it wasn't a working day, tell her to lie down for an hour.

Ellie found her own job. She and Chrissie went into the city looking for factories with vacancies, and both were taken on in a tailoring firm at eleven and six a week. She came back to Julia elated with the news. 'I start on Monday, me and Chrissie. Isn't that great!'

Julia kissed and hugged her and told her it was great and she a clever girl to have found the work. 'You can keep the one and six for yourself. May God bless you. I'm very proud of you. The ten shillings will make all the difference. I'll be able to get you shoes and you need a coat.'

The neighbours congratulated her on being a working girl. Maggie came with a pair of gold sleepers and with Julia's permission pierced Ellie's ears, holding a thick slice of potato behind each one as she thrust a darning needle through the lobe. 'Turn the sleepers as often as you remember, don't take them out for six weeks and put plenty of spit on them when the ears get sore or itchy.'

Mrs Sheridan hoped Julia wouldn't have an objection, but a daughter had grown out of the coat she proffered. There wasn't a brack on it and it was a shame to let it go to waste. Mrs Doyle slipped her half-a-crown, telling Ellie to buy herself something nice with it. Mrs O'Brien had a maroon handbag, shaped like an oval hatbox. 'I had it for a present but it's too young for me. You'll want a handbag for going to work, would you mind me offering it to you?' With graciousness the gifts were accepted. The Jazzer wished her luck and said he was sure she'd get on.

The factory made men's suits and overcoats, high-class work for shops in Grafton, Westmoreland and Nassau Street. The workrooms were filthy, the lavatories – two for more than forty women – made Ellie retch when she first used them, though eventually she overcame the smell and would linger in the tiny area outside them to gossip and listen to the older girls who came there to smoke rather than to pee. The kitchen where you were supposed to eat your lunch she considered worse than the lavatories. It smelled of grease, gas, mice and dirt. The woman who swept the factory floors and kept the dust down by sprinkling water from a milk bottle was in charge of the kitchen. She made lunchtime tea and again in the evenings if there was overtime.

Sheila, a little older than Chrissie and Ellie, who sat at the same worktable as them, said as she showed Ellie the kitchen, 'No wonder everyone dies of consumption in here.'

'Everyone?' asked Ellie, alarmed.

'Not everyone. You know what I mean – a good few, though. We only eat in here if the boss is in at lunchtime, otherwise we have our sandwiches in the workroom. They're a bit cleaner. He'd have a fit if he knew, in case we soiled the work.'

Ellie thought Sheila very pretty, glamorous. Her hair was blonde, not natural she admitted, her sister peroxided it. She looked like a film star. Chrissie was a hick like herself, for so she considered her appearance – her unfashionable clothes, flat shoes and face naked of even lipstick. 'Not until you're a good bit older,' was her mother's answer when she raised the subject of make-up. She would argue, say it wasn't fair. Not for long, though: it was more to get her mother going than anything else. She'd be in bad humour and need to fight. Her humours seldom lasted and then she'd tell herself, 'I don't really want to wear make-up yet. And never as much as Sheila. Sheila's different. She goes dancing. She has fellas. And big sisters earning, buying her rouge, powder, eyebrow pencils and nailpolish and helping to get her the gorgeous clothes.' What Ellie did yearn for was scent – a bottle of *Evening in Paris*, in its blue bottle with the picture of the Eiffel Tower. That, or *Californian Poppy* with orange and red flowers on the bottle. She had smelled both of them from a trial bottle in a chemist's, and they were gorgeous.

Chrissie was very hickey – seldom put a comb through her lovely brown curly hair. Ellie supposed it was because of her life. Her mother was now very sick, something in her insides, Chrissie told her. She had had an operation but it didn't do much good. Her father was still playing in the pit orchestra of the theatre. He got free passes now and again, and gave them to Chrissie as he had promised. Once she and Ellie went. They saw a variety show and then a film. It was a great night out, her only night out and her mother didn't object.

The three girls sat together at a table which was always piled with finished garments covered in white tacking. Bastings, they were called in the trade. It was their job to pull every piece of thread out then throw the coats, vests and trousers to the pressers. Ellie and Chrissie also did messages, official ones for the manager, like going to other factories to borrow say, a parcel of shoulderpads if they had run out, and unofficial errands for the older girls, men and women, for whom they bought cigarettes, two ounces of cheese for a lunch, fancy cakes from Robert's Café and on Friday fish and chips. From the manager they got thanks; from the men and women, threepenny bits or sometimes a sixpence for running the message, creeping down the back stairs and risking the sack if they were caught.

In time Ellie did all the official errands. These took her all over the city so that she got to know it well: the little streets behind Dame Street leading to the Liffey, Temple Bar, Eustace Street, Crow and Fownes Street, the street where the foundry was and where an old woman in work told her Handel had first played his *Messiah*. She didn't know who he was or what it was he had played, but stored away the information, promising herself that one day she would find out.

In Grafton Street she looked into the windows of Brown Thomas at clothes which took her breath away. Passed Mitchell's, its windows filled with chocolate cakes she found hard to believe were real. Turning into Nassau Street she passed Jammet's the French restaurant, from whence came the aroma of dishes she couldn't even guess at. Then she went back to the factory and if it was lunchtime, ate her bread and butter after toasting the parcel on top of the potbellied stove until the newspaper singed and the bread was crisped, the butter melted.

'Ma,' asked Ellie. 'Can I go up the mountains on Sunday? Two of the girls from work are going. They asked me to come.'

'No, love.'

'But why? You always say no. When I was ten and the Sheridans wanted to take me and after that. Now I'm almost fifteen and I still can't go.'

Julia looked at her daughter with the promise of beauty on her. Her silky brown hair with shades of gold in it, long lashes and brows that looked pencilled darker shades than her darkest hair. And her eyes, Jack's eyes, blue with expressions that changed according to her humour. She adored her. She was her life. A good girl with whom until recently she had never had a cross word. Now Ellie often challenged her views and opinions. She was growing up – it was natural. She welcomed her being spirited.

'Well, are you going to tell me why I'm the only person in the street who's never been up the mountains?'

'Because,' said Julia, 'they can be dangerous. The weather changes just like that,' and she snapped two fingers together. It was an excuse she had used in the past and one that Ellie had accepted.

'Not in May it doesn't. It's the Dublin mountains, not them foreign ones in Switzerland.'

'There's been many an accident on them in the summer. You could get separated from the others – twist an ankle and lie there all night.'

Ellie sighed exasperatedly. 'You're not going to give me the real reason why, that's it, isn't it?'

'Yes, all right, that's it now leave it be.' Julia saw the lovely generous mouth droop and a petulant expression cloud Ellie's face, and she longed to tell her why. To say, 'Your father and me loved the mountains. We went there often. Once on a day I'll remember until I die we lay on the grass and made love. I think it was the day you were conceived. I used to look up to them in all the seasons and remember that day. The cows that watched us pass. The buttercups growing in the field where we lay. The larks that soared and sang and disappeared into the sky. Then on another day, an evening it was, men came and took your father to the mountains. To Glenasmole where we had made love and there they killed him. Tell me now, how can I let you go up the mountains?'

At the table Ellie continued to sulk, and Sarah's thoughts turned to Sarah and Barney, bitter as usual. They had killed her husband, her son and her mother before her time. Now they were responsible for a contention between her and Ellie. One that shouldn't have been necessary. There were many occasions and would be more in the future when Ellie would pit herself against her mother. Growing girls did. Some rebellions could be ignored, some given into. But this about the mountains must seem to Ellie unreasonable, spiteful even. As if she was doing it to deprive her of a harmless pleasure, unlike laying down the law about what time she came in, insisting that she knew where she went and with whom. With tact and patience she was able to make Ellie see the sense in those restrictions, and to promise that when she was a little older she wouldn't be so strict. But with the mountains all she could say was No, offer no hope of relenting later, and provide no satisfactory explanation.

God blast Sarah and Barney for all the sorrow and suffering they had caused her. Until the day she died she would continue to curse them, though she prayed that once Ellie was old enough to be told what had happened to her father, her own wound might heal. Once she had sought solace through Confession but didn't find it. Time after time she was told to pray for the Grace of forgiveness, was given a penance and dismissed with the Sign of the Cross and the Latin intonation of absolution. She didn't go to Confession any more.

Instead she talked to Jack, and sometimes her mother, asking for their help. In the beginning she could sense their presence when she prayed to them, but now she seldom did. And wondered had Heaven changed them so they didn't understand her plight. Sometimes in her blackest moments of despair she wondered if Heaven existed.

'Well, can I have a perm then?' Ellie's voice, no longer sulky, brought her back from her musings.

'Why do you want a perm? Your hair is beautiful.'

'I hate it. And everyone in work has a perm.'

'It'll destroy your hair. It's wired up to a thing above your head with electricity going through it.'

'How would you know? You've never had a perm. They're lovely and all the rage.'

'I'll tell you what – leave it until Christmas and if you still want one, then all right.'

'Oh Ma, that's great. And the winter's the best time, with the damp and that making me look like a drowned rat.'

Thank God the confrontations never lasted long. It was no wonder people loved Ellie, that she was so popular in work, for she hadn't a nasty turn in her body. Julia, watching her prepare the cat's tea, hoped that life would be kind to her.

Mary Flynn's husband didn't get a cabinet post but was in the Dail, his party. Fianna Fail with de Valera as Prime Minister had been the government since 1932. Farmers weren't prospering, but Mary's husband was wealthy, thanks to his sugar-beet factory, property and other investments. He was a generous man, so that Mary made many shopping trips to Dublin over the years. After her first chance encounter with Mrs Bellows she had met her many times since in Bewley's. Gradually the older woman had thawed, and despite her loyalty to the upper classes, became impressed with Mary's new status.

One day after their coffee she invited her home. 'It's very small,' she explained as they walked up Baggot Street, 'but in a lovely house and such a good address.'

'Well, may God pity you,' Mary thought after being impressed by the Georgian house, its beautiful hall door, and the flight of granite steps up to it. She liked the immaculate and well-furnished hall, and the thick red carpet on the stairs. When they reached the first landing, Mrs Bellows stopped at a door, its knocker, letterbox and handle gleaming like gold, and opened it. It was the smallest and most crowded room Mary had ever seen – smaller even than any in the tiny cottage where she had been reared. 'May God look down on you,' she breathed, 'this, and all for the sake of a good address.' Every inch of wall was covered by the bed, a single one, the stove, a press, a half-sized sink, a curtained alcove where she supposed Mrs Bellows kept her clothes, and one armchair. A table filled the centre space, making walking round it a squeezing operation. It would have been, she supposed in the days before the house was let out, a closet. Mrs Bellows had done her best with it : everything was neat and clean. A photograph of Glenivy with Mrs Bellows and Lord and Lady Glenivy stood on the press and a vase with five yellow tulips on the table.

'Would you like a sherry ?' Mrs Bellows asked. Mary said she would and from a beautiful Waterford decanter was poured a sweet, cheap sherry. She admired the decanter and was told, 'It was a present on the twenty-fifth anniversary of me coming to the House.'

That must be thirty years ago or more, Mary reckoned, and wondered where the housekeeper had been before that. Perhaps she hadn't worked before. No doubt it was after she was widowed. They were friendly enough for her to ask the question. Mrs Bellows looked surprised. 'My dear,' she said, 'I never married. The Mrs is a courtesy title. It gave one more authority in a position like mine.' She poured herself a second sherry, Mary having refused the offer of another drink. She talked about the family and the one before the Glenivys, another noble house. 'The happiest days of my life were spent working for the gentry,' she said, and without offering one to Mary, poured herself a third sherry. 'The happiest and the saddest, too.'

'Sad, why were you sad ?' asked Mary.

'I loved a man.' A dreamy expression lay on her face. 'He loved me. A wonderful, wonderful man. I close my eyes and he's there. I hear his voice. Our love affair was doomed from the start, we both knew that. He, being who he was, could never marry me. One day a suitable wife would be found for him but in the meantime we were both single, harming no one. Loving each other so desperately. I was having his child. I never told him – it would have pained him, embarrassed him. I would have gone away but I lost the child. I lost our child and stayed to see him marry, bring a bride into the house. We never were lovers any more. You see, he was a gentleman and a good man. I lost everything except a roof over my head.'

She was drunk. Probably had eaten nothing except the teacake in Bewley's, Mary guessed. Probably ate little at any time. Couldn't afford to, not while paying rent for a good address and buying in bottles of sherry. In future she would bring her one. The poor unfortunate creature. Who had been her gentleman lover – Lord Glenivy, or her previous young Master? She would probably regret having told her secret: it was the sherry that loosened her tongue. Mary had better go. 'Is there a message I could get for you first? How about the sherry – are you all right for that?'

'Oh yes, I'm fine for that. I've another bottle – for my heart, you know.'

'The grandest thing for it,' Mary agreed.

'There is one thing you could do for me.'

'Anything,' said Mary.

'It's just that sometimes lately I find the walk into Grafton Street a little taxing. Not always, you know, just occasionally. And so I was wondering if I wasn't in the café one Tuesday, would you come here to see me?'

'Indeed I will. In fact, let's settle on that. Instead of going to Bewley's I'll come here.'

'You're such a kind girl, such a very kind girl.'

'Then until the next time I'll say goodbye. Mind yourself, now. You have my address and the telephone number. You can write or get someone to ring if ever you weren't well. Now don't forget.'

Mrs Bellows promised not to and they parted.

CHAPTER TWENTY-THREE

Before her seventeenth birthday Ellie had had three permanent waves – always against Julia's advice. After the third she finally agreed that her mother had been right; all they did was destroy your hair. She, Chrissie and Shelia had been promoted from pulling out bastings to machinists, each day sewing up dozens and dozens of sleeve linings for the cheaper clothes now being made in the factory.

Ellie found the work undemanding. You could feed through the sleeves while your mind remained free to think its thoughts, gossip with Chrissie and Sheila who sat either side of her, if the manager wasn't about, or sing in chorus with the other women the latest love songs.

Lately she was very interested in love, imagining what it would be like to meet and fall in love with a gorgeous boy. All she knew about it was from films and the look on girls' faces she worked with, on their wedding days. These were always held on a Saturday afternoon when you could go to see them, watch them come out of the chapel after being married. See how beautiful they looked, even the ones that weren't beautiful. That, she knew, was because they were in love. And on their wedding day, more in love than ever before.

She and Chrissie used to go to dances, then Chrissie's mother got worse and she couldn't go. Her mother died and a collection went round for a wreath. Everyone, even Julia, said it was a happy release. Chrissie cried for two days, then she changed and became crabby. Jumping on you for nothing. Ellie knew it was the grief and one day she'd get over it.

Ellie had enjoyed the excitement of getting ready for the dances: the expectation of what the evening might bring. The last look in the cloakroom mirror before venturing into the ballroom. The smell of the different scents and powders, the nervous giggling and in the dance hall the band beginning to play, the slippery French-chalked floor, the girls huddled at one end and the boys at the other smoking, nudging each other and eyeing the girls. But the night never fulfilled her hopes, for oftener than not she was left standing while girls on either side of her were asked to dance, and when she did get a partner she became tonguetied and awkward so that many times she was told to listen to the rhythm. Occasionally a boy asked to leave her home – usually one who had held her too close to him or smelled of drink. She always refused.

Sheila went to the same dance hall and was asked up for every dance. She told Ellie that the reason she wasn't, was because she had a standoffish air about her. 'I know you're not, but you look stuck-up, and fellas don't like that.'

Ellie didn't believe her. She knew Sheila was being kind, saying she was stuck-up instead of telling her that her frocks were too ordinary, she wasn't a good dancer and she wasn't glamorous. Ellie wasn't sorry to stop going to the dance halls when Chrissie's mother became too sick to be left. Nor after she died, when for six months people in mourning didn't go dancing. Nor at the end of the mourning period, when there was a definite change in Chrissie towards dances and fellas. And when one Monday Sheila whispered that she thought she might be pregnant and later at lunchtime told her and Chrissie how it had happened, Ellie was glad she didn't go dancing any more and that she had never let a fella take her home.

They sat well away from everyone else while with tears in her eyes Sheila told them what had happened to her. 'I met this fella on Saturday night. He took me up for every dance and in the interval bought me minerals. He was a smashing dancer. When we were doing the last waltz he asked to leave me home. It was very romantic and he was nice, not drunk and he never held me too tight. So I said he could. We stopped in a doorway a good bit from my house and I let him kiss me. He could kiss lovely only then he did it.'

'What? What did he do?' Chrissie asked.

'He put his tongue in my mouth.' Sheila started to cry in earnest. 'Nearly down my throat. So maybe I'll get pregnant. What'll I do? My ma will kill me.'

'I don't think that's how you get a baby,' Chrissie said, and her voice was full of scorn.

'How would you know? You've never been out with a fella.'

'I was only trying to help,' Chrissie snapped.

'Lies won't help me,' Sheila sobbed.

'Maybe Chrissie's right,' Ellie said, seeing the hurt look on her friend's face. 'I hope so anyway – only when I started the others that was the one thing my mother warned me about.'

'What?' Sheila wanted to know.

'About fellas putting their tongue in your mouth. She said I was never to let anyone on any account do that to me.'

'Oh, Sacred Heart of Jesus what'll I do,' wailed Sheila.

'Ask one of your sisters – haven't they been courting for ages?' Chrissie suggested.

Sheila glared at her. 'And have them tell my mother?'

'She'll have to know sooner or later.'

'D'ye know what? I hate you, Chrissie. I wish now I hadn't told you anything.'

'I didn't ask you. I don't want to know any more about it,' said Chrissie, and left the bench where they were sitting.

'There's something wrong with her,' Sheila said. 'Letting on she knew the answer. Sure she hates boys.'

'You shouldn't be so hard on her. She hasn't got over her mother's death yet. But listen, why don't we ask one of the married women? They'd be bound to know.'

'They wouldn't talk to us about things like that. We're still single.'

'Nan would. She's not much older than us. She'd tell you. Nan's always hinting she wants to talk about what her and her husband do.'

'She might. Will you ask her?'

'Me?' said Ellie. 'But if you can get pregnant like that she'd think I was going to have a baby. It would be all over the factory. Someone from my street could find out and tell my mother.'

'Couldn't you let on you were asking for a friend?'

'She wouldn't believe that. Chrissie could ask her, though. She'd believe Chrissie was asking for a friend. Everyone knows Chrissie hates men.'

'That's right enough. But after the way I choked her off she probably won't ask.'

'She will if I explain, only you'll have to tell her you're sorry.'

'All right then.'

Ellie called Chrissie back and Sheila apologised. She agreed to ask Nan. And in the afternoon watched for her going down to the lavatory and followed her. She waited until only herself and Nan were in the cloakroom and told her the story about a friend who was worried.

Nan laughed. 'How old is your friend?'

'My age.'

'She must be a right shaggin' eejit.'

'I told her as much but she didn't believe me.'

'You tell her from me to put her mind at rest. He could put his tongue all the way down to her arse and she wouldn't get pregnant. Tell her from me it's not the tongue that's the culprit – it's his mickey.' She threw back her head and laughed. 'Jaysus,' she said. 'Ireland's rearing them yet.'

Chrissie came back with an 'I told you so' expression on her face. 'You're not having a baby. Nan says,' and she whispered what Nan had said, every word. Sheila cried again with relief. Ellie looked sick.

For several days Ellie dwelt on the information Nan had given. Pleased that at last she had one definite fact as to how you couldn't get a baby. But she still wasn't clear as to how you could. She had deduced that a mickey was what men peed from. For she had seen Mrs Sheridan's baby boys being changed and their little worm-like things. What a naked man looked like she didn't know, never having seen one, nor a picture nor statue of one. She supposed that the little thing grew bigger as boys became men. Although she had set Sheila's mind at rest, Nan hadn't made it clear where a man did put it. Was it into your mouth? Where else could it go?

After a while she reasoned that there was more to it than she understood. For why else were there so many beautiful love songs? So many films about people falling in love. And people in love, real people she worked with, looked wonderful when they were in love. On their wedding day beautiful, excited and happy. And after the wedding when they came back to work, by which time they'd know all about it, they still looked happy and glowing.

There was a mystery here that she didn't understand, some magic thing which came about when you were in love. A beautiful thing – nothing at all like Nan said. Everyone knew, though they liked her because she could make you laugh, that Nan was vulgar and common.

She wanted desperately to fall in love. She fantasised about it, imagining who she'd fall in love with. Believing fervently that it could happen any time, anywhere. You could be walking along a street, sitting on a tram, in work and suddenly your eyes would meet and you'd know. It happened like that in nearly all the films she had seen and the stories she had read. And never, ever, was there anything horrible or dirty.

It happened almost as she had imagined, on an evening when she was coming home from work. She was crossing a turn on the lefthand side of the street. A boy was riding a bicycle round and round at the end of the turn as she stepped off the kerb. He almost ran into her. 'You want to mind where you're going, you could have knocked me down,' she said, annoyed.

'I didn't see you,' he said, braking, dismounting and wheeling the bike to her side. 'Sorry.'

'He's gorgeous,' she thought. 'I've never seen anyone like him before.'

'I came to see a fellow I'm in college with. We were going to swot some biology. But he wasn't in. He won't be back for a while – so I was just killing time spinning round.'

'And nearly killing me into the bargain.' This time her voice was easy, bantering. She saw that he was wearing a college blazer.

'Do you live round here?'

'Up the street, and you, where do you live?'

'Kilmainham. Are you in college?' he asked curiously.

'I'd be in uniform if I was – no, I work. I'm at the tailoring.'

'You're lucky. I'd love to be working. I've another six years if I get into University. You've more freedom when you're working. Fellas I know who left last year and have jobs can do more or less what they like.'

'Maybe when you're in University,' she said, fascinated by his voice which wasn't altogether Irish. Here and there words sounded like a film star's.

'I'll be living at home, my nose kept to the grindstone – that's if I pass my entrance.'

'You don't sound Irish. Well, some of the words don't – more like a film star.'

He pretended to preen. 'Like an American, you mean?'

'Yes, that's it. I'll have to go now. My mother'll have my dinner ready.' Between looking at his face, his lovely brown eyes and his smile and his gorgeous funny voice she felt dizzy in the most delightful way. And sad at the same time for she knew she might never see him again. She said goodbye and so did he, got on his bicycle and rode back up the turning.

'You're late,' Julia said.

'I met someone.' Ellie took off her coat and washed her hands.

'You'll never guess what's happened,' Julia confided.

'What?' asked Ellie, her mind on the boy she had just met.

'The Jazzer's bought a wireless and we're asked up to listen tonight.'

'I'm going to wash my hair.'

'You washed it the night before last. I thought you'd have been delighted. A wireless! You're always going on about a wireless – how you could learn the latest songs, not having to be buying fourpenny songbooks or getting someone to write out the words for you.'

'I'll go another time. Have you seen my sachet of Amami?'

'Don't start your hair now. I'm dishing the dinner up.'

Her hair didn't need washing but it was the only excuse for not going to hear the Jazzer's wireless – a way of having time to herself to think about the boy, which after her mother had left and her hair was drying she did. Going back over every word he had spoken, remembering how he smiled. How good-looking he was, the American twang to his words. How her heart had raced . . . it must be love. She had fallen in love with him. Would she ever see him again? Did he like her? Would he ever ask her out?

The fire went down and she hadn't bothered to light the gas. Her thick hair was damp around her, her back and neck chilly. Her elation at having fallen in love gave way to depressed thoughts. She would probably never see him again. He lived miles away. He might never come to visit his friend again, find him out and be spinning round on his bicycle. She wondered how old he was, what he was called. What he wanted to be . . . all the things she might never know.

She became further depressed, remembering a girl from work who was dying in the Hospice. A girl of nearly twenty, not much older than her, who was to have been married on St Stephen's Day. When she had started work she was the picture of health – a great dancer, who won medals for ballroom dancing and only last year in the long passage on the first floor of the workroom had shown her how to foxtrot. Into rapid consumption she went. Sheila was right when she said lots of people working in the factory died. Many had since she started – mostly young people, and all of consumption.

'Imagine if I got it and died without ever seeing him again,' she murmured to herself. 'Imagine falling in love and then that happening.' There wasn't a cure. You were sent to a sanatorium and rested for six months. Maggie said they blew you out on eggs, milk and butter so that you came home looking healthy, but it didn't last for long. You always relapsed and died. It wasn't fair. Not when you were about to get married. Not when you were in love.

She felt hungry. After eating a piece of cake, two cuts of bread and jam and drinking several cups of tea her spirit lifted. She built up the fire, sat close to it, and the shivers left her. More people didn't get consumption than did. Why should she be one of the unfortunate ones? She was as strong as a horse. She began again to think about the possibility of meeting the boy on the bicycle. For one thing she could make sure to be at the same spot at the time she had met him. And another thing, be sure to comb her hair well and powder her face before she left work. She was in a chemist club, she had number seven and that was due to come up in two weeks. She would buy a bottle of scent. Scent was supposed to make people remember you. She wished she had been wearing some when she met him this evening.

In the Doyles' room the neighbours sat spellbound listening to the voice coming out of the wireless. It was a programme about farming, even so each sat with baited breath, stunned into silence by the miracle taking place.

Over the next few days, Julia noticed that something ailed Ellie. At first she worried about her health, for she wasn't eating well. Then the real reason dawned on her – the girl was in love. She wondered who he was. Knew as the weeks went by and her daughter went out no oftener than before, that she wasn't seeing him. It broke Julia's heart to think that Ellie loved someone who didn't love her in return. She longed to talk to her, console her and tell her how with 'first love', it was often that way, though this she only knew from hearsay, herself and Jack having fallen in love in their teens and loved each other until he died.

She asked leading questions: Was Sheila doing a line? Was Chrissie? The answers were short: Sheila was always doing a line; Chrissie never – end of conversation. She told Maggie what she suspected, and her friend grunted, 'She'll get over it – we all go through it. Men are bastards.'

Maggie's sailor was home from the sea and wanting her to marry him. His persistence had her permanently in bad humour. 'The life is tormented out of me,' she said, forgetting Ellie and her being in love. 'It was great the way it was – him coming now and then. I'm used to living on my own.'

'He'd get work and keep you and be company for you in your old age.'

'I can keep myself, thanks very much and as for company in my old age, more likely he'd finish up an invalid in the corner. Haven't you noticed how the men go before the women and want nursing and cosseting before they do?'

Maggie could and did keep herself, turning her hand to everything and anything – laying out the dead, of whom there was never any shortage; delivering babies, also in plentiful supply, the babies of mothers who were frightened of hospitals and wanted to avoid the expense of the local midwife. Maggie charged according to their circumstances. She pawned for people too proud or ashamed to be seen in the pawn office. On Monday morning she went laden with parcels, her arms up to the elbow bangled with bracelets and watches. Every finger was ringed and the pocket on her big coarse apron laden with Communion medals, dancing medals, boxing medals and other knick-knacks on which money could be raised. On Friday nights or Saturdays she redeemed the pledges.

Before Ellie had met the boy on the bicycle she and Maggie used to set out together, she for work and Maggie, who didn't like the local pawnbroker, for one on the way to Ellie's factory. Ellie had always enjoyed the walk, for Maggie was a fount of knowlege about the area through which they passed, showing Ellie where once a river now running underground had been on the surface. It was called, she said, the Poddle. In bygone days women used to do their washing there. In her mother's time a woman crossing the road long after the river was underground fell to Eternity when a crack suddenly appeared and into it she fell. On another occasion, when passing St Patrick's Protestant Cathedral, Ellie asked, 'Maggie, did you ever go inside the door?'

'Many a time.'

'Didn't you care that you were committing a sin?'

'I did not,' replied Maggie. 'I don't believe that nonsense.'

Ellie was amazed that someone didn't believe what the Church taught. Never before had she met such a person. Maggie was great. She herself didn't believe everything the nuns told her – certainly not that the little boy of seven who drowned in a quarry last winter went straight to Hell because it was a Sunday and he hadn't been to Mass! She didn't believe that, but would never have dared to say so.

'What was it like in the Cathedral, Maggie?'

'Freezing. Grey. Brass plates and eagles you could see your face in. Busts of oul fellas. Stone tablets on the walls in a foreign language and flags in flitters. If you never see it you're not missing much.'

'It looks so beautiful from the outside,' said Ellie dreamily, looking back at the Cathedral etched against the sky. 'And Drim and Drew rave about it.'

'They're Protestants – it's theirs, where they do their praying, where they've gone from the time they were children. They'd be bound to love it.'

Ellie did not enjoy the walk with Maggie any more, not since she had fallen in love. Maggie wore a shawl – a beautiful soft black woollen shawl. But shawls were common. Dealers and common women wore them. She lived in dread and fear that the boy on the bicycle might see her with a woman in a shawl and think it was her mother. She began to find excuses for not walking part of the way with Maggie. She had to be in work early. She was meeting someone who lived in a different direction. Neither Maggie nor her mother appeared to notice her frequent excuses or if they did, said nothing.

Walking through every street she hoped to see him. Not knowing where he went to college it was a possibility. She talked less to Sheila and daydreamed more as she fed sleeve linings through the machine. Every love song sung by the women while they worked seemed especially written for her, about love that started with no promise and was then fulfilled.

Looking at her one evening when she was dressing up to go to the pictures with Chrissie, Julia thought that whoever it was she was in love with must be blind if he couldn't see the beauty he was missing. 'She's taller than me and her figure's better than mine ever was,' Julia decided. 'And more important than being beautiful, she's a lovely girl, not an ounce of vanity in her. Quite unaware that people turn to look after her when she passes. Apart from now when she's pining for someone, such a happy-go-lucky girl. Quick with the backchat but never cruel. If only,' she thought, 'it was in my power to grant her wish – him, whoever he is – wouldn't I be the happiest woman in the world?'

In an effort to cheer her daughter up, she said what she knew was the truth. 'You've got style. It's a gift – you either have it or you don't.'

'I always thought it was something to do with being in the fashion,' Ellie said.

'Nothing whatsoever. You could be decked in diamonds, dressed by a court dressmaker and still not have style. Maggie has it – look at her the next time you see her.'

Ellie laughed. 'Maggie wears a shawl.'

'Look at how she wears it, though.'

'Shawls are common,' Ellie replied, and Julia suddenly guessed why it was she made excuses on a Monday morning. The fella, whoever he was, must be uppity. Ellie was worried about him seeing her with Maggie wearing a shawl. Some stuck-up little nothing. She was beginning to dislike him.

As was usual these days Ellie, though loving Julia deeply, believed she knew nothing about anything except cooking, cleaning and making shirt-blouses. She really got in on her nerves. Like the thing about style and Maggie. And as for love – well, maybe years ago she had known what it was but now – her mother was the last person in the world she would confide in about love!

The film she and Chrissie saw was *Snow White and the Seven Dwarfs*. Ellie loved it. She felt the theme song, *Some Day My Prince Will Come*, was written for her alone. Chrissie, however, said she felt like asking for her money back. 'I didn't know it was a cartoon – I hate cartoons. And one that turns out to be a love story with those bloody little dwarfs! I could have strangled them.'

'Don't you ever want to fall in love and get married?' Ellie asked as they walked home.

'No, never. Never in my whole life. I hate men.'

'It's because of her mother dying,' Ellie told herself. 'But she'll get over it. Everyone does. Even my mother got over my father's death. All the same, I won't tell her about me meeting and falling in love with someone. And I was going to. I'm dying to talk to someone about it.' Softly she hummed Snow White's song and after she finished, told herself that some day he would come. Maybe tomorrow.

Eventually she did tell Chrissie, for two reasons. If, and she hoped this would be so, she met the boy again and he asked her out, she would need a cover; also she desperately wanted to be able to talk about him. So walking home from work one evening she said to Chrissie, 'I've been meaning to tell you something.'

'What?' asked Chrissie.

'It's about a fella I met, only don't get smart alecky. I know you've gone off fellas, never have a good word to say of them, but promise if I tell you you won't get all sarcastic.'

'I might think that way.'

'I can't stop that, but don't say it. I've no one else to tell and I have to talk about him.'

'I'll listen and won't open my mouth.'

It wasn't what Ellie wanted. She was looking for encouragement, for whoever she confided in to confirm her hopes, to say : 'I think he really likes you. He sounds gorgeous. This might be the real thing.'

But Chrissie said none of this. She listened to all Ellie had to tell her and at the end said, 'I hope it works out for you,' in a tone of voice that Ellie knew concealed her true thoughts – that Ellie wanted her head tested, pinning her hopes on such a slender chance. And that in any case, she was mad to let any fella have such sway over her. But Ellie understood that the change in Chrissie had only come about since her mother's death. One day she would be all right again.

'The other thing,' said Ellie, 'is that if we do go out, often you'll have to cover for me. I'll be letting on I'm going to the pictures or somewhere with you. So don't forget if you're in the house and the talk comes up about somewhere I was, don't make a liar of me.'

'I'd never let you down,' Chrissie said.

Ellie squeezed her arm in gratitude and hoped that Chrissie would get over her grief soon. Be herself again. She loved her. Sheila was all right, but she didn't feel the same for her. Apart from when she had thought she might be pregnant, Sheila was very sure of herself, whereas Chrissie wasn't. Oh, she pretended to be. She could be very abrupt, but Ellie knew that was just a cover-up. Chrissie was sensitive. In school she had been the cleverest girl in the class. The nuns wanted her to go for further education but there wasn't a chance. Her father wouldn't spend a penny to help, and Ellie, who hadn't been in the slightest bit bothered about leaving school, knew that Chrissie would have loved to stay on. Poor Chrissie was very unfortunate. Ellie hoped that one day she would find someone to fall in love with.

CHAPTER TWENTY-FOUR

He came on the following Saturday. On Saturdays she worked a half-day. She reached the turn in the street about half-past one, thinking about him as usual, and that on Saturdays there were no classes so she wasn't likely to see him, and then she did. He was leaning against a wall, his bicycle propped beside him. She watched him watching her as she crossed the road. They spoke at the same time. 'More swotting?' she asked and he said, 'I hoped to see you. Can we go somewhere?'

'Not far,' she said. 'My mother's expecting me.'

'Come for a spin on the bike – on the crossbar?'

She noticed he was wearing his school blazer and commented on it while deciding whether to go on the bike. She had never been on a crossbar. She thought she was too big, too tall.

'I put on the first thing that came to hand. Will you come for a spin?'

'All right. But not here. Let's walk first, to some of the back streets. I'm afraid I might fall off the bike.'

'I wouldn't let you.'

He turned the bicycle round and they walked up the side street. 'Were you seeing your friend?' she asked. Having wanted to say something bright and amusing it was all she could think of. She was so excited, so thrilled, so nervous. For weeks she had thought about him, imagined this meeting, and now didn't know what to say.

'No, I came just to see you. I came last week and the week before.'

'I stayed late in town shopping.'

'I didn't know your name so I couldn't ask anyone where you lived. Will you ride now or d'ye still want to walk?'

'I'm Ellie, Eleanor really but everyone calls me Ellie. I think it'll be all right from here.'

He got on the bicycle and held it steady while she manoeuvred herself on to the crossbar. 'Keep your feet up. Right then, we're away.' The bicycle wobbled under the extra weight; its unsteady movement throwing her against him. He smelled of scented soap and pencils, his breast pocket a quiver of them, and peppermint. The wind blew her hair against his face. Her heart beat quickly and she felt warm all over, a wonderful warm melting sensation that spread from her face to the tips of her toes. And while they rode round the quiet back streets he arranged to see her that night. She agreed, said it would be grand.

'Half-seven?'

'Half-seven, yes, that's grand.'

'Where?'

'The same place as today,' she said, 'unless you want to go into town.'

'I thought we'd go for a walk.'

'All right, a walk,' she told him as they arrived at where the ride had started from. 'I don't know your name,' she added as they walked towards the corner where he had waited for her. 'Nor why you sometimes talk like a film star.'

'I'm Art, Art O'Leary.'

'Is that short for Arthur?'

'It is not. My father wouldn't call me after a British King, legendary though he may be. My father is passionately Irish – well, Irish-American. I'm called after another Art O'Leary – an Irishman, a hero killed by the English in 1700 and something. His wife Eileen wrote a beautiful poem about him. I'll read it to you some time.' She was mesmerised, watching him and listening to him tell of the poem. Such a thing was like out of a story.

'And as for talking like a film star,' he continued, 'that's my father's doing as well. He grew up in Chicago. His grandparents went there after the Famine. He came here on a holiday, met my mother and they got married. The intention was to go back after the honeymoon to America, but she got sick so they stayed until after I was born. I went to America as a baby and was there until I was seven or eight. Anyway, until after I'd made my First Communion.'

'And then you came back. I suppose your mother was homesick.'

'No,' Art said. 'It was my father. He's years older than my ma and wanted to finish up here. Maybe he knew or had a presentiment that something ailed him. He got multiple sclerosis not long afterwards and he's not great.'

'That's very sad. Can it kill him?'

'Eventually.'

'My father's dead. He was shot in a battle in Westmoreland Street. He wasn't in it or anything. He was just walking down the street when the British and the Republicans started firing. He got shot. There's only me and my mother.'

'You'd have been a baby so you don't remember him?'

'No. It's only in the last few years I've really missed him. Wished that he was still alive. It must be lovely to have a father.'

'One like mine certainly is. I'll have to go now. See you tonight.'

'Tonight,' she said, and watched him ride off.

She came in smiling, her eyes shining, a glow on her face. Julia guessed something had happened. She had been with him. She wanted to hug her and tell her how pleased for her she was. She wanted for the two of them to sit down and for Ellie to tell her all about him.

'You were delayed,' she said, offering her an opening if she wanted to talk.

'I went round the shops. Cassidy's and Macey's have their summer dresses in. Gorgeous.'

'You look grand. I was beginning to get worried about you. Are you hungry?'

'Starving,' Ellie replied. 'Will you press my pleated skirt for me after dinner?'

'I will. Are you going somewhere nice?'

'To the pictures with Chrissie.'

Why, Julia wondered as she pressed the skirt, was Ellie being so secretive? Was there something about the young man of which she thought Julia wouldn't approve? Maybe he was a Protestant. You'd think she would know her mother well enough to understand that she wouldn't be like that. It was so sad being excluded. Not that she wanted to be like a sister to Ellie, only to share in her joy and sorrows. Had it been like this with her and Lizzie? They didn't always agree. Usually, if her memory was right, it was Lizzie who would start contentions – *about Sarah*. Unbidden, the memory came into her mind, the arguments they had had about Sarah . . . For a while now Julia hadn't dwelled on her or Barney, too occupied with worrying over Ellie's obvious distress; her unhappiness had wrenched her heart, but it was a healthier suffering than her black bitterness towards Barney, dead this long time, and Sarah who probably still lived. Julia concentrated on ironing in the pleats and looked forward to the time when Ellie would confide in her. When, please God if things worked out, she would bring the young man to meet her. Telling herself it was no use making comparisons between how her courtship with Jack had been conducted, for there couldn't have been any secrecy even if they had wanted it. From childhood on they had been sweethearts, approved of by all in the Terrace. There were no introductions, no bringing him home for the first time. He had always been in and out of her home. Everything was different nowadays. This boy or man was a stranger. She would have to be patient, wait until Ellie wanted to talk about him, bring him home. She hoped he was right for her, a kind good person who would cherish her. Who he was, what he did, what his religion was, didn't matter so long as he was all of the other things.

Once they were away from the street they walked hand in hand towards the canal, stopping to look at the foaming lock. 'I brought you these,' he said, and gave her a bag of chocolate sweets. He wore a sports coat over a Fair Isle pullover, hand-knitted, and carried a dustcoat. She knew about men's clothes. His were good, expensive. They ate some of the chocolates then went on along the bank, walking slowly, he telling her more about himself. He had lived in many parts of Dublin, as his mother had a mania about moving house. They had lived in Clontarf, from there went to a bigger house in Dunlaoghaire, then on to Blackrock. 'There were so many that I forget.'

'Why did your mother want to move so often?'

'It was to do with my father's illness. Each house was more convenient for him. Wider passages for his wheelchair.'

'He's in one of them?'

'His disease is progressive – all he can get is worse. He can't walk at all now. He has to have a nurse. My mother was a nurse so that's handy.'

'All the same it must be hard on her. Unless another nurse is there I don't suppose she can ever leave him.'

'She was never one for going out much, only into town occasionally for special shopping.'

His father obviously didn't work. Ellie wondered how they managed for money, but you couldn't ask questions like that when you hardly knew someone. She wasn't all that interested, in any case. She just wanted to walk with him along the canal bank, holding his hand, squeezing it now and then to convince herself he was real. That he was by her side. That it wasn't a dream.

They passed under seven bridges, and she told him the name of each one. When they came to Mount Street Bridge he said, 'That name I know, Mount Street. Wasn't there a battle here during the Rebellion in 1916?'

'I'm the Dubliner and I didn't know that. What happened?' she asked.

'According to my father the Rebels scored a great victory here. They killed more than two hundred soldiers on their way in from Kingstown to reinforce the Dublin Garrison.'

'On a lovely night like this that's hard to imagine – the poor men, Lord have mercy on them. Don't tell me any more things like that, not tonight.'

They turned and began the walk back. It was beginning to get dark, a chill wind blew off the water and she shivered. He noticed and put his coat round her. 'Now isn't that better,' he said, keeping an arm round her. She leant against him, feeling as if she was in Heaven, a magical place where there was no one else, only him and her. He moved her to stand with her back against an elm tree and kissed her – the first time anyone's lips other than her mother's had touched hers. 'I love you, said her heart. 'I love your dark brown hair and eyes, how much taller than me you are. I love the feeling of your arms around me. I feel so safe in them. I love you.' All was said to herself.

He kissed her again, this time for longer and she felt faint with pleasure. A man walking a dog came close by, so they moved apart. The dog came and sniffed round them. The man called the dog to heel.

'Will you come out with me again ?'

'Yes,' she said. 'Yes, I will.'

'I can't see you often because of the studying, but I will whenever I can. Saturday evening's a good time – will we say a week tonight at the same time ?'

'That'll be fine.' They walked on, now and then stopping on the towpath to kiss. And she thought how this was a night she would remember for always.

They met on the following three Saturday nights. The weather was fine and they chose not to go to the cinema. Twice they walked along the canal and once they went to the Phoenix Park. 'I don't live too far from here,' he told her as they went in by the Island Bridge Gate. 'You'll see for yourself soon. Once I've got these exams behind me I'll bring you home.'

Eventually she told Sheila and Chrissie about Art. Sheila was delighted for her, Chrissie noncommittal. But both agreed to help by making reference to dances and pictures they'd been to together when they were in her house.

Julia wasn't fooled. She noticed the extra care and time Ellie spent getting ready to go out. Particular though she was, never had she titivated so much when it was an appointment with the girls she was keeping. It grieved her that still she wasn't confided in. After a while worry took the place of grief. Ellie had to have something to hide besides going out with a boy. Supposing, as she had assumed, he wasn't a young man, but was older, married, maybe. Well up in the ways of the world. One who would know how to take advantage of her, and she as innocent as a lamb.

In a clumsy embarrassed manner, she began trying to warn her. Telling her of a young girl in the neighbourhood who had got pregnant and the man was married, though until the last minute she hadn't been aware that he had a wife. Of another case where, although the man wasn't married, he didn't want to marry. The trouble this had caused. The heartbreak for the girl and her family knowing the wedding was a forced one. Going on to explain as well as she could the differences there were in men and women's natures.

Once only did Ellie comment, asking, 'Why are you always telling me about pregnant girls, old men and married men?'

'Because you're now a woman,' Julia replied. 'It's time you knew such things.' But if she hoped for any further response, she was disappointed. Ellie made an excuse about having to slip up to the shops and went. 'At least,' Julia thought, 'she didn't lie to me. She didn't say, "It doesn't concern me. I don't go out with men".' For whatever reason she deceived her, but hadn't as yet openly lied. From this Julia took some consolation.

She talked about it to Jack. Asking what she should do, telling him of her worries that the man might be married or well up in the ways of the world. He told her to be patient, to trust Ellie. Maggie gave the same advice, but more explicitly.

'Leave her alone. She'll tell you when she's good and ready. In any case, you can't go with them on their walks and hold her hand. She's eighteen. They'll do what they do, and please God it won't be what's worrying you. You can't be there standing over them. Maybe he's right for her and in time she'll tell you and everything will be grand. Maybe he's not. He could be all you fear. But if you push her into admitting he exists, into meeting him and then take against him, into his arms you'll be throwing her. She's a lovely girl. A biddable girl. But she has a mind of her own. Don't set her against you.'

One day in work Chrissie asked Ellie, 'Why haven't you taken Art home yet? Your mother's so kind and understanding that I'm surprised you haven't.'

'That's the trouble — she's too kind, too understanding. If I brought him home she'd smother him with kindness, take it for granted we were serious, that an engagement and marriage was round the corner. And maybe even let him know that.'

'He's never asked you to his house either?'

'He suggested it once not long after we met, but his father's an invalid and he got worse so it was left up in the air. Though I think it's more to do with his mother. I've a feeling she wouldn't approve of him doing a line while he's studying.'

'A doctor, isn't that what he wants to be?'

'Yes. If he gets his exams he's going to Trinity. They've had the dispensation from the Archbishop. All Catholics who want to go to Trinity have to have that.'

'I know,' said Chrissie. 'Maybe it's that his mother mightn't take kindly to the idea of you being a factory girl.'

'Why d'ye say that?' Ellie asked, genuinely surprised.

'How many factory girls d'ye know who've married a doctor?'

'None, I suppose. But that doesn't mean it can't happen.' Anger and fear surged in her. All of a sudden she hated Chrissie, remembered how carping she had become. Sneering at the mention of love or romance, making cutting remarks behind the backs of newly engaged girls or ones about to get married. Many a time Ellie had bitten back retorts which she felt Chrissie deserved. Now she spoke them. 'Why have you changed so much? I made excuses for you after your mother, Lord have mercy on her, died. For a long time I made them, but the change in you is more than grief. You've become cranky and bitter. You're like a sour old maid. If I didn't know how you hate men, though God knows why, I'd say you were jealous of me and Art. There's something wrong with you. You're not normal.'

'Shut up,' Chrissie hissed, not looking at her, furiously feeding linings through the machine. 'You know nothing. Nothing about me, so shut up.'

Sheila whispered, 'What was all that about?' The manager came on to the floor roaring, chasing a delayed order. Ellie couldn't answer her.

The finished linings piled up between her chair and Chrissie's. They bent at the same time to pick them up and send them for pressing. Their eyes met. Chrissie's were full of tears. 'Oh God, Chrissie, I'm sorry. I didn't mean it. I'm really sorry,' Ellie said.

'Shut up. Leave me alone. Don't open your mouth to me again.'

It was to be a long time before they made it up.

The girl who was to have been married on St Stephen's Day died. A collection was made in the factory, Mass offerings given to the local priest, the Mass cards to the family and the remainder of the money to her mother. She was buried on a Monday. Time off for funerals, except for those of close relatives, wasn't allowed, so Sheila and Ellie saw her for the last time in the mortuary chapel of the Hospice. 'This place puts the fear of God in me,' Sheila said as they passed under the gilt arch spanning the Hospice gates. Worked into the gilt ironwork in large letters were the words *Our Lady's Hospice for the Dying*. 'Imagine coming in with consumption, seeing that and knowing that you'd never come out again.'

'Maybe if you were that sick you wouldn't care,' Ellie said. She was apprehensive about visiting the chapel and seeing the dead girl, but part of her mind was occupied with thoughts of the outing to the mountains on Sunday. Art had told her to try and borrow a bicycle. He was in great form, having finished his exams. To celebrate he had planned a picnic in the mountains.

They walked up the long drive where, when she was a child, unbeknownst to her mother, the Sheridan girls had often taken Ellie to look at the dead. The marble slabs with pillows hollowed from the same stone always held a body. She never remembered an empty place. They went from corpse to corpse saying a prayer by each one. Some had pennies on their eyes. No one ever stole the pennies. She was fascinated by the coldness of the hands with rosaries entwined in yellow fingers, by the stillness. Never sad nor frightened, only curious. Never thinking of death in relation to herself. The smell was unpleasant. She couldn't describe nor liken it to any other smell, except perhaps to the withered tulips in school which a nun sometimes asked her to throw out. The dead flowers and the stagnant water in the vase was the nearest thing to the smell in the deadhouse. She didn't know the people on their marble slabs so she never cried for them.

But now it was different in the chapel with many lighted tall candles, their smell mingling with that of the other smell. Now she was looking at someone she had known and liked: the girl who was to be married after Christmas, who had her marriage bed bought. Who had taught her how to foxtrot. Tears poured down Ellie's face as she stood over the coffin. The girl wore a blue habit and her black curly hair was laid about her shoulders. She was twenty. She had died. Anyone could die. Everyone died. Beside her Sheila sobbed loudly. Then they prayed and left the mortuary chapel.

Before they had reached the end of the drive, Sheila was describing the dress she was having made and Ellie wondering who else she could ask for the loan of a bicycle. Then they talked about Chrissie who wasn't friends with either of them any more. Sheila said, 'I wouldn't mind, only it was nothing to do with me. I never opened my mouth.' They agreed before parting that Chrissie had become very peculiar lately.

Mary Flynn that was now came up to Dublin once a week to see Mrs Bellows, who she believed was failing. She brought her sherry, flowers and luxury items of food like peaches and grapes, small portions of smoked salmon, chocolate cakes from Mitchell's and Lemon's most expensive assortment of boiled sweets. Unobtrusively she tidied and washed small items of clothing, realising that the time was coming when Mrs Bellows would have to be found somewhere to be taken care of permanently. Her husband was sympathetic, but not to the extent that he would pay bills for a Home for her. She wondered if the Glenivys would be prepared to help, but didn't know where to contact them, though she supposed if she tried hard enough they could be tracked down. In the meantime she had alerted the caretaker of the flats and his wife to Mrs Bellows' plight. Every week she slipped them a few pounds and knew by the condition of the flat and the food in the pantry for which she also paid, that in a rough and ready way they were keeping an eye on her. On every trip to town she thought of Sarah, of how the years had flown, and never gave up hope that one day they might bump into each other.

CHAPTER TWENTY-FIVE

From time to time Chrissie's words came back to torment Ellie : would Art's mother object to her son going out with a factory girl ? When she was with him, being held by him and kissed by him, such a thing was unbelievable, but during the long wait from Saturday to Saturday it seemed quite possible. When that mood was on her, she saw her home and the house as she never had before : two rooms in a tenement house. The street that she had always loved she saw through the eyes of others living in residential areas – the little poky shops; cabbage leaves and cabbage buns walked into the path outside the vegetable shop; the tattered comics and books in the secondhand store; wisps of hay and hayseeds on the pavements; and the pawn office – the biggest eyesore of all – with prams of dirty babies sucking filthy soothers, their noses snotty, lined up like a procession along the pawnbroker's window.

Even her mother came in for a critical survey. Julia was always clean and tidy, but she did run to the shops with her pinnie underneath her coat, her purse clutched in her hand, and only wore a hat when she went to Mass.

But on Saturdays after she had been out with Art, the street became alive again, filled with people she loved and who loved her in return. Her mother's face was beautiful, her pinnie starched and immaculate, the food she cooked delicious. The rooms smelled of polish, the mirror gleamed. The sheets on her bed were blued white. The fire was always bright and the kettle singing. It was her lovely home. And on the mantelpiece stood the wedding photograph with her smiling father and mother.

With Art's exams over and the long summer holidays in front of them, Ellie's doubts about her suitability as the sweetheart of a prospective doctor left her. All that troubled her now was getting the loan of a bicycle, and that on Sunday the weather would be fine. By Saturday she knew no bicycle was available. Before leaving to meet Art, she reminded Julia of the next day's picnic to the seaside with Sheila, and not to forget she wanted sandwiches.

Julia's patience was wearing thin. It was a long time to deceive her, and she asked herself again and again – why, why, why ?' She was still pondering the question when Maggie came bursting in the door, her face jubilant. 'I've seen him!' she said. 'I saw the two of them. He's gorgeous! You haven't a worry in the world. A gentleman – you can tell by the cut of him. A tall handsome young man – I could fall for him meself. Why in the name of God she hasn't told you about him or brought him home, I don't know.'

Julia was crying and laughing with excitement and relief and happiness and at the same time urging Maggie to sit down and tell her all about it, and asking whether he or Ellie had spotted her.

'Definitely not. They had eyes for no one except each other. I think if it hadn't been a public place he would have eaten her. You should have seen their faces – talk about young love. They make a gorgeous couple. You'd be mad about him. Oh, I hope it lasts, I hope something comes of it. I love her as if she was my own. I'd be the happiest woman in the world to see them married.'

'Describe him to me,' Julia said.

And Maggie did – the colour of his hair, his eyes, the clothes he wore. The build of him. Always coming back to how he greeted Ellie. 'Barely stopping himself from throwing his arms round her and kissing the face off her.'

'But Maggie, if he's all you say why has she never mentioned him?' asked Julia.

'Now that, I must admit, puzzles me. She'll have her reasons, and tell you she will when she's ready. Don't you mention what I've told you. And be grateful he's not an oul fella, and not married unless he's one of them Indians that marry as children. He's a fine, good-looking young man that if you'd picked for her yourself you couldn't have done better. The other thing I wanted to tell you is that the Sheridans and O'Briens have now got wirelesses. I saw them carrying them out of that new shop that gives out on the weekly. What d'ye think of that, now?'

'We'll be sure of the latest news anyway.'

'I feel sorry for the poor Jazzer. Having the wireless gave him a sense of his own importance. He's gone to look very old. I think he's pining for love of you.'

It was a longstanding joke between them, Julia having finally convinced Maggie that she wasn't interested in the Jazzer, nor come to that, any man. Now she brought the subject back to Ellie and the young man. 'D'ye remember the night you made me put out Jack's photograph?'

'I do,' said Maggie.

'And that I admitted there was something in my past I was hiding?'

'Yes, I remember that as well.'

'And that I promised one day when Ellie was grown up I'd tell you?'

'You did.'

'Well, please God that won't be long now. I've a feeling after what you've just told me that the day won't be long until I can unburden myself. I suppose by grown up, I meant when she had found the right man. It seems she has. When I'm certain, then she'll learn the truth about her father and you will too.'

'If that's what you want,' said Maggie. 'In all the excitement I forgot to tell you. Your man has at last taken no for an answer. He's signed on another ship, thanks be to God.'

'No one has a bike to lend.'

'It doesn't matter,' Art told her as they walked away from the spot where Maggie had spied on them. 'We can go on the tram. It means a bit of a hike, that's all.' They went into town and had tea in a café.

'D'ye want to be a doctor?' Ellie asked him after he had finished wondering how he would do in his exams.

'I'm not sure really. It's been taken for granted that I would by my parents – my mother mostly.'

'What's your mother like?'

'Plump, dark . . .'

'No, I don't mean that – what's she like as a person?'

'Generous, very. I don't think she could refuse me anything. Sad a lot of the time.'

'That's natural with your father being sick.'

'Yes, but it's not only that. She misses America. She's never really settled here.'

'But you said she was Irish.'

'Yes, she is, though she wasn't born here. Her father was in the Indian Army. She lived there until she was ten or eleven and then her parents died in a cholera epidemic. She came to Ireland then, to live with an old aunt in – where was it? Oh I know, Trim. She became a nurse, that's how she met my father. He came to Ireland on a holiday just after the war. Got pneumonia, went into the Adelaide where she was nursing and that was that. Once he was up and about they got married, were all set for Chicago when *she* got pneumonia, worse than his. She had to have a long convalescence. I happened in the meantime so they stayed until after I was born.'

'Didn't your father have a job to go back to?'

'He did, but it was the family business, so there was no question of being sacked. His grandfather had been a saloon-keeper but his father went further and made it into hotels. Not bad going for Famine Irish. My mother adored America. They had a great social life there. I remember a bit about it. Then as I told you before, he got this bee in his bonnet about wanting to settle in Ireland, so he sold up. But she's never really been happy here. Anyway, you'll see for yourself what I mean. Dad is in one of his remissions – not really any better but not getting worse. If it lasts a bit longer I'll bring you home. D'ye want more tea, cakes, anything?'

'Nothing – it's nearly time for the pictures.'

They walked back after the film. 'D'ye know,' he said, 'if I hadn't met you, I might be in Spain now.'

'What would you be doing in Spain?'

'Fighting against Franco. There's a war going on out there, and Irishmen are fighting in it.'

'I never knew that! I never heard of a war in Spain.'

'Seriously?'

'Honest to God.'

'Don't you read the papers?'

'Very seldom.'

'What about in work – what do people talk about?'

'The men, I don't know. The women, about clothes, dances, weddings, fellas – definitely not about wars in Spain.'

'I can see I'll have to educate you. First I'll tell you about Spain.' Which he did, and to which she only half-listened, not understanding half of the half. It was enough to be walking with him, his arm round her and knowing that he hadn't gone to fight in Spain because of her. Though he spoiled the effect a little when at the end of his explanation he said, 'They probably wouldn't have taken me. Told me I was too young.'

On Sunday she and Art took the tram then hiked the rest of the way to Glenasmole as her mother and father had done years before. Identical cows looked over the same gates at them. Skylarks rose, sang and soared. The fields were spread with buttercups and gorse and broom grew in abundance. Everything was green and gold, and the sky so blue and bright it dazzled the eye to look at it. She had never seen anything so glorious, never felt so lightheaded with the beauty and joy of it.

'It must be like being drunk only nicer,' she said to Art, turning round and round and gulping in the sweet air. 'Imagine, all the years I've been alive and never been up the mountains.'

He looked at her incredulously and asked, 'But why?'

'My mother wouldn't let me. It was the only thing I ever nagged her about. Other people offered to bring me, but the answer was always no.'

'Didn't she ever give you a reason?'

'Lots that I didn't believe.'

'You could have come since you grew up.'

'I'd lost the yen by then.'

They came to a grassy hollow. 'This looks all right,' Art said and Ellie agreed. The picnic basket was laid down and he spread his coat.

'It's so gorgeous,' Ellie whispered, and lay and stretched and he lay beside her. For a while they didn't move or speak then he turned, raised himself, bent and kissed her and kissed her and kissed her. She returned the kisses, her lips opening under his and she took his tongue in her mouth. Nothing else in the world then existed for her except him. Neither the sun nor sky nor the larks rising and singing.

'I love you,' he said and she whispered back, 'I love you,' and reached for his mouth.

'No,' he said. 'I got carried away, we'd better go for a walk.' She lay watching him rise, smiling, tempting him though not consciously aware she was doing so. 'Come on, up you get,' he said, offering her his hand. 'Come on, we'll go for a little walk.'

Reluctantly she rose and leant against him languorously. Gently he pushed her from him. 'I'll race you,' he said, bounding out of the hollow and racing into the distance. She followed and they ran and ran until she got a stitch and collapsed not knowing whether to laugh or cry. He knelt beside her rubbing her side until the stitch went then he kissed her quickly and complained of hunger. 'I'm starving.' They walked back slowly to the hollow, laid out the picnic which was devoured before the kettle on its twig fire boiled.

He talked about his parents – the cottage they had rented in Connemara for several weeks. How, while they were away, the examination results would be out. He was worried as to whether or not he would pass, and he would miss her so much. He promised to write.

'I didn't know you were going. You never said.'

'I meant to. I forgot.'

'How could you forget you were going away?' She was hurt, mystified that he hadn't thought her important enough to tell. 'Sorry!' he said again. The glow went from the day. She remembered what Chrissie had said about factory girls and doctors. Maybe when he went to University they wouldn't see each other again.

'If I do get in,' he said as if to confirm her doubts, 'I'll be studying most of the time. Maybe we won't be able to meet so much. If you weren't working it would be different. We could see each other during the daytime. In Bewley's for coffee or for lunch.'

'Well, I am working and we don't see that much of each other as it is.'

'Eh?' he said. 'Are you telling me off? Are you trying to start a row?' He was smiling at her.

'Why would I want to start a row. If you've time you'll see me. I understand.'

'You're sulking.'

'I am not.'

'Maybe I won't go to University even if I do get in. Maybe I'll go to the war instead.'

'In Spain,' she said mockingly.

'No, in Europe.'

'There isn't a war in Europe.'

'But there might be. Have you heard of Hitler?'

'Look,' she said. 'I told you I'd never heard of your war in Spain. That doesn't mean I'm a complete thick. I was younger then. I've heard about Hitler – who hasn't?'

'Then you'll know there might be a war.'

'I want to go home.' Everything had gone wrong; the day was spoiled. Why was it that something which had seemed so perfect could suddenly change? Such a short while ago she had been happy: while they kissed and he told her he loved her. While they ran and ate and when he made her stitch better. Was it her fault? Had she read too much into his remark about her working? Maybe. But then he hadn't told her sooner about the holiday cottage. That was his fault, so really he started what had gone wrong. And he mocked her. The sarcastic way he asked had she heard about Hitler ... 'Oh God, please don't let there be a war. Don't let him join the army. Don't let him go away. Don't let him be killed.'

She wanted to say this to him. Say, 'I didn't want to start a contention. Let's go back to where we were. Let's begin again. I love you. Don't ever let us have rows.' But she didn't know how to begin. They packed the picnic things and started the hike back to the tram. On the way into town he promised to send her a postcard every day from the West. Before they parted he kissed her goodnight and told her he loved her. Even so the day remained spoiled in her mind.

Later in that summer of 1938 Lord Glenivy and his only son came back to Kildare for the first time since the House had been burned down. Word spread round the village that Master Patrick, who was now his Lordship, was back staying in one of the local Big Houses which hadn't been destroyed. A lot of old people whose families had worked for the Glenivys were excited at the prospect of the young Lord being back. They speculated as to whether or not he would rebuild the House. And Mary Flynn considered what were her chances of meeting him. On the day she decided that she would write care of the House where he was staying to ask for an appointment, telling him that her wish to see him concerned Mrs Bellows the former housekeeper at the House, she met him in person on the road. He was walking with a young teenage boy – a fine, tall boy with fair hair not at all resembling his father. They walked the narrow country road, Lord Glenivy and his son, deep in conversation. She came nearer to them. When they were almost abreast Patrick became aware of her, raised his hat and said, 'Good afternoon'. She noticed that he was balding.

'Good afternoon, sir,' she said. 'You won't remember me but I used to work up at the House.'

He stopped, obviously pleased to be recognised. 'I'm afraid I don't.'

'You wouldn't. I was only a bit of a girl, a dogsbody then but I remember you well.' He was, she saw, as handsome as ever. 'I was terrible sorry about what happened. Everyone was.' She didn't feel hypocritical, expressing her sympathy. She had been sorry.

'Thank you, thank you very much.' The boy fidgeted, eager to be off. 'This is my son, Oliver, and I'm sorry I don't know your name.'

'Mary,' she said. 'Mary Flynn,' telling him her maiden name. Lord Glenivy made the introductions, and Oliver said hello and shook Mary's hand. Whatever else you might say about them, the gentry had beautiful manners, she thought.

'I don't suppose there are many of the servants about?'

'I'm the only one. You see, I married someone with local connections. A lot of the old ones died and the young, well . . .' She spread her hands. 'They could be anywhere.' She wondered if he still remembered Sarah. There was nothing she could tell him about her, however, and it wouldn't be fitting to mention her name.

He was preparing to take his leave. 'There is someone. I was going to write to you today in fact about her – Mrs Bellows. She used to be the housekeeper.'

'Ah, yes, Bellows, I remember her. Formidable-looking woman. The servants were afraid of her.' Through his mind flashed an image of Sarah and the morning room. Something about lighting a fire. Scared of Bellows. Sarah, who had vanished from the face of the earth. 'She must be getting on. How is she?'

Mary told him how she was, the need for her to be in a Home, the problem over money. 'Of course she could go into the Dublin Union – no fees there, but I thought if you knew her circumstances perhaps you could help. The Union would be the killing of her. Her mind wanders but isn't gone completely. If it was, 'twouldn't matter where she went.'

'I'm very glad you brought this to my notice. Poor old thing. You see, my mother would normally have taken care of these things, kept in touch, but unfortunately she never recovered after my father's death. What with nerves, and one thing and another, her heart finally gave out. She died last year.'

'I'm very sorry, sir. I could let you have Mrs Bellows' address.'

'Yes, do that. I'll make a note of it.' He took out a slim book from a pocket and a propelling pencil. 'Fire away then.' She gave him the address and he wrote it down. He thanked her, shook her hand, bid her goodbye and his son did too. She looked after them as they went on up the road, up towards where the House had stood, and felt sorry. 'Gentry they may be, but won't he feel as sad as any other man in the place he was reared and it not there any more,' she whispered to herself as the pair disappeared over the brow of the hill.

Eager to tell Mrs Bellows all the news, she went to Dublin several days before her usual time. The housekeeper was up and dressed, her hair combed, a tidy appearance about her.

'What a lovely surprise,' she said. 'I'm delighted to see you. I'll put the kettle on.'

Mary laid out fresh cream cakes from Bewley's. 'Wait till you hear my news,' she said, and when they were seated began to tell it.

'You'll never guess who I saw the other day.'

'I'm sure I won't. Don't keep me in suspense. Who?'

'Patrick – Lord Glenivy as he is now – with his son, a lovely boy.' To her surprise Mrs Bellows showed no emotion. 'He asked about you,' she lied. '"How is Mrs Bellows?" was his first question.'

'Kind of him,' Mrs Bellows said.

'His mother, Lady Glenivy, died. 'Twas her heart.'

'She didn't have one.'

'She didn't what?' asked Mary, thinking she had misheard.

'That woman didn't possess a heart.' Mary began to say something but Mrs Bellows, looking as imperious as she had years ago, held up a hand. 'You say nothing, just listen. She and I were sworn enemies from the minute she arrived. She was a bold brazen young woman, not a suitable wife for him, not at all. He was the gentlest, kindest, most honourable man that ever lived. She never loved him. Was constantly unfaithful – under his very nose. In his own house! Disgraceful. And as for Master Patrick, he has no right to the title. He wasn't Lord Glenivy's son.'

'Ah, Mrs Bellows,' Mary gasped. 'That's a terrible thing to say. You're taking away her character!'

'She had no character. I heard her many a time laughing with that maid, another flighty one, Rosie or Sarah or some such name. Laughing about her affairs, like two common servant girls. Disgraceful that – the Mistress of the House confiding in her servant!

'And I heard the crying, too, when one of the affairs went wrong and she was pregnant. I wasn't surprised. I had seen them naked as the day they were born in the summerhouse. I didn't sleep well in those days. I used to walk late at night and in the early part of the morning. I saw them, like a pair of animals. No shame. Of course, he was known everywhere for a womaniser. Very charming, very handsome, but a rotter through and through. He had a wife. The child was his, no doubt about that, but she passed him off as the rightful heir, encouraged by the other one, the servant girl.

'Ah yes, she was a wicked, deceitful woman without a heart. How could she do that to him? To the world's loveliest man, the most wonderful man God ever created. How could she?'

'Don't cry, Mrs Bellows. Don't upset yourself. Sure it was a long time ago. They're all dead now.'

'I'm not. And every day I remember him and what might have been, what *could* have been, had he not been so honourable, so aware of his duty to his family to carry on their noble line. And who's carrying it on? A bastard, that's who. The son of a man as common and coarse as you could find. He was no son of a noble line. His father kept a shop in Clapham. He was commissioned in the field during the war, a subaltern in his Lordship's regiment. They struck up a friendship as young men in wartime do. This other fellow, when it was over, hung on like grim death. Got himself invited to the House. Oh, he was amusing. He came to the House parties. It's his son that now carries the title. Lord Glenivy, whose grandfather sold tobacco and newspapers for a living. I made it my business to find out.'

'You never said. Never told anyone.'

'Of course not. What was done was done. Do you think I would have broken his heart?'

'No, you wouldn't. You're a good woman. Have a glass of sherry.' The poor creature, Mary thought as she poured the drink. All the years she had loved Lord Glenivy. All the years knowing that secret. All the years, the lonely years growing old in the House with the woman who had married and wronged him. 'And now I've arranged another torment for her,' she said to herself. 'Supposing Patrick comes to see her, how will she react? If it's one of her bad days, she'll maybe blurt out the truth. Then on the other hand he would probably arrange for someone else to see her. One of those ladies, the British ones still here who do charitable work. There's nothing I can do about it anyway. I can't very

303

well write and tell him not to bother. But I won't mention it to her, she decided.' Anything might happen in the meantime.

After a second glass of sherry, Mrs Bellows dozed in her chair while Mary washed up and inspected the larder. She woke her before she left and kissed her withered cheek, feeling more sorry for her than ever before.

Every day Ellie got a postcard with views of Clifden, Roundstone, Galway Bay, the Connemara mountains and one from an island on Arran. One told her he had passed his examinations. And every one told her he loved her. Julia read the cards which came after Ellie had left for work and rejoiced for her.

After tea, if you opened your door, the Doyles', Sheridans' and the O'Briens' wirelesses could be heard all over the house. Drim and Drew complained to Julia about the noise and Julia agreed it was a terrible nuisance. She promised to have a word with the offenders, which she did. They vowed not to play them so loudly and for a while didn't. When the sound went up again she advised the sisters that, short of buying a wireless of their own and drowning out the others, there was nothing more she could do.

Julia liked the Misses Bruton very much, and wished for them to have a little house of their own. They had lovely things in their rooms – figurines on a finely carved walnut whatnot, a real picture over the fireplace (an oil painting), two armchairs with faded chintz covers and winter or summer, a few flowers or leaves in a crystal glass. No more than she did they never spoke about their past life nor what they did for money. Respecting their privacy as they did hers she asked no questions.

The different ways women lived ... Maggie who had turned down the offer of another husband, happy-go-lucky, drinking, making herself a life without a man. Independent. Mrs Sheridan, who must finally be coming to the end of her childbearing. Fat and sloppy, her legs knotted with varicose veins, as happy as a lark. Always a child in her place – her last, a grandchild or any child who wanted minding. Molly O'Brien who'd never been blessed with one. Not a bad sort so long as she didn't know your business. Always running to the chapel. Waiting hand and foot on him, the poor Jazzer who'd have made someone a good husband if any woman was willing to take on his mother as well. Watching his every move. His dancing days over. Never crossing the door except to work. She was sure he turned his wireless up to drown his mother's voice. And herself. Happier than she had been for a long time. Seldom letting thoughts of Barney or Sarah take a foothold in her mind. Never forgiving them, never. Only God Almighty could forgive such a crime.

But trying and succeeding for the most part in not remembering them. So happy for Ellie that they mustn't be allowed to intrude. She blessed the day her daughter had met Art and longed for the time when she would meet him too. He had brought such happiness into their lives, though at the present Ellie was down in the dumps. That was because he was away. That was natural.

After returning from seeing Mrs Bellows, Mary told her husband what she had discovered about the Glenivys, expecting him to be as interested and as shocked by the story as she had been. He listened until she had finished, then he laughed.

'Why are you laughing?' she asked.

'At you,' he said. 'You always professed a dislike for them and here you are all agog with what you've found out.'

'I am not all agog! I was interested – it was gossip. All women like gossip. Sad I was more than anything else, sad for that poor old woman and her wasted life. Sad for Lord Glenivy, too, having been deceived as he was.'

'Woman,' he said. 'Will you ever get sense? Sorrow for her I can understand, but whose fault is it that she's a lonely destitute woman nearing the end of her days without chick or child? His – the Master. She was good enough to go to bed with, but not to marry. The blood-line had to be kept pure, like brood mares. Well, wasn't it the price of him that he had one slipped over him. A pity he never knew. She was a loyal if stupid woman keeping it from him. After how he treated her he didn't deserve such loyalty.'

'You're right, I suppose,' said Mary. 'But all the same, don't you go telling it to anyone. It was Mrs Bellows' secret. She wouldn't have told me except her mind's failing.'

'Who in the name of God do I know that'd give a shite one way or another about the young Lord Glenivy being a bastard or having a grandfather who had a huckster's shop. We've got rid of them – that's all that ever interested me.'

The next morning she had a telephone message from the caretaker of the flat in Dublin. His wife had found Mrs Bellows dead in the bed when she brought her up a cup of tea. Mary went back to Dublin, arranged the funeral, paid for it and stayed up for the burial. She put a death notice in the *Irish Times*, and went through Mrs Bellows' papers and personal things. There were a few items of jewellery, including an old-fashioned silver bangle with the inscription *For Emily with my love*. No other name, no date. She wondered had it been a gift from Lord Glenivy. Amongst the papers, which consisted of old menus, theatre programmes and the newspaper picture of Glenivy before and after the fire, was a small blurred photograph of a young man in uniform and a slim-figured pretty girl. No names, no dates. She assumed it was Emily and her lover. 'I'll keep it,' she told herself. 'I'll keep it in my prayerbook as if it was an *In Memoriam* card to remind me to say a prayer for her.' She paused as if thinking, and added, 'I'll say a prayer for him as well.'

The bangle and the Waterford decanter were the only articles worth money. In case there were any relatives of Mrs Bellows she would have an advertisement put in the newspaper asking them to contact her solicitor. If there were no replies, the caretaker and his wife should have them, and whatever else they wanted from the flat.

If anyone who had known Mrs Bellows read of her death in the *Irish Times* they didn't come to the funeral. Only she, the caretaker and his wife were present. As the coffin was lowered she promised Mrs Bellows that the secret was safe with her.

Art's last postcard to Ellie reminded her to meet him on Saturday at the usual place. She had missed him so much that all the unpleasant thoughts she had harboured on the day of the picnic were long since gone from her mind. He looked glorious. His face was brown, his teeth gleaming against the tanned skin. 'I missed you so much,' he said, catching both of her hands in his. 'Where can we go?' Although the day was fine and warm it was late to go to the mountains. The only other place where they could be alone though amongst many was the cinema. She suggested that. They got seats in the back row where they could embrace and kiss until the film ended and the variety show began.

Walking her home he talked about Connemara, how beautiful it was, but lonely for him without her. He described the mountains and the lakes how long the light lasted into the evenings. He spoke of his visit to the Arran Islands, to Kilronan on Inishmore, and the sense he had experienced of life having gone on unchanged there for centuries. 'We'll go there together. I'll take you some time to the Islands.'

She asked if his parents had enjoyed themselves.

'I think so – though there wasn't much for them to do. They might have been better in a hotel. It's not the best place, an Irish cottage for a wheelchair. And I was selfish. I should have stayed with them more, instead of walking and fishing, though they encouraged me to go and enjoy myself.'

'I've never been outside of Dublin,' Ellie said wistfully.

'Once I'm qualified we'll change all that. There's the whole world to see. Ireland first, and then bit by bit we'll do Europe. I'll take you to America. I'll take you to the moon.'

He was planning their life, years ahead. He must intend marrying her. How foolish she had been to let Chrissie put a doubt in her mind. Never again would she quarrel with him. And soon she would have to bring him home. Make it clear to her mother that as yet there was nothing serious between them. Make her promise not to speak to him as if there was. In any case, it was time she told her mother he existed. She suspected that there was someone. It wasn't fair to keep her in the dark. She could be imagining he was a person she was ashamed of – afraid to bring home.

'Are you tired? Will we take a tram?' Art asked.

'Not a bit. I love walking in the city at night. I love crossing O'Connell Bridge, looking at the Liffey. With you I love everything.'

'Will we go up the mountains tomorrow? We might as well make the most of the weather. We won't get much more of it.'

'I won't be able to get a bicycle.'

'We'll hike. Start early so we have the whole day.'

'Yes,' she said, 'first thing in the morning.'

It was a beautiful September day, the sun well up, the early morning chill of autumn gone. Cobwebs spun from bush to bush glistened, their silvery thread sometimes brushing Ellie's face as she followed Art to their grassy hollow. They rested awhile on the grass before taking off their coats, then lay down. Turning to each other they kissed. 'You're gorgeous,' Art said. 'I missed you so much. I longed for you to be with me in Connemara. I used to imagine us there. Fishing, walking. You'll have to come with me to see it.' He kissed her again. 'I love every bit of you.' He kissed her throat. He began unbuttoning her blouse. She was excited and afraid. Fear overcame her excitement so that her hands stopped his. 'Don't be frightened,' he said. 'I wouldn't hurt you. Let me see your breasts. I won't do anything else, won't touch you anywhere else, only your breasts. Please. I want to touch them, to kiss them.'

He finished unbuttoning her blouse. She sat up and slipped it off. She wore no brassière, only a silk slip. She slid the straps from her shoulders and displayed her high, rounded pink-nippled breasts. He kissed each one, caressed their contours then easing her back in the grass, lay with his face against them, while she stroked his hair, her heart full of love and her body with an awakening desire. Knowing that if he was to break his promise she wouldn't protest.

But soon he sat up, helped to adjust her straps and assisted her on with her blouse. They ate their picnic, walked on the mountain, chased each other, came back to the hollow, lay in the grass, kissed and talked. He mostly. He wasn't looking forward to starting University, complaining about the six years in front of him. The limitations on his life. She took this to mean that they couldn't be engaged or married until he qualified.

307

'I'll be nearly twenty-four, ancient,' he complained.

'Twenty-four isn't old, not really.' She wanted to say, 'I'll wait. I'd wait for you forever.' Instead she asked was his father still in remission.

'The doctors think so. No one knows much about the disease, so it's anyone's guess.'

'Would he not think of going to Lourdes? You hear of marvellous miracles there.'

'Not Dad, he believes you make your own miracles.'

'What about your mother?'

'No, she's not over-religious either.'

'What's her name?'

'Louise. Lotty, my father calls her.'

'I'm sure they're over the moon that you passed your exams, that you're going to be a doctor.'

'Delighted – they bought me a gold watch. My mother's thrilled that I'm doing medicine. My father wanted me to be an engineer, but he never goes against her wishes.'

They talked some more about his parents. He made no mention of bringing her home as he had a couple of times before – but why should he, she thought. Neither had she.

The weather remained fine and they went to the mountains again. She let him undo her blouse and kiss and caress her breasts. Before the next outing she lay in bed thinking of the next day, of her exposed breasts, of Art stroking and kissing them. Now he took her nipples in his mouth. She yearned desperately for a greater closeness, and she became afraid. Not of him but of herself, remembering things her mother had said: 'Never lead a man on. Men's natures are not like women's. A man that's aroused and then refused can become like a mad thing. Not all men, thank God, but as it's the girl that suffers it's up to her to set the standard.'

Still at going on for eighteen she didn't fully understand all that her mother implied, but did know as she had once thought, that a magic took hold of you when you were in love. A power that could blind you, deafen you to all the half-understood warnings. That on the mountains in Art's arms, her insides melting, she could if he were to persist, refuse him nothing.

That was, she supposed, how girls got into trouble. And as her mother had pointed out, sometimes the man married them, sometimes he didn't. If he didn't, unless you had a loving family to support you, the child had to be put in a home and its mother carried the stigma for the rest of her life. If the man married the woman, it was said he felt trapped.

She didn't want either of those things to happen to her. Her dream was of a beautiful wedding, a veil and long dress, like her First Communion only more special, for this day would be only hers and the man she married. Her day to cherish and remember for ever. She had seen such weddings. The mystery, the wonderment and joy on the girls' faces, and on the faces of everyone who watched them. And not until after the wedding, after their first night would they be real wives, women knowing all the secrets that made them so. For herself, for Art, for her mother and for God she wanted such a wedding.

Tomorrow she had to let him know how she felt, tomorrow before the magic began to work on her.

He was patient and listened to her explanation and promised to respect her wishes, but once they lay down on the grass and began kissing, his hand went to her breast. Her body said yes, a voice in her head said no. She removed his hand and saw a sulky look on his face.

'I love you, you know I do and just now you promised.'

'OK,' he said, sitting up, turning away from her and gazing into the distance.

'Maybe we shouldn't come up here again.'

'In a week or two we won't be able to anyway, but while the weather lasts why shouldn't we?'

'Well, for one thing it's so isolated. You'd think there was no one else only us in the whole world, like Adam and Eve. And for another thing, up here I feel more romantic or passionate – more so even than when we're courting in some shop doorway.'

'It's all the fresh air. It goes to your head.'

She knew he was being sarcastic. Nevertheless she tried explaining. 'You may be right about the air. I told you once it was like being drunk.'

'How would you know? You've never had a drink in your life.'

'All right – what I imagine being drunk is like. It's definitely something about the air, the singing of the birds, the smell of grass and flowers – I get carried away.'

He turned to her then and said cuttingly, 'That's the one thing you don't.'

'What do you want me to do – strip off?' She was annoyed that he was annoyed. 'Anyway, as I said, it isn't that I don't love you or like what we do. That's the trouble. I like it too much. I'm afraid. I don't want anything to happen until I'm married.'

'I never mentioned marriage.'

She was cut to the quick. 'I didn't mean you,' she said, trying to sound nonchalant.

'There's no point in talking any more about it. I thought you'd understand and you didn't. We might as well go home.'

In silence they packed their belongings and still not talking walked to the tram. Before they parted he kissed her, arranged another meeting but didn't as was usual say, 'I love you.'

CHAPTER TWENTY-SIX

She waited by Nelson's Pillar for an hour, but Art didn't come. She was furious that he had left her standing – a peepshow, an object of pitying and leering looks from a small group of men who were there for the hour smoking, laughing, now and then calling remarks to her. How could he do such a thing to her! Why couldn't he have sent a note, a postcard, telling the truth, lying even – anything to save her from the ordeal she had just undergone.

For the first time in her life she went into a café on her own and drank several cups of coffee rather than go home so early in the evening and be questioned by her mother. Be forced to tell lie after lie. Say that Sheila hadn't come, had sent her brother. She was sick . . . she was sorry.

Gradually she calmed down and anger gave way to fear. Art could have been run over on his way to meet her; he could have suddenly become seriously ill! Either of those reasons would account for him not getting a message to her. This frame of mind lasted until a man came and sat at her table. He was, she saw, well-dressed, not very young, but not old either. She could smell drink on him. She even, in her more compassionate frame of mind, wondered if someone had also let him down.

Then he spoke. She didn't hear properly what he had said. 'I beg your pardon?' she smiled.

'I asked if you fancied coming for a drink with me.'

She couldn't get up and get out quick enough. The cheek of him! He thought her a pick-up, maybe even worse. Her face was scarlet as she walked up the café's aisle, convinced that everyone had overheard the man's invitation. Never in her life had she felt so mortified, and it wouldn't have happened except for Art letting her down. She would never forgive him. He had left her standing deliberately, done it on purpose to pay her back for what had happened on the mountain. Made a fool of her. Didn't have the decency to tell her, to write to her, to say, 'We aren't meant for each other. I don't want to see you again.'

She walked home very slowly, dreading her mother's concerned questioning, but to her overwhelming relief, Julia wasn't in. Then she remembered that on Saturday nights she went to listen to the wireless in either the Doyles' or Sheridans'. As she had often told her on previous

Saturday nights when she arrived after leaving Art, 'I've just come in before you, this minute.' She scribbled a note, *Dear Ma, Sheila had a terrible headache so we left the pictures early. I've had my supper. Don't waken me. See you in the morning. Love, Ellie.* She went to bed and cried herself to sleep.

On Monday morning she told Sheila, who was sympathetic, assuring her that there must be a good reason for what had happened. It would all blow over. In the meantime she shouldn't sit at home moping. On Saturday nights there were marvellous dances – why didn't she go to one with her?

Sheila took life lightly, Ellie knew. A dance, a new dress, the latest hairstyle, all brought consolation to whatever problem she had. Only once had she known her genuinely worried – when she thought she was pregnant, but Chrissie had been able to put her mind at rest.

Chrissie hadn't spoken to her or Ellie for a long time. She wished now they were still friends. Chrissie had turned cranky but even then when you talked to her, confided in her, you felt always that she was listening to what you said. Although her answers were not always what you wanted to hear, at least they were sincere, unlike Sheila who said the first thing that came into her mind or what she thought would please you.

Every day when she came from work, Ellie looked to the mantelpiece, hoping for a letter or card from Art, one that would explain how something terrible had happened to prevent him from meeting her by the Pillar. Even one telling her he was sorry, but their love affair was finished. Even that would be better than the limbo she was now in; it might even help her to start forgetting him. And then if her mother wasn't about she would cry and talk aloud to herself: 'But I don't *want* to get over him! I love him. I always will. I'd forgive him even if it was to spite me he didn't turn up.'

'Something's wrong between them, Maggie. I know it.'
'It's only been a fortnight. A lover's tiff. They'll make it up.'
'I hope they do. She's beginning to look terrible – have you not noticed? Her clothes are hanging on her.'
'That's all in your mind. I haven't seen any change in her. It's my guess they had a row and neither will give in first. I wish I could bump into him somewhere.'
'She'd hate it if you interfered.'
'How would she know?'

In work the women as well as the men were talking about the possibility of a war with Germany. The first time Ellie heard them she remembered Art saying the same thing. She became convinced that he had gone to England and joined the army. The thought both consoled and terrified her. It was a perfect excuse for what he had done in letting her down. Joining the army wouldn't have meant he didn't love her, only that like a lot of men, like her father had done, he believed he had to fight evil.

She made more excuses for him. She felt he didn't really want to be a doctor; he had said as much. An engineer, that's what he would have preferred. Six years' studying was an awful long time, he had said so to her on the mountain. After their quarrel he might have felt so fed up between that and the prospect of not earning for years that he just packed the whole thing in and ran off to join the army. He might still write to her.

This new idea kept her going for another week, watching for a letter. Sheila like a gorgeous butterfly flitted from one dance and boyfriend to another and Chrissie looked more despondent daily, her appearance, of which she had never taken much care, worsening. The threat of war became more imminent. The wireless in the house blared out more loudly than ever before when it was time for the news, but no one complained of the noise. Those who didn't go to the rooms to listen to the broadcasts left their doors open to hear.

First, Ellie heard the ominous striking of the hours, a sound with which she was unfamiliar, and which filled her with dread. It reminded her of the tolling of a cemetery when someone was being brought in for burial. Then came the equally frightening voice of the newscaster, measured and solemn, bringing to her mind images of death and war: trenches, mutilated and mangled bodies, which she had seen in a book belonging to the Jazzer. The bodies she imagined were no longer anonymous. Every one was Art's. She was convinced he had joined the army and would be killed in the war that was coming.

She feared she would lose her mind unless she could talk to someone, tell her fears to someone. Talk about the love she had for Art – and still had: a love she believed he had also felt. In desperation she went to Chrissie one lunchtime, knowing she might be rebuffed but prepared to take that chance. 'Chrissie,' she said. 'I've been wanting to make it up with you this long time. It was all my fault and I'm sorry. Will you be friends? Don't say no. I need you. You're the only one I can talk to and I have to talk.'

'Sit down.' Chrissie indicated the chair next to her, her manner not encouraging. 'What ails you?'

'Everything. Art, the war they say is coming, the lies I have to keep telling my mother. The way I'm always biting her head off.'

'Whatever you do don't start crying,' Chrissie said quite brutally. 'Tell me about Art.'

She did. About the mountains, her decision to pull back on how far they were going. How he had stood her up. How she had never heard from him since. Her fear that he had joined the army and would be killed.

'You did right on the mountain. If he finished with you because of that, you're as well off without him. But there may be another reason why he didn't come, and I don't mean joining the army. Maybe there will be a war but not yet. That oul fella Chamberlain is going to see Hitler, to try and sort things out, so don't cross your bridges before you come to them. Have you tried to get in touch with him?'

'I don't know where he lives. If I could bump into him accidentally I'd have an idea by the way he reacted, d'ye know what I mean?'

'If he ran over and threw his arms round you, said he'd lost his memory and the sight of you had restored it, is that what you mean? Or if he ignored you – well in that case he's a lousy bastard and you're well rid of him.'

'Something like that,' Ellie admitted.

'What about friends, the fella he was doing the biology with?'

'I never met him. Never knew his name.'

'You could try the parish church in Kilmainham.'

'From something he said about Lourdes I don't think they are great churchgoers. Anyway, that would be too much like prying.'

'I can't think of anything else to suggest,' said Chrissie. 'But I'll go to the pictures with you, even to a dance if it'll help you to get over him.'

'I don't want that. I don't want to get over him. I love him. I'd rather die than think I'd never see him again.'

'Be careful,' Chrissie told herself. 'She's hurt. Don't hurt her more by dragging the truth in head and shoulders.' 'Listen, Ellie,' she said comfortingly. 'Don't mind me. Cling on to your hopes, he may turn up still. It's only been a few weeks. Something serious could have happened.' Seeing the terrified expression on Ellie's face, she quickly added, 'I don't mean to him, but you did tell me his father's sick. He could have died and his mother be in such a state of shock Art doesn't know what's hit him.'

'I never thought of anything like that. You could well be right. I never read the Deaths column and not having met Art, knowing nothing about him, the name wouldn't mean anything to my mother.' Her face was filled with hope.

'The poor eejit,' Chrissie thought. 'The poor fool. But I'll say nothing for the time being to open her eyes. I'm very fond of her, and would strangle him if I could get my hands on him.'

Julia counted the days, then the weeks. It was three nearly since the last time Ellie had been happy. It must be all over between them. She grieved for her daughter, all the more because as she wasn't supposed to know the boy existed, she could offer no comfort. Only to Maggie could she explain her feelings.

Maggie was mystified as to what had happened between the lovers. 'I can't understand it. If you had seen them together you'd have thought only God Himself could have come between them.'

There wasn't going to be a war. Chamberlain in Munich had fixed it. Germany, France, Great Britain and Italy had signed the Munich Agreement. In the house the ex-soldiers rejoiced. The wirelesses were turned down and Ellie no longer feared the nine o'clock news.

Chrissie came up with a great idea. 'When the term starts, why don't I go into Trinity and ask for him?'

'Oh no, I wouldn't want that,' Ellie said.

'Well, how about if I just asked the porter had he started? At least you'd know he was alive and in Dublin.'

She agreed to that. 'And if he is, he'll be going to Bewley's in Westmoreland Street or Grafton Street for his lunch or coffee in the mornings. I could look there.'

'Not in the mornings. We work, don't forget, but I'd come with you at lunchtime.'

In the first week of Trinity term, Ellie stood outside the gates while Chrissie made the enquiry. She knew by her face something wasn't right. 'A nice little fella, the porter,' Chrissie said. 'But the news is bad. He's on their list but he never registered.'

'Oh God,' Ellie said, and Chrissie took hold of her arm, fearing she was about to faint. 'You go home and I'll tell the manager you got sick in town, too sick to come back.'

'I'd love to. I'd love to go to bed and never wake up again, but I'm all right now. It was just the shock. For a minute I thought he was dead. He isn't. I feel that inside me. He just went away. He doesn't love me any more.'

'He may not be dead,' thought Chrissie as they crossed by College Green, 'but you sound like someone not far from it yourself. Shaggin' men, I hate them.'

'You're not hungry?'

'No,' said Ellie.

'Try a little bit,' coaxed Julia.

'I couldn't. I've a headache. A cup of tea, that's all, Ma.'

She wasn't well enough to go to work the next morning. 'You've got a chill, you're feverish,' Julia said with her hand on Ellie's forehead. 'Stay in bed. I'll get you something from the chemist.' By evening Ellie was coughing. Julia went back to the chemist and bought cough medicine. She coughed all through the night. In the morning Julia took her jug in which she saved money for an emergency from the mantelpiece. This was an emergency, she considered, and no dispensary doctor was coming to Ellie. She sent one of Mrs Sheridan's children, not in school that day, to ask the doctor to call. He diagnosed bronchitis and left a prescription.

'I'm away tomorrow,' he announced, 'but I'd like her seen again. I've a new assistant, a good man. I'll get him to call.'

During the night Ellie coughed up sputum the colour of rust and complained of pains in her chest. Julia was alarmed, knowing that the symptoms could mean pneumonia. People died by the score from that. She stayed up all night, bathing Ellie's forehead, giving her sips of water. Praying to Jack and for the first time in ages, to her mother; remembering many her mother had nursed through pneumonia. Telling her and Jack about Ellie and the young man – how she must have got run-down so the pneumonia could take a hold. Asking for them to intercede with God to spare her. Asking them to send morning quickly with the doctor.

Ellie seemed easier the next day. Maybe it wasn't as bad as Julia thought. Maybe you could cough up rust-coloured sputum with bronchitis. Before ten o'clock, Maggie came to see what she wanted from the shops. Drim and Drew brought a siphon of soda water. Mrs O'Brien said she'd offer up her Mass for her. Mrs Sheridan came with a rub for Ellie's chest and Mrs Sheridan gave Julia three newlaid eggs. 'Laid this morning – I've just been to the dairy for them. Make her an egg flip.' Mrs Doyle told Julia not to worry about sheets. She would no doubt have plenty of changing of them, but she herself had lots – which Maggie, when she came back with the messages, offered to wash. Everyone with a wireless promised there wouldn't be a sound from them until Ellie was better.

Maggie stayed with her, waiting for the doctor and opened the door for him. Julia heard her loud exclamation: 'Jesus, Mary and Joseph, am I looking at a ghost?' Julia saw the man, a fellow in his forties come into the room, and she too saw the startling resemblance.

'You're our landlord's son! I forgot he had a son – a doctor, though God knows he boasted of you often enough.'

'Yes,' he said. 'I am his son, Dr Crystal.'

316

'Did your father ever get to Palestine? We never heard after he sold the house.'

'He did, him and my mother. They died where they wanted to. Now, what about this young lady?'

It was pneumonia. 'I'll arrange for an ambulance, I've beds in the Meath.'

'She's not going to hospital,' Julia said, not crying, not wanting to frighten Ellie.

'She has to. It's a serious complaint.'

'She's not to be shifted. That's the worst thing for pneumonia.'

'An old wives' tale. Your girl is very sick. Hospital's the best place.'

'I'll nurse her.'

'You can't. It's a twenty-four hour job.'

'She's got good neighbours, Dr Crystal. We'll mind Ellie round the clock.'

'I can't force you,' he shook his head resignedly, 'but it's completely against my advice. I'll come back tomorrow.'

Away from the bedroom where Julia gave vent to her tears, Maggie said, 'You did right to stand firm. Shifting more often than not finishes a patient off.'

Through her tears, Julia said how often she had heard her mother say the same thing, though in her heart there stirred a fear that the doctor was right: was it an old wives' tale? For she remembered many who weren't shifted and still died. But Ellie wouldn't. Every minute of the day and night she'd mind her. No hospital could do that. Ellie would get better. Jack and her mother were praying for her. They wouldn't let Ellie die. The hospitals had nothing to cure pneumonia. All they could do was nurse. And that for her own child she could do better.

The doctor came every day. He prescribed medicines. Ellie was bathed and changed, her chest poulticed. Sips of liquid were dribbled through her parched lips, teaspoons of clear soups. The women spelled each other while sleep and food was taken. The doctor was impressed. 'Ellie's holding her own. She has a grand constitution. But we're not out of the woods yet, the Crisis is still to come.' The dreaded word, the dreaded time when the victim fought through or died.

It began and her temperature soared. The doctor came twice through one night. When he left for the second time, Drim the oldest of the sisters, said, 'There was a cure my grandmother believed in. She swore it brought many safely through the Crisis,' and her sister added, 'She had it in a book of medieval folk medicine.'

Hesitantly the older sister explained, 'You have to have the lights from a freshly killed bullock. They are bound to the patient's feet and it's

317

believed they draw out the poisons that cause the pneumonia.'

'What day is it?' asked Julia, who had lost count of time.

'Thursday morning,' one of the Misses Bruton replied.

'They kill today,' Maggie said.

'Will you go to the slaughterhouse?' asked Julia.

'I'll be there before it opens.'

Ellie moaned and coughed, pain creasing her face as she retched up the rusty sputum. Julia bathed her face and moistened her parched lips. Maggie came back with a bloodstained parcel from the slaughterhouse. Rags were found and the big spongey lungs were tied to the soles of Ellie's feet. For several days the Misses Bruton's cure seemed as ineffectual as all the poultices, oils and blessed relics that had been placed on or rubbed into Ellie's body. Everything was as it had been, except for the smell of putrefaction as the bullock's lungs began to decay. The doctor commented on the smell, asking what caused it. Julia told him and said why they were being used. He shrugged but said nothing.

The week was nearly up – the make or break time approaching. Maggie ran to John's Lane chapel to light lamps before the Virgin, lamps for her and Julia who wouldn't leave Ellie's bedside : lamps to the Mother of God asking Her to save Ellie's life.

All of the women who watched by Ellie had experience of the Crisis. All of them knew how few people survived. Strong young men and women had a better chance than most, though.

In their own way they understood what was about to happen : a final battle between the sick person and the disease. They nodded to each other when Ellie's face became scarlet as her temperature rose and her body writhed and her teeth dug into her bottom lip while Julia and Maggie sponged and tried to soothe her suffering. For more than an hour the battle going on within her body that having lost so much weight and strength seemed doomed to lose, raged. Then she screamed.

'Jesus, Mary and Joseph,' Mrs Doyle breathed, making the Sign of the Cross. 'I've never heard the likes of that before and many a case of pneumonia I've nursed.'

'Maybe,' said the older Miss Bruton, 'it's the lights dragging out the poison. It might hurt.'

'Would you not send for the doctor?' suggested Mrs O'Brien. The screams had begun to diminish but still Ellie's body twisted as if she was being tortured.

'He can do nothing,' Maggie said.

Ellie took a fit of coughing. Julia, sitting on the bed, raised her daughter's head and shoulders and said : 'It's all right, love. I'm here. Everything's going to be all right.' Then she opened her eyes and looked at her mother, a look of recognition, smiled and closed her eyes. 'Oh Jesus, oh sweet Jesus, no!' Tears were pouring down Julia's face.

Then Maggie was beside her saying, 'Lay her down. It's over. She's come through it, thanks be to God. Look at her, she's fast asleep. Lay her down.' Julia laid her on the pillows then placed her head on the bed and cried as if her heart would break. While she did the women thanked God and His Blessed Mother. Then they made tea and told each other it was the lights that did it. 'Your grannie was the wise woman. May she rest in peace and get her reward in Heaven,' Maggie told the Misses Bruton, who blushed with pleasure.

Still watched over by her mother and Maggie, Ellie slept peacefully through the night and most of the next day. Slept through the doctor's visit, who declared her to be over the Crisis, but warned that for several weeks to come she would have to be minded carefully. 'Not,' he said, 'that I've any need to tell *you*! Your nursing, Mrs Harte, is a credit to you, and to all of you,' he said, looking round at the other women who were there again. He advised plenty of rest and nourishment, and said that he'd look in from time to time. And he put Julia's mind at rest when she raised the subject of his bill: 'Pay it when you can, unless you win the Sweep.'

Julia made Ellie beef tea. Maggie bought an unheard-of luxury – a chicken – and made soup. All of the neighbours brought titbits to tempt her appetite, like egg custards, milk jellies, junket and out-of-season fruits for which they had paid a lot of money.

Gradually the soups were thickened, crustless bread served and steamed fish and very tender meat and mashed potatoes were introduced into her diet. Little by little her strength returned until after three weeks in bed she asked to be allowed up. Julia and Maggie helped her walk around the room. The next day she ventured out of the bedroom and sat by the fire. 'Oh Ma, it's grand to feel well again.'

'Don't go overdoing it, it's early days yet,' Julia warned, and draped a soft shawl about her shoulders.

'I only remember the start of being sick. All the rest is a bit hazy when I thought I was dying. It wasn't frightening, I just felt as if I was drifting away, all warm and comfortable, just slipping along, like when you float in the sea. Then all of a sudden I had this terrible sensation in the soles of my feet. As if something was sucking the life out of me. I wasn't floating any more. It hurt and I was struggling, trying to shake off whatever it was.'

'That's what saved your life. The lights it was, dragging the poison out of you. You had the pneumonia very bad. God bless the Misses

Bruton for giving me their grandmother's cure. It was them that saved you.'

'What lights? This is the first I've heard of them.' Julia told her about them and how Maggie had gone for them. 'And d'ye believe that?' asked Ellie.

'Didn't I see the proof before my eyes!'

'What did the doctor say about the cure?'

'Nothing. Well, you wouldn't expect him to, but there were cures before doctors. They don't know everything, though they'd never admit that. Anyway, thanks be to God you're well again.'

For the first time since recovering Ellie asked questions. Had anything strange happened while she was sick? Had Sheila or Chrissie called? Was her job safe? The question uppermost in her mind she didn't mention: had Art got in touch? Were there any messages or cards for her, or a note?

In the next week Sheila, beautiful with her painted face and shining dyed blonde hair, came smiling her delight at seeing Ellie up, dressed and looking well. Describing the dress she was having for Christmas. Sympathising with Ellie over the mysterious loss of Art. Consoling her that there were plenty more fish in the sea, and that when she was really better they'd go to dances. 'The halls,' she declared, 'are full of fellas. Did you get the collection?'

'I'm sorry, yes I did. Say thanks for me. I should have sent word in.'

'Chrissie got it up for you. Isn't it fecking awful not getting paid while you're off sick? The very time when you need more money. Talking about Chrissie, I think she's losing her mind. Something ails her and you can't be always putting it down to her mother dying. She takes the head off you for nothing. The girls are afraid to open their mouth to her she's that cranky. Everyone's talking about her. She had a go at the manager the other day. The next thing is she'll be sacked. With all the talking I forgot I brought you a present.' Sheila searched in her bag, found a small package and gave it to Ellie.

Ellie cried with delight when she opened it. *Scent*. Everyone else had brought nourishment, but Sheila brought perfume. A bottle of *Evening in Paris*. 'Give it here to me,' said Sheila, and after undoing the little blue bottle with its silver Eiffel Tower on it, dabbed the scent on Ellie's wrists and neck. 'Now isn't that gorgeous after all the smells of oul medicines and disinfectants.'

The next day a letter came for Ellie. With trembling fingers she opened it while Julia watched and prayed it was the news she had been waiting for, but seeing the disappointment register on her face knew it wasn't.

'Who's it from?' she asked.

'From Chrissie. She wants to stay here tomorrow night.'

'She's a peculiar girl. Never coming while you were sick and now wanting to stay overnight, though she's very welcome if you don't mind sleeping with me. I wonder why she wants to stay?'

'How would I know?' snapped Ellie. The first short answer since before she was sick, Julia noted, and was glad her spirit was returning. 'Sheila told me Chrissie might get the sack, so maybe she has. Maybe she's going away,' Ellie went on, less aggressively.

'Maybe so,' said Julia, and her heart ached that the letter hadn't been the one Ellie wanted.

Chrissie brought a suitcase with her when she came. 'It's only the one night,' she said, noticing Julia's eyes on the case. 'Thanks for getting word to me that it was all right to come.'

'It was no trouble. Lily Sheridan works not far from the factory so I gave her the note to drop in.'

'I'm delighted to see you better,' Chrissie said, turning her attention to Ellie. 'I lit more lamps and candles for you in John's Lane. I was afraid you'd die. Thank God you didn't.'

'And thank God for my mother and Drim and Drew.'

'What did they do?' asked Chrissie.

Julia explained about the lights. 'I didn't tell her about them until she was better. They had to be kept on for a few days, so you can imagine the smell! You tell Chrissie the rest while I make the tea.'

Ellie told her about the strange sensations she had experienced during the Crisis, the feeling of something being dragged out of her. How now, like her mother and the neighbours, she knew it was the lights drawing out the poisons. Chrissie marvelled and said it just went to show that doctors didn't know everything. Look at the way cobwebs could cure the bleeding in a bad cut. While she talked, Ellie watched her face. Saw the dark rings underneath her eyes, the face that looked like that of a haggard old woman.

Julia served the meal, then knowing that they wanted to talk, made an excuse to go and see Maggie. 'Why did you bring a case?' Ellie asked.

'I'm going to England in the morning,' Chrissie said.

'You've given in your notice?'

'No. I've told no one. When I got your mother's note I went home during the lunchhour and packed. A woman I know in the ragstore round the corner from work hid the case until I'd finished.'

'Why are you going all of a sudden, Chrissie?' Are you fixed up with a job?'

For the second time since knowing Chrissie Ellie saw her eyes fill with tears. This time she didn't fight them back. They streamed down her face while she talked. 'I have to go. I should have gone in the beginning, after my mother died. When it first started.'

'But what? What started?'

'My father doing things to me. Only then I thought it was nothing. I loved him. I missed my mother and I thought he was being kind, upset for me, trying to comfort me. After the funeral I was on the bed crying. He brought in a cup of tea. He was crying too. He drank, yes, but that didn't mean he didn't love her. He had drink on him this night. He stroked my face and kissed my cheek like when I was a little girl. He was lovely and kind. He told me to drink the tea and not to be crying. He said, "I'll stay beside you till you fall asleep. Remember I used to do that when you were small." I fell asleep.

'It went on from there. For weeks it was only kissing my face and stroking my hair, but it changed. He was kissing me on the mouth. The awful thing was, I liked it. He was my father – I loved him. It didn't seem a terrible thing to be doing. That's what he used to throw up at me when things changed – that I'd encouraged him. You've got to believe me : I didn't. Or I didn't know I was.'

'Was that how you knew about the tongue and the kissing and that Sheila couldn't be pregnant?'

'Yes, that's how I knew, though I couldn't be a hundred per cent sure. Once he started doing that, though no one ever mentioned it to me like your mother did, you just felt it wasn't right, you know. You thought fathers don't do things like this to their daughters.'

'Didn't you try and stop him? Tell him you'd report him?'

'Of course I did. Then he'd hit me, never on the face or anywhere it would show, and goad me – tell me I wanted it, I liked it. It was only when he was drunk. He never touched me when he was sober. I'd lie in bed and pray for him to be sober when he came home. It's a terrible thing. You feel dirty, ashamed. Imagine that people can tell just by looking at you – men especially, and you hate them all.'

'What about the priest or the police – couldn't you have told them?'

'Ellie, you've no idea what it's like. How mixed up you are. You're afraid they won't believe you. You're ashamed to say such things to a priest. You still love him in a way. You don't want him to go to prison. Ellie, it's a terrible thing to go through, and the worst part is that you keep blaming yourself, thinking that maybe it *was* your fault, that you *did* start it. Then I'd see things clear and pluck up my courage. One night I did threaten him with the police and the priest. What he said frightened me more than anything. He laughed and said, 'Do. Go on –

do! Go now and d'ye know what'll happen? You'll be in the asylum before the week is out. I'll have you committed to Grangegorman. A girl making terrible accusations against her father.'

'Could he have done that?'

'Yes, he could. He drinks, but that's not held against a man. He never misses Mass. Him and the priest are like that,' Chrissie crossed two fingers. 'It has happened. A girl not far from us made an accusation against her father. Said she'd come in and found him assaulting her little sister. She finished up in the madhouse. She was in there for three years until her sister at thirteen got pregnant and he was found out.'

'Oh Chrissie, all the suffering and I never knew. No one knew. They thought in work you were going queer, losing your mind.'

'No one else knows. Don't tell them after I go away. Never. Maybe I'll come back some time and I wouldn't want to be pointed out.'

'You'll definitely go in the morning?'

'I have to. He's started on the real thing now. If I don't go I'll kill myself.'

'Would you like to talk to my mother about it?'

'I couldn't talk to your mother about that, I'd be ashamed of my life. No, no one only you. I'll write and let you know how I get on, and where I'm staying.'

'When you get to England you'll have nowhere to go. You won't know anyone.'

'There's the Legion of Mary women. They meet the train at Euston looking for people with nowhere to go. They'll fix me up for a night or two until I get on my feet.'

'What about money? You won't even have this week's wages. Would you not work the week out?'

'No, not if I was to lose a hundred pounds. I have to get away.'

She had stopped crying and though her face was streaked with tears, she looked less strained than when she came, Ellie thought. It was the relief of being able to unburden herself. Before Julia came back Ellie got Chrissie to wash her face and comb her hair. While she was doing it in the bedroom, Ellie undid the strap on the suitcase and pushed a ten-shilling note down amongst the clothes.

After Chrissie had left Julia asked, 'Well, did you find out anything?'

'Yes,' said Ellie and lied. 'It was like I said – she was sacked. She's gone to England for work.'

CHAPTER TWENTY-SEVEN

Art was on his way to Trinity College walking from Donnybrook into the city. At the top of Harcourt Street he decided to finish the last stage of the journey by tram. He waited amongst a small group at the stop. It was a damp, miserable day, and people waiting complained how the trams never came when you wanted one. It began to drizzle. A woman opened her umbrella and in so doing, poked Art in the back with its end. She apologised profusely. 'It doesn't matter,' he told her. She wanted to talk, he could tell, but he wasn't in the humour. 'I think I'll walk,' he said.

'Now,' said the woman. 'The minute you give up hope here one comes.'

The group surged forward. He stood back, the last one to board and had one foot on the platform when an arm grabbed him and a voice said, 'You bloody young pup. Get off that tram before I drag you from it!' He turned and looked into a ruddy-faced, black-haired, gold-earringed, black-shawled woman with an expression on her face that left him in no doubt of her intentions.

'Let go of me,' he demanded. The other passengers were seated, the conductor with his hand on the bellstrap waiting to signal the 'off'.

'Get down,' ordered the woman.

'I will do no such thing. You're mad, whoever you are.'

'I won't tell you again,' threatened the woman. 'Get off.'

'In the name of Jaysus will you both get off,' said the conductor.

'But this woman . . .' Art began to protest.

'This woman is a friend of Ellie Harte. *Now* will you get down!'

'Why didn't you say that in the first place?' Art asked, jumping from the tram which was now swaying down the street, his face red from the sniggers of the passengers and anger at the way he had been accosted.

'You might have made a run for it.'

'Who are you, anyway? What right do you have to accost me?'

It was now raining heavily. 'Listen, I'm sorry about that. I'm Maggie Simmonds, a friend of Ellie and her mother. I saw you and Ellie together once. I couldn't stop myself when I recognised you just now. We'll get drenched standing here. There's a pub around the corner. Come on and I'll buy you a bottle of stout.'

'I'm sorry, too,' Art said. 'Though you must admit the way you went about it was offputting. Where's this pub, then?'

Before even ordering the drinks, Art told Maggie, 'Now before you start on me you have to hear *my* side of the story.'

'Commere you,' she said, 'I'm not interested in any of your business. It's Ellie that concerns me. I've known her since she was an infant, love her as if she was my own flesh and blood. What I want, what I *expect* from a man that looks as if he was well-reared, well-schooled and into the bargain a man, is for him to put that child out of her misery. Not do a vanishing trick! Do like any decent fella would – face her, tell her it's all off. Tell her to her face. In time she'll forget you ever existed.'

'But it's not like that,' Art said when the stout was on the table and Maggie already into it. 'You don't understand.'

'Nor do I want to. You're not part of my business. Only Ellie's is my concern. Tell me nothing except that before the week is out you'll go and see her. She's home. She's been sick.'

'Seriously?' asked Art.

'You'll find that out for yourself.'

'God,' he said, 'if you only knew what I've been through.'

'Pity about you,' retorted Maggie. 'If you don't heed my words I'll be watching for you.' Yet her tone wasn't as threatening as earlier. She finished her stout.

'Will you have another?'

'No,' she said, 'thanks all the same. And to think what I thought the first time I saw you with Ellie.'

'When was that?'

'Never you mind. I thought you were a decent boy. Don't let me down. I'll say nothing to Ellie or her mother, unless in the long run you don't show up.'

'It's still raining. Will I get you a taxi?'

'Are you mad?' she asked, pulling the shawl over her head and bidding him goodbye. On the way home she kept a conversation going in her head, beginning with: 'I hope you haven't put your foot in it. You've a happy knack of interfering in things that don't concern you.'

'This does concern me. I've watched that child at death's door. A broken heart gave her the pneumonia.'

'Other people – babies, old people, they get pneumonia.'

'She got it because she was unhappy. I saw them that day at the corner. If ever anyone was in love it was that pair.'

'Maybe he changed. Maybe he fell out of love.'

'He might. But if he has, it's better for her to know the truth!'

'Is it, though?'

'I think so.'

'She's not like you – you've a hardened heart. She's only a child. Wouldn't it be better to let her keep her dreams? They'd fade one day.'

'I don't know. How d'ye know anything ever for certain. All I do know is that when I saw him on that tram all the horses in Hell couldn't have stopped me doing what I did. In any case, if he doesn't show up she'll never know that I asked him to come, for the same wild horses couldn't drag from my lips that I met him.'

With not a lot of hope Maggie watched through her parlour window for signs of Art, telling herself that if he ever came it might not be this evening. She would give him another twenty minutes then get ready for a night in the snug. A drink would take her mind off what might not have been a wise move. She was about to leave the window when she saw him cross to the hall door. 'Please God,' she prayed, 'let it all come right for Ellie.'

Ellie had been out for the first time since her illness. The walk, though only a short one, had tired her. She was in bed thinking about Chrissie, thinking about Art, when he knocked on the door. Julia opened it. 'Yes?' she enquired, looking at the young man.

'I'm a friend of Ellie's. I wondered if I could see her.' Then from Maggie's description she recognised him and her first reaction was to say, 'No, you can't. You took too long, far too long coming to see her.' From the bedroom Ellie called, 'Who is it, Ma?' Julia relented. 'A young man, a friend of yours. Will I bring him in?' The note in Ellie's voice as she said yes told her she had done the right thing. 'This way.'

Art banked on Maggie not having spoken of their meeting and as he followed he asked Julia, 'Is Ellie sick?'

'She was, but now she's better, thank God. Only a bit tired.'

How would she receive him? His heart thundered. She was propped on pillows in the double bed, paler and thinner than he remembered her. Her hair, loose about her, had grown longer. 'Ellie,' he said. 'I'm so sorry. I never meant it to be so long. Oh, Ellie.' She held out her hands to him.

Julia left the room, closing the door behind her.

'But you came,' she said as they clasped hands. 'Sometimes I lost hope. I thought you'd joined the British Army, that if the war came you'd be killed. But you came back to me.'

He sat on the bed and put his arms round her. She was so thin. So fragile. 'Why are you in bed?'

She told him about the pneumonia. 'They tell me I nearly died.' He broke down then and cried. She held him like a baby, patting his back, comforting him. Telling him it was all right. She was fine, she hadn't died. They were together. And then when he had composed himself he told her what had happened on the day before he was to meet her at the cinema.

'I'd been in town buying medical textbooks. I wasn't in great form – I hadn't been since our parting. At first I was huffed and hurt, thinking you didn't trust me – that you were preparing to pack me in. Through the week I realised you'd been right: I *was* letting my feelings run away with me. And I was sorry for saying that thing about marriage, d'ye remember?'

'I do,' she said. 'Tell me what happened.'

'I had it all planned. After the pictures I was going to take you for supper and ask if you'd marry me. I thought that if I got that in first, you'd forgive me, wouldn't pack me in. I was all on edge – half-hopeful and at the same time despondent. Anyway, I arrived home from town and put my head round the parlour door to say hello to my mother, and I noticed that there was another woman with her. This was most unusual – in fact, I never remember it happening before. They'd been having tea – I could have done with a cup. I expected an introduction but instead, my ma made it very clear that she didn't want me in the room. She didn't even introduce me. I made myself a cup of tea in the kitchen then went to see Dad, but he was lying down. Through a window I saw the woman go. She was about the same age as my mother – smart, well-dressed. I glanced through a few magazines and then I heard the row. It was my mother rowing with my father. I couldn't hear what it was about. They hadn't rowed for ages, not since his MS had got worse. Not that he ever did, it was always my ma who'd start them off, but they were never serious ones. And then she screamed. I ran to the bedroom. Oh God, it was terrible. My father was having a heart attack.

'I don't remember much, but I suppose I must have tried resuscitating him while she called the ambulance. He was out cold. We went to St Stephen's Hospital, the nearest, but he was dead on arrival.'

'Your poor father,' Ellie interrupted. 'The Lord have mercy on him. Oh Art, I'm so sorry. I know how much you loved him.'

'I couldn't believe it. I kept blaming my mother. If they hadn't had the row. If I'd gone to their room sooner and stopped it. If, if, if ... Anyway, we got home. She cried for hours, told me I'd have to see to everything. The next day I was flying around. I couldn't have got in touch with you. I was worrying about that while ordering flowers, choosing a coffin; in the end I told the undertaker to see to everything. The announcement didn't get into the paper until Monday, the day before he was buried. I hoped you'd see it. It was in the *Irish Times*.'

'We only take the *Herald* and my mother wouldn't have known the name in any case.'

'It was just as well, I suppose. It was such a sad funeral. No one there, only me and my mother and the priest. I should have written to you then that night. I couldn't. I could do nothing. So I said, "Tomorrow," and then again, "Tomorrow". I know there's no excuse but I was stupefied. I knew he was going to die, but I didn't think it would have been so suddenly, though I know it was a merciful end rather than what might have faced him.

'My mother went round like a zombie. The cleaning woman bought the food and stayed on to cook it, though not much of it was eaten. She said I should get the doctor for my mother as she didn't like the look of her. My ma wouldn't hear tell of it. I gave myself until Friday – a week, I thought, was reasonable to stay by her side. And I mean by her side. She had me bring a stretcher-bed into her room. Friday was the day I had planned to meet you outside the factory. A letter, I told myself, wouldn't do. I needed you so much. I wanted to bury my head in your lap and cry and cry. I couldn't cry, you see.'

Julia knocked and put her head round the bedroom door. 'I was wondering would you like a cup of tea?'

'Come in, come in, Ma. This is Art. I've known him a good while. His father has just died.' Julia gave her sympathy. She and Art shook hands and Ellie said they'd love a cup of tea.

'And all the time I didn't know. I didn't even know where you lived,' she lamented.

'On Friday morning my mother had a stroke. It's all so horrible you'd think I was making it up. We were back in the same hospital. I was there night and day for a week. They didn't think she'd come out of it. And when I was at home there was the cleaning woman telling me, "I warned you. I said that woman wasn't right." I felt like strangling her, because sure enough I'd ignored her warnings. You see, Ellie, it was true. Ma *wasn't* right. She hadn't been right, now that I thought about it, ever since the Friday when she'd had that visitor in the parlour.

'I should have found time to get in touch with you, but as the days passed it all became more hopeless. What, I wondered, were you thinking of me by now? The worst, of course. All the same, when there was an improvement in my mother I began to plan again on waiting for you outside the factory. And then d'ye know what happened? My poor ma had another two strokes. The third one left her completely paralysed. She can't talk, can't move. It's terrible to see her. She's not even old.' His voice broke. Ellie squeezed his hands.

'I never even registered for Trinity. I couldn't. All sorts of things had to be done. You take so much for granted. You're hungry and food's put before you. You want clean clothes and they're in your drawer. My mother needed things as well. The woman who came in to clean did her best, but she had to be told.'

Ellie wanted to say, 'Don't talk any more. Lie beside me, you're worn out. Lie still and I'll make it better. I love you. Everything will be all right.' But Art talked and talked, words falling from his mouth, pouring out like a tap left running.

'The stillness in the house, the two of them gone. The big house, all those rooms and not a sound. Always there would be my father's wireless, my mother moving about, making sounds. Doors opening, shutting. Dropping something. All the sounds of a house with people in it. And then silence. Silence you could hear.'

'Did no one from college get in touch with you?'

'They didn't. Like me they wouldn't read death notices. Their parents didn't know me. My mother never encouraged me to bring friends home so I didn't accept their invitations. Sometimes I think I'll wake up and find it was all a nightmare. Then I go to the hospital and see her. That's the real nightmare. Only her eyes move. There's a terrified expression in them. I think she's trying to tell me something. I talk to her. Nothing happens. I still talk, maybe she can hear. I hold her hand. She has to be fed, everything done for her. She's been moved. They advised me in Stephen's Hospital that as her condition was no longer acute they couldn't do anything for her, so she's in the Royal Hospital for Incurables. I had to see to that move as well. Fix up her admission. I never even got round to registering in Trinity.'

'What'll happen about that?'

'It's all fixed up now. It was there I was going earlier on after leaving the hospital when I met ...' he stopped.

'Who? Who did you meet?'

'Oh love, this is going to sound awful.' He shifted the tray of tea things on to the floor and moved nearer to her. 'You have to believe this. All the time I thought about you, wanted to see you, meant to see you. The time kept slipping by. So much passed I became afraid. I'd left it too late. You'd send me away — refuse to see me, not even answer a letter. So I gave up. I'd lost you — I'd lost everyone I loved. Then today I met Maggie.'

'Maggie? Maggie Simmonds, you mean? She doesn't know you. How could you meet her?'

'Well, I did. She knew me all right. She'd seen me with you.' He told her where, how and when he'd met Maggie, leaving nothing out.

Ellie laughed in his arms, so much it turned to crying. 'Maggie,

329

Maggie,' she repeated in between sobbing, then laughing again. 'What would we have done without her? We got a second chance. Weren't we lucky? So lucky. Don't ever leave me. A second time, and I would die.'

'We'll never be separated again, not for a minute. Except now, I have to go to the hospital. We'll get married – I'll buy you a ring tomorrow. But we'll ask your mother first before I give it to you. And we'll tell Maggie, she deserves that. We'll have a party. Now I have to make my visit.'

'You could come back later, have something to eat.' Any excuse to keep him close to her. To see him again.

'No,' he said, kissing her goodnight. 'You need your rest, and sleep. I'll come tomorrow evening and miss the hospital visit for once.'

She called her mother who came and cordially bade him goodnight before showing him out. When Julia came back to the bedroom Ellie was up, looking in the glass, doing things with her hair then taking clothes from the wardrobe. 'What are you doing?'

'Seeing what I'll wear tomorrow night. We're getting engaged. We're having a party! Oh Ma, isn't that marvellous? You'll let me, won't you? You wouldn't try to stop us marrying?' She hugged her mother and then twirled her round the room.

'I'm delighted for you. And why would I ever want to stop you marrying the man you love? But for now sit in that chair while I put the clothes away. Sit there and calm down. I don't want you having a relapse. Then I want to hear what kept him from you for so long.'

Ellie told her. Julia made the Sign of the Cross. 'God rest his father and comfort his mother. What a terrible tragedy! And to think that poor boy went through it on his own. What sort of friends and neighbours had he? Were they human beings?' Ellie explained about his mother keeping people at a distance. 'Even so,' Julia said, 'once she was out of the house, and they'd have known, people miss little of what's going on. Someone should have come. Without our neighbours I couldn't have managed when you were sick.'

'They might be different in Kilmainham.'

'Then all I can say is I'm glad I don't live amongst them. You get back into bed, and I'll bring you a warm drink – milk or cocoa?'

'Milk,' Ellie said happily.

Julia brought back the milk, sat on the bed and talked to Ellie. 'Tomorrow night when he brings you your ring, the three of us will celebrate it quietly.'

'But Ma, he said a party,' Ellie protested.

'We'll have the party next week, you'll be stronger by then. And we'll invite everyone in the house.'

'But what about Maggie tomorrow night? After all, if it wasn't for her there'd be no party to have.'

'I'll go down when I know Maggie's in. I'll thank her and tell her your good news. She can come and see the ring and drink a toast. And next week we'll have the party. The first party since ...' She stopped talking and had on her faraway face.

Ellie left her a few minutes before asking, 'The first party since when?'

'The night your father came home from France. Such a night that was, everyone in the street came.' She told Ellie about it, crying by the time she had finished. Keeping Sarah and Barney out of her mind. Remembering her mother, poor Mag, Cissie and all the friends and her beloved Jack. 'Such a night,' she said again, wiping her eyes. 'We'll have another like it for you.' She took the empty mug, shifted one of the pillows, made Ellie lie down and smoothed the bedcovers over her. Kissing her forehead, she said, 'I like him, even on such a short acquaintance. Go to sleep now and dream about him. It'll be tomorrow before you know it.'

He brought flowers and sweets and a jeweller's box with a ring, clustered with small diamonds. 'It mightn't fit, as I forgot to take your size. We can change it. You can choose the one you like best.'

She held out her hand and he put the ring on. It was only slightly too big. 'I don't want a different one. This is beautiful and once I put back my weight it'll fit me perfectly. I love it and you.' She kissed him.

'I brought you something else.' He gave her a small wrapped parcel. Inside was a slim leather-bound book of Irish poetry. He had written in it, *For Ellie on our engagement, Art.*

'Open it at page fifty-six,' he told her.

She did and said, 'It's the one you told me about – the man you were named after, Art O'Leary. He was killed and you said his wife wrote the poem. You remembered, you promised to get it for me and you remembered.' She was very moved.

Today she was up and dressed, her hair tied back with a blue velvet ribbon, her dress, one Julia had made for her, of grey crêpe wool, very expensive had it been bought, but Julia had found the remnant, greatly reduced in price. The bodice was draped so it fell softly over her bust, and being cut on the bias the skirt flowed round her legs. The remaining signs of her illness, her slenderness and pallor, lent an ethereal quality to her beauty. 'My mother,' she looked up from the book. 'She's left us alone until now, but she'll be dying of curiosity.' She kissed him. 'I love you. I love your ring. Now we'll have to show it to her.' She took his hand and led him from the bedroom.

Julia admired the ring, kissed Ellie, kissed Art, looked at the ring again and hugged each of them in turn. Telling them it was the happiest day she had known for years.

'He bought me this as well, Ma,' Ellie said, holding out the book. 'He's named after a man in a poem, Art O'Leary. You tell her, I don't remember it all.'

Art told Julia how the poem was about Art O'Leary from Kerry who had married a beautiful woman, an aunt of Daniel O'Connell. They were great lovers, she having married him against her family's wishes. 'He was betrayed and shot,' Art told her. 'The poem is Eileen's lament for her dead husband, though it's said there's a doubt she wrote all of it.'

'It sounds as if it is a beautiful and sad poem,' Julia said, studiously ignoring the images his telling of the poem had conjured up. Such images, such thoughts had no place on such an evening.

'You promised, when you told me about it, that you would read it to me. Read it,' Ellie said.

'I will, but not now, it's too long.'

'A bit then, a verse or two,' Ellie coaxed.

'I'll read you my favourite verse.' Art leafed through and found what he was looking for.

My sharp bitter loss
I was not at your back
When the powder was fired
So my fine waist could take it
Or the edge of my dress,
Till I let you go free,
My grey-eyed rider,
Ablest for them all.

Ellie sighed. 'She loved him so much she would have died for him.'

Julia excused herself and ran to Maggie's and in her arms cried uncontrollably. Maggie, not asking what ailed her, let her have the cry out, afterwards insisting she drank a glass of port and put a cold cloth to her eyes. 'I know to the differ, others don't, and might think you weren't so happy with the engagement.'

'I'm crying about something else as well,' Julia confessed.

'Well, tell me, girl. It's better out than in.'

'You know there's this secret in my life?' Maggie nodded. 'Well, I think the time has come to tell Ellie. And I think tonight's as good a night as any.'

'I'd agree with you. That girl's responsible enough to hear it now. And has a right to.'

'But for the time being, Maggie, bear with me. You'll have to wait a bit longer for the truth.'

'Julia, if you were never to tell me I wouldn't be offended. It's your business and Ellie's. Tell her. It'll lighten your heart. And when the time comes and you feel you want to confide in me, I'll be here.' They went back upstairs with Julia smiling and composed. Amidst much laughter Maggie renewed her acquaintance with Art, kissed him and Ellie, admired the ring and while drinking many glasses of wine, wished them health and happiness.

After Maggie had left Julia asked them to sit down. 'I've something I want to tell you,' she said.

'You look awful serious, Ma. I hope it isn't bad news. You haven't all of a sudden taken a dislike to Art?' Ellie said laughingly.

'Far from it. I always promised myself I'd tell you this when you got engaged or married. I'd think to myself, when she has a good man. Well, you have and so I'm telling you what I kept from you for years. It's about your father and how he died.'

Ellie's face clouded. 'He wasn't hanged or anything? He didn't murder anyone?'

'No, love. Your father was a fine good man, a beautiful man. Too kind and soft for his own good. He had a friend, well not exactly a friend, a Librarian who helped him with books. D'ye see, after he came back from the war he wanted to learn about Irish history. Your father suspected the fellow might have been in the IRA, but he never knew for sure. Seamus Harrington, the Librarian's name was. I never met him, though I invited him home. Anyway, he got your father his job in the Club, and at one time, though I knew nothing about it, must have asked him to shelter a man on the run. Those were desperate times – with terrible things happening on both sides. And your father agreed. But this you have to believe, Jack never joined or belonged to anything except the British Army.

'Well, anyway . . .' Then Julia stopped talking. She had been about to tell Ellie and Art how their two closest friends, Sarah and Barney, acting on something she had told them, had concocted a story that Jack was harbouring men on the run and so had led him to be shot. She coughed and cleared her throat, and asked Ellie for a drink of water to gain time. At the very last minute she had decided that she couldn't tell them the whole story, not tonight. Not in the middle of such happiness. How could she reveal to them the rottenness that was Sarah and Barney? They were like two innocent beautiful children. It would be hard enough for

Ellie to accept how her father had died, without having to learn of the treachery involved. The complete story would have to wait for a while longer, after they were married and settled down. Maybe not for several years, when they were better versed in the ways of the world. So she changed her story.

'That's better,' she said after swallowing the water. 'My throat was dry. Now, what happened was that someone, God only knows who – it could have been anyone – found out that your father had sheltered a man on the run, and whoever it was informed on him.'

'Oh, Ma. Oh God, that was terrible,' Ellie said, and began to cry.

'The scum of the earth,' said Art, putting an arm round Ellie. 'I'm not for violence but I'd take pleasure in killing an informer myself.'

'Vile people,' said Julia and she too began to cry as she related the Black and Tan raid, the taking out of Jack, and his body being found next morning in Glenasmole.

'That's why you wouldn't let me go up the mountains. And to think how I tormented you. Oh Ma, how did you manage to go on living?' She left Art's embrace and went to her mother and they cried in each other's arms.

'I can't tell you how sorry I am, Mrs Harte. You're a marvellous woman, and you did the right thing to shelter Ellie from what happened all these years.'

'God,' she said, 'has sent you to love and mind her. You remind me of Jack. I know she'll be all right with you. And now, let's not forget that we are celebrating! Nor that your father's watching and wouldn't want you to be sad, so dry your eyes. Give her a drop of wine, Art, and I'll make you something to eat.'

After Art had gone home, Ellie came and embraced Julia and for the second time said, 'I still can't believe that people could do such a thing. What makes them? What do they do it for?'

'Money,' said Julia grimly. 'Money, that's the reason why.'

'It must have been very hard on you keeping it to yourself all these years. That was the reason, I suppose, why you never talked about where I was born and lived until we moved here.'

'The lies I had to tell. D'ye know, in the beginning when I didn't have the photograph of your father up, word was getting round that you were illegitimate.'

'Honest to God?'

'Honest to God. Maggie put me wise to that. Are you tired?'

'No,' said Ellie. 'Why?'

'Sit down then, and I'll tell you about Springfield Terrace, about the little house we lived in with your grannie. The grand people who lived there – how good and kind they were to me.'

'I'd love that. Always you used to put me off with excuses when I'd ask about the olden days.'

'Another thing, we'll go to Mount Jerome. We were never great ones in our family for visiting the graves. I've never been near your father's since he was buried, though I've gone to many funerals since. But we'll go, bring Art if he wants to come. We'll buy a big bunch of flowers and I'll start saving for a stone.'

'I'll help you,' Ellie promised.

They talked on for a long while before going to bed, Julia remembering things from her past to tell Ellie – things about the street, about her childhood there – the party held on the night Jack came home from France ... and then she was forced to lie again when Ellie asked about the man whose life her father had saved and for which he'd won his medal.

'I never knew. Your father wasn't a boaster. He never talked about the incident.'

In bed she thought back to what she had told Ellie. 'I did the right thing not mentioning Barney and Sarah. Maybe I'll never tell her about them. She's so young and innocent – why should I put poison into her mind? Or maybe even a hatred like mine. I don't want that for her! It's enough for her to know that Jack was wrongly executed. Let her hate the Black and Tans – let her hate an anonymous informer, but never know the whole truth. Never know the extent of our friendship, know that Sarah nursed her, admired her, kissed her. Never know the trust I had in her and Barney. Without a name the one she thinks was the culprit will fade faster from her mind.'

The engagement party was a joyous affair, a double celebration, for Ellie's health was restored. Maggie lent her gramophone. Gunner-Eye played plaintive airs followed by jigs and reels on a tin whistle, to which Mrs Sheridan the mother of thirteen children and weighing fifteen stone, with unbound belly and breasts, danced on feet that were miniature by comparison with the rest of her. She danced a jig so lightly and expertly, her tiny feet faultlesssly excuting the intricate steps, all eyes focused on them, her bouncing breasts and wobbling belly not seeming to be connected, things apart from the dancing feather-light creature. They sang, each one in turn – Victorian and Edwardian ballads, Cockney music-hall songs, songs made popular during the war. The older Sheridan girls warbled the songs of the 1930s brought to them by films and the wireless. Art out of respect for his period of mourning wasn't asked to perform.

He began his course in Trinity and Ellie went back to work, to be regaled by tales of Sheila's latest love, fashion aspirations and awesome admiration of the engagement ring. 'I've never seen one like it in my whole life. Them stones are real. It must have cost a fortune.' Until that moment Ellie had never considered what it had cost since she would have loved and treasured it if Art had bought it from Ma Doyle's shop, from where she had worn many a ring.

Sheila spread word about the ring and at lunchtime everyone wanted to see it. 'You fell in lucky,' one of the women said, 'landing a fella with money,' – something else to which she had given no thought. But as the weeks passed, Ellie realised it was true. Art did have money. He booked the most expensive seats for the cinema, bought boxes not bags of chocolates and if his classes allowed, took her out to lunch in cafés she knew were expensive. Once he took her to Jammet's the French restaurant in Nassau Street, where she ate steak with Bearnaise sauce, not telling him when he asked if she liked it that her mother's steak and onions was nicer.

Julia invited him to have Christmas dinner with them. He brought lavish presents – wines and handmade chocolates, champagne for the meal, another selection of sweets and wine for Maggie and for Ellie another book of modern Irish poetry and a bottle of Worth's *Joy*. She thought it smelled of hyacinths and as she dabbed it on her skin remembered Sheila's gift of *Evening in Paris*, how she had thought it the most wonderful scent in the world then. Thinking about that time, she was reminded of Chrissie and wondered why she had never written, not sent a Christmas card even. She hoped that things were going well for her, that she wasn't lonely on Christmas. Then consoled herself that wherever her friend was, it had to be better than being near her father.

Art left after the meal to go and see his mother. Before he went Julia suggested that Ellie should go with him on Stephen's Day. 'Of course I will,' Ellie agreed. 'I didn't offer before, not sure if she'd want a stranger.

'I wish,' she said to Julia when the door closed, 'you hadn't got me into that.'

'Why?' Julia asked, astonished.

'I hate hospitals. I hate the smell of them. I was nearly sick when I went to see Lily O'Brien after her operation.'

'You'll have to put up with it. You're engaged to him. You couldn't *not* go to see his mother.'

★

There was no smell of ether but Ellie detected another more familiar nauseating one – stale urine. You got it sometimes from women on buses and in Mass. She was surprised that it should be here. The grounds and building were immaculate, and she knew that Art's mother was in a private room: that many of the rooms were private. There were flowers before statues of the Virgin and Sacred Heart along the corridor, and huge radiators full on. The heat was overpowering. She felt sick.

Art's mother was propped on pillows. Ellie was surprised to see that her hair was snow-white. She had imagined her to be as young as Julia. She was also a stout woman. Art went forward and kissed her. 'I brought you these,' he said, showing her a bunch of pink rosebuds, 'and I brought Ellie to see you. Talk to her, she can hear you,' Art told her.

Ellie smiled and said hello. The woman's eyes regarded her with bewilderment or fear, Ellie never having seen anyone like her before, wasn't sure which. 'How are they treating you, all right?' he said and then to Ellie, 'I think she responds to me with her eyes.' Then he spoke again to his mother. 'Me and Ellie have been friends for a while.' In an aside he told Ellie to sit down. She did so and the chair was too close to the radiator. The smell of urine was mixed with the smell of hot metal and paint. She felt weak.

'Ellie's in college. She's going to be a teacher. God, it's roasting in here.' He took off his topcoat and laid it on Ellie's lap, covering her hands. 'Did they do anything special for Christmas? I forgot, I asked you that yesterday.' He sat on the bed and stroked his mother's hair back from her forehead. 'It's freezing out. Snow is forecast.'

Between the heat, the smells Art deliberately covering her hands with his coat so he wouldn't have to mention the ring and her mounting anger at him having said she was in college she felt as if she would faint. 'I'll have to go out for a breath of air,' she blurted out.

'Do. I'll be coming in a minute anyway. Wait downstairs by the door.'

With her hands folded and the coat draped over them she stood up and said, 'I'll say a prayer for you, Mrs O'Leary. I hope you'll get better soon.' On shaking legs she went down the stairs and stood by the door gulping in the fresh cold air. When Art came she turned on him. 'Why did you let on I was a teacher? And why didn't you say anything about us being engaged?'

'Listen, love, you don't know my mother. She'd only start worrying that if I was doing a serious line it would interfere with my studies. And the teacher thing, God help her, she's a terrible snob. She won't change now. And why, when she's so sick, should I aggravate her more? If she hadn't had the strokes I could have got round her. Brought you home, let her get to know you gradually. She'd have loved you in time.'

'I'm sorry she's had the strokes but I don't like any of what's gone on. It makes little of me.'

'It does not. She's desperately sick. She'll probably die soon, and I hope she does because I love her. I don't want to think of her lingering on as she is. You have to understand that I'm doing it out of kindness to her. Nothing between me and you is altered by me telling her a white lie. If she was well, normal, then you'd be right to be hurt, offended, annoyed. Think of her, what she looks like. What her life is, lying there day after day not able to do a thing for herself. Waiting for a nurse to come and shift the pillows so she can lie down. I was wrong though in not warning you beforehand of what I had decided to tell her.'

'So you were,' said Ellie, relenting, 'but I can see what you mean. God help her. Is she very old?'

'I'm not sure. In her forties, I suppose.'

'About my mother's age?'

'About that.'

'I forgive you, but I won't go again, well not until you've told her about us. You can let on I'm going to be a teacher if it'll make her any happier.'

Catching her hand and walking down the drive, he said, 'Is it any wonder I love you?'

His mother lay waiting for the nurse who would lower her in the bed and thinking about Ellie. She was pretty. They were engaged, for she had seen the ring. She spoke nicely but she wasn't what she would have wanted for Art. Her clothes were cheap – good taste for what they were, but obviously there was no money in her family. The coat was readymade from Cassidy's or Macey's. Inwardly she fumed at her helplessness. Had she been well she would soon have put a stop to that romance, ring or no ring. Art shouldn't be entangled with a girl until he was qualified. And then he should pick someone more fitting to his position. She loved him so much. He was her whole life. Still thinking about him she fell asleep.

One evening when Art called at the house, having forgotten that Ellie would be late home from work that day, he talked to Julia about the circumstances leading to Jack's death. 'I keep thinking about it, imagining how it was for you. This may sound silly, but I find myself wishing I knew who it was who informed on him. How satisfying it must be to belong to a Mafia family, to be able to avenge the killing. The Arabs do that as well. I know it's crazy – I'd be as bad as all the other killers. It's just that I love Ellie so much. I love you as well. I'm talking all this nonsense to let you know how I feel for what you suffered.'

'God bless you,' said Julia. 'Ellie made a good choice.'

For Julia and Ellie, 1939 was the happiest year they ever remembered. Ellie was in love, engaged to be married and leading a life she hadn't known existed in Dublin : going with Art to boat races, picnics, parties and once to the Trinity Ball, for which Julia made her a marvellous ballgown in rose-pink taffeta. For Julia, though sometimes fearful that things were going too well, Ellie's happiness, radiant health and obvious love of Art made a pleasure of her days and nights. A weight had gone from her mind with the telling of how Jack had died. Maggie she had also told and the news had filtered through the house.

Now, at last, she could be herself. Talk about her past. She was glad of her decision not to have told the whole truth, of Barney and Sarah's part in bringing about the tragedy. Daily they receded further from her mind. Art had wrought this transformation in her life : he had restored her faith in people. She loved him as if he were her own flesh and blood. He had restored her faith in God, too, and she daily thanked Him for all her blessings.

There was another, more mundane reason for rejoicing. As the months passed more and more people, both men and women, went to work in England, in airplane and munitions factories, preparing for the war that despite the Munich Pact seemed to be inevitable. Postal orders flooded back to Dublin, so mothers had more money to spend on their children. Boys' shirts and shirt-blouses were again in demand, and Julia had plenty of work. Half of her earnings she put aside for Ellie's wedding, probably next year.

Art lived in the house in Kilmainham. A younger woman did the housekeeping now and the older one helped out. One Sunday he took Ellie home to see it. It was the biggest house she had ever been inside. She wandered from room to room, looking at the many photographs on display : his father before he got sick ; Art when a little boy in America ; His mother when she was slim, dark-haired, beautifully dressed and pretty. The kitchen was immaculate and well-equipped, comfort and the signs of money everywhere. But it was a cold house for all that. She didn't like the atmosphere.

'We could live here when we get married,' Art suggested.

The idea didn't appeal to her, though she didn't say so. For as she told herself, her aversion could be no more than the fact that the house wasn't properly lived in – hadn't been since the tragedy.

'Of course you could change whatever you wanted to – the furniture, curtains, anything. It would be your home.'

Envisaging different colours, lighter furniture, fewer photographs and no ugly castor oil plants and aspidistras, the house took on a different aspect. 'Yes,' she said, 'that would be grand.'

'I'll buy a car,' he promised. 'Though if the war comes I mightn't be able to get petrol. They'd have to ration that.'

'Are you serious about a war?'

'Yes, I think there will be one.'

'You wouldn't have to go?'

'No one from Ireland would have to go. Ireland's neutral.'

'Thank God for that.'

'On the other hand,' he said holding her, tilting her chin, looking into her eyes, 'it might never happen. But what must happen is that you and I must marry.'

They kept their bargain. She let him see and hold and kiss her breasts, but went no further. Often she pitied him, pitied herself but knew it had to be endured until they married, knowing if any further intimacies were allowed she would be lost, swept along by the desire and passion which overwhelmed her. The sooner they married the better. Her mother was the obstacle. Art *did* have money – a lot of money. That he was only a student didn't matter, but her mother wanted her to wait for a year, until she was nineteen.

'But why?' Ellie had asked, time and again as she used to about her trip to the mountains.

'I want enough money to give you a good send-off. I want you to have the most beautiful wedding dress in the world. And another, more important thing: I want time for you to be well over the pneumonia.'

'Ma,' Ellie said. 'Are you going soft in the head? That was ages ago. I'm grand now!'

'Please God you are, but pneumonia puts a terrible strain on anyone's constitution.'

'Not half the strain that's put on me and Art when we're courting,' Ellie thought.

Her mother continued: 'Married life's very strenuous. There's the running of a house, looking after a husband and well ... then there's married life itself. And babies. Carrying a child puts your body to the test. Any little weakness which you could have after a serious illness like pneumonia comes to the fore.'

She told Art, scoffing at what her mother had said, but he responded: 'In a way she's right. Pneumonia does put a terrible strain on the system, although you look fine to me. You'll be nineteen in April, so it's not that long to wait. We can do it and keep your ma happy.' They settled for a June wedding in 1940.

Julia was pleased at first, then remembered that time off for a wedding outside the factory's annual shut-down week would mean no wages. She reminded Ellie of this.

'It doesn't matter that I'm giving up work. I never got round to telling you this, but Art's father left him a lot of money. He doesn't want me to work.'

'I'm delighted for you. Working and running a home isn't an easy thing for a woman. Where will you live?'

'In his house. He says I can change everything. I'll bring you up to see it. You could give me ideas for curtains and that.'

She went back to the Sacraments. She thanked God every day for sending Art to Ellie, for bringing him into her life, for the young man that he was. A gentleman. A real man. She watched him with Ellie. Saw how he touched her, her hair, let a hand rest on her shoulder briefly. Laughed with her, made her laugh. He reminded her of Jack. She was sorry she had never met his parents. To rear such a son they must have been special people.

Mickey Mouse was on at the pictures. Art loved him. Ellie said he wasn't bad, and thought about *Snow White and the Seven Dwarfs* and the song *Some Day My Prince Will Come*. She remembered humming it on the way home from the cinema and how Chrissie had hated it and the film. No word had ever come from her. She would like to ask her to her wedding, Chrissie who hated everything romantic and who scorned men, so that people thought she was mad. Poor Chrissie, where was she now? Why had she never written? No Prince for her.

Some Day My Prince Will Come, the refrain began in her mind as she and Art walked up O'Connell Street, but *Doing the Lambeth Walk*, the song she and everyone was singing or whistling these days soon replaced it.

More and more people were going off to work in England. News about the threat of war filled the papers. Ellie read that Poland was prepared for it and on another page, that Ireland was making emergency food plans. England had mobilized the Territorial Army. She skipped to other pages, reading advertisements for chocolate at twopence a bar, the washing power of Rinso, the brilliance of furniture after polishing with Ronuk. A Sale notice – shoes at five shillings a pair, jumpers for nine and eleven. Horlicks for Night Starvation. On another page, Tom Mix and his horse Tony were coming to the Royal. Then news of a proposal

341

to mount anti-aircraft guns on the Mail Boat. She put the paper aside. She didn't want to read, hear or think about war, even though Art reassured her that Ireland would remain neutral, that war would make little or no difference to their lives.

One night she spoke again of her fears that like her father he would join up, as had thousands of other Irishmen. 'I know they did, and so they will if this one comes, but not me. I'm a conscientious objector.' He explained to her what that meant.

'But you could still go as an ambulance driver – you could still be killed.'

He lost patience with her. 'Ellie, for God's sake stop meeting trouble halfway. You're worrying about what may never happen. You have to stop this. Think of something pleasant – of this time next year. We'll be married, living in the house. Having your ma come to tea on Sundays. Lovely times. Will you promise to try?'

She promised. For a time she would succeed, then some other piece of news would send her back to her black thoughts, though she confided them less often to Art these days. She had listened one night to her mother talking to Maggie, saying how often she became afraid that things were going too well for Ellie; that it couldn't last, and she knew she had inherited her mother's nature.

On the first Sunday in September, a beautiful warm sunny day, they went early in the morning to the mountains. On the way back on the tram, they learned that war had been declared. For months she had dreaded this day, but discovered that it passed no differently from any other. So did the days and weeks that followed. In work the war was occasionally mentioned, but Sheila's mind was centred more on what she would buy her latest boyfriend for Christmas. Julia's thoughts were all on the style of Ellie's wedding dress, while Hop the Twig, nostalgically remembering his youth – the camaraderie of the trenches – and forgetting where and how he lost his leg, regretted being too old to join up.

In Julia's one evening when Art was there, the youngest Sheridan, who was still a schoolboy, came on a message from his mother. He stayed to talk and eat the cake Julia gave him, telling how in school his teacher had a map on which to chart the war's progress – 'with flags to stick in so we can see when the Germans are winning.'

'Lord have mercy on my father,' said Art, 'but he'd have done the same. Been delighted to and cheered for every mile the Germans advanced. There's a lot more like him in Ireland.'

'Are they like that in Trinity?' Ellie asked.

'Not in Trinity – the majority there are pro-British. It's full of English fellas come over to dodge Conscription. How they reconcile that with their patriotism I don't know.'

'Maybe like you they're conscientious objectors.'

'You're learning fast,' he said, put an arm round her and gave her a hug.

What little interest there was in the war was diverted in February 1940 to the cause of Peter Barnes and James Richards, who were to be executed on 7 February for a bombing in Coventry. In work, even those with no IRA sympathies were against the hanging. Young girls cut photographs of the condemned men from newspapers and pinned them in their bedrooms. Sheila got up earlier and heard Mass which she offered for their reprieve. The execution went ahead.

On the day of their execution Julia, on her way into Kellet's to buy the wedding-dress material, stopped in Whitefriars Street chapel to pray for Ellie's health and happiness before the statue to which she had prayed when she was carrying her. On the way out she lit two candles for the dead men.

She passed the Long Hall where Jack used to meet the Librarian to learn about Irish history, and she thought about the evenings he and Seamus had spent together. Once an unsigned letter had come, suggesting she might be entitled to claim compensation for Jack's death. Pensions and compensation were, she knew, being paid to ex-members of the organisations who had fought in the Easter Rebellion and the War of Independence. She wondered at the time if it was from Seamus. The letter she screwed up and burnt. She wanted nothing from them. Her Jack had belonged to no organisation. Even in death she didn't want his name linked with them. Not even if the government hadn't three years ago granted all widows the right to a pension.

Six and a half yards of ivory satin and three of art silk for an underskirt would be enough, she had reckoned. She bought the stuff, thread, bias binding, hooks and eyes and patent fasteners. In the display cases of bridal veils and wreaths was a set she particularly liked and was tempted to buy, but she stopped herself. This wasn't for Ellie's First Communion, it was for her daughter's own, special day. The style of the dress Ellie had agreed on and the colour and material, but the veil and garland she must choose herself.

Everyone was banned from the living room on the night Julia cut out the dress, having laid a sheet on the floor first, weighting its edges so it didn't slip and pucker. The cut sections were wrapped in another sheet until the next night when she would baste them together for Ellie to try on. She had ordered the wedding cake. The wedding breakfast would be at home, and Art and Ellie would go to Arklow for their honeymoon. It would have been Paris, he said but for the war.

In bed every night, Julia told Jack of the plans. How sad she was that he wouldn't be there to give his daughter away. 'But I won't be like I was on her Communion Day. D'ye remember, I had to run from the chapel – let on I felt weak. Then my heart was still full of bitterness. Now there's no room for it.'

Maggie's sailor was on a merchant ship. Often after coming home from the public house she put aside her brave face and told Julia how she feared for his life. Merchant ships had already been sunk. If she had married him he wouldn't have rejoined a ship. She'd never forgive herself if anything happened to him.

Julia listened and consoled as best she could. 'Please God he'll be all right. And don't blame yourself. Married or not he might still have gone. Mine did. Not because he didn't love me. It's just something about men and war. Look at the thousands gone from here. I know a lot of them went because they had no work, but not all. They've gone from all walks of society – Jews and Gentiles and well-off Protestants. Drim and Drew were telling me about a relation of theirs, a young fella with a good home, job and plenty of money – gone after the first week to join up in Belfast. Men, their ways are not like ours.'

Julia nagged Art and Ellie, reminding them that they were to be married in two months and should book their week in Arklow. It was a popular place and you couldn't leave it until the last minute. More important still was going to see the priest to put in the Banns.

'Monday night, Ma,' Ellie promised. 'Tomorrow we'll have another look at the house to see what changes I'll make before the wedding. Art will be visiting his mother while I'm deciding. Would you like to come with me?'

'I don't think so. I'm stuck into your dress. It's making up lovely, and while it's going well I want to get on with it. I won't rest easy until it's finished. Now, don't forget about the priest on Monday. I'll have your Baptismal Lines ready and tell Art to bring his.'

After the visit to the priest Art went to see his mother. Julia came home. 'Well,' she asked. 'How did it go?'

'Art couldn't find his certificate and you won't believe this, but he doesn't know where he was christened.'

'And his mother no doubt told him a thousand times. Fellas don't listen, so what's happening now?'

'Father Byrne told him to get a copy of his birth certificate.'

'That won't do for getting married. It's proof of being a Catholic you need. Only your Baptismal Lines can give that.'

'I know, I know. So does the priest. What he said was, the certificate will show where he was born, then it wouldn't be hard to find his parish church.'

'Couldn't he ask his mother? I forgot, sure the poor creature can't talk. What about writing, though? She could scribble the name down.'

'She can't talk, move, write, maybe not even hear.'

'Still, someone will know – he must have had someone stand for him.'

'He must have, but he knows not a single soul from that time before he went to America. He wouldn't. He went as a baby.'

'The birth certificate will sort it all out. I forgot to ask what changes you were planning in the house before the wedding.'

'For the time being only the bed. And I've put away some of the photographs. There were dozens.'

'That's a good idea. Then at your leisure you can make the rest. I'll give you a hand.'

'They couldn't trace a certificate for me. In case the dates were wrong they went forward months, back months, forward a couple of years, back a couple of years and still nothing. What'll I do now? And why isn't there one?' Art looked helplessly at Julia and Ellie.

'There was the burning down of the Customs House – your certificate could have gone up with it. Go back and see the priest,' Julia said. 'He'll know what to advise.'

'It's all sorted out,' Julia was told by Ellie after their second visit to the priest. 'You know that Art made his First Communion in America?'

'I do,' said Julia.

'So they'd have had to see his Baptismal Lines, right?'

'Right.'

'And they'll have proof of the sighting, as Father Byrne calls it. So he's writing to Art's parish in Chicago and once he gets it, that will be that.'

Julia wasn't very happy about the arrangement. Letters were taking a long time to get to and fro. Supposing the ship was sunk? There were only six weeks to go now to the wedding, and the Banns had to be called three times. She said nothing of her fears to Ellie, however. God could be with them and the letters arrive and come back in time. Nothing must be allowed to cause one moment of doubt, one moment of unhappiness in her daughter's mind.

Sheila was to be the bridesmaid and a fellow doing medicine with Art, his best man. The hotel in Arklow accepted the honeymoon booking. Ellie and Art bought the new bed. Sheila had started the

346

collection in work for the wedding present and during a lunchtime when Ellie was meeting Art, it was decided amongst the girls that the present would be an eiderdown and matching bedspread.

Ellie's dress was finished; it fitted perfectly and Julia told her she looked like a princess in it. The gown was draped in a sheet and stored in Maggie's second biggest wardrobe which had been emptied to accommodate it. Sheila's dress, a pale pink satin, was in the making. Everything was going to plan except the producing of Art's confirmation of Baptism from America.

Julia wracked her brains. There must be some way of finding what was necessary to prove that Art was a Catholic, otherwise the wedding – now only a month off – could not take place. Then she thought of something that was so obvious she had overlooked it. His mother, like herself, like every other woman she knew and had known, kept important, precious documents. She kept hers in an old handbag. Other women had boxes, or drawers; people like Art's mother might have them in a bank, but have them she would. Death, marriage and birth certificates. Communion certificates. Grave receipts and insurance policies, locks of hair, a baby's first curl to be cut. Her mother had amongst her special things locks of hair cut from her dead mother. Art being a man wouldn't be aware such things existed. And his poor mother couldn't remind him.

'Start searching,' she advised him after explaining her thoughts.

'You're right! A thought like that never crossed my mind. I'll go to the bank first thing and check there.'

'And tomorrow evening pick me up from work and I'll help you search the house,' added Ellie.

His mother didn't have a safe deposit box, nor had she left any documents in the bank's keeping. Convinced that they'd find what they were looking for in the house and that in any case the letter from America was bound to come before the Banns had to be in, Art and Ellie went to Kilmainham, stopping on the way to buy fish and chips to take out. After eating they went and lay on the new bed, delivered that afternoon. They kissed and caressed each other and when Art undid her blouse and his hands and then his lips were on her breasts she almost yielded to temptation, telling herself that in such a short while they would be married. She wanted to strip naked, for Art to do the same and lie in their new bed and love each other. It was Art who broke the spell, reminding her why they were here. And when she showed signs of lingering, pulled her off the bed.

They began in that room, searching every drawer, every inch of the wardrobe, dressing table and his father's tallboy. They found nothing and went from room to room, even to a lumber room where there were suitcases, but they didn't find what they were looking for. Downstairs they were no more successful. 'There's nowhere else. Maybe my mother is the exception to the rule and didn't keep precious papers,' Art said, vexed. Ellie told him not to worry – the letter from America was bound to come.

Julia was bitterly disappointed, but didn't voice to Ellie the thought uppermost in her mind – that there might not be a wedding, at least not when they had planned. It wouldn't, she knew, be the end of the world if it had to be delayed, but a terrible disappointment all the same. So preoccupied was she with her worries, that Ellie had been home an hour before she remembered that a letter had come for her.

'I think,' she said, handing it to her, 'that it's from your friend Chrissie. There's an address on the back and what looks like her surname. But there's that many letters and numbers it's hard to tell.'

Ellie looked at the back of the envelope. *S.A.G.* – St Anthony Guide – was printed across the envelope's point. He was Chrissie's favourite saint, to whom she prayed whenever she lost anything – personal things, like a pair of sleeve-linings. He always found for her what was missing. It was so well-known in work that others seeking lost articles asked her to pray. The manager, a Jew, also came to her when parts of expensive suits were mislaid, like pocket flaps or facings and there was no more stuff left to cut others. He used to say, 'Chrissie, say a prayer to your private detective.' St Anthony never let her down.

Dear Ellie,

I'm sorry for not writing sooner. And by the way in case I forget, thanks very much for the money. As you can see from all the numbers and abbreviations, I'm in the ATS. That's part of the army, the women's part. It stands for Auxiliary Territorial Service, though the soldiers have another name for it which when I see you again I'll whisper in your ear.

I've only been in a few weeks, doing my basic training. Then I'll go on a course and learn how to be a cook. Imagine me in clogs, white overalls and a turban – that's what cooks wear. I didn't really fancy cooking but had no qualifications for anything else nor the right education either. I was advised that cooking is a trade, so you get extra pay and are sure of a job when the war is over.

It's early days yet but I think I'll like it. But you should see the uniform! It's desperate. God knows I was never much for clothes but at least I knew about them. Anyone would think the uniform was made from a blanket. And the stockings. The colour of diarrhoea and that thick. Long knickers with elastic in the legs. Wrist-stranglers, someone told me the men call them.

The food is terrible, but you're always hungry and eat it. Fancy having boiled cod for your breakfast! I was sitting on my bed the other night feeling rotten. We'd had all these injections. Maybe I was feverish, anyway I heard a train in the distance and for the first time since I came away was so homesick I cried. Not missing you know who, but you, Sheila and the girls in work. Even work – that kip of a factory. I could see it. Smell it, the machine oil, the lovely smell of tweed. I knew then I had to write. And here I am.

Did you and Art ever get back together? I hope so. I'll never forget your kindness. Without you I'd have gone mad. Mind you, I nearly did when I first arrived in London. I stayed in a religious hostel. Too religious for me. I got a bedsit. You wouldn't believe what landladies let in London. Talk about the slums of Dublin. I worked in a Home for mentally sick people, God help them. And the accommodation wasn't bad. I stuck that until I joined up. The lights go out here at ten o'clock so I'll have to finish. Will you write to me? Give my love to your Ma and remember me to everyone in work.

Love, Chrissie

'It was from Chrissie, she's in the women's army,' Ellie told Julia. 'She sounds great. A pity she didn't write sooner – I'd have asked her to be my bridesmaid.'

'You might still have time enough,' Julia mused silently, still worrying about the missing Baptismal Certificate.

She hadn't arranged to meet Art at lunchtime the following day, so was surprised when word came that he was downstairs. She flew down, thinking his plans had changed and they could lunch together. 'God, you look awful,' she exclaimed, dismayed. 'Are you sick or something?'

'Or something,' he said. 'I can't come to the house tonight because there's a lecture that won't finish until all hours. But I wanted to set your mind at rest. I found the bag, and the certificate. Your mother was right – everything was in it. But it's altered everything. That's what ails me.'

'How d'ye mean? Is that what has you looking like a ghost? Tell me.'

'I can't,' he said. 'I have to be back. I'll come up tomorrow night.'

'I wish you'd waited until then. Why can't you tell me now?'

'It'd take too long, and it's too complicated. Too serious to talk about here. Listen, I have to go.' He touched her cheek and hurried off.

'He's illegitimate,' Julia said when Ellie finished repeating what Art had said. 'That'll be it. The poor boy, what an awful drop.'

'It could be something completely different.'

'Like what?' asked Julia.

'How would I know? Anything.'

'You'll see, what he's found out is that Mr O'Leary wasn't his father. His poor mother was probably let down. How old did you say he was?'

'The same age as me.'

'It couldn't be that, then. I was thinking maybe it was a wartime thing, but he's not old enough.'

'It doesn't make any difference if he's illegitimate.'

'Not to me or you, but it may very well to him.'

'Why?'

'How would you feel if suddenly you found out I never married your father?'

'I wouldn't care.'

'Ah, but you would. You'd be hurt. You'd see yourself in another light. And even if not another soul knew you'd always be afraid they'd find out.'

'Ma, Art's not going to react like that.'

'Listen, love. I know more about the ways of the world than you do. Already he'll be worrying that we'll shun him. Not want you to marry him. We'll have to be very careful how we receive him tomorrow night.'

Ellie sighed, but decided to say no more about the subject. All that concerned her was that Art had found his Baptismal Lines. 'I'm going to answer Chrissie's letter,' she said, wanting to escape from her mother; knowing that Julia would go on all night about Art and his supposed illegitimacy.

Julia prepared a special meal for him. She forwent the usual cabbage for a cauliflower with cheese sauce, potatoes, small ones in their skins, and carrots to go with the pot roast.

'If he's feeling like he looked yesterday he'll eat nothing,' Ellie warned her mother.

'We'll see,' said Julia, and reminded her for the second time, 'let him do the talking.'

He looked better than he had the day before, but as Ellie had predicted he wanted nothing to eat. Her mother, despite warning Ellie to remain silent, jumped in before Art had said more than two words.

'Son,' she said, 'whatever it is, you're the same person as you were the day before yesterday. You've nothing to worry about. Nothing to feel ashamed for. Nothing has changed between you and Ellie, nor between you and me.'

'I never thought it had, Mrs Harte.'

Julia looked taken aback. 'No, what I meant to say was that, well, supposing you are . . .'

'Ah,' Art said, and for the first time since entering the room he smiled and looked himself. 'You thought I was a bastard, didn't you?'

'It wouldn't have made any difference what you were. That's what I was trying to say,' explained Julia.

'I told you you were wrong, didn't I?' said Ellie, delighted to see Art if not looking happy, better than he had yesterday.

'The most important thing is I've got the certificate, but there's more to it than that. I still can't believe all the lies and deception there's been in my life. I'd better start at the beginning. When I got back home on Sunday night after leaving you, Ellie, I couldn't settle. You know how it is once you start looking for something – you can't stop. I started again, going over places we'd already searched. Then I remembered a shed at the bottom of the garden. Before my father got MS he used to potter with carpentry. It was a good shed, waterproof because of his tools. They were expensive ones. And I remembered a chest that was in it – a small seachest. It had always been locked. Once I asked him what was in it and he'd laughed and said, "Souvenirs of your mother's childhood. Other than that, I don't know really. I've never seen it open. She bought it at an auction in America and by the time I noticed it, it was packed and locked. You must never touch it." He was like that, a great respecter of other people's privacy.

'I never touched it. I forgot all about it until late on Sunday night. The first thing that surprised me about it was the lightness – as if it was empty. I don't know if there'd ever been a key. I couldn't find one, so I broke it open. And as you said, under sheets of newspaper, wrapped in oilskin, was a handbag. In it were marriage and death certificates, my Baptismal Lines, a curl that must have been mine and newspaper cuttings and ones from magazines.'

He cleared his throat. 'I'm not Art O'Leary. Well, I am – my name was changed by deed poll – but my father wasn't my father. I was born well before he and my mother married. And her name wasn't really Louise. My real father was a Dublin man. And he was shot in London.'

'Oh, Sweet Jesus, let me be wrong. Let me be losing my mind to even contemplate such a thing. Dear God, You couldn't do this me. Tell me I'm mad. Tell me it's not what is coming into my mind,' thought Julia desperately.

Ellie cupped her chin in her hands, leant on the table and listened to Art's tale unfold.

'You can imagine the shock, the hurt at being kept in the dark all these years. All the lies. Why? Why couldn't they have told me? Why

351

didn't my father – he was a great one for the truth. D'ye know what he used to say – "give me a thief any day before a liar". Why did they change my whole name? They could have changed my surname for convenience, but why my Christian name?'

'Don't, please God, don't let it be what I'm thinking,' Julia prayed, and cold sweat trickled between her breasts.

'So you're not Art,' asked Ellie, bemused and fascinated by Art's revelations. Smiling at him. Loving him. Adoring him. Glad that all their wedding plans wouldn't be altered. She didn't care what his name was.

'No, I'm not. I'm Patrick.'

'Patrick Daly,' said Julia, in a strange quiet voice which was unnoticed by either Art or Ellie. 'And your mother wasn't Louise she was Sarah, Sarah Quinlan and your father was Barney Daly.'

'Are you telling me you knew them? You knew my ma and my real da? What a coincidence! That's great. That's Dublin for you. You can fill in the gaps for me.' His face took on an eager boyish expression.

'Yes,' she said, 'I can do that, fill in the gaps.' Ellie now became aware that something wasn't right. Her mother looked as if she'd been turned to stone. Her colour was gone, her voice had a strangeness about it, such as she had never heard before. She'd heard it sad and angry, happy, excited, worried, but never like this. It was a voice she couldn't describe: one that frightened her. Something awful was going to come out of this conversation.

'You were born in Springfield Terrace not long before Ellie. I fed you at my breast when your mother was losing her milk. You and Ellie, one after the other. I loved you. I loved your mother. I'd known her all my life and your father too.'

'Tell me about him – what he was like. There's no picture or anything about him in the bag. I can't believe this is happening. I can't believe we were all so close at one time and didn't know it until tonight. Imagine me going off to America, coming back to Dublin, meeting Ellie and now going to marry her. They say marriages are made in Heaven, well ours certainly was.'

'There won't be a marriage.'

'Ma, what ails you? Are you sick or something?' Ellie was alarmed and appealed to Art. 'Do something. Maybe she's losing her mind. Maybe she's having a stroke. Did you hear what she said?'

'I don't understand,' said Art, and now his expression was perplexed. 'I don't understand what you're talking about. No marriage, but why? Shouldn't you be even more delighted now than ever that you know all about my family?'

Julia looked across the table at him. There wasn't a feature in his face that resembled Sarah or Barney, but she saw both of them in him. An hour ago she loved him. Now she was filled with a revulsion towards him. She wanted him out of her home, out of Ellie's life. 'God direct me,' she prayed. 'Keep me calm. I could so easily kill him. I want to kill him for what he's done. He'll break her heart. She loves him, but I'd rather see her dead too than married to a son of theirs.'

Ellie got up from the table; she was crying. 'I'm going for Maggie. Something's happened to you,' she looked with loathing at her mother. 'You're trying to spoil everything. What does it matter who his mother and father were? A few minutes ago you thought he was a bastard and were telling me that didn't matter. You've gone mad.'

'Sit down,' Julia ordered. 'The night of your engagement I told you the story of how your father died. Halfway through I changed my mind and didn't tell it all. It was too horrible, I thought, for the pair of you to hear. I'm going to finish it now. And then,' she said looking at Art, 'you'll go from here, never come again and never see Ellie again. Her father was informed on. I said I never knew who the informers were but I did: your mother and father. They gave the information that brought the Black and Tans who murdered your father, Ellie. And your mother came with me to the morgue to identify him. She put her arms around me like a sister and consoled me. They came to the wake and the funeral. My good friends. Always grateful to Jack for saving your father's life in France.'

'Don't,' Art pleaded. 'Don't tell me any more. I was broken-hearted for you,' he was crying. 'I would have killed the informer. I fantasised about revenging Ellie's father's death, little thinking it was my parents who were guilty of it.' He and Ellie turned to each other and cried, each held by the other. And remorselessly Julia went on.

'You can forget your fantasies. He got his just desert: he was shot like a dog in a London street. Before that, their house in Springfield Terrace was burned from under them. It wasn't until then I knew for sure they were the guilty ones. They got away, but your grandmother and grandfather were roasted alive. Maybe they couldn't have saved them, who's to say. But knowing what I know now about Barney and Sarah, I'd put nothing past them. I lost the child I was carrying because of them, and to my dying day I'll believe they hastened my mother's death. There's no more to tell except that for years my heart was soured with bitterness. It left me when I got to know you. I thought of you as a son.' Her voice broke. 'I believed you'd been sent from God to atone for all the wrongs. I believed that.

'Your mother and father took everything from me. Oh God, it's not fair. Where are You to let such things happen! They took everything except Ellie, and now he's reaching from his grave and she from where she is to take my child, to join her with you. Well, they won't succeed. You'll never have her. *Never! You'll never see her again!'*

She was becoming hysterical. Ellie screamed and screamed. Art tried comforting her, though it was Julia he wanted to try and console. Julia it was to whom his heart went out. This great woman, carrying that secret round all these years. Telling them part of it on their engagement night, still trying to protect Ellie from the true horror. And then for him to be who he was ... It was like some crazy, terrifying nightmare. Something that never in reality anyone should have to suffer.

Ellie's screams brought Maggie running up the stairs and into the room. 'You can be heard all over the house. What's happened?'

Instinctively Art knew this was no time to go to Julia; that his presence was an anathema to her. 'I'll go now, Ellie. I'll see you tomorrow.'

'No, you won't. Never again will you lay eyes on her. Bred from two murderers and liars, d'ye think I'd let her see you again?'

'Please, please,' Ellie kept screaming. 'You're mad, you made it all up. I hate you. I wish you were dead.'

Art went. Full of anger and hatred he went to see his mother. He would tell her what he thought of her. How he despised her. Loathed the fact that she and Barney had brought him into being. He would tell her who Ellie was, of Julia's undying hatred for her. Tell her that never again would she lay eyes on him.

As so often she was sleeping when he went into the room. He had come empty-handed. No flowers tonight. No trying to amuse her. All the love and pity gone. He went to the bed and looked down at her. As if she sensed his presence she opened her eyes, her eyes which were her only way of communicating. He saw fear in them, which was gone almost as he noticed it. This was how it was always if she was sleeping when he came. Before tonight he had always assumed it was wakening and realising her state, that maybe while she slept she dreamed the stroke had never happened. Now he thought the expression of fear was left from her other dreams – dreams of the murdered Jack; the bereft Julia. Dreams of Hell. And he was overcome with compassion for her so that as usual he touched her cheek with great tenderness and talked to her about the weather. About Trinity. He apologised for not bringing flowers. And all the time her eyes regarded him and his own filled with tears.

By any standards she was an evil woman. She deserved castigation. And if she had been well he would have castigated her, had a blazing row – maybe even parted with her for good. He didn't know; he'd never know. She was his mother. He had always loved her. He always

354

would. 'Ma,' he said, for he couldn't bear to stay any longer. He hated the room, the smells – he hated seeing her helpless. Tonight it was less bearable than usual. 'There's a lecture I have to catch, a special one, from a visiting professor – that's why it's so late. He's been in Cork and is coming up tonight so I'll have to go.' He thought her eyes registered disappointment. 'I'll be up again.' He kissed her and hurried out without looking back.

Julia sat at the table, buried her face in her hands and rocked backwards and forwards, keening.

'In the name of Jesus and His Divine Mother will one of you tell me what's going on!' demanded Maggie.

'It's her,' Ellie sobbed. 'She's gone mad. You should have heard the things she said about Art and his parents. She's lost her mind. She won't let me marry him. I'm telling you, she's gone demented.'

'Will you bloody well stop screaming like a baboon and tell me what she said. Tell me how it all began.'

In between sobs Ellie told the story that had unfolded round the table. 'It's lies, all lies. She must have taken a sudden turn against him and went crazy.'

'Shut up you for a minute,' Maggie said and turning to Julia asked: 'Is it true, love?'

'Every word. I kept it back. I didn't want her to know the true horror and I thought my bitterness was leaving me, so I left it out.'

'I'm so sorry.' Maggie put her arms round Julia. 'God look down on you. It's a wonder the shock didn't kill you. And as for you,' she said, turning on Ellie, 'have you no compassion, no feelings for your mother? Comforting her you should be, not screaming like a lunatic!'

'But it's not fair,' Ellie wailed. 'One minute before he came she thought he might have been a bastard and she was saying it didn't matter, he was still the same person we loved.'

'It's a pity he wasn't,' said Maggie.

'I don't care what he is or who his parents are, I love him. And I'm going to marry him.'

'You do,' said Julia, raising her tortured face, 'and for me you'll be dead. They'll have taken you from me as sure as they did your father. Oh Maggie, Maggie, has God no mercy? Why would He send me this affliction. I loved that boy as much as if I'd borne and reared him. I believed God had sent him for Ellie.'

'Lies, lies! All lies!' Ellie shouted, while tears poured down her face. 'She made it up. She took a turn against him. All my life she's told me lies. I knew nothing about my father, only that I had one, that he was supposed to have been killed in crossfire. Then she told another story the night we got engaged. How am I to know that's not what she's doing now – telling another story?'

'May God forgive you for being so cruel. Your mother's no liar. I'm sorry for you. I know the shock it has been to you, but screaming and crying and hurling accusations at your mother won't help anything. There's nothing I can do here so I'll leave the two of you. Talk to each other. And be kind to each other. You know where I am if you want me. I'll concoct a story to satisfy the neighbours for the time being.'

Ellie splashed cold water on her face. She felt physically sick, dazed with the suddenness of what had started out to be a celebration turning into a nightmare. Her delight that Art had his Certificate, her good-natured scorn of how upset her mother thought he would be if it turned out he was illegitimate, all overturned in a minute: Art ordered from the house, she forbidden to marry him, her screaming. Oh, the things she had said to her mother! Never in her life had she witnessed or been part of such a terrible scene. And Art. Walking home to an empty house. Her heart ached for him. They hadn't even made a proper arrangement to meet the next day.

Julia remained sitting by the table, no longer rocking to and fro, no longer keening, but like someone who has been stunned and has not yet recovered from it. Unable to stay still, Ellie moved restlessly about the room, wanting to talk to her mother but not knowing how to begin. She hung the tea towel on the clothes horse, picked up a knife that had fallen to the floor, moving closer to the table as she found other unnecessary tasks to perform. She was torn between her love for Julia, her pity for her and her feelings for Art, who must be so bereft, hurt and lonely. At last she plucked up the courage to ask, 'Ma, will I make more tea? We never drank the other pot.'

'If you like,' Julia replied in a lifeless voice.

She bustled about making tea, cutting thin bread and butter, trying to restore a sense of normality. Trying to blot out the last hour, make believe that Art hadn't come tonight. Her mother hadn't said those things. He was coming tomorrow, bringing his Baptismal Lines. After tea they'd take it to the priest. Next month they were getting married. Her dress was in Maggie's wardrobe. The honeymoon in Arklow was booked. Everything was all right. Julia was only sitting the way she was because her head was bad. The fresh tea would cure that. But the pretence was too much for her to sustain. Her mother's voice sang in her brain, her voice that hadn't been her own, but one that had struck terror in her. Breaking down again and leaving the tea not wet she went to Julia, put her arms round her and said: 'Ma, I love you. I'm sorry for all the things

356

I said. But I love him too. I love him so much. Tell me Ma, tell me again all about it.'

Julia told her. Repeating what she had related on the night of the engagement. Now adding the details about Sarah and Barney. How in the beginning she had never suspected them, though her own mother had. Her devastation when finally she was forced to believe.

'I never knew,' Ellie said sorrowfully. 'All your suffering and I never knew. You should have told me. I had a right to know. I'd have been kinder to you, more understanding.'

'I did what I thought was right. I didn't want you to know there was such evil in the world.'

'If you had, maybe none of this would have happened.'

'It would. We didn't know who he was. He didn't know himself. They were evil, his mother definitely. Barney was like putty in her hands – not that that excuses him. He was your father's best friend. He should have stood against her! But she had powers – evil powers. How else, with all the men in Dublin, would you meet her son and fall in love with him – be about to marry him! But God, though they even managed to shake my faith in Him, doesn't sleep. He didn't let it happen.'

Wise beyond her years at this moment, Ellie knew she mustn't mention Art's name, or her determination to marry him. Instead she encouraged Julia to talk about Jack. Talk more freely than ever before, recalling the day they married, the day he went to France and the wonderful day of his return. His joy when she was born – how he'd changed her name from Eleanor to Ellie. His delight when Julia had told him she was expecting another baby. She listened and whenever she felt that Julia was about to touch on Sarah and Barney, she steered the conversation to memories of happier times. They sat, with Julia talking and talking, and she listening until exhaustion generated by the emotions of anger and grief and the terrible relevation and its ensuing scene, they grew mortally tired and went to bed.

In the dark, Ellie lay and planned how she would continue to see Art unbeknownst to her mother. They would put in the Banns. Julia would relent, realise that what had happened in the past was nothing to do with Art. For the time being she wouldn't mention his name and if her mother raised the subject, pretend she was going along with her, that she had cast Art out of her life. It would be at least ten days before the first calling of the Banns. By then, when Julia would hear them being read she would have softened in her attitude towards him. After all, what had happened was years ago. You couldn't harp on the past. Nor blame someone who was an infant at the time.

He was outside the factory at lunchtime. They went to a café where he didn't order anything for himself, although Ellie was starving. 'You're upset about last night?'

'Of course I'm upset. For you, for your mother and for me. They were my parents. It's not an easy thing to come to terms with. I lay awake thinking of what your mother told me. Asking myself, was it true? What proof was there, after all? Yes, my father was shot in London, but that didn't mean, as she said, that he was executed: he lived in a rough neighbourhood – it's on the death certificate. So what proof is there, I kept asking myself. And their house could simply have gone on fire, as lots of houses do. I don't doubt that the Black and Tans shot your father: they shot hundreds of people. But that doesn't mean my father or mother had anything to do with it ... Then I thought about your mother, the sort of woman she is. She wouldn't make up such an horrendous story. I remembered her face and her voice, though last night I didn't think I was paying attention to either, and I knew she had told the truth.

'Other things confirmed this as well, like my mother's reluctance to have people in the house. How seldom she would go into town; her unhappiness at being back in Ireland – an unease that was always about her. Then the most damning thing of all – changing my identity completely. Never mentioning my real father. OK, she didn't have to tell me he was shot, but never to know he existed! And all the lies, about her name and where she was reared. Your mother told the truth.'

'D'ye think your father knew, I mean your other father?'

'I don't know. Some of it, maybe. I'll never know.'

'None of it will make any difference to us, sure it won't?' Ellie asked, spearing two chips on her fork.

'I love you, you're so innocent, so uncomplicated, so trusting. Of course it'll make a difference to us.'

'Why?'

'Your mother wasn't performing a piece of drama last night. That was real. So was her ban on me seeing you again. On our marrying.'

'In a week it'll have blown over. She's not hard, not vindictive.'

'She isn't any of those things. She couldn't have reared you to be what you are if she was, but she's a strong woman. One who, I wouldn't think, has ever harmed anyone in her life, and who would find it hard, impossible, to forgive harm done to those she loves. If she does relent it won't be for a very long time. And I can't say I blame her. I'd feel the same way.'

'You're taking her part. That's great. I'm not supposed to see you again, nor marry you. You heard her say that.'

'And she meant it.'

'Then what are we going to do ?'

'It depends on you.'

'On me ? What d'ye mean, on me !'

'I don't think we could go on seeing each other in a hole and corner way for long. I think we should go away. Go to England.'

'I couldn't leave my mother!'

'That's what I meant about it depending on you.'

'And if I don't go to England we're finished – is that what you're saying ?'

'No, it's not. How could it be when I love you so much ? If we stay here and see each other she'll find out. We can't go ahead with the wedding here. You and she will fight, live a terrible life. D'ye want that ?'

Her lunch was pushed aside ; the problems which during the night she had thought were solved loomed again. 'I couldn't live like that with her, I love her too much. We seldom even argued. It would break my heart. It would break my heart as well to leave her.'

'That's the legacy Sarah and Barney left. We don't have to make up our minds now. Have another cup of coffee then it's time to go. I'll pick you up this evening and we'll talk again. Then fix up something supposedly with Sheila for the weekend and we'll thrash it out.'

'If we did go away, what about University ?'

'I was thinking of packing it in anyway. I'm not cut out to be a doctor. Later on I might do an engineering degree or just get a job.'

'You really think it's this serious, I mean about my ma ?'

'Yes,' he said. 'I think it's very serious.'

Maggie spent most of the day with Julia, listening again to the story she had concealed all the years she had lived in the house. Crying with her when she related how Jack had died. Sharing her feelings when she found out that Barney and Sarah were to blame. Julia told her of Mag's part in it – a poor simpleton tutored for her role. How Sarah had her run into a Home for fear she would let anything out. She told her everything.

'And after all that for their son to come into your life !'

'Yes,' said Julia, 'and me not knowing. Loving him like a son. Happy, happier than I'd been since Jack died, believing God had sent him for Ellie.'

'In fairness to the boy he didn't know himself. He must be in a terrible state knowing what his parents were. It's like something you'd see on the Queens, one of them melodramas. If I was told such a story by anyone but you, if I hadn't witnessed the outcome last night I wouldn't believe it.'

'I'm sitting here,' said Julia, 'finding it hard to believe myself.'

'It'll be hard on Ellie, too. What about the wedding?'

'There'll be no wedding.'

'It's all arranged. You've the dress ready in my wardrobe and you've nearly finished Sheila's.'

'She won't marry him. And as for the dress, I never want to see it again. Sell it, pawn it, burn it – anything you like so long as you get rid of it.'

'That's very hard on them, Julia. They're only the innocent bystanders. It'll break Ellie's heart.'

'I know all about broken hearts. You can live with one.'

'It isn't the same thing. You had your man. Not for long, but you had him all the same. You had a child for him. You knew what it was to be a married woman.'

'She'll never marry him, I won't let her. Not marry their son. However nice, however plausible he is, their blood runs in his veins and would in his children's. I wouldn't allow that for Ellie.'

Deciding they had talked enough for today and that there was nothing else she could say at the moment to change Julia's mind, Maggie made an excuse of something urgent she had to do and left. When she did, Julia closed the machine and parcelled Sheila's unfinished bridesmaid's dress in paper and tied it with string.

Driving her home from work, stopping before they reached her house, Art repeated what he had said about going to England and asked Ellie to think it over.

Everything seemed as usual when she got home. Her mother was putting her dinner in front of her and asking about her day. Ellie noticed the parcel on the press and asked what it was.

'Sheila's dress,' replied Julia.

Ellie's heart leapt. She had been right: her mother was relenting. 'That's great – you've finished it?'

'I'm not finishing it. I want you to take it into her.'

'But the wedding, Ma. What'll she wear?'

'I told you last night there isn't going to be a wedding.'

'That's not fair. You can't do that. It's my wedding.'

'I'm going to see the priest in the morning to tell him it's cancelled.'

'You can't stop me marrying Art. I love him.'

'Don't mention his name, never again in my home.'

'I love him.'

'I loved your father.'

'Oh, Ma please. It wasn't his fault.'

'I don't want to talk about it, not now, not ever.'

At that moment Ellie hated her. Wanted to hurt her, to slap her face – take that dead expression off it. 'Art was right,' she told herself. 'Me thinking like this about my mother. It's beginning as he said it would.' She went into the bedroom and wrote a long letter to Chrissie telling her of everything that had happened. Then she went to bed and considered life without her mother, or life without Art, and cried herself to sleep.

During the week she went to the chapel and found out that her mother had put her threat into practice – the wedding had been cancelled. And later that week a letter came from the hotel saying they would be unable to refund the deposit as the notice of cancellation was too short. She was stupefied with grief and anger, with the discovery that her mother had meant every word she had said.

The atmosphere was terrible. Julia was torn between grief for what she considered was right and Ellie's obvious distress. Ellie no longer told lies about where she went at the weekends. She said nothing but went to meet Art, defying her mother, hoping to provoke a scene, one in which she would hint that her mind was almost made up to go to England and marry Art there. Perhaps this would bring Julia to her senses, make her see how wrong she was in forbidding her to marry and barring Art from the house. They would scream and shout but in the end because they loved each other and couldn't bear to be parted, would reconcile their differences. Life would be as it was before. The wedding would take place later. She could stay in Dublin with the two people she loved most in all the world.

Day followed day without a scene or reconciliation. At certain times Julia's resolve weakened, looking at the change in Ellie, the way her eyes were shadowed, her hair dull and lifeless, the picking at her food. She wanted to take her in her arms and say, 'I'm sorry. I know it wasn't his fault.' Always, at the last moment, she remembered who he was. How, like his parents, he had – though at the time he didn't know who he was – deceived her, lulled her into a trust which like Sarah and Barney, he was to betray.

The weeks passed, the time for the wedding, too. One day Ellie told Art she would go to England with him and the next changed her mind, still clinging to the hope that Julia would relent. 'You can't keep doing this,' he told her. 'I love you. I want to marry you. Your mother might never change her mind. We could waste years of our lives. We'll have to put a time limit. I'll marry you here if that makes you happy.'

'But supposing we did and she wouldn't come? I'd die.'

'At least in England you could kid yourself it was the distance that

361

stopped her. I'll have to force your hand. July, we'll go in July.'

'The end of July then.'

Like her mother before her, Ellie now had to resort to lies and evasions. 'But what happened so suddenly?' Sheila asked when she knew the wedding was cancelled.

'I don't really know. Something my mother found out about Art's people.'

'Maybe they've all got consumption. I know my ma wouldn't be keen on me marrying into a consumptive family. Did you never meet any of them?'

'I told you that before. His father died and his mother had a stroke, but I've seen her. She looks all right – well, all right if you don't count the stroke.'

'It must be relations of his, then. What are you going to do?'

'I'm going to marry him. I don't care what ails his family.'

'So will I leave it as it is about the wedding present?'

'I forgot all about that.'

'It doesn't matter. It was never bought. We all decided we'd give you the money and let you choose your own eiderdown and bedspread. I've the list of everyone and what they gave so there's no bother about that. What d'ye want me to do?'

'Give the money back.'

'But you're going to get married!'

'I don't know when, though,' Ellie said, and she thought, 'This is what it's been like for my mother – lies and excuses. It's terrible. An awful way to live. But how could I ever tell anyone the real reason? Never in my whole life can anyone be told that. Me, Art and Maggie – no one else must ever know. Not even my children, please God if I have any.'

The majority of the people she worked with either didn't mention the cancelled wedding or simply said they were sorry. Though Sheila, who couldn't keep anything to herself, told Ellie there were some saying that Art's family must have forced him to throw her over. 'You know, with him being a doctor.'

'I don't care what they say,' Ellie lied. She did. She cared about it all – the lies, the slur put on her and on Art, that he'd throw her over for such a reason. She had a good idea who would have said what, and imagined confronting them with the truth. Wiping the sneers off their faces. Then she realised the truth was more meaty than the conclusions they'd arrived at, and the meal they'd make of it. It was just something else she'd have to put up with. All the same, she'd be glad to leave.

★

The Sheridan boy told anyone in the house willing to listen that the Germans were winning. Their flags were way out in front of the English ones on the map his teacher had pinned on the classroom wall. His father boxed his ears whenever he heard his boast, reminding him how he had fought in the Great War. 'You'll never beat the British soldier. In no time your teacher will be pulling his flags out left, right and centre. The British once they get going will make mincemeat of them Curse of God Germans.' But it wasn't so and by the end of May 1940 Dunkirk was being evacuated. And daylight raids had been taking place over England since the beginning of the month.

Their latest acquisition was a small country mansion complete with croquet lawn, tennis court, stables, a paddock and a walled kitchen garden. Amidst this splendour sat Mary Flynn one morning, reading the *Irish Times*, in which she came upon a photograph of Lord Glenivy in army uniform. 'Master Patrick!' she said aloud, and continued talking to herself. 'You're not wearing well, but maybe it's the oul hat not becoming you. Still, you'll be well into the forties now. All the same, the years haven't been kind to you.' She read the article beneath the picture.

General Glenivy, it said, who had rejoined his regiment at the outbreak of war, was now in charge of Southern Command. It went on to relate the General's connections with Ireland and how in the 1920s his ancestral home had been burned down. 'That long ago, was it?' Mary said, still speaking her thoughts aloud. 'Terrible times they were. God spare us from the likes again.'

The picture and article set her thinking about her time working in the Big House, her and Sarah Quinlan. And then her train of thought took her to Grafton Street and the day after years of wondering and hoping that one day she'd meet her, when she did. She was coming out of Newell's after buying a lovely nightdress, and Sarah was going in. They met in the shop porch, not that she recognised her immediately, for Sarah like Patrick hadn't aged well. She had fallen into flesh and her face had a strained look about it. But you'd never forget Sarah's eyes. Strange peculiar eyes. Deep set and penetrating. Not what you'd call lovely though nowadays you saw many a film star with eyes like them. Sexy, she believed they called them.

Mary remembered how while she stood reminding Sarah that they had known each other previously, thinking she had done well for herself. You could tell at a glance. Her crocodile handbag must have cost a small fortune. It took a while to convince her they had once worked together. Even once she admitted remembering she wasn't over friendly and refused to cross the street to Brown Thomas's to have a cup of tea or coffee. And then all of a sudden she said. 'Why don't you have tea with me. Come up to my place. We can get a taxi at the Green, be home in no time.'

It was as if she couldn't get out of Grafton Street quick enough. She caught hold of my arm without waiting for me to say, 'Yes, I'll come to your place,' and almost marched me to the taxi rank.

Once we were in the cab, she became more herself. Her voice wasn't as la-di-dah, though her manner was still as short as ever it was. A smile flitted over Mary's face as she relived the moment of arrival at Sarah's house in Kilmainham. Her body seemed to swell with pride as they got out out of the taxi and Sarah pointed saying saying, 'That's it. That's where I live.'

It was a fine big house, double fronted, three storyed, red brick. A detached house with plenty of ground in the front, Monkey puzzle trees, laurel bushes and a wide gravel drive. Stained glass in the door. A fine big house that would have cost plenty of money. But a newish house for all that. Edwardian. Not a patch on her own beautiful Georgian gem.

For a minute she was tempted to wipe the smug self-satisfied smile off Sarah's face by describing it, and adding that her husband had bought some of the Glenivy land. That would have killed Sarah who worshipped anything to do with the gentry. And who no matter how she fooled herself with her red bricked house in Kilmainham would know full well no gentry had ever lived in it. Then she had told herself, 'Wouldn't I be every bit as bad as her if I started boasting.' Instead she admired the house and when they went in, its furnishings. Sarah showed her into the sitting room. 'I gave the maid the day off but it won't take me a minute to make tea. Let me take your coat. Make yourself comfortable. Are you warm enough?'

Mary recalled wondering at the time why Sarah seemed so agitated. Why, even though they had never been bosom friends, any two women who had been young together would have been a little bit pleased meeting again after so many years. She had been delighted to bump into the girl she had tried to help when she arrived lost and lonely in Glenivy. And had thought they'd have a lovely chat and a good laugh about the old days. It didn't seem as if that was how it was going to be.

Looking round Sarah's well furnished room, more signs of money, many silver-framed photographs, she wondered what her husband did for a living. Had she married the Dublin fella? After she was sent from the House, supposed to be because she was sick, one of the rumours, and God knows there were plenty of them, was that she married someone from Dublin. She was about to get up and wander around having a look at the photographs when Sarah came back with a trolley laid with a silver tea service, cake stands and exquisite china.

'Ah, you shouldn't have gone to so much trouble. A cup at the kitchen table and a chat about old times would have been grand. I wasn't expecting a Glenivy afternoon tea.'

The look she gave me. And the cutting tone of her voice when she said, 'This is how we always have afternoon tea and as for Glenivy I remember almost nothing about it.'

In other words, Mary told herself as she watched Sarah pour tea you're not going to talk about the past. I forgot in the excitement of meeting you again what a pig's manner you could have. So blather away and I'll listen. It'll be all boasting if the cut of the trolley is anything to go by. And boasting and bragging was what followed.

Sarah's wealthy American husband. The mansion he had taken her to live in in Chicago. The social life they had had there. The travelling they had done. Her motor car. Unfortunately her husband had got sick. And for some reason still not fully understood by her insisted on coming to live in Ireland. It was his health that prevented them buying a place in the country. A Big House. He liked to be near his Dublin specialist.

Recalling her visit to Sarah's Mary could hear the voice that talked non-stop and didn't want to lose touch so quickly. So she suggested meeting the following day. 'I'm staying in town for a few days,' she explained. 'And would be glad to have a chat about old times. 'You don't live in Dublin then?' Sarah asked and when Mary said, 'No I live down the country,' she appeared to become more relaxed. For the first time since they had met she smiled and apologised. 'I'm sorry I didn't recognise you straight away. I hate shops and crowds. My nerves are bad. I think I'm on the change. I seldom or ever come into town. The voice that talked about money, about her own achievements. Her driving, her skiing in America, her brilliant son who was the best student in Trinity. Never once did she pause to ask after Mary. To ask if she was married. If she had children.

Like a mad thing, she was Mary thought, like a creature possessed. I should have listened, said nothing and left as soon as I got the opportunity to do so. Instead I rose to her. I had to get in my twopennorth. Cutting across that voice. Shutting her up. Describing my house, the land, the boys at Stoneyhurst.

'Stoneyhurst!' Sarah said incredulously. 'The Catholic gentry send their sons to Stoneyhurst.' Mary recognised the dart – the unspoken, 'How dare the likes of you, Mary Flynn, the dogsbody, the culchie maidservant from Cork send her sons to Stoneyhurst. As if it was yesterday Mary could hear her own voice saying, 'Ah, well, gentry is as gentry does,' and see Sarah's face puffed up with anger as she asked 'What would the likes of you know about the gentry?'

'A lot more than you, Sarah Quinlan. A lot about Lady Glenivy, her son Patrick and the man who thought he was his father.'

Mary smoothed the newspaper photograph of Patrick Glenivy that lay on the table, the picture that had started her reminiscences and talked aloud as if Master Patrick was there in the flesh. 'God forgive me, I shouldn't have said anything. I shouldn't have let that stuck-up begger rise me. I gave Mrs Bellows, Lord have mercy on her, my word I'd keep her secret. I never should have told it to Sarah, nor your mother's either. She drove me to it though with her boasting and bragging and trying to make little of me. Mind you though, I never expected such a reaction. What difference did it make to her if you were a bastard. She went puce in the face. I thought she was going to have a seizure. "Liar, liar," she screamed. "Every word a lie. You made up every word of it to scourge and torment me." She was having trouble getting her breath. I was getting frightened. Then she got her composure back. At least she had shut up and her breathing had eased. I stood up to go when the door opened and a lovely-looking young man put his head round the door and said, "Hello, Ma." Her son, I guessed, and waited to be introduced. Instead Sarah ran him as if I had the smallpox. "I'm busy can't you see. I'll be with you in a minute. Leave us." I was up and out of there like a shot. Needless to say there were no invitations issued to call again. And d'ye know something else,' she asked of the picture, 'it wasn't until going home in the train the next day that I remembered another of the rumours that had done the round amongst the servants in Glenivy after Sarah had left. That she was expecting a child, your child,' she said placing a finger on Patrick's image. If that was true no wonder she had a fit hearing you were a bastard, for that would make the child she was supposed to have for you a crossborn bastard. Not a drop of Glenivy blood in his body. No wonder she nearly had a seizure. For such a thing to happen to Sarah Quinlan that worshipped the ground beneath the gentry's feet.'

Mary folded the paper and put it aside but continued for a minute to talk aloud to herself. 'Poor Sarah and her delusions of grandeur. One thing is sure and certain if I ever see her in Grafton Street I'll look the other way.'

CHAPTER TWENTY-NINE

They met every day for lunch, even if it meant Art missing a lecture or ward-round. His mind was no longer on his studies. He could think of nothing but extracting himself and Ellie from their present situation. He didn't want to take her to London where bombs fell like rain. He didn't want to take her from Dublin. But he wanted to marry her, and knew that wasn't possible while Julia refused to relent. Then what seemed like a reasonable solution presented itself. He told her about it while they ate.

'There's a fellow I know who's just done his elective in a hospital in Salisbury. He knows I'm thinking of packing medicine in and going away. Apparently, there are a couple of vacancies for lab technicians there. My qualifications would fit me for one of them. What d'ye say, will I apply?'

'What's Salisbury like?'

'Beautiful. A Cathedral town – old, very old – you'd like it, nice small shops that sell expensive clothes. And it's not likely to be bombed.'

'We have to go somewhere,' Ellie said despondently, 'so it might as well be there as anywhere else. Yes, write off about it. Will you tell your mother?'

'That I'm going away, but not about packing in medicine.'

'About us getting married?'

'Not that either.'

'You could have let on you would and I would never have known.'

'I won't lie to you, I hope I never have to, but I'll lie to my ma out of kindness. Can you understand that?'

'The strange thing is,' she said, 'I should hate her and your father, but I don't. It's all too long ago. He's dead and look at the state of her – how could you hate someone like that? In any case, they aren't stopping my wedding to you, it's my mother. Even then that's not true, for physically she couldn't do that. But I want her reconciled to it. I want a happy wedding. I thought by now she might have given in. I'll hope until the minute I leave, but in the meantime, we'll plan to go to Salisbury.'

Art looked relieved. He took her hand and kissed it. 'What would have become of me had you turned against me for who I was?'

'How could I do that! You're you. I'm sorry for my own father, for all my mother suffered. Their lives were destroyed. But not even for her sake will I let it destroy ours. She talks about your mother being evil, having powers, snaring me into the family to scald her heart – I don't believe any of that. And if my mother hadn't been scourged with the bitterness, neither would she. She'd realise that the last thing your mother would want is me for a daughter-in-law. Maybe one day she will see that. But there is one thing you have to promise.'

'What's that?' asked Art.

'You must never tell anyone what we did find out about your parents. Not so much for your sake, though I wouldn't want it known that you were their son, but for the sake of our children, please God.'

'I've thought about all that, the mesh of lies we have become entangled in. For me Simon O'Leary was my father and always will be. He's the one and your Dad Jack that we'll tell our children about. I'll get rid of all the other papers. Just keep their marriage certificate and my adoption papers.' He laughed. 'Jesus,' he said. 'There's no end to lies and deception once you start. One day we'll have grown-up kids wanting to know why I was adopted by Simon. Do I know anything about my real father?'

'One day we'll be dead. Don't look too far ahead. I've already been down that road. We'll try taking life as it comes.'

'You're wise as well as beautiful.'

'And don't be sarcastic,' Ellie said in pretended indignation.

'There was something else that crossed my mind – Sheila's unfinished dress. Who'll pay for the waste of that stuff?'

'Didn't you know that the bride generally supplies the bridesmaid's dress? My mother bought the stuff so nothing's owing.'

'So all I have to do is get the job and tell my mother?'

'And, in case you come back, make your leaving with Trinity OK.'

'That too,' he said.

Sarah woke from her drugged sleep. A nurse was calling her. 'Breakfast, Mrs O'Leary. Hold on there till I lift you up.' Propped on her pillows, through the long spouted cup the nurse dribbled thin liquids into her mouth: a thin gruel, so thin it was like water, followed by tea from the same cup which the nurse rinsed in the handbasin by the bed.

After breakfast they'd leave her a little while before coming to wash and clean her. At first she had squirmed inwardly with the shame of all that had to be done for her. Now she no longer cared. When she woke in the mornings it was always with a profound sense of disappointment that she hadn't died during the night. Her life was a living death; she was able to hear, to understand in the intervals when the sedation wore off, her mind working, full of questions, full of anger when nurses and doctors discussed her condition, the absence of bedsores across her body, as if she was already dead.

Art had something on his mind: she knew his face so well. What was troubling him, she wondered. Had he got the pretty little teacher into trouble? Was he going to have to marry her, and didn't want to? Her darling son, her life. And she was helpless.

His own father hadn't wanted to marry her, didn't marry her. Patrick came into her mind from time to time. Always unbidden. She'd be thinking of something else and there he'd be – handsome, naked, rising from her attic bed or about to get into it. She remembered in detail the things he had done to her. Remembered that she had enjoyed them. But now the memories had no effect on her. Only the one still burned in her brain: his answer when she told him she was pregnant. *'Mama sees to problems with the servants.'*

In that sentence he had denied his child, denied him of what should rightly have been his. She used to make excuses for him – like he was engaged to be married, though when they were cavorting in the attic she hadn't known that. She excused him because he was gentry and they had to marry whoever was picked for them by their parents; and she consoled herself that at least she was carrying a child of the gentry. Simon had cured her of all that nonsense, telling her that their 'aura', their fine physiques generally, their good looks, were nothing more than the result of a technique used by horse-breeders, or dog-breeders. They picked the best specimens to marry and breed from, with money thrown in.

The gentry had proper nourishment, proper housing, and indoor plumbing before anyone else. They enjoyed the best medical attention – Never wracked their bodies with back-breaking work. There was no mystique about them, no divine right. Before the Great Hunger Irishmen and women were tall and well-shaped. Like married like and produced handsome, good-looking children. Before the Famine if it was only potatoes and buttermilk they lived on, they had them in abundance. Good, nourishing food. Fresh air and turf for the digging to keep them warm.

Given the right conditions, food and environment, all human beings reached the peak of perfection. Racehorses, the most beautiful creatures in the world, were the proof of that, and the best of everything was what the Anglo-Irish had enjoyed. *He hated them.* A hatred nurtured by what they had inflicted on his ancestors. Standing by while they and thousands like them starved – died if they didn't take the coffin ships. For the Anglo-Irish gentry there was no forgiveness in his heart. Even so, although Patrick was one of them, in part anyway, it never lessened

369

Simon's love for him. When he adopted him he asked only that the child's name should be changed from Patrick to Art, and Sarah readily agreed.

That was after they married, after he had taken her to America to a life of comfort and security. He was the most innocent, the kindest, the most decent man she had ever met. She had seduced him, trapped him, lied to him. Confessed that Patrick wasn't Barney's son but Patrick Glenivy's, conceived after he had raped her. Simon was enraptured after two nights of lovemaking, for she had seduced him again when he returned to Glasgow after his London trip. He might have married her anyhow, being the upright man he was with his strong views that sex outside of marriage was wrong, and that he, not she, had been the seducer. But she always believed it was the story of the rape and rejection that in the long run made him decide to marry her as soon as possible.

'You were defenceless then, a young girl. You're still defenceless and not much older or wiser,' he had said, drying her tears after she told the rape story. 'I want to marry you, take care of you and the child. Please let me.'

And she had. After crying hysterically, blurting out — although every sob and word was contrived: 'And then when the child was a few months old I married to give him a father. I married Barney. I'd known him when I was a child — he seemed decent enough.'

She recalled how Simon, who by then she knew was a Catholic, responded: 'The Lord have mercy on his soul. He fathered the little boy and if God had spared him, would have been good to both of you, I've no doubt.'

'But it wasn't like that — I had to tell you lies about him. It's true he's dead. How could I let anyone I didn't know and trust hear the truth about him? Not only did he commit a terrible crime, a sin against God, but he put me and my child's life in danger.'

'What could anyone do to bring about such a threat to you?'

She told him what Barney had done; she remembered the colour draining from his face, how for the first and last time in his life he had sworn, calling Barney a bastard who deserved the end he got. And while he ranted and raved about informers, saying that Barney deserved the death meted out to him, she reminded herself to be careful in the future about papers concerning her past.

Poor Simon, he was so good to her. Seldom did he ever go against her. She invented a past for herself — even another Christian name, Louise. A middle-class name for a middle-class past. 'It's for the child's sake,' she told him. 'He must never know anything about me marrying Barney. Imagine when he grows up what that could do to him. Let him believe you're his father. Let him learn a different story as to how we met and came to marry. Not until he's a man will he have to deal with birth or baptismal certificates and long before that we'll have told him the truth.'

So far away in her past had Sarah gone that she didn't hear the nurse come to wash and change her. In her mind she cursed them, the two rosy-cheeked, brawny-looking country girls with starched cuffs at their elbows, smiling and jollying her. Telling her what a grand girl she was. Washing and drying, powdering and creaming her. Pushing the spout of the feeding cup into her mouth. Poisoning her with bromide. Sending her into a drugged trance, into the dreams ... *terrifying dreams*. Oh, why couldn't she just die ...

On the night before he left for Salisbury, Art went to see Sarah again. He brought flowers; there was nothing else he could bring. She was awake. 'Ma,' he said after kissing her and pulling a chair close to the bed. 'I'm going to England this week. Tomorrow, in fact. I wasn't sure until this morning. I'm doing my elective obstetrics in Salisbury.' Unblinkingly her eyes regarded him, reminding him of when he was a child attempting to lie, and that stare would unnerve him. 'I'll write every week. One of the nurses will read the letters to you ... Oh God,' he thought, 'why did You leave her like this? Why didn't You let her die? I'm sorry it's such short notice,' he continued. 'probably because of the war.'

He wondered how much she knew about the war, if at all. They held each other's eyes. He loved her. What Julia had told him the other night couldn't wipe out all the years. The devotion she had lavished on him. His irritation with her as he grew older and saw how snobbish she was, an irritation that never lasted very long. Maybe if she was well, fit, he might have asked for explanations – like what part she had actually played in the betrayal. But she wasn't well and fit. She was the most pathetic of human beings, her mind working, to what extent he wasn't sure, all the same she hadn't the peace of being comatose. She lay aware of being trapped in a body that couldn't obey her slightest wish: a living death. He hoped she would die. He hoped she would die very soon. He would go to England with an easier mind if she died now. He imagined her lingering, waiting for his letters, for a nurse to read them. His eyes filled with tears so that he had to turn away and fiddle with the catch on the window, saying it wasn't properly shut. Then, unable to stay any longer, he went to the bed, kissed her, sat again on the chair and laid his head on her breast. 'I love you, Ma,' he murmured, and then he left.

'He's taking her to England with him,' Sarah thought. 'She's ruined him. He's finished with his studies.' Then her heart began to beat so fast she thought she was going to die, and welcomed it. For she had remembered the handbag hidden in the sea chest. Supposing he had found it! Discovered that Simon wasn't his father? That Barney Daly was. Went poking round making enquiries. Oh, why had she kept the documents, and the cuttings about Glenivy and Patrick's wedding photograph . . . ? They should have been burned years ago. She had meant to, one day. There was all the time in the world, she had thought.

Why had that Mary Flynn, the flat-faced maid from years ago in the House, to bump into her in Grafton Street and tell her what she did – all lies! Still, it had affected her. So much so that she'd gone to Simon's room and fought with him for making her come back to Ireland. Poor Simon, he was her chopping block, letting her vent her spleen. But that day she'd made the mistake of repeating what Mary had said – that Patrick Glenivy *wasn't* the Master's son. 'And you mind about that?' Simon had asked.

'Of course I mind! It means that Art isn't . . .'

'Gentry, that's what's worrying you. After all the years, that's what's worrying you. *Isn't it*? After all I've drummed into you about them, you're disappointed because Art may not be one of them.' Then he lost his temper, something he seldom did. He shouted at her, berated the Glenivys and their like. She was responsible for killing him. Without that scene he wouldn't never have had the heart attack.

Poor Simon, the only person in the world who had loved her selflessly. Her mother, Rosie Quinlan, hadn't. She had wanted her to fulfil her own disappointed hopes. Patrick wanted her body; Barney wanted her body. Even Art, like all children, wasn't capable of loving a mother selflessly. *Only Simon.*

Julia flashed into her mind, as quickly she blotted her out. Thoughts of Julia and Jack were never allowed to linger. She had loved America, where she had a position as the wife of a prosperous businessman from a well-respected family, with a beautiful home, money, clothes, servants, and holidays. She had learned how to drive, how to swim . . . If only he hadn't got sick they would still be in America. He would be alive and she wouldn't have had the strokes. But he did get sick – with all sorts of vague symptoms. The doctors thought it was all in his mind, but he said no. He knew his body. Something ailed it: something that would kill him. And he got this yen to die in Ireland. She brought up the threat to her life. 'That's nonsense. You were guilty of nothing but marrying the wrong man. In any case, no Irishman murders women and children,' he said.

She hated Dublin. Terrified that she'd meet someone from the old days, she shunned all social life, even Mass. Not long after they arrived back, Simon's symptoms went, as mysteriously as they had come. He was in remission then. He wanted to play golf, ride – all the things he had done in the States. She cried and wept that she didn't want new acquaintances, neither did she want to be left alone. And like the saint he was, he settled for their miserable secretive life. And in the end she'd killed him and all because of that Mary Flynn and her lies.

'Time for a snooze now, Mrs O'Leary,' said a bustling nurse coming into the room. 'A nice dry bottom, a nice warm drink and before you know it, you'll be fast asleep.'

'God,' cried Sarah Quinlan in her mind, 'if You do exist, let me die before I wake.'

CHAPTER THIRTY

Until the last minute she hoped for a change of heart from Julia. The boat passages were booked; Art had been given the job as a lab technician at the hospital in Salisbury. Bit by bit Ellie had been secretly taking out her clothes for him to pack when it was time to depart. She was supposed to go without telling her mother. She did a special novena to St Jude that before the time came to leave, her mother would welcome Art back. Sheila was also praying for her. Maggie encouraged her to go if she couldn't change her mother's feelings.

On the morning she was to go, Ellie behaved as if nothing was amiss, as if she was simply going to work as normal and would be home for her tea – instead of which, at about that time, she would be taking the Mail Boat.

Julia chatted about this and that – the lovely day it was going to be; the raids in London and the poor people killed. It was an intolerable way to live. All the naturalness was gone from their lives; they talked to each other like two polite strangers, neither ever saying what was uppermost in their minds. Ellie never mentioned Art or marriage, while Julia studiously ignored what she knew well – that despite her ban, her daughter was still seeing him.

Ellie watched the clock. In ten minutes she would have to walk out of the door, leaving her goodbye letter in the bedroom. Suddenly she felt she couldn't do it. Her mother had to have another chance. Until Art came, she had been her whole life. She adored her, she couldn't walk out. 'Ma,' she said, and began to cry. 'I wasn't going to tell you. I was going away today to England without letting you know. Don't make me go. I love you, I don't want to leave you. Please.' She put her arms around her mother, breathing in her smell, the smell no one else had, the smell she had known all her life. 'Say something, Ma. Make it all right. Make it all right for me to stay. Please.'

Julia didn't return her embrace, nor for a moment say anything. She didn't let the tears that swam in her eyes fall. Then she spoke. 'You're going with him? Well, go then. Go, and as far as I'm concerned, you're dead. I never had a daughter. Go to the Dalys. They took everything else I had, so why not you.'

Ellie ran out of the house and down the street to where Art waited for her, oblivious of those she bumped into. 'I hate her, I hate her! I don't care if I never see her again,' she sobbed against his chest. 'She said I was dead, that she'd never had a daughter. How could a mother do that to her child? How could she? Go,' she said, 'go – drive! Leave the street, I'm not sorry. I don't want to see it or her again.'

Julia took from a drawer her pair of dressmaking scissors and went down to Maggie's. 'Where's the dress? I know you didn't get rid of it. I want it.' Maggie brought it out, wrapped in its snowy sheet. Julia removed it, held the dress aloft for a few seconds then began a frenzied ripping and cutting until the yards of ivory satin and art silk lay in a heap of rags. Then, turning to Maggie she said, 'She's gone. Ellie's gone, Maggie. I've lost her to them. What'll I do? What'll I do without Ellie? She was my life. I lived for her. I said terrible things to her. I meant them. She chose them instead of me.'

Maggie said nothing, knowing that if she opened her mouth it would be to tell Julia what she thought of her – how wrong she was to take the attitude she had. But because she loved her and knew in the long run she would suffer more than Ellie from the parting, she said nothing.

They sat on deck. The sea was calm; the moon threw a path of light on the water. Art cradled her in his arms. From time to time she woke, not knowing for a minute where she was. Remembering, she nestled closer to him. They kissed. At times her sadness gave way to excitement as she thought of their new life together.

From Waterloo they took a train to Salisbury, where Art had booked a room in the Rose and Crown Hotel – a double room, to which she had agreed. There was to be no special day for her now. She would sleep with him without her clothes. Every day people were being killed in England. Art told her not in Salisbury, but you never knew. So they went to bed in the afternoon and she learned the secrets that once she thought would have to wait until her wedding day. When she looked in the mirror afterwards she thought she saw the glow all brides had. She told this to Art and they went back to bed again.

The following day Art had to report to the hospital. 'It shouldn't take long,' he told Ellie while they ate breakfast of porridge, streaky bacon and fried potatoes. Ellie complained about the stinginess of the bacon portion.

'You'll have to get used things like that. Almost all food is rationed. I read in this morning's paper a recipe for banana sandwiches made from mashed parsnips and flavoured with banana essence.'

Ellie made a face. 'That's one thing won't ever pass my lips. I hate parsnips. What'll I do while you're at the hospital?'

'Have a look at the shops. Find an estate agent. We'll walk into the hospital and decide on a place for you to meet me after I've reported.'

'I hope you won't be too long. I wouldn't like hanging about in a strange place. I've never been out of Dublin before.'

'I know,' he said and took her hand, stroking it. 'I won't stay a minute longer than I have to.'

'Supposing we can't find a house or flat immediately?'

'We'll stay here. Maybe that's what we should do. Stay here at least for the time being. Not rush into taking a place we're not really keen on. What d'ye think?'

Ellie shook her head. 'Definitely not. I don't care if it's only one room. I couldn't bear living in a hotel. Eating with people all the time. Not being able to be yourself. I want our own place. I want to look after you. Cook your dinner and wash your clothes. No, definitely not a hotel.'

After leaving the Rose and Crown they found their way through the Close, stopping to marvel at the Cathedral's marvellous spire and admire the beautiful houses, then emerged into a narrow street full of shops and people. They both remarked as they went further into the town how many soldiers and airmen were about. 'It was like that on the train down from Waterloo. I've never seen so many people in uniform before, men and women. Packed in like sardines. The corridors jammed. We were lucky that ours was a short journey. I suppose it's all because of the war. D'ye think it is Art?'

'Oh yes. Salisbury Plain is a great place for camps and barracks. It's been a training area for God knows how long.'

'What are they all doing in here so early in the morning?' Ellie asked.

Art shrugged. 'I don't know. Coming and going maybe. Killing an hour while they are waiting for trains. Maybe on a day off. I suppose even in the army you get some time off.'

'I suppose so,' Ellie agreed as they approached the Market Square.

'This will be a good place to meet,' Art said stopping by the Poultry Cross. 'A pity it's not Market Day, but look, there are plenty of shops. Have a wander round. There might be an estate agent's.' He looked at his watch. 'In an hour I'll meet you here in an hour. Don't panic if I'm not dead on time. Wait. Don't move away from here, promise.'

She laughed at him. 'I'm not that much of an eejit. You go now or you'll be late.'

The estate agent confirmed what they had already seen. The town and surrounding area had had an enormous influx of military personnel. 'It's a bad time to be looking for accommodation. Wives have come in their hundreds to join their men. I haven't a vacant property on my books.' He gave them the address of another agent where the situation was the same. But this one did have a flats in a village outside the town. He gave them the address.

Art again suggested that staying in a hotel might be the best idea at least until something became vacant in the town, pointing out that the village was six miles away. That Ellie might find the days long and lonely. The bus only ran every hour. But Ellie was adamant – no hotel. 'Tonight,' she said, 'please God is the last night I'll spend in one,' as they walked back to rebook their room before setting out for the village.

When they enquired about flats, the estate agent told them the same thing: there was a great shortage of accommodation, what with wives coming down to be with their husbands. He said he would take their name, but at the moment he had nothing to offer them. Further out, in a small village, there was a flat to let. He gave them the address. They rebooked in the hotel for another night before setting out for the village.

The address turned out to be a bungalow at the bottom of a rutted lane. Fields surrounded it where fat cattle grazed, reminding Ellie of the mountains. 'It looks nice,' she said, waiting nervously for the door to open, which it was, by a skinny small woman, wearing a brown knitted beret. Her eyes behind glasses were enormous, her face brown and leathery. 'Yes?' she said, in what was to Ellie a strange accent.

'We've come about the flat,' Art said and told her the estate agent's name.

'The flat went yesterday, to a sergeant and his wife from Larkhill, but I've a nice sunny room. I'll show you.' It was sunny, and packed with furniture – a double bed taking up most of the space. 'Twenty-five shillings a week. Everything's gone up since the war. The bathroom's down the hall. There's an electric cooker, and clean sheets every week.' She held her head on one side like a bird, Ellie thought.

They took it. Mrs Coombs told them where the village was, but warned they could buy little until they had ration books. They went back to Salisbury, had a meal in a restaurant, collected their luggage and returned to their room. The next day Art went to work and Ellie to apply for ration books and an identity card. She bought tea and sugar, bread, milk and cocoa and bacon because she didn't know how to cook anything else. The village was pretty, but everyone in it was a stranger. Strange faces, strange voices. The bed had a single and a double sheet. The table, she discovered, was a green-baize topped card-table which, when she laid it, collapsed, breaking the two cups and saucers she had placed on it. The cows looked over the fence and into the window. It was two o'clock and Art not due home until half-past six. The chairs all had wobbly legs, and the springs in the one armchair stuck in her bottom. There wasn't a sound in the house. She explored the cabinet gramophone – maybe there were some records. There were neither records nor gramophone, only the cabinet stuffed with musty-smelling books. She lay on the bed and cried. She wanted her mother.

She fell asleep, not wakening until Art came home. They made bacon sandwiches, she frying the bacon in a tin pan on a fierce electric ring so that it burned. He told her about work and the awful canteen food, and they arranged to see a priest at the weekend and get married. She forgot the terrible room, the loneliness, the gramophone that didn't work while they talked about their wedding. Then, realising there would be no one to come to it, she cried. 'It'll be like your father's funeral, only at that there were the three of you.'

'There'll be four at our wedding,' he joked, trying to cheer her up. 'There'll be the priest and my best man.'

She suddenly remembered Chrissie. 'If I write tomorrow, maybe she would come and be my bridesmaid!'

'Have you her address?'

'I brought her letter. She's in Guildford.'

'That's not too far.'

'Only she was nearly finished there. She was going to do a cookery course, I don't know where.'

'Write to Guildford – they'll forward it.'

The single sheet got wrapped round them. They laughed and threw it off. He told her her skin felt like satin. He asked her was she sorry she came away.

'Not now. Not when we're like this, when you're here. I was lonely today but not sorry. Never sorry I came with you.'

They were married in the Catholic church in the village, a white clapboard building mounted on a dark green base and surrounded by fir trees. The priest was very old, very fat and very shabby. His soutane was green in places with age. Chrissie came from Guildford to be bridesmaid. Before the wedding she and Ellie cried at being together again and laughed afterwards at the terrible uniform and the thick diarrhoea-coloured stockings. But Chrissie looked so well and happy, and Ellie was glad for her. Then, suddenly struck by the realisation that she had been married and her mother wasn't there, she was overcome by terrible grief and cried again. Chrissie held and hugged her and told her it was homesickness. It had happened to her too but it would pass.

To celebrate, they took a taxi into Salisbury where they had tea in a café in a street leading to the Cathedral Close. Afterwards they walked through the Close, remarking once they went through the entrance how far away the town seemed. How still and quiet and beautiful it all was, and how lovely the houses were. In the Cathedral, someone was playing music she had never heard before – the kind she imagined you might hear in Heaven. She remembered Maggie and Patrick's Cathedral at home, and another wave of grief threatened to swamp her, but she fought it off. Enough tears on her wedding day. She was halfway round the Cathedral before realising what she was doing: walking in a Protestant church for the first time in her life.

They walked Chrissie to the station, waited for her train to pull out and waved each to the other until they could no longer see the platform or the train. The best man, a chap Art knew from the hospital, left them in the town – to go for a pint, he said, and asked if they'd join him. 'No thanks,' Art said. 'We'll push off. Catch a bus before the pubs empty.'

'See you tomorrow then,' the best man said.

'Wouldn't it be nice if him and Chrissie had clicked,' Ellie mused, as with arms round each other they waited for their bus.

'Great,' agreed Art. 'Things like that are supposed to happen at weddings.'

She made a day for herself. Sleeping until late. Going to the shops, or for a walk in the fields. Still she was very lonely. Never before had she spent so much time alone. She watched the clock, counting the hours until Art came home, wondering what Sheila was doing at this minute, or her mother. She pictured Julia at home, maybe drinking tea with Maggie or treadling her machine. She wondered did she think of her. She became sad and miserable but her spirit rose once it was nearly time to walk to the bus stop and meet Art. And as soon as she saw him, she forgot all her loneliness.

She could only fry and boil. The meals, she knew, weren't wonderful – made worse by the meat being rationed: one and eightpence worth a week and no choice. You took what the butcher had on offer. But Art always praised her efforts. He never asked, knowing it was the first thing she would have told him, had a letter come from her mother in answer to the one she had sent not long after arriving in England. Instead he talked about work, telling her how he took blood from patients, stained slides with it and studied them under the microscope. 'For simple things,' he explained, 'like anaemia. Sometimes I help doctors who are taking swabs or sometimes, if the porter has nipped out and I'm not busy, I'll push patients to the X-ray department.'

'D'ye like the work?' Ellie asked.

'It's OK for the time being – not what I'd want to spend my life doing. But there's a great crowd there. I've played rugby against some of them when they were at medical school. They had regular fixtures with Trinity.'

Once she asked him if what he'd found out about his mother had changed his feelings towards her.

He thought for a while before answering. 'I'm very much aware of what she did. Maybe if she was young, or not sick, I'd hate her. But she *is* sick and so I feel sorry for her. And because she is my mother I remember nice things about her, too.'

'I suppose I should be angry because you don't hate her, but I'm not. It's hard suddenly to hate someone you love, isn't it?'

'Almost impossible,' he said, knowing she was airing her own feeling about Julia and the unanswered letter.

Her letter to her mother had gone straight into the fire without being opened. 'I have no daughter,' Julia reminded herself, even as tears scalded her face. Letters continued to come and continued to be burnt. Once Maggie, coming into the room as was her way by tapping and then walking in, saw Julia backing the fire with one. She wanted to reach in and take it out, *force* Julia to read it – but she told herself it was early days yet. Julia was bound to come to her senses in time. So neither woman referred to what had been done, but Maggie kept it as no secret and Julia was talked about in the house.

Maggie said, 'She had a terrible cross to bear losing Jack in the way she did, but that doesn't excuse what's she done to Ellie.'

Not knowing the whole truth, the neighbours were mystified as to why the wedding had been called off. Maggie had told them she thought Julia was having an early Change and it had affected her mind temporarily. That's what had caused all the screaming on the night when she called off the wedding.

'Too many things are blamed on the Change, if you ask me,' said Mrs Doyle, long years past her menopause.

'Whatever the reason, she drove that little girl to England where bombs are raining down. If it was one of my daughters I wouldn't be able to close my eyes at night,' announced Mrs Sheridan.

Even Drim and Drew in the privacy of their own rooms criticised Julia. 'Those lovely children – so much in love. Doesn't she know how lucky she was? How could she go against them – and such a devoted mother, too! Such a good woman. It's hard to credit she could be so harsh.'

'How can she bear their loss? She had a husband. She had a child. Then a son-to-be. Such riches.'

Every week Art wrote to his mother, cheerful letters full of lies. The obstetrics firm was great. He had delivered ten babies. His digs were good and the food not bad, considering there was a war on. As soon as it was possible he would come and see her.

Nurses read the letters to her and said, 'You're very lucky, Mrs O'Leary, to have such a son. Not many boys are that considerate of their mother. It's a pity though he's doing his medicine in Trinity. If he was in UCD he'd have done his elective in a maternity hospital in Dublin.' Then they'd fold her letters and put them in her locker, and she would wonder about England and had he told her the truth? Had he packed in medicine and gone away with the school-teacher? Engineering was what he had really wanted to do, but she had had her heart set on medicine for him. She'd imagined the day his degree would be conferred on him. Now she had no power over him any longer. He was young and impulsive: without her he could become lost. She saw nothing of Patrick in him except the physical likeness, and was glad of that. Simon was more evident in his nature. For that she was also glad.

One morning when Art brought Ellie her cup of tea before leaving for work, she sat up in bed and remembered that she had used up the meat ration. There would be nothing decent for his dinner. She told him this.

'Typical,' he said. 'You're a useless housekeeper.'

'I know you're only joking but don't, I'm not in the humour for codding. Maybe the butcher will have some sausages.'

'Sausages! They've got a nerve calling them sausages. Sawdust with seasoning, more like!' Art was always good-humoured in the mornings, Ellie not so until later in the day.

'I've two eggs, I could make an ... Oh God, I hate this place! I hate the war. I wish I'd never left Dublin. I dreamt last night we were home.' She began to cry. 'It was like being in Heaven. I was so happy. I could make you gorgeous dinners in Dublin.'

'O love, don't cry. I don't care what I have for my dinner. I'd eat brown paper so long as there was enough of it and you were with me. I know you're on your own all day, and that must be lonely, but things will change – they're bound to. We'll go out more. Tell you what, we'll go out tonight! I'll take you to dinner. I've heard of a place where you can get steak and gorgeous chips. I'll book a table as soon as I get into the hospital.'

'That would be fantastic,' said Ellie, cheering up a little. 'But if you don't leave now you'll miss your bus.'

'So I will,' said Art, looking at the time. 'I'll have to fly. Go in early, look round the shops. See if there's anything you can buy to cheer yourself up. Mooch around and meet me outside the hospital. What'll you do with yourself this morning?'

'I'll stay in bed. And this afternoon I won't have to walk round the village hoping to get into talk with someone. I'll be on the way into Salisbury.'

He kissed her and left, thinking as he went in on the bus what a lousy life she had. His job wasn't demanding – sometimes he wondered why he even bothered, since it wasn't for the money. It was, he supposed, for the routine of work, the company, being in a hospital environment, not losing complete touch with medicine. All practical but very selfish reasons in the circumstances. Leaving Ellie all day in Dublin wouldn't have mattered. The time would have flown. But here in an English village, with everything unfamiliar and knowing no one, the days must seem endless. And as for his excuse just now that a hospital environment was necessary, well – it was all my eye. He would probably never go back to finish his medical degree for that had always been his mother's idea. No, he went out every day for the company and for the routine and to escape the house. For though he adored Ellie, a man didn't want to spend every day, all day, cooped up in a house. Worse still in a room. Tonight they'd enjoy themselves and he'd make an effort to take her out oftener.

'It seems very old,' said Ellie, looking round the low-ceilinged oak-beamed bar where they sat with drinks after ordering their meal and waited for their table.

'Hundreds of years,' said Art. 'Three or four at the least. There's a plaque on the wall with its history – I'll read it before we go. Is the sherry OK?'

'Lovely. I could get to like sherry.'

'Do, it's good for you. Who are you staring at?'

'Don't look round now, but there's a man just come in and he's the image of you, except he's a bit bald and has reddish hair. And he's on the old side.'

'You're very complimentary, darling. Thanks a million.'

'Honest to God, he is though the spitten image of you.'

'Where is he now?' asked Art, interested to see his lookalike.

'At the bar. His back's to you. Now he's turning round, waving to someone. He's going to sit down, two tables away from us with the man he waved to. Listen to them – don't the English talk loud!'

'Patrick!'

'George!'

'How lovely to see you. Wasn't it a stroke of luck, me running into

Tubby and him giving me your telephone number. I'd no idea you were settled in Wiltshire. How long has it been since we last met?'

Patrick drank from his glass and thought for a minute. 'More than twenty years,' he announced.

'Good God, that long. I suppose it must be. I was over in Glenivy, Caroline too. You two were engaged soon afterwards.'

Glenivy? Art pricked up his ears: he had heard that name before. It was a famous racing stable, in Kildare he thought. Ellie sipped her sherry and continued to study the red-headed man. A tray of drinks was brought to the men's table. Each drank half of their whiskeys then carried on talking.

'How is Caroline?'

'Fine. We've a son now, Oliver.'

'Oliver – that's a departure from tradition. The Glenivys firstborn sons were always Patrick, weren't they?'

'A whim of Caroline's.'

'Women,' said George. 'Of course, when he inherits the title he'll be known as Patrick.'

'Of course,' said Patrick, 'officially, anyway. I can't see his mother suddenly calling him anything but Oliver.'

'I've never forgotten that summer in Glenivy. You never thought of rebuilding it?'

'I did, but there were too many painful memories.'

Glenivy again. There was something other than racehorses about it, Art pondered. Something recent – or was he imagining that. Had his mother mentioned it? Was it one of the places she lived near, growing up? He was sure she had talked about Kildare. Then he remembered Julia and her revelations about his mother's past: she was reared far from Kildare, in Dublin. In Springfield Terrace. The middle-class past was more of her lies.

'They're a long time telling us the table is ready,' Ellie said, and Art motioned her to be quiet, whispering that he was interested in what was being talked about by the two men.

For a few minutes they reminisced – it meant nothing to Art. Then the one called George said, 'It was an appalling thing burning down Glenivy. No wonder your memories are painful. I heard the House going hastened your father's death.'

'Undoubtedly,' said Patrick.

'I meant to write. I was in India at the time – you know how things are. Moving from station to station, skirmishes with the natives. As I remember, you had a pretty little maid. I took quite a fancy to her.'

Patrick smiled. 'That would have been Sarah. I had quite a fancy for

383

her myself. A pretty little thing indeed. We had a good thing going, me and Sarah Quinlan.'

'Didn't we all, with our mothers' maids. I suppose she married one of the staff or locals.'

'I wasn't sure at the time. We slipped up so she had to be sent packing.'

'Yours ?'

'I didn't know or care then. Caroline was on the scene, the engagement imminent. Mama sorted it all out for me but yes, he was mine. I saw him once : no doubt about who'd fathered him. Everything about him screamed Glenivy – that is, all except his hair. She called him Patrick after me. He must have been about two when I saw him – a bit late in the day, I suppose. I'd got this idea fixed in my mind of adopting him. Tracked her down to Liverpool assuming I only had to put the proposal and she'd jump at it. She didn't. She wasn't the same at all. Still pretty, more so if anything, but now a formidable woman. She threw me and my proposal out in double-quick time, even threatened me with the police. For a while afterwards I fretted, felt that I should have been more forceful. But really there was nothing I could have done. You see, old chap, there was no legal proof that the child was mine. Still, I would like to have at least seen that he got an education.'

'And was that it ?'

'No. I hired dectectives, kept them on for years trying to trace Sarah and Patrick, but no luck. They'd vanished into thin air. In the long run I gave up, though now and then I wonder about the boy, how he has fared. Strangely enough I do it even more so since the war. You see all these strange young men in uniform. He could be one of them, and I'd never know. A queer thing, that. I could pass him by and not know.' He fell into a brown study.

Ignoring Ellie's earlier instructions not to look round, Art did so now. There was something familiar about the red-headed man's face, he thought, and then realised that it resembled his own, or himself as he might look when he was older. And at the same time he remembered where he had encountered the name Glenivy : on the night he went through his mother's papers. Amongst the newspaper pictures and articles was a wedding photograph – he hadn't paid that much attention – but had glanced and skipped through what was written about another picture, two actually. They were of a magnificent mansion before and after it had been burned down. *Glenivy.* His mother must have been a maid there. He was the bastard son of the man sitting behind him ! Art felt like getting up and confronting him. Hitting him. Venting his anger and shame. Shouting, 'Here I am ! Take a good look, you bastard, so you won't have to pass not knowing who I am !'

How much more was there to know about his past! How many other lies had his mother told him? Why did he carry on writing to her – let her rot. He owed her nothing.

Then, because he wished it otherwise, he let reason take over: all he had heard meant nothing. His mother didn't have to be the Sarah at Glenivy, nor the woman in Liverpool with a child called Patrick. The newspaper clippings had no special significance. Lots of people were interested in the affairs of the gentry and his mother was a great snob. That was how she had come to have them.

'You haven't said a word for ages,' Ellie complained.

'I'm thinking,' Art said.

'I hope it's to collar that fella and tell him how long we've been waiting for our table. Those two are going. I've never seen such a likeness to anyone in my life as striking as his to you.'

'Will you shut up about that!'

'Why are you turning on me? What did I do?'

'I'm sorry, Ellie, I'll tell you later on. I shouldn't have snapped at you.'

Just then their table became ready. Ellie wolfed down her steak and chips, but Art picked at his. When she commented, he said he wasn't hungry. He had indigestion – too much sherry on an empty stomach. The meal wasn't a great success.

When they got home he threw himself on the bed. Ellie didn't believe indigestion was the only thing that ailed him. She knew she had annoyed him, keeping on about his resemblance to the red-headed man, but that wasn't such a terrible thing to do. She had never seen him in such a sulky mood before. She put on the kettle and tried making toast over the ring of the cooker. She laid a tray and brought it to the bed, the bed where they spent so much of their time for there was nowhere else in the room as comfortable. They ate many of their meals there, talked, played cards and made love there.

His eyes were closed. 'Are you asleep?' she asked.

'No,' he said.

'Sit up and move over, then. Take the tray while I get in.'

'You heard it all, I suppose,' Art said.

'All what?'

'About Glenivy, Sarah and me.'

'I heard Glenivy mentioned a few times. Is that in Ireland?'

'Were you really not paying attention to what they were talking about?'

'No – my mind was occupied fuming about how long we were being made to wait for our table. What about Glenivy?'

He told her what he had overheard. 'They could have been talking about anyone,' She scoffed gently. 'Your mother wasn't a maid.'

'How d'ye you know what she was?'

'My mother never said anything about her being a maid that night when she found out the truth.'

'No, she didn't. At least, I don't remember her saying it – but that doesn't prove anything.'

'Are you trying to tell me you think that man was your real father?'

'That's what it sounded like. And there's pictures of Glenivy in her handbag. Pictures of a wedding.'

'Anyone could have newspaper pictures. I've often cut things out of the paper that caught my eye. Drink your tea before it goes cold.' Then a smile lit up her face and excitedly she said, 'But all the same wouldn't it be great if he was your father.'

'You'd like that? You'd like me to be the bastard son of a Lord?'

'No, not that you fool, but you wouldn't be Barney's son! D'ye not see the difference that would make to my mother?'

'I'd still be Sarah's son.'

'Yes, but it'd only be half as bad.'

'Where's the handbag with the papers?'

'Under the bed in the attaché case, why?'

'I'm going to go through them thoroughly.'

'Why are you crying? Oh Art, what ails you? I've never seen you so upset.' She pushed the tray away and put her arms round him. 'What is it?'

'What d'ye think? How d'ye imagine I felt, listening to that ould bags. I wanted to smash his face in.'

'Oh don't, love, don't cry. Why did we have to go out in the first place.'

'And another thing, Ellie. If I *do* find out he is my father, you're never to tell Julia.'

'But why?'

'It would be yet another slur on my mother. God knows at the moment I feel like strangling her – let me out, shift your legs, I want to get the case – but she is my mother.'

'Don't,' she said. 'Don't look at the papers. What good will it do? I love you. I don't care who your father was. And I'm sorry for being so selfish, so wrapped up in myself. Never really thinking what all that's happened has meant to you – finding out that Simon wasn't your father, then all my mother told you. Another man would have run away. It's only me and you that matters. And I love you and I don't want you to go through them oul papers. You'd still never know for sure if what that oul fella said was true. It's only us that matters. Me and you, Art O'Leary, whose father was Simon. I'm going to burn all the newspaper things and certificates, all except your Baptismal Lines. In Ireland they'll take you anywhere.'

'You're right, what good would it do? Simon was my father – I loved him. He was my real father. Get rid of them, then. Burn the lot.' He got off the bed, removed the tray. Her heart ached for all he had gone through, all that he had believed about himself wiped out in a few minutes by her mother. And again tonight he was made to suffer. She wondered was her suggestion to burn the photographs and certificates the right one, and her instinct told her it was. The papers might have answered some questions, like where and when Simon and Sarah had married; was she pregnant when she married Barney ... but none of that mattered.

Nothing mattered except their love for each other, and that in time, her mother would become reconciled to that love and their marriage.

From time to time Maggie asked if there was any news from Ellie. Julia lied and said, 'None.' Recognising the lie and hoping to prod her friend's conscience, for she suspected that any letters from England were either returned, torn up or burned (as she had seen her doing before), Maggie talked about the air raids over there. 'If you at least knew where she was, your mind would be easier,' she said.

'You've strange ways about you,' Maggie thought to herself. 'As kind a woman as I ever met, yet capable of going to such lengths. That Sarah and Barney have a lot to answer for. I can understand your hatred for them, and your shock at discovering Art was their son. As one of the women said, 'Fate dealt you a cruel blow.' All the same, it doesn't justify what you did and are doing. The wedding dress – well, that was done in a fit of temper. Anyone could do such a thing. But the letters – that I don't understand. The first one, maybe. But not now. What goes on in your mind, Julia? What are you thinking while you sit there sewing?'

She was thinking of the letter that had come yesterday, postmarked Salisbury. She didn't know where Salisbury was: she didn't know how to find out. It could have bombs raining down on it. She prayed every night that it hadn't. And if thinking about someone was a form of prayer, she prayed for Ellie every waking minute.

She called her face to mind, seeing the shape of her hands, and her feet. The texture of her skin. Remembering the sound of her step, her voice, her lovely laugh. She had never known such sorrow, such loss. When Jack was killed there was Ellie, her baby, Ellie to hold, to touch and love, to mind. Now she had no one. And the hardest thing to bear was that Ellie had chosen to leave her bereft, knowing that when she settled for Art, their life together was finished.

It wasn't her going away. It wasn't her getting married; she had welcomed the prospect of Ellie and a husband. And as for the going, times were changing, had already changed. Young people were not staying in their own neighbourhood, it was happening in the street. Her leaving would have saddened her. She would have grieved and then come to terms with it. It was who she had gone with. She could never reconcile herself to that. Never accept the son of Sarah and Barney for her daughter's husband. Then mad, crazed thoughts would go through her mind. She would go to the hospital where Sarah was. She would go there and kill her. Put her hands round her neck and squeeze the life out of her. Stand back and look at her puce face, spit on it. But first she would have seen the terror in Sarah's eyes when she recognised her. Watch it grow as she reminded her of what awaited her. How she would burn for all eternity in Hell. Then she would strangle her.

These thoughts left her sweating and trembling as if indeed she had killed Sarah. Then she would invoke Jack's help, her mother's. Pleading with them to intercede with God for her. Plead with Him to keep her sane. To banish such thoughts of Sarah from her mind. Sitting by the grate, her head buried in her hands, gradually her self-control would return and she'd tell herself that none of it had happened. Ellie had never gone away. Ellie had never met someone called Art who was the son of Sarah and Barney. It was all a derangement of her mind. It happened to women on the Change. It came and went. It was the buried hurt and anger within her still over Jack's death coming to the surface of her mind. Causing her the derangement. It would come and go. Last for a few days, a few hours, for months even. But it would pass. It might pass by teatime and Ellie come walking in the door from work.

Reality would soon return to dispel her hopes and bring with it her hate and bitterness that twice in her life the Dalys' evil spell had ensnared her. And she would ask where was God, to let such a thing happen? And Jack – didn't he care what happened to their daughter?

'Yes,' said the old, kind-faced doctor beaming at Ellie. 'You are pregnant. Let me see now,' and he looked at the notes he had made and then holding a small cardboard wheel-shaped object indented round the edges like a telephone dial, with a finger he moved one of the circles, saying as he did so, 'It'll give me your date. April the fifteenth – a spring baby. See the nurse on your way out. She'll give you a certificate of pregnancy. Take that to the clinic in the High Street for your orange juice and iron tablets. And keep your appointment at the hospital.'

'Thank you, thank you very much,' Ellie beamed.

'It's a pleasure to see someone so pleased,' the doctor replied.

She felt like telling everyone in the street, 'I'm going to have a baby!' But all the faces were of strangers, who passed her by. In the pretty little village with its pond and shops looking like the ones on old-fashioned Christmas cards, its cottages, their gardens filled with brightly-coloured fragrant flowers and behind the village the plains of Wiltshire gently rising and falling away to the horizon, she became overwhelmed with a longing for Dublin. She ached for the sight of tall houses, the mountains, the familiar smells of baking biscuits, hops, and coffee beans being ground in the cafés near her old factory. She longed for the street. Above all she longed for her mother.

She imagined Julia's face when she would have come from the doctor with her news. That was wrong – she wouldn't have had to come. Her mother would have been with her. You never went to the doctor on your own. England was the quare place. All those young girls, pregnant, some with small children, waiting their turn. Little children with them, cross and no one with the women. No mothers or aunties or neighbours. And now she had to find the clinic. All the things she had had to do alone since she came to England. No one smiled at you. No one got into talk with you. Not like people in Dublin.

But Art would come. Not for a while, but the time would soon pass. She'd make a lovely dinner – spend all her meat ration. He'd be so surprised and thrilled. There were only two rings on the Baby Belling, one for the potatoes and one on which she'd cook the chops, lamb or maybe pork. There was no room for doing a vegetable. She'd make a salad, that was easy. In the greengrocer's she bought lettuce and scallions; the woman serving smiled at her, thrilling her with its unexpectedness and leaning over the counter whispered, 'I've a few lovely tomatoes. Would you like some, dear?' She had looked in the window, on the shelves when she came in for tomatoes and couldn't see any. She remembered then, so many things not rationed were under the counter – though this was the first time she had been offered them. 'Oh yes. Oh yes, please! I'd love them – half a pound please.'

'Two per customer, dear. It's the war, you know.'

'That'll do. That'll be grand and I'll have a bunch of Sweet Williams.'

'One or two?' asked the woman.

'Two,' replied Ellie, glad that the war didn't affect flowers. She settled for pork chops and for pudding bought two custard tarts.

In the room she prepared the card-table, wedging the wobbly leg against the bed, and laid it with the odd crockery and discoloured bone-handled knives, and forks too small for the knives, that were supplied by

Mrs Coombs. Day by day she disliked the woman more. She had rules for everything: no sitting in the garden, no washing to be hung out.

'Not even socks or knickers?'

'Nothing, dear. It isn't that sort of area.'

She washed and changed into a dress that Art liked. 'If you didn't know about the baby you would think I was just getting fat,' Ellie thought, running her hands over her belly. 'This dress won't fit me much longer. I'll have to buy more. My mother would have run up half a dozen by now. I wish she'd answer my letters. Maybe they went astray. The war, you know. Please God once I write and tell her about the baby she'll write back. Maybe she'll ask me to come home. I'd be packed and gone in a minute. I have to stop thinking about her and Dublin. Art's beginning to get fed up with it, though he doesn't say. Jealous. I've heard of men being jealous of their mothers-in-law – but that's crazy. You don't stop loving your mother because you love your husband! There's enough room in your heart to love more than one person. In any case, it's a different kind of love.'

She went to meet him at the bus stop, planning how in the middle of the meal she would break the news. Once they got into the lane where no one was about, he kissed her properly. She couldn't wait, and told him there and then. He lifted her up, swung her round, kissed and hugged her, between kisses telling her how much he loved her. Then she remembered the chops. 'I left them on a low heat – but you know that stove. We'll have to fly!'

He admired the table, the chops that for once had cooked perfectly. 'You're doing all right, Mrs O'Leary. Full marks. A good dinner and a baby all in the one day. I hope you got something to drink. We have to drink a toast.'

'You can have the concentrated orange juice. Here, taste it.' She brought it to the table in its medicine-like bottle. Art swallowed and spat and took a fit of coughing.

'I forgot,' she said innocently. 'I should have diluted it.'

Pretending to be a disgruntled customer he demanded the pudding, saying the wine was foul. 'Yes, sir, certainly, sir,' she said, and gave him a shop custard tart. 'Delicious. I'll have another.'

'Only the one, sir. It's the war you know.'

Then they stopped play-acting. He asked what the doctor had had to say; when was the baby due.

'He said everything's fine. I'm to drink plenty of milk – you get extra for having a baby – and to take the orange juice and iron tablets, and I've to go to the hospital in August for the big checkup – your hospital. The baby's due on April the fifteenth.

'I know the Registrar, I'll fix it so you don't have to wait.'

'April – in the springtime. And you still haven't copped on.'

'What?' he looked mystified.

'That I got pregnant before we were married. So wasn't I right on the mountains?'

'You were indeed, you fair, fat, fertile, beautiful witch.'

'I am not fat.' She threw a crust of tart at him.

'You will be, though. By November you'll be waddling like a duck.' She pretended to be furious, and came to his chair, attacking him. They grappled and fell back on the bed.

'Didn't the doctor say anything about this?' Art murmured.

'If he did I wasn't listening,' Ellie said, wrapping her legs round him. After their lovemaking he brought her tea in bed and they talked seriously about the baby. 'We'll have to move out of here for a start,' Art said. 'It's not suitable for a child.'

'Not unless we put him in the gramophone cabinet,' Ellie giggled. 'We'd have to go anyway – Mrs Coombs doesn't allow babies.'

'How did you find that out?' Art asked.

'I forgot to tell you, I met the sergeant's wife. She's having one. They've got an army quarter in Bulford. She thought I might be interested in their flat, but it's a dump and twice this rent. That oul wan should be prosecuted. No washing, no garden, no babies and a terrible picture over the mantelpiece: a big deer looking at you, you should see the size of his antlers! He'd give me nightmares.'

'That's *The Monarch of the Glen*.'

'That's the name of it?'

'That's the name.'

'Wasn't I lucky marrying a University student. You know everything.'

'Don't be sarcastic. We'll go to the agent on Saturday and see if we can find something else.'

Though she hadn't meant to, the thought uppermost in her mind slipped out. 'I'll write tomorrow and tell my mother about the baby.'

'She won't answer it.'

'The baby'll make a difference. Oh, I do miss her. A girl needs her mother when she's pregnant. I think the child will bring her round, don't you? What would I do if she never spoke to me again?'

'She would like a shot if you packed me in.'

'You're my husband. I love you, how could I pack you in? I'd die without you.'

'I wonder. I think your mother comes first.'

'That's daft – of course she doesn't! She's my mother, that's all. It's nothing to do with you. Loving her doesn't make me love you less. It's another sort of love. There's all kinds of it.'

'I can understand you missing her. It's all strange to you here and you get lonely. She is a nice woman – I was very fond of her – but she's hard. That night I could understand her reaction. Finding out my real identity must have been an appalling shock. I don't suppose it crossed her mind to think how *I* felt, discovering my mother and father were murderers, but it should have done since. She showed no compassion, never mind for me, but none for you.'

'You're wrong. She may be strong-willed but she's not hard. Look at all she did for my sake – lived a lie all those years for my sake.'

'You can hardly claim that what she's doing now is for your sake.'

'Maybe she thinks I'll miss her so much I'll pack you in and go home. She can't bear the thought of you being who you are and me with you. Well, you know what Irish people are like, even me. We believe in fairies, ghosts, banshees, curses, the evil eye, premonitions. She doesn't see our meeting as accidental. And don't sneer. She believes it's the evil power of your mother and father still working. Still wanting to destroy. She's not the only one in the world to believe in them things. Nor the only one to put between a marriage.'

'She's not. It happens. I'll take you to see *Romeo and Juliet*. It happened to them – two families loathing each other, and Juliet and Romeo finish up killing theirselves. Maybe that's what she'd like.' His voice was bitter.

'That's a terrible thing to say!'

'I'm sick of your mother. Sick of what she's doing to you – to us!'

'Don't you ever talk about her again – not a word. Never about my mother.'

They were silent for a while, thinking their thoughts. Then Art reached for her and said, 'We're fighting, and it's about her. Even this far away she's coming between us. I promise never to mention her name again. You mustn't, either. We only have each other. Don't let's fight.'

In the hospital's antenatal clinic Art had fixed her appointment and she was called first. She undressed in a cubicle and a nurse helped her into a dressing gown after the doctor had taken her case history. There were so many questions, even about her mother and father. Were they alive? What had he died of? Had she had measles, mumps, everything. 'Only them,' she had told him, 'when I was small, and pneumonia not so long ago.'

'When was not so long ago?' the doctor asked, examining her chest. She was too nervous to remember exactly. Coming out of the cubicle she had seen at the end of the bed in the doctor's room stirrups hanging from poles up in the air. And prayed they weren't for what she suspected.

'Last year, I think, maybe the year before.'

'Say in the last two?'

'About then,' she said.

Her belly was felt and her legs put in the stirrups. The doctor and nurse chatted to her, taking her mind off what they were doing, making her forget the blood they'd taken from first her thumb and then her arm, the terrible pumping up of the bandage or something like a bandage round her arm. Having to pee in a glass, afraid she'd get it on the floor.

'Everything's fine,' the doctor said. 'You can get down now.' The nurse helped her. The doctor returned to his desk and began writing.

'Will I put my clothes on?' Ellie asked. The doctor and nurse whispered across his desk. She stood feeling foolish.

'No, not yet. We have to go to X-ray. It's only down the passage. We'll send you your next appointment. In the meantime, keep going to your local physician.'

The Registrar sought out Art and asked if he fancied a coffee. 'Sure,' Art said. The doctor knew Trinity, he'd rowed against them. They talked of the University and Dublin. Then he said, 'There's a problem with your wife. A shadow on her left lung.' Art knew little about shadows on lungs, even less about tuberculosis, so that he wasn't unduly alarmed.

'Your wife is very young and nervous, so knowing you I thought I'd have a word first before we call her back to speak officially. You can explain things to her, put her mind at ease.'

'It's not serious, is it?'

'TB can't be treated lightly.'

'What's the treatment?'

'Rest, mostly. There are some drugs – but bedrest is essential. She'll have to go to a sanatorium.'

'When?'

'After her next appointment. There's one in the Bournemouth area. Not too far for you to visit – a good climate, too.'

'How long will she have to stay?'

'Six months, I'd say, if she wasn't pregnant. But pregnancy places a great strain on the mother's body. Twelve, more likely.'

'And the baby?'

'The baby'll be fine. She'll go into a hospital for delivery and brief contact with the child – infection, you know – then back to the sanatorium. If you've difficulty caring for the infant we can help.'

It wasn't as simple as he had first supposed, assuming that a course of injections, some medicine, a few weeks in bed was all that would be needed. 'Can you cure her?'

'I'd say yes. There's still no miracle drug for her complaint, but it's in a very early stage. If she does what she's told there should be no problem. Play down the no-miracle-drug thing. Sometimes pregnant women dig their heels in over their babies being taken away, but they have to be. Get that through to her.'

'I checked with the postman. You've been getting her letters, so why haven't you answered them?'

'That's my business, Maggie.'

'She wrote to me. She's having a baby. She wrote and told you! You've been destroying them. You never even read them. You didn't know she was pregnant!' Maggie was beside herself.

'If she is, it's a Daly she's carrying.'

'It's hers and yours and Jack's and all who went before you. She's desperately lonely. She asked me to beg you to write, even a line.'

'I won't. I can't.'

'You're a bitter, black-hearted woman.'

Julia heard the voice of her mother before she died. 'Don't let bitterness corrode your heart.' She wavered in her resolve not to discuss Ellie, asking Maggie, 'When is the baby expected?'

'Mid-April. What d'ye think Jack would think of you?'

'He's dead. I don't know. It's because he's dead I'm like I am.'

'He's been dead for more than twenty years! The man responsible for his death is a heap of bones somewhere in London and the woman, crippled, speechless and powerless. You've had revenge: the ones you're hurting now have nothing to do with what happened. Can you not see that?'

'That husband of hers was sucked out of them two. Nothing was too evil for them to attempt. D'ye think he wouldn't be capable of putting her up to let on she's pregnant, to get round me. For me to say, "Come back. It's all right, I forgive you." Well, I don't!'

'I'm sure he's breaking his neck to come back here. Another man would take her to the ends of the earth away from you. Maybe he will, after the war. And as for forgiving, they're the ones with the only right to forgive. To forgive you.'

'You can go. I don't want to fall out with you. I know you love her and that's why you're doing this, so you write to her: tell her I wish her well on the child, and tell her not to be wasting her time and money on stamps.'

'I will, too,' said Maggie. 'I'll tell her every word you said. The sooner she realises the bitter pill you are the sooner she'll put you from her mind.'

'I'm getting huge. Look at my stomach – and see my breasts. Look at all the veins in them. I never had those before.' Art traced the veins with his finger. 'They aren't like they were on the mountains,' Ellie said regretfully.

'They're different. On the mountain you had the breasts of a girl. Now you have the breasts of a beautiful woman carrying a baby.'

'I love you. You always say the right thing. Will they ever be like they were on the mountain again?'

'No,' he said. 'Never. Why, d'ye want to go back to being a girl?'

'Of course I don't,' she lied. Though she did want to be a girl again. Not because of her breasts, but because she was frightened. Of having the baby. Of not knowing how to look after a baby. Of not finding another place to live soon.

'I was talking to that fellow I know. The Registrar, the one who examined you. They've brought your appointment forward.'

'See what influence can do.'

'That wasn't the reason. There's a bit of a problem.'

'The baby?' she asked, alarmed.

'The baby's fine. They're worried about your chest.'

'What's wrong with my chest?'

'Nothing serious. Nothing they can't put right.'

'Is it something after the pneumonia?'

'Maybe. It's a shadow on your left lung.'

'I've got consumption – that's what you mean.'

'No one mentioned consumption.'

'Well, doctors wouldn't, they don't call it that. But it's what I've got. It starts with a shadow and goes on to a cavity. Then you spit blood. You get thin and cough and cough, a little dry cough. You sweat and get red cheeks and are feverish. You go so thin you can see on a man his neckbones. "The number eleven", that's what they call them. And people say, "He's not long for this world." And then they die.'

'Ellie, don't talk like that! Don't look like that!' He shook her. 'You look like a ghost. You mustn't ever think or say such horrible depressing things like that.'

She sat up on the bed. 'What d'ye know about consumption? Who have you ever seen with it? Who have you seen dying with it – gone to see dead, already a skeleton. Tell me. Go on, tell me!'

'I've never seen anyone.'

'You would if you'd known what to look for. They walk round Dublin in their thousands. Maybe not in Trinity or Kilmainham, your part of it. Don't tell me anything about consumption.'

'I know what the doctor told me, what he told me about you.'

'And what was that?'

'You're lucky, you were caught in time. Six months in a sanatorium and you'll be fine. They'll bring you into hospital for the birth. I'll have to find a nurse for the baby, and you'll go back to the sanatorium until you're completely better.'

'Who told you that?'

'The doctor.'

'And you believed him?'

'Of course I believed him. Why would he lie?'

'Because who could bear the truth? D'ye know what they do – they send you into one of them kips, miles from anywhere, so far away your relations can only see you once a week. Sometimes not that, if they haven't got the bus fare. They blow you out on milk, eggs and butter and keeping you on the flat of your back. Then you're sent home and in six months, a year, you're in Mount Jerome or Glasnevin.'

'That probably does happen to the poor. They come home and haven't the nourishment. They can't work and get no help moneywise. We're not poor. You'll have the best of everything. Bournemouth, where the sanatorium is, is only an hour away. I'll visit you all the time.'

'Oh, Art – why did it have to happen to me? Now, I mean, when I have you and am having a baby. At this time, I mean. I'm not special so I could get it as well as the next one, but not now. I was always afraid of it; so many I worked with got it and died – all young. Then I'd tell myself there were plenty of oul wans and oul fellas in work who never got it and that I'd be lucky like them and escape. Only I didn't. I don't want to die. I don't want to leave you. I don't want to leave my baby. Oh God, it isn't fair.' She cried so much, her body shaken by it, that Art got frightened, thinking she could bring on a miscarriage. He made her hot sweet tea and lay beside her holding her close, stroking her hair, reassuring her until she cried herself out. And she disengaged herself from his arms and asked for a wet face cloth for her head, which was aching.

She fixed the pillows behind her, and asked him for another cup of tea. He thought she was more relaxed, accepting that she wasn't well and would have to have treatment, but he would say no more about it for tonight. She had had no food. In a while he would scramble her some eggs. While he was thinking this, she got off the bed. 'What d'ye want? I'll get it,' he offered.

'The suitcase from under the bed. I want to pack. I'm going home in the morning.'

'You can't! You have to go to the doctor. You have to go to Bournemouth.'

'Listen,' she said. 'Maybe I'll die. Maybe I'll get better. I want to get better for your sake, for the baby and because I don't want to die. Here I would. I'm not happy here. I want to be in Dublin, I want my mother. If they take the baby from me so that I can get well, no one, only my mother, can have the baby. Now will you get out the suitcase?'

'All right, all right. If that's what you want, I'll phone and tell the Hospital I'm leaving. I'll pack before I come to bed.'

Maggie didn't hide from the neighbours what Julia was doing. They were aghast though, as some of them said, many a mother and father had done the same before. Jews whose children married Christians considered them dead. Mrs Sheridan recalled an aunt in the country whose daughter married a Protestant, and on the morning she left the house her mother stood and screamed after her: 'I wish it was your coffin going down the path.'

Mrs Doyle blessed herself on hearing this and said: 'What sort of people are they at all! How can they bend a knee under a priest?'

To which Mrs Sheridan replied: 'To look at, ma'am, like me and you – no horns growing out of their heads or cloven feet, though the Divil has a home in their hearts.'

Maggie's sailor had given her as his next of kin. The merchant ship he sailed on went down with all hands after being torpedoed, and at about the time she was to begin Ellie's letter, she was notified of his death. She didn't seek Julia's comfort nor tell anyone in the house. She drank and slept and slept and drank, and to the frequent taps on her locked door called back reassurances. She had the 'flu: she didn't want any messages. By the time she wrote to Ellie, the young girl had been back in Dublin for over two weeks.

On the day of her arrival, as the train left the harbour and went towards the city, Ellie unobtrusively cried with the joy and relief of being home. Driving to the hotel where they would stay until they found a flat, she saw the mountains, and rejoiced at the sight. Only that night after Art was asleep did the terrible realisation overwhelm her that she was in Dublin but with no home to go to. In a quarter of an hour walking she could have been in her mother's. It was up the street and round the corner, up another street and another corner, and she was there. She pictured the walk in her mind, how often she had done it – the welcome she never failed to receive. Now she was afraid to go. Afraid of her reception. Afraid to read in her mother's face that she wasn't welcome. Her pregnancy and all her pleading letters had not wrought the change of heart: a second spurning would have to be final. All doors then closed, and never again could she ask or beg. Her mother had to come to her. She had to let Julia know she was in Dublin. She would write one last letter, not saying that she had a shadow on her lung, but that she wanted the baby looked after. Her mother must come for the same reason that she wanted to go to her: she must come because she loved her. Come because without her, her life wasn't complete.

The house in Kilmainham was empty, their marriage bed in the master bedroom. Art never suggested that they should move into it, certain that Ellie couldn't live in a house that had been his mother's. And doubly certain that expecting Julia to visit there would be an act of cruelty, one bound to infuriate and jeopardise whatever chance of a reconciliation there might be.

They found a flat in a Georgian house by the Grand Canal and there, on their first day, Ellie wrote to her mother. The letter with its Dublin postmark and addressed in Ellie's handwriting went the same way as the others, into the fire. Though it did arouse Julia's curiosity more than the others. Were they back for good? On holidays? Would she come to the house? How could she receive her? Was she really pregnant? 'Oh Ellie, Ellie,' she spoke her thoughts aloud in the empty room. 'Why did such a terrible thing happen between us? Why did you have to meet him? Why, when you had fallen out, did Maggie bring him back? Why did he have to be who he was? That was all that ailed him. I loved him like a son. I rejoiced that you had found such a man. I never had the slightest suspicion. How could I? How would anyone? How could anyone imagine such a cruel trick of fate? I couldn't find a fault in him. And all the time he had the greatest flaw.'

Morning and afternoon from the window of her flat, where she could see the canal flow by, the ducks and swans bobbing past and the children and their mothers who came to feed them, Ellie watched the postman come to the door. She sent Art down and waited expectantly, knowing by his face when he came back that a letter hadn't come for her. Daily she grew more depressed. She wasn't eating, nor dressing. Her hair was unwashed, unkempt. She refused to see a doctor, refused to talk about her illness. Art's moods swung between despair and anger. Ellie had no right to behave this way: she was carrying a child. She had a responsibility to the child. She had a responsibility to him. He was her husband. He needed her. She was slowly committing suicide.

Then despairingly, he told himself, 'She doesn't need me. She no longer, if she ever did, loves me. She loves only her mother. *Only her mother*. More than me, more than the child. An unnatural relationship, surely to God. A married woman should care first and foremost for her husband – a husband, for his wife. It said so in the Bible. Would the same thing have happened had they married when they were supposed to? If there hadn't been the awful revelation of his parents' identity? Was this how girls were, after the honeymoon, their mothers usurping the husbands in their hearts?

And then anger against Julia swept through him. He could kill her if it meant releasing Ellie from her power. As soon as such a thought registered he realised he was falling into Ellie and Julia's way of thinking, about power over another person, spells and wicked intent, when perhaps it was no more than natural grief for the loss of a close relationship, heightened by pregnancy and whatever effect the lung complaint was having on her.

Day by day they waited. Day by day he coaxed Ellie to eat a little, drink a little. He went through the cycle of his moods, and day by day knew the disease was making inroads into Ellie's lungs. His beautiful Ellie. On the mountain with her pink-tipped little girl's breasts. His lovely wife with her heavy blue-veined woman's breasts and inside her, their child.

Maggie and Julia hadn't spoken since the day of the letters. Julia missed her; Maggie longed to talk to her. To tell her about her sailor, how she missed him, how she cried when she realised that never again would he come swinging in the door with his weatherbeaten face and the gleam in his eye. How willingly she would exchange her joyless nights in the public house to sit by the fire with him if he was sick and ailing. And Julia wanted to talk about Ellie. Say how she regretted burning the letter from Dublin, not knowing where her child might be. Maybe round the corner and she not knowing where to find her. Tell Maggie why Ellie didn't come. Tell her how she had disowned her, when she left, said she was dead to her. But didn't she know that she wouldn't turn her from the door?

In their rooms they sat enduring the loneliness, Maggie's great spirit and courage depressed by drink and grief, making her fearful of a first move. Julia, depressed by guilt, experiencing the same doubt.

She talked to Jack, asking his help. Once she thought he came as he had in Springfield Terrace and sat by the table with his back to her. And when she spoke he didn't answer. She was never sure if she had dozed and dreamed it, or if he had come and had chosen to ignore her.

The neighbours spoke to both women as if everything was normal. Not knowing of Maggie's bereavement, they feared something sinister ailed her, and spoke of tumours on the brain changing people's ways and of the first signs of madness. They remembered both women in their prayers and waited expectantly for what the next day would bring, anything out of the ordinary adding zest to their lives.

When three weeks had passed and no letter came from Julia, in an angry swing of mood Art decided that if Ellie was to be saved and the only way of saving her was to bring his mother-in-law to the house, then he would do that. If the price she asked was his renunciation of his wife, he would do that, too. Ellie would surely die, left as she was. He couldn't forcibly take her to a doctor or into a sanatorium, but he could confront her mother.

He told Ellie he was going to visit his mother. Listlessly she smiled and said she'd sleep while he was gone. On the way to Julia's he prepared what he would say. He'd be calm and composed – ask if she had received Ellie's last letter, then make his proposal: he would go out of Ellie's life. He'd join the army or the RAF, not tell her it was final – let her believe in the beginning that like so many young men, like her father in the last one, he couldn't resist the call of war.

'But you,' he'd say to Julia, 'you have my word that I'll never come back. That's what you want as reparation for what my parents did – and that you can have.'

Going up the stairs no memories of similar happier occasions came to his mind, for by now he was half-regretting his decision to face this formidable woman, and needed all his willpower to propel him up the last few stairs. Before knocking, he straightened an imaginary crookedness of his tie and took a deep breath. He knocked.

'Who is it? Come in,' Julia's voice called. He had forgotten the casualness of the house. He knocked again.

Julia opened the door. He was amazed by the change in her, she had aged so much. She was thinner: it didn't become her. There was more grey in her hair and her eyes had a haunted look.

'You,' she said, her voice seeming hostile. Fear made it so, the sight of him conjuring up an injured Ellie, a seriously ill Ellie. Why else would he come?

His carefully prepared speech flew out of his head and he pushed past her into the room. 'Me,' he said, his voice loud. So taken aback was Julia that she forgot to shut the door. Other doors in the house opened slightly and ears leant against the cracks. 'Yes, it's me. What sort of a woman are you? What sort of a mother? Ellie is pregnant. Ellie has TB. She wrote and wrote. You never answered. She cries for you. She won't eat. She wants you. She loves you, God only knows why. If you don't go to her she'll die. She won't have treatment. She won't see a doctor. I don't understand you. My mother did a terrible thing – she had your husband killed. But at least it was quick. You're killing Ellie a bit at a time. I came here to give Ellie back to you. To go away, join up, hoping I might be killed. But I've changed my mind. You won't have her. She's my wife: I love her more than my own life. I'll find a way to make her better. A way while she's in a sanatorium to rear our child.'

He pushed past her again and ran back down the stairs. Past Maggie's room where she lay sleeping off her lunchtime feed of stout and dreaming of her sailor. Distorted facts of Art's conversation went round the house as women moved from room to room.

'Ellie's dying,' Mrs Doyle lamented. 'The lovely little girl.'

'I never heard that,' Mrs O'Brien contradicted. 'But I did hear him saying he was giving her back. Throwing her over in other words. Maybe the child's not his.'

'Trust you to think up that,' said Mrs Sheridan.

'D'ye think one of us should go to her? He's gone. I heard him.'

'If she wanted anyone there it'd be Maggie and they're not talking, Mrs Doyle.'

'I suppose you're right. Did you hear him about the letters? She should have answered them.'

'Indeed she should,' Mrs O'Brien said. 'Later on I'll drop into Maggie's and tell her what went on.'

He ran down the stairs, trembling after the encounter, his heart thundering, sweating. Asking himself as gradually his composure returned, 'Oh God, what have I done? What have I gained for Ellie? I vented my feelings, vented the spleen I've accumulated through jealousy of Ellie and her mother, but for Ellie I've solved nothing. I wanted to get back at Julia, hurt her as she hurt me the night I learnt about Sarah and Barney Daly. It wasn't Ellie I was thinking about. It was me, all me. And the letter, the one sent since we arrived. If Julia got it she may have destroyed it – not opened it. She probably doesn't know where we live. Though after my outburst she'll never come now.' He went into a public house, ordered one whisky after another and tossed them back, then on an envelope he wrote their address and went back to the house. This time creeping up the stairs, praying he would meet no one, he slipped the envelope under the door.

★

It hadn't been a trick. Ellie *was* pregnant. Ellie had consumption. Her beautiful Ellie was sick with a terrible disease. Julia rocked and moaned and talked to herself. 'I ran her into it — sent her away. She couldn't mind herself, couldn't boil an egg and I told her as far as I was concerned, she was dead. I flew in the Face of God. He's punishing me for it. But it's Ellie's life that's in danger, not mine. Oh Jack, what did I do to Ellie? Our Ellie that we conceived on a beautiful day in Glenasmole. A day when Angels flew overhead and gave her the sweetest nature a girl ever had.

'I've destroyed her. She wants me to come to her, to mind her baby when it's born, please God, and I don't even know where she lives. I can't go to her. He'll never come again — who could blame him? He loves her. I brought it all about. It's all my doing. They only, like me and you, loved each other. He wasn't to know who he was. I gave him the bang of it, not knowing or caring how he'd feel. And all through bitterness. My mother warned me about it — told me what it could do. She reminded me that there was Ellie to think about. I gave her my promise and broke it. Nurturing the bitterness. Letting it corrode my heart and brain until it has destroyed the one person I didn't want touched by it. God forgive me.'

For hour after hour she sat. Evening came, it grew dark, she let the fire go out and didn't light the gas. She fell asleep in the chair and didn't find the envelope until morning. Then, running a comb through her hair, splashing cold water on her face and throwing a coat round her she went to the house by the canal.

Her knock woke Art. He let her in. He didn't speak, neither did she. She followed him up the stairs and into the bedroom where Ellie lay sleeping. He left them alone. Julia sat on the side of the bed looking at her daughter, not wanting to wake her. She was prepared to sit all day rather than disturb her sleep. As if she sensed her presence Ellie stirred, opened her eyes, and smiled. 'Ma,' she said, 'I was dreaming about you. I dreamt you came.' She held out her arms. 'I'll be all right now you've come. I'll get better, won't I?'

'Of course you will,' Julia said and held her close.

She stayed all day. Ellie washed and dressed herself, ate the food that her mother made, and she talked and she talked. Telling her mother about England: Mrs Coombs who wouldn't let you hang out washing, who wouldn't let a baby live in her house. Art watched and marvelled as his mother-in-law and wife talked as if nothing had ever happened between them. As if the letters had never been written and ignored. As if Ellie hadn't been banned from her home if she went on seeing him. And he hated Julia. Hated her for the ease with which she walked back into Ellie's life and usurped him. At the same time he was grateful for how her presence was restoring Ellie to normality.

'I'll come back tomorrow. Call the doctor first thing. She'll see him, she'll do what he advises. If it's to be a sanatorium, she'll go. And when the child is born, please God I'll rear it till she's well. Goodnight.' He showed her down the stairs and bade her goodnight.

Maggie had been informed by the neighbours of the latest developments and had foregone her visit to the public house. Sitting by her parlour window watching for Julia's return she guessed, after frequent visits to her room, which was locked for once, that she had gone to Ellie, having put together the garbled version the neighbours gave her of Art's visit.

It was midnight before she came home. Maggie waited for her to be in her room before climbing the stairs. 'Julia,' she said, 'it's me, Maggie,' and went in. 'How is she? How is Ellie?'

Julia told her, and then each said at the same time how sorry they were for what had happened between them. And Julia confessed how sorry she was for being the cause of Ellie and Art's troubles; Maggie not commenting one way or the other, nor telling of her own loss. That could wait.

'I feel that upset for him,' Julia told her. 'He doesn't understand about women, about mothers and daughters. You can see the hurt in him that we're back together as if nothing had come between us. He's mixing it up in his mind: thinking Ellie loves me more than him, the poor boy.'

'What'll happen when the baby's born, please God?' Maggie asked.

Julia explained that until Ellie recovered she'd mind the child.

'That'll be the makings of you.'

'But Maggie, I'm afraid.'

'It'll all come back to you, don't worry. If you reared one you can rear two.'

'That's not what I mean. I'm afraid to look on the face of the child. Afraid that if I see Barney or Sarah in it I couldn't take on its rearing. What'll I do?'

'For the time being, nothing. You'll have to wait till the baby's born, only I hope you're not going to let your imagination run away with you. I never see a resemblance in any infant. The mothers, fathers and grannies do, but I think that's just wishful thinking. And with wishes they can go one way or the other. Don't you be reading something that isn't there. Get it into your head now that Ellie's child will look like Art's mother or father and that's what you'll see.'

'You're right, I'll put it out of my mind. If Ellie goes to the sanatorium you'll come to see her, we'll go together.'

403

'We will. Now I've a terrible thirst on me.'

'I haven't a drink.'

'Don't I know well you never have. Wet a cup of tea.'

They talked on into the small hours before bidding each other good-night.

Two days after the doctor came, Ellie saw a specialist in chest diseases who arranged for her to go to a sanatorium, but not the one in which so many of her workmates had died. She was adamant about this. Whatever her fears, she kept them to herself, looking better than she had for a long time and cheerfully bidding her mother and Art goodbye.

On the bus journey back to town the pair spoke little, warily polite with each other. 'I'd have bought a car,' he said, 'but petrol's not easy to get.'

'It would have been grand and handy for visiting. It's the tea I miss — what can you do with half an ounce a week?'

'There's plenty on the black market.'

'Tons,' said Julia, 'if you're prepared to pay a pound a quarter for it.'

'It's the war, you know, that's what everyone in England used to say, no matter what went short. And if you made the mistake of quibbling, they'd get ratty and ask, "Don't you know there's a war on?"'

They travelled out separately to see Ellie, Art catching a bus later than the one he knew Julia and sometimes Maggie caught. But gradually during the visits his resentment of Julia lessened, for he noticed how Ellie's eyes lit up when he came into the room. How sometimes she was short-tempered with her mother, or unheeding, all her attention centred on him. She was as loving as in the days when they were courting, when they were first married. He recovered his confidence as a husband and acknowledged that the relationship between mother and daughter and daughter and husband didn't need to threaten either one.

Sometimes he hired a taxi and they both travelled together. X-ray after X-ray showed Ellie's condition improving. Her mother's appearance improved with it, though she was still troubled. She had tried to follow Maggie's advice and not dwell on her fear that the child would look like the Dalys. She *willed* herself not to think about it but what if Barney or Sarah's face was the one she saw on the new baby? What then? It was all very well to say she wouldn't rear it — her refusal might cause Ellie's death. Julia believed that Ellie would never hand the baby to anyone else, but would rather leave the sanatorium and endanger her health and the health of the baby. So Julia would take the child whatever happened, and she would rear it, but if her fears were borne out, though she would feed it, watch over it and mind it, all the care would be given without love.

As the days passed and Ellie became accustomed to the routine of the sanatorium and accepted her separation from Art, she thought about Sheila and the other girls in work. She told Art that she'd like to see them. He promised to let them know, but reminded her that too many visitors would tire her. After the birth they could come.

They wrote to her – sent cards and presents and told of the prayers offered for her. A letter came from Chrissie, now a qualified cook, with a photograph of herself in white overalls, turban and clogs. She wrote that things were progressing nicely between her and Art's best man.

Art thought about his future and decided that he definitely didn't want to do medicine. Until Ellie was out of the sanatorium he would make no new commitments, but once she was completely well he would sign up to read for a degree in Engineering. Another decision that he made was to sell the house in Kilmainham.

He found time in between visiting Ellie to go and see his mother, the sight of whom sometimes filled him with bitterness. But then he'd meet her eyes and try to read their expression, wondering what was going on in her mind. Did she feel guilt, sorrow – any regret for what she'd done? Sadness would overcome him – pity for her and her time with Patrick Glenivy ... for the young girl she had been then. For the poor sick creature she was now, fed lies by him – never to know that he had a wife, and never to know that she was to have a grandchild. What a web she had woven for herself. He held her hand, touched her cheek and stroked her hair. And then he would kiss and leave her.

Her eyes would follow him to the door. Her son – who grew more like his father each time she saw him. Only now as her mind began to fail, the image of his father grew more confused, so that more often than not it was a thin bespectacled face she saw – a kind gentle face, with a humorous mouth : her son's father. Art's father, not Patrick's father. And she would wonder, who was Patrick? She didn't know a Patrick, had never known one. Her son was called Art. And Art's father was Simon O'Leary.

One night as Art was leaving the hospital, a nurse asked him to step into the office where the nursing nun now in charge wanted to speak to him.

'Mr O'Leary,' she said, shaking his hand. 'I'm delighted you're home again. Your mother missed you sorely. You're a very attentive son, so you'll have noticed that she's deteriorating rapidly. It'll be a happy release for her, the poor soul. You're still on the canal ?'

Art said he was.

'We'll let you know immediately there's a change for the worse.'

The change came so rapidly that Sarah was dead before Art got to the hospital. He had scoffed secretly when people said of a corpse how peaceful it looked, but observing his mother now, he agreed that there was some truth in it. She seemed younger – or was it only because he could no longer see her haunted, fearful eyes?

She was gone and there was no one with whom he could share his grief, or his good memories of her. No one in the whole world was sorry to see her go except himself. No one in this city in which she had been born and reared, to grieve her passing. No one to stand by her grave except him.

Had Ellie not been sick he would have told her of Sarah's death . . . but to Julia he wouldn't speak her name. He made the funeral arrangements, ordered flowers and buried her with Simon. 'Poor Ma,' he thought as he left the cemetery after refusing a lift from the priest who had officiated. 'Poor lonely Ma, you paid a terrible price. I'll come again and in the years to come I'll bring the child, who'll know only that you were my mother and his or her grandmother.'

Maggie had put the neighbours straight about Ellie and Art, and now kept them informed about her progress in the sanatorium. She told them too about her own sweetheart and they commiserated, saying they would pray for him. It was grand to see her looking herself again. They were also happy for Julia. She gossiped with them in the yard, round the hall door. No secrets any more. She was able to reminisce, say where she went to school, where she had lived. She could delight in the coincidence of them having a joint acquaintance.

The women who knitted made matinée coats, the ones who crocheted, shawls. Drim and Drew with the finest hand-sewing stitched baby gowns and asked would Ellie or her husband have any objection to them visiting her. Julia assured them there would be delight, not objection.

Mr Sheridan sent her cakes and Mr O'Brien, Jacobs' finest selection of biscuits, apologising that they weren't what they were before the war. The Jazzer, who was going to work in England, gave a box of sweets. The youngest of the Sheridans had left school by now and was a messenger boy, riding a bicycle laden with provisions which seemed too heavy for his small frame; these days he never gave a thought to the map in school or where the flags were going.

Two days before her expected date of delivery, Ellie began her labour and was moved to Holles Street Hospital. Art was notified and came in a taxi to collect Julia. Fleetingly she recalled it was the hospital where she had miscarried all those years ago. They sat in the hall and waited. Art attempted to concentrate on a crossword puzzle. 'She's doing fine for a first baby,' a nurse came to tell them after several hours, 'but she'll be a while yet. You could get a bite to eat and come back.' They found a café, had a sandwhich and a pot of tea and walked round Merrion Square. Back in the hospital they waited again, Art looking at his watch, Julia trying to avoid raising her eyes to the wall clock that stared down.

'D'ye think everything's going all right?' Art whispered, though there was no one else near them.

'It takes a long time. She'll be grand,' Julia consoled him as she imagined the pain Ellie was now going through, wishing she could take it from her. And then, when it seemed as if forever they would sit waiting for news that never came, a nurse was there, smiling, telling them in a voice as enthusiastic as if she was announcing the birth of the first baby ever, 'Mr O'Leary, your wife has had a beautiful baby boy – eight pounds five ounces. You can see them both in a few minutes.'

She came for them and they followed her to a nursery with low glass windows. 'You can't come in, but I'll bring him to the window.' She brought him and held him up, loosening the blanket from round his head. Fearfully Julia raised her eyes, dreading what she might look upon. Then so surprised was she, she laughed out loud and she cried, 'He's so beautiful, God bless him! God bless and spare him to you.'

'He's the image of Ellie, isn't he?' Art said.

'The image,' she agreed, without taking her eyes from the baby into whose face she continued to gaze. And said to herself: 'I prayed he'd look like Ellie or like Art, even like me. I begged God not to let him look like Barney or Sarah and all the time I never thought he might look like Jack. Never. Not once did I consider that possibility. And there he is, a replica of him. My lovely grandson with his grandfather's lovely face.'

The nurse wrapped the baby again and indicated he was going back to his cot. 'You have a handsome son,' she said to Art. 'Thank God it is all over.'

He turned to her. 'Is it, Julia?' he asked. 'Is it really all over?'

'All over, Art.' She reached a hand to him. He took it and then put his arms round her and they stood close for a moment. She broke away first. 'Look at us,' she said. 'Crying like a pair of fools. Wipe your eyes.' She wiped hers. 'If we go in there with the sign of tears, Ellie might think there was something up.'

He took her arm and they went to see Ellie, who lay on her pillows asking, 'Well, what did you think of him?' Art went to her first, kissing her, thanking her, telling her how beautiful the baby was. Then he made way for Julia who loved and kissed her. 'She's the image of you, Art, isn't he?' Ellie said.

'The spit,' he said.

They were there no time when the nurse reminded them that Mrs O'Leary must now rest. They could come back again that evening.

'You go home with my mother,' Ellie instructed Art. 'She'll make you a decent meal. And bring Maggie in this evening.'

'I will,' he said. 'And after the visit we'll go and get footless, me, Maggie and Julia.'

'I wish I could be with you.' said Ellie.

'You will,' said Art. 'We've all the time in the world for the three of us.'

'The four of us,' Julia reminded him. 'Don't forget your son.'

'I love you,' said Ellie. 'I love you all.'

Julia kissed her daughter and left her alone with Art. While she waited for her son-in-law in the corridor, she kept seeing the baby's face ... and smiling at her secret.